READER'S DIGEST

CONDENSED BOOKS

FIRST EDITION

THE READER'S DIGEST ASSOCIATION LIMITED
25 Berkeley Square, London W1X 6AB

**THE READER'S DIGEST ASSOCIATION
SOUTH AFRICA (PTY) LTD**
Nedbank Centre, Strand Street, Cape Town

Printed in Great Britain by Petty & Sons Ltd, Leeds

Original cover design by Jeffery Matthews M.S.I.A.

For information as to ownership
of copyright in the material in this book see last page

ISBN 0 340 25269 3

Reader's Digest
CONDENSED BOOKS

TO CATCH A KING
Harry Patterson

"...BUT THERE ARE ALWAYS MIRACLES."
Jack and Mary Willis

SHADOW OF THE MOON
M. M. Kaye

THE TIGHTROPE WALKER
Dorothy Gilman

COLLECTOR'S LIBRARY
EDITION

In this Volume:

To Catch a King
by Harry Patterson (p.9)

It was spring 1940, and Hitler was looking ahead. Once he had conquered Britain he would need a puppet ruler her people would accept. He thought of the Duke of Windsor, then in Portugal, on his way to an unrewarding post as governor of the Bahamas.

The ideal choice! And if the Duke did not want to cooperate, he could surely be persuaded. . . .

"...but there are always miracles."
by Jack and Mary Willis (p.129)

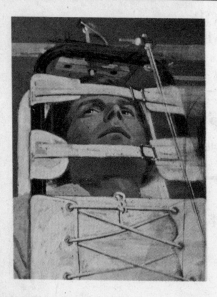

The doctor told him he would never walk again. A broken neck, a damaged spinal cord—the best he could hope for was to be paralysed only from the waist down, and to get about in a wheelchair.

It was a bleak prospect. For Jack, and for his fiancée, Mary, also. They had been planning to get married, to raise a family. What future did they really have together now?

This is Jack's and Mary's story, told in their own words. A story of courage and love, heart-warming, tender, and utterly truthful.

Shadow of the Moon

by M. M. Kaye *(p.223)*

For months Alex Randall had been begging that the women and children be sent to safety in the hills. For months his superior officers had pooh-poohed the notion. And now it was too late. Right across India the Mutiny had burst like a tidal wave, leaving death and destruction in its wake. . . .

The darkest days of the British Raj are brought to life here with rare authenticity—exciting, vivid, passionate. In *Shadow of the Moon* M. M. Kaye has given us a masterpiece of exotic adventure and tumultuous romance.

The TIGHTROPE WALKER

by Dorothy Gilman *(p.417)*

"When I found the note hidden in the old hurdy-gurdy I didn't treat it as a joke. I could smell the terror in the words even before I'd finished reading the first sentence: '*They're going to kill me*. . . .'"

Curiosity is said to have a fatal effect on some animals. But Amelia was no small domesticated feline. She was an unusually determined young woman. And the note she'd found in the hurdy-gurdy raised questions she dared not leave unanswered.

To Catch a King

A CONDENSATION OF THE BOOK BY
Harry Patterson

Illustrated by Kevin Tweddell

PUBLISHED BY HUTCHINSON

Outside top Nazi circles the plot to abduct the Duke and Duchess of Windsor was known to only one person: Hannah Winter, a young American singer working in Berlin.

It was information that had cost many lives already. Now Hannah, and Hannah alone, must somehow evade the Gestapo net and reach Lisbon in time to warn the royal couple. . . .

Much of this story is historical fact. In 1940 there really *was* a Nazi plan to kidnap the Windsors. It failed. Exactly how and why, however, has not officially been revealed.

In *To Catch A King* Harry Patterson compellingly speculates on what may actually have happened. It's an exciting tale, brilliantly told, peopled throughout with real-life characters: the famous, and the infamous.

One

Just after midnight it started to rain and the Portuguese policeman brought a cape from his sentry box and placed it round her shoulders without a word.

It was quite cold now and she walked along the road to keep warm, pausing to look back across the mouth of the Tagus River to where the lights of Lisbon gleamed in the distance.

A long way; not as far as Berlin or Paris or Madrid, but she was here now, finally, outside the pink stucco villa at Estoril. The end of things, more tired than she had ever been before, and she wanted it to be over.

She walked back to the policeman at the gate. "Please," she said in English. "How much longer? I've been here almost an hour."

Which was foolish, because he didn't understand her. Suddenly there was the sound of a car coming up the hill, headlights flashed across the mimosa bushes, and a black Mercedes braked to a halt a few yards away.

The man who got out of the rear was large and powerfully built. He was bareheaded and wore glasses, and his hands were pushed into the pockets of a dark mackintosh.

He said something in Portuguese to the policeman, then turned to the girl. His English was excellent.

"Miss Winter, isn't it? Miss Hannah Winter?"

"Yes, that's right."

"Could I see your passport?"

9

She got it out quickly, her hands fumbling in the cold so that the cape slipped from her shoulders. He replaced it for her politely, then took the passport.

"So—an American citizen."

"Please," she said, a hand on his sleeve. "I must see the Duke. It's a matter of the gravest urgency."

He looked down at her calmly for a moment, then nodded to the policeman, who started to open the gate. The Mercedes rolled forward. He held the door for her. She climbed inside. He followed.

With a sudden burst of power, the car jumped forward, the driver swinging the wheel, taking them round in a circle and back down the hill towards Lisbon.

She had been thrown into the corner, and now the man pulled her upright roughly and switched on the light. He was still clutching her passport.

"Hannah Winter—American citizen? I think not." He tore the document apart and flung it aside. "Now this, I think, would be a much more accurate description."

The passport he pushed into her hands was German. She opened it in fascinated horror. The picture that stared at her was her own.

"Fräulein Hannah Winter," he said. "Born in Berlin on November the ninth, 1917. Do you deny this?"

She closed the passport and thrust it back at him, fighting to control her panic. "My name is Hannah Winter, but I am an American citizen. The American embassy will confirm this."

"The Reich does not acknowledge the right of its citizens to change nationalities to suit their inclinations. You were born a German. I confidently predict you will die one."

The streets were deserted and they drove very fast. Already they were in the city and moving down towards the river.

He said, "An interesting city, Lisbon. To get into any foreign embassy it's necessary to pass through a Portuguese police checkpoint. So, if you'd tried to get into either the British or American embassies, we would still have got you."

She said, "I don't understand. When I asked to be admitted to the villa, the man at the gate told me he'd have to check with headquarters."

"It's simple. The Portuguese police have accepted an extradition warrant to be served on Hannah Winter for the charge of murder—murder three times over."

10

"But you—you're not the police."

"Oh, but we are. Not the Portuguese variety, but something rather more interesting." He switched to German. "Sturmbannführer Willi Kleiber of the Berlin office of the Gestapo." He nodded at the driver. "My colleague, Sturmscharführer Gunter Sindermann."

It was like something out of a nightmare and yet the tiredness Hannah felt was so overwhelming that nothing seemed to matter any more. "What happens now?" she asked dully.

Kleiber switched off the light so that they were in darkness again. "Oh, we'll take you home," he said. "Back to Berlin. Don't worry. We'll look after you."

His hand was on her knee, sliding up over her silk stocking. It was a big mistake, for the disgust his actions engendered galvanized Hannah into life again. She fumbled for the handle of the door, holding her breath as his hand moved higher. The Mercedes slowed to allow a water cart to cross the street. She shoved Kleiber away with all her strength, pushed open the door, and jumped into the darkness. She lost her balance and rolled over twice.

The shock was considerable. When she finally got to her feet, she saw that the Mercedes had pulled up farther along the street and was now reversing towards her. She had lost one of her shoes, so she kicked off the other, plunged into the nearest alley, and started to run.

A few moments later, she emerged on the waterfront. It was raining heavily now and fog was rolling in from the Tagus. Streetlamps were few and far between. There seemed to be no shops, no houses, simply gaunt warehouses rising into the night.

As the fog closed in around her, it was as if she were the only person in the world. Then she heard the sound of her pursuers' footsteps echoing between the walls of the alley behind her.

She started to run again, lightly, in stockinged feet. She was cold—very cold. A light appeared dimly in the fog on the other side of the street. A red neon sign said JOE JACKSON'S, and underneath, AMERICAN BAR.

She hurried across to the building, which backed onto a wharf. She was filled with desperate hope, but there was no light inside and the glass doors were locked. She rattled them in helpless rage. At the side of the building there was another door, with a lighted sign above it that said STAGE. She tried that door too, hammering on it with her fists. At that moment Kleiber ran round the corner, a Luger in his left hand. She screamed.

"I'll teach you," he said softly. "Little Jewish scum."

As Sindermann arrived, she turned and ran along the wharf into the fog.

JOE JACKSON had dark, wavy hair, hazel-green eyes, and a slight, ironic quirk that seemed to permanently lift the corner of his mouth. The weary, detached smile of a man who had found life more corrupt than he had hoped.

He always closed on Mondays. It gave everyone a night off and gave him a chance to work at the books in peace and quiet, which was what he was doing when Hannah first rattled the front doors.

A drunk, he thought, and returned to his accounts. A moment later, he heared her at the side door. Then he was aware of a sharp cry, followed by a murmur of voices. He opened the right-hand drawer of the desk, took out a Browning automatic, and moved out of the office quickly.

He was wearing a navy-blue sweater, dark slacks. A small man, no more than five feet six, with good shoulders. He unlocked the stage door and walked outside. He stood listening. There was a choked cry from farther along the wharf. He went forward, silent on rope-soled sandals.

There was a lamp on a pole at the end of the wharf. In its light, he saw Hannah Winter on her back, Sindermann crouched over her body. Kleiber stood above them, still holding the Luger.

"And now, Miss Winter," Kleiber said in English. "A lesson in manners."

"I don't think so," Jackson called softly.

He shot Kleiber in the right forearm, driving him back against a rail, the Luger falling into the dark water. Kleiber made no sound —simply stood there, gripping his arm, waiting for what was to come.

Hannah Winter, still pinned beneath Sindermann's weight, gazed up at Jackson blankly. He tapped the German on the back of the head with the barrel of the Browning.

Sindermann stood up and raised his hands. There was no fear on his face, simply a sullen rage. Jackson helped the girl to her feet. For the briefest of moments his attention was diverted as she sagged against him. Sindermann charged, head down.

12

Jackson swung the girl to one side and stuck out his foot. Sindermann tripped and continued headfirst over the rail. They could hear him floundering about in the water below.

Jackson leaned over the girl. "You all right?"

"I am now," she said.

He gestured with the Browning at Kleiber, who stood waiting, blood oozing between his fingers. "What about this one?"

"Let him go," she said wearily. "It's not a police matter."

Jackson nodded to Kleiber. "You heard the lady."

The German walked away rapidly. Jackson pushed the Browning in his belt and picked Hannah Winter up in both arms.

"Okay, angel, let's get you inside."

SHE STOOD under the hot shower for twenty minutes before towelling herself dry and putting on the robe he'd given her. The apartment was on the third floor at the rear of the club and overlooked the river. It was neat and sparingly furnished, with few personal belongings. The present resting place of a man who had kept on the move for most of his life.

The sliding doors stood open and Hannah found Jackson standing on the broad wooden balcony, a drink in one hand, gazing down at the river. A foghorn sounded as a ship moved out to sea.

She shivered. "The loneliest sound in the world."

"Let me get you a cognac," he said, leading her inside. "You look as if you could do with one."

His voice was good Boston American. "Where are you from?" she asked him.

"Cape Cod. Fishing village called Wilton. A long time ago." He smiled and handed her the cognac. "And you?"

"New York, although it's a matter of dispute in some quarters," she said, and sipped a little from the glass.

He lit a cigarette. "Those friends of yours out there? You said it wasn't police business."

"True," she said. "But they are police. A variety peculiar to the Third Reich, known as the Gestapo."

He was no longer smiling. He closed the doors and faced her.

"You're Joe Jackson, aren't you?" she asked.

"That's right, but we've never met."

"No," she said. "But I know all about you. My name is Hannah Winter. I'm a singer. Born in Berlin, but my parents took me to

13

America when I was two years old. I returned to Berlin to sing at my uncle Max's club two months ago. You know a piano player called Connie Jones?"

Jackson smiled. "I certainly do. He's in Madrid at the Flamenco with his trio right now. Due to appear here next week."

"Two weeks ago, he was backing me at my uncle's place in Berlin. The Garden Room. He told me about the great fighter pilot Joe Jackson, who now runs the best American bar in Lisbon."

Jackson said, "All right. I'll buy it."

She said, "Have you ever heard of a man called Santo e Silva?"

"Portuguese banker. Has a villa at Estoril."

"Do you know who his houseguests are at the moment?"

"Common knowledge. The Duke and Duchess of Windsor."

"But not for much longer. Not if the Nazis have anything to do with it." She started to shake.

"Okay." Joe Jackson held her arms for a second, then drew her onto the couch beside him in front of the fire. "Now calm down. Take your time and tell me about it—everything there is to tell."

Two

It began in Berlin, if it began anywhere at all, with a man called Erich von Manstein, who at the beginning of 1940 was chief of staff to General Gerd von Rundstedt.

Manstein, who was to become the most brilliant commander in the field that the German army produced during the Second World War, was a superb tactician who constantly challenged the views of his superiors, particularly their plans to invade France and the Low Countries.

Faced with demotion, his career threatened, chance took him to a dinner party given by Adolf Hitler in February 1940. At that meeting he took the opportunity of outlining to the Führer his own alternative plan, an audacious panzer drive through the Ardennes to the Channel coast, aimed at separating the British and French armies.

Hitler became so obsessed with the idea that, in time, he came to believe that it was his own. On the tenth of May, it was put into action with incredible effect. Within a matter of days, the Allied armies were in headlong retreat.

By the second of June, thanks to Hitler's decision to halt his tanks on the Aa Canal, most of the British Expeditionary Force managed to escape from the beaches of Dunkirk. On the twenty-second, the French signed an armistice document in the forest of Compiègne in the old wooden dining car in which Marshal Foch had dicated terms to the Germans in November 1918.

Early the following morning, Hitler, accompanied by a few handpicked companions, arrived in Paris. The most devastating campaign in modern warfare was over.

In the chaos that was the rest of France, particularly in the south, the roads were crowded with refugees pushing desperately for the Pyrenees and the Spanish border, many of them British citizens who had lived on the Riviera for years.

Among them was a convoy of cars headed by a Buick towing a loaded trailer. At a small town west of Arles, a barricade had been erected by gendarmes to prevent any further passage of refugees. As the Buick slowed to a halt, the small, rather slight-looking man seated beside the dark-haired woman in the back leaned out of the window. He smiled with considerable charm, but the authority there was unmistakable.

"I am the Prince of Wales," he said in excellent French. "Let me pass, if you please."

The statement was not strictly accurate, but to millions of Europeans it was the title by which they still remembered him. The officer in charge gazed at him in astonished recognition, then saluted, and barked a quick order to his men. The barricades were hastily removed and the Duke and Duchess of Windsor and their party passed through.

IN BERLIN ON THE following Friday it was raining as Hannah Winter left her apartment in Königstrasse. It was eight thirty, an hour before the first cabaret of the evening at the Garden Room, which was a mile away near the Unter den Linden. Not much chance of a taxi these days, so she'd have to hurry. There was a black Mercedes parked across the street. She glanced at it hopefully, then realized it was a private car and started to walk.

Two young men came round the corner and moved towards her. They were in Nazi Party uniform of some sort, although what it signified she had no idea. They paused, blocking her way, the faces beneath the peaked caps hard and cruel, ripe for mischief. She was in trouble and knew it.

"Papers," one of them said.

She remembered Uncle Max's first rule: Never show fear. "I'm an American citizen," she replied calmly.

"So?" He snapped his fingers.

She produced her passport from her bag and handed it over.

"Hannah Winter—twenty-two. That's a good age." His companion sniggered, his eyes stripping her. The first one returned the passport. "And your pass."

She took it out reluctantly and handed it to him.

The man laughed delightedly. "Well, would you look at this. A Jew." He moved closer. "Where's your star? You know it's a serious offence to be out without it. We're going to have to do something about that."

He was very close to her now, forcing her back towards the mouth of the alley behind. There was the sound of a car door slamming, and Hannah saw a man emerge from the rear of the black Mercedes and start across the street towards them.

"That's enough," he called softly through the rain.

He was of medium height, wore a slouch hat and a black leather coat. A cigarette dangled from the corner of his mouth.

Hannah's interrogator scowled ferociously as the man approached. "Clear off. This is police business."

"Is that so?" the man said calmly. "Fräulein Winter, is that right? My name is Schellenberg. I heard the exchange sitting in my car over there. Are these men annoying you?"

"She's a Jew, out on the street without her Star of David."

"And an American citizen, if I heard correctly. Is this not so, Fräulein?" His smile had a kind of ruthless charm that was accentuated by the duelling scar on one cheek.

"Yes," she said.

A hand grabbed Schellenberg's arm. "Clear off. Unless you want your face kicked in."

Schellenberg wasn't in the least put out. "Oh dear, you are a nasty little boy, aren't you?"

He waved his right hand casually. Two men in black uniforms got out of the Mercedes and hurried across the street. Their cuff titles carried the legend RFSS picked out in silver thread. *Reichsführer der* SS, the cuff title of Heinrich Himmler's personal staff.

Schellenberg said to them, "A lesson is needed here, I think." He took the girl by the arm. "Fräulein."

As he guided her firmly towards the car, there was the sound of a blow, a cry of pain, but Hannah did not look back.

A FEW MINUTES later, the Mercedes pulled up in front of the Garden Room. The doorman opened the car door, and Schellenberg got out and turned to assist Hannah.

"So, this is where you work?" He examined the photographs in the glass case beneath the poster. "'Hannah Winter and the Connie Jones trio, direct from New York.' I must come one night."

She said calmly, "I'm Jewish, and as you can see from the photo, Connie is a Negro. I hardly think we'd be of much interest to a member of the master race."

He smiled gently. "Shall we go in?"

"I use the stage door."

"And I, on the contrary, always go in by the front." He had her by the arm again and she went inside without protest.

Her uncle was talking to the hat-check girl. He was a shrewd yet kindly-looking man, with a shock of grey hair and steel-rimmed glasses. He managed to appear untidy, though, in spite of his dinner jacket.

At the sight of his niece and Schellenberg, he hurried forward. "Hannah, my love, what's happened? You are in trouble?"

"I was, but not any more, thanks to Herr Schellenberg. This is my uncle, Max Winter."

"Herr Winter," Schellenberg said amiably, and turned back to Hannah.

She was a small, rather hippy girl with good legs; her long black hair framed a face that was handsome rather than beautiful, with high cheekbones and dark eyes.

Schellenberg took her right hand, holding it for a moment. "And now, Fräulein, after seeing you in a better light, I am more determined than ever to catch your act—isn't that the American phrase? But not tonight, I regret to say."

He raised her hand to his lips and she was conscious of a hollow excitement in her stomach.

He went out, and when Hannah glanced at her uncle she found that he had turned quite pale. "Uncle Max—what is it?"

"That man," he whispered. "Don't you know who he is? That is Walter Schellenberg, SS Brigadeführer—major general of police. Heydrich's right-hand man."

IN 1920, WHEN Hannah Winter was two years old, her father brought his wife and daughter from Berlin to New York and opened a small restaurant on Forty-second Street. During Prohibition, he turned the establishment into a successful nightclub. But his health had never been good because of chest wounds received as an infantryman on the Somme, and he died in July 1929.

The club, after Prohibition was abolished, once again became a restaurant and prospered under the shrewd direction of his wife. Hannah was raised to be a nice Jewish girl who would one day make a good marriage, have kids, do all the right things.

It might have worked, except for one important point. Hannah Winter had been blessed with an extraordinary singing voice. She discovered her talent by chance, singing with a student jazz band at high school. From that time on, she never seriously contemplated any other way of life.

At seventeen she appeared in Hollywood with Benny Goodman. As a band singer she toured with Artie Shaw and Tommy Dorsey. But she was at her best in the more enclosed world of club and cabaret, preferably backed by a good trio. There she could bring an intensity to her performance of popular songs that perhaps rivalled anything Bessie Smith could do with the blues.

And she would now be in Hollywood doing a film with Bing Crosby if it hadn't been for Uncle Max, her father's younger brother. Though he had been a naturalized American citizen for twenty-five years, in 1937 he had horrified his family by returning to the city of his birth to open a nightclub.

Which was why Hannah was here. To persuade him that it was time to get out of Germany. But events had overtaken her with frightening rapidity. The Nazis were now poised on the Channel coast, with England the next stop and nothing in their way.

HANNAH WAS applying her makeup when her uncle entered. He pulled a chair forward and watched her in the mirror.

"All right—what happened?" he asked.

She told him quickly, then went behind the screen to change.

"Not good," he said. "Perhaps I should explain a few things to you. In Germany today the SS is all-powerful, but within the organization they have their own secret service department—the SD. Reinhard Heydrich is director general, although still under the authority of Himmler."

"And Schellenberg?"

"He's in charge of the counterespionage section, but more important, he's Heydrich's favourite." She made no reply as she slid a long black dress over her head. "Do you understand any of this?" Max asked.

"Not really," she said, emerging from behind the screen and turning so that he could button up the back of the dress. "It's all very confusing. And the uniforms—every second person you meet seems to have one." She sat down. "Uncle Max, let's go home."

"You are going home," he said. "All arranged—tickets and everything. You, Connie, and the boys leave Berlin Monday morning by train for Paris. That same night they've got berths on the sleeper to Madrid and so have you."

"And when was all this decided?"

"Today. The boys have a week at the Flamenco Club in Madrid."

"But I haven't."

"No, you go straight to Lisbon from there. Plenty of boats going to New York. You might even get a seat on the Clipper."

"And you?"

"I've got things to do here."

"Then I'm not going."

"Oh, yes, you are, Hannah." She had never heard that tone in his voice before. He patted her hand and got up. "We've got a crowd tonight. I'd better go and see how the food's working out."

As he reached the door, she said, "Uncle Max, you're mixed up in something, aren't you? Something serious?"

He smiled gently. "I'll see you later."

The door closed softly behind him and she sat there, staring into the mirror, her mind in turmoil. A moment later, there was a knock on her door and Connie Jones came in.

"Are you ready?"

She managed a smile. "As much as I ever will be."

Connie was a large, rugged-looking Negro of forty-five with close-cropped greying hair. Born and raised in New Orleans, he had been playing the piano like a dream since the age of seven and couldn't read a note of music. "Trouble?" he asked.

"Uncle Max tells me I leave with you on Monday."

"That's it. Twelve hours to gay Paree, then the express to Madrid from Austerlitz station, and I can't shake this town soon enough." He paused. "You're worried about the old man, aren't you?"

"He says he isn't coming, Connie, but if he stays here . . ."

"If ever a man knew what he was doing, it's your uncle Max, kid. I'd leave it to him." He took her hand. "You worry too much and that ain't good, because we got a show to do."

She took a deep breath, stood up, and followed him out, immediately aware of the club noises. People talking, the laughter, the hustle. It had an electricity that never failed to affect her.

Two other Negroes moved onto the small stage with Connie: Billy Joe Hale, the bass player, and Harry Gray, the drummer. Hannah waited. Then the spots bathed the stage in white light and Uncle Max's voice boomed from the rear of the room. "And now, ladies and gentlemen, the Garden Room proudly presents, direct from New York, the one and only Hannah Winter!"

As Connie and the boys moved into a solid driving arrangement of "Saint Louis Blues", Hannah walked onstage to thunderous applause and started to sing.

GENERAL REINHARD HEYDRICH, unlike most Nazi Party members, had been born a gentleman. After joining the SS he had been quickly chosen by Himmler as his deputy. His rise to the powerful position of head of the Reich Main Security Office was a tribute as much to his total lack of humanity as to his qualities of leadership and superior intelligence.

He was seated at his desk in the Prinz Albrechtstrasse offices of the SS when Schellenberg entered. "Ah, there you are, Walter," Heydrich said amiably. "You had a busy evening, I hear, playing Galahad to the Winter girl."

"Is there anything you don't know?" Schellenberg said. "It's only just happened, for heaven's sake."

"One survives, Walter, in this wicked old world by knowing everything there is to know about everything and everybody." Heydrich smiled. "Tell me about her. How long has she been under surveillance?"

"Since she arrived. Two months now."

"And she fell for this little drama of yours tonight?"

"I think so."

"What exactly do you hope to achieve? Access to her bed, or information?"

"It's her uncle we're after, remember," Schellenberg said. "The fact that he's an American citizen makes things difficult."

"But he was born a German," Heydrich said impatiently. "The Führer has stated that citizens of the Reich do not have the right to change nationality."

"The Americans might have a different viewpoint on that one," Schellenberg said. "And this is hardly the moment to antagonize Washington."

"So—are we any further forward with this Winter affair?"

"Not really. As you can see from Winter's file, he attended Berlin University as a youth and was a member of the Communist Party. I think he still is."

"A Soviet agent possibly?"

"Perhaps. Certainly involved with the socialist underground and probably also the illegal transfer of Jews from the Reich."

"Then what are you waiting for? Arrest him."

"Not just yet," Schellenberg said. "If we wait a little longer, we get not only Winter but his entire organization. And he is under surveillance at all hours."

Heydrich sat there frowning, then nodded. "Very well. You can have another week." He stood up. "What are you going to do now?"

Schellenberg knew what was coming. "Go home to bed."

"Nonsense." Heydrich grinned. "The night's still young. We'll make the rounds at a few nightclubs. Help yourself to a drink while I change."

He went out and Schellenberg sighed, moved to the drinks cabinet, and poured himself a Scotch.

He had been born in Saarbrücken in 1910, the son of a piano maker. Cultured and intelligent by nature and with a gift for languages, he had entered the University of Bonn to study medicine, but changed to law after two years. Well qualified but penniless, he saw opportunity in the rise of the Nazi party in 1933 and joined the SS. He came to the attention of Heydrich, who recruited him at once into the SD, where his rise had been rapid. A number of successful intelligence operations consolidated his position, and he was soon promoted to SS Brigadeführer and major general of police. He was only thirty years of age.

Of course, Schellenberg had his enemies, but Heydrich liked him, so he moved in the best circles in Berlin. But there was a price to pay, including the occasional night out with Heydrich, who was never happier than when roaming the city's cabarets.

Greatest irony of all was that Walter Schellenberg did not

consider himself a Nazi. Heydrich, Himmler, even the Führer, all came to trust his judgment implicitly on intelligence matters, and yet always in his mind he stood to one side, a spectator of the whole sorry charade, contemptuous as much of himself as of them.

The rain beat against the window in Heydrich's office, and Schellenberg raised his glass to his reflection, in mock salute.

Three

The next morning Schellenberg was working in his office on Prinz Albrechtstrasse when the phone rang. He recognized the voice—Joachim von Ribbentrop, the foreign minister.

"Schellenberg, I'd like you to come to see me at once. It's a matter of the utmost importance to the Reich. I can't discuss it on the phone."

Schellenberg called Heydrich and reported the situation, always aware of his rage at any suggestion of his authority being usurped. For once, Heydrich was intrigued and told him to get on with it. Schellenberg promised a detailed report later.

Ribbentrop received him in his private office at the Reich Chancellery. "Good of you to come, my dear fellow. Sit down and I'll get straight to the point. I am speaking to you on behalf of the Führer himself in this matter, so we are talking of something with the highest security rating."

"Of course. Please continue."

"Did you by any chance meet the Duke of Windsor during his German tour in 1937?"

"No, I didn't have that pleasure."

"What is your opinion about the way in which the English dealt with the crisis surrounding his abdication?"

"It seems to me they handled the problem very sensibly. Tradition and responsibility had to take precedence over emotions." Schellenberg shrugged. "I don't see how the British government could have acted any differently."

Ribbentrop looked extremely put out. "I can see this is one matter about which you have been completely misinformed. The real reasons behind the pressure for the Duke to abdicate were political. He was too determined to change the decadent English society into something forceful and forward-looking. Something more suited to modern needs."

"He told you this?" Schellenberg asked dryly.

Ribbentrop didn't seem to hear him. "The Duke was much impressed with everything he saw in Germany. The Führer received him at Berchtesgaden. They talked for an hour." He paused. "At the moment, the Führer is immersed in planning Operation Sea Lion—the invasion of England—which is why he asked me to handle this most important matter for him."

"I see."

"The Duke, as you know, was serving as a major general with Allied forces in France. After our magnificent victory, he and the Duchess, with a few friends, managed to cross into Spain. They were in Madrid until recently. In fact the attitude of the Spaniards in the matter may be best summed up by a telegram I received from our Madrid ambassador, Eberhard von Stohrer. I have a copy here."

He passed it across and Schellenberg scanned it quickly.

THE SPANISH FOREIGN MINISTER REQUESTS ADVICE WITH REGARD TO THE TREATMENT OF THE DUKE AND DUCHESS OF WINDSOR WHO ARE TO ARRIVE IN MADRID TODAY, APPARENTLY EN ROUTE TO ENGLAND BY WAY OF LISBON. THE FOREIGN MINISTER ASSUMES THAT WE MIGHT PERHAPS BE INTERESTED IN DETAINING THE DUKE HERE AND POSSIBLY ESTABLISHING CONTACT WITH HIM.

Schellenberg handed the paper back. "I don't understand."

"It's really very simple. The English are racially a part of our Germanic brotherhood. The Führer has no wish to destroy them. They could have an important part to play in the greater European ideal. He is convinced that any day now, the British government will see this and will sue for peace. After all, they don't have much choice. They're finished."

"There's still the Channel to cross," Schellenberg said.

"But there won't be any need, don't you see? And once a peace treaty has been concluded, there would be the question of the throne to consider. Much better to see it occupied by a man loved by his people, who is also a good friend to Germany."

It was with difficulty that Schellenberg stopped himself from laughing out loud. "Are you really serious, Minister?"

Ribbentrop seemed mildly surprised. "But of course. I have here a report from Madrid which states that in a conversation with a member of the American embassy staff, the Duke declared that the most important thing now was to end the war before thousands more were killed to save the faces of a few politicians."

"Which hardly makes him a member of our National Socialist Party," Schellenberg pointed out.

Ribbentrop rolled on relentlessly. "The Duke and Duchess arrived in Lisbon recently and are staying at Estoril in the villa of a Portuguese banker, Santo e Silva. On their arrival they found two British flying boats waiting to take them to England. The Duke sent them back. Refused to go. Don't you find that interesting?"

"Did he give a reason?"

"According to our information, he insisted that the British offer him a worthwhile post and assurances that in future the Duchess would be treated in full accord with her status as his wife."

"That seems reasonable. The British have hardly made the best use of his talents so far in this war. Has he had a reply?"

"Apparently Churchill is offering him the governorship of the Bahamas."

"Clever," Schellenberg said, "and practical. Three thousand miles from the war. Do you think he'll accept?"

"No. We feel he would probably far rather stay in Europe, perhaps in Spain or even in Switzerland. Which is where you come in, Schellenberg. The Führer feels you would be the ideal man to speak to the Duke on our behalf. Offer any assistance he may need. Financial, for example, if that is necessary. Whatever happens, the Duke must be given help to reach the country of his choice."

"Even if that proves to be the Bahamas?"

Ribbentrop glanced at him. "My dear Schellenberg, your facetiousness could be the death of you one of these days."

"My apologies, Minister."

"To continue. If the Duke should prove in any way hesitant, the Führer would have no objection to your helping him reach the right decision."

"By force?"

"If necessary. Naturally it will also be your responsibility to see that the Duke and his wife are not exposed to any personal danger. A day's outing into Spain is all it takes. Once you have them over the border, the rest is simple."

"And this is a direct order from the Führer himself?"

"But of course." Ribbentrop passed an envelope across. "You'll find everything you need in there. Total authority. I can only wish you well and envy your inevitable success in this matter."

HEYDRICH SAT by the window in his office holding the document Schellenberg had just handed him.

FROM THE LEADER AND CHANCELLOR OF THE STATE
MOST SECRET

General Schellenberg is acting under my direct and personal orders in a matter of the utmost importance to the Reich. He is answerable only to me. All personnel, military and civil, without distinction of rank, will assist him in any way he sees fit.

Adolf Hitler

"Nonsense!" Heydrich said. "This plan is sheer bloody nonsense and all built on totally false assumptions."

There was a knock on the door and a young secretary entered with a file, which she placed on his desk. She left without a word, and Heydrich tapped it with a finger.

"In here, Walter, is everything you need to know about the Duke of Windsor—everything recorded about him. But what have I taught you to be the fundamental principle of intelligence work?"

"As the Jesuits put it, By the small things shalt thou know them."

"Exactly. It is not what a man says or what people say about him that is the truth. It is how he behaves, for character is action." Heydrich tapped the file again. "And nowhere more so than with this man. How would you describe him—in the world's eyes?"

"A contradiction. Concerned about his fellowmen—his attitude towards the English working classes proved that—and yet fond of luxury and pleasure. A difficult man; reserved."

"Perhaps. Certainly stubborn."

"Because of his stand on the question of marrying the Duchess? Some people might find that admirable."

Heydrich opened the file on the Duke. "When he was serving with the British military mission in France, he managed to make several tours of the Maginot Line. His report, which points out the line's inadequacies, shows every evidence of a first-class military mind. Go through his whole file; then at least you'll know what you're talking about. In the meantime, do the usual departmental report. Everything Ribbentrop said. I want it all down on paper."

26

When Schellenberg returned to his office he called in Frau Huber, Heydrich's confidential secretary. She was thirty-eight, a war widow already, her husband having been killed during the French campaign.

Schellenberg quickly dictated an account of his meeting with Ribbentrop. "As soon as possible, please."

She went out, and he opened the Windsor file and started to work his way through it. Half an hour later, Frau Huber returned with the completed report. He checked it over and signed it.

"The usual copies?" she asked.

"Yes, one for Himmler, one for me, and one for the file."

She left. He sat there frowning for a moment, then picked up the telephone and asked for Admiral Canaris at Abwehr headquarters. But the admiral, it seemed, was out riding in the Tiergarten. Schellenberg ordered a car and left quickly.

WHEN FRAU HUBER went into the copying room, there was a middle-aged woman on duty who was unfamiliar to her.

"Who are you?" she demanded.

"Irene Neumann. I usually work in Central Office."

"I see. Run this off now. Three copies. I'll wait."

The other woman set up the machine. FOR YOUR EYES ONLY— MOST SECRET, she saw at the top of the page. Then the name Duke of Windsor jumped out at her.

Frau Huber paced the room restlessly. "Hurry up, for God's sake."

As the machine started, the phone rang in her office and she hurried off to answer it. It was a routine matter, taking only three or four minutes to handle. As she finished, she turned and found Irene Neumann standing there.

"Three copies, you said, Frau Huber?"

"Yes. Put them on the desk."

The other woman did as she was told and went out. Back in the copying room, she closed the door behind her, then opened a drawer and took out the extra copy of the Windsor report that she had made. She folded it carefully, raised her skirt, and slipped it inside the top of her stocking.

ADMIRAL WILHELM CANARIS was fifty-three. A U-boat commander of distinction during the First World War, he was now head of the Abwehr, the intelligence department of the German armed forces high command. Although a loyal German, like many of the officer class he loathed most aspects of the Nazi regime, an attitude that was to lead to his downfall and execution near the end of the war.

Schellenberg was on close personal terms with him, and they frequently went riding together in the Tiergarten. As he waited beside his car, he could see the admiral now, cantering along the path followed by his two favourite dachshunds, who were having difficulty keeping up with him. Canaris saw Schellenberg, rode up to him, reined in, and dismounted.

"Business, Walter, or conversation?" the admiral asked.

"Interchangeable, I usually find." Schellenberg called to his driver, "Come and hold Herr Admiral's horse."

The two men walked among the trees, the dachshunds waddling at their heels.

"How goes the war, Walter? Do you think the British will sue for peace any day?"

"Not really, Herr Admiral."

"Neither do I. Not with the Channel to cross. And they always do so damned well with their backs to the wall. You heard the gist of Churchill's speech? Fight on the beaches, in the streets. Blood, sweat, tears."

"There's still the Luftwaffe to come."

"I know," Canaris said scornfully. "Fat Hermann Goering boasting again. Reduce London to ashes, bomb them into submission. Wasn't that what he was supposed to do to the British army at Dunkirk? Instead, the Luftwaffe got all hell knocked out of it by a handful of Spitfires."

The admiral's face was stiff with anger, and Schellenberg watched him closely. He liked Canaris, admired him as a man. On the other hand, the admiral was undoubtedly indiscreet.

"Well, what is it, Walter? What do you wish to discuss?"

"I was wondering," Schellenberg said, "whether you had an opinion on the Duke of Windsor."

Canaris roared with laughter. "Has Ribbentrop dropped that one in your lap?"

"You know all about it, then?"

"Of course I do. He approached me personally yesterday. He knows the Abwehr has an organization in Lisbon. He seemed to think we could handle the whole affair."

"And why don't you?"

"Our man in Lisbon has been found to be a double agent. He will be eliminated shortly. Also, I think the whole Windsor affair is nonsense. A number of incidents concerning the Duke have been hopelessly misconstrued. For example: a speech he made some years ago, suggesting that the time had come for British veterans of the World War to hold out the hand of comradeship to German veterans, is taken by our more fatuous leaders as an indication of his approval of National Socialism. Wishful thinking. I also believe the Führer mistaken in seeing in the Duke's tour of our country in 1937 any evidence of similar approval. May I remind you that a distinguished list of world leaders has visited the Reich. Does that make them all incipient Nazis?"

"So—you do not think the Duke would have the slightest interest in our overtures?"

"He has a considerable amount of German blood in him, he speaks our language fluently, and I believe he likes us. But it is my opinion that this liking does not extend to the Nazi Party. There, have I shocked you?"

"Not at all, Herr Admiral. I asked for your opinion and you were good enough to give it. I shall respect the confidence."

They started back towards the car. Canaris said, "My final word. Examine the Duke's record in the World War. Gallant in the extreme. In spite of his father's orders that he was to be kept out of action when on the western front, he loved nothing better than being with the Tommies, which was why they knew him and came to love him. He always made straight for the trenches. Did you know that his aides once made an official complaint? They said it was all right for him, but the trouble was they had to follow him into the shellfire too."

"Now that, I like," Schellenberg said. "That tells me more about the man than anything else."

"Walter, in this matter the Führer is hopelessly wasting his time. Here is a man who renounced a throne rather than betray the woman he loved. Do you really imagine that such a man could betray his country?"

AT ESTORIL, in the Portuguese banker's pink stucco villa above the sea, the Duchess of Windsor sat beside the swimming pool. She was reading *Wuthering Heights*, one of her favourite novels, and was so absorbed in the story that she was not immediately aware that the Duke had emerged from the house onto the terrace and was standing beside her.

She glanced up and removed her sunglasses. "Why, David, you startled me."

The Duke sat down in the deckchair near her.

"Lemonade?" she asked, offering him a glass from a tray on the table.

"I could do with something a little stiffer."

"Nonsense, David, you know you never drink before seven o'clock. What's happened?" She reached over and took his hand.

"You always know, don't you, Wallis?" He forced a smile. "I've had a telegram from Winston. He's finally found me a job. Governor of the Bahamas. Nicely tucked away three thousand miles from the action."

"Will you take it?"

"I'll have to. I won't have them push us into a bottom drawer. It must be the two of us together. Man and wife with the same position. They don't seem to be willing to offer us that in England. So, the Bahamas it is."

"My dear David," she said. "There's a war on, and I'm sure my position doesn't loom very large on the agenda."

"But it does with me, Wallis. I can never alter on that score." He shrugged. "It just hurts that they can't find anything more important for me to do."

He got up and walked to the edge of the terrace, where he stood gazing out to sea. As the Duchess watched him, the sense of waste was so overwhelming that she had to fight back her tears.

Four

Schellenberg was back in his office within half an hour of leaving for the Tiergarten. As he was taking off his coat, Frau Huber entered. She was considerably agitated.

"We've been looking for you everywhere. General Heydrich is very angry."

Schellenberg said calmly, "I thought he knew every move I made before I did. Where is he now?"

"With Reichsführer Himmler. They're waiting for you."

She was trembling a little, because she liked Schellenberg more than she dared to admit, for some reason admiring the fact that nothing seemed to matter to him.

"Be calm, Ilse. I'll manage. Not just because I'm cleverer than they are, which I am, but because I don't take it seriously."

When he was ushered into the ornate office on the first floor at Prinz Albrechtstrasse, Schellenberg found Himmler seated behind a large desk. The Reichsführer was a surprisingly nondescript figure in his grey tweed suit. The face behind the silver pince-nez was cold and impersonal, and it was difficult to imagine what went on behind those expressionless eyes. He was in many ways a strangely timid man who could be kind to his subordinates, loved animals, and was devoted to his children, and yet he was a monster, responsible for almost all of the terror that the Reich visited on its victims.

Himmler removed his pince-nez and rubbed a finger between his eyes, a habitual gesture. "So, General, your conversation with Herr Admiral Canaris was interesting?"

Heydrich had been standing by the window, and now he turned, his face angry. "Playing cat and mouse with that old fool again? You had no authority to do such a thing," he exploded.

Himmler stilled him with a wave of the hand. "What was your primary reason for going to see him?"

Schellenberg took his time in replying, playing it carefully. "A difficult question, Reichsführer. A matter of some delicacy."

"My dear Schellenberg, I respect your tact, but General Heydrich and I are as one in this. There is nothing you cannot say here."

"Very well. You have obviously read my Windsor report. I suspected that Ribbentrop had not been entirely honest with me. It seemed logical that he would have approached Canaris first, since he is head of intelligence, and yet Ribbentrop made no mention of the fact."

"I see." Himmler's voice was very soft now and he smiled in an oddly satisfied way. "And had he?"

"I'm afraid so." Schellenberg then told them everything, holding nothing back, for there was no need to do so.

"So—the Herr Admiral sees no good in this affair?"

"So it would seem."

"And you?" asked Himmler.

Schellenberg knew that he was on dangerous ground now.

Choosing his words with care, he said calmly, "Ribbentrop made it clear that the whole business was to be carried through at the Führer's express command. The Reichsführer must see that I cannot possibly question an order from the Führer himself. My personal opinion doesn't enter into the matter."

Heydrich turned away abruptly to conceal his smile, but Himmler was positively glowing with approval. "I could not have put it better myself," he said. "The Führer carries the burden for all of us. The destiny of Germany rides on his shoulders."

Schellenberg asked, "So, you also wish me to proceed in this matter, Reichsführer?"

"Most certainly. You will travel to Lisbon as soon as arrangements can be made, by way of Madrid. A consultation with our ambassador there, von Stohrer, would be useful."

"One point, Reichsführer," Heydrich said. "Lisbon is alive with secret agents of every nationality, and I think it essential that General Schellenberg have protection. With your permission, I'll assign two or three of my best men."

"Not necessary," Himmler said. "I'll take care of it personally. The Gestapo will provide exactly the operatives we're looking for."

"As you say, Reichsführer."

"Good. You may leave us now, General Schellenberg."

Schellenberg went out quickly and returned to his office. He was sweating slightly and lit a cigarette. A moment later, Frau Huber came in with a cup of coffee.

"See, Ilse?" he said, smiling. "I told you there was nothing to worry about."

But when he raised the cup to his lips his hand was trembling.

AS ALWAYS after such an episode he needed action. He went down to the firing range in the basement, where the targets were of charging soldiers.

"What new weapon have you got, Reitlinger?" Schellenberg asked the SS officer in charge.

"The new Erma police submachine gun, General. Just in this morning."

Schellenberg picked one up and emptied it in short bursts, firing from the waist and cutting a couple of the targets in half. The noise was deafening.

He replaced the weapon. "A butcher's gun," he said. "What I

need is something more subtle—a silent killer, if you like."

The officer smiled and moved to the armourer's cupboard. He returned with a Mauser 7.63 mm, Model 1932, with the latest adaptation, a bulbous silencer.

Schellenberg hefted the weapon in his hand. "Now this is more like it." It held a ten-round magazine, which he emptied rapidly, putting two shots squarely in the middle of five of the targets. The only sound was a series of dull thuds.

"Very neat," Heydrich said, appearing behind him. Reitlinger moved out of earshot, and Heydrich continued. "That was an outstanding performance you gave just now in Himmler's office. Exactly calculated to please."

"And what did you expect me to say—the truth?"

"Which is?"

"That this whole thing is a waste of time," Schellenberg said. "I've read the Windsor file. I've talked to Canaris. The report from Madrid about the Duke's sympathetic attitude is nothing but cocktail gossip by Spanish aristocrats with fascist sympathies who want to believe the Duke thinks as they do. Everyone wants to believe he's on our side and so they manufacture the evidence by wishful thinking. If the Duke of Windsor said Beethoven was his favourite composer, some idiot would take that to be an endorsement of the Nazi Party."

"So, you don't think he'll be interested?" Heydrich asked.

"Not in the slightest."

"Then you'll have to persuade him, won't you?"

"And what on earth is that supposed to achieve?"

Heydrich said, "When we occupy England he will have to do as he's told, for the simple reason that it will be the best way for him to serve the interests of his people."

Schellenberg put down his gun. "Do you mind if I go now? I've work to do."

"Not at all. You can pick me up at eight thirty."

"What for?"

"This Winter girl. I'd like to see her in the flesh. The Garden Room, I think you said?"

"All right." Schellenberg walked to the door. "I'll want one of the Mausers with a silencer," he said to Reitlinger. "And one hundred rounds in ten clips. Deliver it to the office."

"Yes, General."

AT EIGHT THIRTY Schellenberg picked up Heydrich at his house in Berlin's exclusive Zehlendorf quarter. They rode in one of the special department Mercedes with two uniformed SS men up front on the other side of the glass partition.

As they drove towards the centre of the city Heydrich seemed out of sorts. "Uncle Heini," he said, referring to Himmler by the disrespectful nickname by which he was known throughout the SS, "was not exactly being solicitous when he jumped in on my suggestion about providing you with bodyguards. Unless I'm mistaken, you'll have a couple of handpicked Gestapo goons breathing down your neck."

"And reporting every move I make three times a day by long-distance telephone to the Reichsführer," Schellenberg told him.

"I don't know why, but at a time when things have never looked better, I have a feeling that they are beginning to go wrong for us—for all of us."

"And why should that be?"

Heydrich hesitated. "This is in total confidence, Walter, but the truth is I have personal doubts about Sea Lion."

"You don't think the invasion of England will take place?"

"I have a nasty feeling the moment has already passed. The Führer's decision to halt the panzers on the Aa Canal in Belgium, and thus allow the remnants of the British Expeditionary Force to escape from Dunkirk, was a military error of the first magnitude."

"And now?"

"Russia. I think that is the way his mind is turning. I believe he already has a contingency plan in mind."

"And you don't think it's such a good idea?"

"Do you?"

Schellenberg shrugged. "If you want my opinion, I'd say that the trouble with a Russian campaign is the limitless distances, supply lines thousands of miles long, ferocious winter weather. Look what happened to Napoleon."

"I know," Heydrich said. "I have nightmares about that." They were travelling along the Kurfürstendamm now and he peered out of the window. "Not what it was in the old days—nothing is. I was at the Gloriapalast Theatre for the premiere of *The Blue Angel* in 1930. What a sensation when Dietrich appeared onstage. The crowd went wild. Believe me, Walter, those legs of hers were the eighth wonder of the world."

"I can imagine," Schellenberg said.

"One can only hope this Garden Room and your Hannah Winter can supply us with a decent evening's entertainment," Heydrich said. "It would make a nice change."

HANNAH was all ready for the first show, and went in search of Uncle Max, whom she had not seen since the previous evening. She found him working in his office.

She kissed him on top of the head. "Had a good day?"

"Not too bad." He turned and took both her hands in his. "What we talked about last night, Hannah. You'll do as I say? Leave with Connie and the boys on Monday?"

"And you?"

"I'll follow as soon as I can."

"Uncle Max, you're a Jew in a city where Jews are treated as badly as at any time in the last two thousand years."

"I'm American, my dear, and so are you. They don't want trouble with Uncle Sam—so they treat us a little differently."

She shook her head. "There's more to this than meets the eye. Much more."

"Twenty minutes to show time," he said. "Make us some coffee, like a good girl."

She went into the small kitchen that adjoined his office, leaving the door ajar. She lit the gas stove and filled the coffeepot, and was fixing a tray when there was a knock on the office door. It opened, and she heard her uncle say in German, "Irene! Haven't I told you never to come here?"

"I'd no choice, Max. Something rather special happened today."

Hannah moved so that she could see through the partially open door into the office. Irene Neumann unbuttoned her coat, raised her skirt, and took the folded copy of the Windsor report from her stocking.

"I was put on temporary duty in the copying room today. I had to make copies of this for Heydrich. It's a report of a meeting between Schellenberg and Ribbentrop concerning a plot to kidnap the Duke of Windsor."

The kitchen door swung wide open and Hannah stepped into the room. Irene Neumann turned pale. "Oh, God!" she said.

"It's all right. This is my niece, Hannah—Fräulein Neumann. Completely trustworthy. Now, let me have a look at this."

35

He read it quickly, then passed it to Hannah. "So now you know. Go on—read it. This is the sort of thing that keeps me here."

Hannah's brain seemed dulled with shock. She started to read the report while Irene Neumann and her uncle spoke in low tones. She heard the woman say, "Will Moscow be interested?"

"Perhaps. On the other hand, I might be able to pass it on through the American embassy. Difficult, though. The Gestapo watch the place constantly. You'd better go now." He kissed her on the cheek. "Look after yourself, Irene. I'll be in touch."

When Irene Neumann left by the stage door it had started to rain. She paused to button her coat and found an old beret in one pocket, which she pulled on.

There was a street lamp at the end of the alley, giving the SD man on surveillance duty inside a parked delivery truck a clear view of her as she walked towards him. He managed to take several photos before she turned down the main street and disappeared into the evening crowds.

"UNCLE MAX—you're a Communist?" asked Hannah.

"Labels," he replied, "are meaningless these days. The only question that matters is which side you are on. Look, try and understand. In New York, after twenty-five years, I owned a hotel and two nightclubs. Everything paid for, and I had half a million dollars in the bank I didn't know what to do with. So I got involved with a Zionist organization that was trying to do something about our people in Germany. I came back here in '37 to help organize an escape line for Jews. I gradually got drawn into the other side of things. The socialist underground, by its very nature, has links with Moscow."

"And Fräulein Neumann?"

"Irene is a dedicated Communist. Not a card-carrying member. What they call a sleeper. She really believes Karl Marx walked on water and she loathes the Nazis. She's a clerical worker at Gestapo headquarters on Prinz Albrechtstrasse. There are people like her in positions of trust all over the country. You'd be very surprised."

"And this?" She held up the report.

"I told you Schellenberg was important, didn't I?"

"But this business about trying to win the Duke of Windsor over to the Nazi cause. It's nonsensical. He'd never do such a thing."

"I agree, but Schellenberg's instructions seem real enough. If necessary, he's to kidnap the Duke and Duchess." He smiled. "You see, my dear, it's now more important than ever that you leave here Monday and make your way to Lisbon."

"Taking this with me?"

"You'd probably do better to memorize it."

Suddenly Hannah was filled with a fierce exhilaration. "You know, Uncle Max, being a Jew never meant much to me until I came here and saw how Jews were treated. It's been all right for me. Good clothes, position, an American passport. But I've had to walk by while old ladies with yellow stars on their coats have been kicked into the gutter by animals in uniform. It would be nice to hit back for a change."

"You'll do it, then?"

"Why not?" She folded the report, raised her skirt, and slipped it into her stocking as Irene Neumann had done.

There was a knock at the door, and Vogel, the headwaiter, looked in, holding a bunch of red roses. "I thought you'd like to know we've got distinguished company tonight."

"And who would that be?" Max Winter asked.

"Heydrich himself and General Schellenberg." Vogel handed the roses to Hannah. "These are for you, with General Schellenberg's compliments."

THE GARDEN ROOM was not particularly busy. Vogel had given Heydrich and Schellenberg a booth that was usually reserved for guests of the management.

"Champagne," Heydrich said. "Krug. Two bottles and put more on ice."

"Certainly, General," Vogel said, and bustled away.

Heydrich looked the place over. As usual with such clubs, there were several pretty young hostesses available, seated at the bar. He studied them with the eye of a connoisseur.

Vogel returned with the champagne, and Heydrich said, "The blonde, third from the end of the bar. Tell her to come here."

The girl came immediately. Heydrich didn't ask her name. He simply told her to sit down and poured her a glass of champagne. Then he pulled back her skirt and stroked her silken knees while he talked to Schellenberg.

Connie and his boys were playing "Some of These Days", and

37

Heydrich drummed out the tempo on the edge of the table with the fingers of his free hand. Then Uncle Max's voice boomed out, and a moment later, Hannah emerged onstage and started to sing.

Many of her numbers were in English. She worked her way through the popular songs of the day, including "That Old Feeling" and "Time on My Hands", and ended with a beautiful rendition of "These Foolish Things" that had the patrons standing up and cheering.

Schellenberg had been totally absorbed and was on his feet applauding when he glanced down and noticed Heydrich, still sitting, one arm round the young girl, frowning up at him.

As the applause died away, Heydrich said, "Careful, Walter, you're letting your enthusiasm run away with you. I think you like this one—too much, perhaps."

Schellenberg nodded to Vogel, who went to speak to Hannah. She came across to their table.

Schellenberg said, "You were marvellous—truly."

He held her hands tightly for a moment, and she responded in spite of herself. "Thanks—I enjoy singing and that's usually good for the audience."

"General Heydrich, may I present Fräulein Hannah Winter?"

Heydrich didn't bother to get up. "Excellent, Fräulein." His manner was cool, almost offensive. He said to Schellenberg, "Walter, I've decided to have an early night. I'll take the car and send it back for you—if you want to stay on, that is."

"Yes, I think I will."

"Suit yourself." Heydrich got up, clutching the blonde girl firmly by one arm. "Fräulein Winter—a pleasure."

Hannah and Schellenberg watched them go. Then they sat down and he poured her a glass of champagne. "You have another show?"

"Yes, in a little while."

"May I escort you home afterwards?"

She put a hand on her thigh, aware of the folded report that she had pushed into her stocking. It gave her a strange feeling of power over him, so she smiled and said yes, and was aware again of that hollow feeling of excitement.

He took her hand and said gently, "Are you familiar with a song called 'Moonlight on the Highway'?"

"Yes."

"It is a special favourite of mine. Will you sing it for me?"

"If you like." She got up and then walked away.

Max was waiting impatiently in her dressing room. "What happened, for heaven's sake?"

"Nothing much. Heydrich was rude. Schellenberg was rather nice. Gave me champagne and asked to take me home."

"And what did you say?"

"Yes."

"You're crazy."

"Not really. I'm intrigued, that's all."

There was a knock at the door and Connie looked in. "Here we go again."

As she started to leave, her uncle said, "By the way, can I have your passport? I'll get your visa and money in the morning."

"Top drawer of the dressing table," she said, and went out.

Her second show was even more successful than the first, and she ended, as Schellenberg had asked, with the hauntingly beautiful "Moonlight on the Highway".

She went back to her dressing room to change, and when she finally emerged from the club, Schellenberg was waiting for her beside the black Mercedes. "Do you mind if we walk to my place?" she asked. "It helps me unwind."

"Not at all." He nodded to the driver, and as they started down the street, the Mercedes crawled along behind.

"New York, Paris, Berlin," she said. "All different by day, but at night, the same fresh smell. The same rain on the wind."

"And always the feeling that just around the corner something strange and exciting is waiting."

"That's it exactly," she said, and took his arm.

"Twenty was a good age," he said. "One could sniff that cold bracing nip in the air on those autumn evenings and actually believe that life was full of infinite possibility."

They continued in silence for a while, and then she said, "You're not like Heydrich—like the rest of them. I don't understand."

"It's simple really," he answered. "I was a lawyer. I spoke several languages and yet there was no work for me—or for the thousands of young Germans like me. If I could have done what I wanted, I would have gone into the theatre, because I suspect I am a born actor. So, I joined the ultimate theatrical company— the SS."

"That's not good enough."

"It was a job—it was a nice uniform. It was having respect from people where there had been none before."

"Respect for kicking old Jewish women into the gutter? For running concentration camps? I thought that was the prime function of your SS."

They had reached her apartment. He said, "Hannah, it's easy to climb on the merry-go-round. Not so easy to jump off once it starts moving. I'm afraid that's true for most Germans today."

"Then I'm sorry for you."

She turned and ran up the steps to the front door. Schellenberg stood there for a while, then went to the Mercedes and leaned down. "You can go home, boys. I'll walk."

It began to rain again and he pulled up the collar of his coat, shoved his hands into his pockets and started off, his face grim.

Five

At ten o'clock the following morning, Heydrich was at his desk dictating to Frau Huber when Schellenberg entered, carrying a couple of files.

"I'm due at the Führer's weekly conference at the Chancellery at eleven," Heydrich said. "Can it wait?"

"Not really," Schellenberg said. "Priority one, which means a memo is already on its way to Himmler."

Heydrich frowned. He looked as if he had not slept, and the paleness of his face was accentuated by the fact that he was in full black dress uniform. "Go on."

"The Winter affair," Schellenberg said. "As you know, we've had a photographic surveillance team working on his club for some time. Last night they came up with a new face."

He laid a selection of photos on the desk. They showed Irene Neumann leaving the stage door of the Garden Room.

"Do we know her?" Heydrich asked.

"Yes. She's a clerk in Central Office."

Heydrich looked at him in astonishment. "You mean here?"

"I'm afraid so. Here's her file."

Heydrich opened it. There were the usual double identity photos pinned to the inside cover. Frau Huber, who had been sitting quietly at the side of the desk, could see them plainly.

She said, "Excuse me, General Heydrich. I know this woman. I saw her yesterday in the copying room on temporary duty."

"Are you certain?"

"Oh, yes. I'd just done the confidential report on the meeting between General Schellenberg and Foreign Minister von Ribbentrop. I went to have the usual three copies made. As I didn't recognize her, I asked her who she was."

There was a heavy silence. Schellenberg said gently, "You stayed with her while she made those copies?"

"Of course I did, General. Standard procedure with confidential documents." And then she remembered and her face sagged.

"Go on!" Heydrich said. "The truth."

She whispered, "The phone rang and I went to answer it. Fräulein Neumann actually brought the copies into my office."

Heydrich slammed a clenched fist against the desk. "Out of my sight. You're finished—finished. Do you hear?"

She hurried from the room, weeping. As the door closed, Heydrich said, "So, the Neumann woman could have run off an extra copy of the Windsor report."

"Almost certainly," Schellenberg said.

"Then it's curtains for that Jew, Max Winter," Heydrich said viciously. "And that niece of his."

"Oh, I don't know." Schellenberg had spoken as a reflex more than anything else. "There's no necessary connection between her and her uncle's activities. I had her under surveillance as a matter of course, naturally, but—"

"Is that so? Well, I'm afraid I don't share your opinion." Heydrich quickly read through the file on Irene Neumann and shook his head in disbelief. "Clean as a whistle. Her father was killed on the Somme, Iron Cross, First Class. And her uncle, a fighter pilot with Richthofen. Awarded the Blue Max. Lives alone with her mother. Full security clearance." Heydrich was bewildered.

The internal phone rang and he answered it. "At once, Reichsführer." He replaced the receiver with a sigh. "Himmler wants both of us—now. And he wants Neumann's file."

HIMMLER examined Irene Neumann's record in silence while Schellenberg and Heydrich stood before his desk like schoolboys.

Heydrich said, "I just can't understand it, Reichsführer. Full security clearance. An impeccable record."

"Which is hardly relevant," Himmler said. "The fact that she was given full security rating shows a lack of intelligence that I find astonishing. You will determine who the clearance officer was and have him transferred to a penal unit at once."

"Of course, Reichsführer," Heydrich said eagerly.

"Yes, the flaw in the woman's background is evident to anyone with perception. According to the file, she went to Paris in 1921 to do postgraduate work in French. Remember what a hotbed of Communism the Sorbonne was at that time?"

"I see now," Heydrich said. "Of course. She could be a sleeper for our Moscow friends."

"I should have thought it obvious." Himmler turned his attention to Schellenberg. "She'll deny it, of course, but do you think Fräulein Neumann took a copy of the Windsor report?"

"I believe so, Reichsführer. We've had a surveillance unit working on the Garden Room for some months and she's never shown up before. An agent like her must be used with care. The reason for her appearance last night had to be one of supreme urgency."

Himmler said, "I agree entirely. So, Winter may now be taken into custody. And this niece of his, of course."

Again Schellenberg spoke impulsively. "I must point out, Reichsführer, that on the basis of my personal experience, I believe the young woman to be entirely innocent in this affair."

There was quiet in the room for a few moments. Finally Himmler spoke. "Wait outside. I wish to talk to Heydrich alone."

Schellenberg left. When the door had closed, Himmler said, "He has formed an attachment to this girl, am I right?"

"Reichsführer, Walter Schellenberg is the most able officer—"

"I did not ask you for a reference. I asked whether in your opinion he has formed an attachment to this Winter girl."

"Very well. I regret to say that I think he has," Heydrich replied.

"I thought so. Under the circumstances, he must take no further part in this matter. I would suggest that you handle it personally, as well as the interrogation of Irene Neumann."

"With the greatest of pleasure, Reichsführer." Then Heydrich hesitated. Cold and calculating by nature, he seldom cared about anybody—yet Schellenberg was different.

"Reichsführer, I trust this doesn't indicate any change in your attitude towards Schellenberg. His loyalty is unquestioned, believe me, and he has been of great service to the Reich."

"Undoubtedly." Himmler leaned back. "He has all the qualities. A brilliant intellect, gallant soldier, cultured, witty. Humane by nature. In the field of counterespionage, one of the most able minds in Europe. He is also a romantic fool."

"But his record is impeccable. A good party member."

"Which means nothing. Anyone can pay that kind of lip service." He raised a hand. "Don't worry. He's too good a man to discard—yet. Now let's have him back in."

A moment later, Schellenberg was again in front of the desk. "I've decided you will start for Spain tomorrow by special courier plane," Himmler said. "Under the circumstances, you will give all relevant information concerning the Winter affair to Heydrich."

"As you say, Reichsführer." Schellenberg controlled his anger. But the truth was he could do nothing for Hannah Winter now.

IRENE NEUMANN sat on a chair in front of Heydrich's desk, her hands folded firmly in her lap, her face expressionless. Two SS men guarded the door.

Heydrich entered. He sat down behind his desk and opened her file. "So—Fräulein Irene Neumann, you know why you are here?"

"I have no idea."

He pushed the surveillance photos across the desk. "You, coming out of the Garden Room last night."

For a moment only, her iron reserve failed, and what she felt showed on her face.

"Yes, you might well look dismayed. This is the day you've dreaded all these years." He got up and stood at the window, his back to her. "The copy of the Windsor report which you stole. You showed it to Winter, of course. That was the object of your rather injudicious visit, but was his niece with him at the time?"

"I have nothing to say."

"It doesn't matter. They'll both be joining you shortly."

She made no reply, and he came round the desk and took her chin gently in one hand, tilting her face. "You will tell me, Fräulein, in the end. I promise you."

HANNAH WENT OUT for a while during the morning. When she returned to her apartment, there was a telephone message from Uncle Max asking her to meet him at the club. This surprised her, for during the day the club was usually locked up tight.

When she arrived she found the stage door open. As she went in, his voice called, "Is that you, Hannah?" Uncle Max looked out of his office. "Close the door and lock it, will you?"

She did as she was told, then walked into his office. "What did you want to see me about?"

"Arrangements for your trip. What have you done with the Windsor report?"

She patted her thigh. "Still in my stocking, though I spent a couple of hours memorizing it. Do you want me to destroy it?"

"I don't know," he said. "Such a story might not be taken seriously without the evidence. Let me think about it."

"Have you got my passport?"

"Of course." He took a large envelope from his inside breast pocket and produced a passport. "There. You'd better check it."

"But this is French," she said. "There must be a mistake."

"Take a look."

She opened it. The usual photo stared out at her, but her name was given as Rose Lenoir, born in Paris. "I don't understand."

"I had it made up by a friend who specializes in such things. If you have any trouble trying to cross into Spain or Portugal as Hannah Winter, you switch identities. Your French is good. Your real passport is in here as well, plus train tickets and enough money—francs and pesos—to get by on, and a letter of credit for two thousand dollars on American Express in Lisbon."

"You seem to have thought of everything," she said.

There was a knock at the stage door. Uncle Max slipped the envelope back into his pocket, opened the desk drawer, and took out a Walther automatic pistol. He moved to the window and peered out. A young man wearing blue overalls stood there whistling. He was carrying a bulging leather bag of the type used by tradesmen.

Max, followed by Hannah, went out into the passage. He opened the door, leaving the security chain in place. "What is it?"

"Plumbers. . . . Something wrong with the hot water in the kitchen. Herr Vogel called this morning."

Max put the Walther into his pocket, undid the chain, and let him in. "First door on your left is the kitchen."

"All right, leave it to me." The young man had bright blue eyes. He winked impudently at Hannah and disappeared.

Max and Hannah went back into the office. Suddenly there was the roar of an engine outside in the alley, the squeal of brakes, pounding feet.

"Oh, dear God," he said, and grabbed Hannah by the shoulders. "If anything happens, if we get separated, I'll be at a firm of stone-masons called Hoffer Brothers in Rehdenstrasse. It's close to the zoo. Now follow me and do everything I say."

As they went into the passage the young man with the bright blue eyes emerged from the kitchen. He was holding an Erma police submachine gun.

"All right, against the wall. Nothing foolish."

The pounding started on the door, the young man glanced briefly towards it, and Uncle Max flung himself at him. The man reversed the Erma and struck Max under the ribs. The older man went down with a cry of pain.

The young man stood over him, his back turned to Hannah. "You know, I'd kick your head in if you weren't so valuable."

There was a heavy porcelain lamp on top of the filing cabinet by the door. Hannah picked it up in both hands and brought it down with all her strength, smashing it across the man's head. He fell to his knees.

The battering on the door had reached a crescendo. As her uncle looked up at her, his face twisted in pain, Hannah said desperately, "Uncle Max, what are we going to do?"

He was breathing with some difficulty. "Help me to the wine cellar, and bring that with you."

He nodded towards the Erma, and she picked it up gingerly and helped him to his feet. They reached the end of the corridor, and he started to unbolt the metal gate leading to the cellar steps. Behind them, the stage door fell from its hinges, and the entrance was suddenly jammed with SS men.

Hannah turned and swung up the Erma instinctively, her finger tightening on the trigger. She had never fired a weapon before in her life, and the Erma was like a living thing in her hands, ripping plaster from the walls, driving the SS men back into the alley.

She kept on firing convulsively, the Erma bucking so violently that she fell against Uncle Max as he opened the gate. He lost his balance and slid down the wooden stairs.

Hannah had dropped the Erma. She was on her knees now, and screamed, "Uncle Max—are you all right?"

She saw him get to his feet. "Quickly!" he called.

46

A hand grabbed her right ankle as she tried to get up. She half turned and saw that the young man with those bright blue eyes had crawled up to her. "Oh no, you don't," he said. Other SS men were pouring into the passage now, and they ran to help him.

Down below, Max heard the SS men and he knew there was nothing he could do for Hannah. He turned and staggered into the next cellar room, closed the stout oak door, and rammed home two steel bolts. Then he moved on between rows of wine bottles. Behind him, a furious pounding sounded on the door, but they were too late, for he had anticipated just such a situation and had made every preparation.

In the third cellar was a wooden cupboard. Inside were a hat, a raincoat, a large handlamp, and a briefcase containing various false documents and a supply of money in several currencies.

He put on the coat and hat and pushed the cupboard to one side, disclosing a hole in the brickwork. He picked up the hand-lamp and the briefcase and clambered through, then turned and pulled the cupboard back into place. A minute later, he was unbolting a door that revealed steps leading up into a small yard.

He climbed the steps and opened the gate leading out of the yard. The alley was completely deserted. He closed the gate and walked rapidly away.

AT THAT SAME MOMENT in Santo e Silva's villa in Estoril, the Duke and Duchess of Windsor were entertaining Primo de Rivera, the Marquês de Estella, who had driven over from Madrid especially to see them. As the servants cleared the remains of luncheon, de Rivera took out his watch. "Time passes so quickly in good company, but I must start back for Madrid." He turned to the Duke. "I wonder whether Your Royal Highness could spare a few moments' conversation before I go? In private."

The Duke looked faintly surprised, but smiled as courteously as always. "Yes—why not? We shan't be long, Wallis."

It was half an hour before they returned. De Rivera kissed the Duchess's hand, promising to come again soon, and departed. The Duke moved to the terrace and leaned on the marble balustrade, frowning.

"And what was that all about?" the Duchess asked, coming to stand beside him.

"I'm not sure. It was really most extraordinary. He'd heard of

47

my Bahamas appointment from official sources in Madrid. Had even discussed it with Franco."

"But why, David?"

"Do you know, Wallis, he urged me not to go. Said I could still have a decisive role to play in English affairs. He said we'd be better off going to Spain. We would be made officially welcome."

"Would you rather do that?"

"Too complicated. Indications are that the Spaniards don't intend to enter the war on the Nazi side, but they might well use England's present plight as an excuse to demand the return of Gibraltar. I certainly don't want to become a pawn in that kind of game."

"So you don't trust de Rivera?"

"He's a Madrid Falangist, and I trust them no more than I would any fascist. No, there could be more to this, Wallis. Much more."

His eyes crinkled and he put an arm about her waist. "There's a certain excitement to it all, though. I must admit that."

Six

The cell was quite small, the concrete walls whitewashed. There was a light recessed into the ceiling and a small iron bed with no mattress. A cold, white concrete womb.

Hannah sat on the edge of the bed, her mind so numbed by events that she was unable to take any of this in. There was a dreamlike quality to everything, like a nightmare half remembered in the morning. That desperate scramble in the passageway at the club, the submachine gun bucking in her hands, the smell of cordite. And Uncle Max? Where was he now?

Heydrich, watching through the peephole, nodded to the Gestapo interrogation expert, Major Berg. "All right, open up."

The sound of the bolts being withdrawn was of no significance to Hannah. She sat there, staring at the wall, so that Berg had to drag her to her feet.

Heydrich lit a cigarette and stood facing her, legs apart. He was still wearing his dress uniform, a devil in black, but his voice when he spoke was dispassionate.

"You're quite a girl, aren't you? Three of my best men dead. Two more in hospital. They trained you well." He turned to Berg. "Strip her. Thorough search. I'll be back in a few minutes."

When he returned to the cell, Hannah was standing in the centre of the room, naked, her hands folded in front of her. Her clothes were laid out neatly on the bed. She showed no emotion.

"We've struck gold," Berg told Heydrich. "I found this in the top of one of her stockings."

Heydrich unfolded the copy of the Windsor report. "Excellent. Now we're really getting somewhere." Then he grabbed Hannah's hair savagely and swung her head from side to side. "Your uncle— where did he go?"

She felt no pain at all. Her voice seemed to come from a great distance, like a faint echo. "I don't know."

Heydrich pushed her away. "Get your clothes on."

Berg said in a low voice, "She's still in shock."

"Then we'll have to shake her out of it, won't we? You go and see how they're getting on with the Neumann woman. I'll be along in a while."

Berg went out and Heydrich stood there a moment watching as Hannah dressed, still with that vacant look on her face. She really did have an excellent body, he told himself, walking out.

HIMMLER glanced up from his desk when Schellenberg entered his office. "So, a deplorable business, this Winter affair," the Reichsführer said. "Heydrich has just been to see me. Three dead. Two wounded. A surprising young woman. You were obviously wrong about her."

Schellenberg gave him the reply he was seeking. "I'm afraid so, Reichsführer."

Himmler said, "A little humiliation is good for the soul, but I didn't bring you here to discuss that. I have selected two Gestapo men to accompany you to Lisbon as your bodyguards."

He spoke briefly on the internal telephone. A moment later, the door opened and two men entered. They were large and powerfully built and wore conventional grey suits. One was bald and the other wore glasses. Schellenberg recognized the type instantly. Ex-police officers, more used to moving among criminals than anything else.

"Sturmbannführer Willi Kleiber," Himmler said, and the one in the glasses clicked his heels. "And Sturmscharführer Sindermann. General Schellenberg you know."

"A pleasure, General," Kleiber said.

49

"I have explained to Major Kleiber and Sergeant Major Sindermann the purpose of your visit to Lisbon," Himmler said. "I
suggest you show them the Führer's order under which you are
acting."

Schellenberg produced it from his wallet. Kleiber read it, face
expressionless, showed it to Sindermann, then handed it back.

"So you see, gentlemen, any order you receive from General
Schellenberg is an order from the Führer himself."

"Understood, Reichsführer."

"Excellent." Himmler smiled up at Schellenberg. "No need for
you to stay. I'm sure you have arrangements to make."

After Schellenberg left, Himmler turned to Kleiber. "Are you a
religious man?"

"Not really, Reichsführer."

"General Schellenberg is. He had a strict Catholic upbringing.
People like that tend to a moralistic attitude which can cloud their
judgment. They see people as being more important than causes."

"Yes, Reichsführer."

"In this Winter affair, the general seems more concerned with
the young woman involved than with the damage her uncle's
activities have caused the Reich. To be blunt, Kleiber, General
Schellenberg is an excellent officer. However, on occasion he lacks
a certain conviction, and I'm not entirely happy about his attitude
towards the Windsor business."

"I see, Reichsführer."

"There are times, Kleiber, when one must be prepared to go
for the throat if necessary. I'm relying on you to see that Schellenberg does. As your Reichsführer, I have a right to demand your
unquestioning loyalty in this."

"You have it, Reichsführer, I swear it," Kleiber said.

HEYDRICH opened the door of Hannah's cell and went in. She
was sitting dazedly on the edge of the bed again, fully clothed.

"All right," he said. "On your feet. Follow me."

She hesitated, and he grabbed her by the arm and pulled her
out of the door. He pushed her along the white-painted corridor to
another cell door, where he slid back a small metal gate. He put
Hannah's face against the opening so that she had to look inside.

Irene Neumann, her dress ripped to the waist, was sprawled
across a bench while a couple of heavily muscled SS men beat her

across her back with rubber truncheons. The woman arched in agony. Major Berg stood in the cell, watching.

Hannah came back to life then, the horror of it like a blow in the face. "You see?" Heydrich said. "All she has to do is answer a few questions about your uncle. It appears she prefers to die."

He pushed Hannah's face against the opening again, and she struggled to free herself. "No, let her go! Make them stop."

"All right, you answer my questions for her."

"No—I don't know anything."

"We'll see, shall we?" He opened the door and said to Berg, "Hold it." He turned to Hannah. "Now—each time you fail to answer, we start again. You will be the instrument of her pain."

Hannah was terrified now, and it showed clearly in her face.

Heydrich said, "You and your uncle—have you been working together ever since you arrived from America?"

"No," she answered.

"Then how do you explain the copy of the Windsor report?"

"It was an accident. I overheard Fräulein Neumann talking to him." Her mind roamed desperately, seeking the right way to frame her answers. What to give and what to hold back.

"You weren't aware before then that your uncle was working against the Reich?"

"I swear it."

"And the Windsor report? Why was it on your person?"

"My uncle had already arranged for me to return to America via Lisbon. He thought I could take the report to the Duke of Windsor."

"You've read it? You are familiar with its contents?"

Her mind told her that to reply honestly to this question might make him believe her lies also.

"Yes—I memorized it."

"Where is your uncle now?"

"I don't know."

He snapped a finger, and the truncheons started to descend again. She clutched at his arm. "It's the truth, I swear it. He ran away—left me."

And he believed her, staring down into her contorted face, aware, with a fierce anticipatory joy, of the power he held over her. He nodded to Berg. The beating stopped.

"And the Negro musicians. Were they in any way involved?"

51

"No."

"Good." He turned towards Berg. "Put Fräulein Winter back in her cell. Then give the other one any medical treatment she needs. Hot bath, food. You know what to do."

ONE ENTIRE anteroom at Prinz Albrechtstrasse was crowded with the staff of the Garden Room, who were being interrogated individually. Connie Jones, Billy Joe Hale, and Harry Gray were sitting in a corner, talking in low tones. They had already gone through the interrogation process and weren't too happy about it.

"I asked to see someone from the American embassy," Connie said, "but it didn't do any good. This whole thing stinks. All those questions about Hannah and Max."

"The way I see it," Harry Gray said, "we'll be lucky to make it out of here in one piece."

Heydrich entered and walked through into the office. The SS officer behind the desk jumped to his feet.

"Anything?" Heydrich demanded.

"All clean, General. Kleiber interrogated the Negroes and was satisfied they know nothing. They are due to leave for Madrid via Paris in the morning. I have their train tickets and passports."

"Very well," Heydrich said. "Keep them in custody overnight, then put them on the train. Official deportation for associating with enemies of the state." Heydrich turned and left.

He went at once to Schellenberg's office, where he found him signing letters. "So, Walter, you were wrong about the girl. She was going to take that Windsor report to Lisbon to the Duke."

"Not by design," Schellenberg said. "I knew she was going to Lisbon. The travel agents reported the bookings, as they always do in the case of foreign nationals. That was before the report was stolen. Before my interview with Ribbentrop."

"You mean you think she could just be an innocent tool? It's a possibility, but she will still have to be interrogated further. I'll handle that myself."

Schellenberg knew what that meant. Realized that Heydrich was taking a perverted pleasure in telling him, for his sexual habits were well known.

"Actually," Heydrich continued, "I'll do her a favour. You bring her up for me. Talk to her. Make her see sense. She might listen to you. It could save her a lot of grief."

"As you wish," Schellenberg said. "The green room?"

"But of course," Heydrich answered, smiling.

WHEN THE DOOR of the cell was unlocked and Schellenberg entered, Hannah looked up at him without speaking.

"Have you nothing to say?" he asked.

"Not to you—ever again. I thought you were different, but I was a fool. What do you want, anyway?"

"Heydrich told me to bring you to him."

She stood up wearily. "Does that mean what I think it does?"

"Usually."

She followed him into the corridor. He glanced at his watch. "Ten minutes to seven. Just getting dark."

"How interesting."

"Oh, but it is. SS organization is meticulous. Everything on time." They emerged into the foyer, where a guard stood at the main door. "At precisely seven each night, the Chancellery messenger goes out through that door with dispatches for the Führer."

They were climbing the staircase to the first floor now.

"Yes," Schellenberg went on. "The situation reminds me of an astonishing story I heard from Paris recently. It seemed a woman was arrested and taken to Gestapo headquarters at rue des Saussaies. Someone left her alone in an office for a moment. Apparently she picked up a file and walked out. Waited near the foyer till some general or other went out of the front entrance, then followed a minute later, telling the guard she had a file the general had forgotten. Once outside, she was up the nearest alley in a flash."

Hannah stared at him, eyes wide. "What kind of man are you? I don't understand."

He opened a door at the head of the stairs and ushered her into a room that adjoined Heydrich's office. It was painted green and furnished with a desk, some filing cabinets, and a divan. There was a clock over the far door.

"See the time," Schellenberg whispered. "A minute to seven. Two minutes after would be about right." He managed a smile. "I hope you can count."

He crossed to the far door, knocked, and opened it. Heydrich was sitting behind his desk. He stood up and came across the room at once. "Ah, Walter, you've brought Fräulein Winter, I see. Thank you very much. You can go now."

"Herr General."

The outer door closed softly behind Schellenberg. Heydrich stood watching Hannah, a slight smile on his face. He took a cigarette out of his case and lit it. He had all the time in the world. He might as well savour it. Behind and above him the second hand of the clock reached seven and moved on.

Heydrich said, "Come here." Hannah hesitated, panic moving inside her. "I said, come here!"

She started forward, but as she got close to him the phone rang sharply in Heydrich's office. He swore softly, turned, hurried back to his desk, and picked up the receiver.

"Hello? What is it?"

There was a long silence, and then a muffled voice said, "Record department?"

"No, it certainly isn't." He slammed down the receiver and went back into the green room. It was empty.

Such a thing just wasn't possible. It could not have happened—not to him. He wrenched open the door and went down the staircase to the foyer on the run.

"Have you seen a girl?" he demanded of the guard. "Pretty—dark-haired. Tweed skirt and a white blouse."

"That's right, General. She went out just a minute ago."

"Without a pass? How could she?"

The guard looked scared now. "She had a file in one hand. Asked if the Chancellery messenger had left yet. I told her he'd just gone through, and she said she had to catch him, as there was an important dispatch for the Führer."

Heydrich ran down the steps into Prinz Albrechtstrasse. It was quite dark now. Of Hannah Winter there was no sign.

He had no choice, of course. He had to put out a red alert. Then he went in search of Schellenberg, whom he found in his office, dictating a few last letters to his secretary.

"Out!" Heydrich snarled at the woman. "Outside—now!" She went, pale and frightened.

"What is it?" Schellenberg asked.

"She's gone. That little Jewish slut. I went into my office to answer the phone—when I returned, she'd cleared off."

"But how could she get past the front door?"

"Apparently she went out just after the Chancellery messenger. Told the sentry she had another dispatch for him."

"Breathtaking in its impudence, you must admit that."

Heydrich glared at him. "Walter, if I thought for a moment that you had anything to do with this . . ."

"I left her in your care," Schellenberg said. "Since then, I have been dictating letters to my secretary, as she will testify."

Which was not entirely true, for when he had asked her for a cup of coffee it had taken her at least two minutes to go for the thermos she kept in her office, ample time for him to phone Heydrich's office on the internal line.

"All right. All right," Heydrich said. "But what am I going to say to Himmler?"

There was a timid knock on the door, and Schellenberg's secretary peered in. "Well?" Heydrich demanded. "What do you want?"

"I'm sorry, but the Reichsführer is on the telephone. He wants to see you both—now."

ONCE OUTSIDE, HANNAH had walked quickly away, expecting at any moment a voice to call her back. She turned into the first street on her right, only then starting to hurry.

She remembered her uncle's instructions. She had no money for a cab, of course, and had to walk to the zoo, which took forty-five minutes. Once there, she asked directions to Rehdenstrasse.

It was a rather mean street of old decaying warehouses beside the River Spree. Halfway along, a sign on a fence said HOFFER BROTHERS—MONUMENTS. A gate that gave access to the yard was open, and Hannah stepped inside. She recoiled in horror as a row of ghostly figures loomed out of the shadows. And then she realized what they were. Religious images, angels and cherubim of stone, standing amid a cluster of crosses.

She moved on to a warehouse on the other side of the yard. Light showed faintly behind a curtain at an upstairs window. There was a narrow door, which opened to her touch, and she found herself facing a flight of wooden stairs.

EARLY IN THE WAR, German counterintelligence had developed a sophisticated range of mobile radio-direction-finding units, able to search the major cities of Western Europe for the secret transmitters operated by underground organizations.

There was only one such transmitter left in action in Berlin and that existed only because, under Max Winter's orders, transmissions to Moscow were made at irregular intervals and from different places. The present location was Hoffer Brothers, where there was only one brother still alive—Otto, a member of the Communist Party since 1920.

Max had gone straight there on leaving the club and had sent for the radio, which was kept in a separate place. The operator, a new recruit named Haupt, had delivered it.

And then a dreadful error had occurred. Haupt had mistakenly switched the set, which worked on alternating current, onto direct current, rendering it unusable. He was out now trying to obtain replacement parts. In fact, when Max heard the door open, he thought it was Haupt returning. He went to the head of the stairs and saw Hannah.

"My God!" he exclaimed. "I thought you were dead."

HANNAH SAT drinking the coffee Otto Hoffer provided, aware of her uncle's voice on the phone in the next room.

"A miracle," Otto Hoffer said to her. "To walk out of Gestapo headquarters just like that. That's really left those pigs with egg on their faces."

Uncle Max entered the room. "It's all arranged. You leave for Paris in one hour by road. From there, you'll be taken on to Spain by special courier. From Madrid, you can take a train to Lisbon. No trouble."

"But how?" she said. "You make it seem so simple."

"There's an underground route I've used many times before to get important Jews out of Berlin. The people I hire are crooks who do the whole thing strictly for cash. I like that. It means you know exactly where you stand."

"I see."

He took a trench coat from behind the door. "Wear this." He produced the envelope she had last seen in his office. "Your train tickets—no use now, of course. Both passports, francs, pesos, and the letter of credit for Lisbon. Now let's get moving."

They walked through a series of back streets, crossed the river Spree on an iron bridge, and finally turned into a street very similar to Rehdenstrasse. Mainly warehouses.

One faded sign said EAGLE WINE COMPANY. IMPORT-EXPORT. Max knocked at the door. It was opened instantly and a small, bald-headed man looked out.

"Hello, Scherber," Max said, and he and Hannah moved through.

"Five minutes," Scherber said. "Then I want you gone."

"Understood." Max passed him a wad of hundred-mark notes held together by an elastic band. "Are the boys ready?"

"Over here."

They were standing in a large, dimly-lit warehouse. Hannah saw a wine tanker parked at the far end by huge double doors. Two men stood beside it, smoking cigarettes.

"The Dubois brothers," Max said quietly. "Paul is the older one with the bad teeth. Henri is the one who does as he is told."

Henri was no more than twenty-one and wore a tweed cap and leather jacket. "So this is our cargo?" he said in bad German as they approached. "Delightful."

His brother said sourly, "What about our cash, Max? Two thousand francs, that's what we agreed."

Max counted it out. "The boys transport wine in bulk."

"All those krauts in Paris like German wine," Henri said. "And we aim to please."

"Show her where she goes," Paul Dubois told him. "And let's get out of here."

Henri opened the cab door and pulled back the double seat, revealing a trapdoor. He reached inside and switched on a light.

"All the comforts of home—mattress, coffee, sandwiches. Sorry about those boxes. A few items for the Paris black market."

Max kissed Hannah on the forehead. "When you get to Lisbon, go straight to the man himself."

"I won't let you down."

"I know you won't, Hannah. Go with love. Stay well."

She was crying now, as if knowing instinctively that she would never see him again. She clambered through the hatch into the narrow space. She had one final glimpse of him before Henri shut the trapdoor. Then the engine roared into life and the tanker lurched forward.

Seven

It was ten o'clock when Irene Neumann finished the excellent meal that had been served to her after her bath. The greyhaired woman who had attended her had been quite solicitous. "I think they must have made a mistake, dear," she had said.

In spite of the fact that she ached from her beating, Irene, wrapped warmly in a robe, started to come to life again. Then the door was kicked open and Berg and two SS men rushed in and grabbed her. They threw her into the corridor, and Berg pulled her head back by the hair so that she could look up at Heydrich.

"Oh, no, Irene," he said. "Not you. You've done your share. It's the turn of the person in the next cell now."

They dragged her along the corridor to the next door, and Heydrich opened the small metal gate so that she could look inside. An old, grey-haired, frail-looking woman sat on the bed.

"Frau Gerda Neumann, your mother, I believe—age seventy-one," Heydrich said. "Is it true she has a bad heart?"

Ten minutes later, Irene was sitting in front of the desk in his office, telling him everything she knew.

IT WAS just after midnight when Haupt, the young radio operator, returned to the Hoffer Brothers' warehouse with the necessary spare parts. Max Winter had come back from the Eagle Wine Company three hours ago.

"My God, it took you long enough."

"I was lucky to get what I wanted at all," Haupt told him.

Max went to the window and peered out through the curtain. He stiffened suddenly, aware of movement down among the monuments. "Otto," he called to Hoffer, "I think we have company."

"I'll check the front," Hoffer said. He opened a cupboard, took out a Schmeisser submachine gun, and went down the rear stairs to the main warehouse. He walked towards a large double door in darkness. Then the night was filled with the roaring of an engine, and the doors smashed inward as a troop carrier burst through.

The offside front wheel caught Hoffer a glancing blow, bouncing him against the wall. Frantically he squeezed the trigger of the Schmeisser, and at least half a dozen weapons fired at him in reply, tearing him apart.

Max, at the top of the stairs, knew that it was over. He stood there waiting for them, the Walther in his hand. He started to pray aloud, the last prayer a Jew utters on his deathbed: "Hear, O Israel; The Lord our God, the Lord is one."

He shot the first stormtrooper who appeared. Then someone shoved a Schmeisser round the corner and fired a long burst, hitting him several times, so that he fell down the stairs.

The rest of the attack group trampled over his body and went up to the office on the run, followed by Major Berg. A moment later they returned, dragging Haupt.

Heydrich was standing at the bottom of the stairs, looking down at Max Winter. "He's dead, which is a pity," he told Berg. "What have you got there?"

"Radio operator. He was trying to repair a set."

"So, you've transmitted messages today?" Heydrich demanded.

Haupt was terrified and showed it. "No—not a thing."

"Has there been a young woman here this evening?"

Haupt looked bewildered. "A woman? No—no one like that."

"All right, Berg. Take him back to Prinz Albrechtstrasse and see what you can get out of him. I'll see what we can turn up at the other address the Neumann woman gave us."

But the Eagle Wine Company was in darkness and there was no sign of Herr Scherber, the proprietor, at his apartment nearby.

The interrogators at Prinz Albrechtstrasse worked on the unfortunate Haupt for most of the night. He told them nothing because he knew nothing.

It was seven a.m. when Scherber was finally located in a steam bath off Kurfürstendamm. Once caught, he sang his heart out.

THERE WAS quite a crowd in Himmler's office for nine o'clock in the morning: Heydrich, Schellenberg, Kleiber, and Sindermann.

Himmler was speaking. "So, we know Winter didn't have time to pass on any information about the Windsor affair by radio, and the missing copy of the report is in our hands."

"Which means that the only other source of information on the subject is that damned Winter girl," Heydrich added.

"Who, according to Scherber, is now on her way to Paris in the company of two French black marketeers," Himmler said.

"We have the address where they are to deliver her at the other end," Heydrich said. "A café called the Golden Coin in Montmartre. The Paris Gestapo office could provide a reception committee for her."

"I have a better idea." Himmler turned to Schellenberg. "You leave for Spain this morning, don't you, flying by way of Paris?"

"I was under the impression that you didn't want me to have anything further to do with Hannah Winter."

"True, but Major Kleiber could take charge at the Golden Coin most adequately, and I am sure he would welcome your presence as an observer." He looked at Heydrich. "Kleiber will need additional men. Arrange it with the Paris office. Schellenberg, when does your plane leave?"

"Eleven o'clock, from Tempelhof."

"I wish you luck, then. Naturally I shall expect daily reports."

"Of course, Reichsführer."

"Kleiber, you will please stay."

When Schellenberg and Heydrich had left, Himmler said to Kleiber, "In the matter of the Winter girl's escape last night. The fact that she knew about the Chancellery messenger shows she had inside help."

"General Schellenberg, Reichsführer?"

"Watch him closely, Kleiber, and report to me daily. Here is the necessary authority." He passed Kleiber an envelope.

"I understand, Reichsführer."

"Let's hope you do," Himmler said. "You may go now."

HENRI DUBOIS turned the wine tanker into the parking area beside a small café in Clichy, north of Montmartre, and braked to a halt. "Are you going to phone, or shall I?" he asked his brother.

"Leave it to me," Paul said, and jumped to the ground.

Inside the café, he went into the telephone booth and dialled the number of the Golden Coin. The receiver at the other end was picked up instantly.

"Yes, this is the Golden Coin. What can I do for you?"

It was Mme. Bonnet, the proprietor, all right, but there was something in her voice. He was sure of it.

"Is it possible to book a table for seven tonight?" he asked. "Chicken paprika and a good Muscadet, if you could manage it?"

"No, I'm sorry, monsieur. I'm afraid we shall not be open for business tonight."

Paul said calmly, "Many thanks, madame. Another time."

AT THE GOLDEN COIN, half a dozen customers sat at the tables, trying to look as if they were enjoying their drinks. Three Gestapo agents waited behind the curtain leading to the kitchen. Walter Schellenberg, leaning on the bar, thought about Hannah Winter and the trap waiting for her. Unhappily there was nothing he could do this time—he was already in too deep.

Angélique Bonnet was seated behind her desk at the side of the bar, a small elderly woman in a severe black dress who ruled the establishment with a rod of iron.

She put down the telephone receiver, and Kleiber, who had been monitoring her conversation, nodded. "Good," he said.

"But of course. Soon I will have no customers left, and still I do not know what all this is about."

"A tanker filled with good German wine to be delivered here by two brothers named Dubois, together with an even more interesting consignment, eh?"

Angélique Bonnet's bewilderment looked extremely convincing. "But I know no one of that name, monsieur, and as for German wine, well, with the greatest respect, there's just no call for it here."

Kleiber looked uncertain and glanced towards Schellenberg, who said, "Have you considered the possibility that the Dubois brothers don't actually have any connection with the establishment, but with one of the customers?"

"Yes, that had occurred to me, naturally."

"And the local police. Do they have details of the tanker?"

"A full description," Kleiber said stiffly.

"Then there should be no cause for concern." Schellenberg turned to Angélique Bonnet. "My dear madame," he said in fluent French, "I'm afraid I must trouble you again for another glass of that excellent cognac."

PAUL DUBOIS leaned into the truck. "Get her out, quick," he said to Henri. "Something's up at the café."

His brother opened the trapdoor and pulled Hannah through. She looked tired and bewildered after the long twenty-hour drive, with only one stop. "Where are we? Paris?"

"Yes," Paul told her. "In Clichy. I think we're in trouble. Whenever we have a passenger like you, we always phone the Golden Coin before arrival. A prearranged code. I order a special meal for a certain number of people. If things are okay, the woman who runs the place accepts the booking."

"And she didn't just now?"

"Said she was closed tonight, and I've never known the Golden Coin to close before."

"So what do we do?" Henri demanded.

Paul Dubois frowned, then made his decision. "If things have gone wrong at the Berlin end, this tanker could be hot. We'll leave it here and go the rest of the way on foot. We'll see for ourselves what's going on."

They made their way to a small church on a hill above the square in which the Golden Coin stood. From the church cemetery they could see the café clearly, the striped awning above the tables on the pavement.

"There's a black sedan parked in the alley," Henri said.

His brother nodded. "Oh-oh!" he exclaimed, as a man wearing a dark overcoat and soft felt hat walked out of the café.

"Know him?" Henri demanded.

"I certainly do. Name of Ehrlich. A Gestapo major from rue des Saussaies. That does it." Paul turned to Hannah. "Sorry, kid. I don't know what went wrong, but they're waiting for us. You're on your own." He nodded to Henri and they hurried away.

She was alone, standing there in the cemetery, caught for a moment by the suddenness of it all. But that would never do, and she, too, turned and walked away.

She knew Paris well, thanks to a six months' cabaret engagement before the war. She hurried through the streets of Montmartre, not stopping until she reached the Place de la Concorde.

She found a coffee stall with tables arranged around it. She bought a cup of coffee and sat down to take stock of her situation. She spoke French tolerably well and she did have some francs, thanks to Uncle Max's forethought, plus the two passports. And there was something else—something she'd forgotten until now.

With fingers that trembled slightly, she took the railway tickets from the envelope. One was for Berlin to Paris, but the other was the important one. The berth on the Madrid express, leaving Austerlitz station at six p.m.

She glanced at her watch. It was five fifteen and Austerlitz was a good three miles away. She jumped to her feet and, as she turned, saw a small delivery truck swerve into the kerb. The driver, a middle-aged man with a drooping white moustache and wearing blue overalls, tossed a bundle of newspapers onto the pavement. Hannah ran to the truck and scrambled into the passenger seat.

"Hey, what's this?" the driver demanded.

"Please, monsieur, help me." She pulled out her passport and held it up. "See—I'm an American citizen, on my way home. I've got a seat on the Madrid express leaving Austerlitz at six. I did some sightseeing and got lost and I'll never make it on time now, unless you'll drive me there." She pulled out a wad of francs.

"Keep your money." He grinned. "American, eh? My son lives in Los Angeles. I'll have you there within fifteen minutes."

WHEN THE PHONE rang again, Angélique Bonnet answered it as before. "For you," she said to Kleiber as he reached for the earphone. "Police headquarters."

The expression on Kleiber's face was like a shot in the arm to Schellenberg. The major replaced the phone. "They've found the tanker," he whispered. "Abandoned about a mile from here."

"So," said Schellenberg calmly. "A wasted afternoon. My commiserations. Now I must visit SD headquarters. I'll see you back at the airport at eight o'clock."

He left, and a moment later Kleiber stalked out, crossing the square to where Sindermann and Ehrlich waited by a Citroën.

"The French police have found the tanker," he told them. "No sign of the Dubois brothers or the girl."

"They could be anywhere by now," Sindermann said.

It was Ehrlich who suggested the obvious. "We know her intention is to reach Spain. There is a night train to Madrid leaving Austerlitz station at six o'clock."

"Ridiculous," Sindermann said. "She'd never dare."

But Kleiber's face was ablaze with excitement. "She had a booking on that train made in Berlin by her uncle. A sleeping-car berth. So did those Negroes."

Ehrlich glanced at his watch. "Thirty-five minutes, that's all we've got. We'd better get moving."

JUST AFTER FIVE THIRTY, the newspaper deliveryman dropped Hannah at Austerlitz station. It was very busy—a mixture of civilians and German soldiers—and police seemed to be everywhere.

She found the correct platform for the Madrid express and approached the gate. There was a passenger list posted on the board beside the ticket collector. Her name was in the first-class section, in a private compartment with Connie and the boys. But if she presented her ticket, the collector would mark her off on his list.

She moved some distance away to consider the matter. At that moment, two porters passed her, pulling a chain of carts piled high with mail. They pushed open a wide gate giving access to the platform, and Hannah walked through with them, staying on the left-hand side so that she was hidden from the ticket collector.

There were many people on the platform, boarding the train. She walked towards the sleeping cars, moved past the steward, who was busy with another passenger, and then ducked in through the door at the far end of the first-class coach. There it was, only a step away: compartment A.

She tried the handle, but the door was locked. With a sinking heart, she tried knocking. There was a muffled voice inside, then the door opened.

"What is it . . ." Connie Jones started to say in French, and then his face seemed to split wide open. "Hannah baby."

And then she was inside, the door closing, his arms around her, Billy Joe and Harry laughing in astonished joy, and for some reason she started to cry.

THE THREE GESTAPO men reached Austerlitz at precisely five minutes to six. Harry Gray was at the small platform kiosk by the gate buying cigarettes. He recognized Kleiber at once, turned, and hurried back to the compartment.

"We got trouble," he said as he closed the door behind him. "That guy who interrogated us at Prinz Albrechtstrasse—he's at the gate checking the passenger list with the ticket collector."

"But I didn't come through officially," Hannah said.

"That doesn't mean a thing. Any second they're going to knock on that door. The question is where do we put you."

There were four berths, two on either side, and a small lavatory. Connie shook his head. "Man, you can't hide a cat in here."

Billy Joe turned to Harry with a grin. "Remember that time on the Chicago-Hollywood run? That fat white you-all from Alabama who didn't mind sharing with black folk if they was clean?"

"And we drove him out with disgust." Harry was all smiles as he started to unbutton his shirt.

Billy Joe was doing the same. "You heard the story, Connie. Now get her into bed real smart."

Hannah looked bewildered. Connie said, "Do as you're told, kid, and whatever happens, keep real still."

Billy Joe and Harry were stripping off their shirts as Connie shoved Hannah down onto one of the bottom bunks, pushed her against the wall, and pulled the blanket over her.

Harry lay down on the bunk against Hannah, and Billy Joe sprawled across him. There was a thunderous knocking at the door.

"Come on, open up! Police!"

Connie opened the door, leaving the chain on, and peered out at the sleeping-car attendant. "Hey, man, what's the beef? You have our tickets. We'd like a little privacy."

"There is a fourth reservation here, for Hannah Winter."

"It wasn't taken up, man—last I heard she was in Berlin."

"But you've no objection to us making sure." Kleiber appeared behind the attendant. "Open the door or we'll break it in."

Connie slipped the chain off. Kleiber shoved him back across the compartment and crowded in, followed by Sindermann and Ehrlich. The first thing he saw were two black men embracing on the right-hand lower bunk.

Harry said, "Whoops, we got company."

Billy Joe turned. "I thought the reason we paid first class was because privacy was guaranteed."

Kleiber stood glaring at them, his face pale. He kicked open the lavatory door, gave one quick glance inside, then went out into the corridor. The others followed him and Connie slammed the door behind them.

"May the train leave now, Major?" the attendant asked.

"Not until we have checked every passenger," Kleiber said, the disgust on his face plain.

They inspected each compartment, but finally had to admit defeat. As the whistle blew, Kleiber, standing by the gate, saw Connie lean out of a window.

"Anytime, Major." He waved cheerfully, then ducked back inside.

Harry and Billy Joe, now fully clothed, were sitting on one bunk, Hannah opposite. All three were laughing helplessly.

"Okay, children. Joke's over." Connie sat down beside Hannah. "I heard some bad news, kid. It's about your uncle Max."

Eight

The train had to stop for a customs inspection on the Spanish side of the border at Irún. Hannah stayed in the lavatory while a customs officer came round to check passports. After a short delay, they moved off again.

She came out and lay down on one of the lower bunks, her eyes swollen from weeping. Billy Joe and Harry simply sat there looking troubled. After a while, Connie came in with sandwiches and coffee from the dining car and sat beside her.

"Have something to eat. Do you good," he said. "You've got to pull yourself together."

"You just don't understand."

"Is that so? Well, let me tell you something. I served with the Harlem Brigade on the western front in 1918. I lost my only brother, two cousins, and pretty near every friend I had in the world, and you know what it taught me? That life goes on. Now your uncle Max—those pigs killed him. Right?"

She nodded, hands clenched.

"You gonna let them get away with that? He gave you a job to do, girl. Are you gonna do it, or are you just gonna cry all day?"

She hugged him. "Oh, Connie, you're right. What would I do without you?"

"That's my girl. Now, I've spoken to the attendant. We arrive in Madrid at nine o'clock in the morning. There's a train leaves for Portugal at nine thirty-five from the same platform. You can get your ticket on board. You get in at six thirty in the evening."

"That's fine," she said. "Couldn't be better."

"There's the Portuguese border," Harry Gray pointed out. "Could be trouble there."

"I don't see why," Hannah said. "I'll use the false passport Uncle Max gave me, just in case."

"When you get to Lisbon," Connie said, "if you need any help, go to Joe Jackson's American Bar. It's on the waterfront. Any cab-driver knows where it is. We're due to play there next week. He's an old friend and a great guy. Fought against Franco in Spain and flew fighters against the Condor Legion. Nothing happens in Lisbon that Joe doesn't know about. Now get some sleep, kid. You're going to need it."

She turned her face to the wall, trying to blot out every thought of Uncle Max. When she finally awoke to Connie's hand on her shoulder, they were in Madrid.

THE JU-52 German transport in which Schellenberg and his two bodyguards were travelling to Spain stopped at San Sebastián for refuelling. But there was some trouble in the port engine and they were delayed there for some five hours. It was almost ten in the morning before they swung in over the old city of Madrid and landed.

There was a car waiting to take them to the German embassy. As they drove into the city, Kleiber asked, "When shall we be continuing on to Lisbon, General?"

"Sometime this afternoon, I think," Schellenberg replied. "It depends how long my business takes with Ambassador von Stohrer."

"With your permission, General, I'd like to check the railway station."

"That train was due in an hour ago." Schellenberg shook his head. "You're obsessed with the idea of that girl roaming across Europe when she's probably holed up in some attic in Berlin."

"Or she could be here in Madrid at this Club Flamenco, where the Negroes told me they are to appear."

The car turned into the courtyard of the German embassy and braked to a halt. "Very well," Schellenberg said. "You can take the car. Be back here to pick me up no later than two o'clock."

A short while later, at Chamartin station, Kleiber discovered that the Madrid express had arrived on time and that a train had left the same platform for Lisbon at nine thirty-five. He also determined at the taxi stand that three Negro passengers had been delivered to the Club Flamenco.

Half an hour later, Kleiber was closeted with Madrid's chief of police, who was only too pleased to assist the Gestapo.

"I believe," Kleiber said, "that there could be a woman named Hannah Winter on the Lisbon express, travelling on a false American passport. She is a German citizen, wanted for murder. Once she is in custody, we shall apply for extradition, naturally."

The chief of police glanced at the clock on the wall. "The train stops at Talavera one hour from now. I will have the local police board it and search for this woman. In the meantime, perhaps we can enjoy a glass of wine together, and you can tell me how it is in Berlin these days."

WHEN THE TRAIN stopped at the Spanish city of Talavera, Hannah looked out of the window and saw the police. She didn't panic—simply settled back in the corner and returned to her magazine. She was wearing dark glasses, and a scarf tied round her hair, items Connie had bought for her at the station kiosk in Madrid.

The only other passengers in the compartment were a priest and a young woman with a baby. They all waited. Finally the door was pulled open.

Hannah kept on reading the magazine, aware out of the corner of her eye of the uniformed legs.

"Señorita. Passport."

She looked up at the young police officer as if startled, then produced her French passport and handed it over.

"Rose Lenoir. You are travelling to Lisbon, mademoiselle?" he asked in halting French.

"Yes," she replied.

"May I ask the purpose of your visit?"

"Business. I'm a singer. I'm to appear in a cabaret in Lisbon next week." She crossed one leg over the other, allowing the hem of her skirt to slide well above the knee.

The young policeman swallowed hard and handed back her passport. "*Bonne chance, mademoiselle,*" he said, and went out.

The priest looked shocked, the young woman amused. Hannah smiled at her and returned to her magazine.

AT THE GERMAN EMBASSY in Madrid, Schellenberg found himself in impressive company. There was Ambassador von Stohrer, a career diplomat and a Nazi with unquestioning allegiance to the Führer. His close contacts at every level of the Spanish government were of tremendous importance, especially at a time when negotiations between Spain and Germany about the future conduct of the war were at a delicate stage. Also present was the minister of the interior, Ramón Serrano Suñer, brother-in-law of Franco.

"Let's take our coffee on the terrace, gentlemen," von Stohrer said. "Much pleasanter out there."

They sat round a small, white-painted iron table and one of the servants brought the coffee. Then von Stohrer waved him away. "So, now we can get down to business. Perhaps, Minister, you would care to say something about the present problem?"

Suñer nodded. "Very well. So far, we have used Primo de Rivera as an emissary to the Duke. They are old friends. De Rivera has no idea of our mutual interest. He believes he is acting purely for the Spanish government in the matter and takes his instructions from me on behalf of our government."

"Are you implying that he only has the welfare of the Duke at heart?" Schellenberg asked.

"Exactly. It is now common knowledge that the Duke doesn't relish his appointment as governor of the Bahamas. It would be understandable if he felt insulted at its lack of importance."

"So, what has de Rivera suggested to him?"

"That he move to Spain, where the Spanish government would gladly grant him asylum, there to await events."

"And does de Rivera think the British would sit idly by while the Duke and Duchess packed their bags and moved out?"

"No. De Rivera is on his way to Lisbon again to visit the Duke at Estoril. His intention is to arrange a day in the country at some convenient spot near the border. An obvious opportunity for the Duke and Duchess to step across before the British, or anyone else, know what is happening."

"And if they choose not to?"

"But that, my dear Schellenberg, is where you come in," von Stohrer said.

Schellenberg nodded. "I see. Abduction. And de Rivera is aware of this possibility?"

"No," Suñer admitted. "As I've indicated, he is acting only out of concern for what he believes to be the best interests of an old friend. I should also point out that there is a rumour in Spanish society circles that it is the plan of the British secret service, once the Duke is in the Bahamas, to do away with him. Naturally de Rivera will convey this information to the Duke."

Schellenberg laughed out loud. "And do you seriously expect the Duke to believe this rumour?"

Von Stohrer stiffened. "I have it from Ribbentrop himself. His Swiss informant has close contacts with the British secret service."

"De Rivera will soon return with details of the trip to the country, the date and so on," Suñer said. "These will be communicated at once to Ambassador Huene at the German legation in Lisbon, who will, General, pass them on to you."

A servant appeared through the french windows and bowed. "Berlin on the telephone, Excellency."

"Excuse me, gentlemen," said von Stohrer.

He went out and Suñer offered Schellenberg a cigarette. "You looked sceptical, General, about this report from the Swiss agent concerning British secret service designs on the Duke."

"One of the problems of intelligence work is to sift the truth from the lies, or at least to recognize the distortions," Schellenberg said. "There are informants in every capital in Europe, wondering what story they will tell to satisfy their masters with this week."

The Spanish minister of the interior went on. "General Schellenberg, I will be frank with you. We are anxious, here in Madrid, to see a successful conclusion to this Windsor affair for one reason only—to accommodate the German government."

"Why would that be important at this time?" Schellenberg asked. He could guess, but preferred having the cards on the table.

"The Führer would like nothing better than for Spain to enter the war on the side of Germany. At the moment, Britain is still supreme in one respect—her navy. Our entry into the war would give Gibraltar to Germany and strike a crushing blow against the British navy by denying entry to the Mediterranean."

"In return, what would General Franco require?"

"Arms, petrol, manufactured goods that are in short supply here because of the devastation by our civil war. Also the French colonies in North Africa. You understand the situation now?"

"Perfectly," Schellenberg told him. "General Franco is willing to enter the war on Germany's side, but only after Operation Sea Lion has been concluded with the successful occupation of England. In the meantime, the abduction of the Duke of Windsor, in accordance with the Führer's wishes, serves to show that Franco's heart is in the right place, thus keeping everyone happy."

Sũner smiled broadly. "I see that we understand each other, and to be honest, I think that abduction will be necessary. I do not believe His Royal Highness would come willingly."

"Have you any special reason for believing that?"

"Yes, I think so. When the Duke was in Madrid recently, he dined with the Infante Alfonso, his cousin by marriage, who fought in the Spanish Civil War and saw the massive aid Spain received from the Reich. The Infante made a great deal of German military might, making it clear he thought Britain finished."

"And what was the Duke's reaction?"

"He became incensed. Asked the Infante if he'd never heard of the English Channel." Sũner shrugged. "You may not think this important, but to me it indicates the Duke is anything but favourable to your cause."

Von Stohrer returned. "That was Ribbentrop on the telephone from Berlin, gentlemen. I reported your safe arrival, Schellenberg. He trusts that you will carry on to Lisbon with all speed."

Schellenberg glanced at his watch. "Yes, indeed. I must get moving. The car should be back to pick me up at two. I'll be in touch at the earliest possible moment."

It hadn't gone too badly, he told himself as he went out. He certainly knew more than when he went in. The great game, some British intelligence chief had once called it, and what a game. Walking the razor's edge of danger. How many years of his life had he lived that way?

And to come so close to throwing it all away for the sake of a girl he hardly knew. Who most certainly despised everything he stood for. A cynical smile came to his lips. Ah, Walter, he thought. Your impulse to constantly try to do the decent thing will be the death of you one of these days.

When he went out to the courtyard there was no sign of Kleiber and Sindermann or the embassy car.

The porter emerged from the lodge. "May I help you, General?"

"Have you seen Major Kleiber?" Schellenberg asked.

"He hasn't returned yet. His driver phoned in some time ago to say they were at the Club Flamenco. Apparently the major is waiting for someone."

Schellenberg cursed softly. "Get me a car, quickly."

CONNIE AND THE BOYS had left their musical instruments at the Club Flamenco and had gone off to find a hotel. When they returned, Billy Joe's double bass was neatly set up on the small stage beside Harry Gray's drums.

"Hey, somebody unpacked for us," Billy Joe said. "I call that real friendly."

The curtain behind the stage parted and Kleiber stepped through. "That was me. I admire order in all things." Sindermann then emerged from behind the stage door and blocked it.

Connie glanced over his shoulder at him, then back to Kleiber. "What is this?" he asked.

"I'll tell you," Kleiber said. "I have a feeling you've been playing games with me. I think you know where Hannah Winter is."

"We're not in Naziland now," Connie said. "Why don't you just push off?"

Sindermann moved in very fast and punched him in the back, putting Connie on his knees.

"Expensive this, eh?" Kleiber indicated the double bass. He

72

stamped hard, splintering it, then put his foot through the large drum. Billy Joe and Harry cried out in anger and started forward. Kleiber drew a Luger from his coat pocket.

"Come on. Try it. I'd like nothing better than a chance to rid the world of such vermin."

They stayed where they were, crouched, watching, and Kleiber called to Sindermann. "Make the other one talk, Gunter."

Connie was still on his knees, and Sindermann kicked him in the spine. He was enjoying himself now, and he flexed his huge arms, then picked Connie up and threw him across the bar.

"He plays the piano for a living," Kleiber said. "How would he manage without a few fingers?"

Sindermann grinned. Holding Connie's right hand flat on the bar, he leaned across and took a full bottle of brandy from the shelf, gripping it by the neck.

He had raised it like a hammer poised to strike, when a quiet voice said, "Enough, Sindermann. Now let him go."

Sindermann turned his head slowly. His face was bathed with sweat, and there was a vacant look in his eyes.

Kleiber said, "General Schellenberg, these men have information of the greatest importance."

"These men, as you term them, are American citizens in a neutral country, and you, Kleiber, are promoting an incident which in the international press could do the Reich nothing but harm."

"General, I must protest."

"Get your heels together and stand at attention when you speak to me, Major, and put that gun away."

Kleiber did as he was told; slowly, but he did it.

"You would agree that I am your superior officer, appointed by the Führer?" Schellenberg said.

"Yes, General."

"So, remember in future, you do as you're told." His voice was very cold now. "Do you understand?"

Kleiber stared rigidly ahead as he spoke. "Yes, General."

"Good." Schellenberg turned to Sindermann. "Let go of that man and stand at attention."

But Sindermann had gone beyond reason now. "No!" he said.

"I could shoot you," Schellenberg told him. "But I'll teach you a lesson instead. When I look at you, you fill me with disgust. What are you, after all? Two hundred pounds of bone and muscle.

Brute force, and what good is that with a mind the size of a pea?"

Sindermann let go of Connie and charged, arms raised to destroy. Schellenberg pivoted to one side and delivered a left to Sindermann's kidneys as he lurched past. Sindermann fell to one knee, and Schellenberg picked up a chair and smashed it across his back. As Sindermann got up, Schellenberg sank a left under his ribs, followed by a right hook that landed on the cheek. Sindermann went down and stayed down.

Schellenberg said, "Next time, I'll kill you. Understand?"

Sindermann's voice was low, but his reply was quite clear. "Yes, General."

"Good." Schellenberg turned to Kleiber. "Get him to the car and let's get moving. The pilot will be wondering what's happened."

Kleiber did as he was told. Billy Joe had Connie in a chair at one of the tables and Harry brought brandy from the bar.

"He may need a doctor," Schellenberg said. "He could have a couple of cracked ribs."

Billy Joe shook his head. "Man, I can't figure you out, but thanks anyway."

Schellenberg started towards the door. He paused and turned to face Connie. "Just for the record, a matter of personal interest. She did make it? She is on her way to Lisbon? Am I right?"

Connie opened his mouth and said hoarsely, "General, why don't you . . ."

Schellenberg smiled. "Thank you, Mr. Jones, for answering my question."

The door closed softly behind him.

━━━━━━━━━━━ Nine ━━━━━━━━━━━

The Duke of Windsor had been closeted with Primo de Rivera for almost an hour, and the Duchess was in the garden cutting roses when her husband found her.

"What happened?" she asked.

"You know, Wallis, this whole business is beginning to assume rather farcical elements. I hear from de Rivera that, according to Madrid society gossip, the wicked British secret service would like to get their hands on me."

"Oh, David, what nonsense. Why?"

"Well, the logic behind it is really quite simple. Everyone knows

I'm not too happy about the Bahamas appointment, and many people seem to think that I might refuse to go. Stay here in Portugal or go to Spain instead."

"So they send the secret service to drag you off to the Bahamas by the scruff of the neck? How absurd."

"De Rivera seemed more concerned that I wouldn't get there at all. Over the rail one dark night and so on."

"That's terrible. How could he think such a thing?"

"Now, Wallis, you must admit I've been a considerable nuisance in certain people's eyes for quite some time." He was teasing her.

"I don't like it, David, this sort of talk. It isn't funny." She shivered. "I'm not even sure that I like this place any more. Too many policemen around."

"Well, we're going to change all that." He put his arm round her shoulder. "You shall have an outing. A day in the country. De Rivera has a friend who owns a bull farm at Niña. You know, fighting bulls for the ring. He says they'll stage a couple of fights for us and we can have a picnic. How does it sound to you?"

"Marvellous."

"Good." He smiled. "Let's go in now. Getting a little chilly."

THE POLICE ATTACHÉ at the German legation in Lisbon was named Egger. He was only too happy to help Kleiber in any way when the latter arrived from the airport.

"How good are your relations with the Portuguese police here?" the major asked.

"Excellent," Egger told him. "There is a considerable amount of political sympathy for National Socialism in Portugal."

"There's a possibility that this woman could turn up in Lisbon at any time. Here's her description." Kleiber handed him a sheet of paper with a photo of Hannah pinned to it.

"Hannah Winter," Egger said. "What has she done?"

"Shot three security men dead in Berlin, so we want her very badly indeed."

"She is a citizen of the Reich?"

"Of course, but she's been using an American passport."

"That won't do her any good, once I communicate these facts to the Portuguese security police. They mount a guard on all foreign embassies. I'll give them the details. If she tries to approach the American embassy, they'll have her."

As he reached for the phone, Kleiber said, "By the way, the Duke of Windsor is at Estoril. I don't suppose anyone can get in to see him without passing through the security police also."

"So I understand," Egger said.

"Good. My thanks." Kleiber turned to leave. "I'll see you again, I'm sure, while I'm here."

Sindermann was waiting for him in the anteroom. He had a black eye and his right cheek was badly swollen.

"The Portuguese security police are on the job now," Kleiber said to him. "The moment she shows her face, she's ours."

BARON OSWALD von Hoyningen-Huene, the German ambassador in Lisbon was a very different man from von Stohrer, his Madrid counterpart. He was a genuine aristocrat, a man of culture and refinement. He was also, as Schellenberg well knew, no Nazi.

Huene examined the Führer's order, which Schellenberg passed across the desk to him. "Naturally I shall give you every assistance I can, General. The terms of the Führer's letter give me no choice."

"Which means that you don't approve of this whole affair," Schellenberg said.

Huene sat there, staring at him calmly for a moment. "General Schellenberg, what exactly are you trying to say to me?"

"That I don't think much of the idea myself. It's nonsense. There, I've said it, Baron. Do you now place a call to Ribbentrop?"

"No," Huene said. "What I do is get a bottle of the cognac I keep in the cabinet over there, and two glasses, and we talk, completely off the record, of course."

Schellenberg sampled the cognac. "Excellent. But to the Windsor affair. Do you honestly think the Duke is on our side?"

"Frankly, no," said Huene. "Oh, he's not happy about this Bahamas post and he's certainly pro-German, but with his family background one would expect that."

"Which is a very different thing from being in favour of National Socialism."

"Exactly. So—where does that leave you, General? With only one choice, as I see it."

"Abduction?" Schellenberg shook his head. "I don't think so. In my opinion, there would be nothing gained by such an action. But if the Duke indicates a desire to go to Spain, then I shall give him every assistance in the matter. Otherwise . . ."

"Good. I'm glad we are in accord on this thing," Huene said. "The abduction of the Duke would hardly rebound to our credit, however much the Portuguese government are in sympathy with us." He stood up. "Will you have dinner with me tonight?"

"Another time, if I may," Schellenberg said. "I've an old friend to see. What about accommodation?"

"Rooms have been booked for you and your two Gestapo associates in staff quarters. I've also provided a car and a driver for your personal use."

"Then I'll have the driver take me there now."

IN 1938, ONE of Schellenberg's first pieces of active espionage had involved intelligence gathering at Dakar, the chief French naval station in Africa. Most of his preparations for the task had taken place in Lisbon, where he had been introduced to a Japanese businessman, Kajiro Taniguchi. A genuine friendship had developed between the two men, and Taniguchi had been able to assist Schellenberg with the African adventure. Taniguchi seemed to have a finger in all sorts of schemes and had close contacts with the local criminal fraternity. Schellenberg had long ago decided that he was probably an agent of the Japanese government.

Taniguchi owned an import-export agency on the Alcantara docks. Schellenberg drove there himself in the legation car. The offices were dark when he arrived, but when he drove into the yard of the adjacent warehouse, there was a light on at an upper window. He parked, and crossed to the warehouse door.

As he opened it, a voice called in Portuguese, "Who's there?"

The warehouse was crammed with boxes. High above was a glass-walled office reached by an iron staircase. Taniguchi stood at the top of it, a mountain of a man, built like a sumo wrestler.

He peered down into the shadows and then he smiled broadly. "Walter Schellenberg, by all that's holy."

Later, as they drank sake in his office, Taniguchi asked, "Business, Walter? It must always be so with you, I think."

Schellenberg said, "The Duke of Windsor is staying at Santo e Silva's villa in Estoril."

"Common knowledge," Taniguchi replied.

"I want to find out everything there is to know about that villa. The layout of the place, the servant situation, just how good the security is and so on. I would like to have someone in the house to keep me posted on the Duke's comings and goings. I should stress that money is no object. Can you handle it?"

"But of course," Taniguchi said tranquilly. "I know everyone in this town who matters, and in Lisbon money talks very loudly indeed."

"When will you have something for me?"

"Tomorrow afternoon. Let's say two o'clock. But now, my friend," he asked abruptly, "do you think you will win the war?"

"Let's look at the facts," Schellenberg said. "We control more of Europe than Napoleon did. Most neutral countries tend to sympathize with us, and America, let's face it, doesn't want to know."

"So, you think the panzers will soon be driving along the Mall to Buckingham Palace?"

"It's up to the British. The Führer made it clear he's willing to settle for an armistice. Of course, they may want to do it the hard way. They usually do."

"A saying of oriental wisdom—Chinese, actually," Taniguchi said. "If men are not afraid to die, it is of no avail to threaten them."

Schellenberg got up. "I must be off. I'll be in touch tomorrow."

JUST AFTER the Lisbon express crossed into Portugal, there was an inspection at Marvão. Hannah used the French passport and had no difficulty at all. She slept for the rest of the journey, arriving in Lisbon later than expected because of lengthy delays.

At a cab rank outside the station, she found a driver who spoke English and knew the villa of Santo e Silva in Estoril. She got into the cab, leaned back against the seat, and closed her eyes.

She came awake quite suddenly as the car drew up. They had stopped outside an ironwork gate set in a high wall. A policeman, a carbine over one shoulder, sauntered forward and spoke to the driver in Portuguese. The driver turned to Hannah. "He'd like to know what you want, senhorita?"

"To see the Duke of Windsor."

"And now your papers."

She produced her American passport and passed it across. The policeman took it to the gate and handed it to a sergeant who had emerged from a small lodge. He went inside, and after a few minutes came out again and gave the passport back to the first policeman, who returned it to Hannah.

"Can I go in now?" she demanded eagerly.

There was a further conversation in Portuguese, and the cab-driver said, "I'm afraid not. No visitors are allowed through without permission of police headquarters. He has made the telephone call. Now he must wait for a reply. Shall I stay, senhorita?"

"No—I don't think so. I could do with some fresh air." She paid him and he drove away.

Through the trees, she could see lights in the villa and there was the sound of music. It started to rain, and the policeman brought a cape from the sentry box and placed it round her shoulders.

It was quite cold now and she walked along the road to keep warm, pausing to look across the mouth of the Tagus river to where the lights of Lisbon gleamed in the distance.

Finally she went back to the policeman. "Please," she said. "How much longer? I've been here almost an hour."

At that moment, there was the sound of a car coming up the hill. Headlights flashed across the mimosa bushes and a black Mercedes braked to a halt a few yards away from her.

RAIN SWEPT IN across the Tagus and rattled the windows of Joe Jackson's apartment as he threw another log on the fire.

"That's quite a story, Hannah. Will you excuse me for a minute? I'll be right back. Help yourself to another drink."

She poured a little more brandy into her glass and sat in front of the fire, staring into the flames.

When he returned, she glanced up. "Do you believe me?"

"Let's just say I like you and I don't like those guys on the wharf, Kleiber and Sindermann. And the Duke of Windsor is in Santo e Silva's villa at Estoril. That's a fact."

"But we must get to him somehow, don't you see that?" she said urgently. "We can't just stand by and let the Nazis take him."

"It all sounds pretty wild to me," said Jackson. "It could be the invention of a frightened young woman who'd say anything rather than be sent back to Germany, where she's wanted for murder."

She stared at him. "How can I make you believe me?"

The telephone rang in the next room. "You can't, but Connie Jones might be able to. That'll be him now. I placed a call to the Flamenco in Madrid."

He went out and closed the door. She could hear the murmur of his voice for some time. Finally he returned, grinning. "So, it's all true. On top of that, according to Connie, you can sing like Billie Holiday. He'd like a word with you."

She hurried to the phone, and Jackson stood frowning down into the fire. When Hannah returned she looked as if she'd been crying.

"Did he tell you about what happened at the club?" she asked.

"Sure. Three cracked ribs, but he told me it hadn't affected his playing. They've managed to borrow some instruments."

"But Schellenberg?" she whispered. "Why did he do what he did? I just don't understand him."

"Yes, I thought that was one of the more improbable parts of your story—the way he helped you escape in Berlin. The guy really put his head on the block when he did that."

"Then why?"

"I don't know. Maybe he doesn't even know why—maybe he just likes you, angel." He smiled. "That's not hard to understand. But never mind that now. We've got to get you out of here, in case those goons come back."

"Or the Portuguese police," she said.

"Ah, I can handle them." He smiled again. "Some of my best friends are policemen, especially the variety who patronize my gaming room. They seem to win pretty regularly, so everybody is happy. Now get your coat and let's move."

======================================= Ten =======================================

The run along the coast road in Joe Jackson's silver Mercedes sports car seemed to be taking them back towards Estoril, so Hannah asked, "Where are we going?"

"A fishing village named Cascais," Jackson told her. "A friend of mine has a house near the beach. She's away at the moment, but I've got the key. Nice and quiet and secluded. She won't mind."

It was a fine night now, the rain long gone, and there was a full moon in a clear sky. Far out to sea, dozens of lights bobbed in towards the harbour of the small village down below.

"Lanterns on the prows of the fishing boats," he said. "It attracts the fish in great shoals, rather like moths to a flame."

They were close to a wide beach with sand dunes backed by pine trees, and he swung the car into a narrow drive, halting at a gate in a white wall. He unlocked the gate and they drove through into an enclosed courtyard.

The house was one storey with a red pantile roof and a veranda, and surrounded by a garden. Hannah was aware of the perfume of mimosa on the night air. Jackson led the way through the front door and into an enormous living room furnished with startling simplicity: white-painted walls, a huge stone fireplace, the wooden floor polished and scattered with oriental rugs.

"Bathroom, kitchen, bedroom. Plenty of canned food in the kitchen. I'll be back tomorrow with a few other things."

They went out onto the veranda. In the distance, Hannah heard music, sad and strangely exciting. "What is it?" she asked.

"A local café. Somebody's playing a *fado* record."

"*Fado*—what's that?"

"Can't be explained, only experienced. Part of the Portuguese way of life."

The trees around were heavy with olives. She could smell them in the night. It seemed incredible that, two nights before, she had been in Berlin, and now here she was on the most westerly edge of Europe, facing towards America, across the Atlantic.

She put a hand on Joe Jackson's arm. "You will do something, won't you? Promise me?"

"Sure I will. Look, we can't go marching you in to see the Duke personally, not with this extradition thing hanging over your head. I'll see your story gets to the right people myself."

"When?"

"Tonight—in Lisbon. I know the man to speak to."

She stood there, staring up at him, and suddenly kissed him on the cheek. Then she went inside without a word. Jackson stayed on the veranda for some time before going back to his car.

WITHOUT DOUBT, the most beautiful area of Lisbon is the old Alfama quarter. Towering above it are the high walls of the Castelo de São Jorge, in whose moats swim ducks, swans, and flamingos.

Joe Jackson parked his Mercedes and plunged into the maze of narrow alleys. Usually Alfama was like a rabbit warren, teeming with life. At this late hour it was silent, a place of shadows, with only an occasional pool of light from one of the huge iron lanterns bracketed high on the ancient walls.

Finally he turned into a square at the back of the cathedral and paused outside what had once been a nobleman's house. There was a coat of arms set in stone above the archway, and the old oak door was bound in iron.

He pulled on a bell chain. After a while, a bolt was withdrawn and the door opened. A small, dark-haired man in a white tuxedo stood back to let him in. "Senhor Joe—a pleasure," he said.

"Hello, Tomás." Jackson walked through into an enclosed courtyard floored with Moorish tiles. A fountain played in the centre. He followed Tomás across and through an archway into a comfortable little bar with a number of small tables.

"I heard there's a big poker game on tonight," Jackson said, "so Major Frear must be sitting in on it."

Tomás nodded. "Yes—for two hours now."

"Tell him I'd like to see him. I'll be on the terrace."

Tomás went out, and Jackson said to the blonde girl behind the bar, "Bring me the usual."

He opened the french windows and went outside. The vine-covered terrace offered a spectacular view over the Tagus River, lights twinkling in the darkness below the Alfama rooftops. The waitress brought him a brandy and soda, and he leaned on the balcony, wondering suddenly what he was doing here.

Joe Jackson was thirty years of age, son of a Methodist minister. The greatest influence on his life had been his uncle, who'd flown with the Lafayette Escadrille in France during the First World War. The boy had been raised on talk of Spads and Fokkers and his heroes were flying aces like Richthofen and Rickenbacker. At nineteen Jackson dropped out of Harvard and joined the Air Corps, where he trained as a fighter pilot. But the discipline of service life irked him, and he finally resigned. He went on to fight for the International Brigade in Spain and flew against the Nazi Condor Legion. He shot down five planes, which officially made him an ace, before he was blasted out of the sky over Barcelona one fine April morning. Afterwards, thanks to a bullet in the chest, he came to Lisbon to convalesce.

He had stayed and prospered as the owner of the best nightclub in Lisbon. Some mornings, when he watched the Clipper flying boat take off from the Tagus for America, he wished with all his heart that he was on board, but by the evening—

He turned as Frear came onto the terrace. The major wore a crumpled white linen suit. His hair and moustache were snow-white, though he was only fifty. He looked petulant and annoyed.

"What is this all about, Joseph? I'm in the middle of the best run I've had in months."

Frear was a compulsive gambler, his sole vice. He was also an agent for MI6, that branch of the British secret service concerned with espionage in foreign countries.

Jackson said, "The Duke of Windsor. Were you aware that the Germans have more than a passing interest in him?"

"Good heavens, Joseph, is that all? Rumours flying round Lisbon ever since His Royal Highness arrived."

"Earlier tonight I ran into a young woman just in from Berlin who had something more concrete to offer," Jackson said.

Frear sighed. "Name of Winter? Hannah Winter?"

"How did you know?"

"My dear Joseph, I pay a certain Portuguese police lieutenant a handsome stipend to phone me each evening to convey any information worth having. This evening he told me that top of the list on every police blotter in Lisbon is a young German woman named Hannah Winter, wanted for murder in Berlin."

"American," Jackson said. "Not German. If you call rubbing out three Gestapo hit men murder, then she's guilty, but that isn't the reason they've chased her across Europe to Lisbon. It's because a man called Walter Schellenberg's in town, and she knows why."

"Walter Schellenberg here? You sure, old boy?"

"Why, do you know him?"

"Yes, I think you could say that. All right, Joseph, tell me what the young lady has to say."

WINSTON CHURCHILL became prime minister on May 10, 1940, but continued for some weeks to live and work at Admiralty House, in the rooms he had formerly occupied. That evening, a meeting with the Joint Chiefs of Staff had dragged on past midnight. He had retired shortly after, falling asleep instantly: a trick learned during the campaigns of his youth.

He was awakened at two a.m. by Alexander Cadogan, head of the Foreign Office.

"Now what?" the prime minister demanded.

"A signal has been received from our MI6 station in Lisbon," Cadogan replied.

The prime minister lit a cigar, then held out his hand for the report. He read it, then sat in silence for some time.

"What do you think, Prime Minister?" Cadogan asked finally.

"The suggestion that His Royal Highness might actually deal with our enemies, I treat with the contempt it deserves. I have known him all his life and he is a man of finest honour."

"But the other aspect, Prime Minister? The possibility of his abduction? General Schellenberg's presence in Lisbon can only constitute the gravest of threats."

"The Portuguese dictator, Salazar, may lean more towards the Nazis than to ourselves, but he could never tolerate such an act of aggression on his own soil. The international repercussions would be tremendous."

"Then what do we do?"

"Our fears must be made plain to Salazar, and the British ambassador must inform His Royal Highness of the situation."

"And then?"

"Pack him off to the Bahamas as soon as possible. Find out the first available ship, and get hold of Walter Monckton for me."

WALTER MONCKTON, roused from his bed, arrived at Admiralty House just after three a.m. He was of medium height, with thinning hair and thick glasses. A brilliant barrister and friend of the Duke of Windsor when they were at Oxford together, he had been his most valued aide during the abdication crisis. At present, he was director general of the ministry of information.

"Walter," the prime minister said, when Monckton was shown in, "I want you to go to Lisbon as soon as a flight can be arranged. I've just learned that an American ship is leaving for Bermuda on the first of August. From there, we can then escort the Windsors to the Bahamas. I wish you to use your best offices to see that His Royal Highness and the Duchess are on board that ship."

"And if he will not go, Prime Minister?"

"He must, Walter. Look at this signal and judge for yourself."

Monckton read it through, his face calm as always.

"You will do this for me, Walter?"

"Of course, Prime Minister."

"Good. I leave it to you, then." Churchill turned his head into the pillow and was instantly asleep again.

ANTONIO SALAZAR, prime minister of Portugal, was fifty-one years of age. He had been virtual dictator of Portugal since 1932 and his

84

greatest achievement had been to keep his country out of the Spanish Civil War.

Today he had summoned Colonel Fernandes da Cunha, the commander of the Portuguese security police, to the presidential palace. Da Cunha, who had once studied to become a Jesuit priest, now held one of the most powerful police posts in the country.

"Not for the first time, I have called you here because I have a problem of some delicacy," Salazar began.

"In what way may I serve you, sir?" asked da Cunha, who was a small, but powerfully built man with a flat, peasant face and a heavy black moustache.

"The Duke of Windsor. A tiresome business. You may have heard that the English wish him to take up the post of governor of the Bahamas. The Germans, on the other hand, would prefer him to stay in Europe. If they successfully invade England, they may have a use for him."

"And the problem?"

"The English seem to think the Germans might try to spirit the Duke away before he leaves for the Bahamas. In fact, the German counterintelligence chief, Schellenberg, is here in person. I've had a message from Churchill in which he says he has confidence in our ability to see to the safety of the Duke. On the other hand, there are certain political pressures from Germany and it does rather look as if they're going to win the war."

"But if the Duke were abducted from our soil, the repercussions in the world would hardly be favourable," da Cunha said.

"Exactly. So I have decided that if the Duke comes to a private decision which takes him to Spain, well and good, but I cannot permit any act of force in the matter. I make you, Colonel da Cunha, personally responsible for his safety. You will contact the British ambassador this morning, accompany him to Santo e Silva's villa and satisfy yourself as to security there."

"At your orders, sir." Da Cunha saluted and left.

"YOU KNOW, this whole affair is becoming ridiculous," the Duke of Windsor told the British ambassador, Sir Walford Selby, as they sat together in the library. "Primo de Rivera brings me this non-sensical story that the British secret service intend to take me off to the Bahamas whether I want to go or not. Now you give me the same sort of yarn with the Nazis as the villains."

The ambassador tried to contain his exasperation. "With all due respect, sir, the presence in Lisbon of General Schellenberg should give us cause for thought. There are those who suggest that, in the context of an England under occupation, a position would be suggested to Your Royal Highness that you might feel compelled to accept, in the belief it was in the best interests of the people."

The Duke stood up, his face dark. "That, Sir Walford, is a Judas gate through which I would never enter."

He turned away angrily, took a cigarette from a silver box, and lit it. After a moment, he was in control again. "Anyway, what's the time schedule?"

"There's a suitable American ship leaving on the first of August, sir. For Bermuda. The *Excalibur*. We can then provide an escort on to the Bahamas."

"Which gives us what, three or four days? You'll just have to see that our intelligence people here keep a jolly good eye on me."

"Sir, the sole representative in Lisbon of the secret service is Major Frear, who merely acts as a channel for paid informants."

"Do you want me to sleep with a gun under my pillow?"

There was a polite cough, and they turned to find Colonel da Cunha standing in the open french windows.

"No, sir," Sir Walford said. "The Portuguese government have assigned Colonel da Cunha to take charge of all your security arrangements until the *Excalibur* leaves."

"I have inspected the grounds here," da Cunha said. "Extra men will be drafted. I foresee no problem. Of course, it would help if Your Royal Highness would stay within the walls."

"Now there I really can't oblige," said the Duke. "Having a day in the country tomorrow. Place called Niña. Bull farm."

Colonel da Cunha glanced at the ambassador. "Sir, may I point out that you would be within ten miles of the Spanish border."

"The whole affair's being laid on by my good friend Primo de Rivera," replied the Duke. "You're surely not suggesting that he's going to try to run away with me!"

"No, Your Royal Highness," said da Cunha diplomatically.

"Good. Of course, I don't mind your sending a few of your chaps along to keep us company if that will make you happy. But now, you really must excuse me. The Duchess is waiting."

He went out, and Sir Walford turned to da Cunha. "As I said, it isn't going to be easy."

As soon as da Cunha returned to his office, he phoned the German legation and at ten thirty saw Schellenberg, by appointment, in a small café near the Tower of Belém.

"General, I'll come right to the point," da Cunha said. "At the present time, our relations with the Reich are of the friendliest, and you are a welcome guest in our country."

"But?" Schellenberg said.

"The Duke of Windsor is a special case. We desire nothing more than to see him board ship on the first of August and sail away. Until then, Prime Minister Salazar has made me personally responsible for his welfare. I have increased the guards at the villa and they have orders to shoot intruders. Do I make myself clear?"

"As crystal," Schellenberg said. "And now, my dear colonel, a cognac to sweeten your coffee."

"My pleasure," Fernandes da Cunha told him.

JOE JACKSON telephoned Major Frear at his apartment just after ten in the morning. Frear sounded as if he'd just been woken from a sound sleep.

"It's Jackson. What has happened since our talk last night?"

"Nothing new, old boy. I've reported what you said to my people and I'm sure they'll take appropriate action. There's no need for you or that girl to get involved. If you want my advice, tell her to keep her head down or she might get it knocked off."

Jackson put down the receiver and sat there thinking for a while. Then he dressed and went quickly downstairs and got into his Mercedes. He turned into the main road and started along the waterfront.

Soon after, a car pulled away from the kerb. Schellenberg said to the driver whom the legation had provided, "Take your time, stay well back. Don't lose him."

THERE WAS NO SIGN of Hannah in the house at Cascais. Jackson left the car in the courtyard and walked down to the beach. The car that had followed him pulled into the pine trees a hundred yards away, and Schellenberg watched through field glasses.

It was a fine, warm day, and the beach was stacked with fishing boats painted in vivid hues. Fishermen sat mending their nets, children playing around them, and beyond, the long Atlantic combers rolled in.

Jackson saw Hannah walking towards him barefoot, carrying a bucket. When she noticed him she started to run.

"What a marvellous day," she said. "And this place. The people are so friendly and courteous, and the boats . . ." She turned to look at them. "Why do some have eyes painted on the prows?"

"That's debatable," Jackson said. "Some say to ward off the evil one. Others, so the ship can find its way through any storm. I see you've been buying fish."

"Yes. Let me cook you lunch." She took his arm, and as they strolled back towards the house, she said, "You told me you'd see the right people—did you?"

"Yes. My contact with the British passed your story along, and he sees no reason for you to continue to get involved."

She said nothing, and they walked the rest of the way in silence.

At the house, she proved to be a good cook. The fish was delicious, but Hannah did no more than pick at it.

"All right, what is it?" he asked.

"I don't get the feeling that anyone's taking this thing seriously enough." She leaned across the table. "It's no good, Joe. I want to see the Duke myself. Tell him to his face the danger he's in. What he does then is his affair, but unless I do it, I'll always feel that somehow I let Uncle Max down."

"Okay." He sighed. "There's someone I can try. A man I know called Taniguchi, who can fix most things. I'll get in touch with him, but it could cost money."

"I've got a letter of credit for two thousand dollars."

"For that he'd probably kidnap the Duke himself. I'll run into town and see what I can do. I'll be back soon."

She watched him drive away and, on impulse, went down again to the beach, kicked off her shoes, and walked along the sand again. The sun was very warm now. She flung herself down in the sand next to a fishing boat and closed her eyes.

She heard footsteps. A familiar voice said, "Hello, Hannah."

When she looked up, Schellenberg was standing beside her.

"I must say you're looking very well indeed, all things considered," he said.

"What do you want with me?" she demanded.

"Cigarette?" He bent to offer one, and she took it without thinking. When he gave her a light, there was a curious intimacy to the gesture.

"I asked you what you wanted."

"Nothing," he replied. "Or rather, I wish you to do nothing from now on. You can no longer alter the course of events, Hannah. The game is in progress and the players know the score."

"Is that how you see it? Just a game?"

"Of course. A terrible game that, once started, is impossible to stop. It's like a carousel. Once it's in motion, that's it."

"You could always try jumping off."

"Too late for that now. I'm trapped along with thousands like me. Do you honestly think that I believe in that madman in Berlin —in even one word of his lies? Blacks are inferior, which means I can't enjoy the music of your Connie Jones. Einstein can't count to ten, and the fact that Hannah Winter has a voice to—"

"I don't want to hear any more of this." Hannah stood up. "You got me out of Prinz Albrechtstrasse. I don't know why, but you did, and you helped Connie and the boys in Madrid. But you killed Uncle Max. It doesn't matter who held the gun. You killed him."

They stood there, confronting each other. There was only the sound of the sea on the shore, a gull's cry. And then it was as if something broke inside her. "Why?" she whispered, and there was pain in her voice. "I don't understand."

He put a hand under her chin and smiled gently. "Life, my Hannah, has a habit of seizing one by the throat and refusing to let go. It's really very sad."

He kissed her gently on the mouth, turned, and walked away. For a long time after he had gone, she simply sat there, staring out to sea. Then she got up and walked slowly back to the house.

Eleven

Unlike on the previous evening, the warehouse was a hive of industry when Schellenberg entered and went up the iron staircase to Taniguchi's office.

"Anything for me yet?" Schellenberg asked, as he sat down opposite the huge man.

"But of course." Taniguchi unlocked a wall safe and took out a manila folder. "Everything you need, Walter. A plan of the villa and the grounds. A list of the servants. I have already arranged that a footman, a maid, and a gardener will be replaced by people in my pay. They all speak reasonably good English."

"Excellent—and the police?"

"Slightly more difficult," Taniguchi answered. "Colonel da. Cunha, head of security police, has been placed in charge of security at the villa. He is a first-class policeman, beyond any bribe, and in my opinion will follow his orders to the letter. Luckily the officer who is actually stationed at the villa is a different specimen entirely. One Captain José Mota."

"Is he on our side?"

"If you're referring to ideologies, no, but he does have expensive tastes, particularly in women. So, what are your orders?"

"For the moment, what I require is general information about what's going on in the house itself. Any conversation your people can overhear would be useful."

"About the Duke's future plans? And what if he decides to go to the Bahamas after all, Walter? What then?"

"I wouldn't blame him really." Schellenberg got up. "I hear the climate's delightful."

Taniguchi laughed uproariously. "Life really is most amusing. Now take something as abstract as information. A commodity as subject to the forces of the marketplace as any other. Something which may, for example, be sold not only once, but twice."

"An interesting hypothesis," Schellenberg said. "Let's discuss it." He sat down again.

AT THE German legation Ambassador Huene was having coffee when Schellenberg was shown into his office.

"Ah, there you are, General." Huene poured coffee into another cup, then pushed a message across the table. "There's something for you from the Foreign Office which you may not appreciate. I've had it decoded."

It was from Ribbentrop, and very much to the point.

At a suitable occasion, the Duke must be informed that Germany wants peace with the English people, that the Churchill clique stands in the way of it, and that it would be a good thing if the Duke would hold himself in readiness for further developments. Germany is determined to force England to peace by every means and upon this happening would be prepared to accommodate any desire expressed by the Duke, especially with a view to the assumption of the English throne by the Duke and Duchess.

There was more in the same vein, including Ribbentrop's belief that the Duke's host, Santo e Silva, was sympathetic to German aims. There was also a reiteration of the rumour that the British secret service had designs on the Duke's person.

"Well, that's certainly explicit enough," Schellenberg said.

"I've heard from Primo de Rivera," Huene told him. "Tomorrow he's taking the Windsors out to visit a bull farm at a place called Niña. Only ten miles from the Spanish border. What do you intend to do?"

"Wait to see the outcome," replied Schellenberg. "If de Rivera persuades the Duke that to flee to Spain would be in his best interest, then the border is a fast drive from Niña. Ribbentrop and the Führer will be delighted and we can all go home."

"And if the Duke decides otherwise?"

Schellenberg smiled. "The coffee, Baron, was really quite excellent. I'll see you later."

JOE JACKSON'S American Bar was a popular rendezvous at lunchtime, and it was crowded when Kajiro Taniguchi entered just after two o'clock. Jackson came over to him at once.

"Have you got the information I asked for?"

"I think you could say that," Taniguchi replied.

Jackson led the way upstairs to his office and closed the door. "All right—what's the deal?"

"A busy man, this Duke of yours. Tomorrow he goes to visit António de Oliveira's bull farm outside Niña."

Jackson frowned. "Niña is awfully close to the Spanish border."

"Yes, isn't it? However, to stick with the villa. Although Fernandes da Cunha has overall responsibility for the Duke, the officer in charge at the villa is one Captain José Mota."

"And he's bribable?"

"Corrupt as a week-old corpse, but it's going to cost you, Joe. One thousand dollars in American money—in advance."

"What do we get for that?"

"Every night at ten o'clock, the Duke has a final cigar while walking alone in the garden. I've got a plan." He took a square of paper from his wallet and unfolded it. "Down here, below the swimming pool, there's a summerhouse. The Duke always ends his walk sitting in there for five minutes, finishing his cigar."

"So?"

"Just a few yards away, some shrubbery conceals a door in the garden wall. Usually, there's a policeman discreetly on guard, but tonight, if you're interested, there won't be. What's more, the door will be unlocked."

"Thanks to Captain Mota?"

"Exactly."

"Who expects his cash in advance?"

"I'm afraid so."

Jackson went to the large, old-fashioned safe in the corner, unlocked it, brought a cash box to the desk, and counted out ten one-hundred-dollar bills.

"One more thing," Taniguchi said. "The young lady goes in alone."

"Now look here . . ." Jackson began.

"Part of the deal, Joe. Either you agree, or it's all off. She leaves the car halfway down the hill and walks the rest of the way. That's so the gate sentry doesn't hear her."

Jackson shrugged. "Okay," he said reluctantly. "But if I don't get service, old buddy . . ."

"Trust, Joe—one of this world's more saleable commodities. You must learn to value it."

Taniguchi was smiling as he went out of the door.

AN OFFICE at the German legation had been placed at Schellenberg's disposal, and he was working at the desk when there was a knock at the door. Kleiber entered, very pale and carrying his right arm in a sling.

"Well, what do you want?" Schellenberg asked.

"I assumed there would be work to do."

"As I understood it, your task was to act as my bodyguard," Schellenberg told him. "When you lost Hannah Winter on that wharf and allowed the American to shoot you in the arm, you became totally unfit for that duty. So, my orders are that you go back to bed until fully recovered."

"And Sindermann?"

"Is of no use to me whatsoever."

"But the Duke of Windsor, General?"

"Is none of your affair, so do as I order. Do you understand?"

"Yes, General," Kleiber replied, but when he turned to the door there was murder in his eyes.

A moment later, Sindermann at his heels, he entered the office of his friend Egger, the police attaché of the German legation. With some difficulty, Kleiber took out his wallet with his left hand, extracted Himmler's letter of authority, and gave it to him.

"As you can see," Kleiber said, "I act in the name of Reichsführer Himmler himself."

"Of course, Major," said Egger in alarm.

Kleiber sat down. "I have doubts General Schellenberg is pursuing his orders as regards the Windsor affair with the vigour he should. Have you heard anything that should be reported to me?"

Egger looked strained, but replied in a low voice. "Yes, I think so. A contact of mine with the Portuguese police tells me that no more than an hour ago the general received a brief visit from Captain José Mota of the security police, the officer in charge of the detachment at the villa where the Duke is staying."

"I see. Have you any idea of the substance of his talk with General Schellenberg?"

"No."

"But you could find out from your friend Mota?"

"I could try, Major."

"Then do so, by all means," Kleiber told him.

IT WAS just before ten that night when Hannah turned into the hill road leading up to the villa. Following the instructions Taniguchi had given to Jackson, she parked under the trees halfway up the hill and walked the rest of the way.

A couple of minutes later, with the softest of clicks, the car's passenger door opened and Joe Jackson, who had been crouched on the floor, slid out. He wore black trousers and sweater, and a balaclava helmet pulled over his face so that only his eyes showed. The Browning automatic was tucked into his belt.

He followed her, keeping close to the trees. The door in the wall was clearly visible because there was a small light above it. He saw her pause, then try the handle and pass inside.

Some distance farther along there was a tree whose branches overhung the wall. Jackson climbed it quickly and poised on top of the wall. He saw the dim bulk of the summerhouse only four or five yards away, and Hannah approaching it from a path through the shrubbery.

Hannah could see the glow in the darkness and smell the aroma

94

of a good Havana. "Your Royal Highness," she whispered. "Please, I must speak with you. My name is—"

"Hannah Winter," Walter Schellenberg said. He moved out of the shadows and stood on the porch of the summerhouse.

"Oh, my God," she said, and turned to run, only to find her way blocked by a young police officer.

Schellenberg said, "It's all right, Mota. I'll return the young lady to her car now."

He had a hand on her elbow, taking her back down the path to the door. They went out, and Mota closed the door behind them.

Flat on top of the wall, Jackson heard Schellenberg say to Hannah as they passed, "I'm afraid Taniguchi wasn't exactly honest with your friend Mr. Jackson. The Duke doesn't turn up for another half hour yet. What am I going to do with you, Hannah? Didn't I tell you to stay out of this thing?"

Jackson would have slipped off the wall to follow them, but Mota had paused only a few yards away to light a cigarette. The match flared, illuminating a handsome, rather weak face.

Mota peered around furtively, then whispered in Portuguese, "All right, you can come out now."

Kleiber and Sindermann emerged from the bushes.

"You saw what you wanted?" Mota asked.

"Oh, yes," Kleiber answered. "The General will certainly have some explaining to do when we return to Berlin. However, let us discuss tomorrow's events. When do you leave for this bull farm?"

"Nine thirty. Two police motorcyclists lead the way one mile in advance. I follow with half a dozen men in a police truck. The Duke and Duchess with Primo de Rivera and their driver are the last in line, in the Buick."

"So?"

"Three miles before you reach Niña there is a village called Rosario. An inn and a few houses—nothing more. I'll arrange for my truck to break down before we get there. When the Buick catches up with us, I'll tell them to carry on and wait for us at Rosario."

"Which the motorcyclists will already have passed through?"

"Exactly. Around eleven is the time I estimate the Buick to arrive at Rosario. You and your man should be there waiting." Mota shrugged. "A simple matter to take over at pistol point and drive them to the border. Twenty minutes and you'll be in Spain."

"Excellent," Kleiber said. "You've done well."

"And General Schellenberg?"

"Is to know nothing."

"So what about my money?"

"You'll get it, you have my word on that. Twenty thousand American dollars, just as we agreed."

Jackson didn't wait to hear any more, but slid gently off the wall and dropped into the grass. He started back down the hill to where Hannah had left his Mercedes, but it was gone.

The contingency plan had been simple: if they lost touch, they were to rendezvous at the beach house at Cascais, two miles away. He started off at a trot along the side of the road.

WHEN HANNAH and Schellenberg reached Joe Jackson's Mercedes, he held open the door for her, then went round to the other side and got into the passenger seat.

"I came by cab myself. You don't mind giving me a lift back to Lisbon, do you?"

She started the car. "Only as far as the first cab rank."

Schellenberg lit a cigarette. "You must see now what nonsense it is for you to continue to interfere in this business. The fact that you found me waiting for you in the summerhouse tonight, instead of the Duke, must prove that I have more influence in Lisbon than even your Mr. Jackson."

As they neared the Tower of Belém, they came to a cab rank and she stopped. She didn't say a word and Schellenberg got out, closed the door, then leaned in at the window and smiled. "We really can't go on meeting this way, you realize that, don't you?"

She swung the car round in a U-turn and drove away rapidly.

LIGHTS WERE ON in the beach house when Hannah parked the car in the courtyard. As she went up the steps to the veranda, the door opened and Jackson appeared.

"What happened?" he asked, and she quickly told him.

"You missed the best part of the show," he said as she followed him inside. "After you'd gone, your two friends from the wharf turned up, Kleiber and Sindermann. Seems they don't exactly see eye to eye with Schellenberg. They've cooked up a plot with Captain Mota to snatch the Duke and Duchess on the way to the bull farm at Niña tomorrow. That Mota seems to be holding his hand out to everyone."

"Can we stop them?"

"Oh, yes, I think so. Meanwhile, though, we must somehow get you to see the Duke. So I've found out who is putting on the show in the ring tomorrow—a friend of mine, José Borges, one of the greatest *toureiros* in the game. I've just phoned him and he has agreed to take us with him tomorrow at eight o'clock. Now, make me some coffee while I change."

He went out to the car for his suitcase, then changed into a white tuxedo and a black tie. "Working clothes," he told her. "After all, I *am* a nightclub owner."

Hannah handed him his coffee. "I've been thinking. That Japanese friend of yours who set things up for us at the villa didn't exactly come up with value for money."

"Oh, I don't know," Jackson said. "The Nazis have not only been printing their own money lately, but other people's as well. Their British five-pound notes are excellent and their American one-hundred-dollar bills aren't bad. Someone tried to pass a few off at my gaming tables the other month. I confiscated them, naturally, and tossed him out on his ear. Not worth bothering the police, and it did seem the bills might be useful sometime."

"You scoundrel," she said.

"I like to think so."

They left the house and drove to the American Bar, where a great many cars were parked outside. Jackson took Hannah upstairs to his office.

He slid open a panel in the wall, revealing a black grille through which they could look down into the gaming room. Dice, black-jack, poker—they were all doing well, but the crowd around the roulette wheel was especially heavy.

Jackson said, "Good, there he is. You wait here."

He went downstairs and approached da Cunha, who was not doing particularly well at roulette. "Hello, Fernandes," Jackson said quietly. "I always thought twelve was your lucky number."

"Did you, Joe?" Da Cunha smiled. "Then twelve it is."

As the wheel stopped, the ball slotted neatly into the number twelve place. Jackson said, "I'd let it ride if I were you."

"Who am I to argue with the proprietor?"

This time, when twelve came up again, da Cunha picked up the chips the croupier pushed towards him. "You're being excessively generous tonight, Joe. I wonder why."

"Oh, I haven't even started yet," Jackson told him. "Come upstairs and have a drink. You might find it interesting."

Hannah was standing at the grille, looking down into the gaming room, as they entered. She turned, and Jackson said, "Fernandes, I'd like to introduce Miss Hannah Winter. Now, you could arrest her. On the other hand, if you're as smart as I think you are, you'll listen to what we've got to say first."

Twelve

It was a fine bright morning as the old truck rolled along the dusty road between the olive trees. Women in black dresses and straw hats were already at work in the fields.

Hannah and Jackson were in the front seat beside the *toureiro*, José Borges, who was driving. The other members of his bull-fighting team were in the rear.

Hannah was in a black peasant dress and headscarf which Jackson had procured for her. He wore a tweed cap, a collarless shirt, an old jacket many times patched.

"You and Joe—have you known each other long?" Hannah asked the *toureiro*.

"Since Spain, senhorita. We fought together against Franco. It was a bad time, I can tell you. Sometimes we didn't see a loaf of bread for weeks."

Jackson was dozing in the corner. Hannah looked at him and said, "Hardly worth the money, I should have thought."

"Money?" Borges laughed hoarsely. "For the last year of the war we didn't get a peso—not any of us."

"Then why did you fight?"

"I ask Joe that question once. For me, it's simple. I'm a Communist, but Joe just said he didn't like Franco." At that moment, they rumbled past a small inn with tables outside. "Ah, we're in Rosario. We'll soon reach the bull farm."

"You know something?" Joe Jackson said, without opening his eyes. "You talk too much."

In the rear of the Buick, Primo de Rivera was seated next to the Duke and Duchess.

The Duke said, "It really is too much. Wallis received a bunch of flowers this morning. Anonymous, mind you. The card said,

'Beware of the machinations of the British secret service. A Portuguese friend who has your interests at heart.' Have you ever heard such rot?"

"Such talk is common in Madrid," de Rivera said.

"Good Lord, Primo, it's absolute nonsense. I mean, there is hardly any British secret service in Lisbon at the moment."

The Buick slowed as they came alongside the police truck parked at the side of the road. Captain Mota approached and saluted. "I regret the inconvenience, Your Royal Highness. A minor breakdown and soon rectified. If you would continue to Rosario and wait for us there."

"Very well, then," said the Duke, and nodded to the chauffeur. "Drive on."

KLEIBER and Sindermann arrived at Rosario at ten thirty in a rented car from Lisbon. The inn there was a poor place—rough walls, stone floor, and wooden tables—and there were no other customers.

An old woman appeared from a room at the rear to serve them. They ordered red wine and a plate of olives and sat at a table by the window to wait.

"Check your gun," Kleiber said. They had both obtained Walthers from the legation armoury.

The two police motorcyclists roared by, raising dust outside. Kleiber glanced at his watch. "Not long now. I'd like to see Schellenberg's face when he hears about this."

"Why wait?" Schellenberg said, walking in from the kitchen followed by da Cunha and two policemen with automatic pistols.

"I see you've beaten us to it, gentlemen," da Cunha said. "We, too, are here to see the Duke drive past."

"Colonel da Cunha is head of the security police," Schellenberg explained. "He's just had the distressing task of arresting one of his own officers, Captain Mota."

"A most corrupt young man," da Cunha said.

At that moment, the Buick appeared and slowed to a halt. Da Cunha straightened his tunic and went out. They saw him salute and lean down at the window. When he drew back, the Buick continued on and da Cunha returned. "I'll follow them to Niña personally, just to make certain the rest of the day passes uneventfully. You are returning to Lisbon now, I presume, General?"

"Yes, I think so," Schellenberg said. "My thanks, Colonel."

He went out through the kitchen, and Kleiber and Sindermann followed. The major's face was contorted with anger.

BULLFIGHTING in Portugal when performed in gala dress is a spectacular sight. The de Oliveira farm boasted its own ring and mounted a dazzling performance for the royal party.

The first two bulls were fought from horseback in the Portuguese style, de Oliveira himself taking part dressed in cloth of gold, with satin breeches and a tricorne hat with ostrich plumes.

The spectacle which followed, *las pegas*, was even more interesting. The gates were opened and a bull launched himself like a black thunderbolt into the sunlight of the ring. He stood there, pawing the ground. A line of men, in traditional costume, moved into the arena, headed by José Borges.

The Duke asked, "What do they intend to do?"

Primo de Rivera said, "It's rather fascinating. Your Royal Highness has visited Greece, of course. On Cretan vases you will see depicted the dances of the sacred bull, in which young men did handsprings on the bull's horns."

"Are these chaps going to do something similar? Astonishing!"

The men advanced to meet the bull. Borges, supremely arrogant, head thrown back, hands on hips, offered himself as a target.

As the bull charged, the Duchess cried out in alarm; but at the last moment, Borges flung himself at the animal's head, grabbed the horns, and did a handspring onto its back, leaping to the ground as it thundered on. Two companions repeated the trick and finally Borges performed again, this time standing on the bull's back after his somersault and staying there for a full minute while the animal cantered round the ring. When he jumped down, he bowed to the royal party, who applauded. The gates were re-opened and the bull was driven from the ring.

"What happens to the bull now?" the Duchess asked their host, de Oliveira, who had joined them.

"Sometimes he is slaughtered, or if he is brave, he is returned to the pastures and kept for breeding. A bull may never be put into the arena twice. Once he has learned the ropes, so to speak, he would be too dangerous."

"So I can imagine," the Duke said. "Remarkable performance."

Luncheon was served on the terrace of the main house. A

eucalyptus tree scented the air. De Oliveira had deliberately kept the meal traditional. Cold gazpacho, salty smoked sausages, crisp salads and fresh ewe cheese. The one sophisticated concession to the occasion was the plentiful supply of champagne.

The Duke smiled at the Duchess. "Enjoyed it, Wallis?"

"Oh, yes, David, the most wonderful day we've had in ages."

Primo de Rivera seemed about to say something, but at that moment, Fernandes da Cunha approached across the lawn.

"We're ready to go back, Colonel," the Duke said.

Da Cunha saluted. "If Your Royal Highness would be so kind as to spare me a few minutes in private. A question of security."

"Certainly." The Duke smiled at the others. "Do excuse me."

He walked across the lawn, da Cunha keeping pace with him.

"Now look here, Colonel," the Duke said. "I don't know what sort of wild rumours you've heard, but when I leave here, my car will be pointing in the direction of Lisbon. I have no intention of making a dash for the Spanish border."

"Earlier today, Your Royal Highness avoided, by a hair's breadth, a situation which would have given you no choice in the matter."

They were crossing the courtyard and had reached the small stone chapel which served the estate. The Duke paused and said, "Colonel, what on earth are you talking about?"

Da Cunha opened the chapel door. "If Your Royal Highness would care to step inside, there is someone waiting who can explain the situation better than I."

It was a simple chapel with a stone floor, whitewashed walls, and the plainest of altars, with a carved wooden crucifix. At one side, candles flickered before a statue of the Virgin.

Two peasants, a man and a woman, were sitting on one of the rough wooden benches near the front of the chapel. They turned and stood up, and the Duke saw that the woman was young and rather pretty. When she started to speak and it became apparent that she was American, he was quite astonished.

AFTERWARDS, they sat there on the bench, the three of them together, da Cunha standing close at hand.

"It really is the most extraordinary business I ever heard of in my life," the Duke said.

"But true, sir, every word," Hannah told him.

"Oh, I believe you, my dear, never fear. The colonel's account

102

of the near miss at Rosario this morning confirms it." He turned to da Cunha. "You say General Schellenberg told you there was no question of abduction in his mind?"

"Yes, sir, he assured me that as far as he was concerned, the choice of what action to take in this affair was entirely up to Your Royal Highness."

"And you believe him?"

"Yes, sir, I do. There can be no doubt that Kleiber and his man were acting on their own initiative in the matter. As Senhorita Winter's story has indicated, General Schellenberg is an unusual man in many respects."

"Indeed he is." The Duke looked up at da Cunha intently. "Colonel, can I rely on your good offices?"

"Sir, Prime Minister Salazar has made me personally responsible for your safety in Portugal, with my life, if necessary."

The Duke smiled faintly, then turned to Joe Jackson. "And you, Mr. Jackson? May I also rely on you?"

"Of course, sir."

"Good." The Duke turned to Hannah and took her hands. "As for you, my dear, how can I ask for more when you have done so very much already?"

She fought to control the tears, as his hands tightened on hers for a moment.

"May I inquire as to your plans, sir?" da Cunha asked.

"Easily answered, Colonel. I intend to leave on the *Excalibur* the day after tomorrow. I shall take up my appointment in the Bahamas as requested by Mr. Churchill."

"And in the meantime?"

"Back to Estoril. May I ask, Colonel, if you will be at the villa later in the day?"

"I shall make the lodge at the main gate my headquarters," da Cunha told him. "I shall be available to Your Royal Highness at any time of the night or day."

"Excellent." The Duke was frowning slightly. "I may need you. There's something stirring at the back of my mind. And now, I think, I'd better be getting back to the others."

IN BERLIN later that day, at a special meeting held in the Reich Chancellery, Hitler announced that he was issuing the order to prepare for the air attack on England preliminary to invasion. He then outlined Operation Sea Lion, the plan that would culminate in his own triumphal drive into London.

After the meeting, Hitler ordered Ribbentrop to remain. The foreign minister was closeted with him for an uncomfortable five minutes. When he left, he found Himmler waiting in the hall.

"You don't look too happy, Ribbentrop."

"The Windsor affair, Reichsführer. Now that Sea Lion has been settled, the Duke is more essential to our plans than ever. The Führer has instructed me to order his immediate abduction."

"Then you'd better get in touch with Schellenberg as soon as possible, hadn't you?" Himmler said.

Ribbentrop was angry and a little frightened. "Damn the man. I haven't heard from him once since he's been in Portugal."

IN HIS OFFICE at the German legation, Schellenberg was drinking coffee when Kleiber burst in, waving a message angrily.

"You received this an hour ago."

Schellenberg took the message from him and glanced at it quickly. It was a copy of a signal from Ribbentrop.

"My goodness, Kleiber, you certainly have influence. This was supposed to be confidential and for my eyes only."

"It's a direct order from the Führer to abduct the Duke of Windsor. What are you going to do about it?"

"I'll let you know, if and when I think it necessary. On your way out, would you please close the door without slamming it."

Kleiber returned to the anteroom where Sindermann waited. "Nothing!" he raged. "Nothing!"

Kleiber made his decision. He hurried to the communications room, where he asked the officer on duty for a signal pad, and wrote, with difficulty, because his right arm was still in a sling:

> General Schellenberg shows no serious intention of completing mission as instructed. Please confirm with Ambassador Huene my powers to take over in this matter.   Kleiber

He handed it to the officer. "Encode that now. Priority one. Most immediate and for the eyes of Reichsführer Himmler only."

AS DUSK was falling that same evening, the Duchess went into the garden in search of the Duke. She found him sitting by the fountain, gazing pensively into the water.

"There you are," she said. "There's a letter for you from London."

"Thank you, my dear." He opened it and read the contents quickly. "Walter Monckton's due in by plane sometime tomorrow."

"How nice to see Walter again," she said, "but why?"

"Oh, Winston making sure nothing goes wrong at the last moment. Walter, after all, has always been the government's general-purpose man where I am concerned. You are right, though, Wallis. It will be nice to wave goodbye to a friendly face as we sail away into oblivion."

"St. Helena, 1940," she said. "Now I know how Napoleon must have felt."

"I wanted to do something useful in this war, but they won't let me." He laughed softly. "Rather ironic, but the only people who seem to want me are the Nazis."

And suddenly he was no longer smiling, his face tense and excited. "Wallis, I wonder how far they'd be willing to go. If they want me badly enough, that is."

"David," the Duchess said, shocked. "You couldn't."

"No, you don't understand, my dear. What I'm talking about is a possibility, a faint one perhaps, that I might be able to extract something of value from this situation. Not to me, you understand, but to Britain." He seized her hands. "Wouldn't it be marvellous if I could play these Nazis at their own game and beat them?"

She hadn't seen him so alive in years. "Oh, David," she said. "It could be dangerous. I'm frightened."

"I'm not. To be honest, I'm rather beginning to enjoy this. The person I need now is Colonel da Cunha."

Five minutes later, in response to an urgent phone call to the lodge, da Cunha hurried up to the house, where he found the Duke and Duchess waiting for him in the library.

"Your Royal Highness sent for me?"

"I did indeed, Colonel. Earlier today you were kind enough to say that I could rely on your good offices."

"If there is any way I can be of service, I will, sir."

"Go to see the German ambassador, Baron Huene, this evening. Tell him I wish to meet with General Schellenberg."

Da Cunha was unable to conceal his surprise. "When would you wish this meeting to take place?"

"Tonight. I thought it might be fun to repeat his exercise of last night in the garden. I'll have my usual cigar in the summerhouse.

105

You could bring him to me. And I'd appreciate it if Mr. Jackson could repeat his role as well. It would make the Duchess feel easier if he were there. Will you ask him to do that for me?"

"Yes, sir. Would you wish me to be present?"

"Yes, but I think you might find our conversation embarrassing. For your sake, I suggest that you stand a little way off."

Da Cunha hesitated. "Sir, forgive me for any impertinence, but does this mean that you contemplate a move to Spain after all?"

"Now what would you think, Colonel?"

"Why, sir, I think you will sail on the *Excalibur* the day after tomorrow. It also occurs to me that Your Royal Highness is placing himself in a position of extreme danger."

The Duke lit a cigarette, blew out a feathery trail of smoke, and said, with that inimitable smile of his, "Difficult decisions, Colonel, are the privilege of rank."

WHEN SCHELLENBERG arrived at Huene's office later that evening, it was quite crowded. Fernandes da Cunha was by the window, and there was the ambassador himself, but the real surprise was Kleiber, who stood at one side of the desk. The look of pale triumph on his face should have warned Schellenberg to expect the worst.

"Colonel da Cunha is here on behalf of the Duke of Windsor," Huene said.

"Is this true?" Schellenberg said in astonishment, turning to da Cunha.

"His Royal Highness would like to see you tonight. Secretly and informally. He'll be having a cigar in the summerhouse at ten thirty. I'll let you in by the garden door."

"I can't believe it. Why?"

"Thirty-six hours only and the *Excalibur* sails." Da Cunha shrugged. "Perhaps this is the moment of truth for him."

"All right," Schellenberg said. "I'll be there."

"And I'll be with you," Kleiber said, his voice trembling with emotion.

Schellenberg had not sought a public confrontation, but he had no intention of avoiding one. "I don't think so, not after this morning's débâcle at Rosario."

Huene said. "I'm sorry, General, but I have here a signal, received within the last hour from Reichsführer Himmler himself."

He read it aloud. "'General Schellenberg will pursue his present task with the utmost vigour. Failure is unacceptable. At every opportunity he must avail himself of the assistance of Major Kleiber. Any deviation from this order must be reported at once.'"

There was a silence for a moment, then Schellenberg turned to da Cunha with a smile. "So, Colonel, it appears that when you open the door in the garden wall tonight, you open it to Major Kleiber also."

WHEN DA CUNHA was admitted to Jackson's office, the American was seated behind his desk, dressed again in a white tuxedo and a black tie.

The colonel sniffed the air. "Chanel Number Five. You can come out, senhorita. I've left my handcuffs at home."

He went to the sideboard and helped himself to a Scotch as Hannah emerged from the bathroom.

Jackson asked, "What do you want?"

"I've got a job for you," da Cunha told him. "Or rather the Duke has. He's arranged to meet Schellenberg and Kleiber in the summerhouse tonight. He'd like you to repeat your performance, Joe, up on the wall."

"You don't mean he intends to make a deal with them?" Hannah said. "It's not possible."

"Don't be silly, angel," Jackson told her. "If that was his game, then why would he want me on hand?"

"You'll do as he asks?" da Cunha said.

"Sure—I'll be there."

"Good," said da Cunha. "An interesting night lies ahead."

He went out, and Hannah said, "I'm frightened, Joe. What can the Duke be thinking of?"

Jackson went and poured himself a drink. "Perhaps he's started to fight back."

Thirteen

Jackson was on the wall again just after ten, dressed, as he had been the previous night, in black, the Browning ready in his hand. After a while, da Cunha appeared, walking along the path through the shrubbery. He checked the door, then waited. A little later, the Duke arrived. He wore evening dress, and a light tweed coat hung over his shoulders. He took a Havana cigar from a leather case and lit it.

At the same moment, Jackson heard footsteps approaching on the road outside. There was a tap at the door, da Cunha opened it, and Schellenberg entered, followed by Kleiber.

"General Schellenberg and Major Kleiber." Da Cunha made the introductions and withdrew to a discreet distance.

"Ah, the gentleman who was waiting for me at Rosario this morning," the Duke said, nodding at Kleiber.

"An unfortunate error, Your Royal Highness," Schellenberg told him.

"An unnecessary one. Especially if you'd made a direct approach to me in the first place. Suggestions, veiled hints, that's all I've had. What exactly is your government offering, General?"

"It is well known, sir, that the post of governor of the Bahamas has few attractions for you. In the circumstances, you would perhaps prefer to stay on in Europe. In Spain, for example, or Switzerland. I am authorized to say that if you find yourself in financial difficulties by making such a move, a sum of fifty million Swiss francs could be made available on deposit in Geneva."

"Nonsense, General," the Duke replied. "The Führer doesn't want me in Spain or Switzerland. He wants me in Germany, to be on hand for the day the German army enters London. A familiar face to give the British people confidence. Is this not so?"

"What can I say, sir?"

"My ship sails the day after tomorrow and I admit I don't want to go. The British government have treated me badly—and if my services matter so little to them . . ." He shrugged. "Thirty-six hours, that's all I've got, but if I'm to throw myself into the game on your side, I must know exactly what I'm getting into."

Kleiber started to speak, but Schellenberg cut him short. "May I ask Your Royal Highness a direct question? If necessary, would you be prepared to ascend the throne again?"

"Certainly," the Duke said. "I would naturally expect the Duchess to be accepted as my consort."

"I foresee no difficulty there, sir."

"Of course, if I am to take so drastic a step, an action that would cause something of a stir in the world, I shall require some evidence of cooperation on the part of the Führer."

"And what would satisfy Your Royal Highness?" asked Kleiber.

"If the Duchess and I are to make plans to return to England, we must know when the Führer thinks we should be ready to go."

Schellenberg saw it all then, or thought he did, but contented himself with saying, "I understand your interest in the timing involved, sir. I shall convey the substance of this conversation to Foreign Minister von Ribbentrop, who will no doubt communicate it to the Führer without delay."

"You have only tomorrow, General," the Duke said. "It would distress me to leave on the *Excalibur*, but I will go if I must. Any communication you have for me, put through Colonel da Cunha."

"I'll be in touch soon," Schellenberg said. "Good night, sir."

He moved to the door, followed by Kleiber. Da Cunha opened it for them and locked it after they had passed through.

The Duke waited a few moments, then called, "Mr. Jackson?"

"Yes, sir." The American dropped down into the shrubbery and approached the summerhouse.

"Well, you heard. What do you think?" asked the Duke. "Will they play ball—isn't that the American phrase?"

"That depends on how badly they need you, sir."

"If they occupy England, very badly indeed. Still, thank you for coming." The Duke held out his hand. "May I count on you when the Germans are ready to meet with me again? For obvious reasons, it would be unwise for me to approach our own intelligence people at the moment."

"Yes, sir."

"Excellent. Good night, then," and the Duke walked away.

"HE'S LYING," Schellenberg said. "I don't believe a word of it." He was in Huene's office again. The ambassador sat behind his desk, and Kleiber stood facing Schellenberg.

"I was there too," said Kleiber, "and I believe him. Why not? They threw him out on his ear, didn't they? Now we're giving him a chance to regain his throne and with the Duchess at his side. That's all he really wants."

"He wants Sea Lion laid out on a plate for him," Schellenberg snapped. "It's as simple as that."

Huene shook his head. "I don't agree. We'll be landing in Britain in a matter of weeks, the whole world knows that. As I see it, the Duke is just being practical. A timetable isn't an unreasonable request. And if he gives his word . . ."

"I know," Schellenberg said. "A man of finest honour. But it occurs to me that there may come a time for any honourable man to act dishonourably for the sake of a cause he believes in."

"We're going round in circles," Kleiber said. "Are you going to get in touch with Foreign Minister von Ribbentrop or must I do it for you?"

"No," Schellenberg replied. "That won't be necessary. I'll get a signal off right away. I'll leave you to impart the glad tidings to Himmler. You'll enjoy doing that."

AT TEN THIRTY ON the following morning Himmler received Kleiber's lengthy signal, which had been routed through the Madrid embassy. He read it over, lips pursed, then sat there waiting for Ribbentrop to make the first move.

It was just after eleven when Ribbentrop entered his office and said, "I've had a signal from Schellenberg, Reichsführer. Rather remarkable. I'm not sure what to do about it. I wondered whether the Führer—"

"No," Himmler said firmly. "The Führer is particularly busy at the moment, as you well know. There are some burdens we must carry for him. I, too, have received a signal from Lisbon. I know the Führer placed the Windsor affair in your lap particularly, but if you think it helpful, I will be happy to discuss it with you."

Ribbentrop sat down, and Himmler proceeded. "If we give the Duke our time schedule for Operation Sea Lion, what exactly is it that we're giving away?"

"Are you suggesting we show him the entire plan?" Ribbentrop said in horror.

Himmler smiled. "The whole thing is quite academic. Look at it this way. A few weeks ago, the British army left most of its equipment on the beaches at Dunkirk. They have less than two hundred tanks left and they are desperately short of fighter planes." Himmler paused for a moment. "Conditions for a landing are at their most favourable in the period between September the nineteenth and the twenty-sixth. Anyone with a Channel map and a tide schedule knows that. The Luftwaffe will have crushed all opposition in the air by then, and without air support the Royal Navy is most effectively neutralized. No, even if Winston Churchill had the entire plan of Sea Lion in his hands at this very moment, he has neither the resources nor the capability to stop it."

110

"So, you think we should meet the Duke's demand?"

"My dear Ribbentrop, the Führer has entrusted you with the Windsor affair. I can only advise you, but I must say that I don't see how you can go wrong under the circumstances."

IT WAS just after noon when Walter Monckton was shown into the library, where he was greeted with real affection by both the Duke and Duchess.

"I suppose Winston's sent you to make sure I get on board the *Excalibur* tomorrow?" the Duke said.

"Well, sir, the prime minister and indeed His Majesty have been concerned at the delays in the matter. There have been rumours of an unhealthy German interest in your presence here."

"Walter, you're behind the times. It's our own secret service I have to worry about, according to Madrid gossip."

"But that's absurd, sir."

"Walter, my friend Primo de Rivera, who is highly connected with the Spanish government, has assured me that there is considerable substance to these rumours. The idea seems to be that if I refuse to go to the Bahamas, the British secret service would take me by force."

"You've no idea what it's been like, Walter," the Duchess added. "Anonymous letters . . . Policemen everywhere."

"Now, Wallis." The Duke took her hands in his. "You worry too much. Go and get ready for lunch."

When she had gone, the Duke went to the sideboard and poured himself a Scotch. Monckton said, "Good Lord, sir, I've never seen you take a drink before seven in the evening."

"I know, Walter, but I need it today. Tell me, old friend, have I ever been less than honest with you?"

"No, sir."

"Then I ask you to trust me now. Walter, when the *Excalibur* sails tomorrow, I shall be on board, I promise you, but for the moment, it's essential that certain people still get the impression that I'm vacillating. De Rivera is coming to spend the day. Talk to him for me. Tell him how shocked I am about these plots he speaks of. Say that I'm threatening not to leave on the ship."

Monckton said gravely, "And am I not to be permitted to know what's really going on, sir?"

"No, Walter. Not for the moment."

111

There was a knock at the door. A footman appeared and announced the arrival of the Spaniard, Primo de Rivera.

A SIGNAL from Ribbentrop was received at the German legation just after five o'clock, and Huene sent for Schellenberg and Kleiber at once.

"From Ribbentrop," the ambassador told them. "It simply says, 'Demands acceptable. Details requested follow.' "

Kleiber turned to Schellenberg, his eyes ablaze with triumph. "So, you see, General, I knew my man. Better than you did. I'll go to the communications room and wait for the next signal."

When the door had closed, Schellenberg laughed out loud. "This isn't just Ribbentrop. It's Himmler too. A champagne salesman and a chicken farmer. An unbeatable combination!"

"General Schellenberg," Huene said, "I can listen to no more of this. I have a family to consider. Relatives back home."

"Of course," Schellenberg said. "I should not allow emotion to take over. It's just that I detest stupidity."

A few moments later, the door opened and Kleiber entered with a sealed envelope. "They just put it through the decoder, General. It's marked for your eyes only."

Schellenberg weighed the envelope in his hands. "And for the Duke of Windsor's also, I presume."

"Shall I get hold of da Cunha?" Huene asked.

Schellenberg nodded. "Tell him to arrange another meeting with the Duke. Same time and place as last night will do."

Kleiber went out, and Schellenberg followed. At the door, he paused and turned to Huene. "I leave you with one happy thought. I think we've just lost the war."

STANDING on the steps beside the Duke, Walter Monckton heaved a sigh of relief as Primo de Rivera was shown to his car.

"Sir, I don't think I've ever heard such nonsense in my life. I asked him for some sort of evidence of these British plots, and he could show me nothing. He then had the cheek to inform me that within ten days he'd have all the evidence we'd need."

"And he asked you to postpone my sailing tomorrow? Poor Walter. I really am most grateful."

They went into the drawing room, where the Duchess was sitting with their host. "Now, who's for a drink?" asked the Duke.

At that moment, there was a discreet knock at the door and a footman came in. "Colonel da Cunha to see Your Royal Highness."

"Do please excuse me, everyone. Security arrangements for tomorrow. See to the drinks, there's a good chap, Walter."

THE DUKE SAT IN the summerhouse, examining the envelope's documents with a small flashlight. Schellenberg and Kleiber waited by the door.

"Very interesting," the Duke said finally. He returned the papers to the envelope." Quite brilliant. I can't fault it."

Schellenberg asked, "You are satisfied, then, sir?"

"Yes," replied the Duke, putting the envelope in his pocket.

"And the sailing tomorrow."

"Simply can't take place. The Duchess isn't at all well. We'll have to get the doctor first thing in the morning. The *Excalibur* leaves at noon. After she's gone, we can make other arrangements."

"Of course, sir."

"Good. Then I'll say good night, gentlemen."

Da Cunha, who was standing by the garden door, let them out. Joe Jackson, on the wall, waited, then dropped to the ground and walked to the summerhouse.

"Wait here for me, Mr. Jackson," the Duke said. "I'll be back quickly with something of supreme importance."

He hurried away and went directly to the library of the villa, where the Duchess waited. "What are the others doing?" he asked as he spread the papers before him on the desk.

"Playing cards. What have you got there?"

"The most astonishing thing you ever read, Wallis. Operation Sea Lion—the German plan for the invasion of England, supplied by Ribbentrop in the fond hope that it might make me see on which side my bread is buttered."

She locked the door and came back to the desk.

"Look at this," he said. "Eagle Day, August the thirteenth. The Luftwaffe will launch a devastating strike on the airfields of the south of England aimed at destroying the RAF."

"And the invasion?" she asked.

"Must take place between the nineteenth and the twenty-sixth of September. A question of moon and tides. After that, it's no good because they'll be into the autumn and much more unpredictable weather."

"Can anything be done?"

"Yes, I think something can. The whole thing hinges on air superiority. As long as the RAF still functions, the Royal Navy commands the Channel and no invasion can possibly succeed. But the Luftwaffe has orders to eliminate the RAF as a first priority. Goering estimates accomplishing this in two weeks. This brings us to the flaw in the plan," the Duke went on. "The contingency section. If the Luftwaffe has not succeeded in crushing the RAF by the seventeenth of September, then Operation Sea Lion will be cancelled."

"And what happens then?"

"Hitler will turn on Russia, and that, my love, will be the end of him. I'm sure I saw a typewriter in the cupboard over there the other day. Not that I'm any expert, but two fingers should suffice."

"For what, David?"

"To make a copy of the lot, Wallis. For Mr. Jackson."

In forty minutes the Duke was back at the summerhouse. He gave Jackson the envelope. "What that contains is of supreme importance to the British government at this time. I've addressed it to Mr. Winston Churchill and marked it for his eyes alone. After I've sailed tomorrow, I'd be obliged if you would pass it to Sir Walford Selby, the British ambassador, with my compliments. The original I shall give to my good friend Walter Monckton to pass on to Mr. Churchill personally when he returns to London."

"A case of hedging your bets, sir?"

"Accidents do happen. You know, Mr. Jackson, once, in France during the World War, I got out of my staff car and walked forward to view a trench. A few minutes later, the car was riddled with machine-gun bullets, killing the driver. I've often wondered why I was spared on that occasion. Perhaps tonight provides some sort of answer."

"Sir, it's been a privilege to know you."

"And you, Mr. Jackson." The Duke shook his hand.

Da Cunha, still standing guard at the wall, showed Jackson out and locked the door. The Duke approached him. "Not long now, Colonel, and you'll be rid of me."

"A new world, sir, new plans. Something to look forward to."

"Yes, of course. Surf beating on the shore, palm trees swaying, and three thousand miles away from the war. Who could ask for more? Goodnight, Colonel," and he walked away quickly.

Fourteen

The next morning Walter Monckton and Santo e Silva waited in the library. It was almost ten and Monckton paced up and down anxiously. The door opened and the Duke entered, his face grave.

"Well, sir?" Monckton asked. "How is she?"

"Not too good, I'm afraid. Some sort of virus, the doctor thinks. There can certainly be no question of her travelling."

"But sir, the *Excalibur* leaves in two hours. We cannot possibly delay its sailing. Your luggage is already on board."

"There will be other ships, Walter. A delay of a week or two is not going to matter." He turned to his host, Santo e Silva. "I really must apologize for this last-minute contretemps. We've imposed enough on your generosity as it is."

"Your Royal Highness, I am entirely at your disposal. My house is yours for as long as need be. If you will excuse me now, I will make sure the staff is aware of the change of plan."

As the door closed behind him, Monckton said, "Really, sir, is the Duchess so ill that an ocean voyage wouldn't prove beneficial?"

"To tell you the truth, Walter, she's as fit as a fiddle." The Duke took him by the arm and led him out to the terrace.

"But I don't understand."

"You will, Walter, but tell me, is da Cunha on hand?"

"No, sir, he's at the docks. Police headquarters had an anonymous phone call saying there was a bomb on board the *Excalibur*. The work of some crank, perhaps. The ship is being searched from stem to stern. Look, what is going on, sir?"

The Duke leaned on the balustrade with both hands. "Walter, I'm afraid I have not been completely honest with you. I had a meeting with Schellenberg here in the garden last night."

"Sir!"

"Yes, the Germans think I'm on their side now. That I'm not going to the Bahamas after all. In return, I gained this." He took the envelope from his inside pocket. "A present for Winston." He smiled. "With my love, of course."

Monckton took the envelope, a dazed look in his eyes. "But what are your intentions now, sir?"

"To sail on the *Excalibur*. Now this is what you do. Tell our host you're going to the docks to inform Colonel da Cunha we won't be sailing and to retrieve the luggage. Then return here at precisely eleven thirty. The moment you arrive, Wallis and I will join you, and we'll make a dash for the ship. If the timing is right, we should arrive just as they're taking up the gangplank."

"And you wish me to inform Colonel da Cunha of this plan?"

"Yes—most certainly." The Duke smiled again. "We're into the home stretch, Walter. We'll beat them, you'll see."

He went inside and climbed the stairs to his wife's bedroom. The shades were drawn and the room was in half-darkness.

"Wallis?" he whispered, and sat on the edge of the bed.

"David, is anything wrong?" She sat up against the pillows.

"Not a thing, my darling, we're exactly on course. Your performance with the doctor was perfection. I'm sure by now the news has reached the German legation that we're not leaving. In other words, that I'm doing exactly as promised."

"And what happens now?"

He took one of her hands in his and explained quickly.

SCHELLENBERG had slept late for once. When his bedside phone rang at ten thirty, it was Ambassador Huene.

"Good morning," Schellenberg said. "How are things?"

"We had a report that a car turned up at the docks earlier this morning with their luggage. It was put on board immediately."

"What!" Schellenberg pushed himself up on one elbow.

"No need to panic. I've just heard from the house that the Duchess is unwell. The doctor's confined her to bed. They definitely won't be sailing." There was a silence. "Will you be coming in, General?"

"Yes, I suppose so," Schellenberg said. "There's the next move to work out now. When to get them out and how."

He put down the phone, lit a cigarette, and leaned back against the pillow. Strange, but he felt disappointed.

JUST BEFORE eleven thirty, the Duke was waiting at the bedroom window, the Duchess at his shoulder, fully dressed.

"Come on, Walter," the Duke whispered, glancing at his watch. "Don't let me down now."

A moment later, the Buick came up the drive and braked to a halt at the front door. Walter Monckton got out and looked up at the bedroom window.

"Here we go, Wallis." The Duke took her by the arm. "Don't stop for anything."

They hurried down the stairs, and a surprised footman ran to open the front door for them. Just then, Santo e Silva came out of the library. He stopped, a look of astonishment on his face.

"But Your Royal Highness—"

"So awfully kind of you to have put up with us for so long," the Duke said, and kept on moving.

"But Her Grace . . ."

"Feeling better now. Sea air will do her a world of good."

They were into the rear of the Buick in an instant. Monckton followed, slamming the door, and called to the driver. The wheels spun, churning the gravel, and they were away.

WHEN KLEIBER went into Huene's office, he found the ambassador pacing up and down, obviously very agitated.

"Ambassador. You sent for me?"

"I've tried to get hold of General Schellenberg, but he's already left his hotel. Bad news, I'm afraid. I've just heard from the villa that the Duke and Duchess left in a considerable hurry for the *Excalibur* some ten minutes ago. He's tricked us. He's going to the Bahamas after all."

"But he can't do that." Kleiber was very pale. "He gave his word, made a bargain. We kept our part."

Huene said, "A disastrous situation, but there's nothing any of us can do about it."

Kleiber turned, tight-lipped, and went out. Sindermann was waiting outside. "The Duke," Kleiber told him grimly. "He's sold us out. They're sailing on the *Excalibur* after all."

"So—we've lost? He must be laughing at all of us."

"I'm sure he is, Gunter, so let's make sure he dies laughing, shall we? Get the car started. I'll be with you in a few minutes."

"And General Schellenberg?"

"To hell with General Schellenberg."

Kleiber raced downstairs to the legation armoury, and the startled sergeant in charge leaped to attention.

"I want a rifle," Kleiber demanded. "Any decent one will do."

The sergeant picked up a Walther semi-automatic. "An excellent combat weapon," he said. "Astonishingly accurate on rapid fire at up to a thousand yards." He rammed a magazine into place.

"Good. I'll take it." Kleiber made for the door.

"Please, Major," the sergeant called. "You must sign for it."

But Kleiber was already gone. The sergeant picked up the internal telephone and asked to speak to Ambassador Huene.

AS SCHELLENBERG'S car entered the gates of the legation, the driver had to wrench the wheel sharply to one side as a black Mercedes sedan hurtled past. Schellenberg had a glimpse of Sindermann at the wheel, Kleiber beside him.

The driver pulled up at the entrance. As the general got out of the car, Huene appeared on the porch. "Thank heaven you're here."

"What's happened?" Schellenberg demanded.

"The Duke," Huene said, "is leaving on the *Excalibur*. He's fooled us. Fooled us all."

"And where was Kleiber going in such a hurry?"

"I've just been informed he's drawn a rifle from the armoury."

Quickly Walter Schellenberg turned back to the car. "The Alcantara docks," he told the driver. "The pier the *Excalibur* is leaving from, and drive like you never have before."

THE ENTRANCE to the docks was heavily guarded, and all approaching vehicles were being closely inspected. The *Excalibur*'s gangplank had already been pulled in and her lines were being cast off. Kleiber noticed da Cunha standing by the gate.

"What are you going to do?" Sindermann asked. "We'll never get through."

"I've just had a thought, Gunter. Wasn't that the American's bar we passed a couple of minutes ago?"

"Yes, Major."

"Then if he's at home, he could be the solution to our problems."

JOE JACKSON and Hannah were standing on the balcony of the apartment above the club, looking towards the *Excalibur*, whose funnels towered above a jumble of dock buildings.

"We'll get a much better view when the tugs have pulled her out into midstream," Jackson told her.

The door of the living room was flung open, and as they turned, Kleiber and Sindermann entered, both holding guns.

Kleiber said, "What I say, I will say only once, Herr Jackson. I desire to gain entrance to the Alcantara docks, but the gate is heavily guarded."

"So?"

"Colonel da Cunha is on duty there. It occurs to me that he will allow you to pass through on the excuse that you wish to watch the *Excalibur* leave. Only natural, after your part in the affair. I shall be crouched under the canvas cover of the rear seat of your sports car. I could say that I'll blow your spine out if you give me away at the gate, but there's no need. Sindermann will be here with Fräulein Winter. Do you follow me?"

Sindermann then grabbed Hannah by the hair and rammed the muzzle of his gun under her chin.

"Okay," Jackson said. "We play it your way."

AS SCHELLENBERG'S car neared the docks, his driver braked suddenly and pointed at the black Mercedes sedan parked by Jackson's bar at the end of the wharf. "General, it's them. I know the car. It has embassy plates."

"Pull over behind it," Schellenberg told him.

No one was in the car. Schellenberg tried the side door of the club and it opened to his touch. He paused for a moment, then went upstairs cautiously, his hands in his pockets.

SINDERMANN sat on one side of the table, Hannah on the other. She reached for the coffee pot.

"Careful," he warned her.

"I only want a cup of coffee," she said, then hurled the scalding contents of the pot into his face and started for the door. As he cried out in pain, she tripped over a rug and fell. A second later, he had her by the hair, jerking her to her feet.

"Now then, you slut, I'll make you pay."

"I don't think so," Schellenberg said quietly. He was standing just inside the door, the Mauser with the bulbous silencer in his right hand.

Sindermann pushed his gun into Hannah's side. "Drop it," he ordered, his scalded face contorted with pain. "Now—or she dies."

But Schellenberg was quicker. His arm swung up and he shot him through the head. The bullet sent Sindermann backwards, out across the balcony and over the rail. He landed in the river below.

Hannah had fallen to one knee, Sindermann's blood across her

119

hair and face. As Schellenberg helped her to her feet, he said urgently, "Kleiber? Where is he?"

"The docks," she said. "He forced Joe to take him there. He's hidden in the back of Joe's sports Mercedes."

He took her hand, and they hurried down to his car.

When they swerved into the dockyard entrance, da Cunha was standing at the gatehouse, talking to Walter Monckton. The colonel looked at once into the car and frowned at the sight of Hannah Winter sitting beside Schellenberg, blood on her face.

"What's happened? Explain yourself, General."

"Has Joe come through in his sports car?" Hannah demanded.

"Why, yes, several minutes ago. He told me he wished to catch a last glimpse of the Duke."

"Kleiber was with him," Schellenberg said. "Hidden in the back, and he has a rifle."

Walter Monckton said in horror, "Good God, what can we do?"

There was a sudden cheer. As they turned, the Duke and Duchess appeared on the upper deck of the *Excalibur* and waved to the dockworkers below. Monckton ran forward, shouting frantically, "Go back, David! Go back!" The Duke and Duchess, unable to hear what he was saying, waved, smiling.

It was Hannah then, who, looking wildly about her, saw the silver Mercedes parked outside a warehouse a hundred yards away.

"There!" she cried, pointing. "Joe's car."

As Schellenberg's driver gunned the motor, da Cunha jumped on the running board and the car surged forward.

The sports car was standing beside a green door marked FIRE EXIT. Schellenberg flung it open and found stone steps ascending into darkness. He pulled out his Mauser and, followed by da Cunha, went up on the run.

KLEIBER stood behind Jackson at the warehouse parapet. The *Excalibur* was now moving out into the river. As she sounded her horn, the Duke and Duchess entered a railed-off enclosure in the stern which had been specially set aside for them.

"Beautiful," Kleiber said. "I can get two for the price of one."

"Don't be a fool, man," Jackson told him. "There's nothing to be gained now."

"He made fools of us—all of us," Kleiber answered. "Even the Führer himself. Now, he pays."

He rammed the butt of the Walther rifle into Jackson's side. The American went down with a groan and Kleiber knelt, resting the Walther on the parapet. He took careful aim at the Duke.

As he squeezed the trigger, Jackson, though half unconscious, grabbed his legs. The ship's horn blared again at that moment, drowning out the sound of the shot, and the bullet ploughed into the deck several feet from the Duke and Duchess, who were totally unaware of what was happening. Kleiber kicked out at Jackson, pushing him away, and took aim again. The door to the stairs behind burst open, and a familiar voice cried, "Kleiber!"

Kleiber turned, hate taking complete possession of him as his rifle came up. Schellenberg shot him in the right shoulder, the heavy bullet turning him around. The next two shots shattered his spine, driving him against the parapet, the rifle flying away.

Colonel da Cunha went to him and knelt down, but no examination was necessary. He glanced up. "You are a difficult man to understand, General Schellenberg."

"Something I live with every day of my life."

Hannah rushed through the door and dropped to one knee beside Jackson, who was trying to sit up.

"Did the Duke make it?" he asked.

"Yes," she said. "Thanks to General Schellenberg."

Schellenberg was moving towards the door. As he started down the stairs, Hannah caught up with him, grabbing him by the sleeve. "You're going back to Berlin, aren't you?"

"Yes. Today, if I can manage it."

"Why?"

"Because I have no choice, and I think, in your heart, you know this. For me, it is too late."

He started down the stairs again. She called, "Walter!" and there was desperation in her voice, a kind of rage at life and the cruelty of it.

"Did I ever tell you that when you sing, you sound like Billie Holiday on one of her better days?" he said.

His footsteps echoed hollowly for a while as he descended; then the door banged and he was gone.

As the *Excalibur* moved out to sea, the Duchess went in search of the Duke and found him still standing in the stern.

"I've brought you a scarf," she said.

"Why, thank you, Wallis."

She took his arm and they stood there at the rail together. "It could be worse, David—the Bahamas, I mean. We'll make it work, so try not to be too disappointed. After all, we have each other."

"Of course we do, and I'm not the slightest bit disappointed." He smiled that wonderful smile which illuminated not only himself but everything about him. "In fact, to be honest, Wallis, I feel rather pleased with myself."

"But will anyone ever know, David?" she said.

"I will, my love." He kissed her gently on the brow. "And so will you. That's all that matters."

SCHELLENBERG arrived at his Prinz Albrechtstrasse office at three o'clock the following afternoon. He had been travelling for just over twenty-four hours. His suit was rumpled and he needed a shave. His office door opened and Heydrich entered. "You look as if you haven't slept for a week."

"I only feel that way."

"He knows you're back, Walter. Wants you upstairs right away. What a mess this thing turned out to be. I'm sorry, but I can't help you now. This time, you're finished."

"Oh, I don't know," Schellenberg said, and went out.

He delivered his report, standing in front of Himmler's desk, holding back nothing of any consequence.

When he had finished, there was silence for a moment, then Himmler said, "You were right to execute Kleiber as you did. There was nothing to be gained from assassinating the Duke at that stage."

Schellenberg said, "There is, of course, the question of the information passed on to the Duke. . . ."

"By order of Ribbentrop." Himmler sighed. "Yes, I do feel he has been a little injudicious."

"Will you inform the Führer?"

"On another occasion, perhaps. One that is more suited to my purposes."

Schellenberg was silent a moment, then asked, "And the details of Sea Lion, Reichsführer? What can we do about that? The Duke will certainly have had them passed on to Churchill, probably using Walter Monckton as his messenger."

"But to what avail? There are only two periods before the

autumn gales when the tide is right for a landing. The British know that as well as we do. The important point is that there will be nothing they can do about it. In the same way, the fact that they now know the date of Eagle Day, when the RAF will be destroyed, makes little difference. The British are hardly in a position to defend themselves against the might of the' Luftwaffe.''

"But they will also know, now, that if we fail in this task, if the RAF can hold out until the seventeenth of September, Sea Lion will be aborted and the Führer will turn his attention to Russia."

Himmler said, "Are you seriously suggesting that the Luftwaffe, the mightiest air force the world has ever seen, a force that has total control of the skies of Europe, can be held back by a handful of RAF Spitfire pilots with virtually no combat experience?"

"Yes, Reichsführer, put that way, I suppose it does sound rather absurd."

"You're tired, General. You've been through a great deal. I suggest you take a week off, and when you return, you'll see things in perspective again."

"Thank you, Reichsführer."

Schellenberg went out, closing the door quietly behind him. He said softly, "Am I really the only sane man in a world gone mad?"

Epilogue

Hannah Winter returned to America a month later on the same ship as Connie Jones and the boys. Joe Jackson stayed in Lisbon until October, but news of the air war, the Battle of Britain, proved too much for him. He sold his bar, took passage to England, and joined the RAF.

By April 1942 he was a squadron leader with two DFCs to his name. That same month he was reported missing, believed killed, having been last seen pursuing two Messerschmidt 109s across the Channel.

Hannah arrived in England at the beginning of 1944 to tour American air force bases with the United Services Organizations. During the spring of that year, the Luftwaffe renewed its night attacks against London, and Hannah Winter, along with forty-two other people, was killed instantly when the club in Curzon Street at which she was appearing received a direct hit.

Heydrich was assassinated in Prague in June 1942 by a team of

Czech agents recruited for the job. By way of reprisal, the Nazis destroyed the village of Lidice and murdered the entire male population.

Himmler, captured by British forces after the war, took poison when his identity was discovered.

Walter Schellenberg became head of the Combined Secret Services of Germany in 1944, playing out the farce to the end. In 1945 he was imprisoned at Landsberg and later tried on the charge of having been a member of the SS. He was sentenced to six years, but perhaps because a surprising number of witnesses had spoken in his favour at his trial, he was released in 1951 after only a two-year imprisonment. He died of cancer at the age of forty-two.

The Duke of Windsor, who served as governor of the Bahamas until 1945, had already made his contribution. Probably one of the most important of the entire war.

At the height of the Battle of Britain, on the fifteenth of September, 1940, Winston Churchill visited Air Vice-Marshal Keith Park at Group Operations, Number 11 Fighter Group, at Uxbridge.

Fighting the strongest concentration of planes the Luftwaffe had ever sent over, the RAF was stretched to breaking point. The prime minister asked what reserves there were to bring in.

"None, sir," Park told him. "Everything's up there."

"Hold on," the prime minister said. "Two more days, that's all, and it will be over."

Park looked at him in amazement. "But how can you be sure, Prime Minister? Is this information from a trustworthy source?"

Winston Churchill smiled. "I have it on the most impeccable authority," he said.

Where the Eagle Has Landed

Harry Patterson was borne to fame on eagle's wings. Four years ago, despite several highly praised novels, he was but one of many talented authors on the threshold of world acclaim. With his wife, Amy, and their four children, he was living comfortably in a big Victorian house in Leeds, England—proof, in fact, that his five-year gamble to give up teaching for full-time writing had paid off.

Then, with the publication of *The Eagle Has Landed*, written under his pen name, Jack Higgins, everything changed. The book became an international bestseller and later an all-star film. Other successful novels followed, and today Harry, in his fiftieth year, is a millionaire, basking unashamedly not only in the limelight but also the sunshine. The Victorian house in England's industrial north has given way to an ultra-modern residence on the island of Jersey.

As we sat by his avocado-shaped swimming pool, I asked him about *To Catch A King*. "The Duke of Windsor was my inspiration," he said. "I have always thought that he has been badly misunderstood by historians. The more I looked into the details of his life and behaviour, the more I realized what an honourable and brave man he must have been."

There are, of course, many other historical figures in *To Catch A King*. In real life, Walter Schellenberg rose finally to be head of German Intelligence, while both Hannah Winter and Joe Jackson bear resemblance to real-life espionage agents at the time. Once again, and certainly not for the last time, Harry Patterson has written a book in which the reader must decide tantalizingly for himself how much is fact and how much is speculation.

N.D.B.

"...but there are always miracles."

A CONDENSATION OF THE BOOK BY
Jack and Mary Willis

ILLUSTRATED BY MITCHELL HOOKS

PUBLISHED BY FUTURA PUBLICATIONS

For Jack Willis and his beautiful fiancée, Mary Pleshette, the summer of 1970 held every promise that life can offer a young couple in love. Then came Jack's freak surfing accident and, as the fateful wave receded, so did all their dreams of happiness. If Jack survived, it would surely be as a paraplegic, paralysed from the waist down.

Here, in their own words, is Jack's and Mary's unflinchingly honest account of those endless weeks when Jack lay immobilized in a Long Island hospital. While doctors fought stubbornly to restore some movement, and progress was measured by the twitch of a toe, the couple were confronted by some agonizing questions: Could they have children? What meaning would marriage have for them now?

Jack

I realized I might die, but I wasn't afraid. It seemed painless, even tolerable. I tried to get my legs underneath me, but they wouldn't go. I fought slipping off into unconsciousness. Which way was up? I rolled over and over in the surf, looking for the sunlight through the water. But I couldn't find it, and I was running out of breath. How long had I been under? It seemed like hours, and I knew I couldn't hold out much longer. What a dumb way to die, I thought, and suddenly my head came free and I yelled for help as loudly as I could.

I felt arms grab me, drag me out of the water along the sandy bottom. I screamed at them to be careful, that I thought I had broken my neck or back. I had no feeling in my body. I was paralyzed from my chest down. They laid me on the sand near the edge of the water and someone went to call for help. While we were waiting for the ambulance, the police arrived. They asked my name and questioned me about the accident and the lack of feeling and movement in my body. Then, while one went to report in, the other scratched the soles of my feet with a pencil. I could feel it, but it was numb and dull. I felt as if I'd been given a massive dose of novocaine.

I tried moving my arms. They seemed all right, although the left one was weak. Mary was kneeling in the sand next to me.

"Move your fingers," she said.

"I can't move them."

"Here. Squeeze my hand," she said.

"I can't move my fingers," I said. "It's as if they were asleep."

"Try your legs."

"They won't move. I can't move anything but my arms."

She looked at me almost in disbelief. Then she reached down, grabbed my legs, and tried to prop them up. They flopped down on the sand.

She looked around as though expecting an answer from the crowd that had started to gather. The people just stared back. Two ambulance men arrived. They also questioned me and tested my feet for feeling. They didn't want to move me until a doctor came.

Thoughts came rushing in, confused and uncontrolled. I was happy to be alive. I had fought a terrific battle in the water and had won. But that was over, and now I wanted to go home. Now. But I couldn't move. This couldn't be happening to me. I wanted to go back in time. I wanted another chance.

I had been bodysurfing since I was a kid. I should have known better. I shouldn't have taken that wave. I should have waited for a less dangerous one. At least I should have gotten my arms out in front of me. I should have protected my head. It was frightening . . . the one act . . . an accident.

All I could see was faces staring at me. I felt like some strange fish that has washed up on the beach, a subject of concern but also of wonderment. I looked at those faces, and tears welled up in my eyes. I may have been touched by their concern, but I may have been crying for myself.

Mary got up to talk with the police, and a little blond man with soft hands shielded my eyes from the late-afternoon sun and tenderly wiped the sand off my face. He told me not to worry, that I'd be okay. More tears. I couldn't control them.

I don't remember much that Mary said to me on the beach that day. I do remember that when I was first pulled out of the water she was nervous, but slowly became calm and comforting and finally helpful to the police and doctor. We must have said to each other, "Don't worry, it will be all right." But I don't remember. It was so unreal. A nightmare.

I again tried to move my right arm and found that I could. I tried my left. It was weaker than the right, but I could move it. I tried my fingers and the rest of my body. I still couldn't make them move. I saw all those people looking at me in a way that

I had never been looked at before—as an object of pity. What more were they thinking? That it could have been any one of them? Maybe. But serious accidents always seem to happen to somebody else.

I'd never really been seriously hurt, even seriously ill. And I hardly knew anyone who had even been in a bad accident, certainly no one who had been paralyzed. I was seized with fear—a freaky accident, one in a million, and it was happening to me. I didn't want to panic. I didn't want to scare Mary. I tried to tell myself that maybe it wasn't serious. But I knew better. And then I thought, One second I'm healthy, work is challenging, I'm in love; the next second I'm hurt so badly that I might be a basket case for the rest of my life.

THE DOCTOR arrived about fifteen minutes after the ambulance. He was wearing horn-rimmed glasses, and he looked to be in his middle thirties, about my age. He had on black-and-white checked cotton pants and an open-necked polo shirt. He fit right in with the scene. He told me he was from Southampton and had been called while on late rounds at the hospital.

"Can you feel this?" he said as he scratched my feet just as the ambulance men and police had done. He then bent my big toe and asked me what I felt. I told him that he'd bent the toe up. He bent it down, and I said, "Down." Then he did the same with my other foot, and I responded correctly. He said that was "a very good sign." Next he asked me to move my arms, which I did, but I couldn't move anything else, no matter how intensely I willed it.

The doctor told me his name was Dr. Spinzia. For some reason I couldn't call him Doctor. He was my age and somehow, in this situation, formality seemed ridiculous. I asked him his first name, and he answered Joe. From then on I called him Joe.

He cradled my head in his hands while four men lifted me gingerly up onto a board to carry me to the ambulance. When we got to the sand dunes Joe lifted my head just a little, and I felt shocks shoot down from my shoulders through my arms into my hands. I felt as though I were being electrocuted. I screamed in pain. Raw nerves were being violated by bone. It was the most intense pain I'd ever felt. I thought I might vomit, but as Joe lowered my head a little, the pain ceased. They gently placed me

131

in the ambulance, and Joe and Mary got in with me. On the way to the hospital Joe kept telling me that he'd seen worse accidents than mine, accidents men had walked away from. Mary asked him what he thought it was. He said it looked like a broken neck and that the vertebrae were pressing against my spine, causing prolonged paralysis.

When we arrived at the hospital they pushed me right into the X-ray room. I had an eerie feeling that I was lying on an incline, but Joe said I was perfectly horizontal.

The first X rays were of my lower back. "Looks fine so far," Joe said. "Just terrific—no dislocation, nothing broken."

A few minutes later, after more X rays, he said they could find nothing wrong with my neck either. The news seemed good, I thought, but Joe looked troubled. "I don't know why you're paralyzed if there is no fracture or dislocation. Maybe your spine snapped out of place and back in again, causing serious abrasions. We're just going to have to wait to see what happens. In the meantime, we're going to put you in traction."

By now I was feeling high from a shot of Demerol. It helped me get inside myself and view all that was happening with a curious objectivity and interest. "Okay," Joe said. "I'm going to drill holes in either side of your head and insert a pair of tongs— they're like ice tongs—into the holes. It won't hurt. You don't have nerves in your skull, and the novocaine will take care of your scalp. Then I'm going to hang weights on you to immobilize your back and neck."

I was wheeled out of X ray into another room. Joe shaved my head around the ears, and then I felt him make pencil marks on each side of my head for the holes. He shot my scalp full of novocaine. I looked out of the corner of my eye, expecting to see a high-speed drill. Dismayed, I saw him pick up an old hand drill with what looked like a quarter-inch bit. I braced myself for a shock. I felt the pressure of the drill, but felt no pain as it chewed its way into my head. He finished one side, then the other. Then with something like toggle bolts he clamped the tongs into my head and suspended big black weights from them. When he finished, two nurses wheeled me down a long hall to a hospital room. All I saw was ceiling.

It had been about three hours since the accident, but I had no idea whether it was day or night. I was still in my swimming trunks, still covered with sand. I felt no pain, and the pull of the weights in my head was not uncomfortable. I still couldn't believe what was happening to me, and I was scared. Mary was waiting for me in my room. She told me that she had called her parents in New York City. When they arrived I couldn't tell from their eyes how badly off I was. I didn't have to. I knew. We tried to talk, but I drifted off to sleep.

I was awakened by the groans of a man in the bed next to mine. I tried to concentrate on him but couldn't. There was a nurse with him, and when she saw that I was awake, she came over and cleaned a little of the sand off me. She kept calling me chief. "Hold my hand, chief. Now squeeze my fingers." I ordered my fingers to move, but nothing happened. I felt disappointed. She wiped the sweat off my face and smiled. "Don't get down, chief. Sometimes it takes a while."

I tried to smile but couldn't. "Good night, chief," I said, and fell back to sleep.

I HIKED UP four flights of stairs that night of our first date, and Mary opened the door. She was pretty and looked even younger than I had expected. Back on the street, while we waited for a taxi, she took my arm easily, as if we were old friends. My confidence soared. "She likes me," I said to myself. Her simple move quickly did away with the awkwardness of a blind date. She seemed to be saying that we'd make it.

I don't remember what we talked about, but we talked a lot, not rushed, but still afraid of pauses. Sometime during dinner I realized I was eating mechanically, not tasting. I was working hard to impress her. She remembers that after dinner we went for a short walk and that later we went to a bar on the East Side and talked.

I suppose we talked about all the things people normally talk about on a first date. She'd been raised in New York and I in Los Angeles. She'd gone to private schools and on to Sarah Lawrence; I to public schools and to UCLA. She was a researcher at *Newsweek*; I made documentary films. She was twenty-two and I was thirty-four. And we were both Jewish.

Our second date was on a Sunday in Central Park. It was late March and the first warm day of the year, the kind of day before the trees begin to blossom, when the sunlight is thin and winter is still present but mixed with the promise of spring. The strollers and children were out sharing the day with kite fliers, athletes, and lovers. We ate hot dogs. Mary looked beautiful to me, slim and young. She talked almost compulsively about herself, the way people do who have been lonely for a long time.

By summer we were what my Aunt Edith would call "an item." That summer was only a few years ago, but it seems like twenty. What I remember most clearly is an overwhelming sense of joy and completeness when we were together that got stronger as time went on.

That first summer we spent long, hot weekends on Long Island. We bodysurfed together. We began with the tiny waves that break late but roll a long way, high onto the shore. I taught Mary how to get out in front of them, to keep her head up and then ride the wave all the way onto the beach. Then I taught her to go after the big ones, the wave outside, the wave beyond the others. I showed her how to spot the dangerous ones, the waves that have no water underneath them, that crush down on you or flip you around so that you hit the sand instead of being cushioned on a bed of water. When we saw the right one we'd run to catch it while it was still swelling. Then we'd swim madly with it, on top and a little out front so that when it crested and broke we would fall what seemed a hundred feet and bounce along toward the shore. No matter how many times we rode the waves, we'd jump up and laugh when it was over and race out, hurdling the tiny waves, diving under the big ones to get to the one outside.

The days passed quickly, rich with experience, but in retrospect they seem to have gone slowly because there was so much to remember.

In the fall Mary moved in with me, and neither of us was seeing anyone else. We both thought about marriage but didn't talk about it—not until the following spring.

It was a beautiful day in San Francisco. We were on the last leg of a month's holiday—three weeks in Mexico, a few days in L.A. with my family, now San Francisco.

We took the cable car to Fisherman's Wharf for a lunch of cracked crab. I had planned this day to pop the question to Mary. During the meal I tried projecting how it would feel to ask her to marry me, but I didn't know what I should say.

Finally I couldn't wait anymore. I took my wineglass, raised it toward Mary, and tried to catch her eye. I coughed, and she looked up and put some crab in her mouth and waited for me to speak. "I—" I began. "Mary—will you marry me?"

She blushed and, still with her mouth full of crab, said, "Yes." We both started laughing like crazy people, and we both had tears in our eyes.

Mary

It had been so perfect that Sunday, July 12—clear blue sky and a sun so hot that you could actually feel your skin burn. Jack and I were already tanned from a holiday in Mexico and California six weeks before, and the hot July sun had deepened our color. We arrived at the beach at eleven thirty and, looking for a comfortable place to camp, saw a group of friends, who greeted us warmly and congratulated us on our engagement.

I was relishing this summer in Southampton, our plans to get married in the fall. I had never been so happy, completely secure, and yet, in a peculiar way, acutely aware of life's fragility, as though intense happiness reminded me of our mortality.

Within twenty minutes we decided to go in for a swim. Both Jack and I loved to bodysurf. I had been frightened by a riptide the day before, but that was yesterday, and today the waves were big, there was no undertow, and the tide was low so that the water wasn't terribly deep. It is rare to be able to bodysurf off Long Island, because the contour of the beach is irregular and precipitous. Generally the waves break much too close to shore to give you even a tiny ride.

Today was different. There is nothing more exhilarating than riding a wave, catching it at the perfect moment just before its swell turns into a cascading crest, fighting to stay out in front. I had always admired Jack's talent for catching the biggest wave, swimming with it, and then riding it to the shore. I'm lazy and usually dive under as many as I ride in. I also chicken out. But today we were drunk with the ocean and sun. We stayed in the water until we were chilled, then baked on the beach. By four thirty we were ready to go home, to rest and shower before a Sunday night cookout.

We decided to take one last swim before leaving. The waves were getting bigger, and we both had one or two perfect rides.

Then I dove under a breaking wave and, when I surfaced, turned to see where Jack was. I saw nothing but foam. Then his head popped up and he cried for help. I tried to run toward him, but the water fought my efforts to reach him quickly. For a second I felt panic.

It made no sense. It made no sense. It could have been me or one of our friends who had been swimming with us all day. Thank God for the people on the beach. I could never have pulled Jack out by myself. And the irony, I found out later, was that the curly-haired man did not know how to swim. And then there was Stanley, an elf of a man with sun-bleached hair and skin the color of molasses, who maternally brushed the sand away from Jack's eyes and kept telling him that everything was going to be all right.

The trip to the hospital was a nightmare. I remember looking down at my smooth, brown body in the shade of the ambulance. Then, walking into the hospital in my bikini, I felt naked and vulnerable. Everything was so medicinal and sterile inside, but not unkind. An X-ray technician, realizing I was uncomfortable, handed me a white coat. I watched them wheel Jack's stretcher into the X-ray room, and waited, petrified.

The X ray showed nothing. Possibly, the doctors said, the vertebrae in the lower spine had dislocated and snapped back into place. Possibly. But Jack still couldn't move. There is such a thing as contained panic, a condition akin to calm and born of ignorance, impotence, dread, and hope. Jack and I stared silently at each other as he was wheeled out of the X-ray department, through the emergency lobby, and into another room.

I had to speak with the policeman who had accompanied us from the beach to the hospital. I saw the curly-haired man who had helped me pull Jack out of the ocean walking toward me with our car keys and my red beach dress. I thanked him.

The policeman rechecked the information I had given him on the beach. This same policeman, blond and baby-faced, was the first to diagnose Jack's "problem" as a broken neck. He wished us luck, mentioned a case of a man whose house had fallen on top of him; the man had been paralyzed, and was walking a year later. I was touched by the policeman's concern.

They shaved Jack's head around his ears. He was describing to a nurse what he could and couldn't feel. I couldn't believe he was unable to move. He looked so healthy, his chest a dark rust color and his arms and shoulders muscular. On the beach, when he told me he couldn't move his legs, I had refused to believe him and in a frantic gesture had tried to prop his legs up. But the legs had collapsed.

They were going to put Jack into traction, and Dr. Spinzia explained that he might have to stay in the hospital for as long as six weeks. Six weeks! Jack was supposed to teach a night course at Columbia. What about his work . . . ? And I would have to arrange something with the office. I was still part of a scheduled existence where time is punctuated by plans. I tried to call my father from the hospital, but he wasn't home. He is a doctor, and I left a message with his answering service: "Call immediately. There's been an accident."

A tall, horsey-looking blonde asked me to fill out an admission form for Jack. "I wonder how long Jack'll have to stay here," I said. "We're supposed to be married in October."

"Oh, don't worry," she said. "I bet you'll be a beautiful fall bride." She paused, but I didn't say anything. "Dr. Spinzia's a superb orthopedic surgeon, really outstanding."

My father called. I told him that we had been bodysurfing, that Jack had been thrown by a wave and couldn't move, that the attending physician was Dr. Joseph Spinzia.

"Are you all right?" my father said in his scratchy voice.

"I'm fine," I answered. I felt better just hearing his voice. I trusted my father, always went to him to discuss my problems. He was direct and honest but never cold.

"Mama and I will drive out tonight," he said. "You stay at the hospital. We'll be there in around three hours."

A nurse warned me that Jack would be bleeding where the tongs were drilled into his head, but that everything was all right. Visiting hours were over, but no one said I had to leave. I walked to where his room was and saw two nurses wheeling him toward me. For some strange reason the blood didn't disturb me. He was asleep but woke up for a moment. He was too drugged to speak. I told him I would be close by.

I waited for my parents to arrive. When I saw them walking toward me I felt my throat constrict and my eyes fill up with tears for the first time since the accident. There was nothing to say. We just embraced.

I led Papa into Jack's room. Jack's eyes slowly opened and he

137

smiled. My father put a hand gently on his arm. "Wow," he said softly, "you're really done up good. Are you in a lot of pain?"

Jack told him no and tried to explain what had happened. Papa told him not to speak, that he had looked up Dr. Spinzia before driving out and that he was a good man, and also that Southampton Hospital was very good. His presence, his gaze, his tone were comforting. My mother came in for a short visit, and then my father said we should go, that Jack should get some sleep. I kissed Jack good-by and he told me not to worry. I told him not to worry. I would see him in the morning. As we walked down a long, quiet hall my father put his arm around my waist and my mother held my hand.

Jack

I awoke and a young black man in a white uniform was standing next to me. I asked him what time it was. He told me eight o'clock in the morning. I was still in my swimming trunks, still sandy, but it didn't matter. I was lonely and depressed and felt totally disoriented. It was Monday morning. I should be at work in New York City, but here I was in a Long Island hospital with no idea of how seriously I was hurt.

I couldn't turn my head sideways, and my neck was stretched so far back by the tongs and weights that I could only stare up at the ceiling. The young man was leaning over me so that I could see him.

"What's your name?" I said.

"Clive. I'm a nurse's aide."

"Can I have something to drink? I'm thirsty as hell."

"I don't know," he said. "I'll ask. In the meantime this will help," and he rubbed my parched lips with a cotton swab that had been soaked in a sugary lemon substance. I licked my lips; it quenched my thirst a little.

A nurse came in and said it was all right for me to have liquids, so Clive held a container of milk for me to sip and then a glass of orange juice. He couldn't give me anything to eat, he said, but I didn't care because I wasn't hungry.

Another nurse came in and asked me to squeeze her hand. I held it but couldn't squeeze. She scratched the soles of my feet, and I told her I could feel it. She said that was good. At the time,

138

it never occurred to me to ask her why it was good. Did it mean the paralysis was not serious or that it was only temporary? So far I hadn't asked Joe many questions either, but somehow I knew he wouldn't commit himself this early anyhow.

I wished Mary were with me. I was scared, lying there, waiting to find out what was wrong and what they were going to do with me. I stared at the ceiling, not fully comprehending what had happened, still replaying the wave in my mind, waiting and wishing that someone would pay more attention to me.

The room I was in was very small. The walls were light green, the ceiling made of white perforated plasterboard. I was next to the door and on my right was a large window that faced the corridor. I could vaguely see the window but couldn't see out of it. My roommate was moaning softly.

I thought it would be easier on Mary and her parents if I were moved into the city. And I'd be closer to work. The thought scared me a little because of all the horror stories I'd heard about the lack of care in New York City hospitals. But then I realized that I had no idea whether Southampton Hospital was any better or even if Joe was a good doctor. I dropped it. I was sure that Mary's father, Norman, was taking care of everything.

Joe came into the room. "How do you feel?" he said.

"About as good as anyone can feel under the circumstances, I guess." It was true. I didn't hurt. I didn't feel sick. The tongs in my head didn't bother me, although they did feel a little strange. And I had no urge to go anywhere since I couldn't move. I was worried that they hadn't identified the trouble yet.

"What do you think is wrong with me?"

Joe pressed his hand on my belly. "Why you can't move? I don't know. But gas is accumulating in your belly. We're going to have to put a tube down into you to suck it out."

A few minutes later another doctor came into the room. "Relax," he said. "This might be a little uncomfortable, but it won't hurt." He began pushing the tube into my nostril, but he hit a membrane and the tube got stuck. He started to push harder.

"That hurts!" I yelled. He kept wiggling and pushing the tube. I started to panic. Then the tube somehow cleared the nasal passage and he shoved it down my throat and into my stomach. As soon as it was in, a brownish fluid began to flow out of me into a jar near my bed.

Then the doctor pulled out another tube and told the nurse to take down my swimming trunks. "Relax," he said again. "This won't hurt. I'm going to insert this tube through your penis and into your bladder so that it will automatically drain."

I tensed as he began inserting the catheter. In a way I wanted it to hurt, but at the same time I was afraid. I felt the tube go in. I waited for the pain. There was none.

I did *feel* something though. I thought, that's good.

Then a nurse brought in a bottle with a tube attached to it, and inserted a needle in my arm—intravenous feeding.

The doctor and nurses disappeared. I tried to stay calm. The tube in my throat was a little uncomfortable, but it didn't really bother me.

About midmorning Clive and a couple of nurses came in. They covered me from my chin to my toes with what looked like soft and furry sheepskins.

"What are you doing?" I said.

"We're going to turn you onto your stomach. If you're on your back too long you'll get bedsores."

They placed a large metal frame on top of me. My face was exposed except for my chin and forehead, which were covered by canvas straps. Then they strapped the top frame to the one I was lying on. "Just like a ham sandwich," one nurse laughed. "Okay, now, we're going to turn you."

With Clive at my head and a nurse at my feet they slowly began turning the entire frame like a spit. I tensed and my body slid a little sideways. My neck moved and I screamed as I felt the pain shoot through my shoulders and into my arms. When I was on my stomach the pain stopped. I was staring down at the floor, my head supported by the two canvas straps, which were cutting into my chin and forehead.

"Get me out. Hurry!" I pleaded, as they took the top frame and sheepskins off my back.

"How do you feel?" Clive asked.

"I slipped when you turned me. I think you hurt my neck. The straps hurt."

Clive tried to adjust them for me, but it didn't help.

"Turn me back," I grunted. "I can't take any more."

"You've got to try it a little longer," one nurse said. "You're supposed to stay on this side for at least two hours."

141

Two hours. The straps were killing me, and the stomach tube was pressing against my larynx so I could hardly talk. I tried to relax but couldn't. The sweat was pouring off me.

"Don't leave. Turn me back."

"Five more minutes."

I tried to wait but couldn't. "Turn me!" I screamed. I felt Clive putting the sheepskins on my back and strapping me into the frame. "Tighter," I ordered. Then they began turning me. I slipped again. The pain was excruciating. Finally I was on my back and the pain stopped. They unstrapped me and lifted off the frame and sheepskins. I lay there, exhausted, gasping. "The pain is incredible," I said to one nurse. "I want to see Joe."

"He'll be by later." They all began to leave.

"Clive, how do I ring for help if I need it?"

He placed a buzzer in my hand and told me to push it. I couldn't. I couldn't squeeze that lousy little hospital buzzer.

A nurse came in and told me that I was purposely put in this room because it was across from the nurses' station, and that if I needed anything I just had to yell. Then she left.

I waited for Mary.

Mary

It was ten thirty p.m. when my parents and I finally left the hospital. The house was black, and when I turned on the kitchen lights I saw a half-eaten English muffin, the remains of a late breakfast. The place was exactly as we'd left it, and I felt strange being there without Jack. On the night table in our bedroom were Jack's keys, wallet, and black notebook. Something horrible had happened at four thirty that afternoon, and I was beginning to relate to it as one relates to a death.

I was glad my parents were with me, and yet their presence seemed strange. The little farmhouse in the middle of a green lawn in the middle of potato fields was Jack's and my first house together, and it embodied all my hopeless romanticism about being in love, getting married, and having babies. My father and mother in city clothes looked pale and tired. I realized that all I was wearing was my bikini and beach dress and that my tanned skin had a film of salt on it.

My father wanted to go to bed. He had to drive back to the

city early that morning (it was almost one o'clock by now). He still had two babies to deliver before July 20, the date he and my mother were to leave for a vacation in France.

My mother and I went to make up a double bed in one of the extra rooms. It was a perfect house, simple, old-fashioned, and big enough to have weekend guests. It even smelled like the house I had lived in for fifteen summers on Cape Cod. Jack loved the place, but he loved my childish joy about having it even more. It seemed ironic that now my mother and I were making hospital corners for a hideous emergency.

I gave my father an alarm clock and kissed him good night. He didn't tell me not to worry. Mama and I went into the living room to talk. I had stopped smoking a year before, but found myself chain-smoking my mother's cigarettes. She told me I shouldn't start again. I told her I didn't care. I suddenly realized I hadn't called Jack's parents in California.

I looked up their number in Jack's black notebook. As I stared at his notes, the names, addresses, and phone numbers, I thought, Now he can't even move his fingers. I dialed his parents' number and his mother answered. She was so happy to hear my voice that my immediate response was good-natured calm, as if I had forgotten why I was calling. "There's been an accident," I heard myself telling Libbie. "We were bodysurfing this afternoon and Jack was thrown by a wave and hurt himself. . . ."

There was no hysteria or dramatic silence from her end of the line. I told her that he was in traction, that the X rays showed no fractures, that he wasn't in pain, but that he couldn't move. I told her my parents were with me, that Papa had investigated the hospital doctor, and I would call her the next morning to keep them posted.

I hung up and went back to the living room to rejoin my mother. The phone rang and it was Libbie again. Something had begun to sink in. I went over the details again, de-emphasizing the paralysis and re-emphasizing how good the care had been so far. The more rational I became, the more removed I felt from crisis. But as soon as I hung up for the second time, I was swept up in a sea of exhaustion. I had to sleep.

Lying there in bed, I could smell the sea, could even hear the waves breaking on the beach. The sea. It had always been a haven to me. Now I hated it. I went over the events of our last

143

swim in slow motion. Why did we go in? Why didn't Jack dive under the wave? Why did it happen? My head was pounding.

I thought of Jack in the hospital fastened by his head to a contraption that looked like a giant spit. I knew he was safe in the hospital, that I would see him in the morning, but I knew, too, that something had come to an abrupt end. I started talking to myself. "Everything's going to be all right; Jack, I love you. Please, God, let everything be all right."

As I said the words I started to cry. I tried to visualize the inside of Jack's neck, to *see* his spinal cord, to understand what had happened. Dr. Spinzia had said that if Jack's condition didn't change, he was going to call in a neurosurgeon.

IT WAS JUST beginning to be dawn when my father woke me on Monday morning, the day after the accident. He wanted me to lead him to the highway back to New York City. I walked outside. The air was clean and cold, and my senses seemed anesthetized. I had an incredibly empty feeling in the pit of my stomach. The morning was beautiful but joyless. I methodically wiped the dew from the windshield, started my car, and led my father to the Montauk Highway. We waved good-by and he shouted that he would try to drive out the following day. On the way back to the house I saw the sun rise over the potato fields.

When Jack and I had first started coming out for weekends in late May, the potato plants were tiny green specks in perfectly straight rows, rushing like a series of railroad ties toward the sand dunes and seeming to converge at a point in the distance. As the plants got fuller the geometry of the landscape softened.

The kitchen was now filled with sunlight, and the early chill had disappeared. I was so depressed that I resented the beautiful day. I knew that I wouldn't be able to see Jack for hours and that it was still too early to call the city, so I tried unsuccessfully to fall asleep again. I thought about what I would say to Jack's boss and how I would manage to complete the files I was preparing for *Newsweek*. Just three days before, I had spent a hot, sticky day interviewing some actors for a story on Czech film directors in New York. That day felt millions of miles away.

I heard my mother puttering around in the kitchen, so I joined her. Then I looked at the plastic clock over the icebox and realized that Jack's boss at NET (National Educational Television) was probably at work. So I called him. Bill's voice on the phone was friendly, almost welcoming.

"Jack's had an accident," I said. "He's in Southampton Hospital in traction. They don't know exactly what's wrong—we don't know how long he'll be away from the office."

As I was mouthing the words I started to shiver, not from cold but from nervousness. I knew how excited Jack was about the new show that was to debut in January. He had a concept for a new type of television format. It was important to him.

"Oh, my God," Bill said over and over. He kept telling me to tell Jack not to worry about work, that everything would be taken care of, and that he would let the rest of the staff know what had happened. "Please tell Jack not to worry," he repeated. "And for God's sake, if there's anything I can do, please call me. We're in our house in Westhampton every weekend and . . . well, anything we can do, just let us know."

AS A CHILD I would occasionally imagine with terrible guilt what I would do and whom I would turn to if my parents died. There was no doubt that I'd be excused from school and that when I returned the teachers would be sympathetic. These hideous thoughts always led to the same conclusion—to tears and to the desperate hope that nothing would happen. For I loved my parents and wanted to live with them forever, or at least until I got married. Now my life, our life, was being threatened by an inexplicable catastrophe, a nightmare that I knew I couldn't wake up from to find everything warm and safe again.

I knew exactly how I felt about my responsibilities to work. I would tell the office what had happened, would somehow finish my work on the story, but would stay near Jack for as long as I had to.

At that point I truly believed that there was a good chance that I'd be back in the city in about ten days, working at least on a part-time basis. I heard the *Newsweek* operator answer the phone. My immediate boss, the chief of researchers, wasn't there. So I talked with another editor.

"This is Mary," I said. "I'm out on Long Island. My fiancé has been badly hurt and is in the hospital . . ."

Dead silence on the other end.

"I will finish my files today and give them to my mother to

drop off at the office early tomorrow. But I will not be in until we know more."

At this point he responded with a hollow "Yes?" I could tell that he thought I was making up the story to get out of work, so I went into more detail, hoping he would believe me, but not really caring. I refused to play for sympathy, but I heard my voice crack and felt my eyes well up with tears.

"Listen, Jack can't move, and I don't think I will be back in New York for a week—maybe not for longer than that."

There was another silence, but shorter and a little less suspicious than before. "Well," he said matter-of-factly, "at least he's not a paraplegic, is he?"

"No, he's not a paraplegic. He's a quadriplegic."

VISITING HOURS didn't start until one o'clock, but by noon I felt an overpowering urgency to see Jack. I drove past the beach on the way to the hospital and recognized the spot where the ambulance had waited the day before. "This time yesterday . . ." I thought out loud.

I started to walk down the long, green hospital corridor and realized my legs were moving faster and faster, until I actually broke into a trot. I peered into Jack's room. There was a tube in his nose, and I hesitated a moment before going in.

Jack called my name. Somehow he knew I was there even before he saw me. I bent over him and kissed his lips. His wonderful blue eyes looked tired, and his healthy color seemed a fraud of nature. He had a sheet draped over him, and as I lifted it I thought it strange that he was still wearing his bathing trunks. I saw a tube that drained into a plastic sack partially filled with urine. Nothing had bothered me before—not the blood, not the tongs in his head, not even the tube in his nose. But the sight of that catheter made my stomach sink.

I didn't want him to think I was upset, so I casually asked him whether the catheter hurt. He said it didn't, and I pretended I was glad. My mind started to race. It *should* have hurt him. A friend's father who had had kidney stones had described the excruciating pain of having a catheter inserted.

I quickly told Jack that I had spoken to his boss, who had been wonderful. Jack's eyes looked straight ahead. He was not depressed, just thinking.

146

"Maybe they should get someone else," he said. "They need a healthy producer."

I told him that he was being stupid. There was always that possibility, but now it was much too early to know and he shouldn't torture himself thinking about it. Jack smiled at me and again I bent down to kiss him. I didn't care about the roommate behind the curtain. Jack and I spoke to each other in whispers, blocking out the sterile world that surrounded us. We looked so deeply into each other's eyes that we fused.

I spent a good part of the day compiling a list of things Jack wanted done—making calls, breaking dates, taking care of a world we were no longer a part of. I was tense with waiting. The doctors had taken new films of Jack's neck but still couldn't tell what was wrong. Not knowing made the wait more trying.

I had to call Jack's parents. I never felt panicked around Jack, but as soon as I entered that dirty, cream-colored phone booth my heart seemed to beat at twice its normal rate. There was nowhere to sit, and I clutched the dimes, a tattered piece of paper, and the stub of a pencil, all the while trying to dial the operator. When she didn't answer I waited patiently. My life now was made up of waiting, and the fury I usually felt at the telephone company was buried under self-control.

At last I got through, and Jack's brother, Dick, answered. I was happy to hear his voice, but the sadness in his tone frightened me. I told him what was going on—nothing—but that the doctor seemed extremely capable. Dick hardly spoke. He seemed numb. I wanted to hang up the phone.

NIGHT FINALLY came, a clear night, cold for July. I walked into Jack's darkened room.

"Hi, doll," he whispered. "How ya doin?"

"I love you, Jack. Everything is going to be all right."

He closed his eyes and smiled. I didn't want to leave him, but he had to rest. Anyway, the loudspeaker in the hospital was already announcing the end of visiting hours. I kissed his cheek and told him that I would soon be back. He heard me but kept his eyes closed. I knew he wasn't in pain and that he wasn't really sick, but his stillness spoke to me of danger.

Suddenly I heard my name being announced on the loudspeaker. Someone was calling me long distance. I didn't recognize

147

the voice or the name on the other end of the line, but whoever it was, was nervous and excited.

"Look, Mary, I'm a friend of Jack's brother, Dick. I'm a psychiatrist, and my brother-in-law is a neurosurgeon. I don't like what Dick tells me. It sounds like Jack's in bad shape and time is crucial now."

My head began to pound. Who was this person and why was he trying to shake me up? Why was he intruding?

"Listen, I know you're under a great strain, but why haven't they done a myelogram?"

I didn't know what a myelogram was, but I said curtly, "My father has been checking up on everything that's going on, and they are doing all they can."

He was three thousand miles away, had no idea what was happening, and was trying to tell me that I should be scared. I *was* scared. I was petrified. I knew that his intentions were good, but his call seemed rude and pointless.

"There is nothing we can do now," I said, trying to gain control. "Jack can't be moved, and the neurosurgeon is coming tomorrow."

When I hung up I was shaking. I looked up to see who had put his hand on my shoulder and saw my older brother, John. He had come to the hospital with my mother. The surprise and gratitude that he was near me made me want to cry. "Oh, John," I heard myself say, "it's all so awful."

I felt myself beginning to weaken, as much from exhaustion as from the lurking fear that Jack wasn't going to be all right. As we drove toward East Hampton to find a place to eat, Mama lovingly put her cardigan around my shoulders.

We stopped at a restaurant that had been decorated to look like a barn. The place was almost empty, and the candlelight and flowers on the tables suggested a dinner party where half the guests had forgotten to come. I wasn't hungry, but Mama insisted I eat. The sight of the food made the lump in my throat swell, until I could no longer hold in the tears.

"Oh, it isn't going to be all right," I sobbed. "I just have a terrible feeling that Jack's in danger. I just know it." I tried to wipe my eyes with a napkin.

My brother and mother listened calmly. They seemed to know that silence was a greater solace for me than optimistic words.

"Why do you feel so sure?" my mother finally asked.

"I know . . ." I hesitated and tried to control my crying. "I know, because they don't catheterize a man unless it's serious." I hesitated again, frightened to admit what I knew was an even worse sign. "And Jack said it didn't hurt him when they inserted the catheter."

At that point I noticed a young couple sitting at a table close to us. The woman was pretty, with short blond hair, and she was about six months pregnant. Jack and I had planned to start a family soon after our marriage. Now, I thought, we might never be able to have children. For a brief moment I hated that couple for their seeming happiness. I knew they were aware that I was crying, but they never stared, and if they were uncomfortable, they never let on. I liked them for that.

When we got home I remembered that I had to type up the files for *Newsweek*. I was exhausted and couldn't have cared less about work, but I had promised, and that was that. John offered to type for me if I read the interviews aloud. I hoped they would take my mind off Jack, but they seemed so irrelevant. How differently I felt then, I thought. How close I was to what was going to happen that weekend, yet how unsuspecting. It takes only a second to change or end a life. The thought must pass through a billion mothers' and wives' minds when they hear that their husbands and sons have been killed in war, but there the injustice is attributable to something, no matter how ugly, wasteful, or worthy the cause. I couldn't blame anyone, but I found myself cursing a God I hardly believed in.

There is a special conceit that lovers share, as though their happiness makes them superior to the rest of the world. And, in a way, this superiority is both real and illusory. Jack and I had felt protected by our love, almost immune. Yet there was an early awareness that even in our love we were separate human beings, strong and vital, who had chosen each other because life was fuller that way. And we knew that if something happened to one of us the other would go on; the thought of having to survive without the other was disturbing but not frightening.

WHEN I AWOKE THE next morning I started to weep. I felt alone and frightened. No matter what my dreams had been the night before, sleep had come as a relief, a momentary escape from the harshness of the days that I knew would stretch before Jack and me. When I'm happy I welcome each morning as if it were a rebirth, a new chance. But when I opened my eyes that morning, my very soul seemed weighted in yesterday and the day before, until my thoughts took me back to the ocean on July 12. Oh, why did it have to happen? I asked myself.

I walked into the kitchen, and the sunlight hurt my eyes. Mama had left early in the morning. She had scribbled me a note: "Darling, try to eat some breakfast. The car's at the station. See you tonight." I was glad she'd left the note, just as I had always been glad to have her notes when I was a little girl. Somehow her absence in those days had been more tolerable if I knew where she was. I remember that I used to call her name automatically when I walked into the house after school, and if she didn't answer I felt a rush of disappointment. Now, in an almost child-like way, I looked forward to her return.

John came into the kitchen. He saw that I was crying. He put his arm around my shoulders, and the gesture, so simple and wordless, seemed to say, "Cry, go ahead. It's good." I bent over the kitchen table, my hair covering my face. "I'll be all right," I kept repeating. "It's just so hard. . . ."

Jack

Mary had been smiling when she came in and gave me a kiss. If the tubing bothered her she didn't show it. She said she'd called the office for me and that Bill had been wonderful and had said not to worry about anything. I asked her to call my secretary and have her cancel my appointments or shift them to someone else. She left to make the call, and I thought about work.

The show wasn't due to go on the air until January. This was only July, but we'd already been working on it for six weeks. Maybe they should get somebody else for the job.

That afternoon Joe came in. "I want to take another X ray," he said. "There's an area of your neck we haven't been able to get a clear picture of. We'll do it in here so we won't have to move you."

A machine was wheeled into my room. Joe stood at my feet and grabbed my hands, which were lying by my sides. "You're thick in the shoulders," he said. "I'm going to try to pull them down and out of the way, so we can get pictures of C six and C seven, the two lowest cervical vertebrae. Ready?"

"Ready."

I tensed as he pulled on my arms. I felt those shocks of pain and I screamed. But Joe kept pulling while the X ray was taken. Then he let go. He left with the technicians. A few minutes later he returned.

"We still can't get a clear picture," he said. "But as far as I can tell, nothing's broken."

Later Joe told me that if nothing changed by evening he was going to call a neurosurgeon in on my case. "If you want to call your own doctor," he said almost apologetically, "I won't mind, but I have complete confidence in this man."

"What's his name?" I asked.

"Dr. Sengstaken. Dr. Robert Sengstaken."

I told Joe about the pain in my neck and arms when they turned me. He said it might be painful, but that it wasn't doing any damage and that I had to get off my back and onto my stomach every four hours.

"But I know the turning is doing further damage to my spine," I said.

"As long as you're in traction, Jack, it's impossible for the turning to hurt you. . . . But if it's so bad, I'll hold off on the turning until we find out exactly what's wrong."

That night my roommate was alternately moaning and delirious. I couldn't see him because the curtain around his bed was drawn. I tried to talk with him, but it was impossible. So I just shut up and tried to sleep.

Mary was in my room when Joe came in to see me the next day. He looked different, as if he'd made up his mind about something. "I've talked to Dr. Sengstaken," he said. "He's coming out here tonight. We're going to try to get a better X ray, and if we can't, we'll take a myelogram. We inject a fluid into the spine and then trace it."

Neither Mary nor I said anything, and I think our silence made Joe defensive. He repeated that we could still call in our own doctor if we wanted. After he left, Mary said she had already spoken to her father and that he had heard of Sengstaken and thought he was excellent.

Sengstaken was supposed to arrive at four o'clock. Mary read to me and we talked. I tried to be cool. I didn't want to scare her or me. But as the afternoon wore on, I got more and more nervous. I wasn't scared that they might have to perform an operation or do a myelogram. I just wanted to get on with it, whatever "it" was. At five o'clock Sengstaken still hadn't arrived. Mary and I were both tense as we waited for him.

Mary

We continued to wait anxiously, knowing that the longer the mystery lingered in everyone's mind, the more painful the waiting was—maybe even dangerous. When Sengstaken still hadn't arrived by five I found myself praying that he'd come soon. I was afraid Jack would see that I was nervous, even though I was calm on the surface.

"Don't worry, baby," he said softly. "He'll be here. Are you tired? Maybe you should go home and rest."

I said that I was fine and wanted to wait.

Soon after five my brother, John, came in. He was talking with Jack when I saw a man I thought must be Sengstaken. He looked tremendous, maybe six feet three inches tall, and handsome in a rough-hewn way. When I saw him go into the nurses' station and look at what I thought was Jack's chart, I was sure it was he. I wanted to introduce myself. I wanted him to be nice, but he seemed different from any doctor I'd ever met. He was wearing an ugly summer suit, the type that shines too much, a yellow-brown fabric that looks cheap even though it isn't. But even from a distance he commanded respect. He hardly spoke and seemed to move with incredible swiftness, but never seemed harried or rushed. When he was alone I walked over to him. "Dr. Sengstaken," I said. "I'm Mary Pleshette, Jack Willis's fiancée."

I felt dwarfed by him as his huge hand enveloped mine. He didn't smile. "Excuse me," he said, and shifted his attention to Jack's chart. I watched him scan it as if he already knew what had to be done. He never sat down, never wasted a move. Everything about him seemed to say, "Let's get going."

There was no more waiting now. Things happened so quickly that we hardly knew what was going on. I felt at times that the doctors would have preferred my not being so close. But they seemed to understand that I needed to be there and that Jack wanted me. I didn't mind if Sengstaken ignored me, just so long as he didn't ask me to wait outside.

Joe arrived from nowhere. He was nervous, as though Sengstaken's authority disturbed him. I wasn't allowed inside the X-ray room, but I tried to stand close by so I could hear what was happening. Sengstaken's voice was serious but kind. I thought I heard him tell Jack to relax. When he walked from the X-ray room to a small office nearby I tried to accompany him at a distance. I dreaded their telling me to go away. They never did.

They had taken two films and still couldn't get a good picture of Jack's neck. Sengstaken was annoyed with the X-ray technician. "You'll have to do better than this," he said.

Then they smiled when they clipped the third X ray up against a lighted milky glass frame. "We really got it," Joe said.

I thought everything was fine. They couldn't be so happy if it was bad. But I didn't really know. I thought I would burst with tension.

Finally Sengstaken turned to me and said, "Would you mind coming in here?"

John and I followed him into a small blue conference room and watched him clip the X ray of Jack's skull and neck onto a lighted board. It was a side view. Joe stood next to me.

"It looks very bad," Sengstaken said. "He's broken and dislocated his sixth and seventh vertebrae." He pointed with the tip of a pencil, helping me count as he moved the pencil downward. "One, two, three, four, five are all in place."

He didn't have to help me any more. Six and seven were at least a half inch out of place, shoved forward toward Jack's jaw. There was a brief silence, and I could feel everyone's eyes glued to me. I was sitting now, and I was numb, frightened.

"Will Jack be able to walk again?"

Sengstaken was sitting on a desk top. His eyes were cold. "No. He will probably never walk again."

The words seemed to echo in my head. I felt lost, completely alone. I felt as if I were drowning, or maybe I had already died.

"Why? Why are you so sure?"

Sengstaken came over and sat down next to me. He pointed to the X ray and said in a soft, calm voice, "The spinal cord runs through the vertebrae. When Jack hit his head those two vertebrae were pushed forward against the cord and hooked onto each

153

other. The cord was probably severed or, if not, irreparably bruised and torn." He waited for me to say something. But I didn't. "You see, the spinal cord is like a telephone cable, and, like the individual lines that run through a cable, the nerves carry messages from the brain to the muscles." Again he paused and then went on. "But unlike a telephone cable, once the spinal cord is torn, it can't be mended. . . . The result is permanent paralysis."

It was irreversible. Jack was paralyzed from the neck down. Quietly, almost politely, I asked Sengstaken to stop. "Please. Just let me cry."

I buried my head in my arms and for the first time in three days wept without any desire to hold back. I held on to Sengstaken's left hand that was resting on the table in front of me. No one spoke, and Sengstaken made no effort to draw away from me. I felt him hold the back of my head in his right hand, and at one point he smoothed my hair. I told him I'd be all right. John, next to me, kept mumbling, "Horrible. Horrible."

"Is there any chance he will recover?" I asked meekly.

Sengstaken shrugged and said, "I seriously doubt it . . . but there are always miracles."

NOBODY said anything for a few moments. Then Joe said, "I don't agree with Dr. Sengstaken." I looked up in surprise and saw that he meant it, that he wasn't trying to ease my sorrow. "I can't tell you why I feel this way, but I don't think the cord has been severed."

"What are you going to tell Jack?" I asked.

Sengstaken said they wouldn't tell him anything, not unless he asked. "We won't lie to him. We will tell him everything he wants to know when he asks. But you can't tell a man, *unless* he asks, that he will never walk again. If you did that, you would destroy any hope. And that's the only weapon now." Sengstaken paused and looked sternly at me. "He can't see you cry, Mary. He mustn't see that you are upset."

He explained that they would try to unhook the vertebrae with traction, that they would try using up to sixty pounds of weight to avoid having to operate. I waited while he disappeared into the X-ray room. He came back with another X ray and quickly stuck it up on the lighted glass. Sengstaken and Joe studied the picture in absolute silence.

154

"We need another ten pounds," Sengstaken said. He went back into the X-ray room. Ten minutes passed. He came back with another X ray. "One of the vertebrae snapped back," he said. He had marked every X ray with a red wax pencil in the order it had been taken, and I could see the difference in the latest picture.

"Let's add some more weight," Sengstaken said. "Maybe we can get the second one back in place." It seemed like an endless, monotonous parade into the X-ray room and out again.

I was aware that someone had walked into the room. I turned and saw my father and mother. Sengstaken shook my father's hand and stuck a new X ray up against the light. I half listened to the conversation between Joe and Sengstaken, but nothing seemed to register anymore. It all sounded like a foreign language, but I was beginning to understand that the second vertebra hadn't snapped back, that whatever they were doing wasn't working. Finally Sengstaken slowly turned to us all.

"We'd better get going. We have to operate."

I WAS STANDING in the ladies' room, staring at my face in the mirror. I was still suntanned, and my hair was stiff with the salt water I hadn't washed out for three days. I splashed some water on my face, and it seemed to soothe my burning eyes.

As I approached the X-ray room, I saw Sengstaken talking with my father. I went up to them and said that I wanted to see Jack. Sengstaken led me into the room. Jack's shoulder muscles were bulging from the stress of all those weights.

"They're going to have to operate, baby," Jack said.

He asked Sengstaken to explain to me what was happening. He didn't know what I knew, and I didn't want to tell him.

Everyone seemed to be scurrying around. Joe and Sengstaken had disappeared to get something to eat before the operation, and Jack was wheeled back to his room. A nurse came in and gave him an injection. "This will relax you," she said. The hospital seemed deserted; the visitors were gone, the hall lights had been dimmed, the place stank of silence. Jack asked me to get my father.

"Do you think they're doing the right thing?" Jack asked.

"They know what they're doing," Papa said. "They have to clean you up and straighten out those vertebrae. They have to get the pressure off the cord." He paused. "Nobody goes into the neck unless they have to. I have confidence in Sengstaken, and Spinzia's an excellent man."

Papa asked Jack if he wanted him to send for his parents. Jack seemed frightened for a minute, as though the realization of his parents' coming meant that the operation was dangerous. "I guess you'd better," he said, and the fear lingered in his eyes.

A nurse came in with another injection. They started to wheel Jack toward the operating room. I walked next to Jack, and a second before they pushed him behind two heavy swinging doors, I asked the nurses to stop. "Please, just let me kiss him good-by," I said, and didn't really understand the "good-by." I told Jack I would see him when he woke up from the operation. I told him I loved him. I told him everything was going to be all right. I watched them push him into a large, cellarlike room, and I saw a group of people dressed in green wheel him out of sight. I felt an empty hole where my stomach was, and the forbidding doors closed.

As we walked out of the hospital, my father put his arm around my shoulders. I started to cry without knowing it. "Could Jack die?" I asked.

I felt my father's hand tighten around my arm. "Yes."

We waited in the silence of that tiny farmhouse living room. My father looked at me solemnly. "You mustn't feel guilty if there's a part of you that wants Jack to die," he said. "Jack's an active, alive man, and if he's completely paralyzed for the rest of his life, that could be worse than dying."

I nodded but didn't say anything. I thought of life without Jack, and my stomach twisted itself into a knot. I pictured myself alone and saw myself, a specter of a person, putting Jack's suits and ties into huge suitcases. I felt myself sinking into my past, a past that had never been so happy until I'd met Jack. "I don't want Jack to die," I said. "I want more than life for Jack to live." As I uttered the words, I felt immediate relief, and with relief I felt hope, and with hope a surge of strength.

Jack

I dreamed I was calling for Mary. Then I realized I was awake and Mary was next to me. She bent down and kissed me.

I don't remember feeling pain, but Mary says that the first

thing I said was how much I hurt. I asked her what time it was, and she told me it was after midnight.

"The operation went well. Everything's okay," she said.

"Where's Joe?" I asked.

"He went home."

I was hurt. I didn't understand why he wasn't there. Didn't he care? I had a lot of questions to ask him. A nurse came over to us, and Mary said she had to go. She kissed me good-by, and I fell back into a drugged sleep.

I was awakened by two nurses. It was still night, and they were covering me with the sheepskins. When they placed the metal frame over me I began to get frightened. They were going to turn me onto my stomach.

"Joe said I wasn't to be turned. I've just been operated on."

"This won't hurt you, Mr. Willis."

"Call Joe. Please. Just call Joe."

"It's doctor's orders," they said. "Four hours on your back, Mr. Willis, two hours on your stomach."

Two hours! I hadn't lasted ten minutes the first time. Now I gritted my teeth and waited for the pain as they turned me. But there was none this time, and I realized the operation must have relieved the pressure on my spinal cord.

I stared into blackness. The straps cut into my forehead. I couldn't sleep. I tried thinking about work, but I couldn't concentrate. All I could feel were the straps. I heard the nurses quietly move around the darkened room.

"Turn me back!" I yelled. "My head is killing me!"

"You've only been over five minutes, Mr. Willis," one of the nurses said, and the other one came over and rubbed my back and said I had to try to take more.

For the first time I felt the total impotence of my position. I understood what it really meant to be paralyzed. My frustration gave way to rage. "Turn me! I can't stand it!" I screamed.

From the darkness came the answer. "We can't. Doctor's orders. Two hours on your stomach."

Orders. It was like the army. Would those automatons let me suffer for two hours? I tried to wait but finally screamed again, "Get the doctor. It's crazy. I hurt. I can't stand it."

And then, miraculously, the nurse who had rubbed my back came out of the darkness and began placing the sheepskins on my back. "Hurry," I said. She put the frame over my back, strapped me in and, without a word, rolled me over onto my back. "Get the frame off me fast."

She did, and I relaxed and fell asleep. I dreamed I was running full speed down a hill. About halfway down, a fist materialized and smacked me full force right in the face. I took a few more steps, and it hit me again and again and again.

I woke up dripping wet from my own sweat. I waited a few minutes until I calmed down and then went back to sleep. The same dream began again. I was running downhill and got hit in the face again and again. That dream is clearer to me today and more frightening than the accident itself.

I couldn't get back to sleep. I tried to piece together the events just before the operation. Sengstaken had told me that two vertebrae in my neck, the lowest two, were fractured and dislocated. They had been pushed forward and had locked together, causing pressure on the spinal cord, which accounted for the paralysis. To snap them back into place and relieve the pressure on the cord, they first had to be unhooked.

"We don't want to operate," Sengstaken had said. "We're going to add more weight to your head. We're hoping to stretch you out and pull the vertebrae free of each other." He walked behind me and added weights to the twenty pounds already suspended from my head. "That's ten more pounds," he said. I felt the added weight pulling on my body, but felt no pain. Then I heard a snap and said, "I think it's back in place."

They took a further X ray. "Only one vertebra's snapped back," Sengstaken reported. "Let's try another ten pounds."

He added the weight, and we waited, expecting another snap. When nothing had happened after ten minutes they took another X ray. Then Sengstaken stepped behind me and put his huge hands under my shoulders. He tried to stretch me out farther by lifting and pulling my head toward him. I could feel the desperation in the effort and knew we had reached the end of the line. "I guess we've had it," I said.

"I guess so," he said. "I think we have to operate."

"Let's get on with it," I said. But first I wanted Mary to know what was happening. I made him bring her in to explain what was wrong with me and why they had to operate. She had to know what was happening, because at some point we should have to make a decision about whether or not we were still going to be married.

Joe brought her in. We smiled at each other, and then I said, "Hon, they're going to operate. You tell her, Doctor."

He explained. Her expression didn't change and she didn't ask any questions. Then she held my hand. I felt very close to her, and I was proud of the way she was handling everything. So was Joe, I guessed, because he suddenly said, "You kids are very brave. Don't think we haven't noticed. You're going to need to be even braver in the next few days."

THE SUN was finally up, and now I found myself looking objectively at all that was happening to me, and not quite believing it. The day before, I had been happy to see Sengstaken. It meant that two days of waiting were over. I was even relieved when they took the X rays and found the fractures. At least we knew what was wrong. And as crazy as it seems, I was relieved that they were operating. At least we were doing something.

But now it was the morning after the operation, and I still couldn't move. The night before, Sengstaken had told me that if my spinal cord had been severed, the operation could relieve the pressure but could not bring back any movement.

I waited for Joe and framed the questions I would ask him. But when he came in I just blurted out, "Will I walk again?"

"Sengstaken doesn't think so," he said.

The blood rushed out of my head and I felt my heart sink.

"What are the odds?" I asked.

"About ten percent," he said.

"And you. What do you think?"

"I don't know," Joe said. "I'm more optimistic."

I didn't really hear him. I rushed on. "Can I make love?"

"Probably. But you wouldn't feel anything."

"Can I have kids?"

"I don't know." Joe smiled. "Those were the same questions Mary asked."

Mary. So she already knew. I was glad because I didn't want to have to tell her. I sank lower and lower. I couldn't speak.

Joe began talking quietly. "The odds are against you," he said. "But there's some room for hope. When we opened you up we could see that the cord was intact."

159

I pressed him. "Well, then what's wrong?"

"Sengstaken's pessimistic because of the paralysis and because he ran his finger down the cord and felt an indentation. He thinks that means a whole group of nerves within the cord have been severed . . . but I don't know. It could just be a temporary indentation."

"When will we know who's right?" I said. "When will movement begin to return if it returns at all?"

"In around two to three weeks," Joe said. "Not before then." He paused. "Even Sengstaken doesn't know for sure if the cord was severed. If it's only badly bruised, you should begin to get feeling when the swelling goes down. Give yourself a chance. If you still can't move after three weeks, then . . ."

Then? What then? What would I do? How would I deal with it? I couldn't even commit suicide. I couldn't move. Would Mary help me? It was all too dumb, all beyond comprehension.

Mary

When I opened my front door on a Tuesday evening in March, two years ago, Jack looked older than I imagined he would. But I was immediately comfortable with him and almost inadvertently took his arm as we waited for a taxi. When I realized that my hand was neatly resting on his, I made a conscious effort to keep it there. I was testing myself, testing Jack. I was saying, "This is the way I am, and I'm sick of first-date protocol."

I had suspected from his phone voice that Jack wasn't from New York, and now I was sure that my suspicions were right, from the thin black tie and cloddy shoes he wore. I was disturbed that I even noticed, much less cared about his clothes, but he was unlike anyone I had ever dated. I'd always had a fantasy that the man I'd marry would speak fluent French and that we'd have lots of beautiful, bilingual children. Jack didn't fit that mold.

We had dinner in Greenwich Village and I talked about how bored I was with my job, how I longed for one that would utilize all my energies. Jack seemed interested, leaning forward on his elbows to listen. I talked about the newness and the difficulty of learning to be on my own. I talked about my family and he spoke about his. California seemed very far away. I had never been to California. After dinner we walked around the Village and Jack

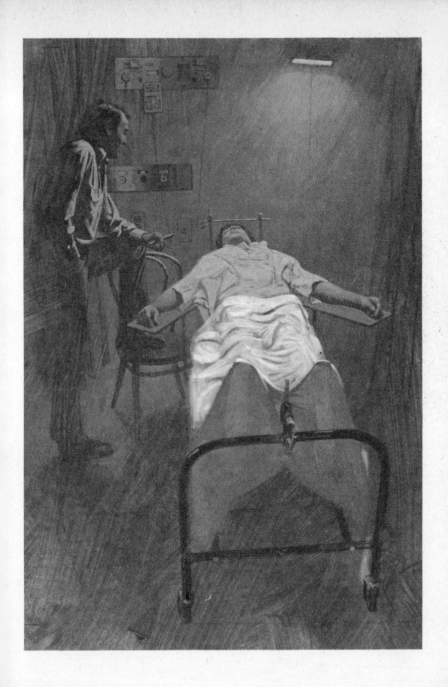

casually put his arm around me. We took a cab uptown and stopped at a bar near my apartment. Jack described his experiences, making films in the South. Mississippi, Kentucky—America. He didn't fit the ideal image, but I liked him. I really liked him.

We walked back to my apartment and climbed up the four flights of stairs. Before I had time to worry about the usual first-date good-night awkwardness, he grabbed me and kissed me. I remember I felt like a comic-strip character with a big WOW! hovering over my head. When I closed the door I was smiling.

I was smiling now. We were different people then, but those two strangers were a part of us. I was at the house, waiting to be called to go back to the hospital. By midnight I still hadn't received word, but I decided to wait no longer.

Jack was in the intensive care unit, a large room with only a few beds. It was so quiet that even the sound of a footstep seemed an intrusion. A nurse led me to where Jack was resting. He looked as though he had been beaten; his cheeks were swollen, his eyes puffy and bruised. He could hardly speak, and I tried to quiet him as he struggled to talk to me.

"I hurt. Oh, Mary, I hurt so much," was all he said.

I hesitated before kissing him, afraid of hurting him more.

"You're okay, Jack. Don't talk. Everything is going to be all right. I love you. Just try to sleep."

It was after midnight. I wanted to hold Jack's hand, to sit quietly by him and stay the rest of the night. But a nurse said I had to leave.

Jack was alive. The panic and fear had vanished. In its place was a calm, so real and solid that I understood I had passed through the nightmare and was now so firmly rooted in the present that nothing seemed to scare me. The knowledge that Jack was alive steered me like an invisible rudder.

I drove slowly back to the house. The air was misty, and everything was quiet, still, soft. My mother had left the kitchen light on. I parked the car and stared at the house.

I thought about how happy everyone had been the night we announced we were getting married. It was my birthday, a ridiculously special day every year, with a family celebration that included gifts, poems, and my favorite dinner of roast beef and strawberry shortcake. But this twenty-fourth birthday was golden. Jack and I had decided to surprise everybody with the news.

162

Jack raised his glass of champagne. "A week ago today on Fisherman's Wharf in San Francisco, over a plate of cracked crab, I asked Mary to be my wife. . . . And she said yes." No one knew whether to drink the champagne or kiss us. There was a happy commotion—my wonderful Aunt Mabel cried, my brother kissed Jack, my mother kept repeating, "Oh, how marvellous." My father glowed. And once the gleeful surprise had passed, I was bombarded with questions of when and where.

At times I felt a strange urgency to be married right away, as though I were scared that waiting was an invitation to some unknown interference. I told Jack that I wished October weren't so many months away. But it was ironic, as I was the one who had always wanted to be married in the fall. Jack laughed and rocked me in his arms. We were sitting on the lawn in back of the house. We waited for the sun to disappear and watched the colors of the country gently fade into the cool grays of dusk.

The memory of that quiet, starless evening stayed in my mind like a lost photograph you discover in a pile of old letters and cannot stop staring at. How I wanted to go back to stop what had happened from happening! It was three o'clock in the morning by now, and Jack's parents had probably arrived at Kennedy Airport from Los Angeles and would be at the house by six. I went to bed and told myself I had to sleep.

THE LAST TIME I had seen Libbie and Lou was in Los Angeles, at the tail end of our Mexican vacation. I'd been uncomfortable before, speaking to them long distance, but I discovered that being with them in their environment, lolling around the pool, wandering into the kitchen for a snack, was another story entirely. I began to relax with them. When Jack spoke I'd watch his father's eyes. To say they filled up with love is corny, but that's just what I saw. Libbie reminded me of my own mother, except that she was more solicitous of me because I wasn't her daughter.

I heard the car on the gravel driveway and then its doors slam shut. Another sunny day that hurt my eyes. I ran downstairs and wrapped my arms around Libbie. She was sobbing, and we stood in the kitchen quietly cradling each other. I realized how much taller I was than she, and that for the first morning in days I wasn't crying. When Libbie pulled away she seemed a little embarrassed, but that didn't matter and we both knew it. Then I

163

saw Lou, who gave me a big hug and said, "Hiya, my little doll. It's going to be okay." I looked into his eyes—round blue eyes with thick black lashes. He was scared but believed what he said. I was just beginning to accept that Jack might not get better, and there was Lou, saying that everything was going to be okay.

My mother came into the kitchen to fix coffee. She looked totally drained—her mouth was tense and she moved in jerks. I could tell that Lou made her nervous and that she felt on the verge of screaming. I noticed that she had sponged the same counter three times and washed the morning coffee cups twice instead of taking clean ones from the cupboard.

We moved out onto the porch, which was filled with sunlight. Libbie sat quietly on the swinging couch. She clutched a handkerchief with a big L embroidered on it and occasionally wiped her eyes behind her big light-blue sunglasses.

Lou talked nervously. He didn't care what the doctors' prognoses were. "I've seen Jack fight," he said. "I've seen him put his foot through a shower door in anger after he lost an important ball game. He'll play ball again. He won't give in."

I wished that Lou would shut up. The image of Jack kicking anything now, much less a shower door, was like a sick joke. The doctors had said he wouldn't walk. How could Lou be so sure they were wrong? I tried to ignore him and remember what Joe had told me when I called him after the operation. I had asked him if Jack was better, and he said, "Mary, this is going to take a long time. If you go into the hospital every day expecting to see improvement, you'll go crazy. You can't expect any change, you can't expect anything."

I said I was going upstairs to dress. Visiting hours weren't for two hours, but maybe they'd let us in early.

I HAD TRIED to warn Libbie and Lou that Jack would be wired with tubes and tongs, but I knew that nothing could soften the shock. I knocked on the door of the intensive care unit, and a stocky, round-faced nurse opened it a crack. "I know we're here early," I said, "but Jack's parents just arrived from California." The nurse whispered that I should come in first and tell Jack they were here. I turned to Libbie and told her I'd be just a second and then she could go in.

Jack's eyes were open, and the swelling had begun to go down.

He tried to smile. I told him that his parents were here and wanted to see him. The tube in his nose made talking difficult, but he indicated he was glad they were here. I kissed him gently on the forehead and said he shouldn't try to talk much. We looked at each other for a second longer, and then I left.

Lou and I didn't speak as we waited for Libbie to come out. He just put his arm around my shoulders, and I wrapped mine around his waist. We stood quietly together like two old friends. The door opened, and as soon as Lou went in, Libbie embraced me, crying, "What have they done to my little boy!" I had never once thought of Jack as a little boy, even though he had been robbed physically of everything that made him a man. And though I realized that for Libbie, Jack would always be her "little boy," the infantile reference annoyed me. It seemed for an instant to threaten the intense attraction I still felt for him.

When Lou emerged from the intensive care unit his eyes were brimming with tears, but he seemed almost buoyant. "I told him that he's going to be all right," Lou said positively. "I told him he had to fight, that he couldn't believe everything the doctors said." He hesitated and looked at me. "I didn't say that the doctors weren't good, but they're going to be wrong. Look, I was told by some specialist that I had cancer. He wanted to operate. Well, I said, just wait a minute. You're not just going to cut into me and mess around. I went to another doctor, who said, 'Lou, you're as healthy as an ox!'"

We walked toward the cafeteria, and I saw Joe Spinzia approaching us. He was in a hurry, and it seemed to me that he really wanted to avoid us but knew he couldn't. I introduced him to Libbie and Lou. He spoke quickly, as if speed would mitigate the horrible prognosis. Lou could hardly ask him a question, and after a while I realized Joe was talking about hand surgery. "Amazing things can be done," he said. "Jack has some return in his flexors and extensors, so we could possibly transfer a muscle to his thumb so he could pinch. That's the most important function of the hand."

He talked almost compulsively, as though he didn't want to have to answer any questions, and I could tell that Libbie and Lou disliked him. He had been so direct and helpful to Jack and me, but this directness was all wrong for Libbie and Lou. They've just arrived, I thought. They're tired and upset. Do they really want to be told about the miracles of hand surgery when they can see what terrible shape Jack's in now? I wished Joe would be gentler with them.

He excused himself to answer a phone call. Seconds later he told Lou that Sengstaken wanted to speak to him. "Dr. Sengstaken is more pessimistic than I," he said. "I still think there's a chance." I was glad he said that. I heard his voice soften and realized that he knew that he had been mishandling the situation, but that he couldn't help it.

When Lou came back after talking with Sengstaken he was pale and angry. "He says the odds are ninety to ten against Jack's recovering. He's full of baloney."

Jack

The tube in my nose and throat made breathing difficult. I tried to disregard the discomfort and think about what Joe had said. I couldn't clear my mind. Paralysis, wheelchair, Mary, sex, marriage, children, job, friends, pity. I couldn't begin to deal with it. I sank deeper and deeper into mindless depression.

A pretty young nurse came over and flirted a little, which made me feel better. Then she disappeared. When she returned she had a flower in a glass. She told me she'd gone outside to pick it for me, but I figured she'd probably swiped it from another patient.

Over on my back again. Drugged, dozing, depressed. I opened my eyes. Mary was there. We kissed. She seemed nervous and excited. She said my parents were outside, waiting to see me.

The night before, right before the operation, when Mary's father, Norman, had asked me whether we should tell my parents to come, I'd been torn. I wanted to see them, but was afraid they might make things more difficult. I prepared myself to comfort *them*.

My mother came in first. She looked fine but controlled. I had no idea what I looked like to her, except that outwardly I appeared pretty healthy. I could tell she didn't know how to start. She couldn't very well ask, "How are you?"

"How was the plane trip, Mom?"

"Oh, fine, a little tiring. But we're fine. Your brother and Cece drove us to the airport. I think they'll be here soon. . . . Jack, do you hurt very badly?"

"No, Mom. It was a freaky accident, but hell, I'm going to be okay. Don't worry. I'm just very tired, and it's hard to talk."

When she left I saw my father, grinning, coming toward me with that crazy Groucho Marx lope of his. It was the same run, grin, and excitement he always had when he picked me up at the airport on my visits to Los Angeles. Now he stood at my bedside and grabbed my hand and said, "Hiya, Jacko. Listen, I don't care what the doctors say. You'll beat it. You've been a scrapper all your life, and no matter what else, you'll fight."

I tried to smile. I tried to answer, but I couldn't. Just a few hours before, the doctor had told me I might not ever move again. And here was this incredible man, telling me that *he* knew that I'd beat it. I felt my eyes well up with tears. I didn't want to break down in front of him. He started to leave.

"Dad . . . I'm glad you're here." I took a deep breath and began to choke up. "It means a lot to me . . . and I'll fight."

"I know you will," he said, and left. I broke down and cried.

That night they rolled me out of the intensive care unit and back to my room. My brother, Dick, and his wife, Cece, were there. I was happy to see them. It didn't occur to me until later that the family suddenly being there meant I could have died—it just seemed so natural for them to be there.

Dick is four years younger than I and is a dentist in L.A. We have always been very close. I am also crazy about Cece.

"Hey, how'd you get away from work?" I said.

"I'm not working this summer," Cece said in her soft voice. She is a teacher.

"And I just left," Dick said, flashing me that big toothy grin of his.

Mary had first met Dick, Cece, and my parents when we'd been in L.A. our first year together, after our Mexican vacation. I had been raised there, but left for New York after I got out of school. I left L.A. because I didn't like it, but being there with Mary was different. I got a kick out of showing her around and explaining what it was like growing up there. She loved it.

We stayed with Dick and Cece in their old frame house in Santa Monica. We went to the beach, drove through Beverly Hills and Brentwood, looked at movie stars' homes, and saw L.A. at night from the hills. And we shopped at boutiques on Hollywood Boulevard.

Now, in hospital, we were all back together again. Dick and I stared at each other for a long time. I wondered what I must look like to him. He looked serious and upset. He didn't feel the need to say or do anything. I had the impression he knew exactly what I was feeling and that a part of him was attached to the tongs with me. "It took less than a second to change my life," I said, breaking the silence. Dick just nodded.

THE FOURTH NIGHT in the hospital I had nightmares again. This time I dreamed of the wave, tumbling over and over, falling and smashing my head on the sand. I could feel my head jerk and the horrible spasms in my neck and back. I woke up scared. I thought I had lifted out of the tongs, but I hadn't. That was impossible. I went back to sleep and had the same dream, falling, falling, crashing down, and the pain. It was like diving into an empty swimming pool.

I awoke and called for the nurse. Like a kid scared of the dark, I asked her to turn on the light. She said the dreams might be caused by the Demerol. Then she turned me on my stomach, and for the first time I relaxed in that position. I let my arms hang down and asked one of the aides if she had time to give me a massage. I lay there staring down at the floor, the straps supporting my head. I didn't think of anything. I just let myself feel her hands kneading my shoulders and back muscles. The fear caused by the dreams slowly disappeared. I'd been so relieved when the nurse came in and turned on the light, I realized that I'd lost my fear of being turned over onto my stomach. I didn't notice the straps cutting into my forehead and chin. I just went limp, and stared mindlessly down at the floor. I felt more relaxed after she turned me back. "I'm better. You can turn off the lights," I said.

This time I dreamed I was running. I tripped and fell forward, my neck jerked, and the pain woke me up.

Next day I told Joe about my nightmares.

"Sometimes Demerol can do that," he said. "We'll try morphine instead. Also, I'm going to change your roommate. There's a young guy down the hall who'll be better company for you. The old man is out of it too much of the time, and I think you'll like this other guy."

"It's okay with me."

Out of the corner of my eye I saw someone being rolled in.

Rather, I saw an arm and leg in a cast suspended from a metal frame above his bed. "Hi," I said. "Welcome."

"Hi," he said as they wheeled him past me, "I hear you're in really bad shape. . . . Hey, sweetheart, Patti," he called to a nurse as soon as his bed was in place. "Where is my table and the radio? And don't forget my Bermuda shorts and my shirts." Then he turned to me. "Hi. I'm Mike Guerin."

"Hi. I'm Jack Willis. Where you from?"

"The Bronx."

I had guessed from his voice that he was around thirty years old. Then he said, "Hey, Jack, man, what happened to you?"

"I was flipped by a wave and broke my neck."

"Wow." He half laughed. "Man, I've never heard of *anyone* getting his neck broke by a wave."

"Me neither," I said. "What happened to you?"

"It's crazy, man. We got this place in Hampton Bays, always something doing. Three weeks ago my buddy and I went out for dinner and some fun. We were driving home when this guy stepped out into the road. My buddy swerved, and that's the last thing I remember."

"You were in a coma?" I said.

"A coma! Man, I didn't wake up till ten days later. I think we went off an embankment and I was thrown out of the car. And then the car rolled over onto me. They told me that when they found me, I had so little pulse they gave me the last rites."

"What happened to your friend?"

"Nothing, man. Do you believe it? He walked away without a scratch. All he lost was his car. And I've been here three weeks." Mike paused for just a second. "Hey, sweetheart," he yelled to a nurse in the hall. "Can you turn the TV around so I can see it? What good is it doing facing the door?"

Mary

Dick, Cece, and I went into the conference room across the hall from Jack's room. The bright lights bounced off the flat yellow walls, making all our skin look a sickly jaundice color. I looked out the screened window into a black night and could hear the sprinklers click on the hospital lawn. The sound irritated me, but I was too tired to care. I wanted Spinzia to talk with Dick so Dick could explain to Libbie and Lou. And I wanted to hear it all again. Maybe I still didn't believe it myself.

Spinzia came into the room and sat down. He was tense, but acted casual. He wasted no time getting into hard facts. "Have you thought about a rehab hospital?" he said, and seeing the look of dismay on our faces, he went right on. "Jack is going to need a lot of care. And that costs money. You can't put it off."

Dick's words came quickly, without hesitation. "Before we talk about rehabilitation, I want to know why you say you're more optimistic than Sengstaken."

"I don't think Jack's cord was severed. I think there's a chance it was badly bruised. If I'm right, he'll get return in around two to three weeks."

He paused. "We never know with these spinal injuries," he went on. "There can be complications." He looked at me. "I just want you to know that I think Jack is an incredible man. I could never go through what he's going through."

I wasn't listening. "Complications? What kind of complications?" I blurted out.

"I guess the most dangerous is pneumonia. If a quadriplegic begins to collect fluid in his lungs, he has no way of getting it out, because he doesn't have the muscles to cough. And then there's the catheter. . . . If it stays in too long, he could develop strictures which could cut off his ability to urinate."

The chance of pneumonia didn't frighten me, but the mention of strictures in the penis terrified me. I wished Joe hadn't mentioned them. "How long can the catheter stay in before it's dangerous?" I asked.

"A pretty long time," he said, trying to be understanding. "That's the least of my worries. We can always catheterize him by inserting a tube right into the bladder."

I pretended to be relieved.

Dick asked a few more questions, and then Joe got up to leave.

"Do you have any children?" I asked.

"Yes. Two girls."

JACK AND I had often talked about the children we would have. Now I felt defiant and angry, more anxious to get pregnant than ever before. We would have a child as soon as we could. Sengstaken said we could still do that. I fantasized about walking into his office one day, big-bellied and glowing. The thought of Jack not being able to run or play with a child didn't frighten me. I tried to picture him in a wheelchair, surrounded by a family, our family. I focused on this idealized vision the way one looks at a painting, not concentrating on the individual parts but looking at the work as a whole. I didn't think about details; I couldn't imagine what life would be with a man in a wheelchair—the ramps, the special bars and equipment for bathrooms and halls. I didn't try to imagine how we would make love. "Somehow we will make it work," I said to myself.

My great desire to be pregnant was totally illogical, but my life seemed to have no relation to rational planning. I felt removed from the neat schedules of *Newsweek*, from the normal schemes which had marked the days and months and years of my previous life. I had been left on an island with no clocks or calendars and had only the rhythms of nature to tell me that time was passing. I felt stripped of anticipation, and the future didn't seem to matter. I felt strangely natural, unprotected, yet strong. Having a baby somehow echoed my feelings of naturalness. It seemed a beautiful metaphor for feeling life, being totally, physically alive.

Jack

Like a baby, I was totally dependent upon others for everything. I had to be fed, cleaned, made comfortable. Unlike a baby, I had the brain of a man and the memory of what I had been and also the understanding of what I might be.

I tried to scratch my nose, but, as if spastic, I missed it completely. I knew Mary was watching, and I wondered what she was thinking. I tried not to think of the jokes we used to tell about spastics. Now I even felt a kind of pride in just getting my hand close to my face. Why hadn't I tried it before?

When lunch was brought to me, I asked Mary to place my sandwich in my hand so I could try to feed myself. They had taken me off intravenous feeding two days before, and since then either Clive or Mary had fed me. Now she placed the sandwich between my forefinger and thumb, but it fell out. "Try again," I barked. I got a better grip and started to move it toward my mouth, fighting gravity. The ham and cheese started to slip out. It didn't occur to me to use my other hand to help. I rushed the

171

whole thing toward my mouth, but all the ham and cheese fell onto my chest, and I hit my cheek with the bread.

After a couple of tries I got a small bite. The effort exhausted me. But I started thinking ahead to the next meal and for a moment forgot that the rest of me was paralyzed.

I tried to concentrate on other things I could do. Lying on my stomach, I thought maybe I could read. I asked Clive to get a newspaper and lay it flat below me, on a stand that was attached to the underside of my bed. I tried to turn the pages but my hands were useless. I discovered that if I bent my wrist forward, I could force my forefinger and thumb into something resembling a pinch. I tried turning the pages that way, but because my fingers were numb, I couldn't feel the paper. The head nurse, Janet LaVinio, suggested I use the heel of my hand to push the page and crumple it. Then I would have something to pinch. It took me forty-five minutes to read a quarter of the *Times*. Janet stayed with me and massaged my back and shoulders. She brought me some juice and, exhausted, I waited for her to feed it to me.

"Try it yourself," she said, and placed a straw in the cup.

I tried gripping the cup between my hands. But it was heavy to lift, and I couldn't coordinate lifting the cup and placing the straw between my lips. So I picked up the straw, put that into my mouth first, then lifted the cup around the straw. When the cup was empty I put it down on the stand, both elated and depressed by my accomplishment. How weak and uncoordinated my arms were—and they weren't even paralyzed. I wondered how weak the rest of my body would be, even if I got return.

That night, after all the visitors had gone, Joe dropped in to say hello. He was relaxing, his foot propped up on the chair next to my bed, puffing on a cigar. I could tell he wanted to stay and talk but was afraid to get too close to me, to strain the doctor-patient relationship. But *I* wanted to get as close to the guy as possible. I needed continual reassurance that he really cared for me. To do that, he had to understand me. So what I really wanted to talk about was me, but I knew that to keep him there we'd have to talk about him.

"Pretty tough racket?" I began.

"Yeah. But I love it. The hours don't bother me, and I'm really my own man. I live only five minutes from the hospital, and my office is across the road. I work hard, but I can run home and see my kids. If patients get on my nerves, I can just knock off work a few days." He shifted his legs on the chair, unwinding a little more.

"Baloney," I said. "I've seen you here over the weekend and almost every night. You don't relax."

"Well, summer's the big season around here. All you dumb city folk come out here and get hurt—auto accidents, swimming accidents. But winter's soft. I get to work on my car."

"Car?"

"Yeah. I rebuild old cars. I buy them cheap when they're piles of junk. Then I transform them into collectors' items. I like working with my hands. Be a lot tougher on me if I was in your position."

I heard my voice rise. "What do you mean by that?"

"My work depends on my hands. You work with your head."

"Yeah, well, I also work with my hands and legs. And what do you think I'm going to do if I'm stuck in a wheelchair the rest of my life? I wasn't sitting still—I made films, and I love sports, and what about a family?"

"Well, sports aren't important," Joe interrupted. "And maybe you can still have a family."

"Maybe. Maybe," I said, but felt depressed. He wasn't telling me anything he hadn't told me before. "Last night," I went on, "I talked to Phyllis, the evening nurse, and she said that usually when there's feeling there's motor control and that eventually there's return. I can feel texture, like my top sheet or the sheep-skins or the pressure of a hand, even though I can't feel pain or hot and cold." I wanted Joe to tell me that Phyllis was right—I'd get back control.

"Every patient asks the same questions," he said. "But there are no rules. Each case is entirely different, and just because somebody else had the same symptoms and recovered doesn't mean that it'll be the same for you."

After he left I thought about what he'd said. I'd dropped that sandwich because my hands felt as though they had gone to sleep. That's the way the rest of my body felt—asleep.

I thought of my numb hands. I thought of trying to caress Mary or to type a letter or to play catch or to carry an envelope home from work. I thought of how unfair it was for Mary that I was racked up like this. But, strangely, I didn't feel a need to talk with

173

her about it, because I knew her well enough to know that she would be totally honest with me and with herself. If she was with me, it was because she wanted to be with me, because she still loved me, not because she felt pity for me or had some misplaced sense of duty. And I also knew that when she felt that she could no longer stand it or that she didn't love me, she would leave. But for the moment I was confident—confident of the fight in her and of the love we shared.

Then I began thinking about all the good times Mary and I had had. Once again I thought about the accident itself. I tried to imagine not taking that wave. I imagined myself diving under it and the two of us coming out of the water together, going home to a barbecue dinner. We would have sat outdoors and watched the sun set, and after dinner we would have gone down to the beach to stare at the stars.

During the past week or so I would have worked on the new show. I knew from my secretary, who'd come out to visit, that it wasn't going well. I'd had a lot of ideas that I thought would help make it work. But now I didn't care. Now it was the weekend, and if I hadn't taken that wave, we'd be back out there at the beach.

But I wasn't on the beach with Mary. I was staring up at the tiles on the ceiling in Southampton Hospital, waiting for the morning shift to come on, for somebody to feed me my breakfast. I really was like a baby. If there was no return, I'd probably need a full-time nurse. And where I had been confident just half an hour before of Mary's and my love, I now couldn't imagine her staying with me, changing the catheter, pushing me around in a wheelchair. If the roles had been reversed, I couldn't have done it, and I didn't want her to. She was young, healthy, and alive. If I were in a wheelchair, I couldn't see how I could satisfy any of her needs.

I thought of the future and of being alone. Maybe I could teach, not in New York—how could I get around the city in a wheelchair? Maybe somewhere in California. I pictured the campus and being pushed to class and home again, being pushed up and down special ramps.

I remembered a guy in college who was in a wheelchair and managed to push himself around. He was big and good-looking, very strong through the chest and shoulders, though with withered legs. He was bright and lively and appeared to have a lot

174

of friends. But who knew what went through his mind when he was alone? Did he brood, as I did, about the past? Did he have the same dark thoughts about the future?

I didn't know how he'd been hurt. But now I wished I'd taken the time to talk with him. I wondered what he was doing and if he was happy. I thought again about teaching and knew I didn't want to do that. It sounded so dull after making films. But what else could I do? I tried not to think about it. I tried to fall asleep.

Mary

I watched Jack sleep. The blood around the tongs was dry and black, and the hair around his ears was already beginning to grow back. I looked over his body, big and silent, and tried to convince myself that he really couldn't move. I pinched his thigh, secretly hoping that it would twitch. But it stayed in place, heavy and dead.

I longed for the time when Jack and I would be in control of our lives without the advice or hopes of all those who now surrounded us. I thought of helping Jack kill himself. I wondered how we'd do it. Then I thought, What if it had been the other way around? Maybe it would have been better, at least easier. If I had been the one, if I were paralyzed. I could still have a baby. I couldn't feel, but . . . Other thoughts flooded my mind, mixed-up thoughts, thoughts that frightened me. I wouldn't be able to dance, to run. My legs would wither, and I wouldn't be able to wear pretty sandals or short skirts. But the worst, the very worst, would have been their shaving off my hair. I didn't think about the pain of having holes drilled into my head. My thoughts were all cosmetic, all vanity.

I stopped projecting. It hadn't happened to me. It had happened to a part of me, to the one person from whom I didn't want to separate myself. I knew that the future couldn't be tampered with, that what lay ahead nobody could know. Meanwhile it almost seemed a miracle that Jack was alive.

Jack opened his eyes and smiled at me. "How you feeling, baby?" he said. "Come here and kiss me."

We kissed and I noticed that Jack was beginning to smell like the clean but stagnant air of the hospital—a different smell, one of inactivity, of no sun and no fresh air.

"How did you sleep?" I asked.

"Okay. I had some bad dreams, but I slept soundly from around five till eight. . . . What about you?"

"Pretty well, I guess. It's just . . . Oh, Jack, I miss you so." I rested my head on his chest and closed my eyes. I felt him rub his arms over my hair. We didn't speak, and I wanted to crawl up and lie down with him.

"Time for your pills, Mr. Willis," a pimply-faced nurse with a twangy Midwestern voice said gaily. "Now, you get the yellow one, two whites, and an orange. There we go," she said, bending the straw into Jack's mouth. "How we doin' today, Jack?" And as soon as Jack said, "Fine," she was off with a squeak of her rubber-soled shoes to dispense pills to somebody else.

Then a mousy girl in a pink nurse's aide uniform wheeled in a tray filled with aluminium-covered dishes. I timidly removed a cover and stared at Jack's lunch—a ham-and-cheese sandwich on white packet bread. Off came another cover—limp iceberg lettuce, topped with some tired slices of tomato and dripping with neon-orange dressing. Dessert was a piece of cake and some canned pears. Every meal began with a large glass of cranberry juice, which cleaned out Jack's kidneys and staved off infection. I broke the sandwich into quarters and began feeding it to Jack. The salad required more care. A precariously balanced piece of tomato fell somewhere between his mouth and cheekbone. Jack and I began to laugh. The whole operation seemed so ridiculous that neither of us could have stood it without laughing.

Jack was usually turned onto his stomach shortly after lunch. I was just beginning to be able to watch this procedure without feeling panic or nausea. I knew how painful it had been a week before, and the sound of Jack's cries had made me shiver with fear and helplessness. Now he gave the nurses instructions.

"Strap me in tighter," Jack said. "That's it. Can't you put a piece of sheepskin between my chin and the strap? Great. Okay, I'm ready."

Squashed between the sheepskins, metal frame, and straps, Jack looked like a grotesque human sandwich. The moment they turned him, I froze. Reflexively I waited for him to cry out in pain, even though he hadn't for a week.

As he lay on his stomach, Jack's back still looked muscular and tan. A bandage covered the incision which ran almost seven inches

177

from the nape of his neck down the center of his back. I'd seen it. The surgeons had cut with such artistry that the skin was healing perfectly and the scar looked like a delicately painted line.

I sat down in the corner—hardly roomy enough for a chair— picked up the *Times*, and started reading aloud. I felt so far away from the news, so distant from the rest of the world. I looked over to Jack and put my hand on his arm. I felt a wave of love wash over me. I felt strangely at peace, settled, almost cozy. Jack may have been waiting for signs of change, secret signals of improvement, but I didn't dare wait. I had expected to be married in the fall, to be pregnant by spring, to live happily ever after. Now I was wary of expectation; I mistrusted the future, or maybe I was simply terrified of more disappointment.

THE WILLISES HAD finally moved into a house of their own. For the first emergency nights both families had lived at our farmhouse, eating numerous meals together, but things had been difficult. The accident had pulled everyone together, but we couldn't really feel close. There was a growing need for privacy.

It was the first meal in a week that the two families hadn't eaten together. I stared at the food in front of me. My mother had done all the work, and I'd been called to the table from a nap upstairs. "You have to eat something," my mother said. "You need your strength."

My strength. Getting through the evening meal seemed an extraordinary effort, but I managed to finish some chicken and a few teaspoons of rice.

After the dishes were washed (I was excused from that task, too), I walked into my bedroom and climbed up on the bed. Facing it was a long mirror, and I stared at my image, no longer comforted by my lingering suntan but cynically amused by my loneliness. "What a waste," I said to myself. "I thought I'd finally made it. I'd found the right guy."

Mama came into the room and immediately looked to see if I was crying. She sat down on the bed and took my hand. Before she could say anything she started to weep. She tried to stifle her sobs, but she was too exhausted to control herself, and I wished she would stop trying to be so strong. "Cry, Mama. Let it all out," I said, wrapping my arms around her.

"It's so unfair." She shook her head. "You're so young and

beautiful—" And then she stopped herself, embarrassed to say what was really on her mind. "I shouldn't be crying. I'm your mother. I should be comforting you."

"But you are comforting me. Don't hold back. Talk it out. Then you'll feel better."

My coaxing seemed to work, and Mama let herself cry freely. We were more than a mother and daughter grieving together. We were two women who understood each other, because we knew what it was to love a man so deeply.

"I guess it upsets me so to see you hurt because I know how hard it is," she said. "There was a time in my marriage when Papa was sick and we were pretty miserable." She hesitated. "I guess if I hadn't loved him so much, I wouldn't have been able to stay with him. But the one thing a mother hopes is that her children will be spared that pain." She began to cry again. "I just hate to see you go through this. You shouldn't have to deal with these problems now."

"I have no choice," I said. "I love Jack and he loves me. We still don't know what's going to happen."

Mama looked at me and tried to brace herself against more tears. "If Jack doesn't improve, he won't want you to . . ." She stopped.

"To marry him," I finished her sentence. "We're not there yet, Mama. We don't have to decide anything now."

I could see she felt guilty for thinking she *hoped* he wouldn't marry me, even though she never said it. But I wasn't angry with her, and I didn't have to say that the decision to get married would be Jack's and mine, would have nothing to do with her hopes or fears. "Do you feel better?" I said.

"I'm fine. Now you get into bed. You can't let yourself get exhausted. Your face looks pinched." I climbed into bed and let her tuck me in. She kissed me good night. "You're a wonderful girl, Mary. I love you very much," she said.

THE NEXT DAY I hesitated before entering Jack's room. At first I thought he was asleep, but then I saw that he was just staring at the ceiling. I went over to his bed and kissed him. His eyes looked cloudy and his mouth turned gently downward in an angerless frown. "What's the matter, Jack? What are you thinking about?" I asked, and tried to ignore the mounting queasiness of fear. There was a sadness, a depression, that I'd never seen in him before.

"What if I don't get return?" Jack said in a monotone. "They said two to three weeks. It's almost two. I haven't let it get me down. This is the first time I've really been depressed."

"I don't know what you'll do . . . what *we'll* do," I said. "I wouldn't have known what I'd have done if someone had told me a year ago that you'd be in an accident, in a hospital. I guess I wouldn't have believed them."

"But if I'm paralyzed? If I can never walk? If we can never make love?"

I realized how contagious fear was. I tried to fight the dizziness, the swirling feeling of doubt and questioning. I couldn't give in. *We* couldn't give in. "Jack, I don't know what will happen. It will never be the same. But the most important thing is us. Not letting our personalities change. It's all now, all present. All I know is I love you now, that I'm here, not because it's my duty but because I want to be here. Because I want us. I can't think about the way we were. What's the point? You can't give in to the ifs—if you hadn't taken the wave, if I hadn't wanted to go in for that swim, if you don't get return."

"What do you mean, not let our personalities change?" Jack asked.

I knew what I was thinking. I was fighting, fighting back the fear. If Jack had doubts, they infected me. "I mean if our life together became unbearable, unhappy, joyless, I couldn't hide it from you. I *wouldn't* hide it from you. I mean, we can't ever play games. We never have. I can't imagine being your nurse, living a life without sex. Don't you see, Jack? Maybe one day I won't love you, but now I can't imagine that because I do love you. I don't see you as a cripple because you don't see yourself as a cripple. That's what I mean about personalities changing. Maybe we won't make it. Maybe one day I'll leave you or you'll want me to go, but that thought now makes me sick. If we change, we'll be two different people. And we'll know. But now I can't even imagine those people."

I felt flushed and excited. It was the fight that saved me from the dejection of hopelessness. It was the deep conviction that comes from loving someone that made me rebel against the odds. Jack was smiling at me and I smiled back. What a crazy time to feel lucky, to feel proud and strong.

Libbie and Lou had come into the room. They usually came in the afternoon, and their presence made me feel awkward. I could tell that Jack was disappointed they had picked that moment to visit. They knew they'd interrupted something, but they didn't know how to leave.

"And how's everything today?" Lou said in a mock-casual singsong. "And how's my little doll?"

"I'm okay," I heard myself say, and watched Libbie caress Jack's face as she kissed him on the cheek.

"I brought you some fruit Jell-O," Libbie said. "I thought something light might refresh you."

Jack thanked her, and some more small talk ensued. I knew they wanted to ask Jack if there'd been the slightest movement, the tiniest sign of inward or outward improvement. Their faces silently begged for some good news and I wanted to cry out, to ease the tension. At the same time I wanted to send them away. There was so much I wanted to tell Jack, now, right this minute.

"Is everything all right?" Libbie asked, sensing the tension.

"I'm just hot and uncomfortable," Jack said. "And we were talking. That's all."

"We'll go," Libbie said. "We just stopped in to say hello."

"Don't be silly," I said. "Why should you go? I'd like a break anyway. I didn't have a chance to buy the paper this morning. Stay awhile. I'll be back in a few minutes."

For the first time I felt trapped. I couldn't go back into that room. I couldn't go home. I wasn't hungry. I'd already read the paper. I wished I could run away, from families, from problems. . . . No. I just wished the accident had never happened.

Jack

I was so involved with myself that Mary was really the only person to whom I could talk. My roommate, Mike, and I kidded a lot, but we didn't really talk. And there just wasn't that much I could say to either Mary's or my family. My parents would always ask me how I was coming along, and when I said nothing was happening, they tried to hide their disappointment. The question annoyed me. It was a reminder that nothing had happened so far. I began shutting them out in self-defense.

I knew how difficult it was for my parents. They had to adjust to

181

the idea that Mary was the person I needed most. She controlled the traffic of visitors, dealt with the doctors and nurses, and, with our close lawyer friend, Duff, took care of my outside affairs. My parents were forced to trust and listen to the advice of a twenty-four-year-old woman simply because that was what I wanted.

I could tell that they were confused. There was not much they could do. Yet just having them there was good for me, though in actual fact I saw them very little. They would drop by at lunch-time with my favorite sandwich, and would come by after dinner, usually with a malted milk or a snack of some kind. There was nothing else I wanted them to do. They had to suffer the frustra-tion of not even being able to be with me when they wanted, because I needed Mary more.

Mary's parents were different. Obviously they felt awful about my tragedy. They had canceled their trip to Europe and had moved into our farmhouse to be with Mary and to help me. Norman had done everything he could to make sure I got the best care possible. Like my parents, they were with me almost every day. But there was the difference in attitude. My father was eternally, overwhelmingly confident, my mother had quiet hope (shored up by my father). On the other hand, I felt Mary's parents were pessimistic, a pessimism born of a sense of reality and of real concern for her own best interest.

They had to be thinking about Mary's happiness first. I was a guy whom they hardly knew, who was engaged to be married to their daughter. And who now was almost certain to be paralyzed for the rest of his life. Who could blame them if they thought it would be better if Mary and I split up? And that the sooner she saw this and started a new life of her own, the better? They had to be thinking that. Hell, I was thinking it.

I thought about our breaking up, but I never reached any con-clusions. I was giving myself from two to four weeks to see if I would get any return. If I didn't get it, then we would have to decide what to do. But until that time, all judgments and decisions were suspended while we waited it out together.

One morning, just before the two weeks were up, Joe went through his usual flexing, twisting, and bending of my limbs. "Try to move your toes," he said. "Concentrate on them. You've got to get the message down from your head through your central nervous system to your toes. Just try. Keep on trying."

I closed my eyes and concentrated as hard as I could on moving my toes. I felt nothing and nothing happened. It was as though my head were separated from my body. Finally Joe told me to relax and walked out of the room.

A few minutes later I tried to move my toes again. I tried to get a mental picture of the nerve circuitry, to picture the location of my toe. Suddenly I heard Mike hollering. "Your toe, your big toe is moving!" It was. I could feel the connection. I couldn't see it, but if I concentrated, I could will it to move. Mike called Joe back into the room, and I moved it for him. Then all the nurses crowded in to look.

"What does it mean?" I asked Joe.

"I don't know," he said. "It could be the beginning of return or it could be nothing more than the fact that you can wiggle your toe."

"Come on. Commit yourself, damn it. I'm doing it. The two weeks are almost up. The swelling in my spine is going down."

"I don't know," Joe said, controlling the excitement in his voice. "Don't kid yourself. Waiting is the name of the game. I can't predict what will happen. Just keeping trying to move that toe. We'll see."

Mary

"We've all been waiting for you," Janet the head nurse said with a big smile on her face.

I didn't know what she was talking about, but I rushed into Jack's room. I didn't have time to suspect anything. Jack gave me a glowing smile. "I have a surprise for you," he said, almost laughing. "I can move my toe."

"What?" I said, not believing. "How? Tell me everything."

I listened, still not believing. I was laughing at the ridiculousness, the hugeness, the sheer beauty of a wiggling toe. "Tell me again. Tell me everything that happened."

"I just told you." Jack was laughing too. "Mary, it's all so crazy. I can't see my feet, but I can tell when the toe moves. It's like I'm making a connection. I can't explain it."

I ran around to the foot of Jack's bed. "Let me see. See if you can do it again."

I stared at Jack's feet. I was concentrating so hard that my eyes hurt. Nothing happened. And then it happened. The big toe on his left foot made a little bow and I could hear myself yelp with glee. "Oh, my God! It moved. Oh, Jack. You really moved it. Do it again." I watched his foot, hardly breathing, the way a crowd at a circus watches a tightrope walker, silently praying, immersed in excitement and fear.

"I'm not moving it, am I?" Jack asked.

"No. It's not moving."

"There it goes," Jack said, his eyes wide with joy, his whole face proud with accomplishment.

"You're right. Oh, Jack. You moved it again. I really saw it. Tell me what it all means."

"Well, you know Joe," Jack said with a smirk. "He said it might mean that I'm beginning to get return. But it might just be that I can wiggle my toe and that's it."

"He doesn't say more than that?" I asked.

"No."

Janet LaVinio had come in behind me to give Jack his little yellow pill. From the first day she'd told me what was going on with Jack. The morning after the operation she'd told me that he was running a high fever, and when I looked upset, she'd put her arm around me and said, "Mary, Jack has just undergone major surgery, and I can't tell you not to worry. But his whole body is fighting. The fever is expected."

Now I asked her, "Janet, is the toe really something we can afford to get excited about?"

"I think it's worth getting excited about," she said. "Any movement is good. It means that some signal is being sent through the cord."

I wanted to run home to tell everyone what had happened.

MY MOTHER was in the kitchen preparing lunch. I burst into the house like the kid who has no cavities in the toothpaste commercial. "Jack moved his big toe. Papa? Did you hear?"

They were happy but not jubilant, and I felt the same kind of letdown one feels after telling a great joke which elicits only a polite chuckle. "But it really *is* great news," I said to myself. "I just didn't tell it right."

I couldn't be certain what it was in their eyes that disappointed me. I knew how fond they were of Jack, but that their affection was measured by my happiness. It was as though I were viewing the movement of that toe through the magnifying lens of a telescope, while they were viewing it all through the long lens where the same objects looked razor-sharp and far away. To me, that toe took up the whole picture. To them, it was the tiniest dot in a frame so large that it almost didn't exist.

I didn't dare be hopeful. If I let myself think about how wonderful it would be if Jack's legs continued to come back and he might walk again someday, I was overwhelmed by a terrible dread that some unseen force would punish me for those happy thoughts. Wishing became synonymous with bad luck—if I think about it or want it, it won't happen. What if Jack's toe were all that was coming back? In the days that followed I began to build up childish, superstitious conditions to ensure safety for my wishes.

As I left the hospital every night, I looked up at the sky and picked out the biggest and most glittering star. I would try not to blink, to keep my eyes glued to the flickering light for as long as it took me to make my wish. "Oh, please, let everything be okay. Let Jack walk again, let us be able to have babies, let him be able to use his hands." I'd try to make sure I wasn't forgetting anything. If people passed me and saw me mumbling to myself and staring transfixed at the sky, I wasn't even aware of them. After I finished my prayer, I felt tremendously relieved and not in the least bit silly.

Jack

Every chance I got I tried to wiggle my toe. Sometimes it worked, sometimes it didn't. I was stretched out flat on the frame and couldn't raise my head to see my feet, but I knew it when I moved my toe. I'd test myself by checking with Mike or Mary. I could tell when I made a connection, no matter how weak. Somewhere inside my spinal cord there was a bruised nerve or ganglion that was healing, and if I concentrated I could locate it and send a message from my brain down through the cord to the muscle that controlled my toe.

The night I first moved my toe, my legs began doing a Saint Vitus's dance, as if they were possessed. I would lie there, my legs outstretched, perfectly straight, and then a leg would jump.

185

Sometimes just a foot moved; other times my whole leg would bend at the knee, as though I had developed a giant tic.

Joe didn't know what caused the spasm, and he didn't know whether it really meant anything. It still excited me because, even if it was involuntary, at least I was moving. But days passed, and nothing else seemed to be returning. I had only sporadic control of my toe. The meagerness of the return began to get me down. Joe was right. I couldn't expect anything.

FOR A FEW DAYS I thought I'd been getting feeling in my hands. One night I thought I could pinch my thumb and forefinger together without bending my wrist. I showed Joe. He grabbed my wrist and held it tightly. Then he told me to try to bend the forefinger. I couldn't.

Joe just laughed. "I think you're kidding me."

He was right. I had been kidding him and myself. There was no more feeling in my hands. I began to get depressed again. Mary, too, was disappointed, I could tell, though she never said anything about it. She never asked if there was any more return. She knew I'd tell her.

One afternoon I was lying on my stomach when my father, who had been off on a short trip, came barging into my room. He was full of enthusiasm because of the movement in my toe. He wanted to hear all about the return, but I just turned him off by telling him it was hard for me to talk on my stomach. Anyway, I wanted to sleep. I told him I'd see him that night.

When he and my mother came back to visit that night, I was talking with Mary and her sister, Annie, who had recently returned from Europe. My father prowled around them like a trapped animal, impatient and angry. Finally I asked everyone but him to leave. He immediately wanted to see me move my toe. His optimism annoyed me. I knew it shouldn't, but I couldn't help it.

"Look," I said angrily. "You can't get too excited. It's not realistic. Just because I've got a couple of muscles doesn't mean I'll get any more. I may never walk again, and you and Mom have to accept that. Calm down. You're not helping anybody."

He didn't say anything; he just looked at me. I knew I was being obnoxious. But I couldn't stop. "You have got to be realistic, Dad. You can't expect improvements every day. You've

186

got to expect the worst." I took a deep breath and waited. He outlasted me. "I'm sorry, Dad. I'm down and it's hot. It's not your fault."

He apologized for pacing the room and said it was just because he was so concerned about me. After he left, I lay there thinking about him and realized I'd never really explained anything to him, had never shown him how I could move. I'd shut him out.

He came back the next day as if nothing had happened the night before. "Hiya, Jacko. How're you feeling?"

"Dad. I've been thinking about last night. Let me explain to you what I know. If the cord isn't torn, the reason I can't move is that it's badly bruised and swollen. That's putting pressure on the nerves. It may take up to four weeks for that swelling to go down. Understand?"

He nodded.

"But we don't know whether the cord was torn or how badly it was bruised. So we're just waiting. The toe coming back is a good sign, because it means that at least one nerve is intact. But it's possible that that's the only nerve or that there are just a few others. Nobody knows."

I realized I was lecturing, but he had to be made to understand. "Mary and I are hopeful, Dad. But we're afraid to get too hopeful, because we've got to be prepared for the worst. We've got to live each day as it comes. I'll tell you as soon as anything happens. In the meantime all we can do is keep our cool."

He nodded, his blue eyes sparkling. I knew I was getting through. Finally. He was pleased we were talking with each other. But I knew his way of dealing with it was not to admit to himself that I might not make it. He was expectant each day. He needed that as much as Mary, and I needed to take each day as it came.

A couple of days later Joe came into my room while I was over on my stomach. He bent my right leg up from the knee and then down again, taking me through the range of motion exercises he usually performed in the mornings. Then he grasped my foot and swiveled the ankle, first to the right and then to the left. "Okay, move your toe," he said.

I tried. I concentrated on the toe on my right foot, the one that had never moved. Nothing happened.

"Relax," he said. "Try moving the left toe."

I tried and felt it move slightly.

187

"Good," he said, and then bent my left leg at the knee. As he started to lower it, I tried to resist him. I felt something. Joe was pulling my leg down and I *was* resisting him, I was consciously holding my leg up.

"Are you trying to do that?" he said.

I could only grunt "Yes," I was concentrating so hard on holding my leg back.

"Relax," Joe ordered, and set my leg down on the frame. Then he bent it up again. "Okay, I'm going to pull the leg down and you try to hold it back." He gripped my ankle with one hand and placed his other hand behind my knee.

I held back with everything I had. Slowly but steadily he was forcing my leg down, but I was resisting him—I could feel it. And then Joe slapped my leg on the frame.

"I felt it!" Joe cried. "I could see it flex. You've got your hamstring. It's only a quiver, but it's a beginning, Jack, it's a real beginning."

After Joe left, the nurses rolled me onto my back and turned out the lights. I tried sleeping but couldn't.

"Mike. You awake?"

"Yeah. Man, I thought Joe was going to buy champagne for the house."

"I can't believe it, Mike. I've got the leg. It's okay. I just know it."

I lay awake for another hour and said to myself over and over. "I'm going to walk. I know I'm going to walk."

Mary

"What did you say? You moved your left leg? The whole leg?"

Jack was laughing as he described what had happened the night before. His lips trembled and his eyes filled. He never said the word "walk," but that's what we both were thinking. This was more than a toe, the faint hint of life; this was a whole leg, a real promise. I wanted to hear it described again, just as I had when Jack first moved his toe. As Jack began to re-create the excitement and discovery of the previous night, it hit me.

I bet he's really going to walk, I thought to myself. And then I felt like weeping, as much from my recurrent, superstitious fear that I had tempted fate, as from joy. I wrapped my arms around

Jack's torso and kissed him. I pressed myself against him, careful not to hit the tongs with my arms, nervous about jerking his neck. I felt Jack awkwardly trying to caress my back and hair.

"Can I feel the muscle?" I asked. I pulled the sheet back, and Jack's right leg began to shake violently.

"A spasm," Jack said, and waited for the jerky movement to subside.

I slid my right arm underneath Jack's left leg and lifted it. I was shocked at how thin his legs were.

"Grab my ankle with your left hand," Jack ordered. "That's it. Now I'm going to try to push down, but don't you move."

"Okay, I'm ready when you are," I said, and watched Jack's face strain and redden in effort. Then I felt a delicate flutter in his leg. "I felt it move!" I almost cried the words.

As I drove home for lunch, I realized I was actually happy. Our close friends, the Wardenburgs, were coming out to visit, and I couldn't wait to tell them the good news. Jack had known Fred Wardenburg for ten years and had made his first film with him. I also knew that my parents, too, would be happy, despite their quiet pessimism.

I saw Chris Wardenburg sitting on the lawn talking with my mother. She was holding her baby, Jason, on her lap. I ran over to them, bursting with excitement. "I have wonderful news," I said, bending over to kiss Chris and the baby. "Jack moved his left leg last night."

My mother's face broke into a smile. "How wonderful," she said quietly.

Both Chris and Fred were anxious to see Jack, but I sensed they were also frightened. They had no idea what to expect and, like so many friends who had been in touch only by phone, were still stunned by the first horrible reports.

Jason wasn't allowed in the hospital, so Fred stayed outside with him while Chris and I went in to see Jack. Chris hesitated at the door as though she wanted to turn and run. But Jack's face lit up with a huge grin when he saw her, and Chris seemed pulled to him like a magnet. She bent over and kissed him.

"You look great," Jack said, completely at ease, as though he were sitting in the Wardenburgs' living room in Brooklyn.

"Oh, I'm so glad we finally got here," Chris said in a hospital whisper. I could tell she was upset by the tongs and Jack's pallor,

189

though she was really happy to see him. I also realized how strange the dark, claustrophobic room must have felt to her.

Chris stayed only a short time. "I know how badly Fred wants to see you, Jack," she said. "I'll wait outside."

I watched Chris leave, and I knew she was confused. She must have forgotten what I had said about good news—the beginning of return—the moment she saw Jack. Her uninitiated eye had seen only human devastation.

I waited for Fred to come in before going out to join Chris and the baby. Fred was less timorous and clasped Jack's hand in his. "I hear you moved a leg," he said. "That's really great."

"Only the hamstring," Jack said, "but it's a beginning."

"I'll leave you two alone for a while," I said, and went out to sit with Chris and Jason.

"What's going to happen with Jack?" Chris asked.

"Seeing him really upset you, didn't it?" I said, trying to sound understanding. I didn't want Chris to feel embarrassed, yet I was disappointed that Jack obviously looked so bad to her.

"I guess it did," she admitted. "I feel physically drained. What a joke that *I* feel tired! Oh, I hate myself for that."

"Don't hate yourself," I said, laughing. "What did you expect? I'm with Jack every day. I'm not aware of the change. Neither of us knows what's going to happen. Originally the doctors said he'd never walk again, but now I'm not so sure. To tell you the truth, Chris, we don't talk about what we're going to do . . . because we just don't know."

I knew that Chris couldn't really understand. I think the accident was so frightening and incomprehensible that it was a threat—the worst thing anyone could imagine. That it had happened to Jack, to a close friend, meant it couldn't be easily pushed out of mind. It had to be dealt with. But how?

The despondency many people felt after seeing Jack came simply from a lack of preparation to deal either emotionally or imaginatively with all the horrors Jack *was* dealing with. Every individual had his own secret dread, and I discovered that in an odd way Jack became a human mirror to the deepest emotions and nightmares of others. It hadn't happened to them . . . yet. Ironically, because it *had* happened to Jack, he was freer than the rest. He had been reduced to the most basic honesty, to the purest openness . . . and many people weren't prepared for that. They came wanting to help, and left realizing that Jack had helped them, that in some unexpected way they had learned something new about themselves.

I WENT back to Jack's room. And as I approached Fred and Jack, I noticed how big Fred looked. I'd known before the accident that they were about the same size, but now Fred seemed a giant. I couldn't keep my eyes from darting back and forth between the two. And as I did so I saw Jack's thinness and pallor more clearly. I simply hadn't realized how much weight he'd lost (it was more than twenty-five pounds). It was as though his whole body had shrunk a size.

For the first time since the accident the outside world had squeezed its way into the protected world of the hospital. For the first time I was seeing and judging Jack through the eyes of the past, and I was shocked by what I saw. Earlier that morning I had been elated by the movement of his leg and had allowed myself the luxury of thinking about his walking. Now, compared to Fred, to normalcy, that movement seemed such a tiny thing.

Jack

It was incredible. And I showed off for everyone.

Clive said he had to see for himself before he would believe what he had heard. He turned me over onto my stomach, held my leg, and told me to resist him while he bent it downward. He yelled and whooped and carried on just as Joe had.

"Stop it," I said. "You knew we'd do it."

He stopped laughing and turned to me. "You don't know what it means to us," he said. "We work so hard with you. We're always hoping you'll be okay, and then suddenly it happens."

FRED AND CHRIS Wardenburg visited the hospital the day after I got return in my hamstring, and Mary showed me off as though I were a child prodigy, made me wiggle my toe and had them hold my leg so they could feel the hamstring quiver.

"Gee, that's great," Fred kept saying. But I could tell he was more upset by what I couldn't move than excited by what I could. Other friends had the same kind of reaction. They hadn't seen me when I couldn't move anything, hadn't spent the three

191

weeks with us in desperate waiting. They only saw me as I was—head shaved, tongs in my skull, immobile. They couldn't imagine what an achievement that toe and hamstring were.

And there were other signs. The next day Joe tried my left leg again and said it was a little stronger. He grabbed my ankle and told me to move my foot. I tried, but it wasn't moving. I tried thinking about turning my *knee*. I tried "right" and then "left," but I wasn't making any connection there either. Then I thought about my heel, and I tried moving *it*. Again, I felt nothing, but Joe said, "I think you moved it. Try again." So I thought about my heel again and tried to remember what I had just done. "You did it again," he said. "I saw it move."

"Put my leg down, Joe. I'm tired." He put it down and picked up the other foot. But I couldn't make it move, so he tried the left one again.

"Okay, move your heel," he said. I concentrated on my ankle and heel. "You did it again," he said excitedly. "That muscle is an extension of your hamstring. It all figures. You've got three down and only nine hundred muscles to go."

Mary

After Fred and Chris's visit with Jack, they went back to the house with me and we talked. "Do the doctors think Jack'll be able to have sex?" Fred asked.

I was shocked by his directness but tried to hide my feelings. "They say we'll be able to," I said. "But it's still too early to know about children."

I couldn't completely blame Fred for his curiosity. Sex was probably the first thing everyone wondered about. But the question presumed a separation or distance between Jack and me, as though I were an objective bystander who could comment coolly on the fate of his friend. Of course I *wasn't* an outsider. I was part of that fate. What would happen to Jack was what would happen to me. To the outside world I was a free agent, a young woman capable of forming new relationships. But to me freedom without Jack meant nothing.

I tried not to be angry with Fred, who, I knew, was asking out of love and concern. Anyway, I reacted more violently to people who did a bad job of suppressing the same questions, like the mother of a friend who asked whether we were still planning on getting married. "What do you mean?" I said.

"Well . . . ." she stuttered. "It's such a big decision."

"We're not rushing into it, if that's what you mean."

At least Fred came right out with it, but I realized I was more sensitive to these intimate questions than I had been earlier. Much more sensitive. I felt that my innermost privacy was being invaded, but my possible lack of sex life had become a matter of public concern. Right after the accident I had never thought about what others might think. I hadn't had time. Now I hated the idea of people viewing me as a victim. I imagined women at work and the mothers of friends sitting at lunch wondering out loud, "Well, how can she marry him now? It would be tragic for a young girl like Mary to be saddled with a . . . a . . . cripple."

When I told Jack about my sudden sensitivity, he said, "Maybe you're upset about what they're saying because that's what you're thinking but can't say. You *have* to be questioning all the things they are. I know I am. Sex is an important part of life."

I realized I needed Jack as much as he did me. We were bound by an inexhaustible devotion. We knew we had lost a certain carefreeness, but that's all we knew. Neither of us was ready to settle for anything less than normalcy at this point. We shared a special intimacy which in its greatest intensity is sex. And mixed with our fear was hope.

Jack

Though I never mentioned it to Mary, I was worried about the catheter. Did it mean I would never have control over my bladder? Could it do permanent damage? And most important, how had the accident affected my reproductive organs?

I was scared to consider the possibility of impotence. So, like everything else that had to do with the accident, I had tried to put it out of my mind and wait to see what would happen. But I couldn't totally block it out.

And now that it looked as if my leg was coming back, what worried me most was sex. I could imagine a relationship where we couldn't have children. It would be disappointing, but we could always adopt kids. But I couldn't imagine a relationship without sex. The only "information" I had was that a few times I'd felt the

193

catheter being inserted, although it had never been really painful. That I felt something gave me hope, but I didn't dare hope for too much.

Joe asked a urologist, a Dr. Weir, to examine me. The night he was expected I was tense, afraid the news would be bad.

Dr. Weir came into my room pushing a rack with a half dozen bottles suspended from it. The first thing he did was push his finger hard up into my scrotum.

"Does that hurt?" he asked.

"Hell, yes, it hurts."

Then he stuck my scrotum with a pin. I felt that, too. I was quietly thankful for the pain. Then he stuck me around my thighs and belly. It all felt dull. I could feel the pressure of the pin sticking me but felt no pain.

Next Dr. Weir squeezed my prostate. It hurt. He said my penis had reacted. "That's very important. It means you can have erections. The long nerves that run down into the penis and the prostate are intact."

"How come I have sensation there but not over the rest of my body?" I asked.

"I don't know. We really don't know much about spinal injuries. Each case is different," said Dr. Weir. "You know I was once paraplegic. I caught a bullet in the spine in Korea."

"But you're fine," I said. "You can walk beautifully."

"I've still got a brace on my leg, and I limp a little."

I hadn't noticed the limp. It was good to know he'd been hurt like me. But it was also the first time I'd thought of myself as a paraplegic. In fact, I wasn't quite a paraplegic; I was a quadriplegic. But the sudden realization shocked me.

Maybe I didn't have to be a basket case. My left leg was coming back, and Weir said the signs in my genital area were good. I pressed him about paraplegics, and he told me he had a couple of spinal-injury patients.

"One of them was a quadriplegic like you," he said. "He can walk now and has a normal sex life."

Finally he ran some tests on my bladder. He pumped fluid into it, measured the amount I could hold, and then asked if the water was warm or cold.

I couldn't really tell, but I thought it felt a little warm. "Warm," I said, unsure of myself.

"That's right. Good."
"I really couldn't tell," I confessed.
"It doesn't matter," he said. "You were right."

Mary

I knew Jack was going to be seen by a urologist, and I was simultaneously anxious for him to have and not to have the prescribed tests. Not knowing was less and less of a comfort as time went on, but the possibility of knowing definitely that we could never have a normal sex life was unbearable. "Sex isn't everything," I remembered Joe saying. Of course it wasn't everything. But what did that mean?

I walked into Jack's room one morning and saw an extra bottle attached to his bed with a cord leading ominously in the direction of his crotch. Oh, my God, I thought. This is it. It's worse than I imagined.

"The urologist was here last night," Jack said.

"Well, what happened?" I almost shouted.

"Calm down. I'm telling you. He said he was very hopeful, but it's still too early to know. We'll have to wait."

I felt myself flush and weaken at the knees. I sat down and took a deep breath, not sure of my reaction to what Jack was telling me. It was neither as bad as I had dreaded nor as good as I had hoped. All I knew was that I wanted to be totally reassured that sex would be perfection.

"Tell me what he did."

I listened intently as Jack described the series of tests. "What did he say about the catheter? Will they take that out soon? Is it hurting you to leave it in?"

I knew I was being too insistent and perhaps asking too many questions, but I couldn't help it. Jack seemed to understand my need to be reassured. I hated my obsession, my minimally disguised panic. I'd lived through a month not knowing whether Jack would ever move a muscle again. I'd watched the slow return of his left leg and waited patiently for the progressive stirrings in his right. A month before, I'd been able to imagine living with a man in a wheelchair. My idealized picture of us surrounded by children had even been a comfort. But now that picture frightened me.

As I walked out of the hospital I met Joe. "Jack tells me Weir's report pleased you," I said.

"Yes, it did."

I waited to see if he'd say something reassuring.

"You know, Mary, your feelings about Jack might change. You can't be too hard on yourself if they do. Jack is going to be a big responsibility, and you're very young."

"Don't all relationships change?" I said, feeling the bile rise in my throat. "And don't you think that Jack and I know this?" I resented Joe's depersonalizing Jack by thinking of him more as a big responsibility than as a man.

"I'm just telling you this for you," Joe said. "Very few people really know what it's like."

"We don't pretend to know," I said. "So there seems no point in worrying now about how I'll feel a year from now. Who would have thought Jack would have come this far three weeks ago?"

"You're right about that," Joe said. "But remember, I was the one who had hope."

"I haven't forgotten," I said. "So why lose it now?"

Joe bit on his pipe and forced a smile. He turned and walked up the steps toward the hospital.

Jack

One day, while Mary and Norman were visiting with me, Joe came in. "You need another operation to stabilize your neck," he said. "We'll take some spongy bone from your hip and fuse it to the vertebra that's been damaged in your neck."

"When?" I asked.

"In about ten days. Afterward I hope we will be able to move you within five or six weeks to a rehabilitation center, depending on how quickly you recover."

The idea of another operation didn't bother me. "It doesn't sound as dangerous as the first operation," I said. "You won't be working so close to the spinal cord."

Joe looked at Norman and then me. "All operations are dangerous. But I'll have the top specialists in the field working with me, and we'll cut the risk as much as possible." He paused. "But I really have to tell you there have been a number of deaths from this type of operation."

There was a silence. "What do you mean?" I said finally. "People you've operated on? How many? What caused it?"

"We don't know," he said. "It's never happened to one of my patients. I've just read about it in the medical literature."

I looked at Mary, who was watching me carefully. Her doctor father was looking at Joe but didn't say anything. Joe said, "Don't worry. We'll take care of you. And the odds are in your favor." He turned and left the room.

"Are you scared?" Mary asked me.

"Hell, yes, I'm scared." What I didn't say to her was that I was afraid of dying. I'd never thought of dying before the first operation. I wouldn't have thought of it now if Joe hadn't mentioned it. I figured the doctors knew what they were doing. Why did Joe go out of his way to frighten me?

I lay there panicked. I thought about the operation and about death—death from unknown causes that doctors had no control over. I was getting angry. So the odds were in my favor. They were in my favor when I took the wave. After all, how many people break their necks bodysurfing?

Mary

How they would take a tiny piece of bone from Jack's hip and fit it carefully into his spine like a piece in a jigsaw puzzle fascinated me. I knew all operations were risky, but I was almost smug that this one would be okay.

What a stupid ass Joe had been to mention death right before Jack was to be operated on. It was at moments like this that I resented Joe as a doctor, even though I liked him as a person.

The flat voice of the head nurse came over the loudspeaker: "Visiting hours are now over. All visitors must leave."

I grabbed Jack's hand and brought it to my lips. I didn't want to leave. I felt helpless to soothe his fear, and seeing it in his eyes made me frightened. "It'll be all right, Jack."

"I know it will, baby. Don't worry. I'll be okay. Give me a kiss and go home and get some rest."

Papa and I walked toward the car. "What do you think of what Joe said—about death from unknown causes?" I asked.

"He was a dope to say that," my father said in his gruff voice. "But he's young and insecure, especially around me. We all know

197

that any time you take a general anesthetic you're risking death, but what's the point of saying it? This operation isn't nearly as dangerous as the first. They won't be working on top of the spinal cord, and Jack's in better shape than he was the first time. And we know Joe's extremely capable technically."

"So you're not too worried?" I said, needing to be reassured.

"No," my father said. "It's amazing he's come this far. As long as he keeps improving . . ."

I didn't ask Papa, "What if he doesn't improve?" I didn't want to know what he thought about that.

THE ALARM went off at six thirty, startling me out of a deep sleep. I wanted to get to the hospital by seven—a full hour before Jack would be wheeled into the operating room.

As I walked into the hospital I was struck by the amount of movement and noise at such an early hour. Like a wind-up clock, the hospital seemed to run on its own time.

I could tell that Jack had been waiting for me to arrive. He looked tired but alert with anxiety and fear.

"You're scared, aren't you?" I said.

"Yeah. I've been awake half the night. It's crazy. Last time everyone was scared, and I didn't know it. Now they're all running around like they do every morning—same jokes, same everything—and I'm terrified."

I held Jack's hand. It felt cold. "It *is* crazy," I said. "Because I think it's going to be okay, too. I know that's no help, but—"

"Yes, it is," Jack said. He looked at me and tried to smile.

A nurse came in with a hypodermic needle. She pulled the sheet off Jack's right leg and jammed the needle into his thigh.

"I felt that," he said excitedly. "That's the first time I've felt anything in my right thigh."

"That's great, Jack," the nurse said gaily. "You come out of that operation feeling a lot, too. Okay?"

Two more nurses dressed in green came in and began to wheel the bed out of the room.

"This is the first time the morphine hasn't worked," Jack said. "I guess I'm really scared."

"It's going to be okay," I said, walking alongside the moving bed. "I'll be here when you wake up."

"I love you, Mary. I'll be okay."

198

I watched the bed move into the operating room—a frightening, forbidding place to me. I stood dumbly for a while, the way you stand after someone you love has boarded a plane and you've watched the last traces of exhaust disappear in the sky after take-off. I snapped out of my daze and repeated the words, "It's going to be okay," and left the hospital.

When I reached the parking lot Jack's mother was getting out of her car. She was by herself, as Jack's father had had to return to Los Angeles.

"They just wheeled him into the operating room," I said.

"Oh, no," she cried. "I didn't think the operation was till eight thirty or nine."

I couldn't see her eyes behind the dark glasses, but I knew they were filling with tears. I felt sad for her. I wrapped my arm around her waist. "Let's go inside and get some coffee."

Libbie hooked her arm around me and drew herself close as we walked back toward the hospital. Neither of us said anything, and for the first time in a long while I felt comfortable with a silence we shared. I remembered what my mother had often said to me: "You'll never understand the pain a mother feels when her child is hurt or disappointed until you have your own children."

Libbie had been so controlled and considerate all this time, and I felt ashamed that my tendency was to condemn her self-control instead of appreciating her consideration. For the first time since the day she arrived, I felt close to her, felt the love we both felt for Jack.

"THIS PICTURE OF Jack was taken when he was three and a half years old," Libbie said over coffee in the hospital canteen. She was fondling a tattered photograph of a smiling boy with red hair and masses of freckles splashed across his cheeks and nose.

"He really looks like an advertisement for the milk companies—the wholesome American boy," I said.

"We were still in Milwaukee then . . . I must have been pregnant with Dick." Libbie sipped her coffee and seemed to relax with her memories. I asked her to tell me more.

"Oh, Jack was a great little boy," she said. "He could be a devil, but we all had such fun."

"How old was he when you moved to California?"

"Jack was nine and Dick was five. Jack always had a mind of

199

his own. If I tried to keep him indoors, he'd always find a way to get out and play baseball." She pulled more snapshots out of her wallet—one of Jack and Dick on the beach, both of them all teeth and spindly legs; their senior prom formal pictures; the one of Jack in a white dinner jacket and black bow tie, his hair cut short, his teeth white and even, his smile a little "1950s sincere."

Libbie and I both laughed. It was easy to remember the good times. "Jack didn't know I existed when that picture was taken." I was thinking out loud. "I remember all those nights with girl friends, wondering who we'd marry, knowing he existed somewhere, but not knowing who or where. Pretty crazy, isn't it?"

"I guess it is," Libbie said, lighting a cigarette. And I realized we were serious again, and sad.

"I think we should both go home and get some rest," I said.

Jack

The afternoon before the operation Joe had agreed to let Mary be with me right up to the time they wheeled me in. "There's not much to be afraid of," he'd said.

Not much for *you* to be afraid of, I thought.

Time dragged. I got more nervous. I developed a pain in my side. That night I dreamed I was going to be operated on, but first I had to get over a high fence. I started to climb over it. When I got to the top, I froze with fear, unable to move. I awoke thinking about the dream and death from unknown causes. It was two in the morning. I fell asleep again.

I awoke too early—about six o'clock—and lay there thinking nervously about the operation until Mary came in about seven. She walked beside me as they wheeled me out of my room and down to the operating room, and she kissed me before they pushed me through the big swinging doors.

Joe came by and introduced me to Dr. Farrell, who was going to assist him. Then they went off to have coffee and study my X rays. A nurse with a checklist asked if I had any false teeth or allergies. I felt I was in a Marx Brothers movie.

The longer I waited, the more nervous I got. I hated just lying there like a lump, while people were walking by me. I wondered if they thought I might die? Did they try to imagine the pain I might feel?

Once I was actually wheeled into the operating room, I felt better. Now I could participate. An intravenous tube was stuck in my arm, and a mask was put over my mouth and nose. I closed my eyes, took deep breaths of anesthetic, and went under.

FROM A distance Joe was saying to me, "The operation was successful." I think I smiled, and then he said something about my legs which, if I heard, I didn't remember when I finally came out of the anesthesia and was fully conscious in the intensive care unit. But by that time Joe was gone.

I hurt a little. But the operation was over and I'd come through. I was almost smug. No thoughts now about death from unknown causes.

Janet LaVinio came in smiling. "I know this is against the rules, but I had to come by and say hello."

Her smile was like a sunburst. She showed me a pretty little lace hankie. "I carried this when I got married," she said. "I brought it today for good luck for you. I told Mary I wanted her to carry it when you two get married."

Mary

"Jack wants you to know that he can still wiggle his toe," a kindly, round-faced nurse told me.

"When will I be able to see him?" I asked.

"He's still pretty groggy. Give him a couple more hours. We'll move him back to his room by then."

I was excited. The operation was over and Jack was alive, wiggling his toe. I saw Joe and ran up to him. He was still wearing his operating shoes and gown. He was glowing.

"It went beautifully, Mary. Dr. Farrell is very optimistic."

At that moment I felt nothing but love for Joe, and instinctively kissed him on the cheek. He was surprised and pleased. He led me over to a taller man who was also wearing a surgical gown. Dr. Farrell looked older than Joe, and his manner was friendly and relaxed. "I think Jack's going to make it," he said. "I think he's going to walk. I'm not as sure about his hands—but there's still a good chance they'll come back too."

I felt elated by his positive prognosis. "Thank you so much," I said. "I can't tell you how much I appreciate your help."

Farrell smiled at me. "You don't have to thank me," he said. "Jack's an extraordinary guy. Joe's told me how well you both have been handling this. It's you who should be thanked."

Jack was still half asleep when they wheeled him back into the room. He had a small bandage on the front side of his neck. I found out later that the incision was only two inches long and ran along a natural crease in his neck. When it healed, the scar would be no more than a vague reminder of hard times.

Jack moaned and tried to move his hand toward his bandaged right hip. I couldn't understand what he was saying, so I bent forward to hear him more clearly.

"My throat," he whispered. "My throat is killing me."

"Don't talk," I said. "You'll be fine. Just rest. The operation was a success. You'll be okay."

I offered him a glass of cold water. The straw slipped out of his mouth as he weakly sipped it. As he swallowed, his face tightened with pain, and I remembered my own first excruciating taste of water after my tonsils had been removed ten years before.

I watched Jack fall back to sleep. It was getting dark. The whole day had passed, and I felt strangely removed from time. The early-morning drive to the hospital, the operation, the talk with Libbie could have happened months before. I wasn't even sure what day of the week it was.

As evening wore into night, Jack's discomfort increased. I stayed by his side as much for my peace of mind as for his sake. At eight a group of Mike's friends barged into the room. I'd seen them all before.

They were always loud, but they hadn't bothered me before—in fact, they'd been something of a diversion. But this night they really got to me—hysterical laughter, dirty jokes told in grating tones. I wanted to scream at them to shut up. Jack was beginning to wake up again. He wasn't moaning anymore, but I knew he felt rotten.

I stuck my head out from the curtains. "Listen," I said to Mike's visitors, "could you be a little quieter? Jack's just come out of a big operation and he feels pretty bad." There was immediate silence, and everyone stared at me.

"Sure," Mike said. "I'm sorry."

I didn't just hate them for their noisiness, I realized. I hated them for their health.

Jack

When I awoke the euphoria had worn off and I ached all over. The next few days were awful. I felt that up to the time of the operation I was beginning to make progress, but that now I was so sick and sore I couldn't stand it. It seemed like a real setback, which depressed me, which in turn depressed Mary. Joe said that by Sunday I would feel better. And on Sunday I did feel better, at least well enough to start thinking once again about the future. Now that the fusion was successful Mary and I both wanted to know how much longer I'd have to be in traction and when we could look forward to going to the Institute of Rehabilitation Medicine in New York City—Dr. Rusk's institute.

"We better get these strong because you're going to need them," Janet said. I was lying on my stomach, and she was massaging my shoulders, arms, and fingers and talking to me about what rehabilitation would be like. "Even if you've got only one leg, they can get you up and walking," she said. "But you can't get impatient. You may need braces and crutches at first, and you'll need your arms to push yourself around in a wheelchair and your shoulders to carry you on crutches when they get you on your feet. It'll be harder than anything you've ever done, Jack."

I didn't think so. It couldn't be harder than lying here and waiting for return. At least I'd be helping myself. I was exercising now, but there weren't many muscles to exercise—only those few in my left leg.

When I asked Joe how much longer he thought I'd have to stay in Southampton, he said four weeks. "Just as soon as the fusion has taken and they've got a bed for you at Rusk."

The waiting became interminable. Now that the danger was past and we thought I'd walk again, Mary finally began to let down. The tension of being constantly with me, of handling our financial affairs, of dealing with doctors, families, and friends was beginning to show. Her easy laughter didn't come often anymore. She looked tired and drawn and began to worry about details, especially money. Blue Cross and Blue Shield paid for my hospital and part, but only a small part, of the doctors' bills. We already owed five thousand dollars, and were told that the Rusk institute would cost about a thousand dollars a week and wasn't covered by Blue Cross.

I tried to assure her that it would be okay, that only we mattered, and that we had the rest of our lives to pay off our debts. I wasn't putting on an act either; I really wasn't concerned about money. I had touched bottom. But now I was on my way up again. I didn't know how far I could go, or how hard it would be to return to a somewhat normal life. But getting there was the only thing that mattered. I couldn't worry about things like money. I could always borrow from friends and family and pay it back when I was on my feet.

I persuaded Mary to spend more time at the beach and to nap. I was hardly ever alone. If she didn't come herself, she always made sure one of the family, hers or mine, was with me.

The physical therapist I had never gave me a real workout. So Mary and I began working together on the sly. I showed her how to give me the resistance exercises Joe had taught me. Every day we worked for half an hour. She resisted while I pushed and pulled my arms and wrists, left leg and ankle, against her weight. Each day I'd get a little stronger.

We'd work to the point of exhaustion. Lifting my leg nine or ten times gave me the same sense of mental and physical well-being that jogging a mile had before. I was again enjoying a physical existence. I was no longer just an object people did things for and to. I began to get a better image of myself, and when I exercised I fought off the boredom and depression.

One day I suddenly wiggled the toes of my right foot. Then I lost the connection, and for two days I couldn't move them at all. I began to lose confidence and even doubted that I'd ever moved them. But Joe said it was possible that I'd only temporarily lost contact with the nerves, and in time would be able to move the foot again. I spent all my spare time concentrating on those toes, trying to find the nerve circuitry to the muscle that could make them move. Slowly I found the nerves and began to wiggle the toes on command. But I soon realized that that was all I could do with the right foot.

I was worried but tried not to show it to Mary. Then one day she picked up my right leg and bent it at the knee. I began pushing it out, the way I had the left leg, and it suddenly straightened. I had to ask to be sure. "Did my leg straighten out?"

"Yes," she said.

"Did I do it?"

"You must have. I didn't."

I wanted to try it again immediately to make sure I had done it. I couldn't feel the actual movement, but I was able to straighten the leg again. When Joe came in on rounds he began playing with my left leg. Then he picked up the right. "Wiggle the toes," he ordered.

"Forget that," I said. "Pick up the leg and bend it at the knee —one hand on my heel and one behind my knee."

He did what I said.

"Watch," I said, and straightened out my leg. Joe got a funny look on his face. He then tried other things with my right leg. All of a sudden I had movement in the ankle and calf. "It's there, Joe. I can feel it."

"Thanks for telling me," he said, as he kept working my legs. Then he told me to move my fingers, but I couldn't. There was nothing there. "I can't believe they're not going to come back soon," he mumbled. "It looks as if you might get it all back."

I realized that was an incredible statement for him to make, but it didn't really excite me. I was now so used to waiting. Also, my hands were last on my personal priority list. I was already teaching myself to pinch by manipulating my wrist. And even if there was no return in my hands, Joe could transfer tendons from my elbows or wrist to my fingers, giving me at least partial use of my hands. What I cared most about now was my legs.

I wondered about my leg. Had the nerves just suddenly healed or had they been there for some time without my knowing it? Were there other nerves in my body that were okay? Were there muscles that I could be using but wasn't? If so, would I have to rediscover every nerve circuit and relearn every movement? Everything I did, every move I made, would be a first time.

And that meant that I not only had to discover the correct circuitry to move a muscle, I also had to repeat the movement constantly to establish it firmly in my body's memory again. Often the muscles tired quickly, so that even though I'd established a pattern of movement, I couldn't always keep it up.

One morning my legs spasmed. I got a terrible cramp as they contorted. I asked Mike to call for a nurse to straighten my legs out. He rang but there was no response. I was getting more cramps, so I tried to move my legs myself. All of a sudden I did it. I lifted my left leg up in the air and bent it at the knee at the same time. Then I moved it to the left and straightened it out and set it down.

I got so excited that I practiced until my leg was too tired to move. If I can do this, I can walk, I thought, because all walking is is picking up your leg and putting it down. This new discovery made me even more anxious to get out of the hospital and into Rusk. I wanted to find out what muscles I did have. I couldn't know the extent of nerve damage to my abdomen, back, or internal organs while I was still in traction.

That night I ran my hands under the sheet and up along my body. It was the first time I had done that since the accident. I didn't know why I was doing it, but suddenly I realized that for the first time in six weeks I somehow had a sense of my entire body. I felt connected from head to toe. I felt like a person.

With the feeling of wholeness came another phenomenon. The spasticity that had occurred only in my feet and legs now racked and jerked my entire body. It seemed to begin in my lower back and extend downward through my hips and legs to my feet. I would be lying perfectly still and suddenly my whole body would spasm and the lower part of me would lift off the bed.

For the first time, being in traction became a nuisance. As long as I was paralyzed it didn't bother me, because I never felt motivated to move. Nor did I get uncomfortable if I lay in one position for a long time. But now, lying in traction, fastened by the tongs, became hell. I ached from being in one position, and I couldn't move to alleviate the pain. And worst of all, I now *wanted* to move, to get up, to go somewhere, and I couldn't.

It seemed an incredible paradox—the better I got, the worse I felt. I remembered a picture of Gulliver tied down by thousands of tiny ropes, arms at his sides, his neck stretched out. That's how trapped I felt.

I became more sensitive to the moods of the nurses and aides. One day there seemed to be something tense and frantic in the air. When my brother came to visit me he said he had just bumped into Joe and that there had been another accident.

"What happened?"

"Some guy, twenty-two, was tossed by a wave. He's paralyzed from the shoulders down."

When the nurses came in I asked them about the kid, but they knew nothing except that he was now on the operating table.

Around three in the morning a nurse told me that he was out of surgery but in pretty bad shape. He'd fractured the two vertebrae higher than the ones I'd broken. The higher the fracture and injury to the cord, the more extensive the damage and less likely the possibility of recovery.

Joe looked exhausted when he came in the next morning.

"How's the kid?" I asked.

"Pretty bad. He's going to need a lot of help. Maybe you can talk with him in a couple of weeks."

"Sure. I'd be happy to." But I wondered what I could tell him except to wait and see what happened.

I couldn't put him out of my mind. I'd never met him, but I was getting progressively more depressed about him. It was tough enough to be thirty-six and have to face paralysis, but to be in your early twenties and have that happen . . . I remembered how confused I'd been at that age, in school, worrying what to do with my life. I couldn't imagine having to face all those problems and be paralyzed on top of it.

Thinking about him made me think about myself. I thought I was getting better, and I thought I knew what I wanted out of life. But deep down I wasn't any more prepared to face paralysis than he was. And now that I was beginning to get movement, I wanted to cry, thinking of what was ahead of him.

Mary

I walked slowly down the hall. It was early afternoon, and everyone, including Jack, seemed to be dozing. I stopped outside the room of the young man who'd broken his neck. Everyone said he was in very bad shape, that he was paralyzed from his neck down and would never get better because he'd severed his cord. How did they know? I'd asked one of the nurses who had watched him being operated on. "You could see the spinal fluid spilling out all over the place," was the answer.

I stared into the room, which looked dark and airless. I wondered what he was thinking as he lay there motionless.

The next morning I saw the boy's mother in his room. She was a squat woman with a warm face; she looked Italian. I watched her fuss around her son, dusting and adjusting every object in the room. She had transformed the impersonal hospital room into "the sickroom" merely by her presence. I could see that she occasionally asked her son questions which he seemed to ignore.

One afternoon we literally bumped into each other in the tiny Surgical One kitchen, where I stored the fruit Jell-O Libbie made for Jack. The woman was cooking soup for her son. "He just won't eat anything," she said with gentle exasperation. "I've tried as many of his favorite things as I can . . . but he's so depressed." She paused. "I hear your husband is doing well. Maybe it will be the same with my boy."

"I hope so," I said.

A few days later she came over to me. She'd heard that Jack was going to the Rusk institute. "Oh, I hope Jimmy can go there . . . but Mrs. LaVinio says it's very expensive. I also heard the waiting list's very long and you need connections." She looked up at me and smiled. "I know your father's a doctor," she said, not quite pleading. "I thought maybe he could help us."

"His connection isn't direct," I said. "We'll certainly try to help, but—"

She patted my wrist. "I just heard they can do such amazing things with them. Can teach them how to feed and care for themselves."

The discussion was making me so uncomfortable that I felt sick. I walked back to Jack's room, trying to figure out why the short talk with her had upset me. I knew I had been cold-hearted, and I felt guilty. Why couldn't I even allow myself to feel sorry for her, to empathize, to help? Maybe it was because I couldn't think of Jack as a cripple.

The next morning when I came in, Jack looked unhappy. I knew that he'd been feeling better the night before.

"What's the matter?" I said. "You look terrible."

"That kid died last night. He's dead."

I was shocked. How could he be dead? "What happened?"

Jack stared straight ahead. "He must have developed pneumonia very quickly. They did a tracheotomy on him, but it got worse. Joe came in and tried to save him. But there was nothing anyone could do."

"I don't believe it," I said dumbly. "His mother seemed so optimistic yesterday. She asked me to help them get him into Rusk. Was she here when he died?"

"I don't know," Jack said.

"Maybe it's better . . . I don't know. They knew he'd severed his cord."

"How can it be better when a twenty-two-year-old kid dies like that?"

"I didn't mean that," I said defensively. "I just meant . . ."

"I'm sorry." Jack looked sympathetically at me. "It's just really upset me—more than I would have thought."

I was thinking about the mother. I wondered where she was. The boy's death seemed real only when I walked past his room and saw his empty bed.

Jack

Mike was improving rapidly. His doctors had finally removed the cast from his arm. With his arm out of traction, he was now able to get up out of bed and into a wheelchair for an hour or so each day.

I watched as he sat on the edge of the bed, apprehensive and dizzy. Janet would help lift him onto his feet, where he'd stand briefly and then pirouette into the chair. He was much stronger than I was, yet the struggle into the chair was tremendous, and he got very dizzy the first few times he tried to get up. I wondered how it would be for me.

Scotty, a night nurse, told me of a paraplegic they'd had in Southampton several years before. He said that when this guy got to Rusk, he had a great deal of difficulty adjusting to the place. One day they just dumped him onto the floor in a room with nothing but his wheelchair and told him that he'd have to stay there unless he could lift himself into the chair.

I didn't know if the story was true. But I did know that the Rusk institute was tough. Howard Rusk was an old army doctor, who was supposed to run the place very much like an army hospital. Nobody was babied, and just as soon as possible you were forced to get dressed and up into a wheelchair to begin exercises. I was afraid of what I might find out about myself when I got there. Would my back support me? Could I walk without braces? How whole would I be?

But the Rusk institute was supposed to be the best and, in spite of my fears, I was ready to get out of Southampton and to start rehabilitation. Janet LaVinio, the head nurse, also thought I was ready. But for some reason Joe kept putting off the decision. At first, right after the operation, he said it would be four weeks, but now two weeks were up and he'd still said nothing about when I might leave, even though he knew how anxious I was to get back to New York.

The days dragged as we waited. I was bored and getting irritable. I wanted more than anything else to get out, to get up and be with Mary, to have a family, to go back to work.

Friends asked me if I thought about living my life differently now. To my amazement, I realized that I didn't want to do anything differently; I just wanted to get back to where I was. I knew people tried to make trade-offs, like "Please, God, just let me walk and I'll be a better person." But I didn't believe it would work, and even if it did, I knew I could never live up to my end of the bargain. So I'd lose either way.

But others were praying for me. Janet told me she said daily prayers for me. And one morning a priest came in to visit Mike. He was short, wore glasses, and, though he looked about my age, was almost completely bald. He had to go around me to get to Mike, so he stopped to say hello and ask what had happened to me. I told him. Before he left, he asked if I'd mind his saying a prayer for me. I didn't mind, and he made the sign of the cross and prayed for my recovery in the name of the Father, the Son, and the Holy Spirit. A few days later when he came in, he said, "What religion are you?" I told him I was a Jewish atheist.

"Impossible," he said. "You can't be Jewish and an atheist." We argued religion for a while, and before he left he asked again if he could say a prayer for me. I said, "Please," and he began to pray, "In the name of Abraham and Isaac . . ."

The priest stopped by often after that. It didn't seem to bother him or Janet that I didn't believe in God. I realized that if their faith was the source of their strength, I was too grateful for that to care where it came from. I looked forward to their visits and prayers as much as I welcomed the warmth of friends who either visited or took the time to write me.

We must have gotten between five and ten letters a day, and on weekends the room was always crowded with friends. I wondered what effect I'd had on the lives of people who wrote to me. A friend of Mary's said, "Your friends become spectators in a situation like this, but that shouldn't disqualify them from cheer-

210

ing you on." A woman from the office whom I hardly knew sent me cards every week. I tried to remember if I'd ever been particularly nice to her. In a way it was like being at one's own funeral and hearing the eulogy and praise of all those who knew and cared for you.

Mary

The beaches emptied after Labor Day, the first Monday in September. Long Island belonged once again to the locals and to a few hangers-on.

Janet LaVinio had been urging Jack to get started with his rehabilitation as soon as possible, but Joe was more conservative. "Just want to make sure that fusion is taking," he said. We'd received word from the Rusk institute that a bed would be ready about September 10, and my family was already making plans to leave Southampton.

Libbie had wanted to stay until we left, but we convinced her that she was needed more in Los Angeles, where Lou had been alone for a month. There was a tearful good-by, mixed with relief on both sides. We were all going home.

I WAITED a moment outside Jack's open door. Clive stood near him and poured a glob of white lotion on his back. I watched his huge, strong hands work the liquid into Jack's back, slowly and evenly. Then Clive rubbed lotion into Jack's legs, which were so thin that I was sure Clive could have wrapped his whole hand around the thigh. I watched him lift Jack's leg and bend it at the knee, gently bouncing it back and forth toward Jack's back. The muscle was so tight that I could see it twitch under the smooth skin of Jack's knee.

"Got to keep those muscles loose," Clive said. "Okay, Jack. You bring that leg up without me."

The hamstring muscle began to strain like the taut string of a bow. Clive looked on patiently, excitement and real pride filling his eyes. Jack's leg started to fall to one side.

"Come on, you can do it. Just keep it comin'," Clive said.

Jack struggled silently to keep the leg from falling. Once past the halfway mark, he was all right. I thought I saw the muscles in his lower back begin to share the leg's weight. The leg swayed but stayed at a right angle, the toes pointing toward the ceiling. It seemed so little, but I felt tremendously excited.

I came into the room. "I can do a new trick," Jack said proudly.

"I know. I saw it. It's fabulous." I bent down and kissed his shoulder, still slippery and sweet with body lotion.

With me in the room, Clive was immediately more formal. In a way, I wished I'd stayed outside longer. There was a bond of love and unarticulated loyalty between them, the kind of friendship I imagine men share fighting a war together.

"Guess I'd better get you over on your back," Clive said, as he placed the sheepskins on Jack's back. Then he easily lifted and placed the frame on top of the sheepskins, quickly strapped Jack in tight, and turned the whole contraption over without the slightest bump or jolt.

Jack let his left leg hang over the edge of the bed. "Watch this, Mary," he said, and began to swing the leg back and forth, building up momentum. Then, with one big heave and a sigh, he lifted it up onto the bed.

"When did you discover you could do that?" I asked.

"I've been working on it," Jack said. "I've started to try it with the right, but it's still too weak."

"Let me see it again." As I watched, I realized I'd never seen him move so dramatically. Whenever I spoke to Joe or asked him questions, I always saw how far Jack still had to go, and I always felt dispirited. Joe could never tell me simply what I wanted to hear—that Jack would walk.

"We still don't know if he has back muscles or how strong his hips are," was Joe's guarded professional response.

But watching Jack now, I didn't think about all the muscles he might not have. When I helped him do his exercises and felt him push against my arm, I felt real pressure, the twinges and jerks of muscles. His legs were alive, as though they'd never lain on those clean, white hospital sheets like deadwood.

I took real pride in Jack's physical accomplishments and liked him to show off for friends. I didn't realize that part of my motivation was to *prove* to the world that *my* man wasn't a cripple. For, as anxious as I was to leave Southampton, I was also scared about resuming a life in New York. Showing people what Jack could do was a way of warning them, warning myself, of the difficulties that lay ahead and of our desire to conquer them.

Jack

The harder I pushed Joe to set a firm date, the more stubborn he seemed to get. Finally he told me I could be moved the Monday after Labor Day. I panicked a little. What if I wasn't really ready to be moved?

I should have been laughing at myself. For three weeks I had pushed Joe to commit himself to a date and let me out of the hospital. Now that he had set the date, I was scared *he* was making a mistake. But I couldn't laugh; I was too scared.

It was Friday, three days before I was to be moved to Rusk. Joe held a small screwdriver in his hand. "This is the day," he said. "How'd you like to sit up?" He began unscrewing the toggle bolts in my head. I didn't feel any pain. One side came loose, then the other. I sensed rather than felt that the weights, too, had been removed.

"Don't move," Joe ordered. "Don't move your head."

Janet handed him the neck brace that I had been fitted for two weeks earlier. Joe slowly and very slightly lifted my head and slid part of the brace behind my neck. Then he gently laid my head back and fitted the front part under my chin and strapped the back and front together.

"How does that feel?" he asked.

"Okay, I guess. Maybe a little loose."

He made a couple of adjustments. "How about now?"

"Better."

I still hadn't lifted my head. But I could tell that with my chin held high and the back of my head supported and pushed a bit forward, my movement would be limited.

"Okay," Joe said, "get him into a bed."

There was some scurrying while nurses went searching for an empty bed. Clive pushed my frame into the hall and placed it near the regular hospital bed. There was a brief conference about how to transfer me. Then Clive and three nurses grabbed the sheepskins on one side while Joe held my head, and they pulled me, sheepskins and all, onto the bed.

I felt funny in the bed. It was so soft after nine weeks in the frame, and I was so used to being forced to stare at the ceiling that I hadn't moved a muscle.

"Smile," Joe said. "You're out of traction." Everyone stood

213

around me and grinned proudly. Then they wheeled me back inside the room. Joe pulled up the sides of the criblike bed so I wouldn't roll off.

"Can I sit up? Roll over?"

"Anything. Just take it easy."

"Does Mary know?"

"No." Janet smiled.

I gingerly tried to roll onto my left side, but the neck brace was awkward, and without wrenching myself over, I didn't have enough strength to do it. So I reached out my left arm and grabbed a bar on the raised side of the bed; slowly I pulled myself over onto my left side and rested my head on the pillow. I looked up and found myself staring directly into Mike's eyes. For what was probably ten seconds but seemed like ten minutes, we silently stared at each other as if we were trying to be sure we were really the same two people who had shared that room for nine weeks. We were like blind men who could suddenly see.

I broke the silence first. "God. Are you thin!"

"You look worse," Mike said. "We both look like we just came out of a Japanese prison camp."

We laughed together, but I was shocked. If I looked worse than Mike, I was in poorer shape than I'd imagined. Suddenly I realized I hadn't seen my own face since the accident. I felt frail and weak, like a wounded animal in that crib of a bed. I asked Mike to ring for Janet.

"How much do you think I weigh?" I asked her.

She looked at my body, put her arm underneath my hips and lifted me just a little.

"Maybe a hundred and twenty-five," she said.

"I don't believe it. I couldn't have lost forty pounds."

"Well, maybe you weigh a hundred and thirty," she said, trying to make me feel better.

"Janet, let me try to sit up."

"Okay. But not too far. We don't want you passing out."

She went to the end of the bed and slowly began to crank me up. I tensed, expecting to feel dizzy or nauseated. At about a thirty-degree angle, she stopped.

I was more reclining than sitting, but it felt good to be "up." The neck brace weighed heavily on me and didn't seem to fit quite right, but I hardly noticed it as I looked around at the room

214

I'd never really seen. From my new vantage point, it seemed even smaller and dingier than I'd thought it was. I could now see the bright sunlight through the window, and without too much trouble I could imagine being out in the sun, lazing in the sand, or jogging along the beach. I tortured myself with those memories until Mary came in.

I was struck again by how thin and tired she looked. Her face was drawn, and most of her tan was gone. But she still looked lovely to me. Her face lit up as she practically ran into the room to hug me. I grinned. "Baby. It's so nice to see you at eye level again."

Mary

"The tongs. They took the tongs out," I said, looking straight and level and incredulously into Jack's eyes.

"Well, what do you think?"

"I think . . . I can't believe you're actually sitting up without those meat hooks in your head."

Jack was smiling and opened his arms to embrace me. He was wearing a neck brace and was so thin that he looked lost in the regular-size bed.

"It's okay, doll, I won't break," he said, as I leaned forward and gingerly hugged him.

I felt as though I were hugging a young boy. I could feel his bones. His chest was narrow, almost concave.

"I'm skin and bones, aren't I?" Jack said. "They let me look in the mirror and I hardly recognized myself."

I burst into tears, overwhelmed by this strange new physical closeness. I was sitting near Jack on the bed, feeling his body near mine for the first time in two months, and I was both happy and horrified.

"It's not that bad, is it?" Jack said, laughing, smoothing my hair with his tightly fisted hand.

I tried to bury my head in his shoulder, but the neck brace got in the way. Then I took a deep breath and smiled back at him. "I'm just not used to seeing you face-to-face, that's all. It's so good not to have to look down at you. I'll be all right. Just give me a few minutes to get used to you." I got up and walked around the bed to see him from all sides. "I guess you *are* pretty

215

skinny," I said. "You look like the ninety-eight-pound weakling who gets sand kicked in his face."

Mike started to laugh, and soon we were all laughing.

I LAY AWAKE listening to the chirps and creaks of the country. I saw Jack's long, thin, pale face—not the face of memories, not even the face I'd grown accustomed to staring down at for nine weeks. I hadn't realized how much weight he'd lost. When he was flat on his back he'd looked fatter, maybe because his weight spread him out a little.

I thought about Jack's description of the silent moment when he and Mike first looked at each other. And then it really hit me that these two men who'd been sharing their room and their lives so intimately had never seen each other face-to-face.

"I thought I really looked bad," Mike had said. "Then I got a look at him and I felt a little better."

There had been a hysterical quality to the laughing and joking, a need to overcome the shock of seeing Jack without being solemn. But now, lying alone, I was haunted by his thin face and sunken eyes. He looked terrible, really emaciated; admitting that to myself made me feel guilty and afraid.

I wanted to run back to him right away. I wanted to get used to him so I could feel attracted to him again. That's what was upsetting me. I wasn't attracted to this shrunken-looking man. I closed my eyes tightly.

"Oh, please, let everything be okay," I prayed out loud. "Let everything be happy and normal again." And then I reiterated my ritual list of wishes, the way most people count sheep, and tried to fall asleep.

Jack

Mary and her mother arrived early with a box of little gifts for the hospital staff. We were going back to New York. As usual Clive fed, bathed, shaved me, and brushed my teeth. But this was the last time. It felt like graduation day.

Joe had come in earlier to say good-by. "Good luck and come back to see us. I think you're going to be okay," he said as he left the room.

"Thanks, Joe. Thanks for everything."

216

Now the room was packed with nurses and aides who had come to say good-by. Some had even come in on their day off. There was lots of kissing and hugging as all of us nervously killed time, waiting for the ambulance to arrive.

"I told you he'd get out of this place before me," I heard Mike say.

"What do you expect?" one of the nurses quipped. "We can't lose both our dreamboats at the same time."

"Break it up," Janet LaVinio said as she sailed into the room. "Time for some nursing." She pulled the sheet up, exposing my right buttock, and swiftly gave me a shot. "You're going to need a little morphine," she said. "It's a long drive in a neck brace. This will relax you." Then she turned on her heel. "Doesn't anyone have any work to do around here? Mrs. DiMaggio needs her bedpan emptied, and it's time for Mr. Simpson's pills."

The staff started to respond, but they all took their time leaving the room, everyone coming up to say good-by. "Stay in touch," they said. "We want to see you on your feet."

Janet came back with two ambulance men. I was a little nervous, but she supervised their moving me from the bed to a rolling stretcher. As they wheeled me out of the room, Janet tucked the rough gray ambulance blanket around my legs and waist. She smoothed my hair and ran her fingers around the neck brace to make sure I was comfortable. Her touch was a mother's touch. I glanced up and saw that Mary's mother was watching. There were tears in her eyes.

As they wheeled me down the hall, I could hear Mike complaining about the injustice of being left behind. Janet carried the pole with the bag attached to the catheter, and Clive helped Mary with our belongings. Outdoors, Janet gave me a kiss good-by. Her eyes were smiling but moist. I looked up, saw the sky and breathed deeply, and then smiled up at Mary. Clive stood around awkwardly watching me. For the first time in nine weeks there was nothing for him to do. I grabbed his hand just before they lifted me into the ambulance.

"I'll miss you, Clive. Thank you."

He looked at me, and finally he just wished me luck. Mary kissed him good-by and then climbed into the ambulance with me. They closed the doors, and as we pulled away from the hospital, I tried to wave to Clive.

217

I HAD BEEN at the Rusk institute for two weeks when I got return in the thumb and forefinger of my left hand. Shortly afterward I could also move the fingers of my right hand. Three months later, just before Christmas, Mary met me in my room at Rusk. I'd been waiting for her. We were going home. She carried my bag, and we walked out together. I was using aluminium crutches, like the kid in the polio charity poster.

For the next five months I attended Rusk in the mornings and went to work in the afternoons. Slowly I got stronger; sex, bowel, and bladder control became more normal.

A year after the accident I quit Rusk altogether, threw away the crutches, and started to get around on a cane. I joined an exercise class and had hopes of a slow but almost total recovery.

Jack and Mary

On September 26, 1971, one year and two months after the accident, we were married. On June 26, 1973, we had a beautiful baby girl. Her name is Sarah.

Jack and Mary Willis

Today, Mary and Jack Willis exude a strength and happiness which they believe is partly the result of the accident that temporarily blighted their lives. "We learned," says Mary, "that the most important thing is to take each day as it comes, drinking up everything you can. You just don't know what is going to happen tomorrow.

"The most painful time for both of us was Jack's stay at the Institute of Rehabilitation Medicine in New York. In Southampton Hospital his rate of improvement, once he got a hint of return, had been dramatic—movement in a toe, a hamstring . . . hope. But the second he got to the institute everything changed."

Only there did Jack fully realize how much he had lost: he would have to relearn every bodily function. "My progress was frustrating," he recalls. "Days went by without any improvement. Also, I was the only ambulatory patient on my floor, and I felt guilty knowing that none of the others would ever walk again."

By Christmas, Jack was convinced that for his own emotional well-being he had to get back to work, even though his doctors were not sure he was ready. Each morning he would go down to the institute for physical therapy, then uptown to his office at Channel 13. Often he was exhausted to the point of nausea. But he persevered.

Jack is now a producer at CBS Television, Mary a freelance writer. Together they have written several successful TV dramas. Jack exercises every day, and has achieved an almost complete recovery. But what matters most to both of them is the joy they find in their little family. They have two daughters now. Tate is three and Sarah, now six, is already big enough to have made up her mind that what she wants to be in life is a dancer.

Shadow of the Moon

A condensation of the book
by M. M. Kaye

TITLE-PAGE AND DRAWINGS BY NEVILLE DEAR

WATERCOLOURS FROM
THE AUTHOR'S COLLECTION

Published by Allen Lane

"There was a ball at the Lunjore Residency that night to celebrate Queen Victoria's birthday. The band stood smartly to attention, their dark faces creased with concentration. *God save our gracious Queen* . . . the familiar tune, the National Anthem of an alien race, blared out through the open windows across the dark parade ground.
'Two more days to go,' thought Captain Alex Randall, remembering Ameera's warning.
But there were no more days. Only hours . . ."

In *Shadow of the Moon*, M. M. Kaye vividly recreates all the passion and splendour of Victorian India, and the horrors of the Mutiny that so savagely engulfed it. And against this background she tells a tumultuous story of bravery, devotion, and enduring love.

Part One

The Shadow Before

"*WINTER*! Whoever heard of such a name? Do pray be sensible, my dear Marcos. Think how it will sound. Winter de los Aguilares—you cannot call the poor mite anything so absurd."

"She will be christened Winter," insisted the distraught young father. "Sabrina wished it."

"Winter!" repeated kindly Lady Barton. "Poor Sabrina must have been out of her mind."

But Sabrina—poor pretty Sabrina—dying in childbirth in the merciless heat of an Indian May, had not been out of her mind. She had been thinking of the snow and dark December woods of Hertfordshire, where she had been brought up: of her grandfather's great house at Ware . . . .

IN THE YEAR 1837, at the age of twenty-one, Sabrina Grantham, the orphaned granddaughter of the fifth Earl of Ware, had travelled to India in the care of her uncle and aunt, Sir Ebenezer and Lady Barton. There she had met and fallen in love with Marcos de los Aguilares.

Marcos was dark-haired and romantically handsome, the son of a wealthy and eccentric Spanish nobleman, the Conde de los Aguilares, who had visited India with his wife on his early travels and never left it. The rich, barbaric kingdom of Oudh had become his home, and on the outskirts of Lucknow, surrounded by groves of orange and lemon trees, the Conde had built himself a house, a vast Spanish castella, the Casa de los Pavos Reales, the House of

223

the Peacocks. It was here, in its cool white halls, that the two young people met and fell in love.

The year of 1838 dawned over Oudh in a blaze of saffron-yellow light, and for Marcos and Sabrina it was filled with sunshine and happiness. But the year was to darken swiftly, for in the first week of February Marcos's mother died and the old Conde himself, stricken with years and grief, took to his bed and did not rise from it again. Three days later his body lay beside that of his wife in the Casa's marble mausoleum.

The Indian winter, however, soon gave way to the warmer days of spring, and Marcos and Sabrina were married. Sabrina wore the wedding dress that had belonged to Marcos's mother. Her ring, too, had been the old lady's. But this was not a sad thing. Rather it gave her a sense of timelessness, and of life's continuity.

The following April Marcos was forced to ride away south on business concerning his estates. Not wanting to leave Sabrina alone, he sent her to stay in the care of his sister, Juanita, who had married one of the princes of Oudh and lived in the Gulab Mahal, a little pink stucco palace in a corner of Lucknow. With his departure, despite her deep affection for Juanita, Sabrina's shining world of beauty and contentment shattered. She was pregnant now, and she missed her husband with an intensity that grew rather than diminished as the stifling days of summer wore on.

Unlike the Casa de los Pavos Reales, the "Rose Palace" was full of noise, and the rooms with their painted and carved walls were stiflingly hot. Immediately in front of Sabrina's room there stood a mosque, its bulb-like dome crowned by an iron horned moon, the symbol of Islam. The sun rose directly behind it and every dawn Sabrina would see it silhouetted against the saffron sky. As the sun rose, it cast the curved shadow of that horned moon across the floor of her room.

That shadow came to symbolize for Sabrina the fear and loneliness of those long days. No longer did India enchant her. She knew now the grinding heat, and was aware of the filthy streets and squalid hovels lurking below the minarets and gilded domes of the palaces. She was aware, too, of being alone in an alien country, surrounded by people of an alien race . . . .

And then, one terrible day, news came that Marcos had contracted cholera. Sabrina had only one thought. She must go to him. She ran towards the stairs, fell . . . fell into a hot spinning darkness that reached up and engulfed her.

Her daughter was born a few hours later, and the dying Sabrina, looking at the tiny, white-skinned creature, called her Winter.

MARCOS DID NOT die of the cholera. He recovered and returned home, but by that time Sabrina had been two weeks in her grave. To stay at the Casa was suddenly intolerable. Marcos yearned for work, and there was always work in the army. So he obtained a commission in the army of the East India Company, which now controlled the whole of Oudh. He placed his tiny daughter in the care of his sister Juanita and the prince. Already a wet-nurse, Hamida, a strong and healthy slave-woman, had been engaged to feed the child.

Winter grew and thrived in the pink stucco palace, her playmate Juanita's daughter, Ameera, a year and a half her senior. Ameera was her father's child, with golden skin, and sloe eyes, and hair as black as jet. Winter, as well, had inherited *her* father's dark good looks. She would lie in the room that had been her mother's, her eyes on the colourful walls where formalized trees and flowers were moulded in high relief. And as soon as she could crawl she would spend hours running her small hands over the flower and bird designs, her especial favourite, a parrot with a wise expression and an upraised claw. As she grew older she would talk to him as if he were a friend, speaking to him in his own language, the language of the palace, which she was never to forget.

WHEN MARCOS DIED fighting in Afghanistan, Winter, now the Condesa de los Aguilares, but only eight and a half years old, was sent home to Ware. The old earl, her great-grandfather, crippled by years and gout, greeted her but distantly. So, too, did his heir, her Cousin Huntly and his forbidding wife, Lady Julia.

After the colourful life of the Gulab Mahal, the gloomy rooms and Victorian discipline of Ware, coupled with bitter pangs of homesickness, reduced the child to a state of dumb misery. She was tiny, small-boned, unappealing. Her dark velvet-brown eyes, the sun-warmed ivory of her skin, and her rippling blue-black hair, were pronounced foreign and ugly by Lady Julia, who possessed a jealous nature and did not relish the appearance of a rival to her own adored small daughter, Sybella. She resented also the tiny Condesa's sonorous Spanish title.

Winter was eleven years old and a lonely child, driven in upon herself by the circumstances of this new life, when Conway Barton, Commissioner of Lunjore in India, came on a visit to Ware. He was a nephew of Sir Ebenezer and Lady Barton who had originally taken Winter's mother to India.

Conway was at that time in his thirty-seventh year and still a personable enough figure of a man, powerfully built, blond and blue-eyed, with the sun-tanned skin of one newly arrived from the East. Ambitious and not too scrupulous, the idea occurred to him that this sallow and unprepossessing child, with her great estates, would one day make a most eligible wife for an ambitious man. He was only thirty-six. He could afford to wait a few years. He therefore talked to her, flattered her, and she thought him wonderful.

The earl, old and tired, and anxious to safeguard his ward's future, failed to mark the signs of weakness and dissipation in Conway's face, and took a fancy to him also. This admirable young man, who was so sensible and whom Winter herself was so fond of, was surely a right and proper person to care for her.

No formal engagement was entered into, but the earl's solicitors called at Ware and drew up various legal documents, her great-grandfather signing on Winter's behalf.

On the day he left, Conway slipped an unpretentious little ring onto Winter's finger. "It is only a token," he said. "One day, when you are grown up, I shall put another one there. The brightest diamond I can find for you in all India." He patted her on the head and rode away, well satisfied with himself.

THE YEARS that followed dragged by very slowly for Winter and as they passed, her memory of Conway became romanticized. One day he would come riding up the long oak avenue with the sun glittering on his blond head, and would carry her away, back to the lovely land of her birth where, like the princess in the fairy tale, she would live happily ever after . . . .

It was not until the summer of 1855, when Winter was sixteen, that Lady Julia awoke to the fact that the ugly Anglo-Spanish duckling had turned into a swan.

Julia gave a party for her daughter, Sybella. A summer dance.

Ware was filled with young ladies of title and eligible gentlemen of quality and wealth. Julia had every reason to be proud of Sybella but Winter had a success also, and Julia was not slow to note how men turned to look at her again and yet again.

Lord Carlyon, handsome, wealthy, bored—thirty-five and still a bachelor—had inquired who the beautiful creature in white might be.

"You mean Winter?" demanded Julia, astonished.

"Winter! But how perfect! She is so cool and mysterious. And yet—" He laughed on an odd note. "So this is the plain cousin from the East. I have heard of her. Pray introduce me."

But his confident approach and suavely experienced manner made no impression on the young Condesa Winter de los Aguilares. She dismissed him with a cool grace that was an entirely new and salutary experience to Lord Carlyon, and an unpleasant one.

But he had by no means been the only man to comment on her unusual style of looks, and the dark, expressive eyes. Lady Julia, coldly angry, decided there was only one thing to be done. Conway Barton must come home and marry the girl. She would be seventeen in the spring and old enough to be married. And the old earl, who knew his doctors held out small hopes of his surviving for another year, agreed with her.

MEANWHILE, CONWAY BARTON was still occupying the post of Commissioner of Lunjore, a district bordering on Oudh. He had expected to be promoted before now, but indulgence had begun to take its toll and his work had deteriorated with his figure.

Fortune had been kind to him in that it had sent him as an assistant Captain Alex Randall, a brilliant soldier and one of those younger officers who had perforce become administrators—some of them the best administrators the world has ever known. Randall was content to do the work and let his chief take the credit: an arrangement that suited Conway perfectly.

The earl's letter frightened him. Now fat and middle-aged, he dared not go to England. To go would mean to lose the fortune he had come to look upon as his own. The girl must come out and marry him in India. Once let her arrive in Lunjore, alone and without friends, and the marriage could be hurried through before she had time for thought. It would be easy.

He wrote to Ware, pleading pressure of work. Winter must come to him. And Alex Randall, about to go on leave, could take the letter and escort the bride back to Lunjore in the following year. Who better to be trusted than his personal assistant . . . ?

ALEX HAD NOT taken to his chief. Neither to his sallow, puffy features, nor to his nicotine-stained moustache, nor to his bumbling ineptitude. Reluctantly now he accepted the unusual commission . . . but with certain inward reservations. There were two alternatives before him. On the one hand, he was asked to convey a gently nurtured woman to an unknown land and hand her over to the care of a drunkard and a libertine. On the other hand, were he to warn Lord Ware of these aspects of the affair, he would be betraying the trust of his superior officer, and stand guilty of disloyalty.

In the event neither alternative was possible. The earl died five days before Alex Randall's arrival at Ware. By then, however, a third possibility had occurred to Alex. India was in a state of serious unrest: surely that alone might prevent the girl's journey? But the new earl and his wife blandly ignored his inconvenient attempts to inform them of the situation's dangers. Such views, in their opinion, were faint-hearted and alarmist.

They were careful, also, during the remainder of his short stay, before returning to London to complete his leave, not to permit him a moment alone with the young Condesa.

On his final evening at Ware, therefore, Alex reluctantly gave her the small sealed packet entrusted to him by the Commissioner. She broke the seal. The firelight gleamed on an enormous emerald in a setting of Indian gold, and Alex, recognizing it, was unprepared for the shock of anger and disgust it aroused in him. He had seen that stone before, many times. Three years ago it had adorned the hand of a member of a princely house, by name Rao Kishan Prasad. Alex knew a good deal about Kishan Prasad. There were odd whispers about him, and the subsequent appearance of that ring in the possession of the Commissioner had caused Alex to wonder just what piece of bribery the fabulous stone represented. It had been flaunted thereafter by an Indian dancing girl, who was the Commissioner's latest favourite at the Residency.

Lady Ware's eyes widened with astonishment at the ring's barbaric splendour, but to Winter it was as though a small chill wind had momentarily breathed upon her. Conway's promise to give her the brightest diamond in all India—he had forgotten it! But then she reproached herself. He had remembered her, and sent her a jewel of great beauty and price.

WHEN, ON HIS last morning at Ware, Alex's conscience prompted him to make one final attempt to prevent her journey to India, he contrived therefore "accidentally" to come upon her out riding in the park. He found Winter in no mood to be put off lightly. She demanded plain speaking of him.

He cleared his throat. "I do not wish to offend your ears with matters that cannot be within your comprehension," he said awkwardly. "However, if you will have it, your betrothed is no fit husband for any young and decently bred woman. He—"

Savagely Winter cut her riding whip across his face. Did she not know Conway? Did she not know him to be great-hearted, the soul of chivalry? A man who surely would have scorned thus to speak against another behind his back?

A thin trickle of blood ran down Alex's chin. Suddenly and unexpectedly he laughed. "I see I have misjudged you," he said. "You may well be a match for him after all."

Bright colour flamed into the girl's face. She brought the whip down again, this time on her horse, and galloped away down the avenue into the morning mist.

FIRM IN THE BELIEF that he would receive no further communication from Ware, Alex was surprised and annoyed by the arrival in London, some three months later, of a letter from Lady Ware. A passage had been procured, she wrote, for Winter on the *Sirius*, sailing on the twenty-first of June. Mr. Barton would meet his betrothed in Calcutta and the marriage would take place immediately. She would be travelling in the company of a Mrs. Abuthnot who, with her two daughters, was proceeding to India to rejoin her husband who commanded a regiment of Bengal Infantry at Delhi. The ladies would be pleased to avail themselves of Captain Randall's protection and assistance on the voyage.

Captain Randall scowled at the letter and tossed it into the waste-paper basket, mentally consigning all women to the same receptacle. He had, anyway, other things to think of. The news from India was not good.

Part Two

Followers of Kali

FLO MAYNARD

CHAPTER 1

Mrs. ABUTHNOT was kind, stout and talkative. Lottie and Sophie Abuthnot, in contrast, were slim and silent. Sophie, the younger by two years, shared a cabin with her mother, while eighteen-year-old Lottie was to share an adjoining one with Winter.

The rain that had been falling as they drove to the docks gave place to blustering gusts of wind that whipped the water of the Thames Estuary to a white froth. Lottie, Sophie and Mrs. Abuthnot retired to their berths while the ship was still in sight of Sheerness, but Winter returned to the deck to watch the coast of England fade into the wet greyness of that June evening.

It had been raining, thought Winter, on that long-ago day when, cold, wet and shuddering with seasickness, she had landed at Southampton. She had not been nine years old; and now she was seventeen and sailing away again, sailing back home, for she felt India to be far more her home than England could ever be. She'd spoken the tongue of Oudh before she spoke her own. She spoke it still . . . . Sailing away to be married and to live happily ever after.

The ship rolled and pitched and Winter began to feel distinctly uneasy. Soon it was impossible to do anything but cling to the rail, wet, chilled, and racked with nausea. She did not hear the footsteps behind her, she was beyond caring. She only knew that arms were around her, holding her, and that she need no longer cling to the rail. Someone lifted her easily, and a man's voice with a hint of a laugh in it said: "I suppose this is included in the duties of a courier?" And then she was being carried down to her cabin.

She was aware of the cabin door being thrown open, and above the creaking pandemonium of the ship she heard the moans of Lottie Abuthnot. Winter buried her face against the man's shoulder. She heard him say, "Good God!" in tones of half-humorous resignation, and then he closed the door on Lottie's woe and turned away.

A moment or two later he laid her down and Winter opened her eyes and found herself looking up into Captain Randall's face. He appeared to be amused, and she closed them again, and pressing a hand over her mouth managed with an enormous effort to say: "Please go away. I—I fear I am about to be very unwell."

"I've seen worse things," remarked Captain Randall philosophically, reaching for a basin. And presently it ceased to matter to Winter whether he went or stayed.

It was morning when she awoke, a cold wet morning. The small cabin rose and fell alarmingly before Winter's eyes and she shuddered and closed them again quickly. Presently, struck by a sudden thought, she opened them once more. She was in a strange cabin. Captain Randall's, of course!

Winter lay still, remembering the details of yesterday's collapse with horrified dismay. She had a distinct recollection of him holding her head over a basin. He had laid her back on the pillows and washed her face in cold water, removed her spray-sodden cloak and bonnet and forced brandy down her throat with a competence and a total lack of embarrassment that surprised her.

Winter did not realize that the life of a political officer in the India of that day called for a great degree of proficiency in dealing with the unexpected. A young woman in the throes of seasickness was nothing so unusual. Winter could only be surprised that he had not also thought fit to remove her dress. She moved cautiously, and discovered that he had in fact done so. The voluminous folds of her grey batiste travelling dress and the whalebone hoops of her crinoline were flung over a chair-back, and the blankets that had been drawn up over her concealed only petticoats and pantalettes. Further investigation revealed the horrifying fact that Captain Randall had unlaced her stays.

The indignity of this discovery impelled her to sit upright, but it proved an unwise move. The cabin swam unpleasantly before her eyes. Someone rapped on the door and it opened to disclose Captain Randall himself, looking, thought Winter resentfully, almost offensively well. He encountered her hostile gaze, and smiled. It was a disconcertingly pleasant smile.

"I've brought you some food," he said. "It's only hot soup and biscuits."

Winter glanced at it and shuddered. The soup in the thick china mug slopped over the rim onto the tray. "Go away!" she said. "Take it away and go away!"

Alex sat down on the edge of the berth. "If you intend to go on being seasick, you will find it is far better to have something to be sick with," he remarked prosaically. And then, she did not quite

233

know how it happened, he was holding her against his shoulder and feeding her with soup and dry biscuits as if she were a sick child.

The soup was hot and sustaining, and she managed to swallow a fair proportion of the biscuits, and felt considerably better. She considered the matter and came to the conclusion that Captain Randall's point of view was a practical one. A dimple broke the smooth curve of her grave young cheek and she smiled.

It was the first time that Alex had seen her smile. He sat looking down at her, no longer seeing her as a forlorn child, but as a young woman. The small, heart-shaped face was unusually pale, and the shadows under the great dark eyes made them appear even larger. The crumpled whiteness of petticoat and corset cover served to turn her bare arms and shoulders to a warm shade of ivory, and the loosened hair glinted with blue lights in the cold greyness of the cabin.

Alex had a sudden and disturbing vision of the moist, unsteady hands of the Commissioner of Lunjore sliding over those smooth ivory shoulders, and his face hardened. He stood up abruptly and, retrieving the tray, said brusquely: "The captain appears to think that we shall run out of this bad weather by sunset. You had better stay where you are for today at least. I have this cabin to myself as far as Gibraltar."

"But—what about you?" asked Winter hesitantly.

"I can manage," said Captain Randall briefly.

Winter did not see him again for some time. It was a steward who knocked at her door with a tray of food at midday, and towards the late afternoon she felt sufficiently recovered to resume her dress and find her way to her own cabin.

FOUR DAYS LATER the *Sirius* finally ran into sunshine and blue seas, and even Mrs. Abuthnot was able to appear on deck. Captain Randall presented himself to them then, but remained discreetly aloof.

Their fellow passengers included several other ladies, in addition to officers of all ranks—most of them returning to India from leave —and a pleasant-mannered Indian who spoke excellent English and was accompanied by several dark-skinned servants.

Kishan Prasad was an entertaining conversationalist and was soon on good terms with the majority of his fellow passengers.

"Who is he?" Mrs. Abuthnot inquired of the ship's captain one day.

"No one of any special importance, ma'am. He is merely a wealthy Indian who has been visiting Europe. Doing a grand tour of the continent, I imagine."

"One wonders what he made of it," remarked Mrs. Abuthnot. "Our great cities must cause such visitors the greatest amazement! Lottie, dear, pray move under the awning. The sun is so strong, and freckles are *so* unbecoming!"

"Yes, Mamma," murmured Lottie dutifully, her eyes under their soft lashes busy with one particular member of a party of gay young officers lounging on the deck rail. Freckles might be considered unbecoming in a young lady, thought Lottie, but on a man they could be strangely endearing.

Lieutenant Edward English was a large young man who possessed a generous supply of freckles, red hair and charm. He also possessed a susceptible heart, upon which Lottie's fairness and fragility had made an instant impression. He had lost no time in making her acquaintance, but Mrs. Abuthnot had no intention of allowing any young man to fix his interest with her daughter at such an early stage of the voyage. There was plenty of time—and plenty of other men on board. So she continued, for the moment, to keep Lieutenant English at a safe distance.

As for her charge, the young Condesa de los Aguilares, although Mrs. Abuthnot herself could see little to admire in the girl's unusual beauty—so sallow, and with such very black hair that she feared such colouring would be misunderstood in the East—there were on board a great many others, principally male, who were only too ready to make themselves agreeable to her.

There was, indeed, only one gentleman who appeared to be wholly uninterested in her. Captain Randall had not addressed more than a dozen words to her since her emergence from her cabin. Mrs. Abuthnot came to the conclusion that he was deliberately avoiding her.

Winter herself, remembering that this was the man who had dared speak against Conway, found his avoidance completely understandable. She felt, nevertheless, a vague and irrational resentment. He was slim and deeply tanned and undeniably good-looking. He might at least speak to her! After all, had he not been deputed to look to her comfort and safety?

THE LONG, HOT, monotonous days passed slowly enough for Winter, but to Lottie Abuthnot and Edward English they were all too brief.

The voyage had been less than half over when Lieutenant English approached Mrs. Abuthnot to ask her permission, in the absence of Lottie's father, to pay his addresses to her daughter. He was so earnest and engaging—and, she had discovered, of such good family—that Mrs. Abuthnot's heart quite melted. Although the last word must of course lie with Lottie's father, she ended by assuring him that if Lottie reciprocated his feelings, she herself would not stand in the way of her daughter's ultimate happiness.

For Alex Randall, however, as for Winter, the days were long and tedious. He took to brooding over the presence on board of the Indian, Kishan Prasad, and the thoughts that must go on behind his bland, inscrutable mask. Alex knew him well. He was a member of one of the great families of Rohilkhand. An exceedingly clever man, and an embittered one—always a dangerous combination. He had been to one of the better Indian colleges and taken top honours in all English subjects. He studied engineering and passed out as the senior student of his year. But because he was not a European he was only nominated to the humble rank of *jemadar* in the army of the East India Company, where he was actually subordinate to a European sergeant—a stupid man who lost no chance to insult him. Kishan Prasad had found the position intolerable and resigned. The Company had lost a good man when it allowed that to happen—and gained a dangerous enemy.

Prasad had then gone on a tour of Europe a year ago: a strange thing for a man of his caste to have done. He had been to the Crimea, where he had seen the British fail in the assault on the Redan at Sebastopol, and met Russian agents. And now he was returning to his own country . . . It should never have been allowed for any Indian to see the British army in the Crimea. Or, having seen it, to return and tell of what he had seen . . . .

Alex thought then of Winter. The girl had probably never thought of India as a conquered country. She imagined herself to be coming home, and the realization that many of its inhabitants could hate all those of British blood with a savage and implacable hatred would be like a blow in the face to a trusting child. He had warned Julia and Huntly Ware that this was no time to send any young woman out to India, but they would not listen. None of them would . . . .

And yet, when the day came, towards the end of the voyage, that Kishan Prasad fell overboard, it was Alex who went after him.

ALEX had not known that it was Kishan Prasad who had fallen. Perhaps if he had done so it might have altered the course of a great many lives.

The day had been hot and still. The sea was blue with the intense midnight blue of the Indian Ocean, and so clear that floating squadrons of jellyfish far below the surface appeared as though embedded like bubbles in blue glass.

It was after four o'clock and the decks were comparatively deserted while the passengers changed for dinner. Lottie had come up early, intending to meet her Edward, and she had seen Kishan Prasad standing on the paddle-box gazing out to sea. Even as she looked, the ship rolled suddenly in the trough of an unexpectedly deep swell and Kishan Prasad, taken off guard, slipped and slid under the rail. Lottie shrieked and ran.

Two of the lascars, together with a ship's officer and a Major Rattray, had also seen him fall, and they ran along the deck shouting. Major Rattray heaved two deckchairs overboard into the creaming wake, where they were joined almost immediately by an empty hen-coop thrown by one of the lascars.

"*Man overboard!*" bellowed Major Rattray and the ship's officer.

Alex, who had been lying asleep in a patch of shade, woke at Lottie's shriek. Racing aft along the deck, he caught a brief glimpse of a despairing hand that reached up from the foaming wake.

"It's all right, m'dear fellow!" panted Major Rattray. "Only one of those blacks. He'll be drowned by now—they can't swim."

A flash of pure rage hit Alex; he kicked off his shoes, and in the next second he had vaulted over the rail and dropped feet first. The rush of the sea closed over his head, sucking him down. Just when it felt as though his lungs must burst, he was shot to the surface like a cork. He gulped deep draughts of air and struck out strongly.

It was, he presumed, one of Kishan Prasad's servants who had fallen overboard, for had it been a member of the crew Major Rattray would have said "a lascar". He saw a struggling shape

237

ahead and then it disappeared. Alex filled his lungs and dived. The man struggled feebly, and for a minute that seemed endless they sank together through the blue water; then Alex got a grip on him, kicked strongly, and they were rising once more.

Even then he did not realize who it was. He swam with the half-drowned man towards the heavy wooden hen-coop that was lifting to the swell not twenty yards away. After several fruitless efforts he managed to heave his limp burden face downwards across the coop and hold him there.

The swell that had been barely perceptible from the decks of the *Sirius* was very different when viewed from the level of the sea itself—in the troughs the sea appeared to be empty and the *Sirius* to have vanished. It would take a long time for them to heave-to and circle back, thought Alex. They would lower a boat as soon as possible but it would be a long wait. The distant ship vanished as the burdened hen-coop slid once more into the glassy trough of a swell, and the Indian coughed, retched, and moved feebly.

"Lie still, fool!" said Alex in the vernacular, and the man obeyed, but presently he turned his head and Alex saw for the first time who it was he had rescued.

The two men stared at each other and Alex was conscious of a twisting wrench at the pit of his stomach: a futile, sick anger against fate and himself. He, fool that he was, had risked his neck to save the man whom he regarded as among Britain's most dangerous enemies in India.

The salt seawater was bitter in Alex's mouth. Kishan Prasad looked into his face and laughed in complete comprehension. "Whom did you think you had saved—*Sahib?*" The appellation was nearer an insult than a term of respect. "One of your own kind? The General Sahib, belike?"

"No," said Alex, treading water. "I had thought it was one of your *nauker-log* (servants)."

He saw the flare of astonishment in the dark eyes.

"My *servant?*"

"Yes," said Alex shortly. "Had I known it was you—"

"You would have let me drown," finished Kishan Prasad, fighting for each breath.

"Yes," said Alex bluntly. "Do not talk. You will tire yourself and the boat will not reach us for some time yet."

Kishan Prasad was silent for a long while. The slow swell lifted them up lazily so that at intervals they could see the distant ship and the small speck that was a boat rowing towards them. Then it would slide them down into a long blue-black hollow and the ship would vanish. Until finally, when Alex felt he had lost all powers of movement, he was aware, as though through thick fog, of noise and shouting voices; then hands were pulling at him, dragging him up over the boat's gunwale, and Kishan Prasad after him. Absurdly sleepy, knowing only the miraculous fact that they were both alive, he collapsed gasping among the feet of the boat's crew . . . .

The following morning, after twelve hours of uninterrupted sleep, he awoke early, feeling refreshed but still confused. Pulling on a pair of trousers he went up on deck. The sea lay colourless in the dawn light. Leaning against the stem rail, idly watching the long white track of the wake, he heard footsteps behind him and turned to see Kishan Prasad. The two men looked at each other for a moment in silence.

Kishan Prasad said slowly: "I wish to thank you—"

"You have nothing to thank me for," interrupted Alex curtly.

"You mean because had you known that it was I you would not have saved me? Is that indeed the truth? Because in the past I have intrigued against your race—you would not have gone after me?"

"No. I would not have lifted a hand to save you."

Kishan Prasad bowed gravely. He said: "It is for that reason I come to thank you. Not for what you did for me, but for what you would have done for one of my servants. There are few who would have risked their lives for a black man and the servant of a black man."

"Are you by any chance telling me," said Alex brusquely, "that you have suffered a change of heart because I risked my neck to pull you out of the sea?"

Kishan Prasad smiled and shook his head. "Alas, no. I have suffered no change of heart. In the name of my country and my gods I will do all in my power to pull down your Company's Raj."

"And I," said Alex, "will do all in my power to get you hanged."

"It is good," said Kishan Prasad. "We understand one another, and we are not children."

He pulled off a small ring that he wore on his right hand and held it out. It was a trumpery thing, fashioned out of twisted silver set with three small rubies. He said: "Will you wear this for me? As a token of my gratitude? It is a talisman that may one day save you from much evil. If ever the day comes, as I pray it will, that the Company's Raj falls and its charter for robbery is destroyed, look on that ring and remember Kishan Prasad. For in that day—who knows—it may repay my debt."

Alex hesitated. Then, taking the ring, he slid it onto the little finger of his right hand. He said slowly: "I will wear this because it is the gift of a brave man."

Kishan Prasad bowed gravely, and walked away.

CHAPTER 2

"WE SHALL be in Calcutta tomorrow," thought Winter. "Only one more day—and then I shall see Conway!" Only one more day, and the long waiting that had begun six years ago at Ware would be over at last . . . .

The *Sirius* was anchored off the Sandheads awaiting the first light and the turn of the tide when, with the pilot on board, she would begin the slow journey up the Hooghly to Calcutta. Winter turned restlessly in her narrow berth and wondered if Conway would meet her at the mouth of the river or at Diamond Harbour. He might take a launch down the river and board the ship on her way up. Mrs. Abuthnot seemed to think it possible.

Dawn came. Winter had completed her packing on the previous afternoon, except for the last few necessities, for she could not bear to waste a moment of that wonderful day. Every foot of the way was wonderful and exciting to the girl who had passed there as a child so many years ago. The tangled thickets of bamboo, the thatch-roofed huts surrounded by groves of tamarind, jackfruit and custard apple, the low brown land. While every approaching craft might be the one that carried Conway . . . .

The sky was ablaze with sunset by the time the *Sirius* reached the Calcutta anchorage, and boat after boat shot out from the shore bringing relatives and friends of those on board or coming to fetch the passengers away. Winter stood apart from the turmoil, her eyes anxiously scanning every boat, but none contained a familiar face. She had seen Kishan Prasad leave, loaded with garlands of flowers and tinsel, and had watched a tubby little gentleman come aboard, who proved to be Colonel Abuthnot. After the introductions had been performed, he and his family retired to shed happy tears of reunion in the privacy of their cabin.

The crowded decks emptied; boat after boat drew away laden with passengers for the shore. At last someone touched Winter on the arm and she turned quickly. But it was only Alex Randall. He said bluntly: "He has not been able to come. My orderly has brought letters from Lunjore."

Winter took the proffered packet with a hand that was not quite steady. She could feel tears prickling behind her eyelids, and she forced them back. If she let Alex Randall see tears in her eyes she would never forgive herself. Or him. She said: "Thank you," in a small cold voice, and Alex turned away abruptly.

Winter caught at the rail to steady herself. The disappointment was almost too bitter to be borne. After a moment she broke the seal of the letter.

Pressure of work, wrote Conway, had made it impossible for him to meet her in Calcutta. A great disappointment, but duty must come first. As the Abuthnots were proceeding to Delhi, she had better remain under their protection and travel as far as Delhi with them. He himself would have occasion to go there in the near future and would be staying with the Commissioner. They could be married in Delhi and spend their honeymoon in that historic city . . . .

The writing was straggling and uneven. He must have been very tired when he wrote it, thought Winter with loving compassion. How like him to put duty before personal happiness. Dear, dear Conway!

Fighting her selfish disappointment, she walked down to the Abuthnots' cabin with her face calm and composed.

Mrs. Abuthnot was sympathetic. Dear Alex had already informed her of the state of affairs. So disappointing! But then life in India was sadly full of such disappointments. One had to learn to bear them. Naturally dear Winter would remain in her care. It would be delightful to have her—although she feared that it would mean some delay, as Colonel Abuthnot had official business to transact in Calcutta which might keep them here for a little time. He had arranged for them to stay with a friend—Mr. Shadwell, a Calcutta merchant . . . .

The Shadwells' house proved to be a palatial two-storeyed mansion on Garden Reach surrounded by lawns and gardens, and to Winter's relief she was given a room to herself, a huge, high-ceilinged room with whitewashed walls and windows opening onto a deep veranda. An Indian room. A room utterly unlike an English bedroom. The tight band tied about her heart relaxed.

She walked slowly out onto the veranda. Below her a lawn sloped down between thick groves of trees to where the river ran gold in the brief twilight. The sky was a wash of clear pale green and the evening air was full of sounds: half-forgotten and yet wholly familiar sounds. Conches blaring in a temple; a distant throb of drums; peacocks calling and a jackal pack wailing; the barking of pariah dogs; all the many noises of an Indian city. The air smelt of sun-baked dust and cow-dung fires; of wood smoke, marigolds and jasmine; the rank scent of the river. A myriad fireflies spangled the gathering dusk with glinting pin-points of light, while overhead a dark flight of fruit bats flapped silently across the garden.

Winter leaned on the broad veranda rail and drew a long, long breath of happiness. It did not matter any longer that Conway had been unable to come to Calcutta to meet her. She could wait. She had come home.

INCREDIBLE AS IT SEEMED, Lottie was to be married within a few weeks of their arrival.

There was a rumour in Calcutta of tension brewing between Great Britain and China, and Edward had received information that his regiment, who were Queen's and not Company's troops, might be sent to augment the British forces in China early in the New Year. In the light of this information he desired to get married as soon as possible, in Delhi.

Edward's arguments carried weight. Colonel Abuthnot withdrew all opposition, and the entire party repaired to the drawing room where Mr. Shadwell called for champagne.

It was at this point that a servant announced Captain Randall. Informed of the wedding plans he congratulated Lottie and Edward in a somewhat preoccupied voice, and announced that he had only called in order to make his *adieu*. He regretted that he could not delay his return to Lunjore any longer.

Winter spoke a few stiff words of thanks when he said goodbye to her, and a formal message of affection to be delivered to her future husband, to which Alex replied briefly that he was happy to have been of any assistance. He was quite obviously in a hurry, and having swallowed half a glass of champagne, shook hands with the assembled company and left. The rattle of his carriage wheels died away on the long drive, and Winter was disturbed to find that the sound brought her a sudden feeling of being alone and unprotected. Which was of course absurd, for was not Colonel Abuthnot here to take his place and see that she came to no harm?

Edward English left for Meerut on regimental business the following day, and Lottie thereafter found much comfort in planning her wedding, which was to take place late in October. Winter's stay in Calcutta was by no means spent in idleness either, for the kindly Shadwells arranged numerous entertainments for their guests, and cards of invitation for balls and assemblies, including a state ball at Government House, arrived at the house on Garden Reach in an apparently never-ending stream.

Calcutta, as the capital and headquarters of the Governor General and the council, and seat of the supreme government, had a reputation to keep up in the way of gaiety, and the state ball was a revelation to Lottie, Sophie and Winter, who had never attended such a function before.

Men in gorgeous dress uniforms—the pale blue and gold of the Light Cavalry, the canary yellow of Skinner's Horse, the green of the rifle companies and the scarlet of infantry regiments—vied with the shimmering silks and frothing tarlatans of feminine ball-gowns in richness of colour and glitter of gold lace.

Moving among them in more sober attire, crows among a flock of peacocks, were the rich Calcutta merchants—men such as Mr. Shadwell—or, distinguished by ribbons and orders, the members of the Governor General's council and high officers of the East India Company. Indian guests, many of them ablaze with jewels and wearing brightly coloured brocades and muslins, mingled with the company but did not dance.

As for the new Governor General, Lord Canning, he was having a troublesome time. A remarkably handsome man in his early forties, he had taken over the reins from the dynamic Dalhousie less than eight months previously, and had early discovered that his predecessor's confident prediction that all was well with India was unfounded.

The annexation of Oudh had been one of the last acts of Lord Dalhousie's reign, but the settling of the province had fallen to Lord Canning, and his appointment of a Mr. Coverley Jackson as chief commissioner of this newest of the Company's possessions had not proved a happy one. Oudh—the main recruiting ground for the Company's Sepoy Army—was in chaos. Grievances were not attended to. Half the younger officers didn't even know their own men. And there were dangerous ideas stirring among the sepoys.

Lord Canning watched his carefree guests waltzing in the ballroom of Government House with an abstracted eye, and as soon as was polite removed himself to an anteroom some distance away. His appearance was hailed by a tall handsome man with cold blue eyes and a marked air of fashion.

"You're looking fagged, Charles," remarked Lord Carlyon. "India don't appear to agree with you. Too many social functions and too much heat."

"And too much work," Lord Canning smiled. "You should try it, Arthur. It would at least have the charm of novelty."

"That is too bad of you, Charles," protested his lordship indolently. "I work like a demned nigger."

"You surprise me. At what, may I ask?"

"Keeping boredom at bay. And here I am flogging round the globe in proof of it!"

"Stay here awhile and try some real work instead," advised Lord Canning. "We can even use someone as ornamentally useless as yourself."

"Then you must be devilish hard up for hands, Charles!"

"We are. The annexation of Oudh has stretched our resources to the limit." The Governor General took Lord Carlyon's arm and moved back in the direction of the ballroom.

"What's on your Excellency's mind?" inquired Carlyon, his lazy-lidded eyes unexpectedly observant. "Do you think that there is going to be trouble?"

"No, of course not! Nothing wrong with the country. Some people enjoy croaking of doom. The effects of this prophecy, I suppose. It is quite astonishing how superstitious even the most level-headed can become."

"What prophecy?" inquired Carlyon, interested.

"Oh, it's an old tale now. It cropped up after Plassey. The Company's rule was to last for a hundred years after the battle that established it. And Plassey was fought in 1757."

"So the hundred years are up next year," commented Carlyon. "Very interesting. But surely you cannot take this seriously?"

"Naturally not!"

The Governor General looked down upon the crowded ballroom and spoke in an undertone that was barely audible above the chatter of voices. "But it would be of use to me if you were to decide to go on an extended tour of this country—in an entirely private capacity, of course; as a casual sightseer only—and give me your impressions. It is this question of Oudh. The ex-king is here in Calcutta, and he deafens me with his complaints as to the behaviour of our people in Lucknow. They are doing our reputation a great deal of harm and providing fuel for the malcontents." Canning paused, frowning.

Carlyon's languid gaze rested without interest on the dancers. He had no intention of prolonging his stay in the East. He intended to reach England by the New Year. The prospect of proceeding to Lucknow in order to test the accuracy of charges brought against the British administration of the newly acquired province by its deposed king did not appeal to him.

"You could not, of course, proceed direct from here," Lord Canning went on, "but were you to go first to Delhi and return via Lucknow, it would give the appearance of a sightseeing tour, and—"

He became aware that Carlyon had ceased to lounge and was gripping the balustrade and watching someone in the ballroom below.

"By Jove!" said Lord Carlyon under his breath. "It *is* the ugly duckling!" He turned to his host with an unwonted gleam of animation in his eyes. "Forgive me, Charles. I see an acquaintance

246

below. Perhaps we may continue this conversation at some other time." He descended a flower-decked staircase and was lost to view.

Lord Canning sighed and retreated to his study, leaving his wife to do the honours. He emerged in the grey dawn, when carriages were drawing away laden with yawning men, sleepy dowagers and excited, laughing girls, to find Carlyon escorting a stout matron in a crimson opera mantle across the hall and into a carriage with a display of affability that was most unusual in him.

"Who was that?" he inquired as Lord Carlyon made his way back across the hall.

"No one of interest. A Mrs. Abuthnot . . . . By the way, Charles," he added, "you will be interested to hear that I have decided to take your advice. I intend to extend my stay in India. I shall visit Delhi, and I may even return by way of Oudh."

CHAPTER 3

*A*LEX AND his orderly had been moving north for some days, in the company of a morose major on his way to rejoin his regiment at Benares. Now the major had left them to go his own way, and Alex and his servant rode alone.

"When there is work to do it is better to travel alone," said Niaz, his dark face blandly expressionless.

Alex nodded. He had had few opportunities for private conversation with Niaz since he had landed.

Niaz was a Punjabi Mussulman who had served in the same regiment of cavalry as Alex Randall, and fought at his side at Moodkee and later at Ferozeshah. Alex's horse had been hamstrung at Moodkee by a Sikh, and Niaz by some miracle of horsemanship had dragged Alex clear as the horse fell. Four days later, at Ferozeshah, Alex had repaid the debt when Niaz had fallen with a bullet through his shoulder, and Alex, his own horse killed, bestrode the wounded man and fought above him in the storming of the Sikh entrenchments. Since then, Niaz had attached himself to Alex as orderly and body servant, and when Alex had been removed on special duty he had managed to gain permission for Niaz to accompany him. Niaz had been granted extended leave during the past year, and Alex had left certain specific and unofficial instructions that he had no doubt at all that Niaz would have carried out. The evening was warm and very still. Alex rode relaxed and silent through fields where maize and sugarcane had been planted, the level plain stretching away to the far horizon. He knew that Niaz would speak when he wished to.

At last Niaz said reflectively: "I did as thou asked. I took my leave and went to visit my relatives in Oudh and Rohilkhand and Jhansi, and from them I heard much. And when that was done I went north and then south, listening to much talk in the twilight and hearing many things in the bazaars and by the way."

He was silent for a moment, then he said: "Thou wert right, my brother. There is devil's work afoot, and this time it is not a plague that will break out in one spot only and may thereby be kept from others. This time the infection is carried to all men. Hindu and Mussulman, unbelievers and the Elect of God, plot together in fear and hatred, and the word goes up and down the land."

"And what is that word?"

"That the feringhis (foreigners) are few and their councils are divided, and that the men of the north, the *Russ-log* (Russians), have made a great slaughter of their armies so that there are none left to come to the aid of those in Hind. It runs from regiment to regiment. Men on pilgrimage to the shrines of Kashi and Haramukh; Mussulman, Brahmin, Sikh and Jain; the woman who draws water at the well and the man who drives a plough—all or any of them may be a carrier of the word. They spill the powder, and when the train is laid it will need but a spark to ignite it."

They were riding now beside a *jheel*, a shallow stretch of water fringed with rushes. Alex stared out across it. The rose and saffron of the sunset had faded, leaving the sky awash with clear green light. "Has that spark been found?" he asked.

"Not yet. Those who plot seek for one. It wants only that to set the land alight. But it must be something that touches Mussulman and Hindu alike, for if one rise without the other, the Company, few and weak as they have become, may still triumph. So they search diligently, and wait."

"Yes," said Alex reflectively, "but a thing that will make Mussulman, Hindu and Sikh sink their differences and unite against us will not be easy to find." He shifted restlessly in his saddle. The swift tropic twilight was gone and he could no longer see Niaz's face clearly. He said abruptly: "All this is talk. Have you proof?"

"*Proof!*" said Niaz, and laughed shortly. "Spoken like a sahib— *Sahib!*"—he gave that title the same scornful emphasis that Kishan Prasad had once done.

"Slave," said Alex gently, "were it not that thou art as my brother in all but blood, I would throw thee into the jheel for that word!"

Niaz flung up a hand in mock appeal. "Have mercy—Sahib!"

Alex leaned sideways, caught the upflung hand about the wrist and bent it backwards, and for a moment the two men wrestled silently.

"Is it to be the jheel, then?" inquired Alex.

"Nay, it is enough! Have mercy—brother."

"That is better," said Alex, releasing him.

Niaz rubbed his wrist and grinned. "At least thy sojourn in *Belait* (England) has not softened thee! But what is that gaud thou art wearing? A love token belike?"

"That—?" Alex looked down at the twisted silver ring with its three small red stones, and shook his head. "It was given me by a man whom I would have given much to see dead."

He told the tale and heard Niaz draw a short hissing breath between his teeth at the mention of that name. "Kishan Prasad!" said Niaz. "I have heard of that man. And if all that I have heard is true, it had been better that thou hadst cut off thy right hand rather than have given him his life. Nevertheless that bauble may yet help thee to this proof that thou hast demanded." He glanced uneasily over his shoulder and lowered his voice.

"I have learned that there is to be a meeting of certain men in a place near Khanwai that lies on the northern borders of Oudh. And I have had the thought that it would be well if we two learned what is afoot. It is set for a night but twelve days hence, when there is a fair at Khanwai. I have been to spy out the land. The place of meeting is a ruin; no more than a handful of stones and a broken wall which the jungle has swallowed. There is but one path to it, for the jungle grows thick behind it, and that path leads through a deep nullah where was once a gateway that has fallen. Only one man at a time can pass through, and each as they pass must say a word. That word I have."

Once again Niaz paused to peer into the gathering dusk, and in the silence they heard from somewhere far out across the darkening plains a jackal howling. Niaz's gaze returned to Alex. "Do we go to Khanwai?"

"Assuredly!" said Alex, and laughed. It was a laugh that men hear sometimes in the heat of battle or as the order is given for a cavalry charge. Niaz recognized it and his own laugh answered and echoed it.

TEN DAYS LATER an itinerant toy-seller, laden with crudely painted plaster trifles, trudged down the dusty road that led from Cawnpore into Oudh. He was of a cheerful disposition and soon attached himself to a party of jugglers who were proceeding to the fair at Khanwai, a village on the borders of Oudh.

From the opposite direction, a slim, wiry Pathan sitting astride a bony stallion and trailed by two sorry-looking hacks on a lead rein was also riding towards the fair. His dress and speech, and the hard, light-coloured eyes in the brown face, proclaimed him a son of the border tribe of the Usafzai, and he too was of a cheerful disposition, for he sang the songs of the border—the more questionable ones—as he rode.

He carried a long Pathan knife in his broad waist-belt and an antiquated but serviceable musket slung over his shoulder, and he took for preference the centre of the road. Alex had always been a believer in the old saying that it is darkest under the lamp.

Khanwai's fairground was surrounded by the booths of sweet-meat-sellers, toy-makers and hucksters, and there was plenty to entertain the idle: jugglers, acrobats, fire-eaters, snake-charmers, and fortune-tellers. And as night fell a troupe of firework-makers brightened the sky with a display of their wares. But as the fire-works flared, it might have been noted that sundry men were drifting away from the fairground to the dark barrier of jungle that backed onto the grazing grounds.

Alex, following, could see that there were men ahead and behind him, hurrying forward down the narrow track that finally descended a sandy slope into a dry nullah. To the left it appeared to be blocked by a fall of rock. There was a space between two huge slabs barely wide enough to allow one at a time to enter it, and behind it—Niaz had told him—lay a narrow, walled tunnel. Alex heard feet slither on the path behind him as another conspirator entered the nullah, and he set his teeth and walked between the rocks.

He had taken no more than four steps in the blackness when his outstretched hands brushed against rough stonework. And then he saw a glimpse of greyness and something touched his chest—an iron-bound lathi such as night-watchmen carry—and a voice almost in his ear whispered: "Give the word."

"*A white goat for Kali.*"

"Pass, brother." The lathi dropped and Alex moved on into the open air.

The darkness thinned, torchlight glowed through the undergrowth ahead, and presently the track ran out into a clearing before the ruins of a long-forgotten fort or palace.

The starlight and a half-moon, the flaming torches and the occasional flare of a rocket illuminated roofless walls and fallen pillars half-hidden by weeds and creepers. It seemed to Alex an odd spot to choose for a meeting of malcontents, except that though it lay less than half a mile from Khanwai and the beaten track, its presence would never have been suspected by the casual passer-by. The open space was crowded with shadowy figures and sibilant with whispering voices. At the far side, before the ruined entrance to a roofless hall, stood two men holding torches—country-made things of dried grass, branches and pitch. They stood as though waiting.

Presently there was a stir among the crowd as half a dozen men muffled in dark cloaks entered the clearing and came to a stop before the torch-bearers. They stood for a few moments talking in undertones, then walked between the torches and simply disappeared as though the ground itself had swallowed them up.

Men gasped and shrank back, then began to move forward slowly, and Alex realized suddenly that the torch-bearers stood either side of a shaft that descended into the ground. As he drew nearer he saw that the two men with the torches scrutinized the faces of all who went past them. A hand touched him in the press and he turned to see Niaz, the seller of toys.

"They will never let you pass. Try the ring!" The words were barely a breath against his ear and then the man had melted into the darkness.

Alex moved forward, a step at a time. He was conscious of a cold tingling sensation between his shoulder-blades. Would they let him

stand to one side and wait as others were waiting, or would they—? The light of the torches flared full in his face and his nerves tightened, but the hand he held out was steady.

The three small stones in Kishan Prasad's ring gleamed red. One of the men, bending forward to stare at it, muttered something that Alex did not catch, and salaamed low, and Alex walked between them and down a steep narrow flight of steps, drops of cold sweat on his forehead.

The entrance to the shaft was concealed by a huge flagstone drawn up with ropes. The walls of the shaft were smooth and dry, and the worn steps so steep and narrow that only one man at a time could descend them. When he reached the foot of the steps at last, he was standing in a vaulted chamber, the roof of which was supported by crude stone pillars, its only illumination a single brazier at the far end.

There seemed to be between thirty or forty men squatting on the stone floor between the pillars. Alex squatted down by one, Indian-fashion, keeping his back to the stone. As his eyes became accustomed to the dimness he saw that many of those present were sadhus—holy men of all sects and persuasions; not only Sikhs, but Mussulmans also; followers of the Prophet to whom all Hindus were unbelievers, crouching side by side with the worshippers of Shiva the destroyer, of Vishnu and Brahma and Ganesh of the Elephant Head, of many-armed Mother Kali, the drinker of blood, and of a hundred other gods. It was true, then. Mussulman and Hindu were prepared to unite against the men of the East India Company—against the white-faced foreign conquerors whose dominion had lasted for a hundred years. Alex shuddered. Nothing but a common cause and a common hatred could have brought about this weird gathering.

A man stood up at the far end of the chamber. Alex could not see his face, but the voice and dress told him much.

The man was a Mussulman and probably from Oudh. A tall man with a silver tongue; and the tale he told was the story of a conquered people—oppressed, cheated, robbed and exploited by the men from the west, from the land beyond the Black Water.

His voice rose and sank and the men before him swayed and groaned in unison. Even Alex, listening—Alex who knew just how much of that tale was truth and how much falsehood—found himself stirred to anger by that wild, bitter, sorrowful saga.

He did not know for how long the man spoke—he ended with an impassioned plea for unity: "They of the Company be few! A handful only, scattered up and down the land. We of Hind have risen against them many times, but the risings have always failed because we of this land were divided one against the other. It needs only this—that we hold together with one heart—and we are rid of them for ever. Let us put aside our differences and strike as one!"

He flung up his arms with a wild gesture and the crowd gasped and shrank back. But the spell had snapped for Alex, and sanity returned to him: and with it an icy sense of danger. If this man could sway others as he had swayed this bigoted, caste-ridden, creed-divided assembly tonight, he was more dangerous to the Company than any who had as yet risen against them.

Another man spoke. A Hindu. Then a sadhu. His message was more specific. Spread the word! Carry it into every town and every village. Tell every man to be ready; to procure arms and secrete them. To sharpen his sword, his axe or his knife and to tip his lathi with iron. The coming year was the Year of the Prophecy in which the Hundred Years of Subjection would be accomplished. Man, woman and child, the oppressor would be slain.

"Carry the word! Carry the word!" The hoarse, hysterical voice echoed uncannily under the vaulted stone. "See! Now we prepare a sign as in the old days, so that all men may know!"

A priest threw something on the brazier and the flame flared up. A second priest began a chant that was taken up by other voices. The light flickered up again, and the two priests moved about it, coming and going. A man squatting near the brazier began to beat on a small drum; the chant became a frenzied incantation, and Alex recognized it as a hymn to Kali.

"Kali! Kali! Oh, dreadful-toothed goddess! Devour, cut, destroy all the malignant—cut with an axe! Bind, bind, seize! Drink blood! Secure, secure! Salutation to Kali!"

A dense smoke whirled upward. From the shadows a priest returned, dragging something that struggled feebly. A sacrifice, of course, thought Alex. *"A white goat for Kali."*

He saw the light glint on the long blade of a knife, and a shudder swept back through the crowd. Alex was seized with a sudden sick horror, inexplicable and paralysing.

The smoke from the brazier faded and the flame leaped clear. The drum beat louder and the chant rose to a frenzy. The knife flashed and fell. There was a cry, shrill and high and almost instantly drowned in the last groaning howl of the crowd. But it had not been an animal's cry.

Alex stumbled to his feet and stood pressed against the stone of the pillar. He saw it was not the body of a white goat that lay on the slab below the flickering brazier, but the naked body of a child. A white child, a boy of no more than three or four years of age, his small body startlingly pale against the dark stone and the bright blood.

A blind, killing rage laid hold of Alex, momentarily. He fumbled for his pistol. Then sanity returned. There were more important things at stake than avenging the slaughter of a single child. The lives of other children and of countless men and women might hang upon his ability to leave that underground den alive.

He slid the pistol back into hiding and wiped the sweat out of his eyes. The horrible ritual of the sacrifice had drawn all eyes and no one was watching him. He sank down again onto his heels.

There was some ritual being performed with the fresh blood and flour on a platter. They were making a chuppatti: the daily bread of India. At last the platter was lifted off the fire and the priests of Kali broke up the cake.

"Let the token be sent forth!" howled the taller of them. "Let it go up and down the land. From the north to the south, from the east to the west!" He fell to the ground and writhed upon the stone floor as the second priest flung oil into the brazier and a crackling flame leaped upward to the roof, blazed furiously for a moment and died. The drum crashed and was still. The chanting ceased.

A cold voice spoke softly into the silence: "This that ye have witnessed shall be binding upon all; for were it known, there is not one here who would not hang at a rope's end for this night's work. In the eyes of the Company's government all who have seen it would be held guilty. It were well to remember this, lest any be tempted to speak unwisely."

The voice ceased, and presently man after man rose noiselessly and groped his way to the stair shaft to pass up it and away. Alex joined them.

The torch-bearers had gone and the square with its surrounding wall of jungle was shadowy under the starlight and the waning moon. Alex made his way down the black length of the nullah, and as he was climbing the goat track into the high grass at the edge of the plain a hand touched his arm and a voice whispered: "It is I, brother!"

"Back!" said Alex softly. He caught Niaz by the wrist and dragged him swiftly down beside the path as man after man hurried along the narrow goat track towards the village.

Niaz jerked at his sleeve and whispered: "Why do we wait? It is not good to linger here. Let us go."

"Hush," said Alex softly. "There is a debt to pay. When these have gone we go back. The priests will leave last, for there is work to do. They cannot leave the dead unburied."

"Has there been killing, then?"

"Yes. Quiet—here is another of them—"

At last the procession of shadowy figures ceased, and for a full ten minutes no one passed along the narrow path. Alex stood up with infinite caution. The night was silent and nothing moved.

"It is foolishness to go back into the tiger's lair having once escaped," said Niaz. "Forgo thy revenge and come away. There is more in this than one life."

"It was a child," said Alex. "An English child."

"Ah!" said Niaz. "Let us go back, then."

They crept back down the steep sandy slope that led into the nullah and the huge stone-paved courtyard. Moving from one clump of shadow to the next, they reached the shelter of the tree that straddled the entrance to the shaft.

The block of stone still leaned upright, and from the shaft itself came a dim glow of light and the approaching sound of a man's voice, faintly familiar and speaking in tones of cold rage.

". . . So all are endangered!"

"Nay, all are now bound one to another!" replied another voice, a shrill, hysterical voice. "None dare now betray us, for all are guilty of the blood. They will keep silence for their lives' sake. For such a sacrifice is necessary—yes, necessary."

"A goat!" snapped the first voice. "Had I known that aught else were planned—"

"*A white goat for Kali!*" interrupted the second speaker. "And now is the spell made doubly sure. A child of the Abominable Ones —the eaters of cattle, the defilers of caste!—a male child. May it be the first of many!" Two heads appeared above the hole in the paving. Niaz's muscles tensed involuntarily but Alex's fingers clamped down upon his arm and checked him.

"But to slaughter a defenceless babe in this fashion," said the first speaker, "is an abomination before gods and men!"

"Thou wouldst spare the young of the serpent? *Pho!* That is indeed folly! One such, if allowed to live, will one day sire many. They must be destroyed; leaf and branch, root and seed. Not one must be spared. Not one—*not one!*"

There was a brief silence and then the first speaker said shortly: "Well, it is done now and it cannot be undone. But though this may do well enough for the villages it will not serve for the sepoys. For them it must be something that strikes deeper and that touches every man. They are already as tinder, but there is as yet no spark. No matter; we will find it."

He turned and called down the shaft: "We go now. Close the stone when all is finished." The faint light from below brightened for a brief moment and the speaker's face showed clear. It was Kishan Prasad. The next moment the men by the stair shaft had vanished, and the night was silent again.

A full five minutes after the last faint rustle had died away, Alex crept forward, unsheathing his knife, and Niaz followed him. They crouched on either side of the tilted slab and waited. At last the light below was extinguished and presently feet groped on the stairs and a man's head lifted out of the black well of the stair shaft. Alex waited until his shoulders were clear of the shaft and then he took him tightly round the throat and lifted him clear with one savage heave.

"What is it? Hast thou fallen?" said a voice from the darkness

256

below, and a second head appeared. Niaz jerked the man up and backwards across the rim of the shaft and brought his head down upon the stone with a sharp sound like the cracking of an egg.

"This one at least will cut no more throats," said Niaz. "Is thine sped?"

"Yes," said Alex breathlessly, wiping the blood from his hands on the man's priestly robes.

They tumbled the bodies back into the shaft and sent the stone above it crashing into place. The noise of its fall awoke a hundred echoes from the ruined walls.

"Quick," gasped Niaz. "If there be any within earshot they may return."

They ran together across the courtyard and plunged into the blackness of the nullah, and ten minutes later they had reached the edge of the grazing grounds and the grove of trees where Alex had tethered the horses.

"Where now?" whispered Niaz.

"Lunjore." He looked down at his stained hands. For rage and revenge he had killed a man. Yet if the fear and hatred that men like Kishan Prasad were coaxing into flame were to flare into rebellion, a thousand men would die worse deaths. It must not happen. At all costs a rising must be prevented.

CHAPTER 4

*T*WO DAYS later, bathed, shaved, fed, and once more in his own clothes, Alex presented himself at the Residency.

Conway Barton was engaged with a visitor and sent out word asking Captain Randall to wait. Alex sat down in a veranda chair and stretched his legs out in front of him. After a time he heard the Commissioner's voice raised in affable farewell. Then an Indian came out through the split-cane curtain that hung over the living-room door. It was Kishan Prasad.

He came to a stop in front of Alex and bowed. Alex did not return the greeting. He looked at Kishan Prasad with eyes as cold and passionless as grey granite.

For a moment some of Kishan Prasad's assurance dropped from him. Then he recovered himself and his voice was smoothly urbane:

"Ah, Captain Randall! This is an unexpected pleasure. The Commissioner was telling me that he did not expect you back until next week."

"It was kind of you to come here," said Alex. "It will save me the trouble of sending an escort to bring you in to the gaol—for murder."

"Murder?" Kishan Prasad affected polite surprise.

"What else? *'This thing that ye have witnessed shall be binding upon all, for were it known there is not one who would not hang at a rope's end for this night's work,'*" quoted Alex in the vernacular. He saw Kishan Prasad's eyes widen, and said: "You should be more careful whom you admit to your meetings. I had heard many tales, but until two nights ago I had no proof. Now I have it."

Kishan Prasad sighed and after a moment he said very softly: "That killing was by no will of mine. I do not war on babes, and had I known what was planned I should have prevented it. As for the rest, I have told you before that I desire to pull down your Company's Raj. But you cannot hang me, for this proof that you have is no proof. It is only your word, and it will not be believed. A hundred witnesses can prove that I was elsewhere, and not at Khanwai two nights ago."

Alex said grimly: "I think you will find, Rao Sahib, that my word will be taken against a hundred thousand of your witnesses."

"Even when one of those witnesses is the Commissioner of Lunjore?" inquired Kishan Prasad softly.

Alex came to his feet. "That I will not believe!"

"But you will find that it is so. He does not know that he lies," said Kishan Prasad. "You see, there was a—a little party that night at the house of a mutual friend, and the Commissioner perhaps indulged too freely in perfumed brandy. He does not remember very much of what occurred and he is convinced that I also was present. So you see—"

Alex did see. Kishan Prasad had made full use of both Mr. Barton's drunkenness and his vanity. It must have been so easy. A prearranged party at the house of one of the more disreputable noblemen; drink and dancing girls, champagne laced with brandy and probably opium. A man—any man with a superficial resemblance to Kishan Prasad—and his name repeated until it was impressed upon a fuddled brain. Alex knew his chief only too well.

258

If the Commissioner had admitted seeing Kishan Prasad at such an affair he would never go back on such a statement, because to do so would be to admit instead that he had been drunk enough to be deceived, and at the house of a prominent Indian.

"They will say that you must have been mistaken," said Kishan Prasad softly. "As for this meeting you will tell them of, they will say it was a mere gathering of malcontents. Talk—but no more than talk." He lowered his voice: "You know you cannot win this fight. The Company is only a handful of men and its power is an illusion. I have seen the slaughter at Sebastopol and I know that your Queen has no more regiments to send." He smiled. "I am sorry that our blood makes us enemies. Perhaps in your next life it may be that you will be born a Hindu."

"Perhaps," said Alex, "when I have hanged you in this one."

"That too may come about," said Kishan Prasad. "But the time is not yet."

He saluted Alex with grave courtesy and turned from him into the bright sunlight of the garden.

And the days that followed bore out all that Kishan Prasad had said. Mr. Barton listened with entire incredulity to Alex's story. Alex had made a mistake—all niggers looked as like as two peas when in a crowd. The suggestion that he himself might have been mistaken drove him to blustering and apoplectic indignation. Such an assertion was absurd and insulting!

As for Alex's assertion that an English child had been murdered in cold blood, he could only suggest that Alex had been carried away by the—er—the unusual circumstances; the atmosphere, the fumes from the brazier he had spoken of, or the effects of fatigue. And if Alex took his advice he would refrain in future from play-acting in native dress and mixing himself up in such affairs. It did not consort well with the dignity of a Company's officer, and might lead to a deal of trouble.

The same opinion was expressed by Colonels Moulson, Packer and Gardener-Smith, commanding the three regiments of Native Infantry stationed at Lunjore. Colonel Moulson, who had taken particular pains to be offensive, had done his best to discredit the whole story. Neither did Colonel Gardener-Smith believe that dis-affection was rife in the country and still less that the army was affected. There had been rumours, of course—but then there were

259

always rumours. He too thought that Captain Randall must have been mistaken. Colonel Packer, an earnest Christian, appeared content to leave the entire matter in the hands of the Almighty, assisted by prayer.

The most that Alex could gain was permission to take six *sowars* and three British officers to see if any concrete evidence could be brought back of the murder that he professed to have witnessed. There had been a report of the disappearance of a child a week earlier, admitted Colonel Packer reluctantly. The three-year-old son of a private in a British regiment stationed in Cawnpore; and it was always possible, though hardly credible . . . .

Alex had ridden back to Khanwai with six troopers and three sceptical but enthusiastic officers. They had found exactly nothing. The stair shaft leading to the underground chamber was open to the sky and choked with fallen debris that had the appearance of being there for some considerable time. Ten paces within the jungle behind the ruined fort they uncovered a grave, but it contained only the rotting carcass of a white goat.

CHAPTER 5

*I*T WAS over six weeks since the Abuthnots had left Calcutta on the long journey northward to Delhi. A journey on which they had been accompanied, somewhat unexpectedly, by Lord Carlyon.

Lord Carlyon, having taken a fancy to visit the old Mogul capital of Delhi, had requested permission to avail himself of the pleasure of their company on what he must otherwise find to be a singularly dull journey. Such a pleasantly worded request had been impossible to refuse.

The majority of travellers were apt to find journeys in India insufferably tedious, but to Winter there was interest and enchantment in every mile of the way: in the sun-baked silence of the dusty roads and the cheerful tumult of the bazaars; in the little villages with creaking well-wheels; in the colourful temples; in the scream of peacocks at dusk and the cry of wild geese and cranes at dawn.

But there was one aspect of the journey which she did not find pleasant—the presence of Lord Carlyon. Winter had not been favourably impressed by Carlyon on the occasion of their first meeting at the summer ball at Ware, and although his manners towards her since their meeting in Calcutta had been outwardly unexceptional, his languid gaze had a way of resting on her with a look of insolent appraisal, as though she were a blood horse whose purchase he contemplated.

Carlyon had never previously been in the least interested in raw young ladies. But Winter de los Aguilares was not in any way like the general run of demurely blushing debutantes. Her unusual looks had attracted him sufficiently for him to pay her some attention, and he had been considerably taken aback by her reception of the compliment. To be put in his place by one so young and inexperienced had, by its very novelty, both piqued and intrigued him.

A girl with so sweetly seductive a figure would not, he was convinced, prove anything but an apt pupil in the art of love, and a journey of several weeks had seemed to offer endless opportunities for dalliance by the way.

But Winter kept close to Lottie or Sophie, and however carefully he manoeuvred he found it impossible to speak to her alone. He could not believe it! Winter remained as cool as her name and tantalizingly out of reach, and Lord Carlyon, angry, frustrated and piqued, ended by falling in love. Thus he was the only member of the party who was not inexpressibly relieved by the sight of the rose-red walls of Delhi.

The Abuthnots' bungalow was situated in the cantonments on the stony ridge some four miles outside the walled city, and Carlyon had no difficulty in obtaining an invitation to stay with them, although Mrs. Abuthnot, well aware of the situation, would have given much to get out of it. What a relief it would be to see Mr. Barton, who must have arrived by now and would be staying until the wedding with the Commissioner of Delhi. He would be sure to present himself at their bungalow on the very first evening. She did hope that he would allow dear Winter sufficient time to bathe and change her dress before making his appearance.

There were no less than seven letters from Edward English waiting for Lottie at the bungalow. But there was neither letter nor message for the Condesa de los Aguilares.

But of course there would be none, Winter thought, when within the hour she would see Conway in person. So she took a last anxious

261

look at herself in the looking-glass, wished yet again that she possessed Lottie's blue eyes and yellow curls, and crossing the hall went into the drawing room from where she could watch the gate and see Conway arrive. The servants were already laying dinner so it must be nearly five o'clock. Surely he would come soon! She heard someone enter the room behind her and close the door, and turned, expecting to see Mrs. Abuthnot. But it was not she who stood there. It was, astonishingly, Captain Randall.

"*Alex!*" She was not in the least aware that she had called him by his Christian name.

Alex bowed slightly: "Your servant, Condesa. I am charged with a message to you."

A sudden recollection of stories of risings and the murder of men in outlying districts drove the blood from Winter's face. "Conway! Has there been trouble in Lunjore? Is that what you have come to tell me? Is anything the matter with him? Is he ill?"

"Not as far as I know," said Alex in a completely expressionless voice.

"Then why are you here?"

"The Commissioner found himself unable to come to Delhi after all. He asked me to explain the matter to you and to arrange if possible for you to travel with me to Lunjore in two weeks' time, when I have completed the business here that the Commissioner wishes cleared up."

Winter sat down slowly, the apple-green flounces that had been intended to please Conway foaming about her. Alex looked down at the bent head and the small hands that were clasped together so tightly, and frowned; aware of a disturbing tug at his heart, and thinking again that India was really no place for such women, and that if there ever should be a rising on a serious scale they were going to be a devilish responsibility.

Winter, looking up at this point, caught that frown, and it brought back her courage and a sudden spark of anger. She rose, straight-backed, and said in a cool, composed voice: "It has been most kind of you to trouble yourself on my behalf. I hope you will not think me ungrateful. Did Mr. Barton not send a letter?"

"There was no time. The alteration in plan came at the last moment and I myself left at less than half an hour's notice," said Alex curtly. He considered it unnecessary to explain that the

262

Commissioner had been in no condition to stand upright, let alone write a legible line, when he had last seen him.

If the truth were known, Mr. Barton, faced with the journey to Delhi, had once more been attacked by his old fears—the same fears that had kept him from sailing to England to claim his bride. Supposing—just supposing—that she should not like what she saw of him? Might she not, supported by the Abuthnots, even go so far as to break off her engagement? He decided to play safe and cancel any idea of going to Delhi. He had celebrated this decision by getting exceedingly drunk, and was barely able, on the morning on which he had originally intended to set out, to do more than mumble a few directions to Captain Randall, the gist of which had been that Randall must go on his behalf, and see to that annexation business while he was there—he'd find the documents in the office files . . . .

Sadly, however, Alex's experience led him to believe that a description of this scene would only produce further misunderstandings, so he stayed silent.

LOTTIE WAS TO BE married at St. James's Church in Delhi on the twenty-sixth of the month, and preparation for the wedding kept the ladies of the household in a constant ferment over the mysteries of silks and muslins. There were also expeditions, picnics, parties and balls, and Lord Carlyon received a flattering amount of attention from the garrison, and was even asked to call upon the ragged old ghost who lived surrounded by a tatterdemalion court in the palace within the Red Fort of Delhi—Bahadur Shah, descendant of the House of Timur and last of the Moguls. But Winter remained as elusive as ever and Carlyon's exasperation mounted daily.

His temper was not improved by the frequent addition of a certain Captain Randall to the party, and he found that his first and instant dislike of the man increased with every sight of him. But Captain Randall was not an easy man to quarrel with. He appeared to be entirely uninterested in Lord Carlyon and his proceedings. Nor did he seem particularly interested in the social gaieties of the Delhi season, and Carlyon was frequently puzzled to know why he troubled to accept invitations to affairs that he so obviously found tedious.

Alex was finding it hard to explain this to himself. The business that was occupying him in Delhi on Barton's behalf consisted mainly of the collecting and checking of evidence in a contested case of accession of territory, and the bulk of the documentary evidence was being dealt with by the Company's clerks. He found himself with a fair amount of time on his hands, and the Abuthnots were pressing with their invitations; but he was still not entirely sure why he did not refuse them.

Was it only on account of that irksome feeling of responsibility that he could not rid himself of? Guilt, even? Because he was aware, without quite knowing why, that Winter was frightened and unhappy and that in some way his presence reassured her?

In this he was partly right. Winter had understood and forgiven Conway's failure to meet her at Calcutta but she could not help feeling that just this once he might have arranged things so that he could have left his desk for a few days to come for her. She was conscious of a return of that feeling of loneliness and insecurity that had been so familiar a part of her childhood.

Winter suspected that Captain Randall was inclined to regard her as a somewhat tiresome responsibility, but she could not help feeling grateful for his continued presence, if only because it protected her from Lord Carlyon's more than unwelcome attentions. When Alex was there she could forget about Carlyon and relax from the strain of being perpetually upon her guard.

That she was bent upon avoiding him and was not merely being coy was gradually borne in upon Carlyon, and he began to realize that vanity and self-assurance had led him into making a grave tactical error. At a ball therefore, when she could not avoid standing up with him for a waltz, he abased himself and begged for forgiveness for offending her on their first meeting at Ware. He had not intended to distress her, and he hoped that he might be honoured at least by her friendship. If he could at any time be of any service to her, his life was at her disposal.

She was touched by the humility of his apology, and could not help feeling that she had misjudged him, so she smiled at him shyly when they next met. She was, however, entirely ignorant of the feelings that had prompted his abasement.

Carlyon had apologized with no other motive than the hope that by doing so he might prevent the little Condesa from pressing for his removal from the Abuthnots' bungalow. He had every

264

intention of removing shortly, but he had made up his mind to take her with him. He wanted the girl. Wanted her more than he had ever thought it possible to want anything; and by God he would have her!

His plan was quite a simple one. Make his peace with Winter, and having made a few necessary arrangements, such as purchasing a suitable carriage and pair, carry her off and compromise her so that she would be glad to marry him. Barton might cause a little trouble at first, but the man was obviously only interested in her fortune, and Carlyon was sufficiently wealthy to apply a generous gold-plaster to any wounds he might receive.

AMONG THE various social engagements of the coming week, a moonlight picnic on the walls of Delhi had been arranged by the livelier spirits among the younger officers. There were clouds to the northeast of Delhi on the evening; a threatening bar of greyness that lay along the far horizon and caused Mrs. Abuthnot some anxiety. Alex, however, assured her that their presence merely indicated rain somewhere in the foothills, and that the picnic party stood in no danger of a wetting that night.

Carlyon, Winter and Alex rode to the picnic, while Mrs. Abuthnot and her daughters drove in their carriage. The ride had been a pleasant one, though a trifle dusty, and Carlyon had behaved in an exemplary manner, so that by the time they arrived at the Kashmir Gate, Winter was feeling quite in charity with him.

They rode in under the massive arch of the gate, left their horses to the care of the attendant syces and walked up the sloping stone ramp to the battlements. Alex stopped to speak to a *jemadar* of the guard, while Winter and Lord Carlyon continued on their way with the remainder of the party.

Winter kept close to Mrs. Abuthnot, for try as she would she could not bring herself to share in the universal high spirits. The iron band that had seemed to fasten itself about her heart when she had learned that Conway would not be coming to Delhi had only drawn tighter, in spite of the prevailing merriment. Once on the ramparts above the wide ditch that separated the walls of Delhi from the jungle greenery beyond, she listlessly accepted a plate of cold food. Lottie was seated on her left, and Mrs. Abuthnot's voluminous skirts effectively protected her right. Carlyon, she noticed, was some distance away, studiously devoting himself to the entertainment of young Sophie.

The moon was at the full, glinting pearly-white on the Jumna river below them. When the debris of the picnic had been cleared away, an officer possessed of impressive whiskers and moustache began playing a sentimental ballad on a guitar. The majority of the guests scattered along the ramparts, talking, laughing and admiring the view. Winter could see no sign of Alex. Sophie informed her that he had walked along the wall towards the Water Bastion.

"Winter, my love," said Mrs. Abuthnot, bearing down upon her accompanied by an unknown gentleman, "here is someone whom I am sure you must be pleased to meet. Only fancy! Mr. Carroll here passed through Lunjore less than a week ago and dined with Mr. Barton. So he can give you the latest news of him. Mr. Carroll, this is the lady who is shortly to marry Mr. Barton. The Condesa de los Aguilares."

Mr. Carroll, a large man with a red face, bowed over her hand, and in reply to her eager questions said that he had indeed seen the Commissioner the previous weekend. Mr. Barton had in fact been kind enough to urge him to stay on and keep him company, there being little to occupy him at present; but . . .

Mr. Carroll became aware of the amazement on the faces of Mrs. Abuthnot and the young Condesa, and stopped, disconcerted.

"But that is absurd!" said Mrs. Abuthnot. "Perhaps you did not know that we expected Mr. Barton in Delhi, but pressure of work did not permit him to leave Lunjore. You must be mistaken."

"Oh—er—yes," said Mr. Carroll unhappily. "I must have mis-understood. Yes, of course. I—"

Winter broke in upon his flounderings. "Mr. Carroll, please tell me. Why could not my—the Commissioner—come to Delhi? Is he —is he not well?"

Mr. Carroll, embarrassed and distressed, caught at the excuse. "Yes! Yes, I am afraid that is it. He—er—did not wish to distress you. Naturally wished to spare you anxiety. Most awkward, being taken ill at a time like this—felt it very keenly."

"But—but why did he not tell me?" said Winter, her hands gripped tightly together.

Mr. Carroll was visited by inspiration: "Would not mention it, of course, for fear that you would consider it your duty to proceed immediately to his side. Sickroom no place for a delicately nurtured lady. Fever, you know . . . ." Mr. Carroll had a momentary vision of the bloated face of the Commissioner of Lunjore, and improvised glibly: "A swelling fever. No, no, nothing serious, I assure you. Merely—er—disfiguring. Not catching. But no man of sensibility would wish to meet his betrothed looking so."

"Oh, the poor, dear man!" exclaimed Mrs. Abuthnot, touched. "How *well* I understand! How could he wish to allow you to see him in such a sad state? Perhaps that is also why he could not come to Calcutta? I expect he hoped to be well enough to proceed to Delhi instead, and suffered a relapse!"

Winter said in an eager, breathless voice: "Is that so, Mr. Carroll? How long has he been ill?"

Mr. Carroll looked unhappily at the small, tense face. "Er—not above six weeks," he said. "Or it may be a little more. Slow business. He hopes to be recovered shortly. On the mend now. You will not let him know that I have told upon him? He—he did not wish you to suffer any anxiety on his account."

"No," said Winter unsteadily. "No, I will not tell him. But I am so *very* glad to know—to know that he is better. Thank you, Mr. Carroll. I am truly grateful to you."

She gave him her hand and Mr. Carroll bowed over it and removed himself hurriedly.

"The poor, dear man!" said Mrs. Abuthnot. "How truly noble of him to wish to spare you anxiety. Why, Winter—where *are* you going, my love?"

Winter did not answer her. She was hurrying away down the long stretch of the moonlit ramparts towards the Water Bastion where a lone gentleman was seated in an embrasure of the battlements overlooking the river.

Alex had no wish for company. He was feeling irritable and irrationally guilty. He found himself reflecting that strangling was probably too good for Mr. Barton. But what could he do? He had tried to tell Winter the truth once before, and had been slashed across the face for his pains . . . .

Someone at the far end of the wall was singing to the accompaniment of a guitar. Below him the glittering river wound between wide, ghostly sandbanks. Suddenly he heard quick light footsteps and the rustle of a woman's dress. He rose to his feet.

Winter's small face appeared drained of all colour in the white moonlight. The close-fitting pearl-grey riding habit she wore in place of a crinoline lent her an illusion of maturity and height, but she could not control the childish trembling of her lips or keep the hurt and anger from her eyes, and Alex, looking down at her, felt an odd pain at his heart.

She said in a quick breathless voice: "You knew all the time what was the matter with Conway, didn't you? You could have told me, even if he did not want me to know. I had a right to—"

Her voice broke. But his hurt and anger matched her own and he said curtly: "I did try to tell you once, but you would not listen."

"You never told me! I asked you, on the day that you came to tell me that he could not come, if there was anything the matter with him, and you said there was not."

"I'm sorry." It was at least a relief that somehow she knew the truth at last.

Winter said: "You knew the reason why he did not come to meet me in Calcutta. You had a letter from him too. He must have told you in that."

Alex frowned. "Told me what?"

"Oh, I know that he did not want me to know! Mr. Carroll told me so. He thought it would distress me, and—and he wished to spare me anxiety. And I know he cannot have wanted me to see him looking—" Her voice stopped on a sudden gasp of horror and her eyes widened: "Why—why, he might even have thought that I might turn from him if his illness had affected his appearance! But you must have known that I was not like that. If you had told me—"

Alex cut harshly in: "We seem to be at cross-purposes. I have not the remotest idea what you are talking about. What is it Mr. Carroll has told you?"

"He told me the truth! That Conway has been ill."

"*Ill?*"

Winter's small chin came up with a jerk. "I hope you do not mean to deny having had any knowledge of it?"

"I most certainly do!" said Alex. "Mr. Barton is not ill. Not in the accepted sense of the word."

"What—what do you mean?"

She was right. He should have told her the truth. "I mean," he

268

said with brutal clarity, "that Mr. Barton suffers from over-indulgence in drink, drugs and women."

Winter caught her breath and turned swiftly away, but Alex caught her by the arm and jerked her round to face him.

"I'm sorry, but you are going to hear me out. I told you once before that Barton was not a fit person for you to have anything to do with. I meant it. A libertine and a drunkard is hardly a suitable husband for such a woman as yourself—or for any woman, for that matter. He would not come to England to marry you because he must have been well aware that one look at what he had become would have been enough to ensure that the engagement was broken. I do not know why he did not meet you in Calcutta. Probably for the same reason. I do know, however, that the after-effects of a debauch, if nothing else, prevented him from leaving for Delhi. He was incapable of standing upright when I left him."

He let her go, but Winter did not move. She stood quite still, her eyes wide and frightened, and once again Alex was conscious of that pain in his heart. He said harshly: "Well, now that you know the truth, I can only suggest that you return to Calcutta and sail for England as soon as there is a passage available."

She did not answer him, and the moment seemed to stretch out interminably. In the moonlit silence the words of a melody drifted down the ramparts, sweetened by distance:—

Believe me, if all those endearing young charms,
Which I gaze on so fondly today,
Were to fade by tomorrow, and fleet in my arms . . .

Winter saw Alex's set mouth soften, and she spoke in a whisper: "No! Oh, no . . . I don't believe it. Alex—"

Her small groping hand touched him, and something as vivid and as elemental as a flicker of lightning seemed to shiver between them. The next instant his arm was about her and he was holding her hard and close. For a brief moment her body was taut with shock, and then his mouth came down on hers, and all at once the resistance left her and the ground was no longer solid under her feet . . . .

Her skin smelt faintly of lavender and her body was soft and sweet and fragrant in his embrace; as soft and sweet and fragrant as her lips and her closed eyelids and her shining hair.

269

His mouth moved from hers at last, and his cheek was cool and harsh against her smooth warm one: "*Darling . . . darling . . . .*"

His voice was no more than a breathed caress, but at the sound of it the spell broke. Winter tore herself free, shaking with rage and shame and the shock of a sudden revelation: "So *that's* why you hate him—!" Her voice was edged with scorn: "You're jealous of Conway, and so you made it all up! Mr. Carroll *did* tell me the truth. Why should he lie to me? Conway is ill—and because you are jealous of him you do your best to blacken him to me so that you can make love to me behind his back! I hope—I hope I never have to see you again!''

Her voice broke on a sob, and she whirled about and ran from him, and he heard the sound of her flying feet die out along the wall and lose itself in the sound of the distant singing.

Alex made no attempt to follow her. Presently he felt in his pockets for tobacco and matches, rolled a cigarette with careful concentration and lit it. He appeared to have forgotten about the match, for it burned out between his fingers. He dropped it with a quick grimace of pain.

''*Hell!*'' he said, addressing the moonlight, the ancient city of Delhi and all India.

CHAPTER 6

CARLYON'S PLANS were at last shaping, and in pursuance of the policy of lulling Winter's fears he had seated himself as far away from her as possible, but this had not prevented him from observing that when the singing began, neither Winter nor Randall was present.

He endured his jealous rage as long as he could, but it increased until suddenly it became past bearing, and he rose and walked quickly away in the direction of the Water Bastion. Halfway down the stretch of wall the shadow of a huge neem tree lay across his path, and as he reached it he heard a sound of running footsteps, and someone ran into him and would have fallen but for his arms.

''Oh, it's you—'' Winter, sobbing, had forgotten that she disliked this man, had forgotten everything but the fact that Alex had betrayed her. ''Take me home! Please take me home.''

Looking down at her face, Carlyon saw that it was wet with tears. He said furiously: ''What has he done to you? My dear—don't! I'll go back and break his damned neck for you!''

''No—no, please don't.'' Winter clung to his arm. ''I want to go back to the bungalow. Please take me back!''

''Of course.'' He drew her hand through his arm and turned back towards the group near the Kashmir Gate, but they had not taken more than a dozen steps when he stopped. ''I can tell Mrs. Abuthnot

271

that you have a headache. I do not think, you know, that you should leave without her, but you will not like her to see you like this. May I—?"

He proffered a clean handkerchief and Winter accepted it gratefully. Then she said in a more rational voice: "You are very kind."

"No, I am not!" There was an unexpected bitterness in his voice, and Winter looked up, startled. Carlyon recovered himself: "I told you that if I could serve you in any way it would give me great happiness. I meant it, you know."

Quite suddenly she found herself telling him everything. Conway's illness. Captain Randall's perfidy. Her own doubts when Conway had failed to come to Delhi. "But now that I know the truth, I must go to him at once. I could help nurse him—I would not mind a sickroom. Will you—would you help me to go to him?"

Carlyon knew little of this man that the little Condesa was to marry, but could only feel satisfaction that Captain Randall, by attempting to make advances to his superior officer's future wife, had presented Carlyon himself with an opportunity that appeared to be little less than a gift from the gods.

He said: "I will take you to Lunjore myself. You cannot go unescorted."

Winter drew a quick breath. "Would you? Would you really?"

"Of course. You and a serving woman can travel in my carriage and I will ride. There is only one thing—" He paused, frowning.

"What is it?" Winter said anxiously.

"Well, I do not know," Carlyon spoke doubtfully, "but I think perhaps it would be as well if you did not mention this matter to the Abuthnots. They will not consider it at all suitable for you to travel either alone or in my care."

"No," said Winter slowly. "You are right. But I will not wait. I will not! I—I am my own mistress. No one can stop me."

"They would try," said Carlyon dryly.

"Yes, I suppose so." Her eyes were suddenly dry and bright, and she lifted her chin. "When can we leave? Tomorrow?"

"I could arrange it."

Winter made her decision. She would leave at once. Alex would be leaving Delhi on Monday and if she left tomorrow she would be in Lunjore by then: married to Conway and safe from him. "You are very kind," she said.

272

She did not stop to think why she needed to be safe from Alex, nor to realize that a part of the driving impulse to get to Lunjore arose from a panic desire to escape from him.

THAT NIGHT WINTER slipped out of bed and wrote a long note to Mrs. Abuthnot, then packed a small valise and a capacious carpet-bag. Carlyon would have to devise some means of smuggling them into the carriage. Struck by another thought she scribbled a hurried and loving note to Lottie. Lottie at least would understand!

That done she blew out the candles, and fell into an uneasy sleep.

The following morning at breakfast Carlyon inquired if Winter would care to drive out with him to try his new carriage.

Mrs. Abuthnot was not at all sure that it was quite the thing for dear Winter to be seen driving *à deux* with Lord Carlyon, but consoled herself with the reflection that she was, after all, engaged to be married. Besides, the child really did look remarkably pale after her sudden return from the previous night's party, and a drive, even in the heat of the morning, would doubtless be of benefit to her. As they drove away, she was surprised to see that Carlyon did not intend to sit in the carriage with his guest, but to ride beside it. Winter kissed her with unusual affection and Mrs. Abuthnot, unsuspicious by nature, was touched.

The carriage rolled out of the drive under the shadows of the pepper trees, and ten minutes later, happening to look out of her bedroom window, Mrs. Abuthnot saw Carlyon's bearer and two of his syces riding out of the side gate that led from the stables, taking with them items of luggage and two spare carriage horses. It seemed to her an odd time of day to exercise horses, and for a moment an odd twinge of uneasiness disturbed her.

Twelve o'clock brought no sign of the carriage, and by one o'clock Mrs. Abuthnot was seriously disturbed. Investigation proved that the procession that Mrs. Abuthnot had witnessed leaving the stables that morning had also not returned. "Mamma," said Sophie thoughtfully, "you do not suppose that they can have eloped?"

Mrs. Abuthnot uttered a small shriek. "Dear Winter would never—" She fell back in her chair with a groan, pressing her plump hands to her ample bosom. "Oh no! She *could* not do such a thing! She would at *least* have left a letter!"

Lottie flew for the hartshorn while Sophie, more practical,

273

went to Winter's bedroom. She returned a few minutes later with the two letters that she had found propped up on the chimney-piece.

Colonel Abuthnot, summoned from the lines, gave it as his opinion that Carlyon had behaved shockingly, and that come to think of it he had never quite trusted the fellow.

Someone must set off immediately in pursuit of the runaways. "*Alex!*" exclaimed Mrs. Abuthnot frantically. She dashed off a note requesting Alex's immediate presence, and dispatched it post-haste. But Alex was out, and the bearer of the letter settled down to sleep away the afternoon until such time as the sahib should return.

Alex arrived back barely half an hour before sunset in no very good humour, and was not pleased to receive Mrs. Abuthnot's agitated summons. He was entirely unprepared for the tearful announcement with which she greeted him.

He said: "What time did they leave?"

"Quite early," sobbed Mrs. Abuthnot. "Ten o'clock, I think."

"Good God, ma'am!" said Alex violently. "Could you not have sent for me before?"

"But we did not realize what had occurred until Sophie found this letter—" She held it out to Alex who, having read it with eyes almost black with anger, thrust it into his pocket. "And then you were out," explained Mrs. Abuthnot, "and the stupid man never thought to inquire after you. And George—Colonel Abuthnot—positively declines to go after them!"

"Quite out of the question!" confirmed Colonel Abuthnot, who had caught the end of the sentence. "Far too busy." He entered the room by the veranda door and, having nodded gloomily at Alex, said: "What do you propose to do about it, my boy?"

"Bring her back," said Alex tersely.

"Too late for that now. She'll have been out all night with that fellow Carlyon before you can catch up with her. As far as her reputation is concerned—"

Alex cut him short. "May I take it that you would allow her to remain here when I bring her back, Mrs. Abuthnot?"

"Of course I should! I know only too well that the dear child means no harm. As her letter says, it was only that she was upset by the news of Mr. Barton's illness and wished to go to his side without loss of time. One can understand that so well. The *best* of motives! But she may not wish to come back."

274

"Her wishes," said Alex through shut teeth, "have nothing whatever to do with the matter. I shall hope to be back at a tolerably early hour tomorrow, and if this matter has not been mentioned outside the house I see no reason why it should become known."

The door slammed behind him, and Colonel Abuthnot, who had been giving the matter thought, said reflectively: "Damme if I don't believe he's fallen in love with the girl himself. Now look what you've done, Milly! If he overtakes those two before they reach Lunjore, he'll murder that fellow Carlyon. And if he doesn't, he'll probably murder Barton!"

Mrs. Abuthnot, who had borne enough, took refuge in a strong attack of the vapours.

ALEX'S MOOD was so nearly murderous that Colonel Abuthnot's prediction might have come unpleasantly near the mark had it not been for a chance occurrence on the way.

He had stopped only long enough to collect Niaz, a third horse and his revolver. Then he had left, riding as though in a race. He knew that Carlyon's carriage could not travel at any great speed owing to the poorness of the roads, and he imagined that it would halt at some *dâk*-bungalow (post-house) for the night, so that he calculated on coming up with it well before midnight.

He rode at a hard gallop, paying little attention to the road. But he reined in hard at Niaz's shout of warning as a python slithered across the track almost under the hooves of his horse. Even so, Shalini shied wildly and the low branch of a kikar tree slammed against his arm. He hit the ground with the point of his shoulder and, in the second before his head struck rocks by the roadside, heard his collar-bone snap as he went down into darkness.

CHAPTER 7

*W*INTER LAY back in a corner of the carriage and closed her eyes. The setting sun shone in with a golden glare, the carriage jolted into ruts and out again, and her head was beginning to ache.

She told herself again that she was going to Conway and that in four days' time—less, if the roads improved—she would be with him at last; no more waiting; no more doubts or fears or loneliness. But the journey had begun to lose some of its charm. For one thing, since leaving Delhi, Carlyon's manner had undergone a noticeable change. Now he had handed the reins of his horse to one of the syces and joined Winter in the carriage. She found that she could not look up without finding his eyes upon her. And for another thing, he had not provided the woman servant he had promised.

He did not talk much. His gaze just rested upon her with possessive appreciation. There was, he knew, a *dâk*-bungalow some few miles farther on which they should reach before dark and where they could pass the night. And tomorrow they would resume their journey, not to Lunjore, but to Oudh; and from there to Calcutta. Winter would be unlikely to discover for several days that their destination was not Lunjore, and by then marriage to anyone other than himself would be out of the question.

The *dâk*-bungalow, when they reached it shortly before moonrise, was already sheltering a large party. Carlyon's bearer informed him that it was an Indian lady and her servants who had broken their journey for a few hours at the bungalow and would be leaving shortly for Oudh, and that meanwhile there were rooms in plenty for himself and the Miss-sahib.

"I am from Oudh," Winter thought, "and I too am returning home." The thought gave her fresh courage.

They ate a tolerable meal in the main room of the bungalow, while the moon rose over the plain and someone—the *khansamah* (cook) said it was the Mohammedan lady in the room at the far end of the veranda—played a tinkling tune on a stringed instrument. It was a haunting thread of sound, oddly familiar.

Winter was very tired, and anxious to get to her own room and be free of Carlyon's disturbing gaze, and the meal seemed interminable. She excused herself as soon as it was over, giving her hand to Carlyon, thanking him once more for his help and bidding him good night.

He took her hand: but he did not release it . . . .

Carlyon had imagined that he could keep his passions under control. But the touch of her fingers snapped his resolution.

He held her hand in a hard grasp with fingers that were feverishly hot, and lifting it to his lips, he kissed it.

It was not a light gesture of gallantry, but greedily passionate.

Lifting his head, he stared at her, breathing hard, and Winter turned cold with fear. Then he released her hand, and she turned and stumbled into the safety of her room.

She closed the door behind her, fumbled for the bolt, and shot it home. She should have known—she must have known!—that it was madness to accept Lord Carlyon's offer to escort her to Lunjore. What had possessed her to set off alone with him? What would Conway think of this escapade? There was only one thing that she could do now, and that was to remove herself instantly from the bungalow. No woman's reputation was entirely ruined unless she had slept a night, unchaperoned, under the same roof as a man. By leaving immediately she might still retrieve herself in Conway's eyes.

A sound of wrangling voices and laughter from the compound outside cut across her disjointed thoughts. The other travellers who were to leave tonight! Of course! She would beg help from the lady from Oudh. Surely another woman would not refuse to help her? And Lunjore lay only a mile or so off the road that led into Oudh . . . .

Winter ran to fetch her baggage and eased open the door. The veranda was deserted. A flare of torches and a group of retainers harnessing bullocks to the waiting Indian cart, and a square of orange light from the window of the end room, showed that the Indian lady had not yet left. Winter ran lightly down the moonlit veranda.

The door was not locked. She pushed it open and went in.

There were three women in the room. A strikingly beautiful young woman wearing the silk tunic and full trousers of a Mohammedan lady of good family, and two older women who were obviously servants, the younger of whom uttered a small scream at the sudden appearance of a stranger.

Winter put a finger to her lips, and spoke in a soft, breathless voice, explaining her predicament and begging that they would take her with them. The Indian girl—she could not have been very many years older than Winter—listened in wide-eyed astonishment, and when she had finished clapped her hands like a child and said: "But it is wonderful!" She turned to the elderly serving maid: "Is it not wonderful to hear a feringhi speak as one of us? Who art thou? What is thy name?"

277

"Winter. Winter de los Aguilares. If the Begum Sahiba would . . ."

"*What?* What is that you say?" said the girl sharply. She snatched up the oil lamp that stood on the floor and held it so that the light fell full on Winter's face. "It is!" she said. "*Allah Kerimast!* It is so. Little sister, do you not know me?"

"I—I do not think—" began Winter breathlessly.

"Ameera!—dost thou not remember Ameera? Hast thou indeed forgotten the Gulab Mahal and my mother, Juanita Begum?"

The older serving woman, a stout grey-haired lady, threw up her arms with a little wailing cry: "*Aie! Aie!* It is the *Chota Moti!* It is the baba whom I nursed!"

Winter's eyes widened. Her voice was a shaken whisper. "Hamida? It is Hamida and Ameera?"

And they were in each other's arms, laughing and crying.

The soft silk, the smell of sandalwood, the liquid Eastern vowels. The touch and the scent and the sound of home.

A sudden tumult from the compound outside brought Winter back to her present predicament, and she pulled away, listening.

"Ameera, you will take me with you? I *cannot* stay here!"

"But of course, little sister! We go now. Those are my servants out there. They make ready to leave. And on the road thou shalt tell me of this feringhi from whom thou wouldst escape. Is it thy husband?"

"No. It is someone who—I cannot explain now!"

Ameera laughed. "No matter, Little Pearl—thou shalt tell me later. See! We will put Hamida's *bourka* upon thee, thus!" The older woman, who had once been Winter's wet-nurse, snatched up the voluminous white cotton garment and dropped it over Winter's head. It was a tentlike cloak that shrouded her from head to foot, leaving only an inset of coarse net over the upper part of the face through which the wearer could see but not be seen.

"There!" said Ameera triumphantly. "That is more seemly. Hamida must cover her face with her *chuddah* if she fears that men will attack her for the sake of her beauty!" She donned her own *bourka* and said: "Come now, we are ready."

"No—wait!" said Winter suddenly. "I must leave a message. If I do not, he will think me lost and rouse the country looking for me. He could not just leave me and go back."

Using a sheet of native paper, a bowl of black and gritty ink and

278

a quill pen, Winter wrote swiftly. She thanked Lord Carlyon for his kind assistance, but she had met with a relative, a cousin, and so need put him to no further trouble on her behalf. He need be in no anxiety about her as she would be quite safe, and was continuing her journey immediately.

The paper was taken to her room, where it would be found in the morning. Then they hurried down the veranda steps and out into the night, and a moment later they were in the dark, close-curtained *ruth*. The driver shouted, the bullocks grunted and the *ruth* jolted forward and precipitated Winter into Ameera's lap, where the pent-up anxieties of the last twenty-four hours found relief in a gale of laughter. She clung to Ameera and laughed, and Ameera and the two serving women laughed with her.

"And now," said Ameera, "tell me all! How dost thou come to be here? Art thou not yet wed? And who is this feringhi from whom we escape?"

CARLYON did not discover that Winter had left the *dâk*-bungalow until breakfast-time the following day, and then he rode after her at breakneck speed along the dusty Lunjore road.

He came to a curtained *ruth* accompanied by a motley escort of mounted retainers, but galloped past without a second glance, and it was only after several hours of hard riding that he was forced to realize that Winter had escaped him, and turned back, rage contending with fear for her safety. Whom had she gone with? A *relative*? How could she have met a relative? The Indian woman in the end room did not so much as cross his mind. The bungalow servants could give him no information. Two days later, white with fury and convinced at last that Winter had tricked him, had planned it all, knowing there would be someone here to meet her, he returned to Delhi, and thence to England.

FOR WINTER DE LOS AGUILARES, that journey, going to her wedding, was perhaps the happiest time she had known since the long-ago days of her childhood. Hamida had combed out her heavy silken waves of hair and braided the rippling silken cloak into two long thick plaits, and dressed her in a replica of Ameera's own graceful costumes. "There!" she had said. "Now thou art no longer of England but of Hind."

"And thus," said Ameera, "do I remember thee when we played together in the women's quarters of the Gulab Mahal."

Here at last was a friend and a companion of her own age, and here once more was all the warmth and wonder of the old memories coming alive again. She told Ameera all that had happened to her, and heard in return all the news of the Gulab Mahal.

There were, Ameera said, few left in the Rose Palace who would remember her, for the cholera had taken a heavy toll. Even Juanita Begum, Ameera's mother, had died of it. Ameera had married her second cousin, Walayat Shah, a minor noble-man at the court of the King of Oudh. The Company's annexa-tion of Oudh had dispossessed him of employment and liveli-hood, and he and his family lived now at the Gulab Mahal. The loss of privilege and revenue had enraged him against the feringhis. Men, explained Ameera regretfully, were apt to get hot and angry. She herself would be content to live in the Rose Palace under any government that could be trusted to keep order.

"I have two sons," she added proudly, and she could not wait to get back to them. "When thou art married and have sons of thine own, Little Pearl, thou wilt know how it is with me."

Although Ameera's road lay through Lunjore, when they neared the outskirts of the city some five days later she would not come to the Residency, but stopped the *ruth* and sent one of her servants to fetch a hired carriage.

"I have thought," she said lovingly, "that it were better if thou didst not arrive at thy bridegroom's house with a cousin who is not

of thy own race. I have heard that there are those among the sahib-*log* who do not look kindly on such things. But we will meet again. Surely, surely we will meet again! And now, as thou hast no woman of thine own to attend thee, Hamida here will go with thee. If he has procured another for thee, then she can return."

The two young women embraced, and Hamida collected her own and Winter's belongings and followed her out into the road. A moment later the gaily decorated *ruth* with its mounted escort had rumbled away down the tree-shaded road, and then Ameera was gone.

Winter, no longer in native dress but wearing a light-coloured riding habit, stood by the roadside blinking back tears until Hamida hurried her into the hired carriage, and they were driven away through the hot sunlight towards the Residency.

Part Three
The Calm before the Storm

FLO MAYNARD

CHAPTER 1

*T*HE RESIDENCY, once the palace of a local princeling, stood behind a massive gateway, in extensive grounds on the edge of the jungle. The carriage drew up under a stone porch festooned with flowering creepers, and a startled *chupprassi* gaped at the girl in the close-fitting riding habit who descended from it. The servants had been aware of their master's approaching marriage, but they had not expected the bride so soon.

Yes, agreed the head *chupprassi* cautiously, the Commissioner Sahib was at home. But he could see no one. He was indisposed—far too sick to receive visitors.

"I know," said Winter. "That is why I have come. I will see the sahib at once. Show me to his room." She swept past him and into the wide hall.

Conway's bedroom had curtains drawn across the windows, and smelt unpleasant. A plump native woman dressed in spangled muslin crouched on the floor beside the bed and waved a palm-leaf fan. She seemed an unsuitable sickroom attendant.

"The sahib is not well!" she said in a shrill, angry voice. "He can see no one."

"He will see me," said Winter, and walked to the bed.

The heap on the bed moaned, grunted and stirred and said in a thick voice: "Wha's that? Shurrup, can't yer! Filthy din—"

It turned over on its back, and Winter looked down at a bloated, unrecognizable face. Was this—*could* this be Conway? A reek of stale spirits and foul breath made her draw back sharply. They had been dosing him with brandy! Surely that could not be a good thing for fever?

Conway grunted and opened his eyes with an effort. He stared up at her, trying to focus. Pity and love choked her, she leaned over him and laid a cool hand on his forehead.

"Conway, it's Winter. Conway, dear, don't you know me? Why did you not tell me that you were ill? I have come to look after you—"

At long last the sense of the words penetrated . . . *Winter!* God, what a head he had. It must be the opium or the brandy. And this was the fortune he was going to marry! She was here! How she had got here he didn't know. But he must get rid of her. He was going to be sick again any minute. Must get rid of—

He was sick. But in the more lucid interval that followed he discovered with amazement that she was bathing his forehead with cold water and whispering endearments. Yasmin, standing by in stunned fury, began to protest, and Conway turned his head slowly and spoke a single virulent word of dismissal.

The small, cool hands pressed his head back upon the pillow and he lay still with closed eyes, trying to think, dimly aware of the need for action. Presently he opened his eyes a little, peering at her under puffy, half-closed lids, and said thickly: "Didn't expect you. Good of you t'come. Call Ismail, there's a good girl. M'bearer."

The portly bearer, who had been hovering outside the door, hurried to his master's side, and after a brief colloquy turned to Winter and salaamed. If the Miss-sahib would follow him he would show her to her room, and refreshments would be brought.

When the door had closed upon her, Conway crawled out of bed and dragged himself to the bathroom. He sloshed water over his head and shoulders, shuddering at the shock. Ismail, returning, applied a variety of well-tried remedies, and the Commissioner staggered back to his bedroom, racked with recurrent waves of nausea and futile rage.

Damn the girl! What had possessed her to come gallivanting here on her own? It would ruin all. He had intended to arrange for the wedding to take place within an hour or two of her arrival, so as to allow her no time to change her mind. And now she had arrived unexpectedly and alone, and had found him with Yasmin, suffering from the after-effects of a bachelor party.

"The Miss-sahib, hearing that the *Huzoor* was suffering from illness, hurried from Delhi in her haste to care for him," said Ismail, laying out clean linen.

Illness! She had said something to that effect, so she had. Why, of course! An innocent creature like that could have had no experience of drunkenness. She had imagined him to be suffering from some illness.

The way opened before him. She was here alone and unattended. There was no one she knew in Lunjore and she could not stay the night in his house unless she were married to him. It was all going to be quite easy after all. The wedding must be performed immediately. He would send for the padre . . . and until the knot was tied he must keep up the fiction that he had been suffering from fever. It could not be better! . . .

THREE HOURS LATER, in the cool, dim drawing room, Winter de los Aguilares, Sabrina's daughter, stood before a makeshift altar between burning candles and was married to Conway Barton.

She wore the pale-grey riding habit in which she had arrived, and carried a bunch of white jasmine Hamida had given her.

Hamida was uneasy. She had no knowledge of the ways of white men, but half an hour in the house had left her under no delusions as to what sort of woman it was who occupied the small detached set of rooms that lay behind the main building.

But if Hamida had qualms, Winter had none. When she looked at the gross elderly man with the pale protuberant eyes and the greying hair who stood or knelt beside her, and whose damp fingers were so unsteady that it was with difficulty that he managed to put the ring upon her finger, she thought only that now that she was here to nurse him and love him, he would recover soon and become strong and well and handsome again.

She looked down at the ring that was too loose for her finger, as the first ring that he had given her had been, and her eyes were suddenly full of happy tears.

After the ceremony Conway refused to return to his bed. "Bed? Nonsense! Never felt better in me life! Told you I was on the mend! Don't get married every day of the week. I've sent out to tell some of m'friends, and they'll soon be over. They'll want to see the bride. You're the Commissioner's Lady now, m'dear. You'll have to learn to do the honours. Have some champagne! Capital stuff for putting life inter yer! Hey there, Ismail, bring another bottle!"

He toasted Winter and looked her over with considerable approval. A fortune and a beauty too! He was a lucky man. The champagne slopped down his waistcoat.

And then carriages and men on horseback began to arrive, and the room filled with noisy strangers. There were not many of them —perhaps a dozen in all—and only two of them were women; but to Winter there appeared to be twice or three times that number. The noise, the loud laughter, the congratulations, the bold approving stares of the men disconcerted her, and the women were neither

286

of them of the kind whom she would ever have felt drawn towards.

Mrs. Wilkinson was small, plump and rouged. She jangled a great many bracelets, and smelt strongly of violet essence. Mrs. Cottar was tall and thin, red-haired, green-eyed. She appeared to be a general favourite with the men. Her remarks were invariably greeted with laughter, but as they were mostly delivered *sotto voce* Winter heard few of them, and those she did hear conveyed nothing.

Lucy Cottar possessed a caustic and malicious wit, and little kindness towards her own sex. But something in Winter's bewildered eyes gave her a momentary twinge of compunction.

"You must find it a little bewildering at first," she said, "meeting so many people whom you do not know. But you will soon get to know us just as well as your husband does. Though you must not expect much gaiety in Lunjore."

"Oh, but I never expected it to be gay," Winter hastened to assure her, "and I know that Conway will be far too hardworked, once he is well again, to have much time for entertainments."

"Has he been ill?" inquired Mrs. Cottar in some surprise. "I did not know. But then I have not seen him for above a week ....."

"But Conway has been ill since late August."

"Ill? Feathers! Did he tell you that? He was joking. And you need not be afraid Con will be too overworked to enter into our few entertainments. Why, he is the idlest of creatures! He lets Alex Randall do all the work while he takes all the credit. Quite shocking —is it not, Con?"

"No idea what you're talkin' about, Lou, my witch. But I am ready to be shocked," said Mr. Barton, coming to anchor beside them. "What is it? A new scandal?"

"On the contrary. An old one. It is you I was referring to. I was telling your wife that you allow Alex Randall to do all the work while you take all the credit."

"What's shockin' about that?" demanded Mr. Barton. "Randall likes work. He deals with the business while I take care of the pleasure. Very satisfact'ry arrangement." He drank deeply, then looked down at his wife's white, rigid face. "Mustn't forget I'm a married man now. Have to watch m'self! Not so much straying from the straight and narrow—eh, m' dear?" He pinched his wife's chin and spilled a quantity of champagne down her dress in the process.

287

The rest of the evening was a nightmare to Winter. A dreadful, feverish babble and noise and the clink of glasses. Hours later—or so it seemed—a meal was served in the big dining room, and Winter sat beside her bridegroom at the head of the table, smiling with stiff lips and trying to force herself to eat the food placed before her. Lamps were lit, toasts were drunk and speeches were made; the bamboo screens were rolled up to let in the cool night air, and still the noise went on.

It was midnight before the guests departed. The garden was full of moonlight, and in the drawing room the servants were stacking glasses and removing cigar stubs.

"I am very tired," Winter said stiffly to Conway. "I think, if you do not mind, that I will go to bed."

"Tha's right. You go to bed. I won't keep y' waiting!" Conway laughed uproariously. Winter did not fully understand the allusion, but the coarseness of the laugh that accompanied it made her colour hotly. She turned away and walked slowly and unsteadily to her room.

Hamida was waiting for her, and the sight of the girl's white face filled her with clucking alarm. Winter allowed herself to be undressed and bathed and put to bed as though she were a doll. Her world—the dream world that she had built up for years—was in ruins about her, and she could not even think.

At last it was quiet, for now even Hamida was gone. Now perhaps she could think—could cry, to ease the terrible pain in her heart. And then the door opened and Conway was there.

Winter sat up swiftly, pulling the sheets up about her. She watched stupidly as he began to remove his dressing-gown. And then, quite suddenly, the numbness left her and gave place to sheer panic and horror.

In the dazed nightmare of that terrible wedding party she had forgotten that people who were married shared the same bed.

This man—this gross, repulsive, drunken stranger—was going to get into bed with her!

"Go away! Please go away at once!" Her voice was hoarse with fear and loathing. "You cannot sleep here tonight—not tonight. Go away!"

Conway gave a drunken chuckle. "Coy, are you, my shy little virgin? Tha's as it should be! But yer a wife now." He looked down at her and his red-rimmed eyes lit with a look that she had seen before. A look that had been in Carlyon's eyes.

He reached out and lifted a tress of her hair, and Winter struck at his hand in fury and terror.

"Don't touch me! Don't dare to touch me!"

Conway lunged towards her across the bed and she flung aside the sheets and leaped out. But her husband's clutching hands were on her hair and they gripped it and jerked it brutally, so that she fell back and was caught. And there was no escape.

CHAPTER 2

*A*LEX WAS both strong and healthy, and Niaz had sufficient knowledge of such matters as concussion and broken collar-bones to deal adequately with the situation. Having eased off Alex's coat and set the collar-bone, binding it securely with his puggari, he had ridden back to a small village they had recently passed, where he procured a ramshackle palanquin and bearers to carry it. An hour later Alex had been installed in the hut of the village headman, and under the care of a wrinkled crone well-versed in the use of healing herbs.

Twenty-four hours later he woke to a splitting headache. He could remember nothing of the past few weeks, and he drank the beldame's drugs obediently and slept; woke to a smell of dung-fires and sun-baked earth, swallowed the infusion of herbs and hot milk that he was offered, and slept again.

It was not until the morning of the sixth day that he remembered Delhi and all that had happened there. It took him some time to realize how many days had elapsed since he had ridden in pursuit of Winter and Carlyon, and when he had done so he cursed Niaz with a savage, concentrated fury for having let him lie there; for having given him drugs and for not having put him on his horse and taken him on to Lunjore or back to Delhi.

Niaz observed him with a thoughtful eye and said in a non-committal voice: "I have news. Three days back the Lord Sahib returned with the carriage and horses and his *nauker-log* to Delhi."

Alex looked at him for a long moment, then he said: "Was the Lady Sahib with him?"

"No. But it was said that she had met with friends upon the road and had gone forward with them to Lunjore. I sent word to Barton Sahib that thou hadst met with an accident and would be delayed."

Alex lay back slowly on the string bed and closed his eyes. Niaz could fetch his gear from Delhi and then they would go on to Lunjore. If Winter had indeed met with friends upon the road she would have reached Lunjore days ago, and there was nothing more that he could do about that. And as for Carlyon, Colonel Abuthnot could be counted on to say all that was necessary upon that head. By now Winter would have learned what sort of man Conway Barton was, and would probably be staying with these friends until she could arrange to return to England.

Barely more than a week ago he would have been thankful to see her go. But that had been before he had kissed her. Now he wished her happiness and security more than anything. And, he realized sadly, he was the last person who could offer her either . . . .

HE AND NIAZ accomplished the rest of the journey by easy stages. Nevertheless, by the time he reached Lunjore he was tired and intended to go straight to bed. But the Commissioner sent over to say that he wished to see him that same evening.

Alex walked over to the Residency in the starlight and was ushered into Mr. Barton's drawing room. The room was brightly lit and empty, and there was something unusual about it. The furniture had been rearranged and the place was clean, and there were vases of flowers.

He was frowning abstractedly at an arrangement of orange lilies and yellow jasmine when a door at the far end of the room opened and he looked up and saw Winter.

He was neither prepared for the sight of her nor for what it did to him.

Winter had not known of Alex's return. She had slipped into the drawing room to fetch a pair of embroidery scissors left there earlier in the evening. She had opened the door and seen Alex . . . .

They stood quite still and looked at each other. Alex put out a hand with the groping gesture of a blind man.

"Did you marry him?"

"Yes." The word was barely a breath.

"Why?"

291

Winter moved her head in a slight, helpless gesture that was less a refusal to answer than hopelessness.

That small despairing movement hurt Alex like the touch of a hot iron. "Was it because you had no one else to go to? You could have—"

He stopped abruptly, aware of the futility of questions or answers. What did the whys and wherefores matter now? The thing was done. His hand fell to his side.

"I suppose I must offer my congratulations. Will you make my excuses to your husband? He sent for me, but I have had a somewhat tiring day and I feel sure he will forgive me if I postpone the interview until the morning. Good night."

He turned on his heel, and Winter heard him stumble as he went down the porch steps, and then the sound of his footsteps died away until there was only the clock ticking, and presently a muffled bellow of laughter from the dining room where her husband and his friends were finishing the port.

Alex had gone. There was no one now she could appeal to.

She could not run to Ameera. Indian wives did not leave their husbands—it was unthinkable. Neither could she return to Delhi, for she had no money and no means of getting any. Conway had taken charge of her jewel box and valuables, saying that such things were better under lock and key. Even Hamida had gone . . . .

The morning after her wedding Winter had awakened from the deep sleep of utter exhaustion to the despairing realization of what she had done. There had been a heavy arm lying across her, its inert weight hurting her breasts, and beside her, his mouth open, her bridegroom snored in sodden slumber. She had crept shuddering from under that arm, bruised, sick with loathing and, stumbling into the dressing room, had bolted the door behind her.

Hamida had been there waiting for her, and Winter had clung to her, dry-eyed and shivering. Hamida had crooned over her and petted her, but it was obvious that she considered such things to be a normal part of life. Husbands, she said, were often rough and brutal in the marriage bed, but wives must bear such things and learn to please their lords, lest their lords turn to light women. Winter's hysterical assertion that she intended to leave Lunjore immediately was received with scandalized horror. Wives had their duties and their responsibilities. She was married now, and that could not be undone. She had not even been forced into the marriage. It had been of her own choosing, and she could not now run away from it.

Winter had listened numbly to Hamida holding forth on the duties of wives, but only one thing that Hamida had said made sense to her—she was married now, and that could not be undone. Hamida was right. But within a week Hamida had gone.

It was the plump, painted woman whom Winter had found sitting beside Conway's bed on the morning of her arrival who was responsible: Yasmin, the woman who lived in the *bibi-gurh* behind the scarlet poinsettias and the feathery screen of pepper trees. Yasmin had recognized an enemy in Hamida and had taken steps to remove her. Conway had told his wife that she must dismiss the woman she had brought with her, as an outsider would only cause trouble among the other servants. With Hamida went Winter's only link with the outside world.

In the slow days and weeks that followed, Winter saw Alex only rarely, and never to speak to. He spent most of his time in the outlying areas of the district, and when he was not on tour he avoided entering the living rooms of the Residency. But he was often in the Commissioner's office. Conway had ceased to take even a casual interest in the affairs of Lunjore and was content to leave the greater part of his duties in Alex's hands.

Secure now in the possession of large wealth, the Commissioner entertained lavishly and the Residency was always full of guests. He was proud of his wife's looks and poise, and it pleased him that her dresses and jewels and her youthful dignity made an impression on his guests.

But he had early tired of her as a woman. She had never again screamed and fought him, but the passive, rigid disgust with which she had endured his subsequent embraces had soon robbed them of all pleasure, and he had returned to the coarser and more cooperative Yasmin for his entertainment.

Winter, for herself, had few friends among the British community. Lunjore society found young Mrs. Barton a cold little thing. She had made a friend of Zeb-un-Nissa, the nine-year-old granddaughter of Akbar Khan, the gatekeeper. Nissa was a frail little creature whose enormous dark eyes had a curiously blind look as though they looked through people and not at them. She was

293

reported to be subject to fits and to have second sight, and the servants were afraid of her.

She was a solitary child who spent much of her time among the roots of the big banyan tree near the Residency gate, watching the birds and squirrels, who appeared to have no fear of her and would feed from her hand. Winter had noticed a flock of green parrots fluttering about the roots of the tree early one morning, and had gone out to see what had attracted them. She had stayed to talk to Nissa, and the two had become friends.

Winter became less actively unhappy as the weeks passed. There was still India, and that alone, in the ruin of her dreams, had not betrayed her.

She would ride out every evening, and in the early morning before the sun rose, galloping across the plain and along the banks of the distant river, or riding through the dew-wet crops where the peafowl screamed at the dawn and skeins of wild geese honked overheard on their way to the jheels of Hazrat Bagh and Pari. The glory of the sunrise over the limitless plains and the wide, winding river; the quiet beauty of the evenings when the sun sank with incredible swiftness, dyeing the river and the long silver sandbanks, the city and the plain and every tree and cane-brake to a warm, glowing apricot; the swift, opal twilight, and night unfolding like a peacock's tail, green and blue and violet, flecked with the last gold of day and spangled with stars—these were things that comforted Winter and held for her a never-failing enchantment, daily renewed.

The wide land and the wide river and the enormous sky were beautiful to her. The vastness soothed her. The sense of space—of the plains stretching away and away to the jungles and valleys of Nepal. Here there was none of the sense of being shut in and enclosed behind high walls that she had experienced at Ware.

She loved the city, too. The heaped colours of fruits and vegetables and grain in the bazaar. The rich smell of mustard oil and masala, of musk and spices and ghee. The shops of the potter and the silversmith. The stalls that sold glass bangles as fine and light as silk and as fragile as dried leaves, in glittering, sparkling, burning colours—red and blue and gold and grass green. The silk shops with their gay bales piled high in the shadows. The drifting, jostling crowds and the great, lazy Brahmini bulls, sacred to Shiva, who shouldered through the narrow streets taking toll of the baskets of the vegetable-sellers.

White women were seldom to be seen in the city, but Winter would go there accompanied only by Barton's syce, Yusaf, so at first crowds collected to giggle and stare. But she went so often that they became used to her, and to the fact that she spoke their language with an idiomatic fluency that they had rarely met with in others of the sahib-*log*. She came to have many acquaintances in the city.

It had at first disturbed Alex that Winter should go so freely and so far afield about the countryside and the city, but he had come to the conclusion that her greatest safety might one day lie in such friendships, and he had withdrawn the unobtrusive watch he had set on her.

He seldom saw her, and then only at a distance when he rode abroad, and might never have spoken to her again—or indeed to anyone else!—had it not been for an unexpected drop in temperature on a night early in the New Year.

CHAPTER 3

*T*HE COLD awakened Winter who slept alone in the wide bed, for Conway had moved back into his own room, and seldom visited her. She reached for the quilt that normally lay folded on her bed, but it was not there and she remembered that she had taken it into the dressing room earlier that evening.

She slipped out of bed, shivering, and pulling a light cashmere shawl about her shoulders, crossed the room and pushed open the door of the dressing room. She had left the quilt on the couch by the bathroom door, and her hand was upon it when she became aware that somewhere quite close to her a voice, curiously hollow and echoing, was speaking in a sibilant undertone.

The sound seemed to come from the bathroom. Quite suddenly she realized that the voice was speaking in Urdu, and that the echoing quality was accounted for by the wide stone sluice pipe that carried off the bath water.

Someone was squatting on the far side of the bathroom wall, out of sight and hearing of anyone within the house, but unaware of the fact that the exit of the sluice was acting as a speaking tube. Winter supposed that it must be Dunde Khan, the night watchman, whiling away the hours with a friend. She was turning away when the voice whispered again in the silence:

"He will be riding the Eagle or Shalini. And either will show up far against the crops—"

Her attention was suddenly arrested. Those were Captain Randall's horses. A second voice spoke.

"But what of Niaz Mohammed? It is seldom that Randall Sahib rides without him, and—"

"That has been arranged. By now I think he will be suffering from a little sickness. And the syce has a poisoned hand. I think the sahib will ride alone."

Winter crept forward, and crouched down near the level of the pipe. A voice appeared to speak almost in her ear:

"And what if he does not ride to Chunwar?"

"He will. There is a report that the canal bank has been breached there, and sitting by the office door I heard him tell the Commissioner Sahib that he would go on the morrow, at dawn, to see if the report be true. And as all know, to ride to Chunwar he must cross the nullah near the dhâk trees. There is no other way for a horseman. It will be thought an accident. When a man has been dragged by a foot that is caught in the stirrup of a bolting horse it is difficult to tell which injury caused his death."

There was a pause. Winter heard a man clear his throat and spit, and then a voice said: "But—but this is a good man. He knows our ways, and though at times he is hot and very angry, he is just."

"*Fool!*"—the epithet echoed hollowly in the cold room—"It is not those who spit upon us and treat us as dogs who are of danger to us, for they do but light a fire for their own burning. It is men such as Randall Sahib, who speak our tongues as one of us, and who have many friends amongst us, who are a stumbling block in the path, for many of our people will listen to their words. It is these who must first be slain."

There was a murmur of agreement. Then something evidently startled the group outside, for Winter heard sounds of hurried movements and an unintelligible mutter, and after that there was silence.

She waited for perhaps a quarter of an hour longer, huddled in

296

her shawl and numb with cold, but she heard no more voices. At last she stood up stiffly and crept back to bed.

Chunwar . . . . That was a village to the south of the city. She had ridden out that way before. The first mile or so was crop land threaded by water courses. Beyond that lay several miles of open dusty plain dotted with kikar and dhâk trees; rough, stony ground, full of unexpected potholes and dry nullahs.

The nullah that the man had spoken of cut diagonally across the plain a mile or so short of the village. It was a wide, steep-sided ravine, full of trees, and there was only one practicable place where it might be crossed: where the narrow cart track ran. It would be easy enough to unhorse a man in such a place.

Winter had a sudden vision of Alex Randall's brown, clean-cut face battered into a shapeless mass of blood and dirt, and she shuddered as she stared into the darkness. The hours crawled past and she dared not sleep for fear that she should awake too late and not be in time to stop Alex from riding to his death.

At long last a cock crowed from somewhere behind the servants' quarters. Winter lit a candle and dressed hurriedly, her fingers clumsy from cold. Then she shook awake one of the servants who slept out on the veranda at night, and told him that she wanted her horse brought round immediately.

Fifteen minutes later she was cantering down the long drive in the grey, aqueous light of the early morning. There was a light burning in one of the rooms of Captain Randall's bungalow, and a syce was walking a restive horse up and down in front of the veranda. So he had not yet left! Winter restrained her mount and made him walk sedately past, and down a narrow lane towards the open ground beyond.

She did not know the identity of the men who had whispered against the wall last night, but one, or all of them, must be in the Commissioner's employ. Winter could not believe that Alex's syce could be one of them, but she had been too frightened by what she had heard to take any chances.

The lane came out close to a mango swamp and a deep belt of crop lands. To the right lay the city and the river, while half a mile to the left lay the road to Chunwar. Winter drew rein a little beyond the mouth of the lane, and waited. When she heard the sound of Alex's horse approaching she turned, swinging across the path so that Alex had no choice but to pull up. Winter saw that he was alone. So the conspirators had been successful in that at least!

His horse sidled and snorted. "Mrs. Barton!" he said abruptly. Then he smiled. "Don't look so tragic. What is it?"

"I—I'm sorry—but I had to stop you. I had to stop you from going to Chunwar." Her voice was unsteady. "They were going to kill you," she said. "In the ravine on the road to Chunwar. I heard them talking last night, and I had to stop you—"

Alex said: "Wait a minute. I must be singularly slow-witted this morning. Who are 'they'?"

"I don't know. I only heard voices—" She told him the story of those voices that had whispered in the shadow of the bathroom wall.

Alex listened without interruption, then he asked if she had recognized either of the men. Winter shook her head. "No. They were speaking very quietly."

"No names?"

"None."

He was silent for a moment or two. Then he produced a small five-chambered Colt pistol and said: "It seems I may have need of this. Go home now by way of the cantonments, Mrs. Barton. I do not think that you should ride so far afield without a trustworthy escort. The times are not as settled as some people suppose."

He made as though to ride on, and Winter snatched at his rein. "No! Alex, no!" Her voice was sharp with panic.

He looked down at her white frightened face and the harsh lines of his own face softened. He dropped his hand over hers for a brief moment and gripped it hard and reassuringly.

"I shall be all right. I promise you. Forewarned is forearmed, you know."

But Winter's fingers still clung to the bridle. "Alex—"

Alex wrenched her hand from the bridle and said suddenly and savagely: "For God's sake don't look at me like that!" He saw her flinch as though he had struck her. "I'm sorry. I am very grateful to you for warning me. Now get on—go on back to the house."

He wheeled his horse, and was gone, galloping away across the open ground towards the distant belt of trees, and Winter sat watching him grow smaller and smaller. The sky shimmered in a wash of saffron light that flooded upwards from the east. It was less

298

than an hour since she had left the Residency, but it seemed as though years had passed.

Why had she not known before that she loved Alex Randall? Why was it only now, when he was riding away from her to what might be his death, that she should realize how much he meant to her? Now, when it was too late, because she had married Conway Barton.

She braced herself. Turning her horse she rode back through the brightening dawn to her husband's house.

CHAPTER 4

*T*HE SUN was still below the horizon when Alex left the green crop lands behind him, and gave the Eagle his head across the wide stretch of the open plain towards Chunwar. The horse's hooves clicked against the bleached bones of cattle, and his black body as yet cast no shadow.

Nearing the ravine, Alex drew out his pistol and held it ready as he passed by the dhâk trees. His horse slipped a little on the steep slope and Alex spoke softly. He was riding loosely, sitting relaxed in the saddle, when he heard a faint rustle to one side of the path. He pulled back on the rein.

Almost simultaneously, a man rose from the high grass by the track and clawed at Alex's boot, but Alex had dropped the reins after that one savage jerk and raised his pistol. The explosion and the howl of pain sent the Eagle rearing wildly, and the slashing blow of an iron-tipped lathi from a second man on the opposite side missed its mark and caught the horse's flank, raising a vicious weal. Alex fired again, as with a squeal of rage the Eagle reared up with flaying hooves. The next moment horse and rider had burst out of the ravine and onto the plain beyond with the speed and violence of a thunderbolt.

Alex let the infuriated horse have his head until his pain and panic had subsided. They rode into Chunwar by way of the canal bank, and Alex called upon the *kotwal*—the village headman—and having dealt with the matter of the breached canal, rode back to the ravine accompanied by the *kotwal* and some of the villagers.

A man was discovered hiding in the thickets a quarter of a mile above the track. He had a bullet through the shoulder and was suffering from severe loss of blood. The second man had not gone so far. A smashed knee is a painful thing, and he crouched in the tall grass by the path and groaned. There had been a third man, but he had fled.

Alex saw the two wounded men taken back to the cantonments in a bullock-cart and, having handed them over to the police, he returned to his bungalow.

After breakfast he walked over to the Commissioner's office. Winter had heard Alex's footsteps and his quiet voice, and had gone to her bedroom and wept for the first time since her wedding

night: weeping for relief and thankfulness as she had never wept for the loss of her illusions.

Later she joined Conway. It was a Tuesday, and that evening the "Tuesday crowd" were to dine as usual at the Residency. Winter detested these parties, but she was too worn out by the anxieties of the night to be able to stand up to a scene with Conway, so she agreed to dine with him on the understanding that she could retire immediately afterwards. Pleased, Conway put an arm about her waist, and planted a wet kiss on her cheek. Winter heard footsteps in the hall and put up her hands in an endeavour to thrust him away, so that for a moment it appeared as though she were returning her husband's embrace. The door opened and she found herself looking into Alex Randall's expressionless face.

Conway released her and turned. "Hullo, Alex, m'boy. Walked right in on the turtle doves, dammit! Have a drink. Make yerself at home."

He shouted for drinks to be brought, took one himself and moved to the door. "Don't go. My wife'll look after yer. Why don't yer come t'dinner? Good party on tonight. Capital crowd!"

"I am afraid, sir—" began Alex, and stopped. He looked at Winter's small rigid face, then continued—"that I have been neglecting my social duties of late. I should be glad to."

"Good, good!" approved the Commissioner heartily.

He removed himself, and Winter said stiffly: "I am sorry that Mr. Barton is unable to give you his attention, but there are arrangements to be made. I hope that your business with him will keep?"

Alex was feeling angrier than he had ever felt in his life. An entirely illogical anger, for surely he should be glad that she was not after all as unhappy in her marriage as he had supposed?

He put his glass down on the chimney-piece and said: "I did not come here to see Mr. Barton. I came to pay my debts."

"Your debts?"

"Let us say, my thanks. I think I owe you my life." He looked down at her and smiled, not entirely pleasantly, and added: "I believe that I had intended to say something to the effect that it is now of course wholly at your disposal, but such statements are apt to sound better in a theatre, do you not think so? So I will confine myself to saying 'thank you'. I am indeed grateful."

He took her hand and bent above it formally. Winter snatched it away, bewildered by the derisive note in his voice. She said a little breathlessly: "You have nothing to thank me for, Captain Randall. I did nothing that anyone else would not have done in the same circumstances."

Making a determined effort to appear calm and composed, she sat down, her wide skirts spreading crisply about her, and said: "You have not told me what occurred this morning. Was there no one in the ravine, then?"

"No, they were there," said Alex. He gave her an edited and colourless version of the happenings in the ravine, then finished his drink and excused himself.

That night Winter had the doubtful felicity of observing that he appeared entirely at his ease among the inner circle of the Commissioner's friends. He even refused to be drawn into any argument with Colonel Moulson, who continued to regard him with a hostile eye.

At the conclusion of the meal the guests repaired to the drawing room. There were usually several Indian guests on these occasions: rich landowners who gambled heavily and were on that account on easy terms with the Commissioner and his more raffish friends. Tonight they were joined by Kishan Prasad, whom Winter had not seen since the day of her arrival at Calcutta.

Card play had not yet begun, and Winter had been about to excuse herself on the plea of a headache, when Kishan Prasad drew up a chair beside the sofa on which she had seated herself. He inquired politely where Mrs. Barton intended to spend the summer months, and on hearing that she would not be removing to the hills, advised her earnestly to do so. She would, he assured her, find Lunjore unpleasantly hot from mid-April until the monsoon broke. He then turned the conversation to the forthcoming duck shoot at Hazrat Bagh, a jheel which lay some fifteen miles to the west of the cantonments.

The shoot was being arranged by some of the local *talukdars* (landowners), and food and beaters on an elaborate scale were being provided for the guests, who included most of the British officers stationed in Lunjore. Those ladies invited to attend would watch the battue from the tree-lined bunds, or from an artificial hide to one side of the jheel. A road was in process of construction so that they would be able to drive there in their carriages, for the jheel lay far from any made road.

"I hope that we are to have the pleasure of seeing you there, Mrs. Barton?" said Kishan Prasad. "I am to be one of the hosts, you know."

"I shall certainly be there," she said. "I have never been out on a big shoot yet."

"Good evening, Rao Sahib," said a pleasant voice behind them. "When did you arrive in Lunjore?"

Neither of them had seen Alex approach and Kishan Prasad started slightly at the sound of his voice. But he turned a countenance as bland and pleasant as Alex's own: "I arrived at midday."

"In good time for the obsequies, in fact," said Alex with a grin. "I am sorry to disappoint you."

"Yes?" Kishan Prasad looked puzzled though polite, but Alex's apparently pointless remark was entirely clear to Winter. She could not conceive, however, why he had made it. To suggest that Kishan Prasad had had any hand in the attempt upon his life was absurd . . . . Or was it? She could not be sure, and because she was not, she was all at once afraid.

Kishan Prasad rose and walked away with Alex, amicably discussing the forthcoming duck shoot, and Winter decided that she was letting her imagination run away with her. But she did not, after all, leave the party early that night.

Kishan Prasad himself left at midnight, by which time her husband, who had passed successively through the convivial, the quarrelsome and the maudlin stages of intoxication, finally arrived at the unconscious. Alex managed to get rid of the other guests. He was turning to go when Winter stopped him.

"Captain Randall, did you know that the Rao Sahib would be coming to the house tonight?"

"I had heard that he might be."

"Is that why you were here tonight? To see him? You thought *he* had told those men to kill you?"

Alex shook his head. "No. He will not deliberately take my life, or plot to take it, because I once made the grave mistake of saving his. But if someone else should do it, that would be quite a different matter. He is an extremely clever man, and a dangerous enemy to the British."

Winter sat down a little abruptly. "I don't understand."

Alex looked at her under lowered lashes. "That may be just as well. Are you going to the hills this summer?"

"No. I do not think that I shall mind the heat so much. Why are you changing the subject?"

"I'm not. I think you should go, and I shall do all that I can to see that you do. Are you so particularly anxious to stay?"

"Yes," said Winter. Had that been what Kishan Prasad meant? Had he been hinting there might be trouble in Lunjore in the coming months? But if that were so, how could she go to the hills, knowing that Alex would still be in Lunjore?

She said almost inaudibly: "There are times when—when one would so much rather not be sent away."

Alex misunderstood the hesitant words. He turned sharply. "Are you going to have a child?"

Her face set in a dreadful silent stare and a shudder went through her body. The colour drained out of her face, leaving it pinched and sallow. That could not happen to her—it could not! Children should be born of love—

She steadied herself with an effort. "No."

Alex's gaze wandered to the sofa on the far side of the room where her husband lay and snored. "I'm sorry. I thought that was

304

what you meant, and it seemed to make it even more necessary that you should remove from Lunjore for the hot weather."

Winter did not look at him. She said: "I only meant that I will not run away."

"No," said Alex thoughtfully, "I don't believe you will."

He sat down, stretching his legs out and leaning his head against the back of the sofa, and the silence lengthened and filled slowly with small sounds: the Commissioner's stertorous breathing, the ticking of the clock, the chirrup of a gecko lizard.

Winter sat motionless, her body still rigid from shock. She did not look at Alex's face, she looked at his hands instead: brown, thin, and strong: and she seemed to see beside them the damp, fleshy, unsteady fingers of the man she had married. She knew then that she could not bear children to Conway. To do so would be the ultimate indecency. She would go away as he had suggested, to Lucknow, to the house that had been her only home. To the Gulab Mahal. To Ameera. She would go home . . . .

She saw Alex's body relax. He was still silent, but his silence was as devoid of tension as his body, and the familiar sense of safety and reassurance that his presence could bring to her gradually smoothed out the turmoil in Winter's mind.

Alex was not thinking of Winter. He seldom had time to think of her, or allowed himself to do so. There were too many other things to think about. Too much that needed to be done, and always too little time in which to do it . . . .

So Kishan Prasad was to be one of the hosts at the duck shoot—Kishan Prasad who never did anything without a reason. What then was behind this shoot at Hazrat Bagh? Could there be an ulterior motive behind such an arrangement?

"I must see Packer and Moulson and Gardener-Smith in the morning," thought Alex, "though they will none of them believe a word of it. What the devil *is* behind the duck shoot? I'll swear there is something . . . . Oh, what's the good of thinking of it! It's none of my business . . . ."

The clock on the chimney piece struck one, and he removed his abstracted gaze from the ceiling and looked at Winter. He said slowly: "I didn't mean to keep you up so late. I'm sorry . . . . Riding this morning?"

"Yes."

"All right. Six o'clock, then."

They smiled at each other, their faces dim and peaceful, and Alex
stood up. Winter rose with a rustle of silk and walked beside him
into the hall. He held out his hand:

"Good night. Or good morning! And I suppose I should also say
'Thank you for a very pleasant evening'."

"Was it pleasant?"

Alex considered the question. "Instructive, at all events."

He was silent for a moment or two, looking down at Winter, the
line of his mouth unexpectedly tender. Then he lifted the hand he
held and, turning it palm upwards, kissed it lightly and, folding her
fingers upon the kiss, released it. Then he turned and went out into
the night.

CHAPTER 5

*L*ESS THAN five hours later Alex was waiting for her on the
Residency road, and they rode out through the cantonments and across the rifle range to the open country beyond.

They drew rein on the crest of a lonely knoll that was crowned
by a banyan tree. Doves cooed among its branches, and a flight of
wild duck whistled overhead, making for the jheel that lay ten
miles to the north. Winter watched them as they dwindled into
specks against the pale blue of the morning, and saw that there
were other lines in the sky: teal and geese flying in from a night
spent on the river or among the ploughed lands.

"That is Hazrat Bagh out there, isn't it?" She pointed with her
riding crop across the plain.

Alex, following the direction of her gaze, said: "Yes. They're
making a road so that the ladies from Lunjore can all drive out in
comfort to watch the duck shoot. No expense is being spared to
impress upon your husband and the garrison how friendly and
cooperative our local landowners are, and I should dearly like to
know—"

He did not finish the sentence but turned away from her, screw-
ing up his eyes against the dazzle of the newly-risen sun, and said:
"Listen to those partridges calling. I must bring a gun out here one
evening."

"You had one yesterday, didn't you? A pistol, I mean. Have you got one now?"

Alex nodded.

Winter said abruptly: "Will you give it to me?"

Alex turned sharply. "What for?"

"I should feel—safer," said Winter lightly, affecting an interest in a pair of weaver birds who were fluttering anxiously about their dangling nest in a thorn tree below.

"Thinking of shooting anyone?"

"No," said Winter soberly. "Not even myself."

The Eagle snorted and backed as though he had felt a sudden jerk on the bridle. Alex brought him under control, and inquired shortly if she had ever used firearms before.

Winter shook her head. "No. But I do not suppose it is very difficult, is it?"

"Try." Alex dismounted and, pulling the Eagle's reins over his head, helped Winter from the saddle. The sunlight glinted on the barrel of the small Tranter revolver as he explained its mechanism. "Here—take it. Fire it in the air."

The report sent the horses dancing and snorting indignantly, and startled a peacock and his five demure brown wives who had been roosting unseen on the far side of a clump of pampas grass.

"Well done," said Alex approvingly. "You didn't jump; but you must allow for the recoil." He made her fire the remaining rounds and then remarked: "Not bad. You can keep it."

"Thank you," said Winter gravely. She held it out to him. "Will you reload it for me, please?"

Alex shook his head. "No. Not until I've taught you how to use it. For the present it is safer unloaded. And probably just as effective a deterrent."

He saw the hot colour rise in her face and had a sudden, startled suspicion why she wanted a pistol. But he asked no further questions and they cantered back between the flat-topped thorn trees to the Residency.

Three days later she was able to use the pistol, unloaded but with, as he had predicted, a satisfactorily deterrent effect.

Conway rarely visited his wife's room, but he had done so on an evening as she was dressing for dinner. He had been tolerably sober and therefore more dangerous.

"Now, my dear wife," he said unpleasantly, "you can take that dress off again. You won't need it."

Winter remained unruffled. She opened a drawer of her dressing table and turned towards him with the revolver in her hand. She was perfectly polite. He had not married her for love, but for money, and he had got what he wanted and must be content with that. She would fulfil her duties as his wife in every way except this, but if he ever attempted to force his attentions upon her again she would shoot him.

"Not to kill you, Conway. I shall stop short of murder. But just to hurt you painfully enough to ensure that such a thing does not occur again. I hope you realize that I mean it?"

He blustered and shouted and called her unprintable names, but backed out of her room and never attempted to enter it again. The revolver had served its purpose, but Winter now took early-morning instruction in how to fire it; partly because it amused her, but largely because it gave her an excuse to see Alex.

Once he brought a rifle with him. It was, he said, one of the new issue: the Enfield rifle that was to replace the old-fashioned infantry musket, and he made her lie down to fire it.

Niaz was with them, and regarded the rifle with interest. "Is it true that this will fire a ball many times the distance of the old ones?" he inquired. "How is it done?"

"It has grooved bores," said Alex. "And the cartridge papers are greased."

He took one out of the pocket of his riding coat and, biting off the end, rammed it down the barrel, and fired again.

"May I try?" inquired Niaz.

Alex handed over the gun and another cartridge and Niaz bit off the end and spat it out upon the ground. "Pah!" he said with a grimace. "With what is that greased?" He lay down, cuddling the butt against his cheek, sighted carefully and fired. A fluff of dust showed that the bullet had chipped an anthill over two hundred yards distant, and Niaz laughed.

"*Hai!* This is indeed a good weapon. Now all that we require is a war so that we may try it on an enemy!"

Alex did not answer. He was staring down at the scrap of greased paper Niaz had spat out upon the ground, and there was an odd look on his face. He drew another cartridge from his pocket and

stood looking at it, turning it over in his hand and rubbing his thumb slowly across the greased paper wrapping.

They rode no farther that day, but returned to the cantonments —Alex riding with a speed and recklessness that he had never shown before when he had been out with Winter, and as though he had forgotten that she was there.

An hour later he was ushered into Colonel Gardener-Smith's office.

"Good morning, Captain Randall." The colonel wondered what Randall had come about this time, and hoped that it was no more alarmist nonsense about an armed rising planned for the coming hot weather. Efficient young man, but he had a bee in his bonnet about mutiny. "Well, what is it now?"

Alex tossed an object down upon the table and said without preamble: "That is one of the cartridges for the new Enfield, sir. Can you tell me what they are greased with?"

The colonel stared, considerably taken aback both by the question and the tone in which it was uttered. He picked the thing up, examined it and dropped it, and marked his displeasure by seating himself behind his desk and keeping Alex standing.

He said coldly: "I have no idea. And I hardly think that the composition of cartridge grease lies within your province."

Alex said: "Perhaps not, sir, but it must be within yours. Those cartridge papers have to be bitten, and if there is any doubt as to the composition of the grease, it is a thing that will affect the caste of every sepoy in the army. A grievance that will unite men of every regiment. A common denominator."

"You mean, if it were animal fat—?"

"If it should contain any lard or animal fat," said Alex harshly, "no sepoy should be asked to touch it, let alone bite it. The pig is an unclean animal to a Mussulman and the cow a sacred animal to the Hindu, while the fat of any dead creature is an abomination to both. But no one knows that better than you, sir."

Colonel Gardener-Smith frowned and said uneasily but without conviction: "That is a point that cannot have escaped the attention of the responsible authorities."

"Why not? The method and manufacture of these things was worked out in England, not India, and the men responsible for it are not likely to possess any special knowledge of the Indian caste system."

"I do not believe . . . ." began the colonel unhappily. He wished Randall would leave well alone and stop this continual harrying . . . bees in the bonnet. *Buzz-buzz-buzz* . . . .

He banged the table suddenly with his clenched fist. "What do you expect me to do about it, anyway? It's none of my business—or yours! I'm not Master General of the Ordnance! These things will be issued to every regiment in India shortly."

"I know," said Alex. "But at least it can do no harm to ask for the official analysis of this stuff, and in the meantime it might be possible to manufacture our own wrapping papers here in Lunjore, so that the men can see for themselves what is used."

"That would be impossible," said Colonel Gardener-Smith.

"Nothing is impossible now," said Alex slowly. "Not even a mutiny of the Bengal Army."

Colonel Gardener-Smith stood up abruptly. "That is a point upon which we are unlikely to agree. If that is all you wished to see me about, I must ask you to excuse me, as I have a great many calls upon my time. I will bear in mind what you have said, and will write at once to inquire into the composition of the lubrication being used. You may be quite confident—as I am—that your fears will be proved groundless."

"Thank you, sir," said Alex in a colourless voice, and went out into the bright morning sun.

HE RODE LESS with Winter after that and he did not again take out the Enfield rifle.

Winter missed those early-morning rides in his company, and did not know that the reason for their curtailment was the fact that it is difficult regularly to arrive home in the early hours of the morning and still wake in time to ride before sunrise.

Alex had taken to spending a great many of his nights disguised in the crowded alleyways of the city, and he managed thus to acquire a considerable quantity of curious information.

Niaz, too, spent much of his time similarly occupied. He had friends among the sepoys and was often to be found visiting the lines. Much of his information tallied with Alex's, and none of it was in any way reassuring.

"It is said," reported Niaz, "that it is the purpose of the government to convert all men to be Christians. But they say that as the feringhis are few, to force their faith upon all in Hind would be difficult; therefore they will accomplish it by fraud."

"With what purpose?" asked Alex.

"So that they may use the sepoys to conquer all the world for them. If the army were all of one caste—Christians—they would all eat the same food, and as slaves of the sahib-*log* could fight their battles in a hundred countries. There is even now a tale that to this end the Company have ground up the bones of pigs and cattle and mixed that dust with the flour and with the grain, so that all who eat of it will thereby lose their caste. And being casteless will have to become Christians, and—hast thou heard this then?"

Alex nodded. "I have heard. Do they in the lines believe it?"

"Many believe. What do they say in the city?"

"They have refused the last consignment of government flour," said Alex. "It lies still unloaded in the carts. I have sent for grain from Deesa, so that they may grind it for themselves."

He had brought up at a general conference earlier that day the question of the refusal of the bazaars to accept or handle the flour, but the Commissioner had merely observed that if they didn't like it they could go without, and Colonel Moulson had remarked unpleasantly that he did not know what the garrison was coming to when members of it allowed themselves to be panicked by every petty rumour in the bazaars.

The windy, unconstructive debate had dawdled to an indecisive close, and Alex had flung out into the sunlight in a fury. The cartridges, and now the flour . . . He remembered the devildom at Khanwai. *This may do well enough for the villages, but it will not serve for the sepoys. For them it must be something that strikes deeper and touches every man. They are already as tinder, but there is as yet no spark. No matter, we will find it . . . .* This surely was the spark Kishan Prasad had spoken of.

Beyond the Residency gate an open carriage passed him, bearing a Captain and Mrs. Hossack, their four children and an ayah. Mrs. Hossack was a pleasant woman with a somewhat anxious manner. The two older children, recognizing Alex, waved enthusiastically as they passed, and Mrs. Hossack smiled and bowed.

"Thank God I'm not married!" thought Alex with sudden vehemence. "At least I have not got that fear to face!" And thought instantly: "I must get him to send her to the hills. She will have to go if he orders her. After all, he *is* her husband."

But he was not thinking of Mrs. Hossack.

CHAPTER 6

*T*HE DUCK shoot at Hazrat Bagh was timed to begin soon after eight o'clock in the morning, to allow the guns and the guests to assemble, and breakfast to be eaten on a prepared ground half a mile from the jheel.

The temporary road that the hosts had constructed for the convenience of their guests proved remarkably good, and the carriages that had started from Lunjore at dawn reached the rendezvous in ample time for breakfast.

To Winter's surprise many of the guests proved to be strangers to her, and she found on inquiry that they were officers and officials from Suthragunj, a large cantonment town beyond the borders of Lunjore.

In a direct line Suthragunj lay less than thirty miles from Lunjore, but the main road ran far to the southward for more than double that distance before a branch road to Suthragunj added yet another fifteen miles to the score. So the British residents of Suthragunj and Lunjore seldom met. Now, however, since the new road had been extended to Suthragunj so that they too could attend, at least a dozen members of the garrison there were present.

Winter had seated herself on the hard ground with her back to a tree trunk a few yards from where her husband had taken up his stand, but when the first shot broke the drowsy peace of the morning, to be followed by a crashing fusillade, Winter stood up, staring in horror at the falling birds and their helpless dying flurries. She shut her eyes, trying to shut out the sight, but she could not shut out the sounds.

She turned and fled down the lake shore in breathless panic, and she did not see Alex until she had run into him.

Alex had not been shooting well that morning. He had been thinking of other things, seeing at last and very clearly the reason for this elaborate shooting party, and wondering why it had not occurred to him before, when it was so entirely obvious.

A lone goose swished overhead and Alex fired and saw the bird fall wounded somewhere along the farther arm of the lake. Niaz gave a grunt of disapproval and Alex threw the gun across to him and said: "Damn the birds!" He turned and walked away, feeling in his pockets for a cigarette, and Winter brushed through the grass and stumbled against him.

Alex caught her by the shoulders, and then quite suddenly she dropped her head against him and wept.

Alex stood very still, holding her, feeling the shuddering of the slim body under his hands. Her hair smelt faintly of lavender as it had on the walls of Delhi, and he held her quite gently because he wanted so much to hold her hard against him. At last the sobs quietened, and he put her gently away from him.

Winter drew a deep breath. "I'm sorry," she said, her voice under control once more. "I don't know why I behaved so stupidly."

She considered the matter gravely. "I think it was because it was such a lovely day and, when the shooting began, that seemed to make it worse—because it had been so beautiful before, and so peaceful. I couldn't bear it being spoiled." She sank down onto the ground. "I don't want to kill anything—*anything!*"

313

Alex sat on the grass beside her. "There's no reason why you should. But a sense of proportion is a useful thing to cultivate. Shooting duck takes skill. And it provides food." He jerked his chin in the general direction of the jheel. "Put it in its proper place. I dislike these large-scale battues myself. I prefer to do my shooting on my own, or with one or two people at most, instead of indulging in this type of mass slaughter."

"Then why did you come—if you knew what it would be like?"

"Curiosity. I wanted to see if I could find out why Kishan Prasad and his friends had arranged this elaborate shoot."

"And have you found out?"

"Yes."

Alex looked out across the stretch of sunlit water that lay beyond a narrow belt of grass and reeds. The firing had died down to no more than an occasional shot, and a warm, sleepy silence returned to the morning.

He pulled a grass stem and bit it thoughtfully. "It's quite simple

really. Lunjore lies across one of
the main roadways into Oudh,
and that road crosses an iron
bridge ten miles to the south. If
there was a rising in the Punjab,
or Delhi way, we could hold that
bridge; or if the worst came to
the worst, blow it up and prevent
rebel troops from using this route
into Oudh, which is at the
moment a hotbed of disaffection.
There is an arsenal at Suthragunj,
a very large one. Some of our
local *talukdars* have not missed
that point, and under cover of a
lavish entertainment for the gar-
risons of both districts, they have
constructed a very adequate road
that avoids the bridge and brings
Suthragunj within roughly thirty
miles of us. And we have very
kindly tested it for them. Where
our carriages have gone, guns and ammunition wagons can
follow."

He rolled over on his back and watched a procession of red ants
hurrying along a branch above him. Winter said a little uncertainly:
"Are you—do you really think that there is going to be trouble?"

"Not trouble. A rising. I've thought so for about five years." He
was silent for a moment, and when he spoke again his voice held a
savage bitterness. "We shall see the ruin, in one day or in twenty
days, of what might have been the finest army in the world. We
shall build it up again, but it will never be the same. There will be
atrocities on both sides—all sides. The East drops straight into
barbarism when it is frightened or enraged, and we shall follow its
example and call it revenge. These people have no conception of
the ultimate strength that we can bring out of Europe against them.
Even men like Kishan Prasad have no idea what they are challenging. They do not realize that even if they murder every white man,
woman and child in the whole of India, England will go on sending

out troops until she has smashed them. And the reprisals that follow will leave a legacy of hatred that will be handed down to future generations, from father to son and from mother to daughter. We shall forget—but they will not!"

A breeze whispered across the jheel, ruffling the water. There was another burst of firing from away to the left, and a dozen teal swished overhead, almost brushing the treetops with their wings. Alex came reluctantly to his feet. He glanced down at Winter and said: "Hadn't you better be getting back?"

Winter ignored the remark. "Is that why you taught me to shoot? And why you wanted me to go to the hills?"

"Yes."

Winter stood up and shook out the grey folds of her skirt. Then she said quite lightly, "I will think about it," and turned away.

He heard the tall grass rustle behind her, and stood quite still, listening, his face drawn and bleak in the harsh sunlight.

"Why," he demanded despairingly of heaven, "does this have to happen to me?"

WINTER did not see Alex again for some considerable time. He attended no more parties at the Residency, and he did not ride again with her, for he spent more and more time in the outlying villages, picking up information. He was aware of an ominous feeling of expectant stillness. But it was a stillness that did not last long, and the first warning mutter came from faraway Bengal.

The thing that Alex had visualized in the moment following Niaz's casual comment on the greased cartridge paper had caught the fuel that officialdom had itself prepared. And the fuel was dry and ready.

On that same January morning that had seen the garrison of Lunjore ride gaily out to shoot duck at Hazrat Bagh, a man of low caste, a lascar who worked in the ammunition factory near Calcutta, had stopped a high-caste sepoy during the heat of the day and begged a drink from his *lotah*—the brass water-pot carried by every caste Hindu and religiously preserved from defilement. The sepoy had stared less in anger than astonishment.

"How can that be, fool?" he asked. "I am a Brahmin, and my caste forbids it."

"Caste? What is caste?" grinned the lascar. "The cartridges we

316

prepare here are defiled with the fat of hogs and cattle, and soon ye will be as one—casteless together—when the new guns are given out to the regiments and ye bite the cartridges daily.''

"What is that?" said the sepoy thickly. "Tell again!"

The lascar had done so, with embellishments, and the sepoy had not waited to hear to the end, but had run to his comrades in the lines. Here was proof at last of the duplicity of the feringhis! The hated policies of annexation, the seizure of land and the deposing of kings were as nothing to this; for this struck at the deepest beliefs of men, in that it destroyed their souls.

Hindu and Mohammedan together recoiled in horror from sacrilege and defilement. Panic spread through the lines, and from there, with incredible swiftness, it swept out across India, its progress sped and fanned by those who had been ready and waiting for such an opportunity.

A hundred men—a hundred thousand—picked up the fearful whisper and passed it on: "It is an order from *Belait*, from the Queen and her council, that by means of the cartridges all sepoys, both Mussulman and Hindu, be defiled—as men in the towns and cities are defiled by the eating of bone-dust in their flour—so that being made casteless they shall do the will of the sahib-*log* as slaves for ever! We are betrayed by the feringhis who have stolen our country and now wish to steal our souls!"

It was then that the nocturnal fires started. The thatch of an officer's bungalow would catch fire, set alight, more often than not, by a blazing arrow shot by some unseen hand. The telegraph station of the big cantonment of Barrackpore burned to the ground, and night after night, despite guards and sentries, flames would glow bright in the darkness, spreading up northward from Calcutta and Barrackpore.

There were midnight meetings of men who kept to the shadows of walls where no guards challenged them. There were letters that went out by every *dâk* (post), calling upon the soldiery to resist the attempts to defile them. The news that the 19th Regiment of Native Infantry at Berhampur had broken out into mutiny spread upwards through India and fanned the panic.

But that mutiny died out, and without violence. An inquiry into the question of the greased cartridges was instituted, and proceeded upon its ponderous way, and officers who had begun to eye the men

317

under their command with an anxiety they would not own to, relaxed again.

The rumours died down, and the Commissioner of Lunjore, who had consistently pooh-poohed the possibility of any serious trouble arising, remarked complacently that he had always known it was a mere tempest in a teapot.

CHAPTER 7

*I*T WILL PASS .... *It has passed ....*

In cantonments and offices, in Residences and bungalows, in government houses and council chambers and in the house of the Governor General himself, wherever the British met to talk, the soothing phrase was repeated again and again. And especially since Sir Henry Lawrence, perhaps the best-loved man in India, had now arrived in Lucknow to take over the administration of the city from the contentious Mr. Coverley Jackson. Aged by the recent loss of his wife and failing health, at the Governor General's request he had nevertheless abandoned the chance to some sorely-needed home leave and had hurried to the help of Oudh.

So men who uneasily had been smelling the wind relaxed again, convinced that the peak of the general unrest had passed, and that any serious danger (if there had indeed ever been any, which the majority were inclined to doubt) was now over.

Lottie wrote from Delhi. Edward had been transferred there from Meerut on special duty, and they had been lent a delightful house in the city, not far from the Kashmir Gate. And she was expecting a child, to be born in mid-summer. Sophie was in Cawnpore, visiting friends, and would not be returning until the end of May, but Mama and Papa sent their love ....

The letter disturbed Winter, for she had thought that Lottie at least would be safe. Meerut housed the strongest European garrison in the northeastern provinces, and where there were well over a thousand British soldiers there would have been little danger. Sophie, too, could come to no harm in Cawnpore, where General Sir Hugh Wheeler and his staff had their headquarters. But Delhi ... there were no British regiments in Delhi.

There was also a letter from Ameera, from the Rose Palace in

318

Lucknow. Winter had written to her earlier, suggesting a visit. But even the Gulab Mahal, she learned, was now closed to her.

Ameera's husband, Walayat Shah, had at no time felt any friendship towards the British, but now that they had deprived him of all rights and privileges and put an end to his means of livelihood, his toleration of the feringhis had changed to a corroding hatred. Brooding on present calamity and past glory, he listened to the words of those who preached a jehad, a holy war, and dreamed the Mohammedan dream. For now a jehad meant far more than the spreading of the Faith and the slaying of Unbelievers. It meant revenge: and perhaps, once more, an empire.

"He is changed even towards me, his wife," wrote Ameera sadly. "And therefore I cannot ask thee to enter the Gulab Mahal. Some day, surely—when all this is passed. But for the present it were wiser to keep away."

And then, on the last day of April, another letter came, hastily written, hardly more than a small folded square of paper. It was a brief enough message, and written, save for two words, in Urdu: "*Cara Mia—They have set the auspicious day. Therefore go swiftly to the sea and take ship for England, for though no harm will befall thee before the last day of the new month, after that there will be no safety anywhere. Least of all where there be regiments.*"

There was no signature, but Winter did not need one. Only Ameera would have prefaced the broken script with that single Spanish endearment.

THAT NIGHT Conway gave a party, a riotous affair lasting well into the small hours of the morning. All the usual guests were there, with the exception of Mr. Josh Cottar who had departed to Calcutta on a business trip.

"Nothing has changed," thought Winter. "It is just the same."

But that was not true. She herself had changed. The noisy, raffish party and the sight of her husband with his arm about Lou Cottar's waist no longer had any power to hurt or disgust her, for now she too could feel the wind and hear the thunder.

If Ameera was right, all these people here might die within a few months. The last day of May, Ameera had said—*and after that there will be no safety anywhere.* It was the first of May tomorrow. Thirty days more. Was Ameera right?

Winter did not ride the following morning. The horses needed rest, and she slept late, but when she had breakfasted she wrote to Alex. It was a short letter and the first she had ever written to him. She gave it to a servant to deliver to him, but the man said that Randall Sahib was in camp among the outlying villages. "Then someone must take it to him," said Winter. "Send his servant Yusaf to me."

Yusaf rode with the letter, and Alex read it late that evening by the light of a flaring oil-lamp. There were only two lines, but he read them and re-read them and then folded the paper carefully and put it into the inner pocket of his coat, and said: "Tell the mem-sahib that I return tomorrow or the next day."

Yusaf saluted and slipped back into the darkness, and Alex returned to his tent.

He did not start for Lunjore until early next afternoon, and leaving the servants to break camp and follow, he and Niaz rode hard through the heat of the day and into the dusty sunset and the brief green dusk. As the sun sank below the horizon they stopped to eat, for the Mohammedan fast of Ramadan had begun with the new moon and, while it lasted, Niaz and all other followers of the Prophet might not eat or drink between sunrise and sunset. Alex, too, kept the fast when he was away from the cantonments, for he had found it to be good training. It was dark by the time they reached the bungalow, and Alex took a hot bath to remove the dust and sweat of the long ride, and having changed into a white mess-jacket he walked across in the starlight to the Residency.

The big house was ablaze with lights and there was a trap and a high dog-cart standing on the wide drive. "Moulson again," thought Alex. He went up the veranda steps. A servant lifted the *chik* before the hall door and murmured that the *Huzoors* were playing cards in the small drawing room and the mem-sahib was in the big drawing room.

Winter was sitting on a sofa in the centre of the room, with the slow-moving punkah stirring the air above her. She had a book in her hands, but it was obvious that she had heard his voice in the hall. She was smiling: the smile an actress might employ to indicate pleasurable surprise. Some instinct for danger made Alex return it, and as he took the hand that she held out to him he knew that he had been right, for her fingers were cold and not quite steady, and

320

they tightened warningly upon his for a moment before they were withdrawn.

Winter said gaily: "How kind of you to come so promptly! I hope it was not inconvenient? I have received a letter entrusting me with a message for you from a friend of yours in Lucknow." Her gaze went past him and she spoke to the servant who lingered by the door: "Bring drinks for the sahib, Rassul."

"*Hukkum*," murmured Rassul, and the door closed softly behind him.

Winter said: "Do sit down, Captain Randall. Have you ridden far today? I am afraid my husband is busy just now. A card party, you know. How much English do these people understand? I did not expect to see you until tomorrow." She laughed as though she had made some joke.

Alex's eyes narrowed but he replied without the least hesitation: "There was nothing much to keep me, and camping is hot work in this weather. A good deal more than most people think."

He saw Winter's quick breath of relief, and smiled. Had she really been afraid that he would misunderstand her and demand explanations? She threw an anxious glance at the two doors that opened on to the veranda. *Chiks* hung before both to keep the room from filling with bats and night-flying insects but there were, he knew, at least three servants on the veranda. He shook his head very slightly, and the door behind him swung open silently and Rassul was back with a laden tray.

Winter said: "Yes, I thought it might be so. Mr. . . . Brown wishes to know if there is any good shooting to be had in Lunjore at this time of the year. He has a few weeks' leave soon and is considering coming here. He sent you this—"

She handed him Ameera's note and Alex read it with a half-smile, folded it, and slipped it into his pocket as Rassul poured out a drink and withdrew. Winter talked trivialities for five minutes or so, and then rose with a rustle of starched muslin flounces.

Alex said good night to her and went off to the small drawing room where he was greeted ungraciously by the Commissioner, stayed to watch a hand of whist, and left.

The city was awake and restless; drums throbbed and conches blared. "It is Ramadan," said Niaz, but he said it uneasily, looking over his shoulder.

321

"It is *dewanee*—the madness," said Alex.

That night he lay awake hour after hour staring into the darkness and thinking of those few scrawled lines of broken script that Winter had given him . . . . So he had been right! A day and a date. He was sure that it must be so. Men like Kishan Prasad would not content themselves with stirring up general discontent. It was a general mutiny of the Bengal army, coupled with a popular rising, that was to be feared, and such a thing called for a day and a date . . . .

The last day of May—and it was already the second. Two days gone. Twenty-eight days in which to turn aside the wind that was rising steadily and blowing hot and fitfully through India.

Alex went to see the Commissioner the following morning, and gave him the substance of Ameera's warning—without, however, disclosing the fact that the message had been received by his wife.

"Nonsense!" said the Commissioner. "Auspicious day?—Don't believe a word of it! Probably refers to a wedding. You shouldn't listen to bazaar gossip."

"As you like, sir," said Alex in his most expressionless voice.

He spent another exhausting hour placing his views yet again before the three commanding officers of the Lunjore regiments, but with no better results than before; and leaving them he rode down to the police lines to discuss the possibility of disaffection in that quarter with Major Maynard, who commanded them.

Major Maynard alone confessed to uneasiness, though not on account of his police, whom he believed to be staunch. "There's old Gardener pottering around with his watering can, cherishin' his fellows as though they were tender plants, and Packer looking upon his as erring sheep to be gathered into the fold, while Moulson goes to the other extreme and slings his sepoys into irons if they so much as blink on parade! He'll go too far one day. But I'll bear in mind what you say," Major Maynard finished easily. "Personally I'm inclined to think that the worst is past."

"I envy you your optimism," said Alex dryly, and rode back slowly through the blinding sunlight and the hot shadows of the wide cantonment road.

THE TELEGRAPH did not as yet operate in Lunjore, and so it was not until two days later that the news trickled over the border from Oudh that on Sunday, May 3rd, the 7th Regiment of Oudh

Irregulars had refused to accept their cartridges, and had mutinied. Sir Henry Lawrence had apparently acted with great promptness and succeeded in disarming the regiment—a good many of whom had absconded—and fifty of the ringleaders had been seized.

"It is too soon," said Alex, reading that laconic dispatch. He crumpled up the slip of paper and flung it from him in sudden rage. It was that night that his house servant woke him at one o'clock in the morning.

Alex slept on the flat roof of his bungalow and Yusaf slept across the stair that led up to it. Alex was a light sleeper at the best of times, and the whispers woke him. He was across the roof in less than ten seconds.

"Who is it?"

"Come down, *Huzoor*," whispered Yusaf. "It is Niaz, and I think he is sorely hurt."

Alex ran down the stairs. He caught the dark figure that sagged against the bottom of the stair, and said sharply to Yusaf: "Take his feet."

"No," gasped Niaz with an attempt at a laugh. "I can walk. Give me thy shoulder, brother."

Alex thrust Yusaf ahead of him: "Light a lamp in my room—quickly! Where art thou hurt?"

"In the back. But it has missed its mark. Do not fear."

Alex pulled Niaz's right arm about his shoulder and half-carried him to the bedroom, where Yusaf had lit the oil-lamp. The wound was unpleasant enough, but it had, as Niaz had said, missed its mark, for it had been deflected by the shoulder-blade and Niaz was suffering more from loss of blood than from anything else. He had walked a mile or more after he had been knifed.

"It was in the lines," said Niaz. "I had —"

"Quiet," said Alex curtly. "Tell me later. We will bind thee first." He cut away the blood-soaked clothing, and with Yusaf's assistance washed and bound up the wound and sent him off to brew strong tea.

"I can go no more to the lines," said Niaz ruefully. "It is finished."

"Who was it?"

"I do not know. I went to talk with those who I thought to be friends of mine and to listen. But tonight they would not talk, and

323

they looked at me out of their eyes, sideways, and there was a constraint upon them. There was a sadhu in the lines—I saw him standing in the shadows of a hut. When I came away he had gone, and I put my hand upon my knife and walked as a cat walks in an alley full of dogs."

Niaz grinned to hide a spasm of pain and drank the hot, sweet tea Yusaf had brought. "There is a lamp by the tree at the turn of the lines," he said, "and there was a revolver such as the sahibs carry, lying in the dust. A child's trick that should not have deceived a babe, yet I stooped for it. I heard the step but I could not avoid the blow. Had I not heard it, that knife would have struck true."

Alex said: "Was there nothing to tell who it was?"

"I did not see. I fell, and turned as I fell. But I think it was the sadhu."

Alex nodded. He, too, knew the characteristic smell of the ash-smeared, unwashed ascetics of India.

Niaz had a touch of fever the next day, but the ugly wound had bled itself clean, and he suffered remarkably few ill effects from it. The weather continued unusually mild, and all over India women who had intended to leave for the hills delayed, and the Commissioner of Lunjore informed his wife that he could not arrange for her to leave for the hills before the twenty-second of the month. It seemed that Mrs. Gardener-Smith, Mrs. Hossack and her four children were all leaving on that date, and therefore it would be convenient if she were to travel with them.

Three days later, Alex inquired after Niaz's wound.

"It is healed enough," said Niaz impatiently. "How much longer do I stay here?"

"For another week, I think," said Alex. He smiled a little grimly at Niaz's face of disgust and said softly: "It is in my mind that thou wert so sorely wounded that I must ride abroad with a syce for some days yet, so that all will know that thou art still a sick man and unable to go about."

"Aah," said Niaz, and smiled. "What now?"

Alex explained: ". . . and if thou and one other go, on foot and by night, and while it is known that thou art sick, I think that the thing may be done."

"So do I also," said Niaz. "Give out that I am like to die. That should please those dogs in the lines! Who goes with me? Yusaf?"

Alex considered the matter, frowning, and after a moment or two said curtly: "It will have to be."

Time was running out. But he had to know what feelings were abroad in the surrounding countryside. "We have only one chance," he thought, "and that is that their ringleaders will not be able to hold 'em until a given day. They're too worked up. Something will set them off. Someone like Moulson will put his foot in it somewhere and provoke a premature explosion that will sound the alarm. But if it does go off on time, and in every cantonment in India, they can write our obituaries now."

IN FARAWAY CALCUTTA a senior member of the supreme council finished reading Sir Henry Lawrence's telegraphed report on the mutinous behaviour of the Oudh Irregulars, and picked up his pen.

The sooner this epidemic of mutiny is put a stop to, the better, wrote the senior council member. *Mild measures won't do. A severe example is wanted . . . . I am convinced that timely severity will be leniency in the long run . . . .*

IN A LARGE bungalow in the cantonment of Meerut, forty miles to the northeast of Delhi, Colonel Carmichael Smyth, the commanding officer of the 3rd Light Cavalry, sat at breakfast. The colonel was a man whose views were identical with those expressed by the senior member of council, and hurrying back from leave to set an example he had ordered that fifteen picked men from each troop were to parade on the following morning to learn to use the new cartridges. "I'm not standing any dam' silly nonsense from *my* sepoys!" said Colonel Smyth.

The ninety men were duly paraded—and eighty-five of them refused to handle the caste-breaking cartridges. They were immediately tried by court martial and sentenced to ten years' imprisonment, and a parade of all troops was ordered by the aged divisional commander, Major-General Hewitt, to watch the sentence put into execution. For hour after hour, in the broiling sun of the Meerut parade ground, the regiments had stood in stony-faced silence to watch eighty-five picked men of a picked regiment stripped of their uniforms and fettered one by one with the iron fetters that they would drag with them through ten weary years of captivity.

When at long last the ordeal was over, the terrible clanking file of men were marched away in the bright, merciless sunlight, calling to their comrades. "Is this justice? Because we will not lose our caste so that none of our own will speak with us or eat with us, must we suffer this fate? Is there no justice? Help us, brothers! Help us!"

"Entirely just!" snapped Colonel Smyth, helping himself to scrambled eggs. "Harsh? Nonsense! These mutinous fools need a sharp lesson. This will serve to stop the rot."

"WAIT, BROTHERS! Wait—wait. Have patience! Remember the auspicious day. It is too soon," urged the agents of Kishan Prasad and the other revolutionary leaders.

IT WAS SUNDAY, and Winter had just returned from church. She sat in the small sitting room, writing a letter to Lottie. Her formal dress of grey, white-spotted *mousseline de chine* was fresh and cool, and her discarded bonnet lay on the sofa.

So far her sheet of letter-paper bore only the address. But she did not write. She sat at her desk, thoughtfully nibbling the end of her pen while the minutes ticked by and the ink dried on the nib.

The punkah creaked gently and monotonously overhead and a pair of gecko lizards on the wall behind the desk chirruped a small, shrill counterpoint. It was hot today: hotter than it had been for many months, and in every room the doors and windows had been closed before sunrise to keep in the cooler air of the night, and exclude the burning heat of May. "There will be no more cool nights now until the rains," she had been told early that morning . . . .

Winter sighed, dipped her pen into the standish and added a date below the address that she had already written at the top of the blank sheet of paper. *Sunday, May 10th, 1857—Dear Lottie . . . .*

CHAPTER 8

T HE NIGHT was hot and very still. Winter could not sleep. Somewhere in the dark recesses of the house a clock struck one. Three more hours before she could dress and go out to ride by the river.

"I will go up to the roof," she thought, and she groped for her slippers in the dark, put them on, and slipped her arms into the wide sleeves of the muslin wrap that lay at the foot of her bed. There was a dim light burning in the hall. Winter went along the veranda and up the steep flight of stone steps to the flat roof.

It was cooler here certainly. A shadow moved on the stonework and she looked up, startled, to see a small white figure standing by the narrow parapet. It was Zeb-un-Nissa. She was staring out across the gardens towards the southwest, and her body looked curiously rigid, as though she were straining to catch some faraway sound.

Winter approached her very softly, and laid a gentle hand on the child's thin arm: "Nissa—"

Zeb-un-Nissa moved her head a little. "Hark!" she said in a hoarse whisper. "Dost thou not hear them?"

She began to shiver, and Winter put an arm about the frail little shoulders and drew the child against her: "What is it, *piara?* What is there to hear?"

The child pulled herself free and turned again to the parapet, listening to some sound that Winter could not hear.

"It is the mem-sahibs! They are screaming! Canst thou not hear them scream? Surely thou canst hear them—there be children also . . . . Listen! *Listen!* They are killing the mem-*log*. Thou canst hear the sword cuts—and the flames. There! that was a child!—hark to its mother shriek! *Ai! Ai!*—" She wailed aloud and put her hands over her ears, cowering down below the parapet and weeping. "I cannot bear to hear them scream!—they are killing the mem-*log*—they are killing the mem-*log!*"

Winter dropped to her knees and gathered the small, wailing figure into her arms.

"Nissa—Nissa, it is only a dream, *piara*. Only a bad dream. There is no killing—"

A shadow fell across them, black in the moonlight, and she turned swiftly, her heart in her mouth. Akbar Khan, the gatekeeper, was salaaming deferentially behind her. His face was dark against the night sky, but Winter could see the gleam of his teeth and the glitter of his eyes and, though her first momentary panic had died, an odd flicker of fear went through her, making her pull the child closer.

"Her mother missed the unworthy one from her bed," said Akbar

Khan softly. "She has been sick with a fever these few days past and she must have left her bed while her mother slept. Her mother is anxious, and sent me in search of her."

He took the child from Winter. "It was a fit," he said placidly. "She has always been a sickly child, and I fear that the time of her release is near. Her mother will grieve; but what is written is written." He cradled the thin body of his grandchild comfortably in his arms and said: "Her mother will be very honoured that the gracious lady-sahib troubled herself with the child. Shall I call a servant to light the lady-sahib back to her room?"

"No," said Winter curtly. "I will remain here. Tell Zeb-un-Nissa's mother that I will come in the morning to see how the child fares."

"The lady-sahib is my father and my mother," murmured Akbar Khan politely, and went away, his bare feet making no sound on the warm stone.

Winter watched him go and she shivered in the hot night air. What did Nissa think that she had heard? "They are killing the mem-*log*, surely thou canst hear them scream?" But there was no scream—no sound. Only silence.

"She was dreaming!" said Winter aloud and firmly. But she shivered again and, drawing her wrap tighter about her, returned to her hot, tumbled bed.

ALEX HEARD her running along the veranda of his bungalow at eleven o'clock the following morning, and knew who it was even before she was standing before him, tense and white-faced, her hands clutching at the edge of his desk.

She said in a hard, breathless voice, "Alex, do something! They've killed her! I know they've killed her! Conway won't do anything. He says it's all nonsense. It's her grandfather—it's Akbar Khan. He did it. I know he did it! Alex, you can't let him do that and—and—"

Alex came round the desk and caught her by the shoulders and propelled her forcibly out of the office and into the living room. He pushed her down into a chair, splashed a generous quantity of brandy into a glass and held it to her mouth while she drank it. Winter gasped and choked, but it took some of the shivering rigidity from her.

"Now tell me."

"It's Nissa," said Winter, tears standing in her eyes. "She—she had a nightmare last night. At least I think it was a nightmare. Akbar Khan said it was a fit—" She described the happening on the roof. "Then he took her away, and I went to see her this morning and—and they said she was dead. They didn't want me to see her, but I made them. But I don't believe—I think they smothered her—" Her voice broke.

Alex said quietly: "You can't know that."

"No. They said she had another fit, and—I don't believe it! Akbar Khan heard what she said and he was afraid. I know he was afraid. I knew it last night."

Alex said: "I'll see what I can do."

He walked back with her to the house, and an hour later he sent over a message asking if she would ride with him that evening.

Winter heard the wailing in the servants' quarters for half that hot afternoon, and later a small wooden box was carried out by a side door to the Mohammedan burial ground outside the city.

"There is nothing we can do," said Alex. "The child appears to have been subject to epileptic fits, and Dr. O'Dwyer, whom I asked to look at the body, says that it is quite possible that she died as a result of one of them. He was not prepared to take any further action on it. He said—and rightly—that there was enough tension in the place already, without giving rise to any more alarm and excitement. I'm sorry, but that is all there is to it. The child was buried at four o'clock." He looked at the set white face beside him and said after a moment: "I'm sorry, Winter."

Winter's account of what the child had said last night disturbed him. It seemed to him quite likely that Zeb-un-Nissa was repeating something, or dreaming of something, that she had heard discussed. If so, that would account for Winter's conviction that Akbar Khan had been afraid. If Akbar Khan had imagined the child to be talking of something she had overheard, she might well have been assisted to die. However, as O'Dwyer had not been prepared to interfere, there was nothing further that could be done about it. But the words that the child had said repeated themselves again and again in his brain as they had repeated themselves in Winter's last night—"They are killing the mem-*log!*—they are killing the mem-*log* . . ."

Part Four
The Long Days of Summer

FLO MAYNARD

CHAPTER 1

MEERUT AND DELHI were far away, hidden behind the dust and the dancing heat haze, and the parched, blazing plains. And perhaps that was just as well. For all through that Sunday and the long hot day that followed, the shrieks of women and the terrified screaming of children, the crackle of flames and the howl of the mob, rose up first from the garrison town of Meerut and then from Duryagunj—that once quiet quarter of Delhi where the European and Eurasian clerks had lived and were now dying in terror and agony in the blinding, merciless sunlight.

The frantic officers in Meerut—where the terror had broken out and from where the mutineers, after a night of murder, had ridden for Delhi—ground their teeth and waited, or pleaded for permission to ride after them. There were more British troops in Meerut than in almost any other garrison in India, and not all the native regiments had revolted—only let them follow up the mutineers and save Delhi before it was too late—or at least send warning. But their commander, General Hewitt, was old and infirm and the magnitude of the crisis had left him too bewildered to take any decisive action, while Brigadier Wilson, his second-in-command, left to take the initiative, hesitated and was lost.

"We must protect the remaining women and children," said Brigadier Wilson uneasily. He would not let them go . . . .

All through that long hot day the Delhi garrison waited and hoped, and watched the Meerut road for the help that they could not believe would fail them. And every moment that the help delayed, the mutineers grew bolder, and the tattered court of the aged King of Delhi grew hourly more confident.

Lottie had seen her father cut down by his own men, an expression of utter disbelief upon his rubicund face. Standing with her mother and a dozen other women and children who had taken refuge at the Main Guard within the Kashmir Gate, she had seen him ride up to the gate with his men, placid and confident. She had heard his fussy, fatherly voice raised in expostulation when his men checked before the gate. And a minute later she had seen him dragged from his horse and three bayonets plunged into his body.

His subadar-major and his Indian orderly had fired on the

murderers and been themselves cut down, and Lottie, looking down dazedly from the rose-red walls where she had picnicked and walked in the peaceful autumn days of the vanished year, had thought how red and bright the blood looked on the hot white dust.

"It cannot be happening," thought Lottie. "It cannot be true."

"I DON'T SEE as 'ow we can 'old out much longer, sir," said Conductor Buckley to Lieutenant Willoughby who commanded the Delhi magazine. "The perishers 'ave brought scalin' ladders—" His words were barely audible above the howling of the mob and the incessant rattle and crash of gunfire.

They had been holding the magazine since morning, and now the sun was moving down the sky again. Was it only four o'clock? Nine of them, against a howling, yelling mob of thousands. Nine of them to man ten guns . . . .

"Scully says the train's laid, sir!" yelled Conductor Buckley. "Any sign from the Meerut road yet, sir?"

Young Lieutenant Willoughby ran to the river bastion and strained his eyes for a last look down the hot, empty road, shimmering under a brazen sky. "No. They are not coming. Perhaps they are all dead. We cannot wait any longer."

His eyes were calm and youthful in his powder-blackened, sweating. face, as he glanced down at the swarming thousands who clambered in, monkey-wise, over the walls, hemming the defenders into the last narrow square of ground.

"We shall take a good many of them with us," said Lieutenant Willoughby. "All right, Buckley. Give him the signal to fire it."

The ground and the buildings and the very sky seemed to rock to the appalling crash of sound, and a vast cloud, rose-red and beautiful in the sunlight, lifted up above the domes and minarets, spreading out like a blossoming flower on a tall white stem.

It hung there for hours, an ephemeral memorial to gallantry. But as though the sound of the explosion had been a signal, the sullen hesitating sepoys within the Main Guard turned upon their officers and those who had taken refuge there. Lottie, six months with child, saw her mother fall without a sound, a hole through her temple, saw little Miss Jennings, too, the Chaplain's daughter, and young Miss Clifford, who had sung to the accompaniment of Captain Larribie's guitar, screaming as clawing, bloodstained hands snatched at them and the sabres cut and slashed, and saw a sabre slash down through her husband's head, laying it open almost to the shoulder.

She had screamed then, and fought to go to him, but someone had caught her arms and dragged her struggling and shrieking to the battlements, and then friendly hands were gripping her wrists and she was being lowered down from the wall on a makeshift life-line of hastily knotted belts, swaying and turning against the hot stone, and screaming for Edward. Once in the ditch, she was caught again and dragged on up the steep escarpment, running and stumbling over the rough ground to plunge headlong into the tangled thickets of the Khudsia Bagh . . . .

The crash of the explosion had shivered through the hot stillness, and rocked the Flagstaff Tower up on the Ridge above the city where the terrified families from the cantonments had been crowded together all that long day, waiting for news and straining their eyes towards the city and the empty Meerut road. The women gasped and flinched to the hammerblow of the sound, while their servants waited and the children shrieked in terror.

"We can't wait here any longer," said a haggard-faced officer pacing the Ridge. "What in hell's name are they doing in Meerut? They cannot *all* be dead . . . . For God's sake, why don't we do some-thing to help those poor devils in the city? There's still the river arsenal to draw on. We could have made some sort of a show, instead of just leaving them to be slaughtered!"

"Don't be a fool, Mellish! We've got to think of the women and children. We must consider their safety first."

As the last of the daylight faded, those who had waited on the Ridge for the help from Meerut that never came, prepared to leave at last. "It will be dark in half an hour," said the brigadier. "The women had better go, and they will need protection. You had all better go while the road to the south is still open."

The glare of the burning bungalows in the cantonments made a second sunset in the sky as carriages and dog-carts and men on foot and on horseback streamed away into the gathering darkness to begin that long torment of flight through a hostile land, during which so many were to die. The brigadier waited until they had gone, and then with the last remaining officer on his staff he faced the sullen remnants of his command. "Sound the Assembly," he said, and they heard the familiar bugle call ring out in the silence.

A single figure, a sepoy of the 74th Bengal Native Infantry, answered the summons, standing stiffly to attention, lonely and obedient in the gathering dusk. The only one to remain faithful out of all the men who yesterday would have obeyed that call.

The brigadier turned at last and rode away from the Ridge, leaving the deserted cantonments to the night and the looters, while behind him, high over the darkening city, the last of the daylight lit a fading cloud above the shattered magazine and marked the only decisive stand that had been made in all that terrible day.

WINTER had not spoken during their evening ride and Alex was too occupied with his own thoughts to notice. His various sources of information in the city were becoming less and less easy to get in touch with. They were afraid of being seen near his bungalow, and what news they brought was inconclusive and disturbing.

He looked up at the pale segment of moon floating high above the veil of dust that blurred the horizon. A flight of cormorants drew a thin dark arrowhead against the opal sky. He wondered how Niaz and Yusaf were faring. It would be far hotter out on the plain than in the cantonments, no mean test of endurance, and the knife-wound in Niaz's back was not yet fully healed. "I shall have to go myself tomorrow night," thought Alex. Night work was all very well for Niaz and Yusaf, who could sleep by day, but it came hard on Alex, who could not.

He drew rein before the Residency gate and spoke for the first time in almost an hour. "When do you leave for the hills?"

"On the twenty-second," said Winter listlessly.

"Which gives you a week in which to get there," said Alex. "Eight days to be precise. It should be enough. I expect I shall see you before then. Good night."

He cantered away and Winter went on under the arch of the gateway. She would be leaving Alex, and it was Alex whom she loved. But she felt curiously apathetic. Nothing mattered any more.

She slept soundly that night despite the heat and the creaking of the punkah. As soundly as Lottie who lay exhausted, her thin slippers and frilly skirts torn and ripped by thorns and stained with dust and blood, in a curtained wagon whose kindly owner had found her and her companion, Mrs. Holly, crouching in a ditch by the roadside, and had befriended them.

Somehow Mrs. Holly had escaped from the carnage and reached the Main Guard at the Kashmir Gate, where she had witnessed the final tragedy and escaped over the battlements. Mrs. Holly had taken Lottie under her wing, and it was she who had cajoled the driver of the wagon to take them to Lunjore.

He had finally agreed. "Delhi will be no place for a man of peace for many moons, and I have a brother in Lunjore with whom I will abide until this madness is past."

NIAZ AND YUSAF returned to the bungalow in the dark before dawn and by different routes, Niaz remaining carefully invisible. He was reported to be still suffering from fever and unable to leave his bed.

Alex had hoped to sleep late but he was awakened at sunrise. "*Huzoor*," said Yusaf softly, "there is a red kite caught in the thorn tree by the city road."

"Damn!" said Alex wearily. "Damn and blast! Oh, all right."

He shook himself awake, and twenty minutes later he was riding through the crop lands in the direction of Chunwar. Some two hundred yards from the end of the cantonments a cheap paper kite such as children fly was caught in a thorn tree's scanty foliage. Gaily coloured kites often flew in the sky above the city, and a strayed one that had broken its string was sometimes to be found tangled among the branches of trees on the plain. Alex did not pass the thorn tree and barely glanced at it. He took a narrow side path that skirted a field of mustard, and presently checked the Eagle by a culvert where the elephant grass grew high, and dismounted as though to tighten a girth. There was a rustle in the grasses and a voice whose owner remained invisible spoke in a whisper that was barely audible above the creaking of a distant well-wheel.

"There is word in the bazaar that the regiments have risen in Meerut, and have slain all the *Angrezi-log* and ridden on Delhi, which has fallen also. It is said that they have proclaimed Bahadur Shah as Mogul and put all feringhis to the sword."

"When?" asked Alex, wrestling with the girth.

"Yesterday only. The news was told at dawn by a fakir at the steps of the Pearl Masjid."

"It is not possible," said Alex. "Delhi is far."

"Do not the very birds of the air speak to the holy men?" whispered the voice.

Alex said: "Is there aught else said?"

"Nay. What need of more? The city hums like a hive."

"Will they rise?"

"Who knows? Their leaders call upon them to hold back and to wait for the Word, but it were better that none of thy people were seen in the city today. Thou knowest the temper of the crowd."

Alex said softly: "Go back, Gopal, and bring me word tonight. I will ride by the tomb of Amin-u-din at sunset."

"I will try. But I am afraid—afraid. If it were known, they would tear me in pieces!"

Alex could hear the man's teeth chatter, and he laid a handful of silver coins in the dust by the rim of the culvert, and said: "There will be fifty more tonight," and, mounting again, he returned to the cantonments by way of the rifle range.

He found the Commissioner still abed. His foot struck against a cluster of silver bells such as often adorn an Indian woman's anklet, and he found it an effort to restrain a grimace of disgust.

"Well?" demanded Mr. Barton sourly. "What is it now?"

"There is a story circulating in the city," Alex said curtly, "that the regiments in Meerut and Delhi have mutinied and killed all the Europeans, and that Bahadur Shah has been acclaimed as king."

"What rubbish!" Barton sat up, groaning and putting a hand to his head. "Meerut's crammed with British troops. Strongest garrison in India. Poppycock! Just another bazaar rumour."

"Perhaps, sir. The point is not so much whether it is true, as whether the city believes it to be true. Such a rumour is bound to give rise to a good deal of excitement. We cannot afford any unpleasant incidents. Have I your permission to put the city out of bounds to all Europeans, just until we hear if there is anything behind the rumour?"

"I suppose so," said the Commissioner ungraciously. "Don't believe a word of it meself, but—Well, go on, go on! Do what you like about it, and leave me in peace."

Alex did not linger. He returned to his office and quickly wrote the necessary documents, using the Commissioner's official paper.

He rode out at sundown that evening. He waited but Gopal Nath did not come. He was lying face-downwards among the high grass at the edge of the grazing grounds with his throat cut from ear to ear, and the work that the jackals and the hyenas began that night was completed the next day by the kites and the vultures and the remorseless heat, so that twenty-four hours later no one could be quite sure to whom those reddened, scattered bones had once belonged. Alex rode home in the last of the twilight knowing it was no use to wait any longer.

THERE HAD BEEN a party at the Residency. The last of the Tuesday parties, although no one there knew that it was to be the last. And at noon on Wednesday a dispatch rider from Suthragunj on a lathered horse arrived in Lunjore. He waited only long enough to deliver the sealed letter he carried to the Commissioner's head *chupprassi*, before setting out on the return journey.

Alex was not told of his arrival, and the Commissioner, handed the letter during luncheon, stuffed it into his pocket, unread, and forgot about it until the following morning. It was nearly midday when he read it at last, and then his first reaction was incredulity. The thing was a hoax—it could not possibly be true. But it was written on official paper, and he knew that scrawled signature. His pale eyes bulged with shock and the paper dropped to the floor, where the draught from the punkah sent it fluttering lazily across the drawing-room floor.

It was Winter who picked it up and sent for Alex. He arrived to find the Commissioner gulping down his third glass of brandy, and under its influence returning to his first view of the situation. "Hoax," said Mr. Barton thickly. "Can't be anything else."

"I'm afraid not, sir," said Alex, running his eye down the single sheet of paper. He looked at the quivering bulk that slumped upon the sofa, glass in hand, and said curtly: "Where is the man who brought this? When did it arrive?"

"During luncheon yesterday," Winter said quietly. "I think the man left almost immediately."

Alex said nothing. He looked at his chief with contempt and exasperation and went out of the room.

"Damned impertinence!" said Mr. Barton querulously, and finished his fourth brandy.

Less than an hour later, a hurriedly convened conference of a dozen appalled men met round the Commissioner's dining-room table to decide what measures, if any, might belatedly be taken to safeguard Lunjore from the mutiny and massacre that had overtaken Meerut and Delhi. Alex urged the supreme measure of disarming the regiments, but the suggestion was treated as an outrage.

"If anyone should ever order me to insult my men in such a manner," declared Colonel Gardener-Smith roundly, "he would first have to disarm me, and after me, every one of my officers!"

"Your suggestion, Captain Randall," said Colonel Moulson, "is beneath contempt, and it is not your place to advance it."

Alex gave a faint shrug of his shoulders. "I am sorry, sir. Then may I suggest that we send the women and children to the hills immediately? Today if possible. There may still be time. The mutinies at Meerut and Delhi were premature," he said. "I am sure of it. As I have already told you, I have reason to believe that a date for a general outbreak has been set for the end of this month. There is still time to send the women to safety."

"We cannot do it," said Colonel Gardener-Smith heavily. "It is too late. At this stage it is surely a matter of vital importance not to show any sign of panic. You must see that."

"I doubt it," said Colonel Moulson with a sneer. "It is the sort of thing that Captain Randall has never been able to see. And I agree with you, Colonel. It is, of course, out of the question for any of the women to leave. Their departure at this juncture would be taken as a clear sign that we had lost our nerve."

"I entirely agree," said Colonel Packer. "We must place our trust in the Lord. His rod and His staff shall not fail us."

"Possibly not, sir," said Alex dryly. "But will the sepoys? Are we to take it that the sight of our women and children being sent to safety will unsettle the regiments to the extent of driving them to mutiny? I had understood that you believed them to be loyal."

"The loyalty of my regiment," said Colonel Gardener-Smith quietly, "has never yet been called in question, and to send my wife and daughter away would amount to a public declaration that I had lost confidence in their loyalty. That I will not do. At this time it is doubly necessary not only to show confidence, but to avoid any action that can be construed as alarm."

"Which means," said Alex with shut teeth, "that no precautionary measures whatever can be taken, for fear that any change in the present routine may be translated as panic."

"You exaggerate, Captain Randall," said Colonel Gardener-Smith coldly. "Reasonable precautions will, of course, be taken."

339

"Will you name one, sir?" demanded Alex tersely.

There was a sudden silence about the table.

Alex came to his feet. "May I *beg* you to reconsider, sir? I am well aware that it will give rise to panic if we send them away. Good God, I am not entirely—" He controlled himself with an effort and continued more quietly: "But I feel that it should be possible to explain to the regiments, through the medium of the Indian officers, that the families are only being sent away because the services of every officer and every sepoy may be needed for action, and not for being kept hamstrung in cantonments protecting a parcel of women."

"I reshent that," said the Commissioner. "Wha' d'yer mean, 'parcel o' women'? Sweet creatures! Privilege to protect 'em!"

Alex ignored the interruption: "I beg of you to send them away while there is still time. It is the lesser of the two evils, and our paramount duty at this time is surely not their protection, but the saving of the country. The maximum efficiency cannot be obtained while the garrison is hampered by a horde of women whose personal safety will be placed above military expediency . . . ." He struck the table with the flat of his hand. "Can you not see that if they remain here they will handicap us into virtual uselessness? How can any man make a cool-headed decision, which he knows may involve grave risk, while he is thinking that to take that risk may mean the murder and mutilation of his wife and child?"

He looked about the table at the circle of grim faces and saw hesitation and doubt, and, for a moment only, he was hopeful.

"My dear Captain Randall," Moulson drawled. "You allow your fears to run away with you. It is my opinion that the news from Delhi will be found to be greatly exaggerated. And in any case the Meerut Brigade will have moved by now, and Delhi has almost certainly been recaptured. But even if that were not so, we have three infantry regiments here as well as half a regiment of Military Police, and if we had only one—my own—I would still engage to keep the city in order and protect double the number of women and children without the smallest difficulty. The rabble are notoriously chicken-hearted, and a dose of grape will be quite enough to cool their tempers should they show signs of violence."

"Hear, hear!" interjected the Commissioner.

"So you must really not expect us," concluded Colonel Moulson, "to make a public exhibition of ourselves by ordering a panic-stricken exodus of all the women and children, just because you feel nervous. There is no lack of confidence here, I assure you."

Alex's right hand clenched slowly—and as slowly relaxed. It was no use. They were courageous enough, but they did not even now realize the magnitude of this thing that was overtaking them. They had refused to take any precautions while the emergency was far away, and now that it was upon them they would take none—for fear of showing fear. They had done nothing while they could, and dared do nothing when they would.

"Qui' ri'," said the Commissioner with a hiccough, " 'tirely agree. Mush keep calm!"

Alex sat down, and did not speak again while the conference dragged to its inconclusive close, but when it was over he dispatched a telegram to the Governor General, in the name of the Commissioner of Lunjore, requesting plenary military powers. The nearest telegraph post, in Suthragunj, had until recently been seventy-five miles away, but it was now not thirty by the Hazrat Bagh road, and Alex reflected grimly that Kishan Prasad's road was proving its usefulness in a way that had not been intended by those who had made it.

THAT NIGHT the first of the Lunjore fires started, and the surgeon of the 105th Native Infantry, Colonel Packer's regiment, had his bungalow burned to the ground. It was a thatched bungalow, and an arrow wrapped in blazing oil-soaked rags was fired into the roof shortly before midnight.

Less than fifty miles to the southwest, Lottie and Mrs. Holly were still safe in the care of the kindly wagon driver, and drawing hourly nearer to Lunjore. But behind them, scattered over the sun-scorched countryside that surrounded the captured city of the Moguls, the majority of the British fugitives from Delhi—men, women, and children—hid and starved and died.

A few—a very few—fell into the hands of kindly people who gave them food and shelter and risked their own lives in order to save a hunted, helpless fellow creature. And within the walls of Delhi, from a stifling windowless dungeon below the palace of the aged, timorous Bahadur Shah, newly proclaimed king of all Hindustan, fifty prisoners—the last of the British and the Christians left in Delhi—were about to be dragged out, to be butchered in the harsh sunlight by men whom the sight and scent of blood had turned into beasts: men who cut and slashed and howled in frenzy, until the last scream and the last moan was silenced.

Towards evening the mangled bodies were dragged to the bank of the placid Jumna and flung in: food for the crocodiles and the mud-turtles, the jackals and the scavenger birds . . . .

There could be no drawing back now—the die was cast.

CHAPTER 2

NIAZ HAD reappeared in public and was once again to be seen with Alex on his official rides through the villages.

They were in the saddle for the greater part of every day, for Alex returned each night to Lunjore. He heard cases and gave judgments, sitting on horseback in the shade of a tree, throughout the long, blazing days: seeing in the faces of the villagers the ominous signs of the sickness that was sweeping through India; the open insolence and hostility that must be stared down; the quick-leaping panic that must be allayed.

The quiet countryside was alive with rumours. There were stories and more stories, but no proof—until one day three men arrived in a village not ten miles from Lunjore city and brought the proof with them in the form of two flounced muslin dresses, a sword, and a long tress of silky blonde hair stained with blood.

"We found them hiding in a ditch by the roadside," boasted one of the men. "Two mem-sahibs and a sahib. There was a child also, whose crying betrayed them. The sahib was sore wounded, but when Abdullah here ran his tulwar through the child, he struck at him with his sword; but his arm had no strength and I took the sword from him and slew him with it, and the young woman also. *Arré*—how she shrieked! Like a peacock. I caught her by the hair— see, here is the lock. All the hell-born are dead, and—"

"Not all," said a hard clear voice behind him, and the gaping villagers drew back hastily. Alex rode forward, Niaz at his elbow, and looked long and steadily at the three men, and no one spoke. Then he crooked his finger without turning his head and said softly: "*Kotwal-ji*, bind me these men."

The headman flinched and hesitated, and suddenly there was a revolver in Alex's hand and another in Niaz's. "Be swift, my father," said Niaz pleasantly. "Do not keep the *Huzoor* waiting— or Hell either, which languishes to receive these three."

If Alex had looked away or hesitated, guns and knives and lathis would have appeared, and stones would have been thrown. But he did not look away and his eyes were cold and unpleasant. As unpleasant as Niaz's narrow-lipped grin.

One of the three men turned suddenly and ran, and Niaz fired. The man fell face downwards in the dust, twitched once and was still. "That was too good a death for such offal," said Niaz cheerfully, controlling his horse more by the pressure of his knees than by the reins in his left hand.

When the two remaining murderers dangled at a rope's end, Alex gestured at the third body on the ground: "Hang him beside his friends, so that all may see."

They strung up the corpse without a word and Niaz took up the sword, the stained clothing and the lock of yellow hair, and tying them swiftly into a bundle, fastened it to his saddle, and they rode on out of the village without a backward look.

Alex sent in a brief report of the incident to the Commissioner and was sent for to explain himself. "You had no authority to do such a thing!" fumed the Commissioner. "Disgraceful! It will create a bad impression in the district."

"On the contrary, it will create a very good one," said Alex shortly. He forced his voice to a more conciliatory tone and said: "If you will allow me unfettered action, sir, I can maintain order in the district as long as the regiments in Lunjore remain quiet. At the moment the sepoys *are* quiet, but if they should revolt it would be a different matter, and I would again urge you most strongly to impress upon their commanding officers the advisability of disarming them while there is still time."

"I shall do no such thing!" snapped the Commissioner, his pallid face becoming dangerously empurpled. "What would happen if they did? Why—we'd be left with no defenders and no defence at all! Disarm the sepoys, and we'd be at the mercy of the scum of the city and every villager who could carry a rifle or a lathi!"

There was obviously no point in talking about the sepoys; he could do nothing there, but there were still things he could do among the uneasy, frightened, rumour-ridden population. Things that would have to be done on his own responsibility.

"I shall have to have his authority, or they will stop me," thought Alex; and returned reluctantly to the Commissioner.

"The head of the whole trouble in the city is Maulvi Amanullah, and his nephew, Abdul Majid. If we can get those two, the city will be left with only petty agitators, but no real leaders," said Alex. "But if we try to take them openly we shall have a first-class riot on our hands. I think it would be putting too much strain on the loyalty of the sepoys to ask them to fight a street action at this point. But I think we can manage it discreetly. Call a durbar of all the influential men in the city. It's the only hope."

It had taken an hour and the best part of a bottle of brandy to persuade the Commissioner, and it had proved harder still to persuade the military that the risk was worth taking, but the battle had been won by Alex's deliberate suggestion that Colonel Moulson did not trust his regiment.

A stately conference had been held under the sweltering shade of a vast *shamianah* erected in the coolest part of the Residency grounds. There were speeches and expressions of loyalty—genuine enough at the moment of their making, thought Alex wryly, reflecting that ten minutes' conversation with an agitator could swing the pendulum as far east as it was now west. Views were canvassed and listened to with respect, and the guests withdrew as the sun began to set. All except two of them: Maulvi Amanullah and Abdul Majid were delayed in conversation, and detained.

There was considerable uneasiness in the city that night, and the following morning a proclamation was issued calling upon all inhabitants of the city to give up their arms within twenty-four hours, followed by another, imposing a curfew. It was backed by the appearance of four heavy guns that were plainly to be seen in position at the Rohilkhand Gate and the main road to the city.

Deprived of its leaders, the city capitulated, and the arms were collected—but not destroyed. "For God's sake," begged Alex, "burn 'em. Blow 'em up! There's enough stuff there to fit out an army. Now that we've got it, don't let's take any chances of it falling into their hands again."

"It could be in no safer place than in the care of the Military Police," snapped Colonel Moulson.

Alex was silent. For the moment at least the danger was averted. The villages and the city would stay quiet—for just as long as the sepoys stayed quiet. The thirty-first of May . . . ten more days. If they would only disarm them now!

There had been no reply to the message he had dispatched to Suthragunj to be telegraphed to the Governor General in Calcutta. It had never reached Lord Canning, but was gathering dust in a pigeonhole, while the junior official who had received it occupied himself with panic-stricken plans for evacuating his wife and family on the first ship to sail for Europe.

LOTTIE had arrived in Lunjore at last, accompanied by Mrs. Holly, who had taken charge of her.

"You know, ma'am," she explained to Winter, "it was Miss Lottie 'oo said you was 'ere when the wagon wallah says as 'e was goin' to Lunjore. She said—she said as you'd invited 'er for a visit, poor young thing."

For Lottie remembered nothing. She had been delighted to see Winter, and she had forgotten Delhi. She wondered sometimes, a little hazily, why it was that she should suddenly have decided to come to Lunjore. Something had happened, surely? But then she had always meant to visit Winter one day, and Edward—she must not think. It made her feel ill, and that was bad for the child.

"Edward wants a girl, you know," she had confided to Winter, "but I want the first one to be a boy and just like Edward. He is to be christened Edward—I have quite made up my mind. But he will have to be Teddy, because we cannot have two Edwards . . . ."

"Alex," said Winter desperately, "do you think she will ever remember?"

"One day," said Alex, and added, "She's better off as she is at the moment. When is that baby due?" He frowned at the sight of the sudden colour that burned in Winter's cheeks, and said impatiently: "You don't really suppose that hitching a hoop up higher and carrying a shawl disguises a thing like that, do you?"

Winter had been taught that babies, until they were born, were an unmentionable subject in the presence of gentlemen, but the impatience in Alex's voice made her ashamed of the blush. She said with as much composure as she could muster: "I think she expects it in about two months' time."

"How soon then can you leave?" Alex had talked to Mrs. Holly and had heard the first true account of that last day of British rule in Delhi. The ease with which Delhi had been captured had horrified him.

"*Leave?* I can't leave now! Dr. O'Dwyer says Lottie must have complete quiet. After what she has been through he says he cannot understand why she has not had a — a —"

"A miscarriage," finished Alex, his mouth curving in the shadow of a grin. "Yes, I've heard of those too! Then you will not be leaving either?"

"How could I?"

"No," said Alex bleakly, "you could not. And I think in any case it is too late."

Almost every night now there were mysterious fires in the cantonments, and though extra guards patrolled the area they never made any arrests. It was difficult to allay panic among the families of the officers who lived in bungalows surrounded by large gardens where trees and shrubs provided cover for lurking incendiarists, and few women slept at night.

The Commissioner, however, noticed little in these days, and that little through an alcoholic haze. The whole situation was beyond him. Even Yasmin had deserted him, slipping away in the night. He was afraid, and his fear drove him to his familiar refuge, the bottle. He took no interest in the information a few days later, therefore, that the sepoys of Colonel Packer's regiment had refused to accept their consignment of commissariat flour, saying that it was known to be adulterated with bone-dust for the purpose of destroying their caste. Colonel Packer and his officers had expostulated, lectured and finally pleaded, but the men had remained obdurate. They would not touch the flour, and moreover they insisted that it must be thrown into the river to ensure that it was not returned to them again or handed to any of their comrades in the other regiments.

The flour was duly taken away and thrown into the distant river, and the sepoys, having won their point, became noticeably insolent and out of hand. Many of them, from all three regiments, that same evening openly looted the ripe fruit from the gardens of the cantonment bungalows, and although their officers soon succeeded in putting a stop to it, it was plain that discipline was deteriorating.

346

"They are a little out of hand," admitted Colonel Gardener-Smith reluctantly, "but that is understandable in the exceptional circumstances. We are all only human. It is nothing serious."

That night Major Wilkinson, who had dined at the Residency and returned drunk to his bungalow, fired at and wounded one of a patrol who challenged him. There was an inquiry held on the following day and the major was acquitted of any intent to wound —on a plea of being unconscious from intoxication at the time.

"Bloody fools!" Alex said to Niaz. "They should have cashiered him—sent him off to be court-martialled—anything but this. To acquit him of wounding a sepoy at a time like this, and on a plea of drunkenness—are they mad? If it had been the other way round, they'd have given the sepoy ten years' penal servitude or hanged him! If this doesn't start something, I'm a bigger fool than Packer!"

There was a ball at the Residency to celebrate the Queen's birthday on the first day of the new week. Victoria's birthday fell on a Sunday that year, so the ball was held on the day following. It was the end of the fast of Ramadan, too, and a new slim sickle moon hung in the green of the evening sky, a curved thread of silver, like the crescent of Islam embroidered on the green banners of the Faithful—like an omen in the sky.

"*La Ill-ah ha! il ill-ah ho!*" cried the muezzins from the minarets of the mosques in the city. "There is no God but God!"

The band of the 2nd Regiment of Lunjore Irregulars stood smartly to attention, their dark faces creased with concentration, and watched the conductor's baton fall. "*God save our gracious Queen, Long live our noble Queen—*" The familiar tune, the national anthem of an alien race, blared out through the open windows across the dark parade ground and the sepoy lines.

She was thirty-eight—that dumpy, self-confident housewife who had ascended the throne as a slim self-confident girl in the year that Sabrina Grantham had met Marcos de los Aguilares; the year that Ameera, wife of Walayat Shah, had been born to Juanita in the little pink stucco palace in Lucknow city.

"*Send her victorious, happy and glorious . . . .*"

Sabrina's daughter danced at the Queen's birthday ball in a wide-skirted ball-gown of water-green tarlatan looped up with garlands of camellias. Winter smiled as she danced—the same smile that was on the face of every woman in that flag-and-flower-

347

decorated room. The smile of women who watch their men and strain their ears, and who will not show that they are afraid.

Alex, too, attended that ball and there was nothing in his face to show that he had spent the greater part of the afternoon arguing, urging, pleading with three courageous, obdurate commanding officers for the disarming of the sepoys.

But they were not to be persuaded. They did, however, decide on taking one precautionary measure, for the sake of the ladies. It was the custom among the European families in Lunjore to drive out in the early mornings to get what little fresh air they could before the heat forced them into the dimness of shuttered rooms. Word was conveyed to the families that on the morning following the ball the women and children were to drive instead to the Residency, taking with them such necessities as they would need for a stay of a few days. The Residency was sufficiently large to shelter them all without too much discomfort, and a party of Military Police was to be posted in the grounds as extra protection, while four guns from Colonel Moulson's regiment were to be placed between the Residency and the city.

"The Residency is admirably situated for defence," said Colonel Gardener-Smith. "With that nullah and the jungle behind it, and a wall round the rest of it, nothing could be better."

"I agree," said Alex, "if one was defending it against a city rabble. But if the sepoys should mutiny it will turn into a trap."

"My sepoys will not mutiny!" said Colonel Gardener-Smith obstinately. "I will stake my life on that."

Alex had said nothing more. He was tired of vain repetitions. He had gone across to the Residency instead and spoken to Winter: "What have you done with that revolver I gave you?"

"I have it."

"Good. Keep it loaded and keep it within reach. I've brought you some more ammunition for it. And see that there is always a horse kept saddled, and—" He did not complete the sentence but went away without further words. What was the good of saying anything else? He had done what he could. Had that woman—Ameera—spoken the truth? Had there been a day set, and had the Meerut rising been premature? It had been remarkably successful and its success had touched off a series of localized risings. Were those, too, a mistake? *"They have set the auspicious day . . ."*

"Two more days to go," thought Alex that night, leaning against the wall and watching a quadrille dancing to the music of the sepoy band at the Queen's birthday ball.

But there were no more days. Only hours.

CHAPTER 3

*I*T WAS Major Beckwith, second-in-command to Colonel Gardener-Smith, who informed his commanding officer on the morning after the ball that the regiment had not dispersed after parade, and could no longer be trusted.

"I will go and speak to them," said Colonel Gardener-Smith. "They will listen to me."

But they had not listened.

"We will not harm thee, or permit thee to be harmed," said the ringleader, "for thou art a good man. But we take no more orders from feringhis who have plotted to destroy our caste and to enslave us. Go quickly while there is yet time."

They had shouted down his words, and, seizing their rifles, had announced their intention of marching immediately for Delhi to offer their services to the Mogul. They had fired on their officers, two of whom had been badly wounded, and there had been nothing for it but to leave before worse befell, and the colonel had left.

His bungalow was empty, for his wife and daughter were already at the Residency, and it seemed intolerably dark and quiet. "I am an old man," thought Colonel Gardener-Smith. "An old man and a fool. I have given my life to a lie. They will disband the ninety-third and remove its name from the army list. *My* ninety-third!"

He went to the deserted mess, took down the colours and burned them in the grate. When there was nothing left but a heap of evil-smelling ash, he shot himself.

"The bloody idiot!" said Alex furiously, hearing of it in his bungalow half an hour later. "Just when we need every man who can fire a gun. God damn these sentimentalists!"

Colonel Moulson was breakfasting at the Residency, together with several officers who were engaged in assuring the ladies assembled there that there was no cause for alarm. The Residency was noisy with women's voices and the laughter of children. They felt safer together than they had in their scattered bungalows, and there was a light-hearted atmosphere that even the non-appearance of their host did nothing to dispel. The Commissioner was cushioning his fear, privately, with brandy.

"I always said it!" fumed Colonel Moulson. "Always said that

fool Gardener was too soft with his men. I'll show 'em! Marching to Delhi, are they? Where the hell's my horse? If we double three companies across the *maidan* we'll cut 'em off and cut 'em to bits!"

He galloped off into the glare of the morning, his adjutant and a senior captain riding behind him, and his regiment received him in silence. They listened to his bellowed commands, and no man moved. Then a man laughed, loud and scornfully, and another took aim and fired.

Ten minutes later the adjutant, his arm pouring a bright scarlet flood, slid from his wounded horse onto Alex's sunny veranda and gasped out the news. "They shot him down—and Mottisham too—and Halliwell and Reeves and Charlie and little Jenks. They're all dead. Packer's fellows have broken too. They've killed him—saw his body. Cut to bits. And old Gardener has—"

"I know," said Alex, knotting a strip torn from a curtain with furious haste about the man's shattered arm and shoulder. He called out to Niaz who had ridden full-tilt round the corner of the bungalow from the direction of the stables: "The Lunjore regiment also! Ride for the river. Get the charges from the Hirren Minar. I will meet thee there. Go quickly!"

The ruin that Alex and Niaz had stumbled across three years ago while tracking a wounded leopard had perhaps once been a hunting lodge. Niaz had named it the Hirren Minar—the Deer Tower—for they had found the antlers of a buck by the threshold. They had frequently used it as a base when on shooting-leave, but had kept it a close secret, for over the years there had lurked at the back of Alex's mind the thought that some day a hiding-place for gunpowder and arms such as this might prove useful.

Niaz turned his rearing horse as Alex helped the adjutant back into his saddle. "If Moulson's men have broken, that means the gunners will go," said Alex. "Get over to the Residency and tell 'em to get the women and children away over the nullah and into the jungle at once—*at once*, do you hear! Think you can do it? Good. Yusaf, run with the Sahib—be swift!"

He leaped down the veranda steps and caught at the bridle of his horse. "Where—are you going?" gasped the adjutant, wheeling his own wounded animal.

"Magazine."

The magazine was a square unpretentious building of white-washed stone surrounded by a high wall that stood near the centre of the cantonment area. There was a yelling crowd of sepoys milling round it, and Alex heard the crackle of musketry from within. He reined back in the shadow of a clump of bamboos. Someone was holding the magazine, then! He caught a brief glimpse of a pink boyish face, hatless, the red hair bright against the whitewashed stone above the inner parapet, and recognized young Eyton, new-joined, barely a month out from England.

Another face appeared beside young Eyton—a dark, bearded face that showed a gleam of white teeth; his rifle cracked and a man in the crowd fell. There were some then who had remained true to their salt. But the fight was an unequal one, for already fifty men or more had swarmed over the outer wall, and the gate was creaking under a heavy log of wood wielded as a battering ram.

351

Alex knew that he should go. There was nothing he could do. But he did not move. He saw the boy appear briefly again on the parapet and peer down at the yelling besiegers, duck to avoid the shots, and hold up his hand to give a signal. Alex knew what that signal meant, and he turned his horse and set him at a low wall fifty yards away, cleared it and was racing across a stretch of open ground. As he reached the far side of it he heard the roar of the explosion and felt the shock of the blast like a blow between his shoulders. "Well done!" said Alex, unaware that he was shouting aloud. "Oh, well done!" He spurred across another piece of open ground, leaped a compound wall and found himself among the flowers of Captain Batterslea's garden.

Mrs. Batterslea had been one of five women who had considered the move to the Residency unnecessary and had elected to remain in her own bungalow. "The children are far better off here. Why, my servants adore them! I am quite sure they would die for them."

Mrs. Batterslea's extravagant statement had proved to be no more than the truth. Her ayah lay huddled among the plumbago bushes below the veranda, in death as in life striving to protect the small silent figure in its white frock and blue sash that her arms still covered, while in the servants' quarters the portly butler, Captain Batterslea's orderly and the low-caste sweeper, had all died side by side, fighting vainly to protect the three small boys.

The bungalow was burning and the heat of the flames joined the furnace-heat of the sun and shrivelled the few plants that still brightened the flowerbeds. The beds had been Mrs. Batterslea's special pride, and in them she had striven, not always with success, to grow the flowers that reminded her of home—larkspur and mignonette, pansies, gillyflowers and roses. Of these only the roses now remained, wilting in the relentless heat. The rosebushes and Mrs. Batterslea herself, who lay among the flowers, staring up at the brassy sky. Her frilly pink-and-white wrap had been torn away, and she had been raped before she died. "That means the bazaar scum and the city have broken out already," thought Alex automatically, knowing that no sepoy would have done such a thing, for to do so would have defiled him.

The sight of her mutilated body turned Alex back from the road he had meant to take. Looking down at Mrs. Batterslea's dead face, he saw another face. Winter's. And he turned back and rode for the

Residency, cursing in a breathless, blasphemous whisper, but driven by an emotion and a fear that he could not control.

The heavy, iron-studded doors of the Residency gate had been closed that morning and the police guard ordered to keep them barred, but the door of the wicket in the main gate, through which only one at a time could enter, stood ajar. There was a crowd before the gate: a swaying, yelling crowd harangued by a wild-eyed figure in a white turban—Akbar Khan, the gatekeeper.

"Kill them!" screamed Akbar Khan. "Slay all, and let not one escape! For the Faith! For the Faith! Kill! Kill!"

They scattered like a whirl of dead leaves as Alex rode into them. He fired only once and saw Akbar Khan topple forward, and then he had flung himself from the saddle and was through the narrow wicket. A bullet fired by someone within the gate smacked into the woodwork within an inch of him as he threw himself against the door and dropped the heavy bar into place. He turned, revolver in hand, and saw the faces of the police guard, sullen and unsure.

"Sorry, Randall," said a gasping voice. "Nearly got you. Thought it was another of those swine."

Major Maynard, commanding the Military Police, was sitting on the ground with his back to the wall and one hand pressed to his side in a vain attempt to stem the red tide that welled out between his fingers. He held a smoking revolver in the other.

"Y'r just in time," he said. "Tell 'em up at the house—run for it. 'Fraid these bastards of mine won't stand. I've got—fifteen minutes perhaps—and as long as—I'm here—they'll do nothing. When I'm gone—they'll open the gate, and run for it. Get up to the house— tell 'em t'get out. I'll hold 'em for—a few minutes—"

Alex did not wait. He had told the adjutant fifteen minutes ago to get the women away, and they must have gone already, but he had to be sure. He ran for the house and leaped up the veranda steps with the noise of the mob beyond the gate rising behind him.

But they were all there still. Perhaps a dozen men and more than twice as many women and children, the women in preposterous, wide-hooped skirts and thin, inadequate slippers. "Good God!" he said furiously. "What the hell d'you think you're doing? Go on— get these women away! Wardle, I thought I told you—"

"Safer here," gasped Captain Wardle. "The gunners are loyal and the police'll hold . . ."

"The gunners have broken and the police will run within five minutes—and half the riffraff of the city is out there!" snapped Alex. "Go on—out by the back and over the bridge. Get into the jungle! It's your only chance. *Run!*"

He saw Winter's face across the width of the room. She had one arm about Lottie and her eyes were wide but quite steady. There was a sudden louder burst of yelling and a crash that told its own tale, and Alex was across the room and had flung open the door that led to the back of the house: "*Run!*"

They ran, picking up screaming children, clasping babies, sobbing and panting, tripping over their wide skirts. Winter ran as he had told her to—ran with Lottie and a dozen others who were making for the bridge over the nullah.

But many checked and turned back to hide in the house or, confused by terror and the blinding sunlight, to run helplessly to and fro like panic-stricken animals, dodging behind trees and shrubs.

Winter saw Lottie reach the bridge and cross it and run on towards the tangled thickets thirty yards beyond it. She had reached the bridge herself when a shriek behind her made her check and turn. It was Mrs. Gardener-Smith, running towards her from the direction of the house, her face a mask of terror and her mouth a screaming square. Two men were running behind her, one armed with a grass-cutter's sickle.

Winter's hand went to the revolver in the deep pocket of her skirt. But the sickle swept, and Mrs. Gardener-Smith fell sideways in a foam of gay muslin flounces.

Winter fired then, and the man tripped and fell. The second man, carrying a butcher's knife, ran forward, howling threats and obscenities. Winter fired again, and missed, and then the revolver jammed. She flung the useless weapon in his face. Then she heard a shot and saw him stagger, and then from somewhere Alex appeared, running towards her. He leaped the sprawled bodies of the men on the bridge, stooped swiftly to pick up the fallen revolver, and said breathlessly: "Run—"

"No!" gasped Winter, catching at the rail. "We can't! Look—"

There were screaming women and children in the Residency garden, running across the lawns, blind with terror; dodging like hunted hares while rifles cracked and dark-faced, bloodstained, blood-crazed men pursued them, yelling and laughing.

354

Alex grasped her arm, and dragged her by force across the bridge and down the path into the narrow arm of jungle that lay between the back of the Residency and the plain. He did not keep to the path but plunged off it right-handed, dragging her with him and thrusting his way between the high grass and thin scrub, the bamboo brakes and the dhâk trees; and when he stopped it was only because Winter's crinoline was hopelessly impeding their progress. They could still hear clearly a bedlam of shots and shouts and screams. But they were not, as yet, pursued.

Winter was sobbing and struggling. "Let me go! You can't leave them! You can't. There are children there—listen to them—*listen!*" She struck at him wildly, trying to break his hold.

Alex slapped her across the face with the flat of his palm. It was a hard blow and it jerked her back against a tree trunk and effectively checked her rising hysteria. "I may yet be more use alive than dead," said Alex brutally. "Get those hoops off—quickly!" He released her wrist and stood waiting, breathing quickly and listening, his revolver in his hand.

The pain of the blow had made her head ring and Alex's curt voice did not permit of argument. She pulled up the voluminous poplin skirts and the frilled petticoat and unfastened the hooped crinoline with feverish haste while he unjammed her revolver and gave it back to her. "Come on!"

It was easier to move now but she knew her shoes were not made for rough walking and would not stand up to it for long. Something rustled in the shadows, and two women crouching among a tangle of grass and creepers stood up. Lottie and Lou Cottar.

"*Winter!*" cried Lottie. She ran and clutched her, her eyes wide and glittering: "I thought—I thought—What happened? Why did they make me run? Why? *Why?*" Her voice rose to a scream.

Alex reached out and caught her, pressing her head against his breast. His eyes were anxious and alert but he spoke in an entirely matter-of-fact tone that somehow carried conviction: "We have to go to Meerut, Lottie. You want to see Edward, don't you? The carriage has broken down, so I am afraid we must walk. We were only running to get out of the sun. You do not want to get sunstroke just as you are going to Meerut, do you? This is a short cut."

Over Lottie's small head his eyes met Winter's. He looked away again and down at Lottie. The hysterical tension ebbed from Lottie's body and she lifted her head and smiled her sweet, dazed smile. "I didn't know. I'm sorry. Why, of course I want to see Edward! I thought—let us hurry!"

Alex shut his eyes for a brief moment, then he released her and said quietly: "Are there any more of you?"

Mrs. Cottar shook her head and answered him in a whisper: "Only the two of us . . . ." She broke off. Her face was chalk-white except where a thorn had scratched it deeply, and her hair had tumbled down her back. Her smart morning dress—she, too, had discarded her hooped underskirt—was torn, and she was trembling violently. But her eyes were steady.

Alex looked down at Lottie and said: "She'll have to take those hoops off. And you'd better do something about your shoes, or we

356

shan't get far. Tie 'em up with strips off your skirts." He knelt
swiftly to help Mrs. Cottar, who was already ripping the frills from
her petticoat with quick unsteady fingers. "You've got a pistol, I
see. Can you use it?"

"Yes," said Mrs. Cottar briefly, and sat down to tie the strips of
cloth round her shoes. Alex performed a similar office for Lottie,
while Winter, having tied her own slippers with a ruffle torn from
her petticoat, coaxed Lottie out of her crinoline.

There was a sudden renewed clamour of shots and shouting from
the direction of the Residency and the screaming of someone in
intolerable pain, muffled by the distance but still horribly audible
in the stillness of the morning.

Alex glanced back uneasily, then swung round on the three
white-lipped women and said savagely: "Don't stand there! For
God's sake get on—quickly." He thrust them ahead of him into the
hot, rustling grass and the shadows of the runi trees.

Two AND A HALF hours later they had covered less than four miles.
Lottie had struggled on manfully, but it had soon become obvious
that she could not keep up with them, and eventually Alex had
carried her. Lottie, even seven months pregnant, weighed astonishingly little, but the lightest weight becomes intolerable after a time,
and he was forced to stop and rest at shorter and shorter intervals.

It was Winter who said suddenly, watching his grim, exhausted
face as he rested for a moment, "Where are we going? What is it
you want to do?"

Alex opened his eyes and looked at her and his face was suddenly
bleak. But for her he might still have reached the bridge in time to
destroy it. The bridge was ten miles by road, but barely half that
through the jungle, and he had gone this way on foot often enough
before. But for Winter he would not be here at all . . . .

He said in a parched whisper: "I know this jungle—it runs to
the river—there's a ruin—mile above the bridge. Put the stuff there
—weeks ago." He closed his eyes again.

"What stuff? What stuff, Alex?" Winter knelt beside him.

"Gunpowder," said Alex without opening his eyes.

"*Gunpowder?* What for?"

"Blow up the bridge," said Alex briefly.

Across his body Winter's eyes met Lou Cottar's. She had never

357

liked Lou Cottar, but now something in the older woman that matched something in herself made a sudden bond between them.

Winter looked back at Alex. "How much farther is it?"

"Oh—mile. Get there soon." He dragged himself to his feet.

Winter said with a break in her voice: "Alex, you fool! You should have left us. We'll bring Lottie. Go on as quickly as you can. If it's only a mile we can follow you."

Alex did not argue. He looked at Lottie who lay with her head in Lou Cottar's lap, and said: "Don't rest too long. Keep moving, even if it's slowly. Hide if you hear anyone, and don't fire unless as a last resort. The sound of a shot carries." He turned away, the shadows closed behind him, and he was gone.

All at once the jungle was intolerably still. Winter whispered: "He was right. We'd better keep moving. We can follow him fairly easily if we go now, but the grass stands up again so quickly."

Lottie rolled her head in Mrs. Cottar's lap and muttered: "Water—please. So thirsty."

The two women looked at each other and looked away quickly, their own throats parched.

Out of Lou Cottar's dress they made a rough-and-ready hammock in which they laid Lottie. It was a precarious enough conveyance and an agonizingly slow performance to keep moving. The sun scorched them, the dense shade held no coolness and it became more and more difficult to persuade Lottie to lie still.

Almost an hour later they saw something loom up out of the tangle of scrub: a solid wall of creeper-covered stone, and knew that they had reached the end of that day's journey.

All that remained of the ruin was part of a two-storeyed building topped by a low dome. It was hot and very dark inside, and smelt strongly of wild boar and leopard. The stairway that led up to the top storey had fallen centuries ago, leaving a gaping hole in one corner of the black, bat-haunted ceiling of the single lower room.

The trodden grass showed where Alex and at least one other had passed in, but the ruin was as silent as the jungle.

"There is no one here," whispered Lou Cottar.

"But there is a ladder," said Winter. "Look!"

Hanging from the hole in the roof was a serviceable rope ladder, and they tugged at it tentatively. It appeared to be quite fast. Winter started upwards, and a minute later she had vanished through the broken aperture. Presently her head reappeared. "Can you get Lottie up? There's water here. There's everything!"

Two rough-and-ready beds, a roll of matting, some tin boxes, an oil-lamp and an earthenware *chatti* containing water would not have been considered "everything" a few hours ago. But the world had dissolved during those hours, and the sight of these homely objects helped in some way to solidify it again.

The water was warm and stale and there was not a great deal of it. There was a tin mug, recently used, standing beside it and they watched while Lottie drank, and then drank sparingly themselves.

"There, there, Lottie," said Winter, forcing her voice to placid reassurance. "You'll be all right now. You must rest. We're safe now—we're safe." But for how long?

CHAPTER 4

*B*Y THE irony of fate it was a bullet fired by one of the five British women who had preferred to remain in their own bungalows that brought down Niaz's horse. Laura Campion, standing over the body of her dying husband on the veranda of her bungalow, had fired his musket at a mob of sepoys who had pursued the wounded man from the lines. The bullet went wide, and the horse, neck stretched at a gallop, crossed the line of fire.

Niaz struck the dry grass verge of the roadway, rolled into a ditch and lay still.

He recovered consciousness within a few minutes, and not long afterwards, shaken and badly bruised but otherwise unhurt, he was crawling down the ditch towards the drive leading into Captain Garrowby's bungalow. He must have a horse, and there would be horses in the stables behind the bungalow. There he heard the explosion of the magazine, and did not know if it also signalled Alex's death. If so it was doubly necessary that he, Niaz, should reach the Hirren Minar and the bridge. He would have to do so even if it meant walking.

Crouched behind a prickly cactus hedge he heard a mob of men stream past, coming from the direction of the city—a mob who shouted the battle-cry of his creed: *"Deen! Deen! Fatteh Moham-med! . . ."* He shut his ears to the fierce cry and, as it died away, he ran on to the bungalow, keeping to the cover of trees and walls. But the stable doors stood open and the stables were empty . . . .

An hour later, on the road that led out of Lunjore towards Oudh, he had dragged a portly shopkeeper from the back of a starved-looking pony, and was riding as hard as he could in the direction of the bridge. He abandoned the pony by the roadside when he took to the jungle, and arrived at the ruined hide-out barely fifteen minutes before Alex.

He was descending from the upper room with sundry packages when Alex arrived. Too exhausted for speech, they looked at each other for a long moment and then Alex climbed the ladder, to drink and to fetch the Westley Richards rifle from its hiding-place in the ruined dome above and load it. Niaz returned from below.

"How much time have we?" Alex asked.

Niaz shrugged his shoulders. "An hour—two hours—who knows? I do not think they will come too soon. They are mad from killing and they are breaking into the bungalows to rob and burn."

"When there are no more left to kill they will be afraid and come away quickly," said Alex, filling his pockets with spare ammunition, and reaching for powder-flask and shot. "All but a few of those who were in the Residency are slain. I came away across the nullah with three mem-sahibs whom I left a mile from here. They follow, but slowly. I have marked the way. Let us go."

They descended the swaying ladder and shouldering their burdens went out into the hot shadows of the forest. The river ran past less than two hundred yards from the Hirren Minar, but the banks were steep and overhung by the dense jungle so that none passed that way, and the road and the bridge lay away to the right, a scant mile from the hidden ruin.

They moved with caution as they neared the road, and presently the jungle thinned out and they heard the creek and strain of the bridge and the gurgle of the river running between the boats that supported it. "Wait here," whispered Niaz. "I will go forward and see if the road be clear." He laid down the load he carried and wriggled away like a lizard through the thick scrub.

Alex sat down with his back to a tree trunk and tried not to think of the things he had seen that morning. He wished that he need never think again.

The undergrowth rustled and gave up Niaz who said cheerfully:

360

"I have bound the toll-keeper and the two police guards and locked them in the toll-house. They will not cry out. There remains now those on the far side."

They came out cautiously into the thinner belt of jungle by the bridgehead. The road lay long and empty and the small stone-built toll-house was silent. There was no sound to be heard except the gurgling of the water between the close-lashed boats.

They walked down the slope of the road onto the bridge. The heat shimmered off the wood in quivering waves that smelt of tar, and the glittering river that slid beneath them did not cool it. The river ran deep from a hundred yards above the bridge to a mile below it, for the bridge spanned it at its narrowest point. Except for mud-turtles basking at the edge of the sandbars on the far side of the river, there seemed to be nothing else alive within a dozen miles, and the hollow sound of their footsteps on the planks of the bridge was loud in the hot silence.

A drowsy toll-keeper heard it and came reluctantly to the door of the mud hut that served as a toll-house on the far bank of the river. Seeing a sahib, he salaamed and hurriedly straightened his turban. Alex returned the salute and inquired as to the hunting prospects in the jungles by the bridge. While he talked Niaz moved between them and the hut.

Five minutes later the two men in the hut who constituted the bridge guard, together with the horrified toll-keeper, were sitting gagged and bound in the inner room and Niaz was making fast the door. He carried the two guards' antiquated muskets out and flung them into the water as he and Alex ran back along the causeway and onto the bridge.

They worked swiftly and methodically in the boiling sun, laying charges, tamping and connecting fuses.

"Listen!" said Niaz suddenly. "There are horses on the road."

Alex leaped to his feet and stood for a moment listening intently. He snatched up the rifle and thrust it at Niaz. "Four more charges and we have done. Hold them off for a little—"

Niaz turned and raced back over the bridge and Alex bent to the charges again, working with feverish speed. The sound of horses' hooves was clearer now, but he did not lift his head.

"Only five minutes," he prayed. "It isn't much to ask—only five minutes—!"

NIAZ REACHED the toll-house, unbarred the door and ran to the small window that looked down the Lunjore road, ignoring the groans of the three bound and gagged men.

There were perhaps twelve to fifteen riders, sepoys from Lunjore, advancing at a leisurely trot for the bridge. An advance guard, possibly, to secure the bridge for the main body of the mutineers. Niaz fetched the muskets belonging to the police guard. With these and Alex's rifle he should be able to save time on loading. He waited until the sepoys were within range, and fired, aiming for the leading horse. He saw the horse rear and fall in a dusty smother.

The riders scattered to either side of the road, and conferred together. Presently one of them, evidently thinking that it was the bridge guard who were firing upon them, bellowed that they were friends and urged the guard to join them—the feringhis being dead and all Lunjore in the hands of its rightful owners.

The man moved incautiously out into the road and Niaz shot him and watched his riderless horse bolt wildly away. The remaining horsemen hurriedly dismounted and disappeared into the jungle.

"Now they will come up under cover on either side of the road," thought Niaz, and remembered with dread that Alex, working alone on the empty bridge, would provide an admirable target. He fired again at random into the jungle just ahead of where the men had entered it, discharging each of the muskets in turn and reloading with feverish haste. A bullet entered the open door and ricocheted round the small room. Niaz turned from the window and running to the door fired into the thick scrub on the opposite side of the road. As he did so something struck his chest and he fell sideways, the rifle jerking from his hand to slide along the floor and come to rest against the far wall.

After a moment or two he came dizzily to his knees and crawled towards the rifle, but he could not reach it. He groped instead for his revolver and, dragging it painfully from its holster, raised himself a little and fired at a face that peered through the high grass at the road's edge, and saw a man lurch forward and fall. Then he heard the sound of running feet, a crash of shots, and Alex had leaped the stone step of the veranda, stumbled over him and turning, had fired his revolver at a man on horseback who rode shouting for the bridge.

The shouting stopped. There was a clatter of hooves, and a

moment of silence. Then the crashing blast of an explosion; then another and another that joined together in a single shuddering roar of sound, and the glaring day was dark with the reek of black powder. And then the silence slammed down like an iron shutter. The river gurgled no longer, but ran quiet and unimpeded from bank to bank. The bridge had gone.

Alex spoke breathlessly: "Before they recover—out by the back. Quickly!" He had barred the door behind him and was across the room pulling at the heavy bolts that closed the rear door. He drew it open a crack and said: "There is no one there—quick!"

"I cannot," said Niaz.

Alex whipped round, seeing for the first time that Niaz was wounded. He knelt swiftly and thrust an arm under him, lifting him: "Hold about my neck and I can carry thee."

"No," said Niaz urgently. "This is the end for me. Go—and go swiftly while there is yet time—my work is finished."

Alex looked down at the greying face against his arm and the swiftly spreading stain that soaked the dusty tunic. Pulling back the reddened cloth, he saw that there was nothing that he or anyone could do, and desperation and a rage beyond anything he had felt that day tore at him. He heard dimly, and as though through a roaring fog, the crack of rifle fire, but he did not move.

Niaz said: "Thou has seen how it is with me—go now. I can still —fire a gun—it will hold them—for a little. Get to the jungle— there be the mem-sahibs to be—thought of—"

Lou Cottar—Lottie—Winter . . . Once again, and for a brief moment, he saw Winter's face against the rough stone walls of the shadowed room; as clearly as he had seen it in Alice Batterslea's garden. But it did not mean anything to him any more. She would have to take her chance. He would not leave Niaz to die alone.

Getting to his feet he closed and bolted the back door and dropped the shutters across the two windows. He took up the guns one by one and loaded them methodically. There was an earthen-ware jar of water in the room, and he fetched a brass cup, stepping over the bodies of the three bound men who lay in a terrified huddle at the far end of the room, and filling it, brought it to Niaz.

He lifted him carefully against his shoulder and Niaz's eyes strove to focus him. He drank a mouthful of water and said again and urgently: "Go!"

"We will go together," said Alex. "Has it not been said that 'death in the company of friends is a feast'?"

A bullet struck the heavy wood of the door and another cracked against the stone. He looked down at Niaz and smiled, and Niaz grinned back at him—the old carefree grin with which he had greeted every chance and mischance of life through the twelve eventful years that they had known each other—and he said in a clear strong voice: "We have had a good life . . . . a good life—and though thou art an unbeliever, and therefore hell-doomed, thou has been as my brother. Lift me up, brother—"

His voice failed. A rush of blood choked him, pouring from his mouth and dyeing Alex's coat, and he fell back and was still.

A musket ball struck a leaf of the wooden shutter over the window and filled the room with flying splinters. There were shouting voices and another fusillade of shots from outside, but Alex did not move. He stayed quite still, holding Niaz's body in his arms until aroused at last by a bullet that smashed through the panel of the door and passed within an inch of his shoulder.

He laid Niaz down very carefully and stood up. His gaze fell on the water jar and he picked it up and drank thirstily, and poured what remained of it over his head and neck. He did not know how many men there were outside. A dozen? Twenty? They would get him in the end, but he should be able to account for some of them before the ammunition in the toll-house ran out. He took stock of it. A rifle, five muskets, two revolvers. A pocketful of cartridges. He might hold them off for an hour—perhaps a little longer.

There were two string charpoys in the stifling room and he stooped and, lifting Niaz, laid him on one of them. He took up the rifle and loaded it and, crossing to the window, lifted the bar of the shutter and pulled it aside.

It was nearly five o'clock when Alex fired the last round and dropped the useless weapon to the floor. He closed the shutter again and sitting down on the charpoy beside Niaz, leaned against the wall and waited. For the moment there was silence outside, but he knew that it would not be long before it dawned upon those without that he must have come to the end of his ammunition.

The room stank of sweat and urine, black powder, betel-nut and blood, and the gloom was noisy with the buzz of flies. Alex pulled

Niaz's puggari over his face, and folded the quiet hands across his chest. It must be getting late. He rose and turned the charpoy so that the dead man's head was towards Mecca, and spoke the words of the Du'a over the quiet body—there being no one else who would ever speak them for Niaz.

"May the Lord God, abundant in mercy, keep thee with the true speech; may he lead thee to the perfect path; may he grant thee knowledge of him and his prophets. May the mercy of God be fixed upon thee for ever. Ameen . . . O great and glorious God, we beseech thee with humility, make the earth comfortable to this thy servant's side, and raise his soul to thee, and with thee may he find mercy and forgiveness."

When the murmured words ceased there was only the buzz of flies once more. Alex sat down again, and presently, emboldened by the silence, footsteps pattered on the stone veranda and dragging sounds told him that wood and dry grass was being piled against the doors and windows. They were going to make a pyre of it. Well, he might as well go that way as any other. A funeral pyre for Niaz and himself. He settled himself comfortably against the wall, and as he did so one of the men on the floor stirred and moaned.

He remembered that there were three other men there, and he could not let them be burned alive. "Wait a minute—" said Alex, speaking aloud. "Wait a minute—"

As he dragged himself to his feet he heard a man outside say triumphantly: "Did I not say so? It *is* a sahib! There are sahib-*log* in there!" and realized that he had spoken in English.

A voice immediately outside the door said loudly: "Who is it? Who is within there?"

Alex knew that voice. It was Kishan Prasad's. He said: "It is I, Rao Sahib. Call off your butchers, for there are three in here who are bound hand and foot and who had no part in this. You cannot burn them alive. I will come out."

"Who else is with thee?"

"None but Niaz Mohammed Khan, who is dead."

There was a shouting and a rush of feet and he heard Kishan Prasad say furiously: "Stand back!—stand back, I say!" and a moment later the sound of a grumbling retreat.

"Open then," said Kishan Prasad.

Alex drew back the bolts and opened the door.

365

Kishan Prasad stared at him and then stepped over the threshold and threw a quick look about the room. He turned and stood blocking the narrow door, facing men whom Alex could not see.

"There is but one sahib here," he said. "The other man is dead and the three men they have bound are alive. This sahib I know, and because he once gave me my life at risk of his own, I say that he shall go free. Stand away!"

There was an ugly growl and a rush of shouting men, but Kishan Prasad did not move and his voice rose clearly above the tumult: "Stand back! I am a Brahmin; and if you would kill this man, you will have first to kill me."

The men drew back, for they were Hindus, and to kill a Brahmin would be sacrilege unspeakable.

"Go," said Kishan Prasad, speaking over his shoulder to Alex. "Move out behind me and run for the jungle. I can do no more. The debt is paid."

Alex said tiredly and without emotion: "Rao Sahib, if I had one bullet left in my gun, I would shoot thee now for the things that have been done this day because of men like thee."

"That may yet come," said Kishan Prasad. "Go now—"

He moved out of the doorway, keeping between Alex and the group of snarling men at the far end of the veranda, and Alex backed away behind him and, reaching the end of the veranda, stepped down and, turning, ran for the jungle.

He heard the uproar break out behind him, and a lone shot whistled past his head. And then he was into the high grass and stumbling through the thickets, keeping as close to the road as he dared. The Hirren Minar lay on its far side. The pursuit would imagine him to be making straight for the thicker jungle instead of turning back up the Lunjore road. They would watch to see that he did not cross the road, however, and it ran here as straight as a spear for more than a mile.

He crawled with infinite caution to within sight of the road and lay there for a long time. The sun touched the rim of the jungle and slid slowly below it, and a peacock called from the thickets behind him. A horseman galloped towards him from the direction of the river, raising a long cloud of dust. And suddenly it was simple.

The rider passed him, and Alex leaped to his feet and ran for the opposite side of the road, screened by the choking cloud of dust.

CHAPTER 5

WINTER AND Lou Cottar heard the faint, faraway crack of rifle fire at the bridgehead, and the distant roar of the explosion. All that afternoon the firing continued, and they guessed what it meant and listened—and waited.

For want of anything else to do they set about turning the stone chamber into some semblance of a home. It was large and square, and windowless on three sides. The fourth side consisted of three pillared arches, two of which still retained broken fragments of stone tracery, and led out onto a flat roof surrounded by a low, ruined parapet.

There were several *chiks* in one corner of the room, and Lou hung them between the pillars, remarking that they would keep out the worst of the flies and mosquitoes. They also curtained off a section of the room with sacking for Alex's use, convinced as they did so that he would not return, but denying the fear by that action.

Bamboo and dried grass made primitive but efficient brooms, and they swept and dusted, cleaned and tidied, in a desperate attempt to keep their hands occupied and their minds from thinking of the many things that did not bear thinking of.

Lou Cottar, standing on the open roof, reported that she could see a glimpse of river and would fetch water. She took the *chatti*—Winter lowered it after her on a rope—and set out to find her way through the dense jungle to the riverbank. She did not return for over an hour and Winter received her with breathless relief. "I'm sorry," said Mrs. Cottar apologetically, "but it's so thick out there that I lost my way coming back, even though it is so near."

Winter drank thirstily while Lou Cottar filled a small rusted tin with water and arranged a spray of wild jungle berries in it for Lottie. "I bathed," she said, knotting up her wet hair. "It was wonderful. The bank is very steep, but there is a place where the river has cut in behind a tree and made a little beach. You had better go too, before it gets dark. It—" She stopped. They had heard no shots for some time, and they were both thinking the same thing—that Alex must be dead.

Winter realized that Conway too must be dead. He had been her husband—yet for him she could feel nothing at all.

"I'll take some of Lottie's clothes and wash them in the river," she said abruptly, "and my own. They'll be dry in an hour."

She removed her own clothes and wrapped herself in a length of faded blue cotton cloth that they had found stuffed in among a collection of odds and ends in one of the tin boxes. It made a skimpy though adequate sari, and she wound it about her in the fashion of the Indian women.

"You know," said Lou Cottar thoughtfully, "you could almost pass as an Indian, if you'd get a little more sunburned. It's your hair and eyes. It may be a help yet."

"I should have to learn to walk without shoes," said Winter.

"We may both have to," said Lou Cottar grimly.

They made a bundle of the clothes and Winter took the loaded revolver and went down the rope ladder. The jungle was waking to life as the shadows lengthened, and there were rustlings among the dry golden grass, and birds called from the thickets. A peacock fluttered up to the low bough of a tree, his gorgeous tail glinting in the low rays of the sun, and a chinkara fawn looked at Winter with startled eyes over a tussock of grass before bounding away in the direction of the river. Making her way through the tangle of dry grass and leaves and creepers, her ears were filled with the sound of her own progress, but she could hear the birdsong above it.

The river ran gold in the evening light by the time she reached it, and the far bank was already in shadow. She clambered cautiously down and, removing her makeshift sari, tucked it and the soiled clothing among the tree roots, and let herself down into the water.

It was cool and delicious beyond belief. She did not know how long she lay there, with closed eyes, but presently she opened her eyes, to find that the sun had almost set and the sky and the river were no longer gold, but rose pink. The leaves and flowers of the tree that leaned above her made a vivid pattern against that wash of colour, and in the pattern a parrot moved, with scarlet beak and long green tail feathers . . . .

And all at once the Gulab Mahal was there before her. The enchanted garden of her childhood. The formal patterns of leaves and flowers and brightly coloured birds that moved against a sunset sky, and that had remained fixed in her memory as a bright promise through all the grey, intervening years. Somehow, some day, she would reach the Rose Palace.

She came to her feet and, reaching for the bundle of clothing, washed out the garments in the river. With the heavy bundle she climbed the bank again and wrapped the makeshift sari about her once more, leaving her wet hair hanging loose. Then, picking up the wet bundle and the revolver, she turned from the river to make her way back to the Hirren Minar.

She had stayed far longer by the river than she had meant to do, and now the sun had gone and the swift twilight was closing in. Unsure of her direction, she stopped at the edge of a small clearing.

Something was moving through the dry rustling undergrowth towards her, something or someone.

Winter crouched down, her finger tightening upon the trigger of the revolver as the high grass at the far side of the clearing parted, and Alex walked out—filthy, bloodstained, dazed, but alive.

For a moment she did not believe it. She had given him up for dead! The revolver slipped from her hand. She stood up and took a swift step forward, the bundle of clothing falling unheeded to the ground.

Alex checked, swaying. Through the haze before his eyes he saw a slim Indian girl confronting him in the dusk, the blue of her sari and the blue-black of her long, unbound hair melting into the shadows of the darkening jungle behind her. Then the haze cleared —and it was Winter.

They stood staring at each other for a minute, then Alex stumbled forward and as she ran to him he dropped onto the grass and she knelt beside him, holding him to her, and felt his arms go about her in a desperate grip. Terrible sobs wrenched his body. She held him tightly, and he lifted his head and looked up into her face.

His eyes held an odd, blind anger, and then his arms pulled her down onto the grass. She felt his hands on the thin cotton of the sari, wrenching it away, and he laid his grimed and smoke-blackened face between her breasts. Her skin was cool from the river, and he kissed it with an open mouth, moving his harsh cheek and his aching head against it, holding her closer. Then his hands moved again, and for a fleeting moment the fear and the horror of her wedding night returned to Winter. But this was not Conway, drunken and bestial. Conway was dead—they were all dead. All those people who had lived and laughed in the cantonments at Lunjore and at Delhi. The whole world was dissolving in blood and tears and terror. But here in the quiet forest there were only herself and Alex—Alex's arms and his mouth and his need of her . . . .

At long last his hold slackened and he lay still. The sky darkened above them, turning from green to a violet blue that was strewn with stars. He slept the sleep of utter mental and physical exhaustion, and Winter held him in her arms and watched the stars and was not afraid. Presently a breeze got up, blowing through the jungle with a sleepy, soothing, rustling sound, and lulling her at last into deep and dreamless sleep.

THE SKY WAS paling to the first light of dawn when Winter awoke and felt Alex move and draw away from her.

She opened her eyes. He was standing beside her, and she saw that his torn coat was black with dried blood.

"Alex!—you're wounded! You're covered in blood!"

"It isn't mine," said Alex in a flat, entirely expressionless voice. "It is Niaz's. He's dead."

He looked down at the stained, discoloured coat, and began to remove it, letting it fall to the ground. He said after a moment or two: "I'm sorry about last night."

His voice did not express sorrow, or anything else and Winter's heart contracted with the familiar ache of pain that she felt so often when she looked at him. She wanted desperately to put her arms about him and to tell him that she loved him, that if her cool body had meant no more to him than a temporary forgetfulness, then it was enough that she had given him that. But she knew that she must not. He would not understand.

He said: "I'm going down to the river. I shan't be long. Stay here."

He disappeared into the jungle. Winter stooped and picked up his discarded coat. He would need it, and she could soak the stains out. It was growing lighter every moment and presently a bird began to twitter in the trees behind her. A hint of the terrible heat that the day would bring was already in the air. Winter knotted up her heavy tangled hair, and searched among the tall grass for the revolver and the bundle of linen. A jungle-cock began to cackle in the thickets, and then the stillness was broken by a babble of bird-song. A flight of parrots screamed out of the trees on their way to the river, and other jungle-cocks awoke and saluted the dawn.

When Alex returned, he was clean again. He had washed out his shirt and trousers and put them on wet. But they were already beginning to dry in the heat. He took the revolver and the bundle of clothing from her and said: "What have you done with Lou Cottar and Lottie? What were you doing out here last night?"

"They're all right—at least—at least I think so," said Winter, turning to follow him. "I went to bathe in the river, and I lost my way coming back. It was getting dark—"

Alex appeared to know his way, for he walked ahead of her unhesitatingly, until suddenly the dark entrance of the Hirren Minar was before them.

He said softly: "Lou—are you all right?" and there was a swift movement above his head, and a voice said: "*Alex!*"

Two minutes later they were both in the upper room. Mrs. Cottar said: "What happened to you? I thought—" She burst into tears.

Alex pushed aside the *chik* that she had hung across the open archway, and went out onto the flat roof. Wearily he sat down on the crumbling parapet. All at once he realized that he had not eaten for over twenty-four hours. Presently the sun rose, and the temperature leaped up as though the door of a furnace had been swung wide.

Winter came out onto the roof behind him. Alex turned and surveyed her with a faint surprise as though she were someone he had never seen before. She was still wearing the blue cotton sari, and he thought with an entire lack of emotion that she was the most beautiful thing he had ever seen—and a stranger.

How can she look like that? he thought with a faint twinge of irritation. As if she were entirely content and there were no longer any problems that mattered. Had women no imagination? Had nothing of all that she had seen made her realize that her life from now on—all their lives—was only a matter of living for an hour or a day more, by luck and cunning and the grace of God?

Winter said: "Breakfast is ready."

The incongruity of the statement at that time and in that setting suddenly struck him, and he laughed for the first time in many days.

ALEX LAY FLAT on his stomach in a thicket at the edge of a glade. He held one end of a thin cord in his hand and he was watching the leisurely approach of a peacock and his retinue of wives towards a primitive trap some twelve feet ahead of him.

The Hirren Minar was well stocked with salt and parched grain and a miscellaneous variety of the more durable stores, but they needed fresh food, and Alex did not dare fire a gun for fear of attracting attention. They had fish-hooks and lines, however, which had proved useful, and he had managed to trap birds.

Afraid of showing smoke, they cooked only after dark or before dawn, and in the lower room of the ruin—a hot and choking performance. They had been in the Hirren Minar for over two weeks now, and already it seemed to Winter and Lou Cottar as though they had lived there for months. Lottie's gentle, trance-like daze had survived even her second escape and, though she talked continuously of Edward, her clouded brain accepted the simplest lie, and the presence of Winter and Alex convinced her that all was well. Life in India was so very different from life in England—one must be prepared to make allowances for foreign customs, and when Edward's manoeuvres were over they would be able to live in their own bungalow in Meerut again. She must be patient.

Lou Cottar, too, schooled herself to patience. At first it was more than enough simply to be alive and safe. But as the days went by she began to take the security for granted. Up to then she had lived only for amusement, and she yearned for the society of her own kind again. For lights, music, laughter—all the things that made life an entertaining affair. Josh would be in Calcutta, and she felt sure that Calcutta at least must still be in British hands.

As for Alex, he knew perfectly well that he was tied to the Hirren Minar until he could get the women to safety. And yet, outside the jungle that sheltered them, there must be so much needing to be done. There was Delhi to be retaken. And his own district . . . . But he could do nothing for the moment. At present the women were safe, and he could not move them until he had reliable news.

There was a bundle of native clothes in the ruined dome of the Hirren Minar, and, wearing them, he visited the Residency. But there was nothing to be learned there. The place was deserted, except for the kites and the crows and the scavenging pariah dogs. Apart from the Commissioner and some half a dozen others, very few were still recognizable.

He did not go to the cantonments again. He went out—when he went—by night into the surrounding district and in this fashion he heard the news of the city and villages.

The tales he was told were all of disaster to the British. There was no safety east or west, north or south. Oudh also had risen, and it was said that Lawrence Sahib and all the British in Lucknow would soon be slain. Meanwhile the countryside was in a ferment, with bands of armed sepoys swaggering through the villages.

Obviously it was unwise to exchange the comparative safety of the Hirren Minar for the dangers of a cross-country flight to some district that might well prove to be in a worse state than Lunjore. There was nothing to do but to keep the women in hiding; Alex chafed at the inaction and occupied himself with snaring birds.

Winter alone of the four occupants of the Hirren Minar had no need to pray for patience. The heat did not affect her to the same degree as it affected Lottie and Lou Cottar, and the jungle and the river and the ancient, hidden ruin held a strange enchantment for her. She shut her mind to the memory of all that had happened to her in Lunjore. She would not think of the past or the future, only of the present. And the present was Alex.

It did not worry her that Alex hardly looked at her and rarely spoke to her. She felt as though she had loved him all her life and knew everything about him. It contented her that Alex was alive and within reach of her, and that she could watch him and feel his presence even when she could not see him.

Lottie and Lou Cottar, in spite of the appalling heat, still wore the hoopless dresses they had worn when they fled from Lunjore. Alex had brought back needles and thread from one of his night excursions, and they had mended them neatly. He had also, somewhat unexpectedly, brought a wine-coloured cotton sari with a deep blue border and a narrow cotton bodice, such as the village women wore, for Winter.

"You're letting yourself go native, Winter!" snapped Lou Cottar one hot evening, in an unwonted outburst of irritation. She looked resentfully at the girl, and thought suddenly that she was beautiful; like something out of an Eastern fairytale—a princess from the *Thousand and One Nights*. Surprised at herself for the thought, she said irritably: "You're the only one who doesn't look out of place in this God-forsaken hole—and who doesn't seem to mind it here."

"I don't," said Winter dreamily.

Lou Cottar stared at her with an indignation that changed to sudden comprehension. She said abruptly: "You're in love with him, aren't you?"

Winter smiled and said: "Yes."

"Is he in love with you?"

Winter shook her head, and Lou said tartly: "Then he's a fool!"

"I think he has too much on his mind to bother about anything like that," said Winter reflectively. "Just now he can only think of me as a tiresome responsibility."

"Not only you," said Lou with a twisted smile. "All of us. And I can't say I blame him. If it wasn't for us he could go. And if it wasn't for Lottie—" She glanced towards the bed where Lottie lay asleep, and her thin features sharpened with anxiety. She said with suppressed violence: "That damned baby! It's hanging over us all like—like the monsoon. We must get her away! How much longer has she got?"

"About six weeks, I think," said Winter doubtfully.

"Six weeks! Oh God—and here we are doing nothing. *Nothing!* What in heaven's name are we going to do if she has it here? Do you know anything about babies?"

"No," admitted Winter.

"Neither do I. Not a damned thing. We've got to get her to some civilized place where there is a doctor. Why doesn't Alex do something? We *must* get her away!"

She spoke to Alex.

"Don't be a fool, Lou!" he replied brusquely. "We can't leave yet. Lottie may have a bad time of it if she stays here, but she'll certainly die—and so will the rest of us—if we are mad enough to attempt a cross-country trip just now. The jungle at least will do us no harm."

But he had spoken too soon, for the jungle that had seemed to befriend them suddenly showed its claws.

They had gone down to the river that evening, all four of them, as they did every evening, because it was cooler there and there were always clothes and cooking-pots to be washed and fishing lines to tend. Winter did not see the cobra until it lashed at her, hissing, as she bent to disentangle her sari caught on a thorn. Her foot touched the cold coils, and the fangs bit into her left arm just above the elbow.

Alex swung round as she cried out, and saw the snake slither across her path, and the two small punctures on her smooth, tanned skin. The next second he had leaped at her and caught her; his fingers tight above the wound, forcing the blood down, and his mouth against it, sucking at it with all his strength.

Lou came running, to snatch up a petticoat that was to be washed and ripped at it frantically. She wound a strip of it above Alex's straining hands and pulled it tight in a tourniquet. Alex said hoarsely: "Permanganate—on the ledge at the back—quickly," and Lou turned and ran, while Lottie wrung her hands and wept.

Alex jerked the knife he carried from its sheath, held Winter hard against him and cut the wound across deeply, twice. She did not cry out. The blood poured down her arm and his in a red tide and he lifted her and carried her swiftly back to the Hirren Minar.

Lou Cottar met them with the tin of permanganate crystals, and they filled the wound with them, and got Winter up the rope ladder. Alex let the arm bleed, bound it up and gave her as much opium as he dared.

Winter ran a high fever that first night and Alex held her hands while she twisted and turned, and Lou Cottar bathed her burning body with cool water. "Is she going to die?" Lou asked.

"No. She'll be all right in a few hours," said Alex with more confidence than he felt. "Give me that cloth and go and lie down, Lou. If you crack up too, I swear I'll go out and shoot myself!"

Lou obeyed him, and Alex took Winter's small fever-racked body into his arms and held it close, his cheek pressed to the burning forehead. The night was breathlessly hot and Alex's own body was wet with sweat, but his hold seemed to soothe her, and after a while he felt her slacken and lie still in his arms, and knew that she was asleep at last and that the fever had broken.

"My love!" thought Alex, moving his mouth against the hot smooth skin and the damp waves of silky hair that were as dark as the darkness about him. "My little love . . . ."

Quite suddenly the gnawing restlessness that had lived with him hourly during the last weeks fell away from him, and he no longer cared what became of anyone else—or of India—as long as Winter was safe. She was no longer a burden and a responsibility, but part of his heart, as she had always been. What did it matter if they had to wait here in hiding for months—or years?

One day the British would be in control again and it would be safe to leave the jungle. They could get away then—get married. Barton was dead. It was only a question of waiting.

CHAPTER 6

*W*INTER SUFFERED remarkably little ill-effect from the incident. The wound had healed cleanly and she was soon about again.

She saw very little of Alex after that, and suspected that he was deliberately avoiding her, but she knew that some tension in him had relaxed and that he was no longer impatient or irritable. He had taken to wearing nothing but a loincloth these days. His body was burned as brown as his face and he could have passed anywhere for a Pathan. He had been out less for news of late and, but for the relentless heat, the days passed peacefully enough.

Alex, like Winter, found the heat unpleasant, but bearable. But to Lou, and more especially to Lottie, it was a torture. They watched the skies daily for signs of the monsoon, and longed for rain; but though the clouds would sometimes gather, and they could hear thunder rumble along the horizon, no rain fell, and they lived for the early mornings and the late evenings when they could lie and soak in the coolness of the river.

Alex became afraid of the river, and he drove in stakes about the little beach where they bathed, in case they might attract the attention of a mugger, and that one day one of them might be dragged down by yellow-toothed jaws. But there was too much food in the river these days for the crocodiles to bother with live prey. Often bodies came down on the current, bloated and bobbing to the undertow, and once one had caught in tree roots by the beach.

Alex had been forced to free the body and push it off into the stream, and the others, arriving minutes later, had wondered why he looked so unusually grim. He had not looked like that for some time past; he had looked relaxed and almost contented, and had taken to humming under his breath as he set the fishing lines. But that night he had gone to the city again, and when he returned at dawn his eyes were hot with restlessness once more; for it seemed that the tide was turning at last.

The British were encamped once more upon the Ridge before Delhi. The Guides had marched from Mardan and were now with the Delhi force, and Hodson Sahib, the *"Burra Lerai-wallah"* (great in battle), was also there, commanding a regiment of horse.

"It won't be long now," Alex told Winter, his eyes blazing in the grey dawn light. "We shall have to stick it out here a little longer, but the monsoon must break soon, and then it will be cooler. And when Delhi is taken we'll be able to get away."

Another ten days; perhaps a fortnight—or a month. But what did it matter, now that the end was in sight? They could afford to wait a week or two more. They had been very lucky, luckier than so many others. Perhaps the luck would hold.

But it did not hold.

THAT SAME EVENING Lottie strayed away to pick jungle berries. She heard someone moving through the bushes and turned, expecting Lou, who had been fetching water.

But it was not Lou. It was a native with the marks on wrist and ankle that are made by iron fetters, a criminal released by the mob from the city gaol, and escaping to the jungle.

He stared at her, then grinned evilly, and drew a stained sword from its sheath. He did not hear Lou coming up from the river.

She never moved from the Hirren Minar without a revolver. She dropped the *chatti*, and as the man looked round she fired. The man swayed, coughed, crumpled at the knees and fell sideways with blood pouring from his mouth.

"No!" screamed Lottie. "No! No! No!"

Alex heard the shot and the screams, and ran. He took one look at the man on the ground and at Lou who was holding the screaming Lottie, and said: "Where's Winter?" And then Winter ran through the bushes, white-faced and panting, and he gripped Lou's shoulders and shook her, "Were there any others?"

"No. I don't know," said Lou jerkily.

"Get on, get back—all of you. He may not have been alone."

But Lottie would not go. She struggled and screamed, and Alex had to carry her back to the Hirren Minar, and into the upper room.

Lottie still screamed and shrieked and fought as she had screamed and fought at the Kashmir Gate at Delhi. "Let me go!— let me go! They're killing him! Edward—*Edward!*" she screamed. And then quite suddenly she went slack in Alex's arms and fainted.

Alex laid her down on the narrow camp bed, and letting down the rope ladder, ordered Winter to pull it up after him and went out into the twilight jungle.

He turned the dead man over and, recognizing him, realized that he was probably on the run. He made a cautious circuit of the immediate area but found no one, and returning to the corpse he dragged it to the riverbank and pushed it off into deep water. Then he returned to the Hirren Minar. There was an appalling smell of burned feathers in the upper room. Lottie was still unconscious and Lou and Winter were making desperate efforts to revive her.

"Leave her alone," advised Alex. "If she has remembered Delhi she is better off like that."

He mixed brandy, opium and water, and when Lottie recovered consciousness they were able to make her drink the brew without much difficulty. She sat up, propped against Lou Cottar's shoulder, and stared up at Lou and at Alex and Winter, and her eyes had lost the dazed sweetness that they had worn for so long.

She said at last: "Edward is dead, isn't he? They killed him. I—I remember now. And they shot Mama—and—and Papa. Where is Sophie?"

"Sophie is safe, darling," said Winter. "She is in Cawnpore."

"They killed Edward," whispered Lottie. "They—they cut him with their swords, and there was a man with a knife who—"

Winter said: "Don't think of it, darling—don't!"

"How can you stop yourself thinking of a thing like that? I should have stayed with him but they wouldn't let me. I should have stayed with him—" She turned her head against Lou Cottar's shoulder and wept, and Alex got up and went out.

He slept in the jungle that night, and at dawn he went down to the river and lay in the water below the bank, watching the sky turn saffron, while the birds awoke in the thickets above him and a troop of monkeys came down to drink. He lay there for a long time, until the sun leaped from below the horizon and the burning day was in full flood across the pitiless sky. It was only then that he realized that none of the women had come down to the river that morning. They were usually there well before sunrise.

He walked back to the Hirren Minar, and he had reached the entrance when he heard an agonized moaning, and stopped, knowing what it meant. He turned and sat down on a block of stone. This, at least, was not his affair. There were two women with her.

He could hear Winter's voice and Lou's, and Lottie's moans going on and on. The moaning rose to a scream that was more fear than pain, and suddenly he could bear it no longer. He leaped up the ladder and into the comparative coolness of the upper room.

Lottie was lying on the camp bed, fully dressed and clutching at the side of it, her eyes wide with terror. Winter knelt beside her and Lou Cottar leaned over her. They turned their heads towards him and on both their white faces was the same terror of the unknown that was on Lottie's. Seeing it, Alex realized that not one of them had the least idea of the mechanics of birth.

The suffocating prudery of the age saw to it that the majority of young women were kept in complete ignorance of such matters, and neither Winter nor Lottie had even seen a cat having kittens. In a sudden fury of exasperation he thrust Winter and Lou aside.

"What in hell's name do you think you're doing? Come on—get her out of those clothes!"

Then he saw from their expressions that even in this extremity they felt it unspeakably shocking to remove Lottie's dress in his presence, and his exasperation mounted. He bent over Lottie and took her hands, and said: "Listen to me, Lottie. You've got to think of your baby now and not of anything else. Forget that I'm a man— just try and do what I say. Will you do that?"

Lottie nodded, clinging to his hands, and he released them with difficulty and said shortly to Lou: "Use a fan to keep the flies off her. Have we got enough water in the place?"

"I—I think so," said Lou. Her face was white and assurance had suddenly forsaken her.

"Well, make sure! And if we haven't, get it." He turned to Winter. "Get down there and heat some water. And here—" He reached for a knife from the stone ledge and handed it to her. "Boil that in some water—let it boil for ten minutes and then take it off."

When she had removed Lottie's clothing she turned without a word and descended the ladder and Lou said: "The smoke—"

"We shall have to chance it." Lottie's moans rose once more to a scream and he went to her swiftly, and Winter heard him talking as she fetched wood and dry grass and lit the fire that they had never yet lit by day. He was telling Lottie about the child. What it was doing, and what her own body was doing to help it in its struggle for release, and what she must do to help them both. It sounded, suddenly, entirely natural and reasonable. His words evidently carried reassurance to Lottie, for her moaning ceased.

379

The long morning wore away, and the appalling heat filled the Hirren Minar as though it was a tangible thing: a weight which could be lifted from the shoulders if only the body had possessed sufficient strength.

Lou and Winter took turns to pull the bamboo punkah and sponge Lottie, while Alex sat by her, talking to her, pulling against her as she clung to his hands. But before the morning was out he knew with sick despair that he was fighting a losing battle.

LOTTIE'S DAUGHTER was born just as the sun touched the level of the treetops; and long before the gold had left the sky, Lottie was dead. She had survived the birth, and she might have lived if she had fought to do so; but she had neither the strength nor the desire to hold onto life. She had spoken only once. Lou had washed the tiny, whimpering creature and laid it against Lottie's thin shoulder. Lottie's sunken eyes opened slowly and painfully and she looked at it. A ray from the sinking sun pierced through the bamboo screen and touched its small head, and Lottie smiled.

"Red hair," she whispered. "Like Edward's. Take care of him, Lou." And then she died.

Lou wept, but Winter did not cry. Lottie was with Edward, and she had loved Edward so much. She washed Lottie's light little body and dressed her again, and went out to the river, leaving Lou with the child.

Alex was sitting on a fallen block of stone among the jungle grass, his head in his hands. Winter went to him and put her arms about him, and laid her cheek against his hair. He turned his head against her shoulder with a tired sigh and his arms went round her quite gently. He leaned wearily against her for a long time, not speaking, while the dusk deepened about them . . . .

Later he dug a grave and they buried Lottie in the clear pearly light of the early morning, an hour before the sun rose. Afterwards, Alex went off to bathe in the river at a spot higher up the bank, leaving the narrow beach by the tree to Winter and Lou, and did not return until an hour after sunrise.

The upper room of the Hirren Minar was clean and tidy, and all the nerve-racking torture of those long, agonized hours yesterday seemed a year away. Winter handed him food, and he ate it and watched Lou feeding the baby with water in which she had boiled a little rice. She dipped a clean rag in the liquid and gave it to the tiny creature to suck, and there was a look on her face that Alex had not thought possible for Lou Cottar. A soft, absorbed wonder.

"You'll have to get me some milk," she said thoughtfully. "I wonder if we could keep a goat?"

Alex came over to look at the skinny, wrinkled little object with the fluff of reddish-gold down on its head that had cost Lottie her life, and looking at it he had a sudden warm feeling of achievement. He laughed and said: "You shall have your goat, Lou, if I have to steal it! What are you going to call her?"

"Amanda," said Lou promptly.

"Good Lord! Why? Did Lottie—"

"No," said Lou. "Lottie was sure it was going to be a boy. She never knew it wasn't. It's just that I think Amanda is a nice name for her. It means 'Worthy of love'."

Alex stroked the downy head with a forefinger and Lou looked up at him and smiled. "Still three women on your hands, Alex."

"Four," said Alex with a grin. "You've forgotten the goat. And I can clearly see that a goat is going to be more trouble than the rest of you put together."

It was a prophecy that was to prove lamentably correct.

Alex went out at sunset, and returned at dawn dragging an exceedingly vocal goat procured from the village. The goat had been loath to accompany him, and he had been compelled to carry it for most of the way.

Lou and Winter learned to milk it and the baby throve. The goat gave far more trouble. It evinced a desire to stray and could be trusted to eat its way through any and every rope. Alex constructed a strong door of thick bamboo poles to replace the flimsier curtain of grass over the entrance to the Hirren Minar, and they kept the goat in the lower chamber at night.

THE JUNGLE DRIED and shrivelled and turned brown about them, and the river shrank; but still the monsoon delayed. They never spoke of Lottie, as they never spoke of all those whom they had known in Lunjore, or of anything that happened there. Their life went on as before, except that now there was the baby to look after in place of Lottie, and Lou had lost her restlessness. Her maternal instinct had sprung alight. She had taken the child and looked at it—with a sudden awestruck sense of possession. Now she did not mind how long they stayed in the Hirren Minar.

The news from the outside world was not encouraging. Sir Henry Lawrence had fought a disastrous action at Chinut and been heavily defeated, and now he and the British in Lucknow were closely besieged in the Residency. General Wheeler and the Cawnpore garrison were reported to be at their last gasp in the pitifully inadequate entrenchments they had scratched up out of the earth. In Jhansi the Rani had urged her people to revolt, and had offered terms to the Europeans who had taken refuge in the fort. The terms had been accepted, and they had surrendered—only to be seized, bound and slaughtered; men, women and children together, not one had been spared. Mutiny had broken out in Allahabad, where the sepoys had murdered their officers and massacred all Christians, and the only news that seemed to hold out hope was that the British still clung to the Ridge before Delhi, although their force was as yet more besieged than besieging.

"We must wait," said Alex, as he had said so often before. "We are safe in the jungle."

But the jungle would not let them wait.

382

CHAPTER 7

*A*LEX HAD been setting a snare at the entrance to a small clearing near the Hirren Minar when he smelt smoke.

He had not been feeling at all well that day. His head ached and he thought angrily that Lou or Winter had disobeyed orders and lit an early fire. Then he realized that the hot wind that was rustling the dry grass and dead leaves was blowing towards the Hirren Minar, and not away from it. He turned to gaze up at the sky to the southwest. There had been clouds in the sky all day: dirty copper-coloured clouds which he had hoped might mean rain at last. But there was something more than clouds there. Was the jungle on fire? He returned swiftly to the women.

With evening, the wind died and the smell of smoke died with it. But later, as the sky darkened, a pink wavering glow that was not the sunset grew steadily brighter.

Alex watched it from the roof of the Hirren Minar. "It may miss us," he thought. "Or it may burn out before it reaches us." But he had little hope of its doing either. So little hope that he made a bundle of those few things that seemed to him urgently necessary, and carried them down to the riverbank.

Presently the wind rose again, and now it brought with it not only the smell of smoke, but drifting ash. Soon there would be sparks, and the forest was tinder-dry from the scorching June days. He returned to find the two women standing on the open roof watching the night sky. Looking at them, he was conscious of a confused mixture of emotions that included gratitude, relief, tenderness, a passionate admiration, and a disgust of himself because he had once considered them as a tiresome responsibility. He found that his voice was a little difficult to control and said with unnecessary curtness: "Can either of you swim?"

"Yes," said Winter.

"A little," said Lou Cottar. "But—but Amanda —"

Alex said: "We'll have to make some sort of raft for her." He disappeared again down the ladder and they heard him hacking down the heavy bamboo door that he had built to protect the goat.

They worked with feverish haste, tearing down the split-cane *chiks* and using them to face the raft, and carrying down the box that Lou had been using as a cradle. The door made an admirable craft, and Alex found himself feeling grateful to the goat for the first time since they had acquired it. The air was full of smoke now, and they could hear the crackle of the flames, while the world about Hirren Minar was as bright as though it were bathed in a red sunset.

Alex said: "Bring anything that isn't too heavy. I can manage this. We may have half an hour or so yet, but it isn't safe to gamble on it. Be as quick as you can."

He departed with the raft, and they went back up the ladder for one last time to collect all the food they could carry. Then they were out in the jungle and Lou was hurrying towards the river while Winter followed her, dragging the goat.

The fire was no longer a distant crackling chorus now, but a steady roar, and the sky was a brilliant rose-pink pall of smoke shot through with sparks. The undergrowth was alive with movement. Peacocks, jungle-fowl, porcupine, a fox, three jackals and a chital hind ran past them, making for the river.

Alex was waiting for them on a strip of bank. The makeshift raft floated high and light in the water, and he was lashing the tin box to the centre of it. He laid the baby in the box among an assortment of bundles, and stretched a strip of wet cloth above it as an added precaution. It was less easy to get the goat on board and safely tethered, but they managed it.

Crouching in the cool water under the shelter of the high bank the heat was not so intolerable, but the river looked appallingly wide—the far bank as though it were miles away. A herd of nilghai not twenty yards below them were swimming out steadily into the river, where the current took them down in a long, slanting line towards the far shore. A moment later a wild boar slithered down the bank, and then suddenly there were animals all about them, so that the steep banks seemed alive with terrified forest creatures. From somewhere farther up they heard the unmistakable snarling roar of a tiger, and a troop of frantic monkeys leaped and howled in the tree above their heads. One of them, a mother clutching a skinny, big-eyed baby, sprang down upon the raft and huddled against the bleating goat, chattering and grimacing.

"Come on," said Alex. "If we wait any longer we shall have a cargo-load of stowaways." He had rigged up a tow-rope and would go ahead with it. Lou and Winter were to push from behind.

He struck out from the bank and felt the current catch him and draw him and the raft downstream, as a shower of sparks fell hissing into the river. He did not glance back but swam on steadily, the rope biting into his shoulder. The oil-smooth surface of the water was filmed with ash and charred leaves and full of frantic swimming animals. It seemed to Alex as though they would never reach the other side as though the river were endless. And then quite suddenly there were sandbanks ahead of him, the current no longer pulled at him, and he had reached the shallows.

All about him wet furry shapes were dragging themselves onto the warm white sand, licking their fur and shaking themselves before scuttling away towards the distant line of trees. Alex freed himself from the rope harness and dragged the makeshift raft forward until it grounded.

He turned then at last, and saw that they were all there. The shivering goat, the baby lying placidly in its box, the monkey still clutching its round-eyed offspring. Lou Cottar on her knees, gasping, and Winter lying in the shallows with her chin on the edge of the raft. He walked over to her unsteadily and pulled her to her feet, and kissed her, holding her cool wet body close. He released her gently, and bent to untie the goat.

The monkey, taking fright, leaped from the raft and fled across the sand. And suddenly they were all laughing helplessly, because they were still together and still alive. They had left only just in time, for behind them there was nothing but flame now to the turn of the river that hid the broken bridgehead. The Hirren Minar must be somewhere in the centre of that furnace, and tomorrow there would be nothing but miles of smouldering desolation where yesterday there had been dense jungle.

A hot spark fell on Alex's arm, and he winced. Everywhere the jungle was tinder-dry. The air scorched their lungs with each breath that they drew. A tuft of pampas grass twenty yards from them caught alight and flared up. He knew they might have to get back to the water, and go for miles, hemmed in between two walls of fire with only that makeshift bamboo raft to hold to . . . . Then suddenly, unbelievingly, they turned their faces up to the furnace of the sky, the hot drifting ash and the falling sparks, and felt something warm and wet splashing upon their parched skins.

It was the monsoon at last.

"Get in among the trees; under the thickest stuff you can find," Alex said, as the blessed drops continued to fall. They forced their way into the jungle with the raindrops splashing on their shoulders and the glare from the burning trees on the far bank lighting their way.

Using the raft as a roof, they wedged it at an angle to carry off the rain and make a rough shelter among the trees, stowing the bundles and the baby under it as the first slow drops turned to the full drumming downpour of the monsoon, and the glare behind them faded and died.

Winter awoke hearing Alex stir, and opened her eyes to see him walk out into the pouring greyness. Lou was still asleep, with her arm about the box in which the baby slept. Winter rose to her knees and wringing out her wet hair, plaited it and looked ruefully at her damp sari. But there was nowhere in the jungle that was dry, and this morning it would be no easy matter to find a handful of grass and dead leaves with which to make a fire.

When Alex returned, the baby raised a feeble wail and the sound woke Lou who sat up rubbing her eyes. She looked up at the grey, weeping skies and round at the sodden jungle and said briskly: "We must get the goat so that I can feed Amanda."

"The goat has gone," said Alex sourly. "Don't be silly, Lou! Give it some rice, or boil it some flour and water. No one is going to notice smoke today."

"Will you stop calling her 'it'!" snapped Lou in sudden and irrational fury.

Alex grinned. "You're getting damned maternal, Lou. One day you'll persuade yourself that it—sorry, she—is your own child."

"She is," said Lou, and went to join Winter who was searching the jungle nearby for fuel dry enough to burn.

Alex looked after her with a half-smile that turned into a grimace of pain. He went into the shelter and found the small tin of opium pills and swallowed down a few of them with brandy. "I cannot go sick now," thought Alex dizzily. "Not now—"

But no amount of brandy and opium could keep the fever at bay, and half an hour later Winter, bringing him food, found him lying under a tree a few yards from the shelter, his body jack-knifed with pain and his breathing harshly audible above the steady patter of the rain.

He said in a blurred, difficult voice: "Be all right—only—dysentery. Tell Lou—keep that baby away—dangerous . . . ."

THERE FOLLOWED a nightmare interval of days and nights—none of them could ever say how many—in which Alex's body was burned and wasted with dysentery and raging fever, and it seemed to Winter that he could not live. She stayed with him day and night, doing everything possible, endlessly and tirelessly, while Alex held on to life. It was, in the end, Lou who betrayed them.

The pouring rain had not suited the baby: she wailed heart-breakingly, and vomited up the rice-water and the thin gruel that Lou made with flour and coarse country sugar. And the supply of even those commodities were running low.

"She will die without milk!" said Lou, wild-eyed and desperate. "She must have proper food—she must!"

Winter did not hear her. She had been watching Alex's haggard, burned-out face and dry, cracked lips, and her mind and her heart were as desperate as Lou's. It was only when there was no fire lit—for Lou had been dealing with all the cooking—and no food prepared, that she found that Lou and the baby had gone.

The rain had stopped now and the jungle that had been so brown and brittle only a few days ago was a hot, humid greenhouse in which new grass and leaves and creepers sprung up overnight in lush abandon. The damp heat was less bearable than the dry heat had been, and Alex seemed to struggle for every breath he drew.

The sound of his laboured breathing tore at Winter's heart, and for the first time in the long weeks since she had run from the Lunjore Residency she wept. She did not know how long she lay there on the steaming ground, and she did not hear Alex move, but when his hand touched her she lifted her head and saw that his eyes were open and lucid. He spoke in a voice that was barely a whisper: "What's the matter?"

Winter stared at him incredulously, the tears drying on her cheeks. He had not looked like that, or spoken sensibly, since the illness had struck him down. He said: "Why are you crying?"

Winter brushed away the tears with the back of her hand. "I'm not—not now."

She stumbled away to make a brew of flour and rice-water, sugar and brandy, and took it back to him.

He drank the concoction because he was too weak to refuse it. "I shall be all right now," he said, and closed his eyes and went to sleep with his head in her lap.

Winter slept too; and when she heard voices and someone shook her, she thought it was Lou.

But it was not Lou. It was a party of men armed with lathis and in charge of a man who carried an old-fashioned musket.

"These are not sahib-*log!*" said one of the men scornfully. "They are but the *nauker-log* of the mem."

But one of them peered closer and said: "Nay, they have *Angrezi* blood in them at least. We will take them. Up, thou!" The speaker stirred Alex with his foot, and Winter said furiously and in the vernacular: "Let be! Canst thou not see that he is sick?"

The tone and the quality of the Urdu she used gave the men pause, and they looked at her doubtfully. It occurred to them that this might after all be an Indian lady of good family. The man with the musket said uncertainly: "Of what city art thou?"

"Of Lucknow," said Winter without hesitation. "Of the household of Ameera Begum, wife of Walayat Shah, who is my cousin and lives in the Gulab Mahal by the mosque of Sayid Hussain. This man is of Persia, and my—my husband."

The men observed her owl-eyed and consulted in whispers, and
Winter heard the leader say: "What matter? The order is for all to
be sent to Pari. Send these also."

They rifled the contents of the shelter, and ten minutes later
they moved off through the jungle with Winter and Alex. It took
them surprisingly little time to reach the road where a bullock-cart
waited and a curious crowd of villagers—and Lou Cottar.

She stared at Winter and Alex in horror and said hoarsely: "I
didn't mean—I didn't know this would happen. I thought I might
find a village where I could get milk. And—and they did help me.
They were kind to Amanda, too. I didn't realize they would go back
to see if there was anyone else. I—"

Her voice choked and stopped and Winter said: "It's all right,
Lou."

And then they were thrust into the cart and jolted away down
the long, uneven road towards the little walled town of Pari.

Part Five
Homecoming

D. KAYE

CHAPTER 1

*I*T HAD been dark by the time the captives reached the town. The cart that now carried Alex, Winter, Lou and Amanda creaked to a halt, and they were taken out and hustled across a dark courtyard and into a long, low-ceilinged room lit by a single guttering cresset. The two men who had carried Alex laid him on the floor and the door banged behind them. An iron bar clanged into place, and someone at the far end of the room stood up in the shadows beyond the circle of light and said hoarsely and incredulously: *"Winter!"*

Winter was on her knees beside Alex, and she looked up, startled. A face moved into the range of the lamp and stared down at her. It was, incredibly, Mrs. Hossack who stood there. Mrs. Hossack, whom she had last seen on the veranda of her bungalow in Lunjore. Mrs. Hossack, who she had thought to be dead. The two women had hardly known each other well, but now they clutched each other and wept.

There were other voices behind Mrs. Hossack, and other faces: Captain Garrowby—Dr. O'Dwyer—and yet others whom Winter did not know.

There were charpoys in the room, and Captain Garrowby and Dr. O'Dwyer lifted Alex onto one of them, and after the doctor had examined him he lay there and listened to the story of their escape.

The Garrowbys, Dr. and Mrs. O'Dwyer and Mrs. Hossack and her children had not been at the Lunjore Residency, and had miraculously escaped the massacre in the Hossacks' carriage. Later they had been forced to abandon the carriage and had wandered in the jungle, living on roots and berries, and first one and then another of the party had died. Captain Garrowby and the doctor, with Mrs. Hossack and her remaining child—a baby boy of six months—had been forced to ask help at a village on the outskirts of Pari, and the villagers had taken them in and treated them kindly. But three days ago they were brought to this house—they did not know why, nor how long they would remain there. They had been given food, and had not been ill-used, but the attitude of their gaolers was not reassuring. The other captives had arrived on the following day: the Reverend Chester Dobbie, a Mr. Climpson and a Miss Keir—the sole survivors of a party of fifteen Europeans who had hoped to escape from Oudh and had been attacked and massacred at a village five miles away. They, too, had been fugitives for many days before being captured and brought here.

"What do you suppose they mean to do with us?" asked Lou uneasily, rocking the baby.

"Keep us as hostages, I think," said the Reverend Mr. Dobbie, who thought no such thing but trusted that God would pardon him that comforting lie.

"Hostages for what?" inquired Lou.

Mr. Climpson, a middle-aged magistrate who had escaped from his burning bungalow with the assistance of a loyal servant, said: "The local *talukdar* has been wavering for some time. He cannot decide which side is going to win, and he seems to have given orders that any Europeans found in these parts were to be taken prisoner but not harmed. I think he means well enough, but he is getting nervous. The whole of Oudh is now in revolt, and I think that is why he has had us brought here."

Alex, lying on his charpoy, wondered weakly if the man really believed that. It seemed to him far more likely that they were being kept alive in order to provide a Roman holiday for the mob when a suitable occasion should arise. But he kept the thought to himself.

Yet another bedraggled captive came to swell the ranks of the prisoners the following day—an elderly Eurasian clerk who had been found hiding in a village some five miles to the south. His tale differed little from the story of escape and flight, horror and hardship and final capture, that had been the lot of all of them.

"It is not the country people who are cruel," said Mr. Lapeuta in his soft sing-song voice. "They are like us, you know—veree ordinary people. It is the townspeople and the sepoys who are hot against us. I think that the *talukdar* of these parts, he will not kill us, but I think that he wishes to be rid of us, for he is fearful of the sepoys, who preach against us. If there is better news, then doubtless he will keep us here so that he can show how he has sheltered us, and gain much reward later. But if the news is bad, then I think he will send us away. That is what the headman in whose village I hid told me."

The accuracy of this forecast was proved within three days. News from Lucknow trickled into Pari. Sir Henry Lawrence was dead. He had died in the beleaguered Residency at Lucknow, and all over India men heard the news with a catch of the breath. Now that he had gone it would surely be only a matter of days before the Residency was captured, and its defenders massacred.

The *talukdar* wavered no longer, and hastened to rid himself of the haggard band of British before they were murdered by the mob in circumstances that might involve him in trouble in the unlikely event of the hell-born ultimately regaining power.

He sent in more and better food, permitted the services of a barber and allowed the women facilities for the washing and mending of clothes. And having impressed his excellent intentions upon them, he had them hurried by night into covered carts such as purdah women travel in, and sent them off under guard.

They did not know where they were going, and the unexpectedly good treatment they had received after days of surly neglect raised their hopes. But Alex was taken from the cart in which the women travelled at dawn on the first day, and put with the other men. Their cart rumbled away and there was no sign of it again. The four days and nights that followed its departure were a horror that equalled anything that Winter had yet endured. She had tried to force her way out, and had been thrust roughly back, and the cart had jolted forward on that long, nightmare journey. The cart made slow progress, for the heavy rains had turned the roads into quagmires. The torrential downpour soaked through the inadequate covering and drenched the huddled occupants, and when it ceased the sun turned the hooded cart into a steam bath in which it became difficult to breathe.

The days crawled past without their knowing where the men had gone, or whether they were dead or not. Winter nursed Lottie's baby when Lou fell at last into an exhausted sleep, and longed for the Hirren Minar as a lost soul might long for Paradise. But the Hirren Minar was only a blackened pile of stone standing gaunt among a waste of charred stumps and layers of sodden ash, and if this terrible journey lasted much longer Lottie's baby would die too. Perhaps they would all die—perhaps Alex was already dead . . . .

She heard no news in those days, and did not know that on one of them the last survivors of the Cawnpore garrison had died, and with them, Sophie Abuthnot.

Little Sophie Abuthnot, as small and fair and fragile as Lottie, had been with the two hundred exhausted, hopeless, helpless women and children who were herded like animals in one small building there. And when the guns of the British advance could be heard in Cawnpore the order for their murder had been given.

By nightfall the floor of the building was deep in blood and littered with the bodies of the dead and dying. When the new day dawned, the butchers had dragged out the corpses and flung them into a well outside the house. And half India shuddered in horror and drew back, for that massacre caused many men who would otherwise have fought the British to the bitter end to lay down their arms and return to their homes.

"There can be no blessing on such a deed," said Ameera's husband, Walayat Shah, who had hated the British and rejoiced at the news of the risings, and had himself taken part in attack after attack upon Sir Henry Lawrence's beleaguered garrison in the Lucknow Residency. But on the day that he had heard the news of the murder of the women and children in Cawnpore, he broke his sword in two and threw away his musket, and came back to the Gulab Mahal. "We cannot prevail," said Walayat Shah. "The jehad is dead. To slaughter captive women is a deed to blacken the sun. I will fight no more against the feringhis, for God can no longer be upon our side."

HOW MANY DAYS had they been in the cart? How many times had the sun gone down? Winter could not remember. Mrs. Hossack, cradling her small son, moaned with despairing monotony. Poor Miss Keir suffered from bouts of sickness. Lou made pastes of boiled rice and water as best she could, and fed the baby . . . .

Dimly Winter became aware that the cart was passing through a crowded street. Lights and voices and noise pressed about it and somewhere guns were firing; guns and a ceaseless distant crackle of musketry.

The noises faded and at last the cart stopped with a jolt, and there were more voices. And then the stout cloth that was bound over the end of the cart was unfastened, and the dazed women, Lou and Mrs. Hossack clutching the babies, were dragged out to stumble and fall to the ground, their legs giving way under them.

There was a man with a drawn sword in his hand, shouting, and another man with a musket, and Winter thought numbly: "They are going to kill us," but it seemed a matter of supreme indifference to her. Alex had gone—everything had gone. There was nothing to live for any more. Then someone ran to her and lifted her, and the voices and the lights and the shouting men spun together in a circle and turned into darkness.

CHAPTER 2

*W*INTER AWOKE to find herself lying on a low bed, feeling cleaner and cooler than she had felt for a very long time. She opened her eyes.

And saw again the vision that had come to her once before when she had lain in the river by the Hirren Minar and wished for death. The rose-pink sky and the formal patterns of leaves and flowers and birds. The vision that had once before drawn her back from despair, and the dream that had glowed before her mind's eye for so many cold years . . . .

She lay quite still, not stirring, barely breathing. Thinking confusedly that she was asleep—or dead. It could not be true! When at last she moved, it was to stretch out a hand and touch the green parrot moulded in painted plaster on the wall beside her.

And this time it was real. This was the Gulab Mahal! She was safe at last. Incredibly, she had come home.

From somewhere in the distance there came the sound of gunfire, but she did not hear it. She rose and walked slowly about the room in a waking dream, running her hands over the dear familiar flower patterns, caressing the painted birds and beasts. She did not know that this was the room in which she had been born and in which Sabrina had died. She only knew that every foot of it was familiar and beloved. She saw the crescent-shaped shadow of the horned moon steal across the floor, and remembered it too, and did not fear it as Sabrina had done, for it was linked with love.

She did not know how she had come there, or know that it was the *talukdar* of Pari's determination to play safe that had been responsible. In the unlikely event of the British returning to power he did not wish it said that he had sent his captives to certain death. Remembering what his men had told him of the woman who was

396

no *Angrezi* and who claimed kinship with the wife of Walayat Shah of Lucknow, he had decided to send them to his care, and thus his own hands would be clean. Walayat Shah might spare the woman if she were indeed bloodkin to his wife, and the woman at least would be able to testify that he, the *talukdar*, had only acted for the best.

And when the captives from Pari had arrived at the Gulab Mahal all had indeed been given shelter, for Walayat Shah remembered Cawnpore. He knew that if it should become known in the city that he was housing these people, their lives, and probably his own, would not be worth a moment's purchase. But he took them in.

Winter had been given her mother's old room as by right, and later that morning the heavy curtain over the doorway lifted. She turned at the sound and saw that it was Ameera. They clung to each other and wept and did not speak for a long time, and then Ameera held her off at arms' length and looked at her.

"It is true, then!" said Ameera. "I thought it a dream. So thou hast come home . . . ."

There was much to talk about. Winter learned that the other women were safe, lodged in a secluded wing of the Rose Palace adjoining the zenana quarters. She learned also that the men of the party had reached the palace in safety. Alex was alive! Still a sick man, he was housed in a little pavilion on an isolated square of roof above the main quarters.

As soon as she could, she tore herself away from Ameera and went to him. A split-cane *chik* hung over the open side of the small pavilion, and Alex lay within on a narrow charpoy. He seemed to have shrunk to no more than skin stretched over bone, and there were dark patches like bruises under his eyes. Wordlessly she took him in her arms.

Three of the most trusted servants of the household were put in charge of the feringhis, who had been given native dress to wear in place of their own ragged garments, and were not permitted to go even into the secluded garden except between sunset and dawn. They were kept in complete segregation from the other inhabitants of the Gulab Mahal, and they had little fault to find with this, for they knew it was not in Walayat Shah's power to protect them should they be discovered and their lives demanded by the rabble.

The continuous rattle of musketry, punctuated by the boom of

397

guns, came clearly to their ears all day and for a large part of every night, and was both a continual reminder to them of the peril in which they stood, and that they were not the only British in Lucknow. The garrison in the Residency on the outskirts of the city had numbered barely a thousand combatant British and seven hundred loyal Indian troops when the crisis had arisen, and they were hampered by the presence of well over a thousand women, children and non-combatants, as well as by lack of adequate food, by sickness and appalling problems of sanitation and the disposal of the dead. The position they held had never been intended for purposes of defence. The hurriedly constructed fortifications were flimsy, and the forces surrounding them numbered twelve thousand fighting men, many of them British-trained sepoys, backed by the rabble of the city. But the attacks were never delivered in sufficient strength, and the siege dragged on.

Meanwhile, all hopes of relief were receding. Havelock's army, which had crossed the border into Oudh in the last days of July and had subsequently fought and won two major battles, had suffered heavy losses in the fighting and, finding their communications threatened, had fallen back on Mangalwar to wait for reinforcements. Three times in August Havelock advanced again towards Lucknow, only to be checked each time and compelled to retreat.

Slowly Alex recovered. But he did not move from the pavilion on the roof, for the fever had an unpleasant habit of returning at unexpected intervals. So he lay there day after day, listening to the firing round the Residency and longing, as he had done in the first days at the Hirren Minar, for news. The other men would come up to his roof most evenings—Dr. O'Dwyer, Captain Garrowby, and the elderly Eurasian, Mr. Lapeuta—and the women would usually join them there for an hour or so.

There were only three women now—and Lottie's tiny daughter. Miss Keir had never recovered from that nightmare journey in the covered cart. She died one hot night within a week of their arrival at the Gulab Mahal, and Lou Cottar had moved into Mrs. Hossack's room in her place because Mrs. Hossack, a mother herself, was a mine of information on the subject of babies and could be relied upon to give helpful advice should any crisis threaten Amanda.

Alex, anxious and irritable, hardly welcomed these visits, Lou Cottar's in particular. The witty, acid Mrs. Cottar of Lunjore had vanished without trace, and in her place was a worried woman who appeared to think of nothing but the welfare of a tiny, placid infant with a fuzz of red hair and round, solemn blue eyes.

One morning, when he and Winter were alone together, Alex turned on his elbow to look morosely up at her.

"Lou, of all people!" he said. "I should have thought that she was as unmaternally minded as a goldfish. Why, the child isn't even hers!"

"Yes, it is," Winter said. "Lottie gave it to her."

"I wonder," Alex murmured thoughtfully, "what Edward English's parents are going to say to that?"

It was a thought that worried Lou also.

"Has she been christened?" asked Mrs. Hossack one day.

"*Christened?*" Lou looked up from bathing Amanda in a small metal basin. "No, of course not. How could she be?"

"There's Mr. Dobbie," said Mrs. Hossack. "He could do it."

Fired with this idea, Lou approached Mr. Dobbie, who instantly agreed to perform the ceremony. So Lou Cottar, with her own ideas as to names, had Amanda Cottar English christened "in the presence of this congregation" on Alex's rooftop the very next day: Alex, Winter and Mrs. Hossack standing as godparents. Although the surname English was the child's by law, the ceremony brought a considerable portion of relief to Lou. It seemed to make Amanda more her own, and the claims of the misty and faraway grandparents—Lou was not aware that Edward had been orphaned for several years—faded and became less alarming.

But, only two evenings later, the fact that there was a clergyman available who was qualified to perform Holy Offices was to have unexpected repercussions.

IT HAD RAINED heavily that day, but by sundown the skies were clear and the garden smelt fresh and fragrant in the dusk. They had all gone out to walk under the orange trees, because Alex had been feverish all day, and Dr. O'Dwyer had decreed that he must have quiet.

By now the sound of firing from the direction of the Residency had become an integral part of life in the Gulab Mahal; as familiar as the cawing of the grey-headed crows, the liquid cooing of the doves or the creak and squeak of the well-wheel. It was, to the fugitives, a comforting sound, for it told them that the Residency had still not fallen.

That night Alex slept out on the open roof and the first intimation he received of the returning storm was when he was awakened by what appeared to be a tub of cold water emptied over him. This was not the warm rain of the hot weather, but the colder rain of autumn, and a wind was behind the rain. He was drenched almost before he was awake, and the roof appeared to be awash with water.

"This is where I catch pneumonia," thought Alex, exasperated, wrestling in the darkness to release the sodden *chiks* so that he could gain the shelter of the pavilion. He became aware of someone else on the roof, and of Winter's voice calling his name.

"Alex, Alex, where are you?"

"I'm here," he shouted. "What do you think you're doing? Get on back! Where are you?"

He groped for her in the blackness and caught a wet arm, and as he did so the blast of wind that had driven the storm before it died out as quickly as it had arisen, and there was only the rain falling steadily onto the roof with a soft splashing sound.

Alex said furiously, "Winter, are you mad? You'll be drenched! Get back to your room!"

He heard her laugh a little shakily and she said, "I'm drenched already. And I won't go down unless you come with me. You can't stay up here for the rest of the night. You'll only be ill again, and we've had enough trouble with you already."

"You sound," said Alex, "regrettably like a nurse I used to have when I was about six. All right, I'll come."

The room seemed hot after the wet windy roof, and there was an oil-lamp burning. Alex took the cloth that Winter handed him and rubbed himself dry with it.

Winter was wringing the water out of her hair and twisting it up in a heavy shining knot at the back of her head. He gazed up at her. Her arms were lifted, and her thin cotton sari was drenched with rain and clung wetly to her body, outlining every rounded curve of a figure that was no longer the reed-slim one he had known.

And suddenly he remembered. He remembered that, although the garden was now pleasantly cool before the sun rose, Winter was rarely seen there in the early mornings, and for three evenings

400

running she had failed to join the others on Alex's rooftop. Taxed with it on her reappearance, she had said lightly that the heat and an overripe *papiya* that she had eaten had been responsible. And he had accepted the explanation.

But now . . . . Winter finished knotting up her hair and turned to look at him, and saw that he knew. There was a white shade about his mouth and his eyes were wide and very bright, and she stood quite still, looking down at him gravely, her gaze steady and a little apprehensive.

After a long minute Alex spoke. "Is it mine?"

"Yes."

He held out a hand to her and she came to him slowly. Above them the storm had passed. He drew her down into his arms and said in a voice that she had not known he possessed, "Why didn't you tell me? Oh, my love—my little love!" He laughed suddenly: a laugh that broke on a dry sob, and held her away from him so that he could look into her face.

"Go and tell Dobbie I want to see him," he said.

CHAPTER 3

SO WINTER was married at night, and by moonlight, as her mother had been. And, like Sabrina, with no preparation at all, and in a wedding dress that did not even belong to her. She wore the dress of heavy white silk, yellowed by the years and scented with the neem leaves and tobacco in which it had been kept, that had belonged to Ameera's mother, Juanita.

The moon that had looked down on that strange wedding looked down also on the looted, burned-out shell of the Casa de los Pavos Reales and the blackened paving stones of the terrace where Marcos and Sabrina had stood together on that other moonlit night to watch their guests ride away. But the scent of the orange blossom and the lemon trees remained, and was as sweet on the hot air as it had been on that long-ago night.

The scent of orange blossom rose, too, from the walled gardens of the Rose Palace, and reached the flat rooftop where Winter stood in Juanita's white dress and felt Alex push a heavy ring of beaten gold and silver onto the finger that had once worn Kishan Prasad's glowing emerald. The ring, also, had been one of Juanita's.

Alex wore Mussulman dress, borrowed for the occasion, and only managed to keep on his feet with the assistance of one of the pillars that divided his room from the roof. To Winter there was nothing strange about this wedding. It was the fulfilment of the promise that the Gulab Mahal had always stood for—that once she returned to it, all would be well. She was suddenly aware of an uplifting sense of timelessness—as if she would live for ever in the future in Alex's children and her own, just as she lived in the past in Marcos and Sabrina . . . .

They were allowed three days and nights of unclouded happiness.

Sabrina's room was an enchanted garden a thousand miles removed from the harshness of the warring world outside. They had so much to talk of and to tell. Lying in the crook of Alex's arm, Winter no longer heard firing from the Residency, but only Alex's quiet breathing and the steady beat of his heart under her cheek. She was entirely and completely happy. She knew now that whatever the future might hold, she had touched every one of those stars and held the moon in her hand, and that if she died tomorrow she would die content.

But then, on the fourth day, cruel reality returned. The crackle of rifle fire and the boom of guns began again with the dawn.

They could see the smoke from the cannonade hanging like a haze above the roofs and treetops that hid the Residency. Alex listened, and presently said: "How long have we been here? Four weeks? Or is it five? It feels like months. It must feel like years to them. We know Havelock is in Cawnpore, and Cawnpore is less than forty miles away. *Why* aren't they here?"

He turned away with a groan. If the whole of India was in revolt, it was going to take more than a few months of campaigning to reconquer it and restore order. Months, he thought, perhaps a year —perhaps longer. And he thought again of Lottie. He could not forget her. That agonizing day in the Hirren Minar had burned itself into his brain. He could not bear the thought of watching Winter die as Lottie had died . . . .

And so August dragged out its slow length, and it was September. And still the torn rags of the Union Jack fluttered defiantly from the flagstaff on the topmost roof of the shattered Residency. And still the dying, fever-racked garrison held out—and by doing so occupied and held in check an army which, but for their resistance, would have been free to turn and attack the Delhi force and create havoc throughout the northwestern provinces.

IT SEEMED to the fugitives in the Gulab Mahal that they had lived in their hot, cramped quarters in the little pink stucco palace in Lucknow for a lifetime.

Day succeeded day with an appalling, crawling monotony. The lack of news from the outside world was the worst affliction. Not to know what was happening to the garrison in the Residency, to Havelock's forces, to the regiments on the Ridge before Delhi, to the rest of India and the Empire of the Company, made the long days longer and frayed their nerves to breaking point. Until one night three of them, Captain Garrowby, Dr. O'Dwyer and the ex-magistrate, Mr. Climpson, slipped out through a narrow gate in the enclosed garden and vanished into the maw of the city.

They had told their plan to no one, for they realized that a small party stood a better chance of escape than a large one, and they considered that Lapeuta and Dobbie, both elderly and frail, were better off where they were, while Alex naturally could not be asked to abandon his wife.

But they did not go far. They kept together instead of taking the wiser course of separating, and they lost their way in the maze of streets, so that dawn found them still in the city. They were stopped and questioned, and that afternoon they were shot, and their bodies hung up by the heels for an encouragement to the mob.

Alex was brought the news on the following evening. The men had been tortured but they had died without divulging their hiding-place. But Walayat Shah was frightened and angry, and took immediate precautions to see that none of the remaining feringhis jeopardized his safety by escaping. The doors were locked now at night, and the gardens patrolled, and what little liberty the fugitives had previously possessed was drastically curtailed.

Neither Lou nor Mrs. Hossack, made selfish by fear for the safety of their two small children, would have escaped from the Gulab Mahal even if they could. To them, however, the loss of Dr. O'Dwyer meant more than the deaths of the two others, for he had been a tower of strength, and now that he was gone their anxieties for their children doubled. Until finally, as September was drawing to a close, the sound of heavy guns returned. Havelock's guns.

All that day the sound of the guns shivered through the hot sunlight, coming nearer and nearer until it seemed as though they could only be a few miles from the city. And as twilight fell, the British in the Gulab Mahal gathered on the rooftop.

Alex leaned on the parapet, straining to listen; knowing that men he knew would be fighting out there—pressing on to the relief of the battered Residency whose indomitable garrison had held out stubbornly all through that terrible, burning summer.

"We shall soon be safe!" sobbed Mrs. Hossack. "They *must* be here soon—perhaps tomorrow!"

But Winter did not speak, or Lou. Winter only watched Alex, oblivious of the guns. Absorbed in him as if he were the only person present, as if she were trying to imprint his face on her mind, and never forget it. For she knew that when the army relieved Lucknow he would have to go from her.

Lou was silent also, knowing that she did not want to leave the Gulab Mahal, as she had not wanted to leave the Hirren Minar. She was safe here; she and Amanda. She clutched the small, solemn red-headed creature tighter in her arms.

The wind shifted in the night, and in the morning the cannonade came no nearer. But on the following day the guns were firing from within the city limits, as the Highlanders and the Sikhs and the British and Indian cavalry and infantry under Havelock's command fought their way through the streets.

The gates of the Gulab Mahal were barricaded and every shutter closed and bolted, and none stirred outside while the city shook to the savage din of battle. And as the sun sank, the wind brought from the Residency a new sound, faint but unmistakable. A roar of cheering.

"They've got there!" said Alex with a catch in his voice and a lunatic desire to cheer himself hoarse. "Listen to that! They've got there!"

"They're safe," said Lou, and wept.

They had got there at last. But the garrison of the Residency, though sure now of survival, had not been relieved after all. They had only been reinforced. The regiments who had fought their way through the streets had been too badly mauled for them to be able to do more than join the exhausted defenders in the Residency and to stand siege there themselves. Alex waited anxiously for several days. Clearly the situation was developing into another stalemate. The garrison was hampered by an inordinate proportion of women and children. To fight their way out with them would be no easy task and it might be many months before another and stronger force could be marched to attack and take the city.

On the last evening of September he went down to the painted room. The light of the oil-lamp played upon the rose-coloured walls and the painted plaster birds and flowers as it had on the first night that he had seen that room. Winter was combing out her long hair, and he sat on the low bed, and watched her, and did not speak.

After a moment she laid down the comb and looked at him, seeing in his face what it was he had come to say. And she put her arms about him, standing between his knees with his head against her heart, as she had stood in the dusk outside the Hirren Minar on the day that Lottie had died. Now, as then, he held her gently, and presently he said: "There are troops at the Alam Bagh just outside the city. It will not be too dangerous to get you there."

The Alam Bagh—the "Garden of the World"—was a walled and fortified royal garden some two miles outside Lucknow, where Sir Colin Campbell had left a force under General Outram to hold at least one outpost within sight of the city.

"You can pass as an Indian," Alex went on. "And once you were there you would be safe. After that it would only mean reaching Cawnpore, and then by river to Allahabad and Calcutta. If Havelock is here it means the road must be open."

Winter said, knowing the answer: "Would you come with me?"

She felt Alex's arms tighten about her. "To the Alam Bagh, my darling. Perhaps to Cawnpore."

"And after that?"

"I must go back to Lunjore." He moved as though in pain. "I should never have left. There was so much that I could have done there. It—it is my work; my responsibility. It's my *own* district! And I ran away from it because —"

"Because you were saddled with three women," said Winter with a break in her voice. "But you can't go back there now! They would only kill you. You'd be throwing your life away, and it isn't only yours—it's mine too. It's *mine!*"

Alex's arms were hard about her; he said: "I know, my heart. But it wasn't the villages—or even the city—that created the trouble. It was the sepoys, and they will have gone. There's more than an even chance that I shall be safe. There's no one to keep order there now. Once they see someone in authority again it will quiet them. That is what they need: peace and quiet and assurance . . . . Dear heart, I must go back! Give me leave to go—"

Winter said: "And if I will not? Would you still go?"

"I—I must. But I would go happier if I went with your leave."

She said in a whisper, because she could not trust her voice: "Go with it, my love."

She felt him relax. He leaned his weight against her as though he

406

were very tired. After a while she said: "When are you going?"

"Tonight. In an hour. Can you be ready?"

She did not answer him at once, but began to stroke his hair, quite gently, and presently she said: "I am not going."

She smiled down at him. "Dear, I could not go. They would send me away to Calcutta. Here Ameera will take care of me, and I shall be among friends. I was born in this room, and I have loved it all my life. Perhaps your child will be born in it too. I will wait here for you."

Alex said: "You don't understand, dear love. I can't let you stay. One day we shall attack this city, and take it. You don't know what that would mean. I do. I have seen a city sacked, and—"

Winter's hand covered his mouth so that he could not speak, and above it his eyes looked into hers steadily and for a long time. Then he kissed the warm palm, and did not argue with her any more.

He went before midnight, slipping out by the narrow side door, and there was only his wife to see him go. She stood, pressed against the iron-studded door, listening to the sound of his footsteps as they died on the dusty road outside. Then she turned away.

She cried again in the painted room when he was gone, and Ameera comforted her. But in the morning it was the room that comforted her most. She had woken to find it bright with the dawn, and as the sun rose and the familiar shadow crept across the floor and touched the bed on which she lay, peace and reassurance flowed back, filling her heart. Nothing could hurt her while she was here. Alex would come back. She had only to wait.

FIVE OF THEM LEFT. And the two small children: Jimmy Hossack and Lottie's daughter, Amanda.

Two days after Alex had left, news reached the Gulab Mahal that Delhi had been recaptured by the British. But the price had been high. And still the year wore slowly on, and the ceaseless, familiar sound of musketry and gunfire from around the Residency made a background to each day. It was not until mid-November that another British force fought its way towards a second relief of the Lucknow Residency, and once more the ugly tide of war surged through the narrow streets of the city.

Once again the gates of the Gulab Mahal were barricaded, but fortune was with it, for it did not lie in the line of the advance, and the floodtide of street fighting passed it by. Once again the Residency was relieved. But had Lucknow itself been captured by the British? None dared go forth for news, for the streets were not safe. Until one evening word was whispered in the dusk at the barred gate of the Gulab Mahal that Havelock was dead, and Sir Colin Campbell was at last going to retreat from Lucknow and fall back upon Cawnpore, and that the evacuation would take place that very night. The women and children of the Residency were to leave in carts at midnight while the city slept; stealing out in great secrecy and making for the Alam Bagh, which was still strongly held by the British.

Ameera brought the news to Winter. "My husband," said Ameera, "says that if it be thy wish, it can be arranged that thou and the other feringhis go also. There are *dhoolis* here, and men to carry them, and they will join with the others at a place that is known to them, and take thee to safety. But it must be decided swiftly, for already it is dark."

Winter smiled lovingly at her. "I will tell the others. It may be that they will choose to go. But I will stay here—unless thou and thy husband wish me to be gone. And if that be so, then thou wilt have to send me away by force!"

"That we shall never do," said Ameera, embracing her. "Is this not the house in which thou wast born? Go and tell thy friends to make ready if they would go."

They went.

Lou tried to persuade Winter to go with them. "I know you are safe here now," she said. "But it isn't safe to stay. The place may be sacked. You can't risk it, Winter. You have the child to think of."

"It is Alex's child," said Winter. "Alex knew that Lucknow would be taken, but he let me stay. Don't you see that even if I wished to go I could not? Everyone in this house has risked their lives to save ours. We owe them a debt; a very great one. If I am here when the attack comes, the fact that I am in this house may save it. I could not go. Alex knew that."

Lou wasted no more words. Somewhat unexpectedly she kissed Winter's forehead. Even more unexpectedly there were tears in her eyes. And then they were gone.

Sir Colin Campbell's army—Havelock's army—retreated from Lucknow taking with them to the Alam Bagh the women and children and all who remained of the gallant garrison who had held out so stubbornly and for so long, leaving behind them the empty shell of the Residency where a tattered Union Jack still fluttered in the dawn wind above the broken roof. And in the Gulab Mahal, the little pink stucco palace in Lucknow city, only Winter remained of the twelve fugitives who had been taken in and given shelter on a hot night in July.

And so the tide of war drew out of Lucknow, leaving the ruin and the wreckage behind it, and there were no more sounds of the siege. There was firing still, but it was farther away now. All through the succeeding months the Alam Bagh was attacked again and again, but it was a strongpost that defied capture and waited for the day when it would act as the spearhead of the final advance upon Lucknow.

There had been no word of Alex. But the bearers of the *dhoolis* had returned, saying that the others had reached the Alam Bagh in safety, and had been sent forward with all the other mem-*log* to Cawnpore. So Lou and Mrs. Hossack at least were safe, and Winter hoped that Lou would not find that escape had robbed her of Amanda. Lou deserved Amanda.

The year drew to its close, the mutiny still raged, but within the faded pink-washed walls of the Gulab Mahal the days passed peacefully enough, and Winter sank into the life of the Rose Palace and became part of it—as she had been part of it in the long-ago days when Juanita had been alive, and Winter herself had been a small black-haired child playing with the painted plaster birds in the room that had been Sabrina's.

Frequently the inmates of the palace forgot that she was not one of them, for she spoke in the vernacular as she had done when a child, and busied herself with the same household tasks as they: drying fruits and grinding spices, making jasmine oil and preparing *surma*—the black ore of antimony used for beautifying the eyes. And there was always Ameera, and Ameera's small sons to play with, to fly kites with on the roof, and tell stories to.

Twice a day, morning and evening, she would go alone to the rooftop, and look out across the trees and the lovely battered city, towards Lunjore.

"He is not dead," she told Ameera. "If he were I should feel it; here, in my heart."

And then in January she heard news by a roundabout route that there was a sahib in Lunjore who had brought back order to the district. He had been protected by a bodyguard of men provided by a Sirdar who had reason to be grateful to him, and with this backing he had taken control of Lunjore and put down the malcontents and set up courts again with native magistrates and judges and native police, and life was gradually returning to normal. The rumour gave no name, but Winter did not need one. She knew that it must be Alex, and that he had been right to go.

Towards the end of February a last and desperate assault was launched against the Alam Bagh. Winter heard the opening of the cannonade in the early morning, but the roar meant no more to her than the cawing of crows, for her pains had started before dawn and the guns were only a dim background to the ordeal of birth.

It was not an easy birth but Winter remembered a long, hot, agonizing day in the Hirren Minar, and Alex's voice talking to Lottie—explaining, encouraging, soothing; and it was as if he spoke to her now as he had spoken then to Lottie; telling her not to be afraid. And she had not been afraid.

Through the waves of pain she could see the pink sunset sky that was the walls of her room, and the dear enchanted flowers, and the birds and beasts that had watched her own birth and had been her own first playthings.

The moon had risen and Ameera had lit the oil-lamp when Winter suddenly thought that Alex was in the room. She screamed to him by name—a scream that rang out through the open windows and across the silent garden and awoke the echo that lived within the high, encircling walls—Alex! . . . *Alex!* . . . *Alex!* . . . And to the sound of that echo Alex's son was born.

IT WAS MARCH when the long-expected attack upon Lucknow began. Colin Campbell's army—Highlanders, Sikhs, Punjabis, British and Indian regiments of cavalry and infantry, Peel's Naval Brigade and Jung Bahadur's Gurkhas from Nepal—had stormed the defences and driven the mutineers back from street to street, from building to building . . . .

It was the group of fugitives last to leave the Gulab Mahal that was largely responsible for saving it from the sack and slaughter and destruction that overtook almost every house in that shattered city. Mr. Lapeuta, Mr. Dobbie, Lou Cottar, Mrs. Hossack and the children, had all reached safety. And they had told their stories, and told, too, of Captain Randall's wife who had remained behind in the house with the people who had sheltered them. And later, when the Delhi Column had joined Sir Colin Campbell's force and the army moved to the final attack upon Lucknow, the Gulab Mahal had been granted protection. It had been promised them, and even in the frenzy of the fighting the promise was not forgotten. With the terrible tumult of battle ebbing and surging like a furious sea through the city, riflebutts knocked on the barred door of the Gulab Mahal and men's voices had shouted above the clamour, demanding entrance.

Winter went down to them alone, wearing Juanita's white dress; not knowing who it might be. Then she heard the English voices above the din and opened the gate, tugging at the heavy bars and locks with her small hands, for the gatemen had run away in terror, and opened it at last to see the smoke-blackened, blood-streaked faces of officers and men of the Highland Brigade.

They stared at Winter open-mouthed, and then grinned, transformed in an instant from furious, fighting animals to kindly, ordinary men with wives and children and sweethearts of their own. The door was barred again and an order signed by Sir Colin Campbell himself nailed to it; and while the fighting lasted a guard stood at that gate and protected the Gulab Mahal from the looting and the frenzy of battle-crazed, blood-drunk troops until the last resistance had been crushed and the terrible guns were silent.

But the fall of Lucknow did not bring peace to Oudh. The mutiny was being stamped out, but it would be many months yet before peace was fully restored. Soon it would be May again, and the breathless burning days that a year ago had seen the fuel catch fire would see it still burning, though with a dying flame, in Jhansi and Rohilkhand and Gwalior and Oudh. And there was still no news from Lunjore.

"Surely if her husband were alive he would send word," the women of the Gulab Mahal said among themselves. "It must be that he is dead."

The thought was often clear on their faces and in their kind, troubled eyes, and one day it had been too clear to be borne, and Winter had answered it as though it had been spoken aloud: "No!

It is not true—he is not dead. He will come for me. I have only to wait . . . ."

Snatching up her son, she had carried him up to Alex's rooftop where the heat shimmered on the smooth stonework, and had strained her gaze in the direction of Lunjore as though her love could reach beyond the horizon and pierce the distance that hid him from her.

The withered leaves of the tree below her rattled dryly in a little wind that blew through the garden. A wind that must have blown over Lunjore. Some day, thought Winter. Some day . . . .

They were words she had been saying all her life. She had said them as a child at Ware. "Some day I shall go back to the Gulab Mahal . . . ." And she had come back. Surely some day Alex would come back too.

Quite suddenly she could bear it no longer, and she turned and ran desperately, as she had run before, to the refuge of the painted room. The sunlight filled it with a warm rosy glow, and the birds and the flowers welcomed her.

She sank down on the matting with the child in her arms, and gradually the trembling of her body lessened. Outside the windows the daylight faded. The hum of the city rose up about the palace, and through it Winter could hear all the familiar, friendly sounds of the household. The distant chatter of voices, children laughing, a clatter of cooking-pots and the creak of the well-wheel. The sounds mingled with the no less dear and familiar scent of orange-blossom and jasmine and marigolds, and the smell of warm dust and sun-soaked stone.

The sounds and the scents seemed to weave a web of safety about the painted room, and Winter drew a long, slow sigh and felt the last of the shuddering fear leave her. "Some day," she whispered. "Some day . . . ."

There were footsteps and a murmur of voices in the passage beyond the doorway, and then someone lifted the heavy curtain that hung before it and she looked up.

And it was Alex.

M. M. Kaye

Born in India, M. M. Kaye is the daughter of an Indian Army officer. Her grandfather had been a prominent member of the Bengal Civil Service. She spent the first ten years of her life in Delhi, retiring to the cool of the hills every summer. After her education back in England, which was "an eternity of boarding schools", she returned to India.

There she married Goff Hamilton, an officer in Queen Victoria's Own Corps of Guides. Up to his retirement a few years ago her husband's military assignments had taken them to all parts of India, as well as to Egypt and Kenya. Settled in England now, they have two daughters, and two small grandchildren.

"The Mutiny was part of my childhood," she says. "Stories of the terrible events were told to me by people who could actually remember them, and in our Delhi garden stood one of the plinths erected to mark the sites of siege batteries used in the final British assault. This particular battery had been commanded by a cousin of my grandfather's, and his name, Kaye, was cut into the stone.

"Then, many years later, returning to India, I was shown an unpublished letter from the Government House archives in Lucknow. A girl who had been caught up in the Mutiny had survived to write this letter home to her parents. At once it suggested the basis of a plot to me, and I thought, gosh, what a story that would make!

"*Shadow of the Moon* contains far more truth than fiction. I hardly needed to invent, it was all handed to me on a plate. All that was needed was a hero and a heroine, and a handful of other characters to do the things the real people had done. And to stretch India a bit in order to fit in Lunjore, an imaginary state on the border of Oudh.

"My book has been called a 'Mutiny' novel—and of course it is. But the actual outbreak comes very late in the story, because it always seemed to me that it was something that crept forward very slowly, getting closer and closer until it suddenly exploded. And the prophecy of the Hundred Years—that the rule of the Company would end 100 years after the battle of Plessey—did come true. The Crown took over from the East India Company, and less than eighty years later India gained her independence. The Mutiny had marked the beginning of the end of the Raj."

The TIGHTROPE WALKER

A CONDENSATION OF THE BOOK BY

Dorothy Gilman

ILLUSTRATED BY DAVID BLOSSOM

PUBLISHED BY ROBERT HALE

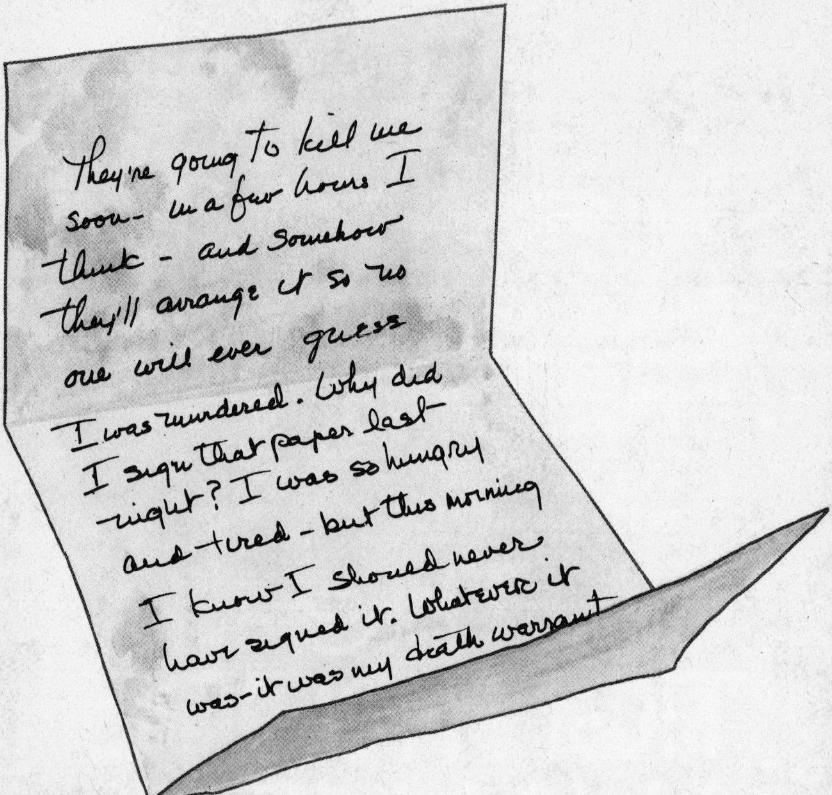

Chapter One

Maybe everyone lives with terror every minute of every
day and buries it, never stopping long enough to look. Or
maybe it's just me. I'm speaking here of your ordinary basic
terrors, like the meaning of life, or what if there's no meaning
at all, or what if somebody pushes the red-alert button, or the
noises in an old house when boards creak and things go bump in the
night. Sometimes I think we're all tightrope walkers suspended
on a wire two thousand feet in the air, and so long as we never
look down we're okay, but some of us lose momentum and look
down for a second and are never quite the same again: we *know*.

That's why, when I found the note hidden in the old hurdy-
gurdy, I didn't take it as a joke. I could smell the terror in the
words even before I'd finished reading the first sentence: "They're
going to kill me soon—in a few hours I think—and somehow they'll
arrange it so no one will ever guess I was murdered."

But perhaps I'd better explain about the hurdy-gurdy and why
at my age, which is twenty-two, I am not out setting the world
on fire, but instead own and tend the Ebbtide Shop, Treasures &
Junk, Amelia Jones, Prop., 688 Fleet Street (not your best section
of town), in Trafton, Pennsylvania.

Actually it's because I'm so free, a word I use not without irony.
I have been quite alone in the world since I was eighteen, and
with a rather strange childhood under my belt as well. When I
was seventeen my father sent me to a psychiatrist named Dr.

Merivale. I think my father knew he was going to die soon, and one day he looked at me—perhaps really saw me for the first time—and packed me off to Dr. Merivale to have confidence and character injected into me in prescribed doses. A few months later my father went to the hospital with his last heart attack and died. He left a rather surprising amount of money, which a bank downtown was to dole out to me month by month until I was twenty-one.

I continued visiting Dr. Merivale for two years, and discovered that I came from a trauma-ridden family and that I was terrified of life. I grew interested in psychology and began reading books on the subject all day and half the night.

It had an effect. One day I looked in a full-length mirror and realized why nobody had ever noticed me—I wouldn't have noticed me, either, in an oversize gray sweater and a gray skirt with a crooked hem. I went out and bought a pair of bell-bottom slacks which swished when I walked, and I liked that; the next week I bought a white sweater and then a blue one. One day I accused Dr. Merivale of being a stuffed shirt! After he recovered from the initial shock he was very pleased with me. I can't say I blossomed physically: I was still thin and freckle-faced, with straight brown hair, but inside I was coming to life. I could almost forgive my mother for committing suicide when I was eleven.

After our big house on Walnut Street was sold, I moved into a boardinghouse—Dr. Merivale insisted I be among people—and fell into a very growth-oriented regime, because I wanted to change as fast as possible. I rose at eight and did deep breathing exercises, then transcendental meditation, and after that yoga, followed by Canadian Air Force calisthenics (aimed mostly, I have to confess, at increasing my bust measurement). And three times a week I went to Dr. Merivale.

But I still had nightmares every night.

It was at the boardinghouse that I met Calley Monahan, who had freckles, too. What struck me first about him was his great calmness. He couldn't have been older than thirty, he had a red beard and red hair, and I knew nothing about him except his name and that he played the guitar. After about three weeks I stopped going into a panic when he said "How are you?" and one evening after dinner we actually had a conversation. He wanted to know what I did all day.

I rather incoherently explained about Dr. Merivale, and Calley

418

looked at me for a long time, gravely. He said at last, "You'd better come and meet Amman Singh."

What's strange about this is that after he took me to meet Amman Singh that evening I never saw Calley Monahan again. Yet if it weren't for him. I would never have met Amman Singh, I would probably have joined the typing class that Dr. Merivale kept urging on me, and I would certainly never have found the note in the hurdy-gurdy.

I was very nervous about going out with Calley. Spending an evening with a young man was a rarity for me, and I was quite unable to decide whether it was a date or not, so I compromised and wore the old gray sweater with the bell-bottoms—half old life, half new. From somewhere Calley produced a motorcycle, and off we roared with me hanging on for dear life. In spite of having lived all my life in Trafton, I'd never seen Clancy Street before. It was a narrow street, lined with decaying old houses and funny little shops. We parked in front of a grimy wooden house with a lopsided front porch, climbed five grimy flights of stairs, and walked into Amman Singh's room.

He was the oldest man I think I've ever seen; a network of fine lines crisscrossed his face. He glanced at me as we came in, and I saw that his eyes were black, really black, like ink, and so soft, so luminous, I felt something inside of me melt. He sat cross-legged on the floor like a Buddha in pajamas; several people were crouched around him talking a language I couldn't understand.

We sat down and waited. Being here struck me as weird and a little scary, and yet I felt a sense of peacefulness flowing over me. It was about ten minutes before Amman Singh turned to me and said, "We have been speaking of violence, the violence inside us all, the angers, the negative thoughts, the resentments, and greeds."

I nodded politely.

He said in his soft, whispery voice, his eyes kind, "When you entered this room I felt your violence."

Now if there is one thing I thought I was *not* at that time it was violent. I was soft, malleable, shy, and timid. I said indignantly, "But I *don't* have violence in me. My psychiatrist is trying to *teach* anger to me. He says I don't want *enough* for myself."

Amman Singh listened with his head cocked like a bird and then he said in his soft, singsong voice, "How blind we are to ourselves. . . ." His eyes met mine and held them. "A tree may be bent by harsh winds," he said, "but it is no less beautiful than the tree that grows in a sheltered nook, and often it bears the richer fruit. In your desperate longing to be like everyone else, you seek to destroy what may be a song one day."

I sat, astonished. Of course what he said was true: I wanted above all else to be—well, normal, homogenized, pretty, popular, not lonely. I had accepted my longing as logical and sane; it was what Dr. Merivale wanted for me and it was what I wanted for myself. Now, suddenly, all my exercises and calisthenics looked like little straitjackets. I couldn't decide whether this funny little man was hypnotizing me or waking me up from a long sleep. I sat staring at him, and then I stood up and walked out, without a word to either Calley or to Amman Singh.

The next morning I telephoned Dr. Merivale and told him that I wouldn't be coming in to see him for a while. I began to walk around town just looking at people and flowers and things. On some days I would stop in to see Amman Singh and he would make herb tea and we would sit very quietly and drink it. When he asked me what I was doing, I said I was waiting, and he nodded.

And then one day, two blocks from Amman Singh's room, I saw this merry-go-round horse in the window of a shop and I stopped, transfixed. I stared at its lines, at the rakish tilt of its bridled head, and a deep sense of pleasure lifted my heart. It was the first time in my life that I admired something not influenced by someone else's tastes.

I went into the shop, which was called the Ebbtide Shop, and I bought the merry-go-round horse from the gnarled little man inside. It was delivered to my room and I spent the loveliest week of my life regilding and painting the horse, which I named—of course—Pegasus. For that entire week I slept without a nightmare.

Unfortunately, the next week there was a second merry-go-round horse in the window of the Ebbtide Shop, and since my room measured only fifteen by fifteen, it was obvious that I couldn't buy this one, too. I went inside to admire it, though, and to explain to the owner, Mr. Georgerakis, why I'd have to pass this one up. He said it didn't matter to him, because his business was for sale, and a merry-go-round horse in the window was a good advertisement.

For the first time I became aware that I had turned twenty-one and had money. I asked him how much he was asking for his shop. He said he had a long-term lease on the building, which was high and narrow, with a two-room apartment upstairs, and in the basement a storeroom and delivery platform. For the business itself he was asking twelve thousand dollars.

I bought the shop that same day. Its more valuable stock consisted of five merry-go-round horses, two player pianos, three antique dolls, a jukebox, piles of old clothes, and a hurdy-gurdy. I scrubbed and swept and painted, had a new sign made for outside, and hung blue-and-white-striped curtains on gold rings at the back of the window. What I could not do was discipline the overwhelming amount of junk that Mr. Georgerakis had bought, so I cut prices and hoped the things would move steadily out the door in the hands of customers.

The hurdy-gurdy I didn't find until later, because it was hidden in a dark corner of the shop. It was in mint condition. It stood on a sturdy maple stick, and the strap for carrying it was only a little frayed. The box itself was glorious: a faded Chinese red with gold edging, and in the center was this bright, rather corny painting of towering blue alps, a river gorge, and a cream-colored sky. When I turned the crank there was a creak, then a twang, and the instrument actually began to play "Tales from the Vienna Woods." After that came a second tune, followed by "The Blue Danube" waltz. I knew I couldn't part with this; I carried it upstairs to the apartment and began playing it in the evenings when I wasn't teaching myself to play the banjo, or doing accounts.

One evening about three weeks later the hurdy-gurdy crank got stuck, silencing "The Blue Danube" on its second note. I found a screwdriver, pried open the back panel, and discovered that a folded slip of paper had worked its way down into the mechanism. I carefully lifted out the wad of paper with a pair of eyebrow tweezers and tried the crank again. "The Blue Danube" resumed playing at once. I screwed the panel back into place and then picked up the slip of paper I'd tossed on the floor. I smoothed it out and met with a terror far worse than my own. I read:

They're going to kill me soon—in a few hours I think—and somehow they'll arrange it so no one will ever guess I was murdered. Why did I sign that paper last night? I was so hungry and tired—

but this morning I know I should never have signed it. Whatever it was, it was my death warrant.

But to die so strangely, a prisoner in my own house? *Why hasn't someone come?* What have these two clever faceless ones told Nora, or even Robin, to explain my silence? Never mind. What has to be faced now is Death. Perhaps I could hide these words somewhere in a different place in the hope that one day someone will find them—that would make Death less lonely. And so—should anyone ever find this—my name is Hannah. . . .

The last *h* ended in a long shaken stroke, as if a voice had been heard, or a step approaching. . . . I pictured this unknown Hannah trembling—as I was trembling now—folding up this paper, wide-eyed as she looked around a room for a hiding place, and then quickly moving to the hurdy-gurdy with its loose back panel.

What kind of person would own a hurdy-gurdy? The paper on which the words were written was the kind of cheap yellow paper that fades fast. The handwriting looked sensible, even if the words ran together a little toward the end. There was that paragraph, too; I didn't think I would have bothered with a paragraph if I knew I was going to be murdered any minute. What kind of person was this? My wanting to know was so strong it astonished me.

She couldn't still be alive. The hurdy-gurdy had been mine for several weeks and before that it had belonged to Mr. Georgerakis. This woman must have gone to her death taking comfort from the thought that she had left these words behind her and that someone would find them. It said so right here—"that would make Death less lonely."

How had they killed her, these people she called the clever faceless ones? Had they really managed her death so that no one knew she'd been murdered?

I felt shaken. I placed the piece of yellow paper on the table and walked into the kitchen and made some instant coffee in a mug. Coffee in hand I returned to the living room, carefully avoiding the slip of yellow paper that I could see waiting for me out of the corner of my eye. I went to one of the two windows and opened it and looked out. The street was silent and empty; this was a street where other people lived over shops, too—the family across the street who ran the secondhand bookstore, the dressmaker next to them. The lights were bright squares; one by one

I watched them extinguished. I thought, "There must be some way to find out who wrote that note."

"Don't be ridiculous," scoffed the contrary half of me. "It could have been written years ago. And the person who wrote it didn't even give her name."

"She gave half of it."

"You *think* she gave half of it. It could just as easily have been written by a man named Hannahsburg or some such. Anyway, she's probably walking around alive and sound at this very minute. Don't be a fool."

"If she's alive, then why didn't she recover the note?"

"Too much trouble. The nightmare was over."

"I'm familiar with nightmares," I pointed out dryly, "and they are not ended so easily. She addressed the note to me. She wrote it to whoever found it and I found it. And there's *no one else to care.*"

I turned from the window and looked at the room before me. In this room I'd affected my environment, as Dr. Merivale would phrase it; he was always urging me to affect my environment. I'd sanded the bumpy old plaster walls and painted them off-white, and a man had come in with a machine to refinish the hardwood floor. This room was my cocoon now; its shining white walls and bright colors gave my life a lovely dimension. I didn't want to lose the sensuous delight of creating more of this—I hadn't even begun on the kitchen. I didn't want to turn my attention elsewhere, which I would have to do if I went plunging out into the world to look for a woman who had written that she was going to be murdered, and who was probably dead now, anyway. But already I knew that I was going to do *something*.

At two o'clock I turned off the light and climbed into bed, and then I got up and turned on the light again and looked up two addresses in the phone book. Feeling better, I returned to bed. I had expected to toss and turn, but I slept serenely until the alarm woke me at seven.

Chapter Two

Mr. Georgerakis met me with a scowl at the door of his apartment. He was wearing one of the Indian blanket bathrobes from the shop, which he must have bought in volume years ago, because there were still a dozen left. I can't say that the garish colors did much for his figure, which was shaped like a Chianti bottle—thin at the top and plump at the bottom.

He gave me a baleful stare. "I warned you business was slow. You can't tell me I deceived you."

I hurried to explain that I had come to ask about the hurdy-gurdy. "Come in and sit," he said, a twinkle in his eyes, as if he found me very funny. "You took the stairs too fast. Sit and have a cup of coffee. Cream?"

"Black," I told him, "and thank you very much."

He peered at me from under his heavy gray brows. "Now what's this about the hurdy-gurdy?"

I told him that a customer was very interested in buying the hurdy-gurdy but first wanted to learn its history from the original owner. I said, "I'm hoping you can remember who you bought it from so I can trace it."

"Remember, no," he said. "But look it up I can."

"You mean you keep *records?*"

He gave me a reproachful glance. "These I offered to you at the lawyer's office. You should yourself keep records, because of the police. Sometimes things that people sell are hot, stolen."

I vaguely remembered his saying something about this. At the time it had seemed unlikely that anything in the shop was worth the fuss, so I had taken only the names of the auction houses at which he'd found the merry-go-round horses, and had let it go at that. I said, "Then . . . you mean there really is a possibility?"

He shrugged his shoulders. "Maybe yes, maybe no." Getting to his feet, he went into another room. I heard the murmur of a woman's voice, which surprised me, because at the time I bought the shop from him he was definitely not married. Maybe he still wasn't; it gave Mr. Georgerakis a new and interesting facet.

A minute later he padded back, carrying a black notebook. "It was six, maybe eight months ago," he said, thumbing through the pages. He nodded. "One hurdy-gurdy, a hundred dollars, November nine . . . Oliver Keene—he's been in before, usually to sell me paintings when he's broke. He's a painter. I don't know where he lives."

"Oliver Keene," I repeated. I took out the small spiral notebook I'd bought on the way and copied down the name, my heart beating faster at this triumph. "This is wonderful—I really appreciate it." Putting away my notebook, I asked innocently, "You live alone here, Mr. Georgerakis?"

He rolled his eyes heavenward. "If I lived alone, would I sell you my business? Of course not. For ten years I climb these five flights courting Katina. With twelve thousand dollars she marries me." He was really a funny man now that I understood his deadpan humor.

"That's very nice," I said, walking to the door with him. "I hope you and Mrs. Georgerakis will be very happy."

I headed at once for the telephone booth at the corner, where I looked through the K's. There was an Oliver Keene living on Danson Street, and I copied down the address. After that I went to the post office and xeroxed two copies of Hannah's note. I'd brought scissors with me, and I took one of the xerox copies and cut out parts of two sentences: "I was so hungry and tired—but this morning I know" . . . and then, "should anyone ever find this—my name is Hannah." After doing this, I walked back to Fleet Street. It was just nine thirty, and there were no customers waiting for the shop to open. I hung a BACK AT NOON sign on the door and walked south to find 901 Fleet Street, the address of a graphologist I'd looked up in the Yellow Pages the night before. I had passed his sign innumerable times and once, out of curiosity, I'd checked the word in the dictionary: the study of handwriting for the purpose of character analysis. In the Yellow Pages the man sounded professional: Joseph P. Osbourne, Accredited Consultant. I was hoping he could tell me something about the person who'd written the note.

The 900 block of Fleet Street had an uncanny resemblance to the 600 block except that it had been shored up, laundered, dipped in paint until it sparkled, and I could guess that its rents were triple that of mine. Joseph P. Osbourne, Graphologist, was on the second floor of 901, over a doctor's office that occupied the first floor. I walked up steps that grew progressively shabbier and dustier until by the time I reached the second floor I felt quite at home. On the landing I was met by three doors, all wide open: one to a lavatory, another to an office with desk and chairs, the third to a sunny back room that to my practiced eye was obviously J. Osbourne's living quarters. Since the office was empty, I knocked on the door to the living quarters. It was at this moment that I felt a prescient stab of terror at what I was getting into. It simply hadn't occurred to me that this quixotic search was going to mean knocking on strange doors and meeting people.

The man who came to the door wasn't much older than I was, and I wasn't sure he was J. Osbourne. He was wearing blue jeans and no shoes and a wrinkled denim shirt. He had a nice open boyish face, with dark hair and blue eyes and a thin, intense look. He stood there running one hand through his hair and frowning at me. "I work by appointment," he said.

"You're Mr. Osbourne then? I thought you'd be older."

"I *am* older sometimes," he said.

I didn't find that surprising; it seemed a very sensible remark to make.

"You might as well come in," he said grudgingly, "and explain your popping in like this. I hope you don't mind if I scramble an egg. I haven't had breakfast yet."

"Of course not," I said. "I've come because it's an emergency."

He moved to the stove and cracked an egg into a frying pan. I looked around me. It was a bright, cheerful room, just disorderly enough to keep me from feeling pangs of inadequacy.

"Okay, show me what you've got," he said, carrying his plate of scrambled egg to a desk and sitting down.

I brought out my envelope and arranged the pieces of cut paper in front of him. "Copies!" he said scornfully. "Bits and pieces. If you want your money's worth—I charge fifteen dollars—I'll need the original."

I said coldly, "I'd rather not show the original."

The telephone on the desk rang. He gave me a curious look as he answered it. He listened a minute, his face thoughtful. "No, I'd disagree with that. I think the child needs professional help. Right. Juvenile court at two p.m. I'll be there."

He hung up, and seeing the look on my face, he smiled. "I hope you don't assume handwriting analysis is fortune-telling," he said. "I have a degree in psychology and I work with the courts and with the schools, Miss . . . Miss . . ."

"Jones. Amelia Jones. If I thought it was fortune-telling, I wouldn't be here."

"Good." He turned in his chair and gave me his full attention, his egg only half eaten. "I don't know why you don't want me to see the original, Amelia, but I have to have more lines for evaluating." He must have seen the stubbornness in my face, because he added patiently, "I need a look at connective forms. I have to look for the clusters of traits, and laterals. The dotting of i's and crossing of t's is terribly important, and so are the marginal patterns, and fluctuations that might suggest ambivalence, the pressure of the pen on paper, the strokes, and interspaces. . . ."

"Oh," I said, blinking.

"With what you've given me, I can't do a decent job."

I sighed and reluctantly brought out the original letter.

"Thanks." He bent over it. "Interesting handwriting," he murmured. "Written under some pressure."

"Man or woman?" I asked.

But he had begun to read the letter now, I could see that. I dropped my eyes and stared intensely at the egg which lay on his plate, cooling and congealing. After a moment he said in an astonished voice, "Where on earth did you get this? Who wrote it?"

"I found it," I said, my eyes remaining fixed on his egg. "I don't know who wrote it."

"But shouldn't you take this to the police?"

I hate explaining. When you're not a strong person, people can take things away from you so easily. I said, "When I bought the Ebbtide Shop at 688 Fleet Street, there was an old hurdy-gurdy included. Last night I was playing the hurdy-gurdy and it got stuck, and I found the note inside. The former owner looked it up and found that he'd bought the hurdy-gurdy six months ago. That's a long time. I don't see what the police could do, do you?"

"No," he said. "But then, what do you have in mind?"

I wrested my gaze from his egg and found him looking baffled but kind. I said, "If I go and see the man who sold it to Mr. Georgerakis, he may know who Hannah is. Or was. I'm hoping you'll tell me more about the person who wrote the note."

He looked at me for a long time. "Right. None of my business, either, is it? Except—" He turned on me angrily. "But if the note should be real, the operative word here is murder, have you thought about that?"

I flushed. "I can't really explain. It's just something I feel I have to look into. Wouldn't you?"

"I don't know," he said, looking young and unprofessional. "Amelia—" He stopped. "Damn it, my egg's cold."

I giggled. "I know."

"Coffee?"

"All right."

I sat and drank coffee while he studied the letter and made a great many notes on a sheet of paper next to it. I learned that graphology couldn't determine the sex of a person but only their masculine and feminine qualities. Hannah appeared to have a fairly equal proportion of each, with perhaps the feminine a shade more persistent. She was somewhat introverted, and definitely a reclusive type. Her writing was sensitive and artistic. She was basically a generous person. She was healthy and educated, had a strong vein of common sense, and along with her flair for the artistic she had considerable executive capabilities.

"No fool, your Hannah," said J. Osbourne, putting down his pen. "I can type up a detailed analysis for you tonight, but I'd say she's a perfectly sane person—I'm assuming she's female. I wish I could tell you she was unbalanced, sick, or mad, the sort who writes notes and hides them in hurdy-gurdies every day. Then you'd go home and forget about her. If you don't . . . well, you've placed me in a lousy position, you know. I'll have to worry about you."

"Oh, you mustn't," I said earnestly. "It's very nice of you, but you mustn't feel that way. An hour ago you didn't even know that I existed. It wasn't your fault that I brought you a letter like this, although I did try to keep you from seeing it," I pointed out.

"Yes, you did," he agreed dryly. "Where are you going to go now?"

"To see Oliver Keene, the man who used to own the hurdy-gurdy."

"Look, Amelia . . . uh, you live with your parents?"

I shook my head.

"Close friends?"

I shook my head.

"Hell," he said, running a hand through his hair again, "then do me one favor, will you? Call me tonight and tell me you're all right." He rummaged in his desk and produced a card. "This is my number, I'll be here." When I looked surprised he smiled faintly. "Look, it isn't only that. I'm curious. I want to know what you find out, okay?"

"All right," I said. "I will." But of course I wouldn't. I counted out fifteen dollars, placed them on his desk, and fled.

Chapter Three

Danson Street was in the warehouse district over by the river. I caught a bus across town and found number 306, where there was a new window set into a dingy wooden front. A really good painting hung there: palette-knife work, the paint thick and juicy and clotted with dizzying whorls of blue. The hand-painted card at its base read: COMPULSION BY OLIVER KEENE.

I rather liked that. I have my compulsive moments, too. It was possible, although I didn't care to admit it, that I would presently find myself growing compulsive about this unknown and mysterious Hannah. I pushed the buzzer. The woman who opened the door was easily six feet tall, an Amazon with a face like a Barbie doll. She wore jodhpurs and a white shirt open almost to her navel, and her curves were breakneck. My eyes must have said "wow," because she grinned.

"Honey," she said, "it's God-given and there's nothing I can do about it except hold out for a man with a million bucks. What do you want?"

"I'm looking for Oliver Keene."

Her grin was as wholesome as cornflakes, but it still left me feeling I'd been a fool to stop my chest exercises.

"Ollie? You'd better come in and wait. He's dashed out for some burnt sienna." She pushed the door wider and I followed her inside. "I'm Daisy," she called over her shoulder.

"I'm Amelia Jones," I answered, feeling about ten years old.

It was a nice studio. There was a huge wooden easel under a skylight, a circular model stand, and paintings stashed in cubbyholes and leaning against walls. The room held a pungent odor of turps and paint. The easel was empty, but there were drawings on the drafting table in the corner, all of them lascivious nudes, and all of them Daisy. They probably paid well.

Daisy looked me over. "If you came to ask about modeling, honey, your bones are great, but this week he's doing sexy calendars, and I don't think—"

"I appreciate your tact," I told her, smiling—it was impossible not to like her—"but I came to ask about a hurdy-gurdy he sold to the Ebbtide Shop. I'm tracing it for a customer."

"Oh," she said. "Yeah, he sold it, and it was mine, not his. We had a fight, and he sold it."

I brightened. "But that's great, I don't have to see him at all, then. Could you tell me where you bought it?"

"I didn't buy it. It was a gift."

"Then who—"

But Daisy was regarding me now with caution. "So if I told you the guy's name, what would you do?"

"Pay a call and ask him where *he* bought it."

She shook her head. "No way, kid. Like I told you, the hurdy-gurdy was a present. Along with a diamond clip and earrings, and a cash award for services rendered."

"Oh." I blinked. "I don't have to know that, do I?"

"Don't be dumb," she said. "If I told you the guy's name, he'd assume I'd just as easily tell his wife or anybody else who came asking. A girl's got to think about these things. I'm really fond of Ollie, but Ollie's going to be doing porno calendars twenty years from now. Sorry, honey. I've got to protect my future. You think this is going to last?" She glanced down at her voluptuous body.

"You'll still be six feet tall," I pointed out dryly. I drew the letter out of my shoulder bag and handed it to her. "I'll tell you the real story. I'm not tracing the hurdy-gurdy for a customer. It belongs to me and I found this inside it last night."

"Holding out on me, kid?" she said good-naturedly, but she moved closer to the light and read the note. "What is this, anyway? Who's this Hannah?"

"That's what I want to find out," I told her. "Does your friend— Has he mentioned anyone named Hannah?"

She frowned. "His wife's name is Sylvia, I know that. Look, whoever this is, she has to be dead now."

"Not just dead," I pointed out. "Murdered."

She was nibbling on her index finger, her eyes on the note. "I'd sure be interested in what you figure *you* could do about it."

"Someone locked her up in her own house," I said, watching her. "They didn't give her food or let her sleep until she signed something. She was a woman and you're a woman."

She looked down at me. "Of course, you're a kook, you know that?" she said.

"Maybe," I said. I put the letter back in my shoulder bag and there were tears of frustration in my eyes.

"Okay, kid, I'll throw in the towel, but on conditions. Have you got paper with you?"

I dug out my notebook, my hands trembling.

"The conditions are as follows," she said. "You tell him Miss Doris Tucci sent you. We keep it formal, very formal. And I *bought* the hurdy-gurdy from him, you hear? I don't even know the man. Promise?"

"Promise," I said. "What changed your mind?"

When she'd written the name and address in my notebook she looked down at me and grinned. "I figure if I'm ever in the same situation—locked up by a guy but *not* for my jewels, honey—it's nice to know I can call on you. Let me know sometime what you dig up."

"I will," I said, "and thank you."

As I left, she called after me crossly, "Try brushing your hair a hundred strokes a day—it doesn't *have* to look like that, kid."

IT WAS half past twelve when I got back to the shop, and by that time some of my triumph and excitement had worn off. Daisy had given me a Park Avenue address in New York City, which meant I was going to have to venture still farther out of my cocoon. I think it was at this point that I came closest to giving up the idea.

However, a decorator from uptown walked in and bought two of the merry-go-round horses and a bolt of pre-war emerald-green velvet. When he left, he said he'd be back with a repairman to look at the jukebox.

A link with a decorator was a pretty dazzling prospect. He was also well on his way to cleaning out all of my good stuff. Obviously I would have to begin going to auctions, and this placed the trip to New York on a practical basis that reduced my anxiety over it. In fact I was feeling quite confident again, when J. Osbourne, Graphologist, strolled into my shop just before five o'clock.

"Hello," he said, looking very neat and professional in a jacket and tie. "I brought over that written report."

"Thanks," I said, taking the two neatly typed sheets of paper and placing them on the cash register.

"I thought I'd find out what progress you made this morning, too."

It suddenly felt like quite a bit of progress. "I have another lead, a new name."

"You're awfully determined. You know," he said, frowning, "you look about sixteen years old, but you can't be."

"I'm twenty-two."

He nodded. "I'm thirty-one. If you weren't so thin," he added sternly, "you'd look older. Do you eat enough?"

"I eat like a horse," I told him. "I don't see what that has to do with anything."

"I was leading up to inviting you to go out with me to dinner. I can offer Italian or Chinese."

I felt a stab of panic. It was happening at last and I wasn't ready. I hadn't even had time to brush my hair one hundred strokes.

THE CHINESE RESTAURANT was full of squat, smiling little Buddhas tucked in niches, and the booths were wicker, painted Chinese red. After Joe had ordered, I told him about my morning.

"I can see this is very educational for you," he said, looking amused. "Daisy sounds like quite a girl."

I conceded cautiously that it could be, and that she was.

He asked me about my family.

"My father died four years ago, my mother when I was eleven."

He winced. "I'm sorry. That must have been rough."

"It was, a little." Casual voice. Bright smile. I *know* I'm not the only person in the world to whom these things have happened, but the memory sits there, a bone in my throat, an undigested pain. "And your family?" I asked.

His family seemed right out of a television sitcom: humorous lawyer father, understanding mother, two mischievous sisters. That's what made him so nice, I suppose, and I was realizing even before dessert how very nice he was. He called himself a casualty of the 1960s—he had been in peace vigils and protests— but, so far as I could see, the only casualty this produced was his law career. He'd veered into psychology instead.

"And then what?" I asked.

"Then two years of graduate school, after which I went to Switzerland to study graphology at the Institute for Applied Psychology in Zurich."

Switzerland, no less. A real sophisticate. And here I was, edgy about a trip to New York, less than a hundred miles away.

Over dessert he asked if I was going to look up Daisy's diamond-earring boy friend.

"Oh yes," I said, "I'll buy some things for the shop, too."

"So when will you go?"

I'd been planning. "Probably Sunday, and come back late Monday. That way I can cover both the weekend and a weekday."

I had realized, thinking about auctions, that eventually I was going to have to buy a car to carry things, so Joe and I spent the rest of dinner talking about cars.

"Do you know how to drive?" he asked.

"Oh yes, that was one of Dr. Merivale's projects."

"Dr. Merivale?"

And so we came to Dr. Merivale, and I managed to keep that very light. Still, I could see the puzzled look in his eyes, so I asked, "Does it shock you about the psychiatry?"

"No," he said, "it's just that I'm glad you've stopped seeing him, because I'd hate to see you lose the kind of quirky quality you have. I like it."

"*Quirky?*"

He grinned. "You keep me guessing. When I met you this morning on your mission you were so confident. And then later, when I asked you to dinner, you looked terrified. Advance and retreat. You strike me as very honest and direct and warm, a bit of a nut basically."

I laughed. He paid the bill and we walked slowly back to my apartment, where I showed him the hurdy-gurdy and he played it a few times. He liked the merry-go-round horse, too. We listened to a few records, and then he said he had to type some reports before morning. When he said good night he reached out and touched my hair, experimentally, sort of, and then he kissed me lightly on the cheek and left.

Chapter Four

Three days later, on Sunday afternoon, I walked under the canopy of the Heathcliffe Arms on Park Avenue, smiled pleasantly at the doorman, and rang the buzzer of apartment 1023, Colonel Morgan Alcourt. I was wearing my high suede boots—rather hot for a May day—and a beige corduroy skirt and jacket, and I was trembling in those boots. A voice rasped in my ear, "Yes, who is it?" and I said over the intercom, "Amelia Jones about a hurdy-gurdy."

"Jones? Hurdy-gurdy?"

"Jones, hurdy-gurdy." I kept it terse, thinking this might be mystifying enough to get me in.

"Get Alphonse," barked the voice. "Doorman."

I fetched the doorman and he took over. "A young woman, sir. Looks very pleasant." He winked at me. "Something about one of those musical instruments you collect."

So the colonel *collected* hurdy-gurdies; no wonder the word hadn't thrown him. "Yes, sir, I'll send her up," said Alphonse, and the elevator soon lifted me silently toward the penthouse.

When the doors of the elevator slid open I stepped out into a lobby—he had a whole lobby to himself—and a man in a white jacket was waiting for me. *Not* the colonel; this chap was Asian and looked very remote, as if he'd wiped away every trace of personality along with the lint on the glassware. "This way, miss," he said, and led me over thick carpeting, through a short hallway and into a huge, uncluttered room with a breathtaking view of the city. And there was the colonel.

He wasn't at all what I'd imagined. He stood about five feet four inches high and the huge room made him look even smaller, a little lost, even pathetic.

"But I don't know you," he said in surprise, sounding aggrieved. I was terribly glad he had money, because in some unaccountable way he looked completely defenseless.

"No," I said in my most reassuring and ladylike voice, "and I'm ever so grateful to you for seeing me. I'm from the Ebbtide curio and antique shop in Trafton, Pennsylvania. Amelia Jones." I put out my hand, which he reluctantly accepted.

"Mmmm . . . I see," he murmured.

"I'm tracing a hurdy-gurdy," I told him, very businesslike. He had dropped my hand and was now regarding my bosom speculatively. When his eyes ran down to my hips I decided not to be so reassuring. "A Miss Doris Tucci gave me your name."

That brought his eyes up in a hurry. He looked astonished, frightened, and then angry, and suddenly he didn't seem pathetic anymore: the anger was quick and nasty. "Miss Tucci has said she purchased it"—I lingered over that word—"from you sometime within the year. Although she couldn't recall just how, or where, she did recall your name."

I felt I'd now preserved Daisy's future for her, although my blood ran cold at the thought of her with this man, and I added,

"I have a Polaroid shot of the hurdy-gurdy." I brought the photo from my shoulder bag.

"Ah yes. . . . Mmmm," he murmured, staring at it. "Miss Tucci. Yes, I think I met her at a cocktail party." He darted a sly, sideways glance at me. "But really, you know, this instrument is of very little value except as a conversation piece. You say you're tracing it?"

I said crisply, "Yes, it's become both an insurance and a police matter. I really can't be more specific except that it's important to us to find its original owner."

"Mmmm . . . I see, yes," he said, blinking. "Well, I'm afraid I can't tell you who the original owner was. For myself, I bought it from Robert Lamandale, the actor. Don't know where he's living now, but he's here in town somewhere. Fine old family."

Having watched me write down the name, he suddenly relaxed and turned arch. "But I must clear up one detail, my dear young lady. That," he said, pointing at the snapshot I held in my hand, "is not a hurdy-gurdy."

"Oh?"

"Come, I must educate you." He grasped my arm, pulling me closer to him than I appreciated. I fell into step with him, and, walking practically thigh to thigh, we passed through a pair of mahogany doors and into a room that looked like something borrowed from a museum. Glass-covered exhibits marched down the center of the room, and the walls were hung with all kinds of exotic objects.

"Now here are your *real* hurdy-gurdies," he said, mercifully releasing me. "What *you* are tracing, my dear, is a hand organ, a mere street instrument, and a complete corruption of the true hurdy-gurdy. *Quite* different."

His lips curled contemptuously, showing small, rabbitlike teeth. Obviously he was a purist, but I could see his point: there *was* a difference. The instruments he was pointing out looked like bulky, foreshortened violins or lutes, and aside from the fact that they appeared to have handles at one end, there was no resemblance at all to my hurdy-gurdy. Or hand organ.

"An incredibly old instrument, the hurdy-gurdy," he said, very much the authority now, "but for most of its life it was called an organistrum. It wasn't called a hurdy-gurdy until the eighteenth century."

436

"I see," I murmured, trying to strike a note of interest.

"You can see the growing sophistication as time went on," he added, darting from one glass case to another. "This thirteenth-century hurdy-gurdy has only three strings. In the eighteenth century the instruments were considerably refined. They were given six strings with a melody compass of two octaves."

"Amazing," I said. I was learning more about hurdy-gurdies than I needed to know. "When did they turn into hand organs?"

"Well," he said, "they were probably corrupted in the nineteenth century by the Italian street boy who strolled through town with it, and in due course discarded it for a form of organ to which he could add a strap and a stick for mobility."

"I see."

We had reached the end of the room and faced some rather appalling objects hung on the wall. He gave me a sly glance. "Interested in torture, Miss Jones?"

Startled, I said, "Not particularly, no."

"Over the years," he confided with considerable relish, "I have collected a very remarkable group of torture instruments and I believe you'd find them quite fascinating. Would you care to join me in a drink?"

"Thank you, no," I told him, taking a step back. "I really have to go—friend downstairs waiting—thanks so much." Leaving him there in the middle of the room, I raced back through his living room, down the short hall to the lobby, punched the DOWN button, and didn't feel safe until I was on the sidewalk again.

I headed for a telephone directory to look up Robert Lamandale, and then I flagged down a taxi.

Mr. Lamandale lived on East Ninth Street, and such was my naïveté that I believed anything *east* in New York was much finer than west; so as the cab drove downtown I kept waiting for an elegant neighborhood to materialize. It didn't. We drew up in front of a line of garbage pails which spilled litter onto the ground. Number 218 was a tall brick building surrounded by rubble. The whole block looked like something out of a war movie. The driver agreed to wait for me.

I scurried up the half-rotted stairs and pressed the buzzer under LAMANDALE, APARTMENT 12. Nothing happened, and I began pressing all the buzzers until someone finally buzzed me in. I started up the stairs and had reached the second landing when a man came racing down toward me, taking the steps two at a time. As he sped past me I said, "Could you tell me where I'll find apartment twelve?"

"Twelve! Who are you looking for?"

"Robert Lamandale."

He stopped just two steps below and looked at me. I saw that he was close to forty-five. He was small and slender and very compact, with a friendly, cheerful face, an upturned nose, and thin, merry lips. But he dyed his hair too dark a shade of brown and there were hammocks of flesh under his eyes, and small lines etched around his mouth.

"Look, dear," he said, "I'm Robert Lamandale, but I've got a call from my agent. I can't stop. What is it?"

"It's about a hurdy-gurdy you owned once and sold. I'm trying to trace it. It's terribly important."

"So is my audition, darling. There aren't that many calls for aging romantic leads. Did I ever have a hurdy-gurdy?"

I handed him the snapshot and he laughed.

"Oh yes . . . *that*. Certainly brings back happier days. A cousin of mine sold off her entire estate at auction in Maine. I bought the hurdy-gurdy as a memento. Purest indulgence."

"Yes, but what's her name?"

He was already six steps below me. "Leonora Harrington," he called over his shoulder.

"Is she still alive?" I called after him.

"Only semi and quasi, the poor girl," he said, turning at the next landing to look up at me. "In a psychiatric hospital near Portland, Maine, somewhere. Try Greenwood Hospital. Green *something*, anyway. Nice meeting you," he added cheerfully, and he was gone.

I followed him out, climbed back into my taxi, and gave the driver the name of my hotel. I hoped Robert Lamandale got the job; I liked him.

Chapter Five

I returned to Trafton on Monday night with, among other things, a first edition of *The Maze in the Heart of the Castle* by H. M. Gruble. I'd counted it a bargain at sixty-five dollars, but I certainly wasn't going to show any profit buying out-of-print first editions of a book I already owned, and had read as a child until its pages were tattered. I knew I'd never want to sell it. I consoled myself by remembering that a box of Bavarian cuckoo clocks was on its way by truck, as well as some cartons of blue willowware—all of which I had just acquired at my first auction.

It was past ten o'clock when I climbed the stairs to my two rooms over the shop. I opened a can of chowder, made a pot of coffee, buttered two slices of bread, and sat down at the kitchen table to thumb through the pages of the book I'd so recklessly bought. Here were the same illustrations I had loved when I was eleven, of Colin meeting the Grand Odlum, of Colin fighting the Wos, and of the Conjurer building a rainbow for Colin.

My favorite part had always been Colin's meeting with the Despas. When he began his search the Grand Odlum had told him, "If search you must, then I can only give you this advice: the important thing is to carry the sun with you, inside of you at every moment, against the darkness. For there will be a great and terrifying darkness."

The Despas were the darkest, which is why I loved it when Colin outwitted them. When he reached them, he was exhausted and ill and the Despas sheltered him in their dark caves, gave him food, and told him that he was naïve and foolish to think of going on, that he really must give up. Colin listened and believed, until one day he remembered the Grand Odlum's words and he realized the Despas had nearly extinguished the sun in his heart because they had none at all in their own.

It wasn't until I met Dr. Merivale that I understood why the Despas had affected me so: I'd lived with one—my mother—for half of my life.

Carefully I put away the book, and then I returned to the pile of brochures I'd collected on cars and vans because I'd decided I was going to drive to Portland. Somehow, I didn't want to call Joe and tell him I was back. I didn't want to expect anything from him, which of course meant that already I was expecting too much: I was looking forward to seeing him again, and terrified that I might not. It is very uphill work being insecure.

I didn't hear from Joe the next morning, and so, during my lunch hour, I doggedly went out and looked at cars by myself. This whittled down my defenses enough to telephone him.

"I thought you would never call," he said. "How long are

you going to play games? You got back last night, didn't you?"

"Yes, but it was late and I thought—"

"You thought I'd say Amelia who?"

I decided to ignore this. I said I'd seen a car and a van, and I hoped he knew something that might help me decide.

"I'll be over at five, but how was New York? Any luck?"

"I saw two people, a hurdy-gurdy collector and an actor," I told him, "and next I have to go to Maine."

"It's like a scavenger hunt," he said. "See you at five."

It was a busy afternoon. The interior decorator arrived with a mechanic and they prodded the insides of the old 1940s jukebox. The bell over the shop door jangled frequently. One of Mr. Georgerakis' weird bathrobes sold, as well as a stuffed moose head with antlers. Suddenly, at two o'clock, the jukebox lit up with flashing neon lights and roared out the "Beer Barrel Polka." Six people were in the shop at the time; it was like a party.

All of this increased the momentum I'd returned with from New York, and between sales I began making plans to go to Maine before I lost my courage. I pondered how to handle four or five days away from the shop. The shipment from New York would arrive Thursday at the latest. Allowing one day to price and sort the new items, I could leave for Portland on Saturday morning. I telephoned Mr. Georgerakis.

"I thought you'd never ask," he said. "Today I read the newspaper all morning and after lunch I ran the vacuum cleaner for Katina. This is retirement?"

"How much will you want for coming in?"

"I'd do it for free," he told me, "but I have my dignity. Pay me ten dollars a day, but no vacuuming. I'll be there Saturday morning, eight o'clock sharp."

When Joe came at five I wondered why on earth I'd felt so afraid; he wasn't even as handsome as I remembered, just bony and nice-looking, cheerful and somehow very real. "You look good enough to eat," he said. "What was the fellow on Park Avenue like?"

"A dirty old man, I think."

Joe grinned. "Innocent Amelia, you are getting around. You handled him skillfully, I trust?"

"I bolted."

"And the actor?"

440

"Oh, very nice, although we only talked on the stairs. *He* bought the hurdy-gurdy from a cousin, a Miss Harrington, when her estate went on the market. She's in a psychiatric hospital in Portland. I suppose she could be mad as a hatter, but I have to try."

He nodded. "Definitely, since one person's definition of mad as a hatter is entirely different from another's," he said with mock solemnity, and reached for my hand as we walked.

We spent the next two hours peering into and under cars, and another hour excitedly discussing them over meatballs and spaghetti, and in the end I owned a van. It was a really weird one; someone had custom ordered it and then walked out on the deal. It was black as a hearse, with a porthole on either side, and on both the sides and the rear, pictures had been painted of a lighthouse in the moonlight. The effect of ghostly blues and white on black was altogether spooky, but the van would hold an entire room of furniture if necessary.

"This will certainly amuse my parents," Joe said. "But I haven't invited you, have I?"

"Invited me?" I had just unlocked the shop; the bells were still jangling as I reached for the light switch.

With the lights on I saw that Joe was looking pleased with himself. "They're celebrating their thirty-fifth wedding anniversary on Sunday and I told them I'd bring you. If you close the shop in midafternoon Saturday, we can be there for dinner. I can't wait to have you meet them."

I looked at him blankly. "*This* weekend? But Joe, I'm leaving for Maine early Saturday morning."

He looked startled. "But you can postpone it, can't you?"

I swallowed hard. "I don't really think I can."

He stared at me incredulously. "But Amelia, this will be fun. We can swim, there's badminton, and you'll enjoy my sister Jenny. You can't be serious."

"But I am," I said helplessly. "Going to Maine is something I have to do. I've already made all the arrangements, and Mr. Georgerakis is coming in to look after the shop while I'm gone."

"Amelia, aren't you letting this get out of hand?"

"I'm sorry," I said miserably. "Truly I am."

"Sorry!" he exploded. "My God, here I am with free time at last and I was hoping—I thought we really hit it off, and damn it, Amelia, this woman's dead. She has to be. But I'm not."

441

"I can't help it," I said stubbornly. "I just can't. I have to go to Maine and look for Hannah."

We stared at each other across a vast chasm. "I don't get it," he said furiously, "but I hope you enjoy your damn trip very much." He stalked out of the shop and closed the door so hard the bells hanging over it jangled for a full minute.

Well, of course I'd known it would have to happen. A part of me whispered, "Hurry—run after him and say you'll go," but I only stood there, feeling numb. This was the thing about people: if you asserted yourself, they went away, which is what my mother had done to punish me, so why not Joe? I had long ago learned that everything I became attached to either went away, changed, or died. Suddenly I felt guilt at daring to do what I wanted, bruised at hurting Joe, and, worst of all, a crushing fear that I might be losing my mind over an insane search for a dead woman.

Frightened, I reached for a sweater, left the shop and locked the door. I hadn't seen Amman Singh for a week.

The smell of curry and spices hung in the air outside his door. He was alone, except for the ubiquitous compatriots whom I could hear poking about in the kitchen. After the five flights of stairs I said breathlessly, "Amman Singh, I have to talk to you. Please?"

"I have been expecting you," he said courteously, and gestured me to sit down beside him.

I sat facing him, my legs crossed under me. I told him about the note inside the hurdy-gurdy and about the people I'd met since I last saw him. He closed his eyes to listen, and I wondered what nuances he would hear in my voice to give away my doubts and my sudden terror. When I finished, I pleaded, "Amman Singh, am I right to do this? I don't understand this—this compulsion. Hannah surely has to be dead by now."

He opened his eyes and reached out for my hand; his grasp felt dry and cool, scarcely flesh at all. "When the wind frees the seed from the flower and the seed is driven on the breeze across the fields it is not compulsion. The seed is obeying laws we cannot see or know. Trust the wind. One day you will understand."

"But will I find her?" I asked.

He said, "You will find something."

"But it's Hannah I must find!" I cried.

He looked at me and his smile was tender. "Is it?" he asked softly. "Is it?"

I FELT BETTER after leaving Amman Singh, although I didn't understand what he meant, not then at least. Still, it was astonishing how impoverished my life suddenly looked without Joe. A grayness hung over everything, like smog.

On Wednesday afternoon my goods arrived from New York, and I rearranged the shop's window display, laid out some blue willowware, and hung price tags on the cuckoo clocks.

On Thursday, after dinner, I dialed Joe's telephone number just to hear his voice, planning to hang up as soon as he answered. I was denied even that; there was no answer. I called again at midnight, and still there was no answer. Obviously he was finding solace elsewhere. A woman, I thought darkly.

If grief can be called a form of insanity, then the next day, Friday, I arose sane. Joe had come and Joe had gone; never mind. I was twenty-two and I had promises to keep. To Hannah. Mr. Georgerakis stopped in at noon to be shown where everything was. We had a cup of coffee together and then he patted my hand and said the shop looked just like me, sunny and bright and cheerful. Since I'd just climbed out of the Black Hole of Calcutta I was inordinately pleased by the compliment.

"See you tomorrow at eight," he said. "It will be a pleasure."

Tomorrow at eight . . . I remembered what that meant—Portland, Maine—and nearly panicked. I had to reread Hannah's note before my sense of mission was restored and my anxieties banished. I packed blue jeans, some heavy sweaters, my windbreaker, pajamas, and toothbrush, and at eight o'clock in the morning, wearing my beige corduroy suit, this time enlivened by a pink and orange scarf, I greeted Mr. Georgerakis. Half an hour later, when I carried my suitcase out to the alley where the van was parked at night, I stopped in my tracks. Joe was leaning against the side of the van.

"Hi," he said cheerfully. "If you'd only left this monster of yours unlocked, I'd have stowed away."

I stared at him, not understanding a word.

"I'm going with you to Maine." He pointed to a duffle bag at his feet that I hadn't noticed in my shock. "Unless you mind?"

"Mind!" I gasped. "But your parents!"

He shrugged. "I drove down Wednesday to wish them another thirty-five years of connubial bliss and got back last night."

I must have looked as dazed as I felt—after all, I'd lost him, mourned him, and buried him by now—because he added patiently, "Look, Amelia, if Hannah's the top priority for you right now, I'll make her mine, too. I may have to be back here Wednesday for a court case, but I'm yours until then. I think this is what's called compromise."

I grinned from ear to ear and said, "I'm so awfully glad to see you, Joe. Would you like to drive, or shall I?"

Chapter Six

There was no Greenwood Hospital in Portland, but there was a private psychiatric hospital five miles out of town called Greenacres. It was a gently aging building of rosy brick surrounded by improbably green lawns. I swung the van into the parking space labeled VISITORS ONLY. "So," I said brightly, "we're here."

"We're here, and it's all yours," Joe reminded me, bringing out his paperback copy of *Astronomy for the Layman.* "Good luck."

He said the last very dryly, because after talking about it for several hours, neither of us had any idea how I was going to get inside to see Leonora Harrington *if* she was here.

I walked up the wide cement steps. As I entered, I could see that it looked just like any hospital. There was a brightly lighted reception counter on the left, with clipboards and a switchboard, and a waiting room on the right. The only person in sight was a nurse in very starched white behind the counter. She looked young, earnest, and new.

I said politely, "Good afternoon, I've come to see Miss Leonora Harrington."

The girl's friendly smile turned startled. "Miss *Harrington?*"

"Yes. Unless of course she's—"

"Oh no, it's just she never has—" The girl stopped, flushed, and began again. "That is, usually no one except—I'll have to check it out. Would you mind waiting?"

A very severe-looking middle-aged nurse was produced next. "I'm Mrs. Dawes. Are you a member of Miss Harrington's family?"

Hers was the cold voice of authority, and her gaze was sharp enough to strip a person of pretentions, illusions, and confidence. I am very familiar with the type. They like rendering people helpless, and I saw no reason to frustrate her. "Oh, I do so hope I can see her for just a minute," I said. "I have no right, of course—not at

444

all—but her cousin Robert Lamandale in New York referred me here. It's a legal matter," I added, gesturing helplessly. "It's so important that she identify this photograph of a hurdy-gurdy."

I've noticed that if someone is about to tell you that you've no right to do something, it confuses them no end if you say it first. Mrs. Dawes blinked. "Dr. Ffolks is in his office," she said coldly. "I really don't know—"

She left me then and returned presently with a man in a white coat. He looked very tired and all the lines in his face sagged, including his jowls, which gave him an uncanny resemblance to a Saint Bernard dog. He nodded to me curtly. "Nurse Jordan will have to accompany you for the visit, and it will have to be limited to five minutes. Miss Harrington's under sedation but she's quite lucid. Miss Jordan?"

"Yes, Dr. Ffolks," said the young nurse. "This way, miss."

I was glad I'd decided on the truth, since I was to have a witness to my interview. In the elevator I asked Nurse Jordan how long Miss Harrington had lived at Greenacres.

"She was here eight years ago when my mom worked nights, and we were all kids," said Nurse Jordan cheerfully.

"Weird," I said, and we exchanged the knowing glances of contemporaries.

"They say she drank all her money away," Nurse Jordan added in a lowered voice as the elevator slowed. "They say she's paranoid, too, but I've never—"

The doors slid open at the third floor. Miss Jordan knocked on the door opposite the elevator, opened it, and I followed her into a room with its curtains half drawn against the sunlight.

"I didn't ring," said a petulant voice.

"But I've brought you a guest," Nurse Jordan said.

In a bed along the left wall of the room a woman stirred and sat up. In the semidarkness it was hard to guess how old she was. She could have been thirty or forty—certainly no older; but her face was an oval from which all emotion and life had been drained. Only her eyes were alive, and they burned like the eyes of someone who looked frequently into hell. She must have been beautiful once, one of those fragile ash blondes; the bone structure was still there. Her hair hung to her shoulders, but it looked as if she ran her fingers through it often, and with anger. Seeing me, she tilted her head questioningly.

445

"This is Miss Jones," said Nurse Jordan. "She's a friend of your cousin in New York."

Miss Harrington's face brightened. "Robin? You've seen Robin?"

Robin. I was so startled I almost jumped. Robin—and her name was Leonora. Of course—Robin and Nora, the two names in Hannah's letter! It was like panning for gold and suddenly bringing up a fortune-sized nugget. I found it hard to suppress my excitement, but I said calmly, "Yes. He sent his best to you, and he said it was all right to ask you about this."

I placed the picture of the hurdy-gurdy on her bed table. She turned on the bedside light and leaned over to peer at it. "Oh, it's Aunt Hannah's hurdy-gurdy," she said softly, tears coming to her eyes. "How we loved it as children!"

She was staring at the photo, bemused, the tears rolling down her haggard cheeks.

"Your cousin Robin said that it was your hurdy-gurdy later, that *you* owned it for a while," I said carefully, really excited now but not wanting to frighten her.

She nodded. "I chose it—as a souvenir, you know—after everything went. Everything. Oh, I hated selling it, but I needed the money," she said with sudden anger.

I said quickly, "Where did you and Robin play with the hurdy-gurdy, Miss Harrington? I mean, where did your aunt live?"

"In Carleton."

"Carleton, Maine?"

She nodded absently, her eyes looking far beyond the picture into a past she'd lost.

"And your aunt Hannah's last name, was it Harrington, too? Or perhaps Lamandale?"

She wrenched her gaze from the picture and stared at me in astonishment. "Of course not. Hannah Meerloo. Why didn't you know that?" she asked suspiciously. "She ought to have known that," she told the nurse pettishly. "I don't like her, I don't like her asking me questions and making me cry. Take her away."

Nurse Jordan touched my arm, and as I followed her out Leonora Harrington called spitefully, "Tell Robin to come himself next time, damn him."

"She'll cry now and fall asleep," Nurse Jordan said as we walked into the elevator. "No harm done. Tomorrow she'll be sitting out on the rear lawn knitting in the sun with all the others."

I said, "But if she's so poor, how on earth can she afford to stay here at Greenacres?"

"Oh, a friend of the family pays her bills. He's the only one who comes to see her, which is why you surprised me. He comes once a month, regular as clockwork."

The doors slid open and there was Mrs. Dawes waiting for us, like a vulture. "Very good." She nodded to Nurse Jordan. "Five minutes to the second." Her eyes rested on me dismissingly. "*Good* day, Miss Jones."

I walked alone up the hall to the lobby and suddenly noticed a bronze plaque set into the wall:

GREENACRES PRIVATE PSYCHIATRIC HOSPITAL
GIVEN IN MEMORY
OF
JASON M. MEERLOO
BY
HANNAH G. MEERLOO

I walked thoughtfully back to the van, and to Joe, who looked at me questioningly and put aside his book. "That didn't take long. Amelia, you look funny."

I said slowly, "Leonora Harrington is Nora—she has to be—because she called Robert Lamandale *Robin*, and the hurdy-gurdy belonged to their aunt Hannah, whose last name was Meerloo. This hospital is the gift of Hannah Meerloo."

"Wow—pay dirt," Joe said, and whistled. "And so?"

"I don't know."

"You looked scared," he said.

I nodded. "Now I know her name and I don't know what to do about it."

Joe grinned. "Then it's a darn good thing I came along, because I know exactly what to do. Climb in and I'll drive."

We looked up Carleton on the road map and found it about a hundred miles to the north, on one of the bays that scallop the Maine coast. I said doubtfully, "Its population is four hundred sixty-three."

"Then someone will certainly remember a woman named Hannah Meerloo," pointed out Joe. "What's the nearest decent-sized town?"

"Anglesworth's the nearest city and *its* population is only four thousand six hundred eighty-seven."

Joe turned onto Route 1 and glanced at his watch. "We'll head for Anglesworth; it's nearly half past two now."

I could guess what he was thinking. Last night we'd stayed at a modest inn and had taken rooms at opposite ends of the building: Miss A. Jones, Mr. J. Osbourne.

But that was New Hampshire. Nothing much was open at this season in Maine, and the smaller the towns, the more limited the accommodation. Soon we would have to become self-conscious about what lay between us.

"Actually," said Joe, pointing to still another motel with a CLOSED UNTIL MEMORIAL DAY sign, "I think we should stop at L. L. Bean's in Freeport and pick up some camping gear just in case. I brought a sleeping bag but you didn't, and we may have to use the van." His voice was so impersonal—like Peary planning a trip to the North Pole—that I couldn't help but relax.

They were having a parade in Freeport on this Sunday afternoon, with a high-school band that marched along briskly, playing "Strike Up the Band" a little off-key, and a procession of men and women carrying placards that read VOTE FOR ANGUS TUTTLE FOR U.S. SENATOR. A small, amiable group followed the parade on the sidewalk, bearing signs reading SILAS WHITNEY FOR U.S. SENATOR. In L. L. Bean's I proceeded to acquire my first sleeping bag, a pair of hiking boots, a flashlight, thermos, and collapsible drinking cup.

Hours later we stopped in Anglesworth for a quick dinner, had the thermos filled with hot cocoa, and headed immediately for Carleton so that we would reach it before the general store closed. That, Joe said, was the place to learn anything in the country, and he was right. There were two gas pumps and a faded sign saying PRITCHETT'S GENERAL STORE, SIMON PRITCHETT, PROPRIETOR. We walked inside and found Mr. Pritchett reading a newspaper behind the counter.

"Evening," he said. "Can I help you folks?"

"We're hoping you can," Joe told him. "My friend here is looking for the place where Mrs. Hannah Meerloo used to live."

"A very dear friend of my family's at one time," I added, seeing him look at me with a sharp, wary glance.

He was silent, mulling us over thoughtfully for a long minute.

448

He finally nodded and said, "That'd be the old Whitney place. It's up for sale again by the summer folks who bought it three years ago. The Keppels."

"Keppel," I repeated.

"Go down the road a piece, far as the fork. Bear to the right— that'd be Tuttle Road—and you'll find it on your left, near the river. Big place; can't miss the 'for sale' sign."

"She . . . uh . . . died. . . . I mean, of course, Mrs. Meerloo is dead but—" I stopped doubtfully.

"Buried in the town cemetery," he said flatly. "Can't be deader than that. You one of those people tracing roots I hear about?"

"Something like that," Joe said easily. "Perhaps you could direct us to the cemetery?"

"Just across the road, behind the Methodist church."

And so at dusk on a warm May evening we wandered through the Carleton cemetery in search of Hannah's grave. The sun was low, turning the grass a brilliant emerald green as it slanted through the trees. We strolled along in the hushed silence and there it was, except there were two headstones, very simple ones, side by side. The stone on the left read:

JASON M. MEERLOO

BORN JANUARY 23, 1920—

KILLED IN FRANCE DECEMBER 1945

BELOVED HUSBAND OF HANNAH

"Good grief," I said, "he was only twenty-five."

The sun had withdrawn now and it was nearly dark among the trees. I knelt beside the companion gravestone.

"'Hannah G. Meerloo,'" I read softly. "'Born May 27, 1925, died July 25, 1965. . . .' Joe, she was only forty."

Joe was doing sums in his head, too. "It also means that when she was widowed in 1945 she was twenty years old. Younger than you are now, Amelia."

But I was staring at the inscription below the dates: AND SO SHE WENT BEYOND THE HORIZON INTO THE COUNTRY OF THE DAWN.

Strange words . . . strange and poetic and somehow familiar to me. "That's surely a quotation," I told Joe. "Do you know it?"

He shook his head. "I like it, though. I think it means—" He hesitated and then he said very quietly, "I think it means there was someone left behind who loved her."

It was at that moment, hearing him say that, and in that kind of voice, that I believe I fell in love with Joe.

"Come on," he said, putting a hand on my shoulder. "It's nearly eight o'clock. I think it's time we find a place to park the van, have some cocoa, and turn in. I'm beat."

I looked up at him and said urgently, "But there'll be records, won't there, Joe? Newspapers keep records, don't they? And a death certificate somewhere?"

"Tomorrow," he said. "Tomorrow, Amelia." And he helped me to my feet and firmly led me away from the grave.

WE FOUND a deserted wood road, drank our cocoa, and curled up in our sleeping bags inside the van, Joe on one side, and I on the other. I fell asleep at once, tired from two days of driving and tension. I must have been asleep for several hours when it began again. . . . I was wandering through long, empty, cold halls, calling "Mother?" and looking into cold empty rooms, and then I was slowly climbing the attic stairs—slowly, slowly, as one does in a dream—and there she was at the top of the stairs, hanging from a rafter, gently turning and swaying, her eyes—

I screamed, and, waking, found the flashlight switched on and Joe struggling out of his sleeping bag. "Amelia, what is it?"

I had long ago stopped crying following this nightmare, but as usual I was shaking all over. Joe stared at me; then he put his arms around me and held me.

When I'd stopped shaking I said, "I had a nightmare."

"So I gathered. Like to talk it out? It helps, you know."

Through clenched teeth I said, "When I was eleven my mother didn't just die, as I told you. She hung herself. And when I have these nightmares I see her hanging there, her neck broken and—"

He said incredulously, "She hung herself and *you found her?*"

"Yes."

"My God." He shuddered. "And you've had to live with this?"

"I'm all right now," I told him. "It's over."

"What do you mean, it's over?" he demanded. "Don't be polite, Amelia. Have some cocoa. There's some left in the bottom of the thermos." He began rummaging about for the cup, the flashlight sending long cavernous shadows up and down the walls of the van. "Have you ever learned *why* your mother committed suicide?"

I said politely, "Well . . . she gave up. On living, I mean."

451

"Yes, but she had an eleven-year-old daughter and a husband, didn't she? What kind of woman would be so careless about *them?*" he asked, bringing me the cocoa.

"A woman with an infinite lack of capacity for living."

"Were you close to her?"

I thought about this while I sipped the cocoa. "Of course I wanted to be close to her, but there always seemed such a high price to pay. I think when I was born she thought, At last, someone to give me unqualified and total love. As it turned out, nothing I could do was enough."

"Then what she wanted was total possession?"

"Perhaps," I admitted. "There was, apparently," I added loyally, "some tragedy in her life. Once I overheard my father tell my Aunt Stacey that my mother had never loved him, that she'd never stopped loving someone named Charles, who'd rejected her and married someone else. She never stopped mourning him."

"Did she try?" asked Joe savagely.

I laughed in a hollow sort of way. "Not very hard, no. I think now, looking back, she had been in love with death for a long time. When I was very young we used to visit graveyards often. And she'd stop and say in a dreamy voice, 'Just think, Amelia, all the people here were once alive, and one day we, too . . .' I guess she found life very pointless."

Joe said harshly, "Didn't your father know or care what she was doing to you?"

"He was away a lot."

"Was he away the day she hung herself?"

"Oh yes."

"So your mother knew you'd find her?"

I looked at him sharply. "Why do you say that?"

"Because," he pointed out simply, "if she knew you would be the one to find her, it was the ultimate rejection for you."

The ultimate rejection . . . No one had ever put it in that way before, so bluntly, but of course that was it, that was what had always mattered far more to me than finding her dead.

"The ultimate punishment, too," I added quietly, "for not being enough to her." And suddenly the tears I'd not cried for so long overwhelmed me and I sobbed in Joe's arms. Finally, reduced to hiccups, I sat up and looked at him, finding him blurred through my lingering tears. "Thanks." I smiled at him.

He laughed. "You're going to be all right, you know—that's the thing to remember, Amelia. In my book you're already okay. The absence of love is very prevalent in this world, but patterns can be broken, you know."

"I hope so," I said, and quoted Amman Singh. "'A tree may be bent by harsh winds but is no less beautiful than the tree that grows in a sheltered nook, and often it bears the richer fruit.'"

He stared at me gravely. "You're a very lovely, special sort of person, Amelia, do you know that?"

I looked at him and then I leaned over and kissed him—flippantly, gratefully—except that when our lips met, our arms somehow curved greedily around each other. I gasped, "Joe!"

He said questioningly, almost desperately, "Amelia?" and a moment later we were inside my sleeping bag, our clothes strewn across the floor, and I was learning for the first time the new and exotic language of love.

Later, smoothing my tangled hair, Joe said, "Let's never be careless with each other, Amelia, promise? Because what happened just now between us is too important."

"Yes," I said dreamily. How amazing life could be, after all! It was almost enough to make me forget Hannah, the Hannah who "went beyond the horizon into the country of the dawn."

I closed my eyes and suddenly, just as I was slipping off to sleep, the source of the quotation surfaced smoothly into consciousness, striking me full force. Except for the change in gender it was a word-for-word quotation from *The Maze in the Heart of the Castle*—the closing lines of the book: "And so he went beyond the horizon into the country of the dawn."

Chapter Seven

"She must have loved the book, too," I told Joe incredulously the next morning at breakfast. We were seated in a diner in Anglesworth and it was ten o'clock. "It's the most astonishing thing."

Joe bit into his toast. "Are you certain the gravestone inscription is the same? It must be years since you've read it."

"But it isn't," I told him eagerly. "I mean, besides rereading it once a year, I bought a first edition of it in New York only last week."

"The book meant that much to you?"

"It saved my life. I was so very young, you know, and so clob-bered. It gave me a kind of philosophy, a feeling that maybe life isn't meant to be easy, that it's a kind of pilgrimage or testing ground, and we have to fight like warriors to live. I mean, to live *well*."

"Like warriors," Joe repeated, sounding interested.

I nodded and said solemnly, "I think I like this Hannah of ours very much, Joe."

Joe brought me down from my trip by saying, "It's certainly convenient you like her, but we're here to establish whether she was murdered or not, remember? And it's Monday morning. Some-time today I'm going to have to call my answering service and see whether there are any messages about being in court Wednesday."

"What happens Wednesday?"

"It's when Griselda's case may or may not come to court," he said. "Griselda is ten years old and she was taken away from her grandmother because her grandmother is seventy-three and can't jump rope with her, for heaven's sake. She was put in a foster home, where she changed so much in two years that they've de-cided she's schizophrenic and ought to be institutionalized."

"Oh boy," I said.

He nodded. "Her grandmother's a smart cookie, and she hired a lawyer, who hired me. We've collected handwriting samples from years back, and think we can prove: one, that the foster parents are the crazies and, two, that Griselda has withdrawn because she has neither stability nor love in her life. She needs her grand-mother." He drank the last of his coffee. "Are you finished yet? We've got a long list of things to do today, Amelia."

"Right," I said, and swallowed the last of my toast. "Death certificate first, or obituaries?"

"I think death certificate first," Joe said. "After all, if it turns out that Hannah died in a hospital of pneumonia, or collapsed of a heart attack in full view of a crowd of people, then we might as well go sightseeing."

"Joe, you don't really think—"

"Verify, Amelia, verify," he said with a grin. "Some of my father's legal mind has rubbed off on me. Verify *everything*."

The diner was shabby, with an eroded mirror behind the counter. While Joe paid the bill I studied its dreary decorations, which included the same kind of political placards we had seen in the parade in Freeport. One read: FOR U.S. SENATOR ELECT ANGUS TUTTLE, FOUR YEARS STATE SENATOR, A MAN OF EXPERIENCE, A MAN OF VISION. The poster carried a photograph of the candidate, wearing tweeds and sitting in an armchair looking like a man in a toothpaste ad. He had a young face, prematurely white hair, handsome brows and a broad, dazzling white smile.

The other poster read: VOTE FOR SILAS WHITNEY FOR U.S. SENATE, A MAN OF THE PEOPLE, A MAN OF JUDGMENT. He looked as if his face had been carved out of granite, long and thin, with steady black eyes and a lantern jaw. I didn't think Silas Whitney had a chance against that enormous toothy smile of Angus Tuttle's.

"What on earth are you doing?" asked Joe, seeing my lips moving silently.

"Counting teeth." I pointed to Tuttle's poster. "His smile shows twelve upper teeth. It's unbelievable."

"So are you," he said, reaching for my hand, and as we walked out into the sunshine Joe looked down and smiled at me. It was a lovely smile, made up of all that we'd shared, and I realized I had never been cherished before, or truly and utterly happy.

The courthouse stood on a side street, a very old building with Corinthian columns. We found the city clerk's office, and then had to buy a copy of the death certificate in order to see it! Trembling with suspense, I paid the two dollars, and we leaned over the document, my eyes skidding past the name Meerloo and down to the cause of death. It read: "Intercranial hemorrhage; basal skull fracture." It was signed by Timothy Cox, M.D.

"*Not* pneumonia," I said flatly. "*Not* heart attack."

Joe shook his head. "Skull fracture."

"Like maybe a blow on the head. Joe, let's get to the newspaper office and see if we can find an obituary."

The office of the Anglesworth newspaper was on the main street, and it was so small that I was afraid they might not have back issues on file. I was wrong: the files were in the basement.

"You might as well come down with me if you're doing some kind of research," the woman clerk told us. "Nineteen sixty-five, you said?"

The Anglesworth *Tribune* was a weekly paper, which explained why the plastic-bound volume for 1965 could be easily carried to the table by one person. The clerk went upstairs, and Joe and I eagerly riffled through the pages.

455

"Obituaries, obituaries," I murmured, running my finger down the index of the July 28 issue.

Joe said in a strange voice, "You don't have to look for the obituaries, Amelia."

I followed his pointing finger to the headline on the first page: NOTED RESIDENT DIES IN BIZARRE ACCIDENT.

"Bizarre accident," I repeated aloud. "Joe, they must have gotten away with it."

And then I saw the subhead: HANNAH GRUBLE MEERLOO, PHILANTHROPIST AND AUTHOR, DEAD AT 40.

My eyes were trapped by the word author and the name Gruble. I wrenched them free to skim the page, my heart pounding, and there it was, down near the end of the column:

> In 1950 Mrs. Meerloo, using her maiden name of Gruble, published a book for young people entitled *The Maze in the Heart of the Castle*, of which *The New York Times* wrote, "a small classic, a book for adults as well as children, full of enchantments and insights." It is the only book Mrs. Meerloo is known to have written.

I whispered, "Joe, she's H. M. Gruble. She *wrote* the book."

"Take it easy, for heaven's sake," Joe said. "You look as if you're going to faint, Amelia. Are you all right?"

I just stared at him, the thoughts inside my head spinning. . . . "If search you must, then I can only give you this advice: the important thing is to carry the sun with you. . . . For there will be a great and terrifying darkness." And Amman Singh saying to me, "Trust the wind. One day you will understand."

I said in a clear hard voice, "I am very much all right." I sat down at the table and began to read the column.

> July 25—Mrs. Hannah Meerloo, noted philanthropist, and resident of Carleton since 1953, was pronounced dead on arrival at Anglesworth Hospital early this morning, following a fall down the cellar stairs in her home on Tuttle Road. Mrs. Meerloo was the widow of Jason Meerloo, killed in World War II.
>
> In the house at the time of the accident were her niece, Leonora Harrington, who had arrived just that day for a visit; a houseguest, Hubert Holton, and her summer chauffeur, John Tuttle, a graduate student at Union College. Of the accident Miss Harrington said, "I heard this terrible scream and when I turned on my bedside

light it was five minutes after one in the morning. I raced into the hall and bumped into Mr. Holton, who'd heard it, too. We knocked on my Aunt Hannah's door and then went in and found her lights burning but the room empty. We began searching for her, not knowing where the scream came from, and then we heard a pounding on the kitchen door.

"It was Aunt Hannah's chauffeur, Jay, who sleeps over the garage adjoining the house. He'd heard the scream, too. We finally found her lying at the foot of the cellar stairs. She must have been going down to the safe—there were canceled checks lying all around her. She was always up late nights, and the safe is in the basement, in the old preserve closet."

Miss Harrington was admitted to the hospital suffering from shock and gave this account upon being discharged.

Joe said in an astonished voice, "It's real then, Amelia: a very odd and disputable death."
I finished scanning the rest of Hannah's obituary.

Mrs. Meerloo was born Hannah Maria Gruble in Pittsfield, Mass., in 1925, the daughter of a carpenter and a schoolteacher. At 18 she married Jason Meerloo, whose father made millions from his various patents and inventions, a fortune his son, Jason, inherited several months before his tragic death in France. Left widowed and wealthy at an early age, Mrs. Meerloo traveled extensively for several years.

In 1953 she purchased the old Whitney house on Tuttle Road in Carleton and lived there in semi-seclusion with her housekeeper. She endowed and built the Greenacres Private Psychiatric Hospital near Portland, established in 1946 the Jason Meerloo Orphanage in Anglesworth, and gave to this city the building which now houses the public library.

She leaves as survivors her niece, Leonora Harrington, of Boston, and a nephew, Robert Gruble, of New York City, an actor professionally known as Robert Lamandale. A formal inquest into the death will be held on Thursday.

"Joe," I said, pointing to the last sentence.
"Inquest," he echoed. "Find the inquest edition!"
In a fury of haste I turned the pages of the August 5 edition. This time it was on the second page of the newspaper and Nora's

age was listed as twenty-four; Hubert Holton, forty, was described as an associate professor of political science at Maine's Union College and John Tuttle as a graduate student, age twenty-seven, who had chauffeured for Mrs. Meerloo for nine summers. A very respectable group.

It was not a long report. Dr. Timothy Cox gave his testimony: death due to a basal skull fracture, with subdural bleeding—a wound, he said, that fitted with the circumstances of her death, in this case the head striking cement, causing instant unconsciousness. She had died in the ambulance.

Nora repeated the story that had been given earlier to the newspaper, and both the chauffeur and the houseguest confirmed it. The only new testimony was from the housekeeper, a Mrs. Jane Morneau, age forty-two, who said it was customary for Mrs. Meerloo to give her servants their vacations during the month of July, because July was "when Mr. Robin or Miss Nora, or both, came to visit her." Mrs. Morneau said that on July 1, the day she left for her holiday, Miss Harrington had already been there for a week, "and very high-spirited she was." The housekeeper recalled vague plans for Miss Harrington and Mrs. Meerloo to be driven to New York City by John Tuttle to see Mr. Robin in a new play on Broadway. Mr. Holton's name was vaguely familiar to her, but she was sure he was no friend of Mrs. Meerloo's. He had never come to the house before, and he was a stranger to her now.

Death by accident was the verdict of Judge Henry Tate, "due to lack of evidence to the contrary."

Joe closed the volume thoughtfully. "What strikes me first is, who is this Hubert Holton? Was he a friend of Nora's?"

"There's something else, too," I pointed out. "Why did the first report in the newspaper say that Nora had just arrived for a visit on the day of Hannah's death when the housekeeper testified she was already there on July first? Where had she been?"

Joe was lost in thought. "Just three people in the house at the time," he said, "aside from Hannah, of course: Nora and this Holton and the chauffeur, John Tuttle. But Hannah writes about the faceless ones. Who could they have been?"

"Her captors might have worn stocking masks when they brought her food," I said.

"But the people in the house were known to her, Amelia. Even in stocking masks she would have recognized them."

458

"There could have been others in the house," I pointed out. "They could have come while Nora was gone. We have to find out how long she was away."

He nodded. "Okay, where do you suggest we start?"

"Why not at the very beginning?"

Chapter Eight

The real estate agent was a nice little man named Bob Tuttle— lots of Tuttles in Anglesworth, he said. He drove us back to Carleton in his ancient Chevy.

At first glance Hannah's house was disappointing; I guess I'd expected a huge brick mansion after reading the word philanthropist in the local paper. It was large—ten rooms, Mr. Tuttle said—but it was just a comfortable, old-fashioned frame house with a big wooden porch. It was an inconspicuous dun color that blended with the overgrown, frost-killed lawn.

We walked up wooden steps, crossed the porch, and entered a very cold house. Every house has its own personality, but this one was curiously neutral. Too many owners in too few years, I guessed. The kitchen was modern except for a very old woodburning cookstove. *That* would have been Hannah's, I decided. There were fireplaces everywhere, even one upstairs in the master bedroom, Mr. Tuttle said, but Joe announced that he'd like to see the basement first, "to have a look at the foundation and the sills." This earned him a look of respect from Mr. Tuttle.

The door to the cellar opened at the end of a long hallway that began at the front door. Wooden steps marched down at a moderately steep angle, but there was a handrail and nothing unusually dangerous about them except for the cement floor waiting at the bottom. I followed Joe and Mr. Tuttle down, feeling a little queasy, and stopped at the last step, staring at the floor where Hannah had been found lying unconscious. Of course there was nothing there. I turned and looked back up the stairs. The accepted story was that Hannah had been carrying a handful of checks, had turned on the light, started down the stairs, lost her balance, and fallen to the bottom. But there was something missing here. If I lost my balance on the stairs, I thought, I would automatically throw out my hands to protect myself. I'd stumble, grope for the handrail, hit a few steps, and possibly break an arm or a shoulder bone when I hit the cement. But I couldn't understand a person being killed by the fall unless that person was moving at some terrific speed. Unless she had been pushed. Or was dead before she went down. Or hurried down the hall blindfolded.

"Let's go upstairs, please," I said, suddenly panicky.

Joe shot me a glance that included the stairs and up we went.

We mounted to the second floor and inspected four bedrooms and two baths before we moved on to the attic. Here the arrangement was curious: the door opened on five shallow steps and a landing, at which point the stairs turned abruptly right to continue up to the attic. At this landing there was another door.

"What's that?" I asked, pointing.

"That's what they called a boxroom," explained Mr. Tuttle.

We went on up the stairs to the attic, where we found two maids' rooms and a lavatory, but I wanted to see the boxroom.

"It's locked," said Mr. Tuttle.

"Just give me the key then," I told him, holding out my hand. "While you and Joe discuss price," I added brightly to make it worth his while, "because we plan a very *large* family. I have to see all the rooms."

As soon as I unlocked and opened the door of the boxroom I *knew* this was where Hannah had been held prisoner. It had no windows; there was just a metal vent high up near the ceiling with a tiny fan set into it. A solitary light bulb hung from the slanted ceiling. The room, roughly twelve by fourteen, was empty except for a rusty iron cot and an old bureau tilted on one leg.

I sat down on the iron cot and looked around me at what Hannah would have seen. A boxroom would have been where they stored trunks in Victorian days; there would have been one or two of those, I guessed, plus the hurdy-gurdy, and perhaps a few other pieces, possibly a rocking horse kept for Robin and Nora. One of the trunks would have been filled with costumes—what made me know this?—for dressing-up fun on a rainy day. But I didn't think it would be a good place in which to be trapped: there would have been no daylight, and the mattress—if it was the same one—was filthy and full of lumps and holes. The room must have been stifling in July, and claustrophobic.

I said softly, "Hannah?" and then, "Hannah Gruble?"

I've never believed in ghosts, although I do believe that we leave some imprint of personality or essence of ourselves behind us. This is my only explanation for what happened to me after I spoke Hannah's name. A feeling of unbelievable tranquillity, almost of communion with someone, flowed through me. It transfixed me until I heard Joe and Mr. Tuttle descending the stairs from the attic.

The sound of their footsteps brought me back to the moment with a start, and I remembered why I was here. Wondering if Hannah might have attempted any other messages, I walked over to the bureau and examined it, but the drawers were empty, except for two dead flies.

Joe and Mr. Tuttle walked in. "It's four o'clock, Amelia. I think we'd better go back to town and talk about the house. Mr. Tuttle feels the owners are ready to come down in price."

We moved out into the hall and I noticed that Bob Tuttle forgot to lock the boxroom. Joe was saying deliberately, "Mr. Tuttle tells me that Dr. Cox is dead, but your mother's old friend Jane Morneau still lives in Anglesworth."

"Wonderful!" I exclaimed—we were turning into a regular vaudeville team, Joe and I. Remarking on the coincidences of life, we left Hannah's house behind us.

Parting with Mr. Tuttle, however, proved less easy. He wanted to give us a good many judicious suggestions about the house, while we in turn wanted to inquire about Hannah's will before the courthouse closed. It made for a tight squeak. It was precisely four fifty when we raced up the stairs of the courthouse again and ran down long hallways to the probate room.

I had the terrible feeling that the clerk would say we needed a court order to see someone's will, but she asked us to write the name on a piece of paper for her, and then presently placed before us a single-page document with a signature at the bottom.

"You just have time to photostat it if you'd like," she said politely. "There's a machine behind you."

"Thank you," I said, incredulous at its being so easy.

We made two copies and hurried out of the building in a stream of departing clerks. We began our reading of the will seated outside on the steps in the fading sunshine.

"Joe, look at the date," I gasped. "July second, 1965, only twenty-three days before she was killed."

"I'm looking," he said grimly.

The single sheet was neatly typed, with the signatures of three witnesses at the bottom. I read:

Let it be known that this is the last will and testament of Hannah Gruble Meerloo, and that being of sound mind and body I, Hannah Gruble Meerloo, appoint as co-executors of my estate my nephew, Robert Gruble, of New York, and my attorney, Garwin Mason, of Anglesworth.

Since the Greenacres Private Psychiatric Hospital has already been endowed by me with a permanent trust fund, and other charities of mine are now self-sustaining, I bequeath to my loyal housekeeper Jane Whitney Morneau the sum of $35,000 and, renouncing all previous wills, ask that the remainder of my estate, once taxes have been removed, be divided equally in three ways: one third of the residual to my niece, Leonora Harrington, of Boston, one third to my nephew, Robert Gruble, of New York, and one third to my protégé, John Tuttle, of Carleton, with the hope that he may see fit to continue contributions to the support of the Jason Meerloo Orphanage in Anglesworth, in which he spent his early years.

Signed on this 2nd day of July 1965,
Hannah Gruble Meerloo

Witnessed by:
Daniel Lipton
Hubert Holton
Leonora Harrington

Joe said, "John Tuttle's the young man who was driving for her."

"Enter chauffeur," I said, nodding. "Enter a witness named Daniel Lipton. Re-enter Hubert Holton."

"And Nora witnessed the will, too," mused Joe.

"Joe, I think we've got to see this man Garwin Mason next, don't you? Hannah's attorney. If he's still alive."

"Let's find out," said Joe.

We drove two blocks to a public phone booth, where I found Garwin Mason's law firm listed in the directory. It was after five o'clock but I telephoned anyway. The secretary said that he'd already left but that I could see him the next morning at half past eight.

I looked up Jane Morneau and found that she lived at 23 Farnsworth Road. I put in a call to her, too, but there was no answer and so Joe and I decided to have dinner.

"AND WHAT do we use for bait for Mr. Mason?" asked Joe. We were in the coffee shop of the Golden Kingfisher Motel, where we had checked in to unit 18. We each had a seafood platter in front of us, a milk shake, and a copy of Hannah's will.

"I think," I said firmly, having already considered this, "that I should visit him alone and tell him I'm writing a biography of Hannah Gruble, author."

Joe grinned. "Your inventiveness astounds me."

"Well," I said, "there's client confidentiality and all that. Joe, this will has to be the paper Hannah was forced to sign before she died, don't you think?"

"The date's wrong," he pointed out. "The will was drawn up the second, and remember Hannah's note? She'd signed whatever it was the night before she was killed, and she was killed the twenty-fifth."

"It could have been typed up the twenty-second or twenty-third of July but dated earlier to avert suspicion."

Joe said patiently, "But Nora's signature is on it and Nora wasn't in Carleton until a few hours before Hannah's death. She'd just come back, remember?"

"Damn," I said, and thought about this. "Then suppose somebody typed up the will on July second, using Hannah's typewriter, persuaded the witnesses to sign it, and sometime after that Hannah was locked into the boxroom until she herself signed it."

I glanced down at the will in front of me. "We have to find out what's different in this will from any others she might have made. I do think it's very odd, her leaving one third of her estate to this John Tuttle, who's not related."

"Okay, so why don't you look in the directory and see if there's still a Jason Meerloo Orphanage?"

"I already did," I told him quietly. "No orphanage. John Tuttle did *not* keep it afloat as she hoped in her will."

Joe looked at me with an odd smile. "But Amelia, aren't you forgetting that if our suppositions are correct, *Hannah didn't write that will?*"

I sat back, neatly floored by this jab. "But that makes it a *very* strange will, Joe. I can't believe Nora's involved. She must have loved her aunt—"

"But her signature's on the will," Joe reminded me.

"I'm betting it was forged or gotten under false pretenses. But if

Nora *was* involved, that makes it even stranger, because she cut herself off from one-third of a lot of money."

"Wait—be patient," said Joe. "Tomorrow we make certain that Hannah's attorney did *not* draw up this will. We verify."

"That word again," I said indignantly, and left him and went to look up Daniel Lipton in the telephone directory. There was a Mrs. Daniel Lipton living at 13½ Pearl Street. I copied the address, stopped at the counter to buy a map of Anglesworth on display there, and went back to the table to tell Joe.

"Okay," he said after a glance at his watch. "I suggest we have a couple of hot fudge sundaes and then go and see if she's related. I'll call my answering service first."

When Joe came back he looked pleased. "Ken says the hearing's been postponed again, so we can relax."

"Beautiful," I said, and felt ten pounds lighter despite the enormous sundae on which I was gorging.

THERE WERE only six houses in Pearl Street, but any differences in their architecture had long ago been erased by apathy: broken windows stuffed with blankets, sagging porches, peeling paint. At number 13½ I noticed a sizable number of empty wine and gin bottles among the refuse.

The bell wasn't working; we knocked and called, and after an interval a woman opened the door and said, "Yeah?"

"Mrs. Lipton?" asked Joe. "Mrs. Daniel Lipton?"

She peered at us suspiciously. Her face was a circle of dessicated flesh with heavy pouches under her eyes and chin. She was wearing a long flowered cotton skirt and layers of sweaters. Her hair was a frizzy blond with gray showing at the roots.

"We're trying to trace a Mr. Daniel Lipton," Joe told her. "Around 1965 he had some connection with Mrs. Hannah Meerloo, and witnessed a will she made in July of that year."

"Danny?" She shrugged. "If you got the price of a bottle, I'll let you in."

Joe took out a five-dollar bill. "Tom?" she called over her shoulder and opened the door wider to let us in.

We walked into a cold hallway and then into a dark living room. The blinds had been drawn and the only light came from the television screen across which a wagon train was traveling. Silhouetted against this ghostly illumination, three men sat stiffly

464

upright. One of them slowly stirred, detached himself, and walked over to Mrs. Lipton. She gave him the five-dollar bill and he glided out of the house.

Mrs. Lipton led us to a couch with broken springs and we sat down. "So?" she said, staring at us.

"You're the wife of the Daniel Lipton, who knew Hannah Meerloo and witnessed her last will in 1965?"

She moved her eyes from us to the wall. "He did yardwork for her sometimes. The big house in Carleton?"

"Yes."

She nodded. "Yep, that's Danny." She sighed and said in a sentimental voice, "He could put it away faster'n anybody I met since."

"Since what?", asked Joe quickly.

"Since he got—" Whatever it was I didn't hear because on the television the Indians were attacking the wagon train.

Joe was sitting closer to her. "You said Danny was killed?" I heard him say. "When?"

"It was 1965," she said. "On Christmas Eve."

The front door opened and Tom glided back into the room carrying a heavy paper bag. Mrs. Lipton sprang to her feet, pulled out one of the bottles, wrung it open, took a long drink, shivered, and handed it to Tom. "Party night." She giggled.

We got up from the couch, too. "Mrs. Lipton," Joe said, and then louder, "Mrs. Lipton—"

She looked at us in surprise. "I got no more to say. Danny's dead, that's for sure, and there's the door." She walked over and held it open for us. We were already on the porch when she shouted after us angrily, "Got his throat slit from ear to ear down by the river, Christmas Eve, that's what, and they never learned who did it or tried very hard neither, the bums."

When we spun around to look at her the door was shut. Christmas Eve, 1965, I thought. Five months after Hannah's death.

We climbed into the van, but Joe made no move to start it. He said grimly, "Amelia—you don't have to go on with this. It happened a long time ago; life has arranged itself around it now."

"I don't think life has arranged itself around this death very happily," I said. "And we're just beginning to get somewhere."

"Yes, but closer to a murderer. A murderer who got away with violence a long time ago, Amelia."

I said, "You're thinking what I am, then? That Daniel Lipton may have been murdered because of something he knew about Hannah's death?"

"And before he could talk," Joe said, starting the van at last and shifting into gear. "After all, he witnessed that will, Amelia, and everything points now to its being a bogus will."

"Still to be verified," I reminded him with a smile, but I considered his words thoughtfully as we left Pearl Street behind. Since morning, when I'd learned that Hannah was H. M. Gruble, all my doubts seemed to have vanished. "I can't back out, Joe," I told him flatly. "Even if you do, I can't now."

He said darkly, "I thought I'd fall in love with some nice wholesome all-American girl whose idea of a good time was doing crossword puzzles and admiring me."

"Isn't life amazing?" I said cheerfully.

Chapter Nine

At twenty-five minutes past eight the next morning I left Joe sitting outside in the van again with *Astronomy for the Layman*, and was shown into the office of Garwin Mason.

Mr. Mason rose to shake hands. He looked far beyond retirement age, eighty at least, but there was nothing frail about him: his face was weather-beaten, and his eyes were an unbleached vivid blue, narrowed now in their appraisal of me. Yet I liked him at once; he was, to use a very old-fashioned word, a gentleman. It was obvious in the soft, courteous voice that suggested I sit down, Miss Jones, and in the courtly manner in which he asked what he could do for me.

"I'm writing a biography of Hannah Gruble Meerloo," I said, "and in my research I've come to the facts of her death." I placed the xeroxed copy of her will on his desk, and added innocently, "This will was, of course, drawn up by you personally?"

He reached for a pair of glasses, put them on, glanced at the will, removed his glasses, and restored his gaze to me. There was an edge to his voice when he said, "No, it was *not*, Miss Jones. I can assure you that no will constructed in my office would read as this one does."

I said with all the ingenuousness I could summon, "You'd written other wills for her, of course."

He gave me a sharp glance. "Yes."

"May I ask why she didn't have you write this one for her, sir? I mean, were you away, perhaps, on"—I took a moment to examine the date, as if I didn't already know it by heart—"July second, 1965?"

"No, I was in my office. Just as I am today. Is this a court of law, Miss Jones?" he inquired with humor.

I looked at him, and I realized Mr. Mason was wary but he was relaxed and waiting. But waiting for what, I wondered.

So I went at once to the point. "Mr. Mason, I realize it's confidential information, but I would like to ask"—I took a deep breath—"how this will differs from Mrs. Meerloo's previous wills."

"Ah . . ." It was like a sigh, and those ancient eyes seemed to go through me. "It *is* confidential information you're asking for." He added, "You are not from these parts, Miss Jones?"

"From Trafton, Pennsylvania."

He nodded. "This is a curious corner of Maine. I have lived here for over fifty years and yet they still say of me that I'm 'from away.' Hannah, too, was from away. We live here surrounded by Liptons, Tuttles, and Pritchetts." He was silent for a moment and then he said, "Her previous wills were similar to each other but not similar to this will of July second, 1965. Over the years that she lived here—first in Anglesworth and then in Carleton—she made half a dozen wills, changing them in only minor ways. In all of them she left a stated amount to her housekeeper, Jane Morneau, and she bequeathed sums to the Greenacres Psychiatric Hospital and to the Jason Meerloo Orphanage. The residual—and we are talking here of perhaps two million dollars after taxes—"

"Two million!" I exclaimed.

"—was to be divided between her nephew, Robin, and her niece, Nora."

"So there was never before any mention of—" I stopped abruptly. "I appreciate your giving me this confidential information, sir."

He bowed courteously, mockingly. "A pity her book is out of print. I've always felt that if the sequel could have been published, it would have firmly established *The Maze in the Heart of the Castle* as the classic it deserves to be."

"Did she ever consider writing a sequel?" I asked.

"I believe she had completed one at the time of her death."

"What?" I gasped. "But what happened to it?"

"I doubt that many people knew of it." He shrugged. "People were accustomed to her scribblings, as she called her writing. I know about it because in her previous will—drawn up two months before this one—she specifically mentioned leaving her niece and nephew the right to apply for copyright renewals on *The Maze in the Heart of the Castle*, and—if it was published—a book entitled *In the Land of the Golden Warriors*. A sequel to the first, she called it."

"And the manuscript was never found? Nobody knew?" And then it hit me. "You say a previous will was drawn up *only two months* before the July second one?"

He nodded, watching me with interest.

"Mr. Mason," I said, "wasn't anyone skeptical—just a little—of this final July will? Didn't it seem strange to someone?"

His smile was approving, like that of an instructor with an apt pupil. "It seemed strange to one person, her nephew, Robin," he said. "Robin insisted on a probate-court hearing."

"A hearing," I repeated, not understanding.

He explained. "A will is filed in probate shortly after the death of the testator. Following this, a legal notice called a citation is issued to all the heirs, listing the terms of the will, and if any heir objects he may ask for a hearing."

"Would records of the hearing be available?" I asked.

"There are always records. I can lend you my copy," he said with his curious little smile, and rang for his secretary. "I couldn't represent Robin because I was named co-executor of the estate, but I followed the hearing closely and took pains to secure a copy for my files. Miss Edmonds," he said when she entered, "will you fetch us the probate hearings on the Hannah Meerloo will—October 1965, I believe."

She was gone and we smiled at each other politely. There were many questions I longed to ask him, but I knew that his courtesy would extend only so far.

A moment later Miss Edmonds was back. Garwin Mason glanced over a two-inch-thick sheaf of printed matter, tucked it into a large envelope, and handed it to me. "Just return this, Miss Jones. It's all I ask."

"I will," I promised and stood up to go. "And thank you."

I had reached the door when he said, "Miss Jones." He was polishing his reading glasses with an immaculate white handkerchief, but now he paused and looked at me, and although his face was stern his eyes were kind. "You are not writing a biography of Hannah Gruble." It was a statement, not a question.

"No, sir."

He nodded. "I am grateful to you, Miss Jones. For years I've lived with the mystery of Hannah Meerloo's last will and I can now exchange that mystery for another: why a young woman has suddenly begun asking the questions about Hannah's will that were never properly answered in 1965."

"Mr. Mason," I said impulsively, "what was she like?"

"Hannah?" His gaze moved to the corner of the room. "I always find it difficult to describe her. I could tell you that she had dark hair, gray eyes, small regular features, nothing distinguishing. I think she would have been called a plain-looking woman. But I will say this," he added with a slight smile. "I have met a great many people in my lifetime and what has impressed me about the majority of them is the smallness of their souls. Pinched, shrunken, undernourished. Hannah Meerloo was—literally—the most beautiful woman I have ever known."

"Beautiful," I whispered, nodding.

"She had an eager, childlike quality which, if I may say so, I see somewhat repeated in yourself. She never lost a sense of wonder; she made one notice things. She was a woman who loved life."

"Thank you, Mr. Mason," I said. "Thank you *very* much."

"AMELIA," Joe said when I joined him in the van, "you look funny again. And what's that enormous envelope you're carrying?"

"A copy of the court hearing that Robin asked for," and I told him breathlessly about the interview with Mr. Mason.

"We've hit pay dirt again." Joe started up the van.

"No, I think we've just entered the maze in the heart of the castle. Joe, where are you taking us?"

"Back to the motel to start reading," he said.

We sat next to each other in unit 18 with doughnuts and coffee on the table beside us. I removed the papers from their envelope and began scanning the first page.

"Well, now," I murmured. "Robin is accusing John Tuttle, boy chauffeur, of exercising undue influence on Hannah. Robin points out that Hannah had drawn up that new will in April, prepared by her attorney, Garwin Mason, but that the will of July second was written without the knowledge of her lawyer, that two of its witnesses are unknown to him, Robin, and that all previous wills made by his aunt were always discussed with him and Nora, and they were sent *copies*."

"Okay, go on."

"That the contents of the July second will were unknown to his cousin Nora when she signed as a witness—hmmm, that's interesting—and that this sudden inclusion of John Tuttle, his aunt's chauffeur—even though his aunt had a very real interest in his career and had financed his college education—has deprived him and his cousin Nora of their rightful legacies."

"The lines are drawn," Joe said, nodding. "The operative word now is 'undue influence.'"

"Oh, boy, here we go," I said, reaching page four. "Hubert Holton testifies, questioned by Robin's lawyer."

Q. Mr. Holton, would you explain, please, how you came to be staying at Mrs. Hannah Meerloo's home during July?

A. Certainly, sir. I was on vacation, touring Maine. Passing through Anglesworth, I thought I'd telephone Jay to say hello. John Tuttle, that is. John was a student of mine—a brilliant student—and I'd become interested in his future, an interest, I might add, that was obviously shared by Mrs. Meerloo, who had seen his potential when he was at the orphanage she founded.

Q. But you had never met Mrs. Hannah Meerloo before?

A. No, sir. I telephoned Jay from Anglesworth on July second. He suggested my coming out to Carleton. I arrived at his apartment over the garage about five o'clock, and we had a drink or two. Before I left for dinner he wanted Mrs. Meerloo to meet me. Mrs. Meerloo insisted that I have dinner there with her and Miss Harrington and Jay—John Tuttle—who apparently dined regularly with them. He was not the usual chauffeur, you see. He drove for her in the summer as a way of repaying her kindness.

Q. Mrs. Meerloo then invited you to remain as a houseguest?

A. It was actually Nora's idea, sir. Nora Harrington. We did have a stimulating evening discussing books and politics—I teach political science—and Nora somewhat impulsively asked her aunt if I couldn't stay the weekend. They had a tennis court, you see. Nora pointed out that with Robin not there she'd need a partner.

Q. But you stayed longer than the weekend, Mr. Holton?

A. Yes. I was there until—until the tragic accident on the twenty-fifth of July. I mentioned leaving, but no one would hear of it, and frankly I was enjoying their company very much.

Q. Mr. Holton, how would you describe John Tuttle's relationship with Mrs. Meerloo?

A. Oh, charming, absolutely charming. He obviously thought the world of Miss Hannah, as he called her.

Q. Would you describe any incident in which, in your estimation, John Tuttle might have exercised undue influence upon Mrs. Meerloo in changing her will to his benefit?

A. I must remind you, sir, that I was asked to sign the will as a witness that very first evening I stayed for dinner. That is to say, I have carefully checked my diary on this matter of dates. But I was after this a houseguest for three weeks—and I frankly cannot imagine on what Mr. Robert Gruble bases this alleged undue influence unless—

Q. Unless what, Mr. Holton?

A. Unless it was the fact that the relationship between Jay Tuttle and Mrs. Meerloo was more like that of mother and son, and some jealousy might have been involved, but that is, of course, only speculation.

Q. Yes, it is, Mr. Holton, and quite unsolicited. The court is interested only in facts, not speculation.

A. Yes, sir. Sorry, sir.

"Ha," intervened Joe, leaning closer to look at the page. "He got that in very smoothly; neat little touch, what? Robin, the displaced son-nephew, jealous of the interloper, charming Jay. Who testifies next?"

"Nora," I said. "Leonora Hannah Harrington of Boston, daughter of Patience Gruble, Hannah's sister."

Q. Now, Miss Harrington. A statement was made by you to the newspapers that you had arrived at your aunt's house only a few hours before her tragic accident on July twenty-fifth. Yet at the inquest it was stated by Mrs. Morneau, your aunt's housekeeper, that you arrived in June, a week early for your usual July visit. You were not with your aunt then for the major part of July?

A. Oh yes, I was there. I joined Aunt Hannah on June twenty-sixth, and was with her until her accident, with the exception of two days, when I drove to my apartment in Boston on July twenty-third, for more clothes. There was talk of going to New York to see Robin in his new play, and I needed city clothes for that. Except we never drove to New York. . . . That awful night happened instead.

"I can't believe it," Joe said, voicing my own thought. "Nora was there all through July, except for two days?"

"She couldn't have been so cruel. Joe, she couldn't have been in on it; there has to be an explanation."

"Like what?" asked Joe.

"They made her a prisoner, too. Or blackmailed her."

Joe took the transcript from me and read aloud.

Q. This will, Miss Harrington. Can you tell us about the circumstances under which it was signed and witnessed?

A. We'd finished dinner and Aunt Hannah asked if Mr. Holton and I would come into her study to witness her signature on a document. We went into the study and there was a typed sheet of paper on her desk. Through the window we could see Danny Lipton mowing the lawn and she called to Jay to ask Mr. Lipton to come inside and be a witness, too. Jay went out and got Danny, and then Jay went off somewhere, and Aunt Hannah explained to the three of us that she'd just written a new will. She wanted me to sign, too, she said, just in case three signatures proved necessary in a home-drawn will.

"Lies, Joe," I said indignantly. "Lies, every word. How did they persuade her to say all this?"

"Hold on," Joe said, "there's more."

Q. But did you not find it odd that Mrs. Meerloo's will had been changed to include John Tuttle as beneficiary?

A. She didn't show me the will, or tell me what was in it. But she was very fond of Jay, and very proud of him. He'd graduated Phi Beta Kappa, and magna cum laude from Union College, and he was doing splendidly in graduate school. I think she looked on him as something of the son she'd never had.

Q. So you feel no bitterness that in this will she reduced your own personal legacy by a third?

A. Well, sir, it was Aunt Hannah's money, and her wish.

Q. Miss Harrington, I would like now to ask you: Did John

Tuttle at any time use undue influence—any persuasion of any kind—on your aunt, to encourage this change in her will?

A. No, sir. Absolutely not.

I sat there digesting the fact that Hannah's niece had been in the house all the time, and therefore must have known what was happening upstairs to her aunt. And in 1965 she had submitted to verifying and even enlarging upon Holton's testimony. By what means had they kept her from going to the police instead?

I said incredulously, "If it weren't for Hannah's note in the hurdy-gurdy, Joe—it all sounds so *plausible*, and yet we know that every word is a lie."

I sat bolt upright as another fact struck me. "Joe, if every word about the signing and witnessing of this will is a lie, then it's possible that Hannah never met Hubert Holton at dinner on July second, *and may never have met Holton at all.*"

Joe whistled. "Not bad, Amelia."

"Wipe it all out, Joe, and Danny Lipton was *not* called in on the spur of the moment. Hannah did *not* invite anyone to her study to witness the signing of a will. And Holton was never invited to stay for the weekend."

"You realize," Joe said grimly, "what that makes of Holton."

I nodded, pleased. "*One of the faceless ones!*"

Joe was silent and then he said softly, "Maybe we should find out what happened to each of these people after they murdered Hannah. Daniel Lipton had his throat cut by persons unknown five months later. Nora's in a psychiatric hospital. . . . I'd like to know what's happened to John Tuttle and Hubert Holton."

"But what about Nora?" I demanded. "Something tragic happened to her back in 1965. That's obvious. But *what?* What did they do to her, what hold did they have over her?"

Joe reached for the phone beside the bed. "There's one person we haven't reached yet and that's Mrs. Morneau."

"Wait. Her testimony comes next," I said, glancing at the records. "And very cautious and wary it sounds, Joe."

Q. Did you know, Mr. Hubert Holton?

A. No, sir. I said before I'd heard the name somewhere, and I've remembered now. When John Tuttle was away at his college he'd write Miss Hannah a letter now and then and she'd mention how taken Jay was with this one professor, Mr. Holton.

Q. Did you have occasion to visit the house after your departure on July first, or to speak with Mrs. Meerloo by telephone perhaps?

A. No, sir. I did call twice, both times on the Fourth of July, just before I left for New Hampshire to visit my friends. I phoned to tell her there'd be fireworks in Anglesworth that night—she always loved fireworks—but there wasn't any answer.

Q. Did you find that unusual?

A. I didn't think about it much, sir. The weather was hot and Miss Nora was a great one for picnics. Mrs. Meerloo always looked forward to July, when Miss Nora and Mr. Robin visited her.

Q. And was it typical of Mrs. Meerloo to invite Mr. Holton to be a houseguest for a month in place of Mr. Robert Gruble?

A. Well, I can't say she'd done anything like that before. She was a—well, a very private person, sir. She wrote her stories, you know, and she—well, meditated is what she called it, something she learned on her travels. She must have thought Mr. Holton would be company for Miss Nora, for tennis and the like, what with Mr. Robin being stuck in New York this year, although Nora usually played tennis with Jay. Mr. Tuttle, that is.

Q. Would you say, Mrs. Morneau, that Mr. John Tuttle ever used any undue influence upon Mrs. Meerloo?

A. Well, it's not the sort of thing I understand, undue influence. But he had the run of the house. He wasn't a real chauffeur, not in the usual way, sir.

Q. Thank you, Mrs. Morneau.

I told Joe, seeing his hand still on the telephone, "You might as well wait for Daniel Lipton's testimony."

"Anything there?"

"Proof that he was in on it, too." I glanced over his testimony. "He says that he was mowing the lawn that evening, was called in to witness a will, and Mrs. Meerloo gave him five dollars for it."

Joe snorted. "And we know that was an outright lie. Danny Lipton perjured himself."

I said, frowning, "I think he did more than perjure himself, Joe. I think he must have been the other faceless one. Hannah wouldn't know him that well, his walk, his gestures. . . . Holton could have done any of the talking."

"Go on," Joe said, watching me. "How do you see it?"

I said, "Everything points to John Tuttle and Hubert Holton

475

having plotted this out together. I think as soon as Mrs. Morneau left on her vacation, Holton moved into the house, and Danny Lipton, too. Just before they arrived, Hannah walked into the boxroom, the door was locked behind her—did you notice the lock is still on the outside of that door, Joe?—and she became a prisoner in her own house. Not on a happy July Fourth picnic, as Mrs. Morneau supposed, but hidden away in a hot little room without food or water." There were tears in my eyes as I pictured it.

"Before you get too carried away," Joe said gently, "grab that phone book. I suggest we telephone every John Tuttle in the book and see if we can zero in on the one who graduated from Union College in the early 1960s. I'll do the calling. I'll say I'm an alumnus. Look up Holton, too, and see if he's around still."

I had already turned to the H's. "No Holtons listed," I told him. I turned to the T's and winced. "Good heavens, there are *dozens* of Tuttles, nearly a whole page of them, and not a John among them. As follows: Jacques Tuttle. Three James Tuttles, Jane Tuttle. Jason Tuttle. Jaspar Tuttle. Jean Tuttle. Jerry Tuttle. Jess Tuttle. Joel Tuttle. Joseph P., Joseph M., and Joseph L. Tuttle. Jules Tuttle." I presented him with the directory to prove it.

He scanned the page unbelievingly. "Incredible—there are always Johns." He picked up the phone and dialed the number I'd scribbled down yesterday. "Let's hope Mrs. Morneau's at home finally. At the least she can tell us where to find Tuttle."

Apparently Mrs. Morneau was at home and while Joe made an appointment for us to see her after lunch—again using a Gruble biography as a cover—I skimmed through the opinion filed by Judge Arthur Pomeroy in December of 1965, *In re* Will of Hannah Gruble Meerloo, to the last paragraph:

> We cannot know what circumstances led Mrs. Meerloo to write a will of her own making on the second of July, 1965, when all previous wills had been drawn by her attorney. But this is her signature, testified to by two experts as well as by those familiar with her signature. The will was also witnessed by three people, among them her niece, Leonora Harrington, a relative of obvious closeness to the legatee. It is a legal will, and must therefore be honored and allowed to pass through probate.

On the bottom of the page someone had written: "Decision made by R. Gruble not to appeal." I wondered why.

I thought, They could never have gotten away with this without Nora's testifying for them.

And this, I realized, was the hell that Nora had faced each morning since July 25, 1965.

Chapter Ten

Mrs. Morneau had said she would see us at one o'clock. It was half past eleven when we finished reading the probate-court records, and we had just decided on an early, leisurely lunch when the telephone rang. Joe picked up the receiver. "Joe Osbourne." He listened and I saw his face tighten. "Ken, I'm way up here in Maine, you know. Couldn't they have decided this earlier? Okay, Ken, I don't know *how* but—right. Okay."

He hung up. "Damn. I've got to be in court at nine tomorrow."

The next forty minutes were spent on the telephone. Blue Harbor Airlines had one seat available on a plane leaving for Boston at four o'clock that would connect with the flight to New York at six, which would connect with a New York flight to Trafton at nine. I would have to drive home alone in the van, Joe reminded me, and he wanted my promise that I would leave for Trafton first thing in the morning, and that after we visited Mrs. Morneau and I'd delivered him to the airport, I would consider all investigations into Hannah's death suspended. Promise?

I promised.

I was to drive no faster than fifty miles per hour on the highway, he said sternly; he would mark my route on the map and I was not to drive too much in one day. It was really very endearing.

By the time the airlines clerk called back to confirm space on all three flights, we just had time to buy two packages of peanut butter crackers in the coffee shop. En route to Mrs. Morneau's we reviewed the questions we wanted to ask.

Number 23 Farnsworth Road was a trim little white Cape Cod house with a picket fence. We rang the bell and the door was opened by Mrs. Morneau. She had a pale, placid face, gray eyes, and iron-gray hair forced into a neat bun at the nape of her neck. Her figure was what would be called full, and so sternly corseted that it thrust out her bosom like a tray.

At sight of us she said, "I didn't expect you to be so young." Her voice held a note of sharpness in it.

477

"Well," I pointed out, smiling. "Hannah Gruble's book was for young people, you know."

We shook hands and followed Mrs. Morneau into her neat, box-like living room. We sat down, Mrs. Morneau very erect, her feet placed primly together on the floor. "Imagine a book being written about her," she said in an awed voice. "After all these years, too."

I brought out my spiral notebook, laid it professionally on my lap, and dug out my pen. "You worked for Mrs. Meerloo a long time, Mrs. Morneau?"

"Oh yes, miss. Since before she came to Carleton. An angel she was to work for, I can tell you."

"You were very fond of her then," Joe said.

"Fond?" Mrs. Morneau approached the word warily. "All I know is, when I heard she'd died, I couldn't stop crying for hours. And though she did leave me a rare amount of money—well, I'd gladly give it all back, every penny of it, to have things as they used to be." Her voice turned nostalgic. "Just her and me living there together and the children coming summers. Her writing in her room or sitting cross-legged on the floor doing her thinking.

"Hearing you was coming," she continued, "I went looking for pictures and I found a few." She handed me two snapshots and a faded cardboard photograph, saying, "I'm sure there are more, but these might look well in your book."

The stiff cardboard photo was Hannah's wedding picture, clear but taken at a distance. I saw a thin, slight girl in a long dress standing next to a tall young man in an army uniform. They looked very young, very happy, and a little frightened. I turned to the second picture, a close-up dated 1950—a small oval face; grave dark eyes with the hint of a smile; odd, slanted black brows. The third snapshot showed a slender figure sitting cross-legged under a tree, reading a book.

"Thank you," I said, grateful that they in no way threatened my own inner picture of Hannah. "By the way," I added as I handed them over to Joe, "we've heard that Mrs. Meerloo completed a new book before her death. Would you know anything about that?"

"Ah, that would be Mr. Mason. He's the one insisted there was a book. Him being co-executor of the estate, and Mr. Robin busy in New York, it was him and me searched the house for it."

"And you found nothing?"

"Not so much as a scrap."

I shook my head sadly. "Well—we have another question. Mrs. Meerloo gave so much money to her projects, but we can't find any record of the Jason Meerloo Orphanage. Is it still in existence?"

A faint shadow crossed her face. "It went bankrupt in 1970, and that would have broken Miss Hannah's heart, I can tell you. The state moved the children to an orphanage in Bangor."

"I understand John Tuttle, the chauffeur, came from the Jason Meerloo Orphanage," I said.

"Yes, he did."

Joe intervened, his voice smooth as silk. "Could you tell us at what point Mrs. Meerloo became interested in John Tuttle—her protégé, as he was called in her will?"

Mrs. Morneau looked startled. "So you've read the will, have you? Well, I had to look up that word protégé in the dictionary. Means 'one under the protection and care of another,' it does."

"That sounds about right," Joe said encouragingly.

"Not to me," she said sternly. "Miss Hannah was not one to treat any of the orphans different from the other. Each summer she hired one of 'em—sometimes two—to do her yardwork. And when they reached high-school age there'd be one of them to stay in the apartment over the garage and drive her car for her. Jay Tuttle was no different, not at first. He started coming to the house when he was twelve or thirteen. First he cut grass for her and burned leaves in the autumn, although I will say they talked about books and plays and things a lot on the porch. He had a good mind, Miss Hannah used to say. When he got his driver's license he began driving for her summers—he was a junior in high school then. After that she paid all his bills at college and saw to it he had the same kind of clothes Mr. Robin wore, and pocket money. In that way he was treated different."

"So he was there at the house," I said, "when Nora and Robin came in the summer?"

"Nora and Robin," she echoed, and sighed. "Seems so natural to hear them names, and so long ago, too. Such a pretty little thing Nora was, a real beauty."

"Which of them chose the words for the gravestone?" I asked.

"Strange words, aren't they? Mr. Robin did that."

I like you for that, Robin, I thought. "Did they get along well together?" I asked. "Nora, Robin, and John Tuttle?"

"Children do," she said vaguely.

"Later as well?" prodded Joe. "When they grew up?"

Mrs. Morneau began to look troubled; she must have imagined herself telling us what foods Hannah liked best, and what colors she loved. The idea of relationships was unsettling to her. Perhaps a lifetime of dusting surfaces was infectious, and surfaces were all that she acknowledged.

"And may we ask your personal impression of John Tuttle?"

Her face stiffened. "You'd do better asking someone else. I thought he took too many liberties, and I told Miss Hannah so."

Mrs. Morneau had not liked John Tuttle. Jealousy? I wondered. The resentment of a native over a local boy being given special status? I remembered to scribble a few doodles to look professional, and then I cleared my throat and began again. "We're delighted to have found you, Mrs. Morneau. You're going to be an invaluable source of material for us, and I'm sure you won't mind us consulting you from time to time—"

"Oh, any time at all," Mrs. Morneau said eagerly.

"But for the moment we hoped—and we wondered if you could help us here—we'd like to talk with people who were with Mrs. Meerloo during the three weeks before her tragic accident."

"Oh," said Mrs. Morneau, and suddenly the expressions that had enlivened her placid face were called back inside of her like children at dusk. She folded her hands in her lap, her lips thinned, and she said, "Well, I don't know about that."

"There was a houseguest, Mr. Hubert Holton."

She nodded. "It comes back to me how excited Jay was about meeting that man. Nora; too."

"Nora? Nora met him before that summer?"

She gestured vaguely. "Visiting Jay at his college, sometimes. Dances, homecoming weekends."

I met Joe's startled glance and looked quickly away. I said, "And John Tuttle was there that July, too."

She said warily, "He was there, yes."

"We've already spoken with Miss Nora," I said.

That surprised her. "Oh? You've been to the hospital?"

"Yes." I shook my head. "It's very sad, isn't it?"

"I can only say," announced Mrs. Morneau, disapproval bringing her back to life, "that it's a blessing Miss Hannah never knew. After she inherited her aunt's money, Miss Nora had a beautiful

480

house built near the water. But when I saw her six months later she looked frightened. Of being alone I think it was, and I should have known then, for she wasn't too steady on her feet. Drinking too much, you see. Frail she was, frail inside, not like Miss Hannah who could stand up to life."

I said firmly, "We've tried to find John Tuttle in the telephone book—"

Mrs. Morneau stared at me in astonishment and then threw back her head and laughed. "Him? You won't find any John Tuttle, miss. Changed his name, he did. Changed a lot of things."

"To what?" I asked, trying not to sound eager.

But Mrs. Morneau's face darkened again. "You'd go to him and say Jane Morneau told you where to find him, I expect. That wouldn't do at all." She looked at her watch. "I think we really have to continue this another time, for I've work to do now." She rose to her feet, and stood over us, massive and implacable.

Rising, I said, "You won't tell us about John Tuttle?"

She shook her head. "I'm sorry, I can't help you."

Joe, rising too, said with a smile, "Surely then you can tell us how to locate Mr. Holton?"

"Any questions about Miss Hannah I'll be glad to answer. Anything else—ask Miss Nora," she said almost maliciously.

I followed her helplessly to the door. "We can appreciate your reticence, of course, but—"

We were at the door now. She said in a harsh voice, "There's no bringing Miss Hannah back. Or Danny Lipton, who had his throat cut, or Miss Nora either, who's as good as gone. The dead are dead. It's the living—" Her voice broke and she added flatly, "I don't want anyone thinking I gossip, miss. It would be best if you send any questions by letter and not come here again." With this she closed the door in our faces.

Joe took my arm, but I shook my head. "Listen," I whispered. From the other side of the door came small sobbing sounds. Abruptly the sounds stopped and footsteps fled down the hall.

We walked slowly and thoughtfully down the walk to the van. I said, "Joe, we frightened Mrs. Morneau."

He nodded. "Badly."

I looked back at the trim white bungalow. "She suspects the truth then, Joe." I drew a deep breath. "And obviously John Tuttle is the threat," I said.

"It's a nice little house," Joe pointed out. "If John Tuttle wrote that last will of Hannah's, he saw to it that Mrs. Morneau didn't get cheated, and I'm sure she got the point. It was a subtle form of payoff. She's safe so long as she doesn't rock the boat."

"But you're implying that she knew from the beginning!"

Joe shook his head. "No, I'm not. All I'm saying is that she knows a good many things about the people involved in this, and I think over the years she reached certain conclusions she's tried to repress. We didn't get much from her, Amelia."

"Yes, we did," I protested. "We learned that John Tuttle has changed his name and that Mrs. Morneau is frightened."

"But we don't know to what name he changed it. Or why Robin never appealed that probate-court verdict."

"Ah, you noticed that, too?" I said, pleased. "That leaves three questions dangling. Who is Tuttle now? Where is Holton? Why was there no appeal?"

"Amelia, is this the right direction for the airport?"

I picked up the map. "It's about nine miles farther. Joe, I have the court records to return to Garwin Mason before I leave, and I'm sure he could tell us about John Tuttle. If," I added cheekily, "I can solicit your permission for one more inquiry?"

"Don't push me, Amelia," he said crossly. "Go to Mason, but if he doesn't want to tell you, put it in the hands of the police."

That sounded reasonable; we were nearing the end, anyway. "Why are you suddenly cross?" I asked.

"Because I don't like leaving you."

I didn't like being left, but I thought it would be a good chance to gain a sense of perspective. Could I still function alone, or was my confidence going to collapse as soon as Joe left?

At the airport we bumped over a dirt road to a parking lot surrounding a wooden building, parked the van, and walked into a room with long wooden benches and a tiny counter. While Joe paid for his ticket I read the same ubiquitous political posters: VOTE FOR SILAS WHITNEY! VOTE FOR ANGUS TUTTLE! A noisy family of six arrived, followed by a well-dressed business man with an attaché case. He wore huge round spectacles and appeared singularly out of place. As if aware of this, he was careful not to look at anyone.

In the interest of seeing Garwin Mason before he left his office, I kissed Joe good-by as soon as he'd bought his ticket, and resolutely walked out. I shed a few tears as I drove away, then reminded myself, You'll be back in Trafton in forty-eight hours, Amelia.

It was at this moment that one of those crazy thunderbolts interrupted my thoughts to prove how industriously the subconscious works over puzzles long after they've been put aside. Now there slipped into my mind four small words from Hannah's letter that I'd never really noticed.

Hannah had written, "Perhaps I could hide these words somewhere in a different place in the hope that one day someone will find them."

In a different place.

Different from *what* place?

I'd read the letter dozens of times, assuming she'd meant the hurdy-gurdy was a different kind of place in which to conceal a note, as indeed it was. Now I found myself looking at these four words from a new angle, and it seemed a very curious phrase to use unless Hannah had *already hidden something else*. It suddenly meant to me, "I will not hide it in the same place."

I put my foot down on the gas pedal and roared into the parking area of the Golden Kingfisher Motel, raced into unit 18, and fumbled through my papers for a copy of Hannah's note. The words were waiting for me; I hadn't imagined them. What might she have wanted to conceal from the faceless ones as soon as she realized that she was a prisoner? Could she possibly have been carrying the manuscript of her second book, *In the Land of the Golden Warriors*, when she entered the boxroom? Could she have hidden it there?

It all depended, of course, on just how she'd been lured there in the first place. It seemed to me quite logical to suppose that she'd gone there of her own volition. Was it where she did some of her writing, or did she use the room for her meditating—for what Mrs. Morneau called her thinking? The latter seemed to hold the more potential: the room was too hot for working, but it was dim and quiet, far removed from the distracting sounds in the house. It would have been a very good place for meditating.

The contrary part of me pointed out that she might have wanted to hide a valuable piece of jewelry. "No," I said, shaking my head, "I know Hannah now and she wouldn't have considered jewelry important enough to hide."

"Well, she certainly wouldn't go around carrying a manuscript with her," retorted that perverse self.

"Why not?" I asked. "She might have carried it the way some women carry around their knitting, or she might have been planning to work on it as soon as she left the boxroom."

"And have hidden it there?" asked that other me.

"Exactly," I said out loud, and felt a lift of excitement. There was the bureau, for one thing, which I'd given only a cursory inspection. There was the filthy old mattress, and there was the floor. I hadn't looked for loose floorboards.

I had convinced myself now that Hannah had hidden the sequel to *The Maze in the Heart of the Castle* in the boxroom. It might no longer be there, but I knew that I couldn't leave for Trafton without looking for it. Even the remotest possibility of finding an unpublished Gruble manuscript left me shaken. If it should be there—Poor Joe, I thought, to miss such a triumph!

I glanced at my watch. It was nearly four o'clock and I'd promised Joe that I'd leave early tomorrow. I didn't think I'd be able to find Bob Tuttle in his real estate office at this hour and, even if I did, how could I possibly explain my interest in taking apart the boxroom? There was only one solution.

Chapter Eleven

I drove first to a hardware store, purchased what I needed, and then headed for Carleton. I passed Pritchett's General Store, veered right onto Tuttle Road, and turned into the driveway of Hannah's house. I drove the van across the grass and around to the rear, out of sight. Climbing out, I grasped the flashlight and the tool kit I'd bought, and prepared to burgle Hannah's house.

I soon discovered certain practical drawbacks to the tidy professional job I'd planned. For one thing the wind was rising in that insistent and menacing way that suggests a brewing thunderstorm, and the back door, which I'd considered removing by unscrewing its hinges, was oversize and built for the ages. Expediency won: I simply broke one of the small panes of glass in the door and reached inside to unbolt the lock. I told myself that if I recovered the sequel to Hannah's book, Bob Tuttle might forgive my larceny, but just in case he didn't see things my way I would mail him ten dollars in the morning.

Once inside the house, the damp cold hit me like a fist. I was surprised at the difference it had made to have companions on my earlier visit. As I left the kitchen and passed the door to the cellar, I could feel prickles run up and down my spine, as if four murderers walked behind me and at any moment I might hear Hannah's scream. The house was not at all quiet, either; every board that I put a foot on sent out a small groan of protest, and the wind outside made whispery moaning sounds. I hurried up the staircase to the second floor and here I found it so dark that I had to turn on my flashlight. Only one thought kept me going: what Joe would say if I found Hannah's manuscript after all these years.

I propped open the door to the attic with a brick, walked up the several steps to the boxroom, which Bob Tuttle had left unlocked after my first visit, and went in. I closed the door behind me to shut out the darkness and the sounds of wind.

Hannah, I thought, I've come back.

It was dim and silent in there. With the screwdriver I'd brought I began to remove the rear panel of the bureau. This didn't take long, because the back had been made of cheap wood that started splintering before I'd removed two of its screws. I felt a little foolish when it was done: the bureau was quite empty.

Carrying the flashlight with me, I went down on my hands and knees and examined the wide oak floorboards. I couldn't find a squeaky board or a telltale scratch, so I gave up on the floor and turned my attention to the bed. I ran my hands over the mattress: there were holes, bulges, and a complete redistribution of whatever cheap mattresses are stuffed with. Suddenly, as I probed a particularly devilish hole in the mattress, my fingers encountered resistance down near the foot. I thought, It has to be, dear God, please let it be . . . My suspense was so unbearable that I gave up my polite tuggings and feverishly ripped the mattress.

And there it was: perhaps two hundred sheets of white paper tightly rolled up and bound by string. I tore off the string, unrolled the pages, and saw neatly typed on the first sheet: *In the Land of the Golden Warriors,* by H. M. Gruble.

I had found Hannah's sequel.

I sank down on the remains of the mattress and began to read eagerly. "One morning in the country of Galt, when the grass was silver with dew and the primroses scarlet in the meadows . . ."

At that moment I heard the lock on the door to the boxroom

485

snap with a strange *ping* sound, and as I looked up in astonishment a floorboard creaked on the landing and I heard the door to the attic steps closing. Someone was in the house with me.

It took a moment to apply intelligence to this improbable discovery. I had entered an empty house; no one had known I was coming here. My mind told me it was inconceivable that I was not alone. My senses knew better: my heart was thudding and my hands were shaking. I laid aside Hannah's manuscript, tiptoed to the door, and gently tugged at the knob. It resisted and I pulled harder—and now there was no doubt about it, I was locked inside. I put my head against the door and listened. A faint sound reached my ears; a crackling noise that I couldn't quite identify, as if someone were crumpling up very stiff paper, and then I heard a floorboard crack some distance away, as of someone leaving. My mind told me that I should call out; it was probably a caretaker or the real estate agent checking the house, but my senses told me to be quiet and think, because I was in grave danger.

I am not proud of the several minutes that followed. I paced, wept, and apologized profusely to Joe, who must have guessed I might do something irrational like this. It did not escape me that my mother had died in an attic and now, irony of ironies, I was to die in an attic, too, and in exactly the room where Hannah . . .

But Hannah hadn't died here, I remembered. Nor had she, I realized, suddenly galvanized by the thought, possessed a tool kit for breaking and entering.

This punctured my spasm of self-pity. I crept to the door and listened again to see whether anyone was waiting to learn what I'd do. This time there was only silence. Pulling the bureau over to the door, I climbed on top of it, carrying screwdriver and hammer, and looked over the possibilities. I found the top hinge of the door and applied my screwdriver to its screws, but they'd been painted over so many times that the tool found no leverage. I hammered the blade of the screwdriver into the dry wood, prized up one corner of the hinge, and at last saw it pull loose from the wall. As the door shuddered from the loss of the hinge I smelled smoke. My hands began to shake again.

It was, of course, a very shrewd maneuver to set Hannah's house on fire; there had always been the possibility that the real estate agent would find me before I died of thirst, and whoever had locked me into the boxroom wanted me dead.

The smoke, I saw, was seeping lazily in under the door now. I realized that this was the crackling sound I'd heard earlier, the kindling of a fire. A very thorough killer, I thought, enraged by his ruthlessness. It seemed a miracle to me now that I'd only broken a windowpane to get into the house; if he'd realized I had a tool kit, he would never have gone off and left me.

I tore off the scarf around my throat, tied it over my nose and mouth, and went to work with a fury on the remaining hinge. When I freed it, the door sagged open, then nearly fell on top of me as it tore away the lock as well. The landing was thick with smoke. Choking and gagging, I grabbed Hannah's manuscript and my purse, went down the steps to the attic door, and pushed it open. Here I nearly fell over the pile of flaming rags on the threshold. Nothing beyond it appeared to be burning, but the stench of gasoline and smoke set me coughing wildly. I made one leap through the fire and raced for the stairs.

I had taken only two steps down when I heard the crackling noises below, and saw an astonishing brilliance illuminating the walls of the living room. I turned back and raced through the second-story hall until I found a bedroom overlooking the sun porch. I wrenched open a window, climbed over the sill, and jumped down to the porch roof. I then crept to the farthest corner of the roof and jumped again, landing in a bush and rolling over once. I picked myself up and ran around the corner of the house.

My van was gone.

As I stood staring blankly at the space where I had parked the van with its ignition locked, a small explosion inside the house— no more than a muffled *blop*—reminded me that at any minute a gas leak could blow up the house; I turned and ran. I had reached the intersection when I heard the scream of the town's fire alarm.

The thunderstorm struck before I had walked a mile, and I had five more miles to go. It didn't occur to me to ask for help or call a taxi. Whoever had tried to kill me must have followed me to Hannah's house in a car. He had taken my van to confuse both firemen and police, but eventually he would have to come back to retrieve his car from whatever hiding place he'd found, and I didn't intend him to see me, still alive, limping along the highway. I walked at the very edge of the road, and ducked behind a tree whenever I heard a car approaching.

I had been drenched a few seconds after the rain began, but

worse, I had twisted my ankle when I jumped from the porch roof and now it began to throb painfully. Nursing it as well as I could, it took me almost two hours to limp to the motel, and it was nearly dark when I reached it. My van was parked precisely in front of my unit. I had planned a hot bath and dinner, but finding the van at the motel, in exactly the right place, pushed me beyond reason. I unlocked the back, made certain no one was hiding inside, climbed into the front seat and drove away. I was leaving behind my suitcase with my clothes in it; I was wet and cold, and my ankle was throbbing, but at least I was still alive.

I stopped at a gas station five miles out of Anglesworth, and while the tank was being filled, I found a sweater and some jeans in the back of the van; I went into the ladies' room, took off my dripping corduroy suit, and changed into the dry, clean clothes. By the time I'd driven fifteen more miles I felt a little safer but utterly wrung out. I stopped at a motel called the Bide-a-Wee that had a restaurant, and after forcing myself to eat a large dinner, I rented a room, and fell into an exhausted sleep.

When I woke up, it was midnight and the rain had stopped. For some reason I was now able to look sanely at what had happened to me during the past few hours. There was no getting around the fact: Joe and I had come to Maine to look for a murderer, and it was just possible that we had flushed him out. Certainly whoever had followed me into the house had murder on his mind. The thought brought a gravelike chill. I resumed my reading of *In the Land of the Golden Warriors*.

The story was startling, to say the least. In the book Colin makes another journey, this time to a country far away, where the people are said to be wise, their strength great, and their wealth so bountiful that their helmets are covered with gold and shine like the sun: the Land of the Golden Warriors. Along the way Colin collects three young people scarcely out of their teens. Their names are Rolphe, Jaspar, and Sara, and this is where I began reading with fascination and then horror.

Rolphe was thin and serious, with "rusty hair like a squirrel." Jaspar was at first glance the heroic figure of the three, a handsome lad, and strong, but ever so subtly it emerged that Jaspar was interested in accompanying Colin to the Land of the Golden Warriors only to steal the gold and bring it back.

And Sara . . . Sara was beautiful and a delight to Colin, but always her eyes were fixed upon Jaspar. She followed him everywhere, trying every means to gain his approval. When they met a witch in a forest, Colin overheard Sara beg for a spell to make Jaspar love her. "Only if you sell me your soul," the witch told her. Before Colin could stop her, the transaction had taken place: Sara had sold the witch her soul in return for a spell that rendered her inseparable from Jaspar.

The ending was poignant: they had many adventures in the Land of the Golden Warriors, but when the time came to leave, a greedy Jaspar was discovered with gold in his travel bags and he was banished to a prison in that country. Because of the witch's spell Sara was doomed to sit outside the prison, perhaps for an eternity, a captive herself. Only Rolphe rode off with Colin.

I walked into the bathroom and ran a steaming hot tub. The book was a revelation. If this was Nora when she was young, if this was what Hannah had seen, had she looked ahead to where such obsession could take Nora, and written of it to warn her? Warn her, too, that the boy she loved was equally obsessed, but with gold?

I had tried so hard to be kind as I struggled to explain Nora's presence in the house while Hannah was being killed, but she had been an accomplice from the beginning, I knew that now. She must have loved John Tuttle with a passion so complete, so blinding, that everyone else had stopped existing for her. Tuttle had totally possessed her.

The horror of it rocked me, and I wondered why Jay Tuttle hadn't married Nora once she was rich. I thought of her at Greenacres, I remembered her ravaged face, and I said aloud, fiercely, "Oh Nora, why couldn't you have gotten angry just once at what was being done to you?" As I was angry now at whoever had tried to kill me in the boxroom.

I climbed out of the tub, dressed, and tied up Hannah's two hundred pages of story. I knew that of the cozy foursome who had killed Hannah, two were now accounted for but two were distressingly not: John Tuttle and Hubert Holton. I had to assume that it was one of them who had tried to kill me, except that I couldn't puzzle out how they'd learned about Joe and me. Unless Garwin Mason had told one of them. Or Mrs. Morneau.

Mrs. Morneau seemed the more likely candidate except for one important detail: Joe and I had left her house at half past two that afternoon and we had driven straight to the airport without stopping at our motel. Considering this, how could I explain the van being returned to the Golden Kingfisher Motel and parked precisely under my unit? It implied an intelligence that chilled me. What I had to do now was get back to Trafton, and to Joe. I also had to find John Tuttle, but under no circumstances was I going to return to Anglesworth and ask Garwin Mason where he was.

"Ask Miss Nora," Mrs Morneau had said.

Very well, I decided. Greenacres was a safe one hundred miles away from Anglesworth on my route back to Trafton. I was fairly sure that Nora would know about Tuttle. I had a hunch that he might be the mysterious friend of the family who paid her bills.

I had driven ten miles before I realized there was one other person who could have betrayed us to a murderer, and that was Mrs. Daniel Lipton, if she had run out of drinking money again.

Chapter Twelve

At half past three I parked in a rest stop beside the highway, locked myself into the back, crawled into my sleeping bag, and slept until dawn filtered through the portholes. After that I drove on to Portland and found an all-night diner, where I ate breakfast elbow to elbow with truck drivers and night-shift workers. At half past eight I visited Western Union to send Joe a telegram. I wanted to write, "I love you, I miss you, I'm scared, but I've got to handle this alone so that I know that I can." The telegram I finally sent was: RETURNING HOME, MAY STOP IN NEW YORK TO SEE ROBIN, REACH TRAFTON LATE TOMORROW AFTERNOON LOVE AMELIA. I would have preferred to telephone him, but I was afraid I might say too much and alarm him. The thought that Joe might have telephoned the Golden Kingfisher Motel to tell me he'd safely reached Trafton simply never crossed my mind—a symptom, I think, of how unaccustomed I was to being tenderly regarded.

In the meantime, at some point during the night, I had decided I must deliver Hannah's manuscript to Robin because it belonged to Hannah's heirs, and Robin was the only one to whom I could entrust it. I was also hoping that I might find a tactful way to ask him why he had never appealed that probate-court decision.

But first there was Nora to see before I turned this search over to the police, this Nora who had given everything, including her integrity, to a man who had abandoned her. *Why hadn't Tuttle married her?* Nora was beautiful, and heaven only knows she'd been devoted. After the murder she was also rich and, as an accomplice, dangerous to him as well. By every law of logic he should have married her, if only to make sure she would never testify against him, but he hadn't. Why? Tuttle had gone to enormous lengths to change Hannah's will before she was murdered, but if he'd simply killed her and then married Nora without that bogus will, he would have married a woman with an inheritance of a million dollars. It implied that Jay Tuttle had wanted seven hundred thousand dollars, but not Nora.

But if this were so, there was another question. Lipton had been murdered because he was an accomplice. Nora, who was more involved and more dangerous, had been allowed to survive. Why?

By half past nine I was circling Greenacres, bumping over the woods roads that surrounded it and keeping my eyes on the rear lawn. I had remembered the nurse saying that Nora would be all right after we left her, and by the next morning would be sitting in the sun in the back with the rest of the patients. By ten o'clock there were a number of people sitting in chairs in the sun, distributed like dolls, each very carefully apart from the others, with a nurse in uniform reading quietly on the rear porch. I parked, and finally saw Nora, off to one side, in a white chair, staring into nothingness; the waste of it struck me as appalling.

I slipped through the hedge and walked across the soft carpet of lawn. No heads turned to watch me. I reached Nora and knelt beside her chair. "Miss Harrington," I said.

She was wearing expensive pale green slacks and a matching blouse that hung loose on her. She wrenched her gaze from some unfathomable dream and frowned at me. "Yes?" she said dully.

"Miss Harrington, where can I find John Tuttle?"

This startled her out of her apathy. "He comes here," she faltered. "Once a month, I think. He comes to see me."

"I'd like to know how to reach him," I said gently.

She peered closer at me. "I remember you," she said suddenly. "You came about the hurdy-gurdy."

"Yes, and now I've come to ask you, please, how to locate Jay Tuttle."

"Dear Jay," she murmured. "But he doesn't have anything to do with hurdy-gurdies. It was Robin and I who played with it."

492

"Yes, and you kept it awhile, and then Robin bought it at the auction and kept it awhile, too."

She nodded. "We took turns choosing things. And that's what I wanted most of all. It was in the boxroom and I chose it." And then she repeated, "In the boxroom . . ." She looked at me. "The hurdy-gurdy was in the boxroom," she whispered, and her eyes grew wider and wider as horror and intelligence filled them. "In the same room as . . ." One hand flew to her mouth. "*Why are you here? Why are you asking me these questions?*"

I said, "Miss Harrington—" But I was too late; she flung back her head and began screaming.

The young nurse reached her first. She gave me a mute, reproachful glance as she leaned over Nora, and then I saw Nurse Dawes running across the lawn to us. "You again!" she shouted. "Out. I'll call the police if you come again. You've no right to sneak in here and harass a patient. *What have you done to her?*"

"Nothing. I'm going now," I said angrily above Nora's screams. Heads had turned dully toward us; my eyes held a picture of green lawn and Dr. Ffolks racing toward us in his white jacket as Nora's screams grew more hysterical. Nurse Dawes was rolling up Nora's sleeve for still another injection to bring her peace.

"I won't bother you again," I said coldly, and I walked back to the van. When I turned, they were all clustered around Nora, whose screams had turned into sobs.

I AM NOT one for marathon driving. I stayed the night in a motel near Westport, Connecticut, and from there I telephoned Robin in New York City. I explained that I was on my way home from Maine, where I'd been tracing the hurdy-gurdy, and could I see him for a few minutes the next day?

He said politely that he would be at home during the morning. I wrote down his directions on how to approach the city by car, feeling cowardly about all those expressways. I think it's a fear in me of getting lost; when a person has felt basically lost for half of her life it is not a situation to be courted.

It was thus with a sense of astonishment and triumph that I pulled up in front of his building on East Ninth Street at eleven the next morning. It was a sultry day, with the sun hidden behind clouds, and the humidity oppressive; I was still wearing blue jeans and sweater, so I noticed. I was also nervous about telling

Robin how I'd found Hannah's manuscript in an old mattress.

He must have been watching for me, because no sooner had I backed into a parking space than he came out of the door and waved. "Good morning," he said. Again he gave the illusion of great youth until the light picked out the lines in his face.

As we began the climb to apartment 12, I could see that he was puzzled by my being there, and too polite to say so. "So you actually went to Maine and visited my cousin," he said.

"Yes," I said, stopping to catch my breath on the third landing. I wanted to ask him if he'd gotten the part he auditioned for on the day I first met him, but I thought it better not to. There was one more landing before he unlocked a door with three locks.

"I've put together some iced tea and peppermint for us," he said. "It's a warm day. I hope my directions worked. No detours?"

"They were perfect," I told him, looking around. It was a one-room apartment, but it was full of light. There was a shabby kitchenette on my right, but the other end was very different: the white walls held a line of well-framed theatrical photographs over the low couch; there was a low square table with one flower in a vase, three square cushions on the floor, and a wall of bookcases. I walked over and saw that one shelf was filled with books on Zen. "I see you're interested in Zen," I said.

"An aunt of mine was," he said almost curtly, dropping ice cubes into two tall glasses. "Shall we sit here?" He carried the glasses to the shabby chrome and plastic dining table.

"Your aunt Hannah Gruble," I said deliberately, "who wrote *The Maze in the Heart of the Castle*."

He stopped short, the glasses still in his hand. He said quietly, "I think you'd better tell me what this is all about. It was a hurdy-gurdy you were tracing last week. Or so you said."

"It *was* a hurdy-gurdy," I told him, "but I was tracing it because of a note I found inside it, a note signed with the name Hannah. No last name."

He looked baffled. "May I ask what on earth the note said to inspire such curiosity on your part?"

I hesitated, wanting to ease into this gently. "It suggested that an accident was being arranged for her, and that she was going to die soon."

"But that's preposterous," he said. "It's absolutely ridic—" He bit off his words, abruptly turned and walked to the window.

There was a long silence; then he turned to face me again. "I'm sorry. That was a stupid thing to say."

"Because it doesn't entirely surprise you?"

He returned to the table. "Shall we sit down?" he said wryly. "I take it that you've been doing a bit of research into my family."

I nodded. "You're Robin Gruble. And your cousin is Nora. The names were in the note." I began digging in my purse for Hannah's note. "My friend Joe Osbourne was in Maine with me until he had to fly home. We visited Nora, and your aunt's house in Carleton, her attorney, Garwin Mason, and her housekeeper, Mrs. Morneau."

"All those people?" He looked startled. "I've never cared to go back, you know."

I said, "Mr. Lamandale, could I ask you why you went to all the trouble and expense of a probate-court hearing on your aunt's will and then didn't appeal the verdict? Was it because of Nora?"

He whistled soundlessly through his teeth. "You really go for the jugular, don't you?"

"Here's a copy of the note." I handed it across to him.

As soon as Robin saw the handwriting he looked shaken. "Oh my God," he whispered, and when he'd finished reading it he carefully placed it on the table, his face white. "This was inside the hurdy-gurdy?"

I nodded and explained how I had found it. Then I handed him the manuscript. "There's this, too," I said gently. "In exchange for information I'd like very much to have."

"Hannah's *book*." He stared at it incredulously. "Do you mind if I have a drink of something stronger? You're throwing shock after shock at me. I've only one shot of brandy left or I'd—"

"Go right ahead," I urged. "I think you need it."

He reached into a cupboard and emptied a bottle of brandy into a shot glass. He put the glass on the table and sat down. "You've brought back a very old nightmare," he said slowly. "But I can at the very least answer your questions. I owe you that if only for the miracle of your finding Hannah's manuscript."

"You knew of its existence?"

"She told me about it when I visited her the Easter before her death. She said once it was typed up she'd xerox a copy and send it to me." He hesitated. "I think you asked about the will."

"Yes," I said, watching him.

"I never quite believed in it, no. And her death happened so *very* soon afterward. . . ."

He picked up the shot glass, tossed its contents down his throat, and made a face. "But everywhere I turned," he said, lifting his eyes to meet mine, "there was Nora."

I nodded. "And everywhere *we* turned there was Nora. Is that why you didn't appeal the verdict?"

"Of course," he said simply. "Garwin Mason warned me that accusing Jay Tuttle of undue influence would fail—had to fail—because I wasn't prepared to go far enough. Do you know what the legal definition of undue influence is in Maine?"

I shook my head.

Closing his eyes he recited, "'Amounting to moral coercion, destroying free agency, so that the testator was constrained to do that which was not his actual will but against it.'" He opened his eyes. "How could I accuse Nora of coercion? I went ahead with the hearing because I thought some piece of testimony might explain away my uneasiness, but it only increased the suspicion that pursuing the matter further could destroy Nora."

I said without thinking, "It destroyed her anyway."

He sighed. "How was one to know? You can't possibly realize how it was with us, or what Nora was like when we were growing up together. We were like brother and sister each summer, living in a magic world that Aunt Hannah created for us. There were picnics, treasure hunts, acting out plays on the sun porch, long evenings reading aloud to each other in front of the fire. Absurd games. A trip to the river to swim every sunny afternoon, and always Aunt Hannah's Tibetan parasol . . ."

"It sounds lovely," I said with a catch in my voice.

"But afterward"—his voice tightened—"Nora would go home to a cold father and an impossible stepmother, and I would go back to my father, who, following my mother's death, packed me off to private schools or camps as hastily as possible. Which I've no doubt that Aunt Hannah paid for. During those dismal months of reality we exchanged letters: Aunt Hannah's tranquil and supportive, Nora's desperate, and mine lonely.

"We were, you see, very close," he concluded. And then he added, "At least until Nora fell in love."

Ah, yes, I thought, now we come to it, and I could feel my pulses quickening. "With Jay Tuttle."

496

"You guessed, then?"

I said, "I have the advantage of you; I read your aunt's manuscript last night. You'll understand what I mean when you've read it, too. Until then I'd hoped she was blackmailed."

His smile was bleak. "I wonder if one can exclude blackmail in an unholy kind of love like Nora's." He shook his head. "It must always have been there, but I never saw. Hannah did, because I remember one day when Nora was about eleven, we were down by the river and I saw Aunt Hannah watching her with a sad expression. I asked her what was wrong and she said, 'Robin, I want you to promise to be very patient with Nora, and very wise. There's an emptiness inside of her, a desperate need to be loved, and there's nothing you or I can do but try and protect her.' A few years later those words came back to haunt me. From the moment that Nora met Jay—she was fourteen, I think—no one else existed for her. She dumped everything she was or could be into his lap."

"Compulsion?"

"Compulsion, obsession, emotional deprivation." He shrugged. "She was so lovely, like a fairy-tale princess. I have snapshots somewhere. I'll show you." He got up and began rummaging in a desk drawer. "She could have had anyone, but Jay arrived first and that was that."

"Did he seem to care for her, too?"

"It was always difficult to know what Jay was thinking or feeling, he was always so damned charming." He came back with a large, bulging envelope. "Certainly he was very attentive the last time I saw them together. At Easter, that was, when Hannah told me—in confidence—about her new book. Several weeks after that Nora phoned me in New York one night, terribly excited, to say that she and Jay were going to be married in the fall."

"Married," I repeated, calculating dates very cynically. In the fall . . . after she had lent her help to a murder.

"Which led," he added bitterly, "to my final rationalization: that Hannah *could* have changed her will on impulse if she felt that it would make Jay and Nora 'equal' enough to marry. The only other possibility was too god-awful to contemplate: that Nora had been unstable enough to—to—" He shivered. "She adored Hannah."

"Do you know why Nora and Jay never married?"

"I never asked," he said. "I remained stubbornly in New York, sinking my inheritance into plays that only proved what poor judgment I had, and nursing a dazzling career that shot down as fast as it had shot up. I buried my nagging little doubts about Nora." He looked at me steadily and took a deep breath. "All right, what do you believe happened?"

And so I told him. His aunt a captive in the boxroom, where I'd found her manuscript. The signing of the will at last, and then her being taken out of the boxroom and led downstairs.

"God," said Robin, going white again. "And then?"

"It's only a theory, but I think she must have been blindfolded. They confused her sense of direction, hurried her along the hall, with the cellar door ahead wide open—and when she reached the threshold of the doorway they pushed her. It was the only way to do it—by trickery—that would leave no marks."

"Who?" demanded Robin.

"John Tuttle and Holton . . . I think with the help of Daniel Lipton, whose throat was cut five months later."

"You're leaving out Nora, aren't you?"

"It's possible that Nora tried to break away, that she couldn't face what was happening. She left for those two days, you know."

"Kind of you," he said with a twisted smile, "but she came back. How was she when you saw her at the hospital?"

I thought about this. "Like someone who had died a long time ago, leaving only a shell behind."

"I wish I could hate her," he said. He sorted through a few snapshots and handed one to me. "Here's the Nora I knew. And loved."

She was sitting in a hammock, probably no older than fourteen, wearing grubby pants and a torn shirt that somehow made her beauty all the more potent. I felt a pang of envy—that long blond hair, the eager, radiant face, the flawless features. She was lovelier than anyone I'd ever seen. "Who's the boy behind her?" I asked. "It's not you, yet he looks so familiar to me."

Robin leaned over and looked. "Oh. That's Jay Tuttle."

"We have yet to find him," I told Robin. "I don't suppose you've kept track of him at all, have you?"

He looked at me strangely. "You mean you don't know?"

"Nora wouldn't tell me yesterday, and Mrs. Morneau seemed too frightened to tell. She said he'd changed his name, and a good many other things, too."

Robin's laugh was harsh. "Morney was never one to go against

498

the establishment, no." He walked over to his bookcase and baffled me by returning with a recent copy of *Newsweek* magazine. "Here." He turned the pages. "Under New Crop of Candidates. They're arranged according to states. Look under Maine."

But of course as soon as he spoke the word candidate, the truth struck me. Nevertheless I leaned over the page and searched for the pictures of the two men who were running in Maine for the U.S. Senate: Angus Tuttle and Silas Whitney.

"Morney was misleading you," Robin said. "Jay changed only his first name, making it Angus. The plainness of his name always irritated him but, believe me, he would *never* consider changing the Tuttle. It brought him too many votes in Maine."

He pointed at the toothpaste-ad smile that had bedecked the telephone poles, the restaurant mirrors, the store windows. "There's your John Tuttle, and Holton is his aide."

I said stupidly, "There are twelve teeth in that smile," but my stomach had tightened. What have I gotten us into? I was thinking. No one on earth is going to believe this man is a murderer.

Chapter Thirteen

It was raining when I left New York, a silvery rain that was already cooling the air. I had telephoned Joe from Robin's apartment to tell him about Tuttle, but there had been no answer; all I could think about now was getting back to Trafton and seeing him.

It was a shock to realize that I'd never given a thought to what Tuttle might have become. I had assumed he would be living defensively, as I would, trembling at the sight of every policeman, with an occasional nightmare from which he awoke drenched with sweat. Now I saw how unimaginative I'd been.

A murderer, I realized, must first of all have a great and consuming ego. He would see other people as satellites to feed and nourish him, not as human beings like himself. He would be cleverer, more resourceful, realistic and intelligent, and after he had successfully murdered he would think of himself as God. He wouldn't tremble at the sight of a policeman, he would smile, his secret glowing inside of him, his superiority reinforced.

As to what to do about Tuttle, Joe would know, as Robin had not. "I'm an actor," Robin had explained. "With Hannah's manuscript I'm on familiar ground. I know her agent. All this I can handle, it's part of my scene. Murder, no."

It was just six o'clock when I entered Trafton. I drove down Fleet Street and slid the van into a parking slot in front of Joe's office. Then I raced upstairs to his door. The first thing I saw was my telegram lying on the floor mat. Unopened.

This was jarring. I'd sent the telegram yesterday morning, on Wednesday, and now it was early Thursday evening—thirty-four hours later. I banged on the door, because there was always a possibility that Joe's phone had been out of order for days and the telegram had just been delivered, but I was only playing for time while my heart adjusted to disappointment. I'd expected to be crushed savagely in a passionate embrace and told I'd been missed. All right, I thought grimly, this is the way life is, Amelia.

I climbed back into the van and headed north to my own block of Fleet Street. I was suddenly anxious to see my shop. It would have closed at six, but I could telephone Mr. Georgerakis and I was sure he would have a warm welcome for me.

I parked the van in the alley and unlocked the door of the shop. It looked cheerful and tidy. I looked around and noted that two clocks and quite a few pieces of the willowware had been sold. To round out this satisfying moment, someone knocked on the shop door and my heart lifted as I realized that it could only be Joe. I eagerly opened the door. It wasn't Joe. It was a well-dressed, gray-haired man carrying an attaché case.

"I *am* sorry," he said, noticing my disappointment, "but I was to pick up a case of willowware. Perhaps the gentleman told you, the one who was in the shop this afternoon."

"He didn't tell me. A whole case?" I repeated.

"Place settings for eight."

This was very nice indeed. Most people in my neighborhood buy a dish or two at a time. "Come in, by all means," I told him, opening the door wider.

He walked inside. I knew I'd seen him before and I wondered if he worked in the neighborhood. The most conspicuous features about him were his round, steel-rimmed glasses and his clothes, which were conservative and well cut. Otherwise he was literally colorless, with parchment-pale skin, thin lips, and a short, fleshy nose. But somewhere I'd seen him before. "I'll be only a minute," I told him. "I'll just open up the case and check for breakage."

500

I reached for the stubby penknife hanging from its hook, hauled the case out from under the rear shelves, and knelt beside it. As I slit open the top of the carton I suddenly realized that I associated that face—those large round glasses and the attaché case—with a background of wooden benches.

I bent over the dishes, my fingers exploring the china. Where had I encountered wooden benches lately? It was with Joe.

I picked up the case and half turned to look at the man again. He didn't see me. He had quietly walked over to the door, where he was clearly outlined against the white shade that I pull down every evening, with CLOSED printed on the street side. Now I saw him reach out and touch the lock, and as I heard it snap—with that crazy *ping* sound they make—I caught my breath. There had been wooden benches at the Blue Harbor airport in Maine, and he'd followed us into the waiting room looking conspicuously out of place with his attaché case, conservative business suit, and large steel-rimmed glasses. I'd watched him with amusement and after that, I remembered, I'd kissed Joe good-by, driven back to the motel and then to Hannah's house and the boxroom, where once before I'd also heard a lock snap unexpectedly.

I didn't hang up the penknife on its hook; I slipped it instead into my pocket.

"Amelia," I told myself sharply, "don't panic. He wouldn't dare try anything here. Surely not on a busy street. . . ."

"Oh no?" sneered a part of my mind. "The two of you are quite alone and no one in Trafton knows you're back. The telephone," I thought. "Somehow I've got to get to the telephone."

I pretended that I'd neither seen nor heard him lock the door. I strolled toward the counter and the telephone behind it with a bright false smile, carrying the carton of dishes in front of me like a shield. As I neared the counter, I saw his attaché case lying there, and I saw the name stamped on it in gold: H. Holton.

Hubert Holton. I had a nearly overwhelming urge to scream, but I shoved my hysteria deep inside me. I said calmly, "I believe Mr. Georgerakis still has these dishes on sale at twenty percent off. I'll just give him a ring and ask—"

"No," he said, equally calm, "I've no time for that."

I threw the box of dishes at him across the six or seven feet that separated us. He ducked and the case hit the floor with a thud and a crash of broken china. Before I could reach the telephone, he picked up the long scissors lying across the dry goods and cut the telephone wire. Following this, he brought a small, businesslike gun out of his pocket and leveled it at me.

"All right," he said evenly, "how did you know?"

"I noticed you in Maine, at the Blue Harbor airport. You're Hubert Holton."

He nodded. "You're a troublemaker," he pointed out in his soft, precise voice, "and I don't appreciate troublemakers."

"No," I said, watching him, "two murders *can* be embarrassing." I shouldn't have said that, of course, because until that moment I don't suppose he was aware of how much I knew.

He blinked at that, and his voice sharpened. "What led you to Anglesworth? So far as I can discover you never knew Hannah Meerloo, or Jay, or Nora."

I countered, "First tell me how you heard about me."

He shrugged. "Mrs. Lipton phoned me—I was in Augusta—and told me that you and a young man, driving a very distinctive van, had visited her to ask about Danny's witnessing Mrs. Meerloo's will in 1965. She thought there might be a few dollars in it for her. I thought it worth attending to personally, and with not many motels open yet I soon found your van. Of course the name of your shop here was on the side of the van. I followed you to Mrs. Morneau's house and then to the airport, and then—" He stopped and added harshly, "And Jay had a hysterical phone call yesterday from Nora telling him about your visit."

"And telling you that I'd survived. You left out your attempt to kill me in Carleton, Mr. Holton."

"So I did," he said smoothly. "Now I'd like to hear what took you to Maine in the first place."

I shook my head. "I'd prefer to let you always wonder how I knew about Hannah. You goofed, you know."

"I do not," he said coldly, "goof, as you phrase it. What you fail to understand is that not even the police would be interested in such ancient deaths. I think you've forgotten—if you ever knew—that there's such a thing as a statute of limitations."

"Oh?" I said. "Then why are you so—uh—upset?"

"Because I simply cannot allow you to jeopardize Jay's chances of being elected to the U.S. Senate. I've worked too hard."

"*You've* worked too hard?"

"Of course," he said. His eyes were like cold gray marbles behind his glasses. "I waited a long, long time to find Jay, and I've taught him everything he knows. He's young; he's only beginning; there's no limit as to how far he can go in politics."

I stared at him. "You killed Hannah for *that?* A woman with more talent, imagination, and intelligence than that precious Tuttle of yours could ever have?"

He shrugged impatiently. "She was only a woman. And you show a tiresome interest in the past that doesn't become a person of your age," he added. "For myself it's the future that matters."

I blurted out, "Why didn't Jay marry Nora?"

I swear that he looked shocked by my question. "*Marry?*" he repeated. "But my dear Miss Jones I had no intention of letting him marry Nora. It was money he needed, a grubstake one might say. I had only a professor's modest salary, and Jay needed money for clothes, for meeting the right people."

"But Nora had money, and Nora loved him."

He smiled forgivingly. "One does not sell a personality like Jay Tuttle's so cheaply. Nora's inheritance, once taxes were paid, was not so large as you might assume. With money of his own Jay could do much better, and he did. Before the year ended he was safely married to Senator Plumtree's daughter Janet, and I can assure you that an heiress to the Plumtree pharmaceutical fortune and the prospects of a father-in-law in Washington made Nora look very small league."

"You arranged it," I whispered.

"Of course. The Plumtrees had always summered in Maine, and I made a point of meeting them in 1964."

I flung at him bitterly, "I'm surprised you let Nora go on living with all she knew."

His lips tightened. "Only at Jay's insistence. The one time he— But it was a mistake, and it's not one I plan to repeat now, Miss Jones. You will be shot beside your cash register."

He means I'm really going to be killed, I thought. Me.

"After which I will empty your cash register, break a window to show how your burglar got in, and exit by the rear door. The dishes you threw will add a good touch to the scene—you put up a valiant struggle before you were killed."

I swallowed hard. "It won't help, killing me, because I wasn't in Maine alone. Joe knows, and do does Robin Gruble."

He made a soft *tch-tch* sound. "A pity. You can see what a

503

nuisance you're proving to me, but I appreciate your telling me this." He smiled. "A few more deaths will scarcely be noticed among all the muggings and robberies these days, but it does seem a bore. Kindly move to the cash register now."

"Kindly?" I echoed, and I laughed. I couldn't help it. I mean, he was going to kill all of us and it seemed a bore? "*Kindly* move to the cash register?" I repeated.

He gave me an impatient glance and gestured with his gun. "Over," he said, and when I didn't move, he came to get me. He could have shot me from where he stood, but he was obviously a perfectionist, wanting things precisely right for the police. This rigidity was his first mistake, because I was waiting for him with my fingers curled around the penknife, my anger as cold as steel now. Just as he reached for my arm, I lifted the penknife out of my pocket and plunged it into his gleaming white shirt. It was a small knife, scarcely an inch in length, but his reaction gave me two seconds to get away. He yelped in pain.

I knew I'd be shot before I could unbolt the lock on the street door. Instead I headed for the stairs; as I raced up them two at a time, a bullet hit the wall behind me. I passed the door to my apartment, opened the one leading to the roof, closed it behind me, ran up the narrow stairs, unbolted the steel door at the top, and plunged out onto the flat graveled roof of my building.

It was a shock to discover that it was almost dark. I raced across the gravel, dodging chimneys and apertures, and pulled myself up to the neighboring roof, three feet higher. I checked the steel door leading down into that building: locked, of course. Over my shoulder I saw Holton's head silhouetted against the sky as he climbed over the parapet behind me. I turned and jumped down to the next roof and stopped to examine the edge of the trapdoor there. No luck. I ran toward the edge of the third roof and abruptly came to a halt. I was facing an alleyway, wide enough for a car and too broad to jump across. I was trapped.

Fifty feet below me traffic passed in a steady stream; I shouted, but no one heard. I turned and saw Holton scrambling down from the roof and I could feel my heart thudding mercilessly. There was a broken brick lying near me; I picked it up.

He was walking toward me slowly, still breathing heavily from the climb, but he was confident now and smiling faintly, and the gun in his hand pointed at me. In that moment I looked clearly and

504

sanely into death and I was no longer afraid; I was angry.

Abruptly I ducked my head and ran toward him, weaving and zigzagging. The first bullet hit me; my left arm felt as if it had been torn away, but it had the effect of shocking me into a deeper fury. The second bullet grazed my temple. Blood streamed into my eyes, but by that time I was under his gun and on Holton, kicking, screaming, biting. I had no thought of myself anymore, only for this man who had the effrontery to kill—kill Hannah, kill Lipton, and now me. In the darkness my teeth found his wrist. The gun dropped to the roof, and I kicked it aside and hit him with the brick. This time, caught off-balance, he fell.

I leaned over him; then, seeing how still he was, I straightened up. I gasped at the pain in my head. I began crying with huge, dry, soundless sobs. Dragging myself across the roof, I managed to pull myself up to the roof of the next building. Nearly blinded from the blood streaming into my eyes, I crept across it and half fell, half jumped to the roof of my own building. I got myself to the open door, sat down on the stairs, and lowered myself, step by step, still sitting—I couldn't have stood—until I reached the second floor and the stairs leading down to the shop.

That was when I stopped to wipe the blood from my eyes and saw him. He was watching me from the bottom of the stairs.

I should have known he'd be here, too. I stared down through a film of blood, recognizing him from his pictures, except that he wasn't smiling now—those flawless twelve teeth were hidden. John Tuttle . . . State Senator Angus Tuttle now. He looked pale, strained, appalled at the sight of me.

"You're supposed to be dead," he whispered.

I shouted at him, "You can't even do your own killing." Still crawling, I reached the top stair and looked down at him again.

He had brought a pistol from his overcoat pocket and was staring at it in surprise. He lifted his eyes to look at me and licked his lips. "Where's Hubert?" he asked, and then he shouted, "Hubert, where are you? Hu, for God's sake, finish her off!"

I wasn't thinking any longer; I was a wounded animal without fear. He was going to shoot me, and all that mattered was to die as quickly as possible, and with dignity. I felt for the railing and pulled myself to my feet, the stairs swaying in front of me. But I stood. It would have to be a real murder this time, not concealed for years and years.

Behind me I heard Holton shout from the top of the stairs and below me I saw Tuttle lift his pistol. I stood erect and gritted my teeth, a great dizziness sweeping over me, until abruptly the dizziness was joined with darkness. I fell just as a gun exploded, fell endlessly, the roar of blood in my ears, until I came to rest on something soft. Dimly I heard a crash of splintering glass, and voices shouting. Then, hearing Joe's voice, I gave myself up to the voluptuous oblivion of unconsciousness.

Chapter Fourteen

It was a long journey, full of darkness at first, and whispering voices and a glacial cold. I was in a labyrinth, turning corner after corner, yet someone was with me, someone whose presence was familiar and peaceful. I stumbled on, until suddenly I felt warmth ahead, and light. Reluctantly I opened my eyes. A lighted room. White walls. The two worlds converged, split apart, the labyrinth receding before certain images of pain and violence, a rooftop and a gun.

A dark-haired young man sitting in a red plastic-leather chair reading a magazine. I was not dead. I was lying in a bed, all white and pristine, the blood wiped away from my eyes, my left arm in a splint. I was alive and it was Joe sitting in the chair. I said tentatively, "Joe?"

"Amelia?" He jumped up and came to my bed. "Welcome back, Amelia."

"Yes," I said, smiling at him mistily.

He said in a funny kind of voice that shook a little, "I love you, Amelia."

"I'm surprised," I said carefully.

"At my loving you?" He sounded startled.

"No," I said, thinking about this, "at being alive."

"You were damn lucky. As the police put it all together," he explained, "Holton shot at you from behind, from the top of the stairs, and at that same moment you lost consciousness and fell. The bullet hit Tuttle at the bottom of the stairs instead. He fell over and you landed on top of him. Which is where you were when I smashed down the door and found you."

How very complicated life sounded, I thought, and how very fast Joe talked. "Weird," I said politely, for it had no reality for me now. "I hope no one was hurt." I was still half clinging to the maze, wanting to discover what lay at the end of it.

"Tuttle's still alive," Joe was saying, "but Holton went back up to the roof and killed himself. Tuttle's been arraigned as an accessory to your near murder, and he's in all the newspapers, but no longer smiling. The police know about Hannah now, too. Robin and I took them all the papers and documents."

"Ah," I said, nodding at the name Hannah. I wondered if it had been she who guided me through the maze. I said drowsily, "I love you, too, Joe, but I couldn't find you. When I got home."

I didn't understand why he looked as if he were going to explode. I watched in wonder as he swallowed his anger. "I spent two days in Maine looking for you, Amelia. *Two days.* I phoned you on Tuesday night at the Golden Kingfisher Motel. You weren't there. The manager found your suitcase there, but not you *or* the van. As soon as I finished in court on Wednesday I hopped the first plane, and by two o'clock in the afternoon I was back in Anglesworth, with the state police."

"Weird," I said, watching him and thinking he had lovely eyes.

"I will not," he said, "go into my reactions when I learned that Hannah's house had burned to the ground, or that the tire marks of a medium-sized van were found nearby. I will only tell you that it was twenty-four more hours before I knew that you were still alive. That's when the state police finally traced your van to the Bide-a-Wee Motel, where a girl answering your description registered at ten o'clock, soaking wet, and checked out several hours later. And then—my God, Amelia, I barely got back in time."

"Back?" I repeated blurrily.

"To Trafton, to find your telegram on my doorstep. In time to rush to your shop and find you lying with Tuttle at the bottom of the stairs. In time to prevent Holton from shooting you again. Amelia, you *are* going to marry me, aren't you?"

"Well," I began, and then hesitated. Perhaps, I thought, I had found the heart of the maze after all. But without finishing either my sentence or my thought I fell asleep, and the next day Joe had to repeat everything he'd said to me all over again.

AND SO IT became just one more sordid story that would titillate newspaper readers all through the fall and winter of the trial. A slightly demented Horatio Alger story of a clever young man,

508

who years ago learned to use a handsome face and a broad smile to charm his way into Hannah's family, and destroy it. And of an older man, frustrated, pedantic, ambitious, who was looking for just such a young man to exploit for his own purposes.

And they got away with it, except that the one thing they never dreamed of in their wildest moments was Hannah's note. Or my curiosity, for that matter.

In the tabloids Hannah was barely mentioned at all, but *The New York Times* reprinted its long-ago review of *The Maze in the Heart of the Castle*, and the book will be reissued when *In the Land of the Golden Warriors* is published. For the latter book Robin is writing a foreword explaining the circumstances of the manuscript's discovery. He is dedicating the book to me, because Hannah would have wanted it, he says. They won't bring Hannah back to life, of course. Or will they? Just a little?

I think now about how our lives all touch each other, gently or violently, for good or evil, as Hannah's life touched mine. People's futures have been rearranged by all this. Robin, for instance, is going to have money again. It's too late for Hannah's will to be upset, but a very good lawyer advised him to sue the senator for damages, and when this became evident there was a hasty and very large settlement out of court to avoid even more publicity.

As for Nora, she is dead. Robin tells me that she died of heart failure at what he believes to be the precise moment that Jay Tuttle was shot on the stairs. As if she knew. I think about this sometimes. . . . Tuttle chose to keep Nora alive and in luxury for years, refusing to allow Holton to kill her; he visited her surprisingly often, too, for such a busy man. Who is to say that Nora and Jay hadn't gone on loving each other all those years? Often I wonder what their lives might have been if Tuttle had been less malleable and Holton less ambitious. I blame Hubert Holton for much more than murder.

From Garwin Mason came flowers: the news of Tuttle's fall from grace must have been very big in Maine. There was no note, only his name on a card, but I knew what he wanted to say.

As for myself, I feel changed in a way that I can't explain except, perhaps, to say that I moved from victim to survivor, a distance of no small import. A balance has occurred that astonishes me: I am turning into a very agile tightrope walker, gliding across chasms without a glance below. I have no more nightmares and, ironically, now that I have come very near to death it no longer haunts me. Joe says I am moving from old age to middle age and he suggests we get married in time for my adolescence.

Amman Singh says that I have begun to walk the path to my original self. He quotes a proverb to the effect that no one can learn to live who has not learned to die.

What Dr. Merivale would say is something else again. As a matter of fact I met him the other day on Main Street. When I said hello, he stopped, surprised. "Why—it's Amelia, isn't it? What have you been doing since I last saw you?"

I like Dr. Merivale, I really do. I mean, he held my hand for two difficult years and I am grateful, but I was feeling mischievous that day. He had been away on vacation, and so he hadn't seen the newspapers. I said gravely, "Well, Dr. Merivale, since I last saw you I've been looking for the murderers of a woman killed many years ago. I found them and was nearly murdered myself, and now one killer is dead and the other arrested. I've found a guru of sorts, and I've fallen in love. I really think I've been affecting my environment, don't you? At last?"

It's possible that the passing of a truck blurred my words, or it's possible that Dr. Merivale is not by nature playful. His glance at me sharpened suspiciously. "Ah," he murmured. "Well, I hope you will still consider that typing class, Amelia. It's so important that we all have purpose in life." He gave me a kindly smile and continued walking down the street.

I watched him go and I laughed. I mean, have you ever stopped to realize—not just the miracle that life is—but how basically comic it is despite its griefs? The wonder of it, as Amman Singh says, is that we take it so seriously. One day, poised on my tightrope, I hope to manage a glorious cartwheel or, at the very least, a pirouette.

In the meantime, however, I bought a flower from the vendor on the corner and carried it home to Joe.

Dorothy Gilman

Dorothy Gilman is a woman of many parts. Born and raised in New Brunswick, New Jersey, where her father was a Baptist minister, she showed great literary talent as a child, winning a newspaper short-story competition when she was only eleven years old. She was clever with her paintbrush, however, as well as with her pen, and, determined to be an artist, studied for several years at the Pennsylvania Academy of Fine Arts in Philadelphia. Then, when she was twenty-two, she returned briefly to her childhood enthusiasm, writing, and published a number of successful novels for young people. Until suddenly yet a third career intervened: that of wife and mother.

More than anything else, Dorothy Gilman had always wanted to travel. But for twenty-five years she stayed at home, raising her two small sons, and dreaming of adventure. And, as soon as her boys were old enough, with the idea of putting her dreams into words, she turned to writing again, this time for adults—creating for her very first heroine that adventurous old dabbler in international espionage, Mrs. Emily Pollifax.

The novel was an immediate success, and was made into a film starring Rosalind Russell. Other Mrs. Pollifax stories followed: Condensed Books have published two of these, taking the redoubtable senior citizen to Mexico and Switzerland.

Nowadays, a successful author, her two sons away in college, Dorothy Gilman no longer has to dream: she has had ample opportunity for adventures of her own, journeys to far-off foreign lands, and a spiritual odyssey as well. Recently she has completed her first work of nonfiction, *A New Kind of Country*, based on her life in her current home, an ancient, wood-framed house on the coast of Nova Scotia, fronting the rugged beach. At last, she says, she has "found her roots" in the isolated lobster-fishing village, and she spends much of her time there, writing and tending her flourishing herb garden. In the harsh, dramatic landscape that Mrs. Gilman describes as "space and sky and water" she is finding good friends and a new and satisfying life.